Also by David Grossman

FICTION

In Another Life

Someone to Run With

Be My Knife

The Zigzag Kid

The Book of Intimate Grammar

See Under: Love

The Smile of the Lamb

NONFICTION

Writing in the Dark: Essays on Literature and Politics

Death as a Way of Life: Israel Ten Years After Oslo

Sleeping on a Wire: Conversations with Palestinians in Israel

The Yellow Wind

TO THE END OF THE LAND

TO THE END OF THE LAND

David Grossman

Translated from the Hebrew by Jessica Cohen

McClelland & Stewart

Originally published in Israel as *Isha Borachat Me'besorah* by HaKibbutz HaMeuchad Publishing
House, Ltd., Tel Aviv, in 2008. Copyright © 2008 by David Grossman and HaKibbutz HaMeuchad
Publishing House, Ltd.

Library and Archives Canada Cataloguing in Publication

Grossman, David
[Isha borachat me'besorah. English]
To the end of the land / David Grossman ; translated by Jessica Cohen.

Translation of: Isha borachat me'besorah.
ISBN 978-0-7710-3634-7

I. Cohen, Jessica II. Title. III. Title: Isha borachat me'besorah. English.

PJ5054.G738I8413 2010   892.4'36   C2010-901577-0

We acknowledge the financial support of the Government of Canada through the Book Publishing
Industry Development Program and that of the Government of Ontario through the Ontario Media
Development Corporation's Ontario Book Initiative. We further acknowledge the support of the Canada
Council for the Arts and the Ontario Arts Council for our publishing program.

This is a work of fiction. Any resemblance to actual persons living or dead,
events, or locales is entirely coincidental.

Printed and bound in the United States of America.

McClelland & Stewart Ltd.
75 Sherbourne Street
Toronto, Ontario
M5A 2P9
www.mcclelland.com

1   2   3   4   5   14   13   12   11   10

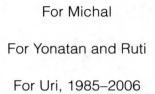

For Michal

For Yonatan and Ruti

For Uri, 1985–2006

TO THE END OF THE LAND

Prologue, 1967

HEY, GIRL, quiet!
  Who is that?
  Be quiet! You woke everyone up!
  But I was holding her
  Who?
  On the rock, we were sitting together
  What rock are you talking about? Let us sleep
  Then she just fell
  All this shouting and singing
  But I was asleep
  And you were shouting!
  She just let go of my hand and fell
  Stop it, go to sleep
  Turn on a light
  Are you crazy? They'll kill us if we do that

Wait

What?

I was singing?

Singing, shouting, everything. Now be quiet

What was I singing?

What were you singing?!

In my sleep, what was I singing?

I'm supposed to know what you were singing? A bunch of shouts. That's what you were singing. What was I singing, she wants to know . . .

You don't remember the song?

Look, are you nuts? I'm barely alive

But who are you?

Room Three

You're in isolation, too?

Gotta get back

Don't go . . . Did you leave? Wait, hello . . . Gone . . . But what was I singing?

———

AND the next night he woke her up again, angry at her again for singing at the top of her lungs and waking up the whole hospital, and she begged him to try to remember if it was the same song from the night before. She was desperate to know, because of her dream, which kept getting dreamed almost every night during those years. An utterly white dream. Everything in it was white, the streets and the houses and the trees and the cats and dogs and the rock at the edge of the cliff. And Ada, her redheaded friend, was also entirely white, without a drop of blood in her face or body. Without a drop of color in her hair. But he couldn't remember which song it was this time, either. His whole body was shuddering, and she shuddered back at him from her bed. We're like a pair of castanets, he said, and to her surprise, she burst out with bright laughter that tickled him inside. He had used up all his strength on the journey from his room to hers, thirty-five steps, resting after each one, holding on to walls, doorframes, empty food carts. Now he flopped onto the sticky linoleum floor in her doorway. For several minutes they both breathed heavily. He wanted to make her laugh again but he could no longer speak, and then he must have fallen asleep, until her voice woke him.

Tell me something
What? Who is it?
It's me
You . . .
Tell me, am I alone in this room?
How should I know?
Are you, like, shivering?
Yeah, shivering
How high is yours?
It was forty this evening
Mine was forty point three. When do you die?
At forty-two
That's close
No, no, you still have time
Don't go, I'm scared
Do you hear?
What?
How quiet it is suddenly?
Were there booms before?
Cannons
I keep sleeping, and all of a sudden it's nighttime again
'Cause there's a blackout
I think they're winning
Who?
The Arabs
No way
They've occupied Tel Aviv
What are you . . . who told you that?
I don't know. Maybe I heard it
You dreamed it
No, they said it here, someone, before, I heard voices
It's from the fever. Nightmares. I have them, too
My dream . . . I was with my friend
Maybe you know

What?
Which direction I came from
I don't know anything here
How long for you?
Don't know
Me, four days. Maybe a week
Wait, where's the nurse?
At night she's in Internal A. She's an Arab
How do you know?
You can hear it when she talks
You're shaking
My mouth, my whole face
But . . . where is everybody?
They're not taking us to the bomb shelter
Why?
So we don't infect them
Wait, so it's just us—
And the nurse
I thought
What?
If you could sing it for me
That again?
Just hum
I'm leaving
If it was the other way around, I would sing to you
Gotta get back
Where?
Where, where, to lie with my forefathers, to bring me down with
sorrow to the grave, that's where
What? What was that? Wait, do I know you? Hey, come back

————

AND the next night, too, before midnight, he came to stand in her
doorway and scolded her again and complained that she was singing in
her sleep, waking him and the whole world, and she smiled to herself
and asked if his room was really that far, and that was when he realized,

from her voice, that she wasn't where she had been the night before and the night before that.

Because now I'm *sitting*, she explained. He asked cautiously, But why are you sitting? Because I couldn't sleep, she said. And I wasn't singing. I was sitting here quietly waiting for you.

They both thought it was getting even darker. A new wave of heat, which may have had nothing to do with her illness, climbed up from Ora's toes and sparked red spots on her neck and face. It's a good thing it's dark, she thought, and held her loose pajama collar up to her neck. Finally, from the doorway, he cleared his throat softly and said, Well, I have to get back. But why? she asked. He said he urgently had to tar and feather himself. She didn't get it, but then she got it and laughed deeply. Come on, dummy, enough with your act, I put a chair out for you next to me.

He felt along the doorway, metal cabinets, and beds, until he stopped way off, leaned his arms on an empty bed, and panted loudly. I'm here, he groaned. Come closer to me, she said. Wait, let me catch my breath. The darkness filled her with courage and she said in a loud voice, in her voice of health, of beaches and paddleball and swimming out to the rafts on Quiet Beach, What are you afraid of? I don't bite. He mumbled, Okay, okay, I get it, I'm barely alive. His grumbling tone and the heavy way he dragged his feet touched her. We're kind of like an elderly couple, she thought.

Ouch!

What happened?

One of these beds just decided to . . . Fuck! So, have you heard of the Law of Malicious—

What did you say?

The Law of Malicious Furniture—heard of it?

Are you coming or not?

The trembling wouldn't stop, and sometimes it turned into long shivers, and when they talked their speech was choppy, and they often had to wait for a pause in the trembling, a brief calming of the face and mouth muscles, and then they would quickly spit out the words in high, tense voices, and the stammering crushed the sentences in their mouths. How-old-are-you? Six-teen-and-you? And-a-quar-ter. I-have-jaun-dice, how-a-bout-you? Me? he said. I-think-it's-an-in-fec-tion-of-the-o-va-ries.

Silence. He shuddered and breathed heavily. By-the-way-that-was-a-joke, he said. Not funny, she said. He groaned: I tried to make her laugh, but her sense of humor is too— She perked up and asked who he was talking to. He replied, To my joke writer, I guess I'll have to fire him. If you don't come over here and sit down right now, I'll start singing, she threatened. He shivered and laughed. His laughter was as screechy as a donkey's bray, a self-sustaining laughter, and she secretly gulped it down like medicine, like a prize.

He laughed so hard at her stupid little joke that she barely resisted telling him that lately she wasn't good at making people roll around with laughter the way she used to. "When it comes to humor, she's not much of a jester," they sang about her at the Purim party this year. And it wasn't just a minor shortcoming. For her it was crippling, a new defect that could grow bigger and more complicated. And she sensed that it was somehow related to some other qualities that were vanishing in recent years. Intuition, for example. How could a trait like that disappear so abruptly? Or the knack for saying the right thing at the right time. She had had it once, and now it was gone. Or even just wittiness. She used to be really sharp. The sparks just flew out of her. (Although, she consoled herself, it was a Purim song, and maybe they just couldn't come up with a better rhyme for "Esther.") Or her sense of love, she thought. Maybe that was part of her deterioration—her losing the capacity to really love someone, to burn with love, like the girls talked about, like in the movies. She felt a pang for Asher Feinblatt, her friend who went to the military boarding school, who was now a soldier, who had told her on the steps between Pevsner Street and Yosef Street that she was his soul mate, but who hadn't touched her that time, either. Never once in two years had he put a hand or a finger on her, and maybe that never-touched-her also had something to do with it, and deep in her heart she felt that everything was somehow connected, and that things would grow clearer all the time, and she would keep discovering more little pieces of whatever awaited her.

For a moment she could see herself at fifty, tall and thin and withered, a scentless flower taking long, quick steps, her head bowed, a wide-brimmed straw hat hiding her face. The boy with the donkey laugh kept feeling his way toward her, getting closer and then farther away—it was as if he were doing it on purpose, she realized, like this was a kind of game for him—and he giggled and made fun of his own clumsiness and floated around the room in circles, and every so often he asked her to say something so he'd know which direction she was in:

Like a lighthouse, he explained, but with sound. Smart-ass, she thought. He finally reached her bed and felt around and found the chair she had put out, and collapsed on it and breathed heavily like an old man. She could smell the sweat of his illness, and she pulled off one of her blankets and gave it to him and he wrapped it around himself and said nothing. They were both exhausted, and each of them shivered and moaned.

Still, she said later from under her blanket, your voice sounds familiar. Where are you from? Jerusalem, he said. I'm from Haifa, she said, accentuating slightly. They brought me here in an ambulance from Rambam Hospital, because of the complications. I have those too, he laughed, my whole life is complications. They sat quietly. He scratched his stomach and chest and grumbled, and she grumbled, too. That's the worse thing about it, isn't it? she said. She also scratched herself, with all ten fingernails. Sometimes I'm dying to peel all my skin off, just to make it stop. Every time she started talking, he could hear the soft sticky sound of her lips parting, and the tips of his fingers and toes throbbed.

Ora said, The ambulance driver said that at a time like this they need the ambulances for more important things.

Have you noticed that everyone here is angry at us? As if we purposely . . .

Because we're the last ones left from the plague.

They sent home anyone who was feeling even a little bit better. Especially soldiers. Wham-bam, they kicked them right back to the army so they could make it in time for the war.

So there's really going to be a war?

Are you kidding? There's been a war for at least two days.

When did it start? she asked in a whisper.

Day before yesterday, I think. And I told you that already, yesterday or the day before, I can't remember, the days get mixed up.

That's right, you did say . . . Ora was dumbstruck. Clots of strange and terrifying dreams drifted through her.

How could you not hear? he murmured. There are sirens and artillery all the time, and I heard helicopters landing. There are probably a million casualties by now.

But what's going on?

I don't know, and there's no one to talk to here. They have no patience for us.

Then who's taking care of us?

Right now there's just that thin little Arab woman, the one who cries. Have you heard her?

That's a person crying? Ora was stunned. I thought it was an animal wailing. Are you sure?

It's a person, for sure.

But how come I haven't seen her?

She kind of comes and goes. She does the tests and leaves your medicine and food on a tray. It's just her now, day and night. He sucked in his cheeks and said thoughtfully, It's funny that the only person they left us with is an Arab, isn't it? They probably don't let Arabs treat the wounded.

But why does she cry? What happened to her?

How should I know?

Ora sat up straight and her body hardened, and she said coldly, quietly, They've occupied Tel Aviv, I'm telling you. Nasser and Hussein are already sipping coffee at a café on Dizengoff Street.

Where did you come up with that? He sounded frightened.

I heard it last night, or today, I'm almost positive, maybe it was on her radio, I heard it, they've occupied Beersheba and Ashkelon and Tel Aviv.

No, no, that can't be. Maybe it's the fever, it's because of your fever, 'cause there's no way! You're crazy, there's no way they'll win.

There is, there is, she mumbled to herself, and thought, What do you even know about what could or couldn't happen.

————

LATER, she awoke from a quick doze and looked around for the boy. Are you still here? What, yes. She sighed. There were nine girls in the room with me, and I'm the only one left, isn't that annoying? Avram liked the fact that after three nights with her he still didn't know her name, or she his; he liked little mysteries like that; in the sketches he wrote and recorded at home on his reel-to-reel, in which he played all the parts—children and old men and women and ghosts and kings and wild geese and talking kettles and any number of other characters—

there were often brainy little games like this, creatures that appeared and disappeared, characters imagined by other characters. Meanwhile, he amused himself with guesses: Rina? Yael? Maybe Liora? She seems like a Liora, he thought. Her smile is full of light, so there must be an *or* in her name.

It was the same in his room, he told her. Almost everyone in Room Three had left, including the soldiers. Some could barely walk, but they still sent them back to their units. Now there's only one other guy with him, not a soldier, actually someone from his class who came in two days ago with forty-one point two, and they can't bring it down, all day long he dreams and tells himself a thousand and one nights— Wait, Ora cut him off. Were you ever in training at Wingate? Do you happen to play volleyball? Avram let out a small yelp of horror. Ora held back a smile and put on a stern expression: Well, isn't there any sport you're good at? Avram thought for a moment. Maybe as a punching bag, he said. Then what youth movement are you in? she asked angrily. I'm not in any movement, he said, smiling. No movement? Ora flinched. Then what are you? Just don't tell me *you're* in a movement, Avram said, still smiling. Why not? Ora was insulted. Because it'll ruin everything for us, he said with an exaggerated sigh. Because I was starting to think you were the perfect girl. Ha! she spat out. I happen to be in the Machanot Olim. He jutted his chin forward and stuck out his lips, and gave a long, brokenhearted, canine howl at the ceiling. That's a terrible thing you're telling me, he said. I only hope medical science will find a cure for your suffering. She tapped her foot briskly. Wait, I know! Weren't you with your buddies at the Yesud HaMaale camp once? Didn't you have tents in the woods over there?

Dear diary, sighed Avram in a heavy Russian accent. At the midnight hour of a cold and tempestuous night, when I, woebegone, at last met a girl who was certain she knew me from somewhere— Ora sniffed contemptuously. Long story short, Avram continued, we examined every possibility, and after rejecting all her horrendous ideas, I came to the conclusion that perhaps it was in the future that we knew each other.

Ora cried out sharply, as though stabbed with a needle. What happened? Avram asked softly, infected by her pain. Nothing, she said. It's nothing. She secretly stared at him, trying to penetrate the darkness and finally see who he was.

. . .

Somehow, in a super-avian effort, he flew to Room Three and landed on the edge of his classmate's bed, and he too was trembling and sighing and scratching in his sleep. It's so quiet here, Avram murmured. Have you noticed how quiet it is tonight? There was a long silence. Then the other boy spoke in a hoarse, broken voice: It's like a tomb in here, maybe we're already dead. Avram contemplated. Listen, he said, when we were alive, I think we studied in the same class at school. The boy said nothing. He tried to lift his head to look at Avram, but could not. After a few minutes he moaned, When I was alive, I basically didn't study anything in any class. That's true, said Avram with a thin, admiring smile. When I was alive there really was a guy in my class who basically didn't study anything. A guy called Ilan. Unbelievable snob, never talked to anyone.

What could he possibly have to talk to you guys about? A bunch of babies, pussies the lot of you, clueless.

Why? asked Avram quietly. What do you know that we don't?

Ilan let out a short, bitter snort of laughter, and then they sat quietly, sinking into turbulent sleep. Somewhere in the distance, in Room Seven, Ora lay in bed and tried to figure out if these things had really happened. She remembered that not long ago, a few days ago, when she was walking back from practice at the Technion courts, she had passed out on the street. She remembered that the doctor at Rambam had asked whether she had been to one of the new army camps set up in preparation for the war, and if she'd eaten anything or used the latrines. She was instantly uprooted from her home, then exiled to a strange city and trapped in total isolation by the doctors, on the third floor of a tiny, miserable, neglected hospital in a city she barely knew. She was no longer sure if her parents and friends were really forbidden to visit her or if in fact they had visited her while she was sleeping, had stood helplessly around her bed trying to revive her, had spoken to her, called her name, then walked away, turning back to give her one more look: What a shame, such a good girl, but it can't be helped, life goes on and you have to look ahead, and now there's a war and we need all our strength.

I'm going to die, Ilan mumbled.

Nonsense, Avram said, shaking himself awake. You'll live, another day or two and you'll be—

I knew this would happen, said Ilan softly. It was obvious from the beginning.

No, no, Avram said, scared now. What are you talking about, don't think that way.

I never even kissed a girl.

You will, said Avram. Don't be scared, it's okay, things will work out.

When I was alive, Ilan said later—maybe a whole hour later—there was this kid in my class who only came up to my balls.

That was me, Avram laughed.

He could never shut up.

It's me.

Always made such a fuss.

It's me, it's me!

I used to look at him and think, That guy, when he was little, his dad used to beat the crap out of him.

Who told you? Avram asked, alarmed.

I see people, Ilan said, and fell asleep.

Agitated, Avram spread his wings and flew down the curved corridor, banging into walls until he finally landed in his spot on the chair next to Ora's bed. He closed his eyes and slept fitfully. Ora was dreaming about Ada. In her dream, she was with Ada on that same endless white plain where the two of them walked almost every night, silently holding hands. In the early dreams, they talked all the time. From afar they could both see the rock looming over an abyss. When Ora dared to glance at her from the side, she saw that Ada no longer had a body. All that was left was a voice, quick and sharp and alert as it always used to be. The feeling of clasped hands was also still there, the fingers desperately clutching. The blood inside Ora's head pounded: Don't let go, Don't let go, Don't let go of Ada, not even for a minute—

No, Ora whispered, and woke up in a start, bathed in cold sweat, I'm so stupid—

She looked at the place where Avram was sprawled in the dark. The vein in her neck started to throb.

He woke up. What did you say? He tried to steady himself on the chair. He kept sliding down toward the floor, a despotic force pulling him to lie down, to rest his unbearably heavy head.

I had a friend who talked a bit like you do, she murmured. You still here?

I'm here, I think I fell asleep.

We were friends since first grade.

But not anymore? Ora tried in vain to control her hands, which suddenly shook wildly. It had been more than two years since she'd spoken to anyone about Ada. She hadn't even said her name out loud. Avram leaned forward a little. What's the matter with you? Why are you like that?

Listen—

What?

She swallowed and said quickly, In the first grade, on the first day, when I walked into the classroom, she was the first girl I saw.

Why?

Well, Ora giggled, she was a redhead, too.

Oh. Wait, are you?

She laughed out loud, and her laughter, again, was healthy and musical. She was so surprised that anyone could be with her and talk with her for such a long time, three nights, without knowing she was a redhead. But I don't have freckles, she quickly clarified. Ada did, all over her face, and on her arms and legs. Does this even interest you?

On her legs, too?

Everywhere.

Why did you stop?

I don't know. There's not much to tell.

Tell me what there is.

It's a little . . . She hesitated for a moment, unable to decide if she could tell him the secrets of the fraternity. You should know that the first thing a redheaded kid does is find out if there are any other redheads around.

To be their friend? Oh, no, the opposite. Right?

She smiled admiringly in the dark. He was smarter than she thought. Exactly, she said. And also so they never stand next to them or anything.

That's just like how I—I look for the runts first.

Why?

That's the way it is.

Are you . . . Wait, are you short?

I'm willing to bet I don't reach your ankles.

Hah!

Seriously, you have no idea what kind of offers I get from circuses.

Tell me something.

What?

But be honest.

Go on.

Why did you come to me yesterday and today?

Don't know. I just did.

Even so.

He cleared his throat and said, "I wanted to wake you before you started singing in your sleep, Avram lied."

What did you say?

"I wanted to wake you before you started singing in your sleep again, lied the ever-scheming Avram."

Oh, you're—

Yes.

You're adding in what you—

Exactly.

Silence. A secretive smile. Wheels spinning rapidly, on both ends.

And your name is Avram?

What can I do? That was the cheapest name my parents could afford.

And that would be like my saying, for example, "He's talking to me as if he were a theater actor or something, thought Ora to herself"?

"You've got it, Avram praised Ora, and said to himself, Dear soul, I believe we've found—"

"So now be quiet for a minute, said Ora the genius, and delved into thoughts deeper than the ocean itself."

"I wonder what she's thinking thoughts deeper than the ocean itself about, Avram speculated nervously."

"She's thinking to herself that she really wants to see him, just for a minute—and then Ora, sly as a fox, revealed to him that apart from a chair, she had also today prepared *this*."

A scratch, and another scratch, a flare, and a spot of light shines in the room. A long, fair, slender arm reaches out, holding a matchstick torch. The light sways on the walls like liquid. A large room with many empty, naked beds, and trembling shadows, and a wall and a doorframe, and in the heart of the circle of light is Avram, shrinking back a little from the glare of the match.

She lights another and holds it lower, as if not wanting to embarrass him. The flame reveals a young man's thick, sturdy legs in blue pajamas.

Surprisingly small hands grasp each other nervously on the lap, and the light climbs up to a short, solid body and cuts a large round face out of the darkness. Despite the illness, the face contains an almost embarrassing lust for life, curious and intense, with a bulbous nose and swollen lids, and above them a wild bush of black hair.

What astounds her more than anything is the way he presents his face for her perusal and verdict, closing his eyes tightly, strenuously wrinkling all his features. For a moment he looks like someone who has just tossed a very fragile object into the air and is now waiting fearfully for it to shatter.

Ora gasps with pain and licks her burned fingertip. After a moment's hesitation, she lights another match and holds it with severe candor in front of her own forehead. She shuts her eyes and quickly runs the light up and down in front of her face. Her eyelashes flutter, her lips protrude slightly. Shadows break on her long, high cheekbones and around the defiant, swollen ball of her mouth and chin. Something dark and imbued with sleep hovers over this lovely face, something lost and unweaned, but perhaps it's just the illness that makes it look that way. Her short hair glistens like burnished brass, and its brilliance glows in Avram's eyes even after the match goes out and the darkness once again envelops her.

———

HEY—

What, what?!

Avram?

What?

Did you fall asleep?

Me? I thought you did.

Do you really think we'll get better?

Of course.

But there must have been a hundred people in isolation when I got here. Maybe we have something they don't know how to cure?

You mean—both of us?

Whoever is left here.

That's just the two of us, and the other guy, from my class.

But why us?

Because we have the complications of hepatitis.

That's just it. Why us?

Don't know.

I'm falling asleep again—

I'm staying.

Why do I keep falling asleep?

Weak body.

Don't sleep, watch over me.

Then talk to me. Tell me.

About what?

About you.

They were like sisters, she told him. People called them "the Siamese twins," even though they looked nothing alike. For eight years, ages six to fourteen, first grade to the end of the first trimester in the eighth grade, they sat at the same desk. They didn't part after school either, always together, at one or the other's house, and in the Machanot Olim youth movement, and on hikes— Are you even listening?

What . . . ? Yes, I'm listening . . . There's something I don't get—why aren't you friends anymore?

Why?

Yes.

She isn't—

Isn't what?

Alive.

Ada?!

She heard him flinch as though he'd been hit. She folded her legs in and wrapped her arms around her knees and started rocking herself back and forth. Ada is dead, Ada's been dead for two years, she said to herself quietly. It's all right, it's all right, everyone knows she's dead. We're used to it now, she's dead. Life goes on. But she felt that she had just told Avram something secret and very intimate, something only she and Ada had really known.

And then, for some reason, she relaxed. She stopped rocking. She began to breathe again, slowly, cautiously, as if there were thorns in her lungs, and she had the peculiar notion that this boy could carefully remove them, one by one.

But how did she die?

Traffic accident. And just so you know—

An accident?

You have the same sense of humor.

Who?

You and her, but exactly the same.

So is that why—

What?

Is that why you don't laugh at my jokes?

Avram—

Yes.

Give me your hand.

What?

Give me your hand, quick.

But are we allowed?

Don't be stupid, just give it to me.

No, I mean, because of the isolation.

We're infected anyway.

But maybe—

Give me your hand already!

Look how we're both sweating.

It's a good thing.

Why?

Imagine if only one of us was sweating.

Or only one was shaking.

Or scratching.

Or only one had—

What?

You know.

You're gross.

It's true, isn't it?

Then say it.

Okay: shit—

The color of whitewash—

And with blood, loads of it.

She whispered: I never knew I had so much blood in my body.

What's yellow on the outside, shakes like crazy, and shits blood? There, now you're laughing . . . I was getting worried . . .

Listen to this. Before I got ill I thought I didn't have any—

Any what?

Blood in my body.

How could that be?

Never mind.

That's what you thought?

Hold my hand, don't leave.

————

APART FROM THE COLOR of their hair, they were very different, almost opposites. One was tall and strong, the other short and chubby. One had the open, glowing face of a carefree filly, and the other's was crowded and worried, with lots of freckles and a sharp nose and chin, and big glasses—like a young scholar from the shtetl, Ora's father used to say. Their hair was completely different too: Ada's was thick, frizzy, and wild, you could barely get a comb through it. I used to braid her hair, Ora said, in one thick braid, and then I'd tie it around her head like a Sabbath challah, that's how she liked it. And she wouldn't let anyone else do it.

Ada's head was truly red, much redder than Ora's, and it always stuck out in acclamation. Ora curled up on the bed now and saw it: Ada, like a match head, like a blotch of fire. Ora peeked at her, peeked and closed her eyes, unable to face the fullness of Ada. I haven't seen her that way for a long time, she thought, in color.

She always walked on this side of me, Ora told Avram as she grasped his hand in both of hers, because Ada could hardly hear out of her right ear, from birth, and we always talked, about everything, we talked about everything. She fell silent suddenly and pulled her hands away from his. I can't, she thought. What am I doing telling him about her? He isn't even asking anything, he's just quiet, as if he's waiting for me to say it on my own.

She took a deep breath and tried to find a way to tell him, but the words wouldn't come. They pressed on her heart and could not come out. What could she tell him? What could he even understand? I want to, she thought to him. Her fingers moved and burrowed into her other palm. That was how she remembered them together, she remembered the togetherness, and she smiled: You know what I just remembered? It's nothing, just that a week before she—before it happened—we were doing a literary analysis of "The Little Bunny." You know, the nursery rhyme about the bunny who gets a cold.

Avram shook himself awake and smiled weakly. What, tell me. Ora laughed. We wrote—actually Ada wrote most of it, she was always the more talented one—a whole essay about how dreadful it was that the plague of the common cold had spread to the animal kingdom, even to the most innocent of its creatures . . .

Avram whispered to himself: "Even the most innocent of its creatures." She could feel him taste the words in his mouth, run his tongue over them, and suddenly, for the first time in ages, her memory was surprisingly lucid: She and Ada. It's all coming back, she thought excitedly. Endless discussions about boys who did or did not have an "artistic personality," and heart-to-hearts about their parents—after all, almost from the start they were more loyal to each other than to their family secrets. Now she thinks that if not for Ada she would not even know that it was possible, that such closeness was allowed between two people. And there was the Esperanto they started learning together but never finished . . . On the annual school trip to Lake Kinneret, she told him, on the bus, Ada had a stomachache and announced to Ora that she was going to die, and Ora sat next to her weeping. But when she really did, you know, I didn't cry, I couldn't. Everything in me completely dried up. I haven't cried even once since she died.

One small road and an alley separated their houses in the Neveh Sha'anan neighborhood. They walked to school together, and together they walked home, always holding hands when they crossed the street; that was their habit since the age of six, and that is how they did it at the age of fourteen. Ora remembered the one time—they were nine, and they had fought about something that day, and she didn't hold Ada's hand when they crossed, and a municipal van came around the bend and hit Ada, tossing her high up—

She could see it again: her red coat opening up like a parachute. Ora was only two steps behind, and she turned back and ran to hide behind a row of bushes, where she kneeled on the ground with both hands over her ears, shut her eyes tightly, and hummed loudly to herself so she wouldn't see or hear.

And I didn't know it was only a dress rehearsal, she said.

I'm no good at saving people, she added later, perhaps to herself, perhaps to warn him.

And then it was Chanukah break, she said as her voice grew smaller. My parents and my brother and I were on vacation in Nahariya, we went there every year, to a guesthouse, for the whole holiday. The morning after vacation I went to school and waited for her by the kiosk where we used to meet every morning, and she didn't come, and it was getting late so I walked on my own, and she wasn't in the classroom, and I looked in the playground by our tree, in all our places, and she wasn't there, and the bell rang and she hadn't come, and I thought maybe she was sick, or maybe she was late and she'd be there soon. And then our homeroom teacher came in and we could see that he was confused, and he stood with his body kind of leaning sideways and said, Our Ada . . . And he burst into tears, and we didn't understand what was going on, and a few kids even laughed, because he let out this kind of sob, from his nose . . .

She spoke in rapid whispers. Avram pressed her hand hard between his palms, hurting her, and she didn't pull back.

And then he said she'd been killed in an accident, last night in Ramat Gan. She had a cousin there, she was walking down the street and a bus came, and that was that.

Fast and hot were her breaths on the back of his hand.

And what did you do?

Nothing.

Nothing?

I sat there. I don't remember.

Avram breathed heavily.

There were two books of hers in my backpack. Two *Youth Encyclopedia* volumes I brought to return to her after the vacation, and I kept thinking, What am I going to do with them now?

And that's how you first heard about it? In class?

Yes.

That can't be.

It can.

And what happened afterward?

Don't remember.

And her parents?

What?

What about them?

I don't know what about them.

I'm just thinking, if something like that happened to me, an accident, my mom would probably go crazy, it would kill her.

Ora sat up straight, pulled her hand away and leaned back against the wall.

I don't know . . . they didn't say anything.

But how?

I didn't . . .

I can't hear, come closer.

I didn't talk to them.

At all?

Ever since.

Wait, you mean they were killed, too?

Them? Of course not . . . They live in the same house to this day.

But you said . . . you said you and her, like sisters—

I didn't go there . . .

Her body started to harden. No, no—she let out a cold, foreign shard of laughter. My mother said it would be better not to go, not to make them even sadder. Her eyes began to glaze over. And it's okay that way, believe me, it's for the best, you don't have to talk about everything.

Avram sat quietly. He sniffed.

But we wrote an essay about her in class, every kid wrote something, I did too, and the composition teacher collected them and made a booklet and said she'd send it to her parents. Ora suddenly pressed her fist against her mouth. Why am I even telling you this?

Did she at least have any brothers or sisters? he asked.

No.

Just her?

Yes.

Just her and you.

You don't understand, it's not true what you're . . . They were right!

Who? Who are you talking about?

My parents. Not my dad, my mom, she knows better than anyone about these things. She's from the Holocaust. And I'm sure Ada's parents didn't want me to come either, that's why they never asked me to come. They could have asked me to come, couldn't they?

But you can go to them now.

No, no. And I haven't talked about her with anyone since, and she— Her head was rocking and her whole body shook. No one in class talks about her anymore, ever, two years . . . She started banging her head back against the wall: bang-syllable-bang-syllable. As-if-she-ne-ver-e-ven-was.

Stop, said Avram, and she immediately stopped. She stared straight ahead in the dark. Now they both heard it: somewhere out there, in one of the distant rooms, the nurse was crying. A quiet, prolonged wail.

After a while he asked, What did they do with her chair in class?

Her chair?

Yes.

What do you mean? It stayed there.

Empty?

Yes, of course empty, who would sit in it?

She sat quietly, cautious. She had already begun to suspect earlier that she'd been wrong about him and his cute teddy bear look, which was slightly ridiculous. This wasn't the first time he'd suddenly asked her a seemingly innocent question, which cut into her in a way she only felt later.

Did you keep sitting next to her chair?

Yes . . . No . . . They moved me back. They moved me, I can't remember, three rows behind her seat, but on the side.

Where?

Where what?

Show me, he demanded eagerly, impatiently. Where exactly?

A new, unfamiliar exhaustion began to spread through her, the weakness of total submission. Let's say our desk was here, she mumbled and quickly drew on his hand with her finger, Then around here.

So basically you could see it right in front of you the whole time.

Yes.

But why didn't they put you somewhere else? Maybe closer to the front, so you wouldn't have to keep—

Stop, that's enough, shut up! Can't you ever shut up?!

. . .

Ora—

What now, what do you want?

I was thinking, maybe one day, I don't know . . .

What?

I was just thinking, maybe we'll go and see her parents one day?

Me and you? But how could we?

If I'm ever in Haifa, I don't know, I can come with you, if you'd like.

A desperate little chick began to beat its wings furiously, deep inside Ora's throat.

And her parents have . . . they have a corner store on our street, and we stopped . . .

What, tell me—

Shopping there.

What do you mean you stopped?

My parents, my mom, she said it was better not to.

And you agreed?

So we go around the block . . .

But how do you—

Avram, hold me!

Repelled by her, drawn to her fear, he felt his way with his hands and bumped into knees, then a thin, sharp elbow, a slight curve, hot dry skin, the moisture of a mouth. When he held on to her shoulder she clung to him with her entire body, trembling, and he held her to him and was instantly filled to the brim with her sorrow.

They sat that way, clutching each other frantically. Ora cried with her mouth wide open, with snot, the way a lost little girl cries. Avram smelled her breath, the smell of illness. It's all right, it's all right, he said, caressing her damp head over and over, her sweaty hair, her wet face. They sat crowded together on her bed, and Avram thought it was fine with him if they had been forgotten by everyone. He wouldn't care if it went on like this for another few days. Sometimes his hand stole down of its own accord and touched her warm neck or accidentally slid over her long thin arms with their walnut-like boy-biceps. With all his strength he struggled to remain merely good and kind, but as he did so, against his will, he also labored to gather supplies for his tortuous masturbation travels. Ora's head leaned back a little as if nestling into his hand. A moment like this, Avram calculated through his fog, would last him a good few weeks. But no, leave her alone, he scolded himself. Not her.

Afterward, long afterward, she wiped her nose on her pajama sleeve. You're very kind, you know? You're not like a regular boy.

We starting with insults?

It's good this way. Don't stop.

And this way?

Also.

———

THE NEXT NIGHT—by now she had lost count of the days and nights—Avram pushed a wheelchair into her room. She woke up covered with cold sweat. She'd had the same strange nightmare again, with a metallic voice that crept around her describing horrible scenes. At times she was convinced it was coming from a transistor radio somewhere in the ward, down the corridor or in one of the empty rooms. She had even identified it as "The Voice of Thunder from Cairo," which broadcast in Hebrew—the kids in class could already mimic the flowery Egyptian announcer, with his ridiculous Hebrew mistakes—and at other times she was certain the voice was coming from inside her, telling only her that the Zionist entity had been almost entirely occupied by the glorious Arab armies, who had "taken the enemy underwears." Waves upon waves of courageous Arab warriors are at this moment flooding Beersheba and Ashkelon and Tel Aviv, the voice declared, and Ora continued to lie there with her heart pounding, bathed in sweat. And to think that Ada knew nothing of this, of what was happening to Ora here. And that it was not in Ada's time anymore. What did that mean, not in her time? How could one make sense of the fact that they once shared the same time, and now Ada's time was over, she was no longer in time at all. How could that be?

Then Ora heard the sound of wheels and sharp, wheezing breath. Avram? she murmured. I'm so glad you came, listen to what happened to me . . . Then she realized there were two people breathing, and she sat up in bed, wrapped in her sticky sheets, and stared into the dark.

Look what I brought you, he whispered.

All day she had waited for him to come back and be with her, talk to her, listen to her as if every single word she said was important to him. She missed him stroking her head and the back of her neck with his soft, hypnotic fingers. Soft like a girl's fingers, she thought, or a baby's. During the few lucid moments between the chills and the nightmares, she had tried to reconstruct the nights she had spent here with him and found that she had forgotten almost everything except the boy himself. Even he was difficult to remember. She could not picture him as someone she had seen and known. But she lay for long hours, asleep and awake, imagining his hand caressing her face over and over, strumming her neck. She had never been touched that way, and so few had touched her at all, and how did he know exactly how to do that if he'd never been with a girl that way? And now, amid the surge of kindness she felt toward him, after waiting for him all day so they could lie down together and have one of their talks, he had to make such a crude mistake, such a boy's mistake, like those guys who make rude noises at the movies when there's a kiss on-screen, like coming to her room with this other guy—

Who was asleep in his wheelchair, snoring lightly, and apparently didn't know where he was. Avram maneuvered him into the room, bumped into a cabinet and a bed, and poured forth apologies and explanations: I feel bad leaving him alone in the room all night. Ilan has nightmares, his temperature is forty, maybe higher, he hallucinates all the time, he's scared of dying, and when I leave the room to come to you, Ilan keeps hearing noises of the Arabs winning, horrible things.

He turned Ilan in his wheelchair to face the wall and felt his way over to her. From afar he could already sense her bristling, and with a delicate wisdom that surprised her, he did not get on the bed but sat down meekly on the chair next to her and waited.

She folded her legs in, crossed her arms over her chest, and sat in angry silence. She vowed not to say anything for all eternity, and she soon burst out: I want to go home, I've had it with this place!

But you can't, you're still sick.

I don't care!

You know, Avram said sweetly, he was born in Tel Aviv.

Who?

Him, Ilan.

Good for him.

He just moved to Jerusalem a year ago.

Whoop-di-doo.

His dad was made some kind of commander on an army base here. Colonel, or something like that. And d'you want to hear something funny—

No.

Avram threw a cautious glance to the edge of the room, leaned forward, and whispered, He talks without knowing it.

What d'ya mean?

In his sleep, 'cause of his fever, he babbles on and on.

She leaned forward too and whispered, But, doesn't that . . . that's kind of embarrassing, isn't it?

Wanna hear something else?

Go on.

Normally, we don't speak.

Why not?

Not just me, the whole class, we don't talk to him.

You blackballed him?

No, it's the other way around. He's the one blackballing us.

Wait a minute, one boy is blackballing the whole class?

It's been like that for a year.

And?

I told you, with the fever, he doesn't shut up . . . What?

I don't know. Isn't that a little . . .

I'm bored, so sometimes I . . . I pull him along, you know, and he answers.

In his sleep?

Well, he kind of half understands, not really.

But that's—

What?

I don't know, it's like reading someone's letters, isn't it?

What can I do, put my hands over my ears? And the truth is, also—

What?

When he's awake I really hate him, like at school, but when he's asleep . . .

What then?

It's like a different person. Let's say he talks about his parents, right? About his dad and the army and all that?

Yeah.

So I tell him about my dad and my mom, and how he left us and what I remember about him, that kind of stuff.

Oh.

I tell him the straight truth, everything. So we'll be even.

Ora adjusted her position and covered herself with a blanket. For the last few moments his voice had contained a shadowed hint, and a slight tension grabbed at her calves.

Like yesterday, Avram said, after I got back from you in the early morning, he was talking feverishly, and he told stories about a girl he saw on the street, he was too embarrassed to talk to her, afraid she wouldn't be interested . . . Avram giggled. So I did, too.

Did what?

Don't worry, he doesn't take in anything anyway.

Wait a minute, what did you tell him?

What you and me, you know, and what you told me, about Ada—

What?

But he was asleep . . .

But those are things I told *you*! Those are private things, my secrets!

Yes, but he didn't even—

Have you lost your mind? Can't you keep anything to yourself? Not even for two seconds?

No.

No?!

She jumped out of bed, forgetting her weakness, and dashed around the room. She moved away from him in disgust, and from the other one, who was asleep with his head drooping on his chest, exhaling fervent breaths.

Ora, don't . . . Wait, listen to me, when I got back from you I was so . . .

So *what?* she yelled, feeling her temples exploding.

I, I didn't have any . . . space in my body, 'cause I was so—

But a secret! A secret! It's the most basic thing, isn't it?

Ora came close and lunged over him as she wagged her finger, and he shrank back a little. This is exactly what I thought of you the whole time, it's all connected!

What, what's connected?

The fact that you're not in any youth movement and you don't play any sport, and all that philosophizing, and that you don't have a group of friends—you don't, do you?

But what does that have to do with it?

I knew it! And the fact that you, you're such a . . . such a *Jerusalemite*!

She leaped back on her bed and pulled the blankets up over her face, and kept on simmering there, in the depths. There's no way she's ever telling him another word about herself. She thought she could trust him, that's what she thought. How did she even let herself be tempted by a pathetic loser like him? Come on, get out of here! Get out of here, d'you hear me? Split, I want to sleep.

Wait, that's it?

And don't come back! Ever!

Okay, he mumbled. Well . . . good night.

What do you mean good night?! Are you leaving him here for me?

What? Oh, sorry, I forgot.

He got up and felt his way over, slow and hunched.

Wait a minute!

What now?

First tell me what you told him. I want to know exactly what you told him!

You want me to tell you now?

D'you have a better time in mind? Should we wait for the Messiah?

But it doesn't come out just like that . . . Listen, I have to sit down.

Why?

Because I don't have the strength.

She considered. Sit down, but just for a minute.

She heard him walk back heavily, bumping into the corner of her bed, cursing and feeling with his hand until he found his chair and collapsed into it. She heard Ilan breathe fleetingly and sigh in his sleep. She tried to guess his voice from his sighs and the way he looked in the dark. She wondered what he already knew about her.

Somewhere out there an ambulance siren wailed. Echoes of distant explosions erupted. Ora exhaled with her lips pursed. A commotion was brewing in her head. She had already recognized that her anger at him was exaggerated, and maybe it was even a show of anger, and she tried to protect herself from the treacherous affection rising within her. She was alarmed to realize how distant she had grown from all the people she loved and cared for. She had hardly thought of Asher Feinblatt all these days in the hospital. She had boycotted him, and her parents and her friends from school. As if her entire world were now the illness and the fever and the stomach and the itching. And Avram, whom she hadn't known until three or four days ago. How did that happen? How had she forgotten everyone? Where had she been this whole time and what had she dreamed?

A new chill iced over her burning skin. Avram slept across the way and sighed shortly, and Ilan at the other end of the room was sleeping in total silence now. She felt as though they were both slightly letting go of her so she could finally comprehend something hugely important that was happening to her. She sat upright in bed and wrapped her arms around her knees and felt as if she were being slowly cut out from the picture of her life, and a faded hole would remain in the place where Ora used to be.

Into her thoughts, into the sleepy rustle that took hold of her, stole a dim, hoarse voice, and at first she did not recognize it as Avram's, and she thought maybe the other one, his psycho friend, had started talking to himself, and she tensed up. From the minute I saw you with the match in your hand I thought I could tell you anything on my mind. But you'll get annoyed at me, I know it, you're a firebrand redhead, with a quick temper, a short fuse, I can tell. You know what, if you get annoyed then kick me. She's not kicking me, maybe she's on a kicking fast today, maybe she joined some order that forbids kicking helpless runts? There, she smiled just now. I can see her mouth even in the dark. What a great mouth she has—

He waited. Ora swallowed. A new layer of sweat erupted from her body at once. She pulled the blanket up higher over her face so that only her eyes glimmered in the dark. She didn't kick this time either, Avram noted, which must mean she's letting me tell her, for example— he hesitated, it was suddenly too close; let's see you, coward, sissy—for example, I can tell her that she's so beautiful, the most beautiful girl I've ever seen, even here in the hospital, with the fever and the illness. And from the moment I saw her, even though it was dark, I felt the whole time that she was light, something bright, pure . . . And she showed me herself with the match, and then she closed her eyes and her eyelashes trembled . . . The more he spoke, the more excited Avram grew. He was burning and erect from his boldness. Ora's heart beat so hard she thought she would pass out. If any of her friends, boys or girls, didn't matter, saw her like this, listening silently to all this talk, they wouldn't believe it. This is cynical Ora? This is bullheaded Ora?

And she shouldn't go thinking I'm such a big hero, Avram added hoarsely. I've never talked to a girl like this, only in my imagination. He held two fists up to his cheeks and focused on the burning embers glowing in his gut. I've never had the chance to be so close to someone so beautiful. I'm just noting that for the minutes, because she's probably thinking, Oh, here's another one of those lookers who has all the girls falling at his feet. Ora stuck out her chin and pursed her lips, but a dimple of laughter was twitching in her cheek. What a strange person, she thought. You can never tell if he's serious or joking, or if he's very smart or a total idiot. He keeps changing. She wiped the sweat off her brow with the blanket and thought that the most annoying thing about him, the truly insufferable thing, which could really drive a person mad, was that he seemed to be constantly stuck under your skin and you couldn't get a second's break from him, because from the moment he had come and sat down next to her two days ago, or whenever it was, she had known exactly when he was excited and when he was happy or sad, and above all she had known when he wanted her. He had such a nerve, he was a pickpocket, a spy—and a tiny eel slithered inside her like a little tongue, supple and flushed, not hers at all, where had it come from? And Ora jumped up in fright: Come here! Stand here for a minute!

What . . . what happened?

Get up!

But what did I do?

Shut up. Turn around!

They felt their way through the darkness until they were standing back to back. They shivered from the fever and other ardors, and their bodies twitched and danced against each other. Ilan sighed, and Avram thought, What lousy timing, please don't wake up on me now. He felt her muscular calves against his own, her springy rear end touching his. After that things got off track: his shoulders were somewhere down there against her back. His head rested against the back of her neck. You're a head taller than me, he noted lightly, himself amazed at such a cruel realization of his fears. But we're still at that age, she said softly, and turned to face him. Despite the darkness, she could see his face and his huge, exaggerated eyes, which showered her with sad, yearning looks, and she quickly looked for Ada to hand her a trace of mockery to hold on to, to unravel his image and his entirety, and generally this whole place, along with the guy drilling a hole in her head from the other side of the room. But her heart was tensing in anticipation of bad news.

Hey, she whispered weakly, can you see me? Yes, he murmured. How come we can see now? she wondered, afraid she might be hallucinating again. He laughed. She examined him suspiciously. What's funny? That you won't let me say bad things about myself. It was when he laughed that his face changed. He had nice teeth, bright and evenly spaced, and nice lips. The whole mouth area, Ora thought feebly, is like someone else's. If a girl ever kisses him, she'll probably shut her eyes, and then she'll just have his mouth. Can you make do with just a mouth? Stupid thought. Her knees felt a little shaky. She was going to fall. This illness was doing her in. Making a rag out of her. She grabbed on to his pajama sleeve and almost fell on him. Her face was close to his, and had he tried to kiss her she would not have had the strength to pull away.

And I want to tell her about her voice, Avram said, because the voice is the most important thing for me, always, even before a girl's appearance. She has a voice that no one I know has, an orange voice, I swear, don't laugh, with a little bit of lemon-yellow around the edges, and it has a spring, it has a pounce. And if she wants me to, I can describe to her right now on the spot something I'd love to write for her one day, and interestingly she isn't saying no . . .

Yes, Ora whispered.

Avram swallowed and shivered. I think it will be a piece for voices, he said. Just voices. I've been thinking about it for a few days, since we started talking, and here's how it will start: there are fourteen notes, you see. Single notes, one after the other, human voices. Human voices are my favorite. There is no lovelier sound in the world, is there?

Yeah? So do you, do you make . . . music?

No, not exactly music, it's more a combination of . . . never mind. Voices, that's what interests me now, in these years.

Oh, said Ora.

But why fourteen? he asked in a whisper, deliberating with himself as if Ora were not in the room. There are fourteen voices when I hear it, but why? He mumbled to himself: I don't know. That's how I feel it. It will start with one long note, you see? A kind of "Ah . . . ," for six beats, and only after it disappears the other voice will start: "Ah . . ." Like ships sailing in the fog, blowing their horns at one another. Have you ever heard that?

No . . . Yes, I'm from Haifa.

And it will be sad. He inhaled through his teeth, and she felt it: all of him, in the blink of an eye, immersed in that sadness, and the whole world was the sadness now, and she too, involuntarily, felt a bitter, heart-sucking sorrow lapping inside her.

She said, Maybe it's because of Ada?

What is?

Because she was, I told you, she was fourteen when—

What?

The notes, like you said, how there are fourteen notes.

Oh, wait—one for each year?

Could be.

You mean—a farewell to each one of her years?

Something like that.

That's nice. That's really . . . I hadn't thought of that. One for each year.

But you came up with it, she laughed, it's funny how impressed you are with it.

But you're the one, Avram smiled, you're the one who showed me what I came up with.

———

YOU INSPIRE ME, Ada used to say with her childish gravity. And Ora would laugh: Me? I inspire you? I'm just a bear of very little brain! And Ada—she was thirteen then, Ora remembers, one year from her death, and how horrifying it is to realize how ignorant she was of that, how she went about her business and did everything as usual and never guessed, but still, deep inside she seemed to be growing more profound, more mature, and more solid that year—Ada took hold of Ora's hand and swung it back and forth with enthusiasm and gratitude and said, You, yes, you. It's like you just sit there quietly, but then you throw out a single word or ask one small question, like it's nothing, and bang! Everything falls into place in my mind and all of a sudden I know exactly what I wanted to say. Oh, Ora, what would I do without you? How could I live without you?

She remembers: they looked into each other's eyes. One year, dear God.

Alive and sharp, this memory was almost intolerable now: Ada reading to her from her notebook stories and poems that she had written, using voices and gestures, and sometimes costumes, with hats and scarves, acting out the different characters, and crying with them and laughing. Her rosy, freckled face is flushed as if flames are leaping inside her head and peeking through her eyes. Ora sits opposite her with her legs crossed, watching wide-eyed.

When Ada finished reading, she was often exhausted and lost and gaping, and Ora would quickly pull herself together. Now it was her turn: to hug, to encircle, to bandage Ada, not to leave her for even a moment without Ora's hand.

And I keep asking myself whether she has a boyfriend, Avram said to himself from somewhere in the distance, in his throaty, daydreaming voice. I know she said she didn't, but how could that be? A girl like that wouldn't be alone for a minute, the guys in Haifa aren't stupid. He paused and waited for her answer. She said nothing. Doesn't she want to tell me about her boyfriend? Or does she really not have one? She doesn't have one, Ora said quietly. How come? Avram whispered. She doesn't know, Ora said after a long pause, unwillingly seduced by his style and finding that it was actually more comfortable to talk about herself this way. She didn't even want a boyfriend at all for a long time, she said, inadvertently playing her words to the slow, tense beat of the pulsations coming from the edge of the room. And then there just wasn't anyone right, I mean, really right for her.

And hasn't she ever loved anyone? Avram asked. Ora did not answer, and in the dark he thought she was sinking deeper into herself, her long neck bending painfully down toward her shoulder, toward the distant side of the room, as if she too were now seized by a tyrannical power like the one gripping his own body. So she did love someone, said Avram, and Ora shook her head. No, no, she just thought she did, but now she knows she didn't. It was nothing, she mumbled despairingly, just a waste. She felt that as soon as she started to tell him about Asher, the truth would rush out in a huge, roiling torrent, the truth of those two years of nothingness, and nothing could be turned back anymore, and she was frightened by how much she wanted to, burned to tell him.

Wait a minute, he whispered suddenly from the doorway, I'll be back in a minute. What? Where are you? Ora was distraught. What are you doing leaving me now? Just for a minute, he said, I'll be right back.

With his last remaining strength he pulled himself away and left the room. Leaning on the corridor walls, he dragged himself on, far away from her, and every few steps he stopped and shook his head and said to himself, Go back, go back now, but he kept uprooting himself until he got to his room, and he sat down on his bed.

She called out to him a few times, first shouting, then softly, but he did not come back. The nurse came and stood in the doorway, demanding to know what Ora was shouting about. A bitter coil wound through her voice. When she was gone, Ora lay terrified and tried to fall asleep, to dive under reason and thoughts, but the illness was playing tricks on her mind. Tendrils of wild dreams climbed up and grabbed hold of her. The air filled again with the thundering metallic voices and military music. I'm dreaming, Ora mumbled, it's just a dream. She covered her ears and the voice that spoke Hebrew in a thick Arab accent echoed inside her head, orating about the glorious Syrian army's tanks that were trampling the Zionist Galilee and the criminal Zionist kibbutzim, and they were on their way to liberate Haifa and obliterate the shame of the '48 expulsion. Ora knew she had to escape, to save herself, but she could not find the strength. Suddenly she was completely awake and sat upright in bed, holding the matchbox like a shield against her face, because she thought someone at the end of the room was moving and calling weakly, Ora, Ora, talking to her in his sleep in an unfamiliar boy's voice.

———

LATER, who knows how much later, Avram came back with his and Ilan's blankets. He came into her room without a word, covered Ilan, swaddled him on all sides, and tucked the blankets under him. Then he sat down and covered himself and waited for Ora to say it.

She said: I don't ever want to talk to you again. You're messed up. Get out of my life.

He said nothing.

She was furious. I swear, you're such a loser!

What did I do?

"What did I do?" Where did you disappear to?

I just popped over to my room.

"Popped over to my room"! Speedy Gonzales! Leaving me here alone and disappearing for hours—

What are you talking about, hours? Maybe half an hour, tops, and anyway you're not alone.

Shut up. You'd better just shut up!

He shut up. She touched her lips. She thought they were on fire.

Just tell me one thing.

What?

What did you say his name was?

Ilan. Why? Was there . . . did something happen here while I was gone?

What could happen? You left and came right back, what—

I left and came right back? Now it's "You left and came right back"?

Stop it, get off my case.

Wait, did he talk? Did he say something in his sleep?

Look, what are you, the Shabak?

Did you turn the light on?

None of your business.

I knew it, I just knew it!

So you knew, you're a genius. So if you knew, why did you leave just when I—

And you saw him.

Okay, I saw him, I saw him! So what?

So nothing.

Avram?

What—

Is he really very sick?

Yes.

I think he's sicker than both of us.

Yes.

Do you think he's . . . I don't know, in danger?

What do I know?

Ahh, Ora sighed from the depths of her heart, I wish I could fall asleep now for a month, a year, *ach*!

Ora?

What?

He's good-looking, isn't he?

I don't know, I didn't look.

Admit that he's good-looking.

Not exactly my taste.

He's like an angel.

Yeah, all right, I get the point.

The girls at school are crazy about him.

Tell it to someone who cares.

Did you talk to him?

He was asleep, like I said! He can't hear a thing.

I meant—did you talk *to* him? Did you tell him anything?

Leave me alone, won't you just leave me alone!

Ora?

What?

Did he open his eyes? Did he see you?

I can't hear you, I'm not hearing anything, *la-la-la-la—*

But did he say anything? Did he talk to you?

". . . *On a wagon bound for market, there's a calf with a mournful eye . . .*"

Just tell me if he spoke.

". . . *High above him there's a swallow, winging swiftly through the sky . . .*"

Wait, isn't that the song?

What?

That's the song, I swear. From when you woke me up.

Are you sure?

Except then you were screaming it so loudly I couldn't even make out—

That's the song . . .

A calf with a mournful eye, yes, "Dona Dona." But you were shouting it, like you were fighting with someone, arguing.

Ora could feel herself lift up out of her own body and float to a distant place that was not a place, where she and Ada walked together and sang Ada's favorite song, and it was Ada's mother's favorite song too, and sometimes, when she washed the dishes, she would sing it to herself in Yiddish. The song about a calf being led to the slaughter, and a swallow that flies up in the sky and mocks him, then flutters away with lighthearted joy.

Avram, Ora said suddenly in horror, leave now, leave!

What did I do now?

Go! And take him with you! I have to sleep now, quick. I want to—

What?

I have to dream her . . .

Later, just before dawn, she suddenly appeared in the doorway of Room Three and called to him in a whisper. He jumped awake: What are you doing here? She said sadly, I've never met anyone like you, and then corrected herself: Any boy like you. He was hunched over, extinguished, and he murmured, So, did you dream about her? Ora mumbled, No, I couldn't sleep. I wanted to so badly that I couldn't. And he asked, But why did you want to? What was so . . . ? She said, I have to tell her something important.

Ora, said Avram tiredly and without any pleasure, Do you want to see him again? She said, Do you have a screw loose or something? I'm talking about you, and all you keep doing is showing me *him*. Why are you, like, purposely— Honestly, I don't know, he said. I'm always like that, it just comes out. And she said desperately, I don't understand anything anymore, I don't understand anything.

They sat hunched in the dark, suddenly very ill. From one moment to the next the burden of bad tidings swelled inside him. What a mistake he had made, what a terrible, destructive complication he had caused by leaving her alone with Ilan.

There's something else I wanted to tell you, he said hopelessly, but you're probably not interested, are you? She asked carefully, something like what? But even before he spoke she knew what he would say, and her body locked up against him. No one knows that I write, he said. I write all the time.

But what, what do you write? Her voice sounded oddly piercing to her own ears. Essays? Limericks? Tall tales? What?

I write all kinds of things, Avram said with slight arrogance. Once, when I was little, I used to make up stories, all the time. Now I write totally different things . . . I don't understand, she hissed, you just sit there and write, for yourself? A desolate revulsion enveloped him. He wanted her to leave. To come back. To be who she was before. The thing that had been woven between them the last few nights, the wonder, the delicate secret cooled and faded away at once. And perhaps it had never existed at all, perhaps it had only been in his head, along with everything else.

Just explain to me, she urged him, suddenly eager for battle, what you mean by "I write totally different things"? But Avram sank into himself, amazed at the sting of betrayal. Ora mumbled stubbornly, And limericks are fun! Let me tell you, they are the ultimate entertainment! She recalled the way he had said earlier that in these years he was interested in voices—"in these years"! From which she was apparently supposed to conclude that in previous years he had been interested in other things, that snob, as if he already knew that in "the next years"—ha!— he would have yet other interests. Smart aleck. But she, she, where had she been "in these years"? What had she wasted herself on? All she'd done was cheat everyone and sleep with her eyes open. That was her big accomplishment. A cheating pro, sleepwalking champion of the world. She slept when she ran and did high jumps and played volleyball, and most of all when she swam, because it was a lot less painful in water than on land. She slept when she went with the team to the stadium in Ein Iron on Saturdays, and sometimes they went to the Maccabi courts in Tel Aviv, and in the back of the truck she roared cheers at the passersby along with everyone else.

She slept while she sang her heart out on hikes, and on the night trek to the beach at Atlit, and at the Machanot Olim all-nighter, and when they all took turns jumping onto a canvas held by the team, and when she did the zip line, and helped build a rope bridge and set up the fire displays. She didn't think about anything when that was going on. Her hands moved, her legs moved, her mouth babbled constantly, she was all noise and bells, but her brain was empty and desolate, her body a desert wilderness.

And together with Miri S. and Orna and Shiffi, her new friends after Ada, she was once again brimming with funny songs and operettas for parties and trips, everything just like it was before. Life really did go on.

It was almost ungraspable how it did. Her body kept making the usual moves—she ate and drank and walked, she stood and sat and slept and crapped and even laughed—it was just that for the whole first year she couldn't feel her toes, sometimes for hours on end, and sometimes she couldn't feel the skin on the back of her left hand, either. There were places on her thigh and her back too, and when she touched them, even scratched them softly, she couldn't feel a thing. Once she held a burning match to the dead spot on her thigh and watched the fair skin singe and smelled the burning, but she did not feel any pain. She didn't tell anyone about that. Who could she talk to about things like that?

There's a hole, she thinks now, and feels cold and chilled. It's been there for a long time. How could I not have seen it? Ever since Ada there's an Ora-shaped hole where I used to be.

She coughed and sprang back to life. She must have fallen asleep in the middle of fighting with Avram. What were they fighting about? What was it about him that got to her? Or maybe they'd already made up? In the darkness she guessed at Avram's sprawled figure on the other end of the bed, leaning on the wall, snoring heavily. Was this his room or hers? And where was Ilan?

He had told her he was going to die. He knew it would happen, knew it had to happen. From the age of zero he'd known he wouldn't live long, because he didn't have enough life energy inside him. That's what he said, and she tried to calm him, to erase his strange words, but he didn't hear her, maybe didn't even know she was there. He shamelessly cried over his life, which had been ruined since his parents divorced and his father took him to his army base to live with all the animals there. Everything had been screwed up since then, he wailed, and the illness was just a natural extension of all that shit. He was burning, and half of what he said she couldn't understand. Fragments of mutterings and whispers. So she just stood very close to him, bathed in his warmth, and carefully stroked his shoulder. Every so often she stroked his back too, and sometimes, with a pounding heart, she quickly slid her hand over his thick hair, and as she did so she realized she didn't even know what he looked like, and perhaps she even vaguely imagined that he looked a lot like Avram, simply because they had both come into her life together. She kept telling him the things Avram said to her when she was afraid or miserable. Thanks to Avram, that idiot, she knew what to say. Ilan suddenly grasped her hand, squeezed it hard, and glided over her arm from one end to the other. She was taken aback but did not pull her hand away, and he leaned his cheek against her, and his forehead, and held her arm to his chest, and suddenly he kissed her, showering dry, burning little kisses on her arm, her fingers, the palm of her hand, and his head burrowed into her body, and Ora stood speechless, looked into the dark over his head, and thought wondrously: He's kissing me, he doesn't even know he's kissing me. Ilan laughed suddenly to himself, laughed and shivered, and said that sometimes, at night, he snuck out and wrote on the walls of the army base huts: "The Commander's Son Is a Fag." His father went crazy when he saw the graffiti and walked around with a bucket of whitewash, and lay in wait to ambush whoever was doing it—but I'm warning you, bro, don't you ever tell anyone, Ilan giggled and shivered. I'm only telling you this. He talked in a hoarse voice about the fat soldier his father was screwing in his office, and how the whole base could hear her, but even that was better than when my parents were together, he said, at least that nightmare is over. I'll never get married, he groaned, and his forehead burned against her chest until it hurt, and she pressed him to her and thought he sounded like someone who really hadn't spoken to anyone for a whole year. He laughed and buried his face in the crook of Ora's arm and inhaled her scent. I'm crazy about the smell in that music shop on Allenby, he said. It's the sweet smell of glue—they use it to stick the plastic pads that plug the saxophone holes. He told her that a year ago he found a used Selmer Paris in good condition there. In Tel Aviv I had a band, he said. We used to sit around on Fridays listening to new records all night long, learning about John Coltrane, Charlie Parker, making Tel Aviv jazz.

His body heat trickled into her. She was overcome by a paralyzing awe of the burning boy leaning on her arm. She wouldn't mind if this went on for a while, even until morning, even a whole day. I want to help him, she thought, I want to, I want to. Her body was prickling with desire, even her feet were burning. She hadn't felt these kinds of currents for so long, and Ilan found her other hand and placed her palms on his closed eyes, and said he knew how to always be happy.

Happy? Ora choked and pulled her hand back for a second, as if burned. How?

I have a method, he said. I just break myself up into all kinds of areas, and if I feel bad in one part of my soul, I skip to another part. His breath licked at her wrists, and she felt his eyelashes tickle her palms.

I just spread out the risks that way, said Ilan, and he put his head back and gave a dry, tortured laugh. No one can hurt me, I skip, I—

In mid-sentence his head drooped and he was swallowed up, exhausted, in a deep slumber. His fingers loosened and slid down her arms until they dropped on his lap, and his head plunged forward.

Ora stood, struck a match, and lit up Ilan's face for the first time. With his eyes closed, and within the circle of light, his face was a drop of beauty. She lit another match and he kept mumbling, fighting with someone in his dream, and he shook his head hard, and his face flinched with anger, perhaps because of the blinding light, perhaps because of what he saw in his mind's eye. His dark, rich eyebrows coiled sternly toward each other, and Ora forgot herself as she stood there and lit up his clear forehead, the shape of his eyes, his gorgeous lips, warm and slightly cracked, which even now still burned on her own.

———

SHE SWORE HERSELF to silence. Anything she said would be a mistake anyway, it would give Avram further proof of her stupidity and superficiality. If only she had the strength to get herself up from his bed and go back to her room and forget him forever, and *the other one*.

I got on your nerves, she said.

It doesn't matter.

But you . . . why did you run away? Why did you run away on me just when—

I don't know, I don't know. I just suddenly—

Avram?

What?

Let's go back to my room. We're better there.

Should we leave him here?

Yes, come on, come on . . .

Careful, otherwise we'll both fall.

Walk slowly, my head is spinning.

Lean on me.

Can you hear her?

She can go on like that for hours.

I dreamed about her before. Something really frightening, I was terrified of her.

Such sobbing—

Listen, it's like she's singing to herself.

Mourning.

Tell me, she said later, when they were in her bed.

What?

Will you write one of your . . .

My limericks? My tall tales?

Ha-ha. Your *stories*. Do you think you'll write about this hospital?

Maybe, I don't know. I actually had one idea, but it's already—

About what? Tell me . . .

Avram sat up with effort and leaned on the wall. He had given up trying to understand her and her reversals, but like a kitten with a ball of
yarn, he could not resist a "tell me."

It's about a boy lying in a hospital, in the middle of a war, and he goes
up onto the rooftop and he has a box of matches—

Like me—

Yes, not exactly. Because this boy, with the matches, in the middle of
the blackout he starts signaling enemy planes.

What is he, crazy?

No. He wants them to come and bomb him, personally.

But why?

I don't know that yet. That's as far as I've thought.

Is he really that miserable?

Yes.

Ora thought Avram had gotten the idea from what Ilan had told him.
She didn't dare ask. Instead she said, It's a little scary.

Really? Say more.

She thought about it and felt the rusty wheels start to turn in her
brain. Avram seemed to sense them too, and waited silently.

She said, I'm thinking about him. He's on the roof. He lights match
after match, right?

Yes, he said, and stretched out.

And he looks at the sky, in all directions, waiting for them to come, the airplanes. He doesn't know where they'll come from. Right?

Right, right.

Maybe these are the last moments of his life. He's terribly frightened, but he has to keep waiting for them. That's how he is, stubborn and brave, right?

Yeah?

Yes, and to me he looks like the loneliest person in the world at that moment.

I didn't think about that, Avram said with an awkward giggle. I didn't think about his loneliness at all.

If he had even one friend, he wouldn't do it, would he?

Yeah, he wouldn't—

Maybe you could make someone for him?

Why?

So he'll have . . . I don't know, a friend, someone who can be with him.

They sat quietly. She could hear him thinking. A rustling, rapid trickle. She liked the sound.

And Avram?

What?

Do you think you'll ever write about me?

I don't know.

I'm afraid to talk, so you don't go writing down all my nonsense.

Like what?

Just remember that if I talk nonsense here it's because of the fever, okay?

But I don't write things exactly the way they happen.

Of course, you make things up too, that's the whole fun, right? What will you make up about me?

Wait a minute, do you write, too?

Me? No way! I don't, no. But tell me straight—

What?

Weren't you planning to call me Ada in the story?

How did you know?

I knew, she said, and hugged herself. And I agree. Call me Ada.

No.

What do you mean no?

I'll call you Ora.

Really?

Ora, said Avram, tasting the name, and the sweetness poured through his mouth and his whole body. O-ra.

Something was flowing inside her, some ancient, measured knowledge: He is an artist. That's it, he was an artist. And she knew what it was like with artists. She had experience with them. She hadn't used it for a long time, but now it was filling her up again. And she'd get better, she'd beat the illness, she suddenly knew for sure, she had female intuition.

She closed her eyes and a slight shock of pleasure hit her as she wondered how, in a moment's urge, she had been emboldened to lean over a strange boy and kiss him on his lips for a long time. She had kissed and kissed and kissed. And now, when she finally dared to remember without holding back, she felt the kiss itself, her first kiss, seeping into her, awakening her, trickling into each of her cells, churning her blood. What will happen now? she wondered. Which of the two will I . . . But her heart was surprisingly light and cheerful.

The truth is, I also write a little, she confessed to her complete surprise.

You do?

Not seriously, nothing like you, never mind, I just said that. She tried to shut up but could not. They're not really songs, never mind, honestly, just hiking songs, for trips and camps, nonsense, you know, of the limerick family.

Oh, that. He smiled with odd sadness, retreating into a sort of politeness that pinched at her. You should sing me something.

She shook her head vigorously. No way, are you mad? Never.

Because even though she knew him so little, she could already tell exactly how she would feel when her rhymes echoed inside his head, with all his twisted, snobbish ideas. But it was that thought that made her want to sing—what did she have to be embarrassed about?

So you want to penetrate the profound hidden meaning of the lyrics? She flashed him a deliberate smile. This is something I wrote ages ago, she said. We wrote it together, Ada and I, for the last day of camp at Machanayim. We had a treasure hunt, everyone got lost, don't ask.

I won't, he smiled.

Then do.

What did you tell Ilan?

You'll never know.

Did you kiss him?

What? What did you say? She was horrified.

You heard me.

Maybe he kissed *me*? She raised her eyebrows and wiggled them mischievously, a shameless Ursula Andress. Now be quiet and listen. It's to the tune of "Tadarissa Boom," d'you know it?

Of course I do, said Avram, suspicious and enchanted, squirming with unforeseen delight.

Ora sang, drumming the beat on her thigh:

> We set off on a treasure hunt, *Tadarissa Boom*,
> Our counselor was a real hunk, *Tadarissa Boom*,
> He said he'd help us find the way, *Tadarissa Boom*,
> And not get lost or go astray—

Tadarissa Boom, Avram hummed quietly, and Ora gave him a look, and a new smile, soft and budding, lit her up inside and her face glowed in the dark, and he thought she was a pure and innocent person, incapable of pretending, unlike him. "The most innocent of its creatures," he recalled. I am happy, he thought with wonder. I want her, I want her to be mine, always, forever. His thoughts skipped, as usual, to the brink of possibilities, a lovesick dreamer: She'll be my wife, the love of my life—

Second verse, she announced:

We solved the clues and found the prize—

Tadarissa Boom, Avram sang in a thick voice and drummed on his own thigh, and sometimes, distractedly, on hers.

But no one cared except the guys—

Tadarissa Boom.

'Cause when the counselor looked at us—

Tadarissa Boom!

He made us swoon and blinded us!

Wait. Avram put his hand on her arm. Quiet, someone's coming.

I can't hear it.

It's him.

Coming here? Is he coming here from the room?

I can't understand it. He's barely alive.

What should we do, Avram?

He's crawling! Listen, he's dragging himself along with his arms.

Take him away from here, take him back!

What's the big deal, Ora, let him sit with us for a while.

No, I don't want to, not now.

Wait a minute. Hey, Ilan? Ilan, come on, it's here, a little farther.

I'm telling you, I'll leave.

Ilan, it's Avram, from class. I'm here with Ora. Go on, tell him—

Tell him what?

Tell him something—

Ilan . . . ? It's me, Ora.

Ora?

Yes.

You mean, you're real?

Of course, Ilan, it's me. Come on in here with us, we'll be together for a while.

The Walk, 2000

THE CONVOY twists along, a stammering band of civilian cars, jeeps, military ambulances, tanks, and huge bulldozers on the backs of transporters. Her taxi driver is quiet and gloomy. His hand rests on the Mercedes's gear shift and his thick neck does not move. For several long minutes he has looked neither at her nor at Ofer.

As soon as Ofer sat down in the cab, he let out an angry breath and flashed a look that said: Not the smartest idea, Mom, asking this particular driver to come along on a trip like this. Only then did she realize what she'd done. At seven that morning she had called Sami and asked him to come pick her up for a long drive to the Gilboa region. Now she remembers that for some reason she hadn't given him any details or explained the purpose of the trip, the way she usually did. Sami had asked when she wanted him, and she'd hesitated and then said, "Come at three." "Ora," he'd said, "maybe we should leave earlier, 'cause traffic will be a mess." That was his only acknowledgment of the day's madness, but even then she didn't get it and just said there was no way she could leave before three. She wanted to spend these hours with Ofer, and although Ofer agreed, she could tell how much effort his concession took. Seven or eight hours were all that was left of the weeklong trip she'd planned for the two of them, and now she realizes she hadn't even told Sami on the phone that Ofer was part of the ride. Had she told him, he might have asked her to let him off today, just this one time, or he might have sent one of the Jewish drivers who worked for him—"my Jewish sector," he called them. But when she'd called him she'd been in a state of complete frenzy, and it simply had not occurred to her—the unease slowly rises in her chest—that for this sort of drive, on a day like this, it was better not to call an Arab driver.

Even if he is an Arab from here, one of ours, Ilan prods at her brain as she tries to justify her own behavior. Even if it's Sami, who's almost one of the family, who's been driving everyone—the people who work for Ilan, her estranged husband, and the whole family—for more than twenty years. They are his main livelihood, his regular monthly income, and he, in return, is obliged to be at their service around the clock, whenever they need him. They have been to his home in Abu Ghosh for family celebrations, they know his wife, Inaam, and they helped out with connections and money when his two older sons wanted to emigrate to Argentina. They've racked up hundreds of driving hours together, and she cannot recall his ever being this silent. With him, every drive is a stand-up show. He's witty and sly, a political dodger who shoots in all directions with decoys and double-edged swords, and besides, she cannot imagine calling another driver. Driving herself is out of the question for the next year: she's had three accidents and six moving violations in the past twelve months, an excessive crop even by her standards, and the loathsome judge who revoked her license had hissed that he was doing her a favor and that she really owed him her life. It would have all been so easy if she herself were driving Ofer. At least she'd have had another ninety minutes alone with him, and maybe she'd even have tempted him to stop on the way—there are some good restaurants in Wadi Ara. After all, one hour more, one hour less, what's the rush? Why are you in such a hurry? Tell me, what is it that's waiting for you there?

A trip alone with him will not happen anytime soon, nor alone with herself, and she has to get used to this constraint. She has to let it go, stop grieving every day for her robbed independence. She should be happy that at least she has Sami, who kept driving her even after the separation from Ilan. She hadn't been capable of thinking about those kinds of details at the time, but Ilan had put his foot down. Sami was an explicit clause in their separation agreement, and he himself said he was divvied up between them like the furniture and the rugs and the silverware. "Us Arabs," he would laugh, revealing a mouth full of huge teeth, "ever since the partition plan we're used to you dividing us up." The memory of his joke makes her cringe with the shame of what has happened today, of having somehow, in the general commotion, completely erased that part of him, his Arabness.

Since seeing Ofer this morning with the phone in his hand and the guilty look on his face, someone had come along and gently but firmly taken the management of her own affairs out of her hands. She had been dismissed, relegated to observer status, a gawking witness. Her thoughts were no more than flashes of emotion. She hovered through the rooms of the house with angular, truncated motions. Later they went to the mall to buy clothes and candy and CDs—there was a new Johnny Cash collection out—and all morning she walked beside him in a daze and giggled like a girl at everything he said. She devoured him with gaping wide looks, stocking up unabashedly for the endless years of hunger to come—of course they would come. From the moment he told her he was going, she had no doubt. Three times that morning she excused herself and went to the public restrooms, where she had diarrhea. Ofer laughed: "What's up with you? What did you eat?" She stared at him and smiled feebly, engraving in her mind the sound of his laughter, the slight tilt of his head when he laughed.

The young cashier at the clothing store blushed as she watched him try on a shirt, and Ora thought proudly, *My beloved is like a young hart.* The girl working at the music store was one year behind him at school, and when she heard where he was going in three hours, she went over and hugged him, held him close with her tall, ample body, and insisted that he call her as soon as he got back. Seeing how blind her son was to these displays of emotion, it occurred to Ora that his heart was still bound to Talia. It had been a year since she'd left him, and she was still all he could see. She thought sadly that he was a loyal person, like her, and far more monogamous than she, and who knew how many years would pass before he got over Talia—if he even had any years left, she thought. She quickly erased the notion, scrubbing it furiously from her brain with both hands, but still a picture slipped through: Talia coming to visit them, to condole, perhaps to seek a sort of retroactive forgiveness from Ora, and she felt her face strain with anger. How could you hurt him like that? she thought, and she must have mumbled something out loud, because Ofer leaned down and asked softly, "What is it, Mom?" For a moment she did not see his face before her eyes—he had no face, her eyes stared into a void, pure terror. "Nothing. I was thinking about Talia. Have you talked to her recently?" Ofer waved his hand and said, "Forget that, it's over."

She kept checking the time. On her watch, on his, on the big clocks in the mall, on the television screens in appliance stores. Time was behaving strangely, sometimes flying, at other times crawling or coming to a complete standstill. It seemed to her that it might not even require much effort to roll it back, not too far, just thirty minutes or an hour at a time would be fine. The big things—time, destiny, God—could sometimes be worn down by petty haggling. They drove downtown to have lunch at a restaurant in the *shuk*, where they ordered lots of dishes although neither of them had an appetite. He tried to amuse her with stories from the checkpoint near Tapuach, where he'd served for seven months, and it was the first time she discovered that he would scan the thousands of Palestinians who passed through the checkpoint with a simple metal detector, like the one they used when you walked into the mall. "That's all you had?" she whispered. He laughed. "What did you think I had?" "I didn't think," she said. He asked, "But didn't you wonder how it's done there?" There was a note of childish disappointment in his voice. She said, "But you never told me about it." He presented a profile that said, You know exactly why, but before she could say anything he reached out and covered her hand with his—his broad, tanned, rough hand—and that simple rare touch almost stunned her and she fell silent. Ofer seemed to want, at the very last minute, to fill in what he had left out, and he told her hurriedly about the pillbox he'd lived in for four months, facing the northern neighborhood of Jenin, and how every morning at five he used to open the gate in the fence around the pillbox and make sure the Palestinians hadn't booby-trapped it overnight. "You just walked over there like that, alone?" she asked.

"Usually someone from the pillbox would cover me—I mean, if anyone was awake." She wanted to ask more but her throat was dry, and Ofer shrugged and said in an elderly Palestinian man's voice, *"Kulo min Allah"*—it's all from God. She whispered, "I didn't know," and he laughed without any bitterness, as if he had understood that she could not be expected to know, and he told her about the kasbah in Nablus, which he said was the most interesting of all the kasbahs, the most ancient. "There are houses there from the Roman era and houses built like bridges over alleyways, and underneath the whole city there's an aqueduct that goes from east to west, with canals and tunnels running in all directions, and the fugitives live there because they know we'll never dare follow them down." He spoke enthusiastically, as if he were telling her about a new video game, and she kept fighting the urge to grasp his head with both hands and look into his eyes so that she could see his soul, which had been slipping away from her for years—although with warmth, with a grin and a wink, as if they were playing a casual game of tag to amuse themselves—but she did not have the courage to do it. Nor could she say to him simply, in a voice that was not drenched in complaint or accusation, "Hey, Ofer, why aren't we friends like we used to be? So what if I'm your mom?"

At three o'clock, Sami would come to take her and Ofer to the meeting point. Three o'clock was the farthest point in her thoughts. She did not have the strength to imagine what would occur after that, and this was further proof of her frequent claim that she had no imagination. But that was no longer true, either. That too had changed. Recently she'd been flooded by imaginings—she had imagination-poisoning. Sami would make the drive easier for her, especially the way back, which would undoubtedly be far more difficult than the way there. They had a domestic routine, she and Sami. She liked to listen to him talk about his family, about the complex relationships between the different clans in Abu Ghosh, about the intrigues in the town council, and about the woman he had loved when he was fifteen, and perhaps had never stopped loving even after he was married off to Inaam, his cousin. At least once a week, by total coincidence, he claimed, he would see her in the village. She was a teacher, and there were years when she taught his daughters, and then she became a superintendent. She must have been a strong, opinionated woman, judging by his stories, and he always drew the conversation out so that Ora would ask about her. Then he would report her news with a sort of reverence: another child, her first grandson, a prize from the Ministry of Education, her husband's death in a work accident. With touching detail he quoted their chance conversations in the mini-market, the bakery, or on the rare occasions when he drove her in his cab. Ora guessed that she was the only person he allowed himself to talk to about this woman, perhaps because he trusted her never to ask him the one question whose answer was obvious.

Sami was a seasoned man, a quick thinker, and his life wisdom was augmented by his business acumen, which had produced, among other things, his own small fleet of taxis. When he was twelve he had a goat, and every year she birthed two kids. And a year-old kid in good health, he once explained to Ora, can sell for a thousand shekels. "When the kid would get to a thousand shekels, I would sell it and put the money away. I put away, and I put away, until I had eight thousand shekels. At seventeen I got my license and bought a Fiat 127, an old model but it worked. I bought it from my teacher, and I was the one boy in the village who came to school with wheels. Afternoons, I did private drives, errands, take this, bring that, go, fetch, and that way, slowly-slowly . . ."

Last year, amid the great upheavals in her life, a friend of Ora's found her a part-time temporary job working for a new museum being built in Nevada, which for some reason was interested in the material culture of Israel. Ora liked the unusual work that had fallen into her lap to distract her from herself a little, and she preferred not to delve too deeply into the museum's ulterior motives or what had led its planners to invest a fortune in the construction of a model of Israel in, of all places, the Nevada desert. She was on the team in charge of the fifties and knew there were another few "gatherers" like her on various other teams. She never met any of them. Every two or three weeks she set off with Sami on delightful buying trips around the country, and out of some vague intuition she avoided discussing the museum and its intentions with him. Sami never asked, and she wondered what he imagined and how he described these trips to Inaam. The two of them spent days roaming the country together. They bought a collection of stainless-steel basins from a kibbutz in the Jordan Valley, an antique milking machine from a moshav in the north, a shiny like-new icebox in a Jerusalem neighborhood, and of course the trivial, forgotten items whose discovery gave her an almost physical joy: an eighth of a bar of Tasbin soap, a tube of

Velveta hand cream, a package of sanitary napkins, textured rubber "thimbles" that Egged bus drivers once used, a collection of wildflowers dried between the pages of a notebook, and vast quantities of textbooks and popular books—one of her tasks was to reconstruct a typical kibbutz household library from the fifties. Time after time she watched as Sami Jubran's warm, earthy charm encircled everyone he met. The elderly kibbutzniks were positive that he was a former kibbutz member (which was true, he told her jokingly: "Half of Kiryat Anavim's lands belong to my family"). In Jerusalem, at a local backgammon club, a few men pounced on him, convinced he had grown up with them in the Nachlaot neighborhood and even claimed to remember him climbing pine trees to watch Hapoel soccer games in the old stadium. And a vibrant Tel Aviv widow with bronzed skin and jangling bracelets determined that he was without a doubt from the Kerem: even though he a was little fat for a Yemenite, it was obvious that he was "with roots," she said when she called Ora the next day for no reason. "And very *charmant*," she added, "the kind of guy who definitely fought in the Etzel. And by the way, do you think he's available for a moving job?" Ora saw the way people agreed, for Sami, to part with beloved possessions, because they felt that these objects, which their children belittled and would undoubtedly get rid of as soon as the old people passed on, if given to him, would in some sense stay in the family. And on every trip, even a ten-minute drive, they always got into politics, keenly confabbing over the latest developments. And even though years ago, after the devastation with Avram, Ora had completely cut herself off from the "situation"—I've paid my price, she asserted with a narrow, distancing smile—she found herself drawn into these talks with Sami over and over again. It was not his arguments or his reasonings that pulled her in, because she'd heard them all before, from him and from others, and she didn't believe anyone had a single unused claim left in this eternal debate. "Who could possibly come up with a new, decisive argument that hasn't yet been heard?" she asked with a sigh when anyone else tried to take it up with her. But when she and Sami discussed the situation, when they argued with little jabs and cautious smiles—and with him, curiously, she frequently veered much further to the right than she intended, further than her real opinions, while with Ilan and the boys she was always, as they said, on the delusional left, and she herself couldn't say exactly what she was and where she stood, "and anyway," she would say with a charming shrug, "only when it's all over, the whole story, will we really know who was right and who was wrong, isn't that so?" Yet still, when Sami used his Arabesque Hebrew to undermine the long-winded, indignant, greedy pretenses of both Jews and Arabs, when he skewered the leaders of both peoples on a sharp Arab saying that often aroused from the depths of her memory the equivalent idiom in her father's Yiddish, she sometimes experienced a subtle latency, as if in the course of talking with him she suddenly discovered that the end, the end of the whole big story, must be good, and good it would be, if only because the clumsy, round-faced man sitting beside her was able to preserve within his fleshy thickness a flame of delicate irony, and mainly because he still managed to be himself within all *this*. There were also times when it occurred to her that she was learning from him what she would need to know, one day, if—or when—the situation in Israel was reversed, God forbid, and she found herself in his position, and he in hers. That was possible, after all. It was always lurking behind the door. And perhaps, she realized, he thought about that too—perhaps she was teaching him something by still being *her*self in all this.

Because of all these reasons it was very important that she observe him as much as she could, to learn how he had been able to avoid becoming embittered all these years. As far as she could tell he was not even suppressing a silent yet murderous hatred deep inside, as Ilan had always claimed. She was astonished to see—and wished she could learn from him—how he managed to avoid attributing the daily humiliations, large and small, to some personal defect of his own, as she would undoubtedly do with great fervor were she, God forbid, in his position—and as she in fact had been doing, truth be told, quite a bit during this lousy year. Somehow, within all the chaos, all the mess, he remained a free person, which she herself only rarely managed to be.

Now it grows and swells and threatens to burst: her stupidity, her failure in the principled and complicated matter of being a gentle human being in this place, in these times. Not just being gentle, or *ladylike*—there are some words she still hears only in her mother's voice—merely because you are incapable of being anything else by nature, but being intentionally and defiantly gentle, being a gentle person who dives headfirst into the local vat of acid. Sami was a truly gentle man, even if it was hard to tell from his size and his heaviness and his thick features. Even Ilan had to admit it, although grudgingly and always with a note of suspicion: "Gentle he may be, but just wait till he gets his chance. Then you'll get to see some gentleness à la Allah."

But in all the years she'd known him, and as much as she observed him—and she constantly did—she was unable to lose the childish curiosity about some congenital handicap she sensed in him, in his condition, in his split or double existence here; she was absolutely certain that he had never failed. In gentleness, he had never failed.

He once drove her and the kids to the airport to meet Ilan, who was coming back from a trip. The cops at the airport checkpoint took him away for half an hour, while Ora and the boys waited in the taxi. They were little then, Adam was six and Ofer around three, and it was the first time they discovered that their Sami was Arab. When he came back, pale and sweaty, he refused to tell them what had happened. All he said was, "They kept saying I was a shitty Arab, and I said, 'You may shit all over me, but that doesn't make me shitty.'"

She never forgot that sentence, and lately she recited it to herself ever more firmly, like medication to strengthen her heart whenever they shat all over her, everyone, like the pair of obsequious managers—*unctuous*, Avram used to call their type—at the clinic where she'd worked until recently, and a few friends who had more or less turned their backs on her after the separation and stuck with Ilan (but I would too, she thinks to herself; if I only could, I would choose Ilan and not get stuck with me), and she could add to the list the son of a bitch judge who took away her freedom of movement, and in fact she could include her kids among those who shat on her, especially Adam, not Ofer, hardly at all, she wasn't sure, she just wasn't sure anymore, and Ilan too, of course, the master of shitters, who once, about thirty years ago, had sworn that his purpose in life was to protect the corners of her mouth so that they would always curl upward. Ha. She absentmindedly touches the edge of her upper lip, the one that droops slightly down, the empty one—even her mouth had eventually joined with those who shat on her. Through all the trips with Sami, all the little unexpected challenges, the suspicious looks people sometimes gave him, the casual comments that were so horrifyingly rude coming from the warmest, most enlightened people they met, through all the tests with identical questions that daily life gave them together, a quiet, mutual confidence had grown between them, the kind you feel with your partner in a complicated dance or a dangerous acrobatic trick: you know he won't disappoint you, you know his hand won't shake, and he knows you'll never ask him for something you are absolutely forbidden to ask for.

And today she had failed, and she was causing him to fail, and by the time she realized this it was too late, when he hurried to open the taxi door for her, as he always did, and suddenly saw Ofer coming down the steps from the house wearing his uniform and carrying his rifle, and this was the Ofer he'd known since he was born. He had driven her and Ilan home from the hospital with Ofer because Ilan was afraid to drive that day, said his hands would shake, and on the way from the hospital Sami told them that for him life really only started when Yousra was born, his oldest daughter. At the time he had just the one; later there were two boys and another two girls—"I've got five demographic problems," he would cheerfully tell anyone who asked—and Ora noticed on that trip that he drove very carefully, smoothly rounding the car over potholes and bumps so as not to disturb Ofer as he slept in her arms. During the years that followed, when the boys went to school downtown, Sami drove the carpool she organized for five kids from Tzur Hadassah and Ein Karem. And whenever Ilan was overseas, Sami helped out with chauffeuring, and there were years when he was an integral part of the family's daily routine. Later, when Adam was older but didn't have his license yet, Sami would drive him home from his Friday night outings downtown, and then Ofer joined in, and the two boys would phone from a pub and Sami would come from Abu Ghosh, at any hour, denying he'd been asleep, even at three a.m., and he would wait for Adam and Ofer and their friends outside the pub until they finally remembered to come out, and he probably listened to their conversations, their army stories—who knows what he heard all those times? she suddenly thinks with horror, and what they said as they kidded around and told alcohol-fueled jokes about their checkpoint experiences—and then he would shuttle the boys to their homes in the various neighborhoods. Now he would shuttle Ofer to an operation in Jenin or Nablus, she thought, and she had forgotten to mention this one little detail when she phoned him, but Sami was quick. Her heart sank when she saw his face darken in a deadly coupling of anger and defeat. He got it all in the blink of an eye: he saw Ofer coming down the steps with his uniform and rifle, and realized that Ora was asking him to add his modest contribution to the Israeli war effort.

An ashen current had spread slowly through the dark skin of his face, the soot from a fire that leaped up and died down inside him in an instant. He stood without moving and looked as though someone had slapped him, as though she herself had come over and stood facing him, smiled broadly with her light-filled joy and warmth, and slapped his face as hard as she could. For one moment they were trapped, the three of them, condemned in a flash: Ofer at the top of the steps, his rifle dangling, a magazine attached with a rubber band; she with the silly purple suede handbag that was far too fancy, grotesque even, for a trip like this; and Sami, who did not budge but nevertheless grew smaller and smaller, slowly emptying out. And then she realized how old he had grown. When she first met him he had looked almost like a boy. Twenty-one years had gone by, and he was three or four years younger than she was but he looked older. People age quickly here—them too, she thought oddly. Even them.

She made things worse by getting into the back of the car, not the passenger side where he held the door open for her—but she always sat next to Sami, how could it possibly be otherwise?—and Ofer came down and sat next to her in the back, and Sami stood outside the taxi with his arms hanging at his sides and his head slightly tilted. He stood by the open door like a man trying to remember something, or muttering a forgotten sentence to himself that had popped into his mind from some distant place, perhaps a prayer or an ancient saying, or a farewell to something that can never be regained. Or perhaps just like a man taking a moment of absolute privacy to inhale the glorious spring air, which was bursting with sunny yellow blossoms of spiny broom and acacia. And only after this brief pause did he get into the taxi and sit down, upright and rigid, and wait for directions.

"It's going to be kind of a long drive today, Sami, did I tell you on the phone?" Ora said. Sami didn't shake his head or nod, or look at her in the rearview mirror. He only lowered his thick, patient neck a little. "We have to take Ofer to the, you know, that campaign, you probably heard on the radio, the meeting point, up near the Gilboa. Let's start driving and we'll explain on the way." She spoke quickly and tonelessly. "That campaign," she'd said, as if she were telling him about an advertising campaign, and the truth is that she'd almost said "that stupid campaign," or even "your government's campaign." But she had restrained herself with great difficulty, perhaps because she knew she would make Ofer angry, and rightly so: How could she forge subversive alliances on a day like this? Besides, maybe it was true, as Ofer had tried to persuade her over lunch at the restaurant, that they had to come down on them once and for all, even if it obviously would not eliminate them completely or dissuade them from wanting to hurt us—on the contrary, he had insisted, but maybe it would at least give us back a little deterrence. Now Ora bit her tongue and pulled her left knee into her stomach and hugged it, tormented over her rudeness to Sami. To quell the commotion inside her, she kept trying to start a casual conversation with Ofer, or with Sami, and kept coming up against their silence, and decided she wasn't going to give in, and so she found herself, to her complete surprise, telling Sami an old story about her father, who had gone almost completely blind at the age of forty-eight—"just imagine!"—and at first he'd lost his sight in his right eye, because of glaucoma, "and that's probably what I'll get one day," she said, and over the years he'd developed a cataract in his left eye, all of which left him with a field of vision about the size of a pinhead, "and if genetics do their job, that's more or less what I'll have, too." She laughed excessively and reported into the space of the taxi in a cheerful voice that her father, for years, was afraid to have cataract surgery on his one almost-seeing eye. Sami said nothing, and Ofer looked out the window and puffed his cheeks out and shook his head as if refusing to believe how low she could go to ingratiate herself with Sami, how she was willing to offer such an intimate story as a sacrifice to make up for her crude mistake. She saw all this, and still could not stop herself. The story took on its own force, because after all it was Ofer, he alone, who had managed, with patience and stubbornness and endless conversations, to convince her father to have the surgery, and thanks to Ofer he had gained another few good years before his death. As she talked she realized that Ofer was the one who kept her childhood anecdotes and recollections in his memory, her stories about school and her friends, about her parents and the neighbors in her childhood neighborhood of Haifa. Ofer had lived those little stories with a pleasure that was unexpected in a boy his age, and he always knew how to pull them out at exactly the right moment, and secretly she felt that he was preserving her childhood and youth for her, and that must be why she had deposited the stories with him all these years. Almost without noticing, she had slowly given up on

Ilan and Adam as listeners. She sighed and immediately felt it was a different sigh, a new one, carved from a different place inside her, with an ice-cold edge. She was frightened, and for a brief moment she was a child again, fighting with Ada, who insisted on letting go of her hand and jumping off the cliff; she hadn't been there with her for years—why had Ada suddenly come back to hold her hand, only to let go? She kept chattering through Sami and Ofer's silence and found it even more depressing that these two men, despite everything that stood between them now, had still managed to unite against her. There was an alliance, Ora finally realized, an alliance at her expense, and it turned out to be deeper and more effective than everything that divided them.

A nose-blowing interrupted her so violently that she stopped talking. Ofer had a cold. Or allergies. The last few springs his allergies had lasted almost until the end of May. He blew his nose into a tissue pulled from the ornate little olive-wood box that Sami had installed in the back for his passengers. He pulled out square after square and blew loudly and scrunched the used tissues into an overflowing ashtray. His Glilon assault rifle sat between them; its barrel had been pointed at her chest for several minutes, and now she could no longer bear it and motioned for him to turn it away. But when he moved the rifle and placed it between his legs with a sharp, irritated gesture, the front sight scratched the car-ceiling upholstery and pulled out a thread. Ofer said immediately, "Sorry, Sami, I ripped this." Sami looked quickly at the unraveling thread and said hoarsely, "Don't worry about it," and Ora said, "No, no, there's no argument, we'll pay for the repair." Sami took a deep breath and said, "Forget it, it's no big deal." Ora whispered to Ofer to fold the butt in at least. Ofer hissed in a half whisper that it wasn't standard practice, he only folded it in when he was in the tank, and Ora leaned forward and asked Sami if he had a pair of scissors to cut off the thread, but he didn't, and she held the thread that danced and spun in front of her eyes and looked, for a moment, like a spilled-out gut, and she said maybe it could be sewn back, "if you have a needle and thread here I can sew it right now." Sami said his wife would do it, and then he added, without any color in his voice, "Just be careful with the gun"—he was clearly addressing them both—"so it doesn't scratch the upholstery. I just reupholstered a week ago." Ora said with a crushed smile, "Okay, Sami, no more damages," and she saw him lower his eyelids over a look she did not recognize.

Last week, on a routine drive, Ora had encountered the new uphol-stery: synthetic leopard skin. Sami had watched her expression closely, and then commented: "You don't like this kind of thing, Ora. This, for you, is not considered a pretty thing, right?" She replied that in general she wasn't crazy about animal-fur upholstery, not even imitation fur, and he laughed: "No, for you this is probably Arab taste, isn't it?" Ora tensed at the unfamiliar bitterness in his voice and said that as far as she could remember, he had never chosen that kind of thing before, either. He replied that he actually found it beautiful, and a man couldn't change his taste. Ora did not respond. She imagined he'd had a rough day, maybe a passenger had insulted him, maybe they had shat on him at a checkpoint again. They both somehow extricated themselves from the gloom that momentarily drifted through the taxi, but an unease gnawed at her all day, and only that evening, when she was watching television, did it occur to her that his new taste in upholstery might have some-thing to do with the group of settlers who had planned to detonate a car bomb outside a school in East Jerusalem. They had been caught a few days before, and one of them described on television how they had designed the car, inside and out, to match "Arab taste."

Now the silence in the car grew even thicker, and Ora was once again driven to fill it with chatter. She spoke about her father and how she missed him, and about her mother, who no longer knew right from left, and about Ilan and Adam who were off having fun in South America. Sami remained expressionless, but his eyes darted around, examining the convoy in which he'd been crawling for over an hour. Once, on one of their first trips together, he had told her that ever since he was a boy he'd had a habit of counting every truck he saw on the roads in Israel, civilian or military. When she'd looked at him questioningly, he'd explained that they would come in trucks to take him and his family and all the '48 Arabs over the border. "Isn't that what your *transferists* promise?" he'd asked with a laugh. "Promises should be kept, no? And take it from me, our idiots will line up to drive the trucks if they can get a few bucks out of it."

Ofer wipes his nose constantly and blows it with trumpeting sounds she's never heard before, which seem grating and alien to his natural tenderness. He scrunches the tissues and pushes them into the ashtray and immediately pulls another tissue out, and the used tissues fall to the floor and he doesn't pick them up, and she gives up on constantly leaning over to put them into her handbag. A "Storm" Jeep passes them, honking repeatedly, and cuts in front. Behind them a Hummer lunges, almost touching them, and Sami keeps running his hand over his large, round bald spot. He presses his huge back against the orthopedic seat cushion and jolts forward every time he feels Ofer's long legs prodding his seatback. His slightly burned masculine scent, always mingled with an expensive aftershave she likes, has been replaced in the last few minutes with a sweet smell of sweat that is worsening, and it bursts through and fills the entire car, overpowering the air-conditioning, and Ora gags and does not dare open the window, so she sits back and breathes through her mouth. Large beads of sweat form on Sami's bald head and run down his face over his puffed cheeks. She wants to offer him a tissue but she is afraid, and she thinks about the way he swiftly dips his fingers in the rose water they bring to the table after meals at his favorite restaurant in Majd el'Krum.

His eyes dart between the Jeep in front of him and the one tailgating him. He reaches up and uses two fingers to pull his shirt collar away from his neck. He is the only Arab in this whole convoy, she thinks, and she too starts to feel a prickle of sweat: he's simply scared, he's dying of fear, how could I have done this to him? One large drop hangs from the edge of his chin and refuses to fall. A thick, teary drop. How can it not fall? Why doesn't he wipe it off? Is he leaving it like that on purpose? Ora's face is hot and red and her breathing is heavy, and Ofer opens a window and grumbles, "It's hot," and Sami says, "The A/C is weak."

She leans back and takes off her glasses. Waves of yellow blossoms sway in front of her. Wild mustard, probably, which her deficient eyes crumble and crush into bright smudges. She shuts her eyes and at once feels the pulse of the convoy burst through and rise, as if from her own body, in a tense, menacing growl. She opens her eyes: the dark pounding stops at once and the waves of light return. She covers her eyes again and the growl picks up, with a heavy drumbeat within, a stubborn, dulled, abysmal sound, a medley of engines and pistons, and beneath them the beating of hearts, pulsating arteries, quiet splutters of fear. She turns back to look at the snake of vehicles, and the scene is almost celebratory, excitable, a huge, colorful parade full of life: parents and brothers and girlfriends, even grandparents, bringing their loved ones to the campaign, the event of the season. In every car sits a young boy, the first fruits, a spring festival that ends with a human sacrifice. And you? she asks herself sharply. Look at you, how neatly and calmly you bring your son here, your almost-only-son, the boy you love dearly, with Ishmael as your private driver.

When they get to the meeting point, Sami pulls into the first parking spot he finds, yanks up the emergency brake, folds his arms over his chest, and announces that he will wait for Ora there. And he asks her to be quick, which he has never done before. Ofer gets out of the cab and Sami does not move. He hisses something, but she can't tell what. She hopes he was saying goodbye to Ofer, but who knows what he was muttering. She marches after Ofer, blinking at the dazzling lights: rifle barrels, sunglasses, car mirrors. She doesn't know where he is leading her and is afraid he will get swallowed up among the hundreds of young men and she will never see him again. Meaning—she immediately corrects herself, revising the grim minutes she has been keeping all day— she won't see him again until he comes home. The sun beats down, and the horde becomes a heap of colorful, bustling dots. She focuses on Ofer's long khaki back. His walk is rigid and slightly arrogant. She can see him broaden his shoulders and widen his stance. When he was twelve, she remembers, he used to change his voice when he answered the phone and project a strained "Hello" that was supposed to sound deep, and a minute later he would forget and go back to his thin squeak. The air around her buzzes with shouts and whistles and megaphone calls and laughter. "Honey, answer me, it's me, Honey, answer me, it's me," sings a ringtone on a nearby cell phone that seems to follow her wherever she goes. Within the commotion Ora swiftly picks up the distant chatter of a baby somewhere in the large gathering ground, and the voice of his mother answers sweetly. She stands for a moment looking for them but cannot find them, and she imagines the mother changing the baby's diaper, maybe on the hood of a car, bending over and tickling his tummy, and she stands slightly stooped, hugging her suede bag to her body, and laps up the soft double trickle of sounds until it vanishes.

It is all a huge, irredeemable mistake. It seems to her that as the moment of separation approaches, the families and the soldiers fill with arid merriment, as if they have all inhaled a drug meant to dull their comprehension. The air bustles with the hum of a school trip or a big family excursion. Men her age, exempt from reserve duty, meet their friends from the army, the fathers of the young soldiers, and exchange laughter and backslaps. "We've done our part," two stout men tell each other, "now it's their turn." Television crews descend on families saying goodbye to their loved ones. Ora is thirsty, parched. Half running, she trails behind Ofer. Every time her gaze falls on the face of a soldier she unwittingly pulls back, afraid she will remember him: Ofer once told her that when they had their pictures taken sometimes, before they set off on a military campaign, the guys made sure to keep their heads a certain distance from each other, so there'd be room for the red circle that would mark them later, in the newspaper. Screeching loud-speakers direct the soldiers to their battalions' meeting points— a *meetery*, they call this, and she thinks in her mother's voice: barbarians, language-rapists—and suddenly Ofer stops and she almost walks into him. He turns to her and she feels a deluge. "What's the matter with you?" he whispers into her face. "What if they find an Arab here and think he's come to commit suicide? And didn't you think about how he feels having to drive me here? Do you even get what this means for him?"

She doesn't have the energy to argue or explain. He's right, but she really wasn't in a state to think about anything. How can he not under-stand her? She just wasn't thinking. A white fog had filled her mind from the moment he told her that instead of going on the trip to the Galilee with her he was going off to some kasbah or *mukataa*. That was at six a.m. She had woken to hear his voice whispering into the phone in the other room, and hurried in there. Seeing his guilty look she had tensed and asked, "Did they call?"

"They say I have to go."

"But when?"

"ASAP."

She asked if it couldn't wait a little while, so they could at least do the trip for two or three days, because she realized immediately that a whole week with him was a dream now. She added with a pathetic smile, "Didn't we say we'd have a few puffs of family-together time?"

He laughed and said, "Mom, it's not a game, it's war," and because of his arrogance—his, and his father's, and his brother's, their patronizing dance around her most sensitive trigger points—she spat back at him that she still wasn't convinced that the male brain could tell the difference between war and games. For a moment she allowed herself some modest satisfaction with the debating skills she'd displayed even before her morning coffee, but Ofer shrugged and went to his room to pack, and precisely because he did not respond with a witty answer, as he usually did, she grew suspicious.

She followed him and asked, "But did they call to let you know?" Because she remembered that she hadn't heard the phone ring.

Ofer took his military shirts from the closet, and pairs of gray socks, and shoved them into his backpack. From behind the door he grumbled, "What difference does it make who called? There's an operation, and there's an emergency call-up, and half the country's reporting for duty."

Ora wouldn't give in—Me? Pass up getting pricked with such a perfect thorn? she asked herself later—and she leaned weakly against the doorway, crossed her arms over her chest, and demanded that he tell her exactly how things had progressed to that phone call. She would not let up until he admitted that he had called *them* that morning, even before six he had called the battalion and begged them to take him, even though today, at nine-zero-zero, he was supposed to be at the induction center for his discharge, and from there to drive to the Galilee with her. As he lowered his gaze and mumbled on, she discovered, to her horror, that the army hadn't even considered asking him to prolong his service. As far as they were concerned he was a civilian, deep into his discharge leave. It was he, Ofer admitted defiantly, his forehead turning red, who wasn't willing to give up. "No way! After eating shit for three years so I'd be ready for exactly this kind of operation?" Three years of checkpoints and patrols, little kids in Palestinian villages and settlements throwing stones at him, not to mention the fact that he hadn't even been within spitting distance of a tank for six months, and now, at last, with his lousy luck, this kind of kick-ass operation, three armored units together—there were tears in his eyes, and for a moment you might have thought he was haggling with her to be allowed to come back late from a class Purim party—how could he sit at home or go hiking in the Galilee when all his guys would be there? In short, she discovered that he, on his own initiative, had convinced them to enlist him on a voluntary basis for another twenty-eight days.

"Oh," she said, when he finished his speech, and it was a hollow, muffled Oh. *And I dragged my corpse into the kitchen*, she thought to herself. It was an expression of Ilan's, her ex, the man who had shared her life and, in their good years, enriched the goodness. *The fullness of life*, the old Ilan used to say and blush with gratitude, with reserved, awkward enthusiasm, which propelled Ora toward him on a wave of love. She always thought that deep in his heart he was amazed at having been granted this fullness of life at all. She remembers when the kids were little and they lived in Tzur Hadassah, in the house they bought from Avram, how they liked to hang the laundry out to dry at night, together, one last domestic chore at the end of a long, exhausting day. Together they would carry the large tub out to the garden facing the dark fields and the valley, and the Arab village of Hussan. The great fig tree and the grevillea rustled softly with their own mysterious, rich lives, and the laundry lines filled up with dozens of tiny articles of clothing like miniature hieroglyphics: little socks and undershirts and cloth shoes and pants with suspenders and colorful OshKosh overalls. Was there someone from Hussan who had gone out in the last light of day and was watching them now? Aiming a gun at them? Ora wondered sometimes, and a chill would flutter down her spine. Or was there a general, human immunity for people hanging laundry—especially this kind of laundry?

Her thoughts flit as she remembers how Ofer presented her and Ilan with his new "tankist" overalls. They had already sold the Tzur Hadassah house by then and moved north to Ein Karem, closer to the city. Ofer came out of his room wrapped in the big, fireproof overalls, approached them with little hops and skips, swayed this way and that, flapped his arms, and shouted sweetly: "Mommy! Daddy! Teletubbies!" Two decades earlier, in the garden at night, in the middle of hanging up the boys' clothes, Ilan had walked through the crowded lines and hugged her, and they had both rocked together, entangled in the damp laundry, laughing softly, sighing lovingly, and Ilan had whispered in her ear, "Isn't it, Orinkah? Isn't it the fullness of life?" She had hugged him as hard as she could, with a salty happiness pulsing in her throat, and had felt that for one fleeting moment she had caught it as it rushed through her, the secret of the fruitful years, their tidal motion, and their blessing in her body and his, and in their two little children and in the house they had built for themselves, and in their love, which finally, after years of wandering and hesitating, and after the blow of Avram's tragedy, was now, it seemed, standing up on its own two feet.

Ofer finished packing in his room, and she stood motionless, dropsi-cal, in the kitchen, and thought that Ilan had won again without any effort: she would not go on the trip with Ofer, she would not have even one week with him. Ofer must have sensed what she was going through, as he always did, even if he sometimes denied it, and he came and stood behind her and said, "Come on, Mom, it's okay . . ." He said it tenderly, in a voice that only he knew how to use. But she hardened her heart and did not turn to him. They had planned the Galilee trip for a whole month. It was her gift to him for finishing the army, and it was a gift for herself too, of course, for *her* release from his army. Together they'd gone out and bought two little tents that folded up into small squares and elaborate backpacks and sleeping bags and hiking boots, but only for her: Ofer wouldn't give up his dingy pair. In her spare time she'd bought thermal underwear and hats and fanny packs and Band-Aids for blisters and canteens and waterproof matches and a camping stove and dried fruit and crackers and canned food. Every so often, Ofer would pick up the swelling backpacks in her bedroom, gauge their weight in astonishment, and comment, "They're coming along well, really grow-ing nicely." He joked that she'd have to find a Galilean Sherpa to carry all the gear she was packing. She laughed heartily, responding to his good spirits, to the light in his face. In the last few weeks, as his dis-charge date approached, she could feel the tastes and smells slowly returning from exile. Even the sounds sharpened, as they do when you get your ears flushed. Little surprises awaited her, wild crossbreeds of sensations: she would open a water bill and feel as if she had unwrapped a package of fresh parsley. Sometimes she would say to her-self out loud, so she could believe it: "One week alone, the two of us, in the Galilee." And mostly she proclaimed to no one: "Ofer is being released from the army. Ofer is getting out. He's getting out of it in one piece."

During the last week she played the words over and over again to the walls of the house, growing bolder and bolder. "The nightmare is over," she would say. "No more nights of sleeping pills," she whispered defi-antly, and knew she was tempting fate. But Ofer had been on his dis-charge leave for two weeks by then, and there was no immediate threat. The general, almost eternal conflict from which she had disconnected herself years ago kept on making its dark circles, here a terrorist attack, there a targeted assassination, hurdles that the soul leaped over with an expressionless face and without ever looking back. And perhaps she was emboldened to hope because she felt that Ofer himself was starting to believe that this was it, that it was over. A few days earlier, when he stopped sleeping for eighteen hours straight every day, she noticed the change in him, the slight civilianness that diluted his military speak, and his expressions, which softened day by day, and even the way he moved around the house once he allowed himself to grasp that he had apparently escaped his three years of lousy military service unharmed. "My boy is coming back," she reported cautiously to the fridge and the dishwasher, to the computer mouse and the flower arrangement she put out in a vase. She knew full well from her experience with Adam, who had been out of the army for three years, that they don't really come back. Not like they were before. And that the boy he used to be had been lost to her forever the moment he was nationalized—lost to himself, too. But who said that what happened to Adam would happen to Ofer? They were so different, and what mattered now was that Ofer was coming out of the Armored Corps—*and out of his armor*, she thought, waxing poetic. These were the sweet drops she had been pouring into herself just the night before, when she took the remote control out of his hand and covered him with a thin blanket, and sat watching him sleep. His full, wide lips were slightly parted in a hint of an ironic smile, as if he knew she was watching him. His rounded forehead gave him, even in his sleep, a slightly severe expression, and his open face, with the bronzed crown shaved down to a stubble, looked, more than ever before, strong and ready for life. A man, she thought in amazement. A total man. Everything in him looked possible and open and propelled. The future itself lit up his face, from inside and out. And now this operation suddenly comes along, and I could really do without it, Ora sighed the next morning as she stood in the kitchen and made herself a particularly noxious cup of coffee. Had she been able to, she would have turned around and gone back to bed and slept until the whole thing was over. How many days could a campaign like this last? A week? Two? A lifetime? But she didn't even have the strength to go back to bed, incapable of taking a single step, and from one moment to the next everything became decided, inevitable. Her body already knew, and her stomach, and her gut, which was melting away.

. . .

At seven-thirty that evening she stands cooking in the kitchen, wearing jeans and a T-shirt, and, for lyric effect, the floral apron of a real, hard-working, eager housewife: a chef. Piping-hot pots and pans dance on the stove top, steam curls up to the ceiling and thickens into aromatic clouds, and Ora suddenly knows that everything will work out.

As befitting the adversary she faces, she plunges into battle with her winning combination: Ariela's Chinese chicken strips with vegetables, Ariela's mother-in-law's Persian rice with raisins and pine nuts, her own variation on her mother's sweet eggplant with garlic and tomatoes, and mushroom and onion pies. If she only had a proper oven in this house she could make at least one more pie, but Ofer would be licking his fingers anyway. She moves between the oven and the stove top with unexpected gaiety, and for the first time since Ilan left, since they locked up their house in Ein Karem and dispersed to separate rental houses, she feels a sense of affection and belonging toward a kitchen, toward the whole idea of a kitchen, even this old-fashioned, grubby kitchen, which now approaches her tentatively and rubs up against her with its damp snouts of serving spoons and ladles. Piled on the table behind her are covered bowls of eggplant salad, cabbage salad, and a large, colorful chopped vegetable salad, into which she snuck slices of apple and mango, which Ofer may or may not notice, if he even gets to eat this meal. Another bowl contains her version of tabbouleh, which Ofer thinks is to die for—that is to say, which he really, really likes, she corrects herself quickly for the record.

She has arrived at the moment when all the dishes have been sent on their way: cooking on the stove top, baking in the oven, bubbling in pans. They don't need her any longer. But she still needs to cook, because surely Ofer will come home at some point and want fresh food. Her fingers flutter restlessly in the air. Where was I? She grabs a knife and a few vegetables that survived her salad assault, and starts chopping and humming quickly, *The tankists set off with screeching chains, / Their bodies painted the color of earth—* She stops herself. How in the world did she come up with that old song? Perhaps she should make a steak the way he likes it, braised in red wine, in case he gets home tonight? And the people who come to make the announcement, she wonders, are they convening in some office now, at the local army center, undergoing training or a refresher course—but what is there to refresh? When would they have had time to forget their job? When have we had even one single day here without an announcement to a family? It's strange to think that the notifiers were enlisted at the same time as the soldiers who take part in the operation, all orchestrated together. She giggles with a high-pitched squeak, and there is Ada again, with her large eyes, resurfacing, always there to observe how Ora acts, and Ora realizes that for several minutes she's been staring at the semitransparent lower half of the front door. There is a problem there that requires a solution, but she does not understand what it is, and she hurries back to the pots on the stove, stirs and seasons generously—he likes his food spicy—and holds her face over the steam to inhale the pots' thick breath. She doesn't taste the food. She has no appetite tonight—if she puts a crumb in her mouth she'll throw up. She watches her hand move wildly over a pot, showering its contents with paprika. There are particular movements that always make the phone ring. She noticed this odd conjunction a long time ago: when she seasons food, for example, or when she wipes a pot or pan dry after washing it, the phone almost always rings. Something in these circular motions seems to bring it to life, and also— how interesting—when she adds water to the flowers in the delicate glass vase. But only that vase! She laughs warmly at the secretive whims of her telephone, empties the pot of rice with raisins and pine nuts into the trash can, and carefully washes and dries the pot slowly, seductively. But nothing happens. The phone is dead (meaning, silent). Ofer is probably terribly busy. It will be hours until anything even starts, and they may not leave until tomorrow or the next day. *And when his tank was hit with two rockets*, she hums, *He was inside the burning fire*— She cuts herself off. She needs to find something to do tomorrow. But tomorrow is one of those days when she has nothing much to do. Tomorrow she was supposed to be skipping among the Galilee rocks with her young son, but there was a slight hitch in the plans. Maybe she should call the new clinic in Rehavia and offer to start working right away, even as a volunteer, even doing secretarial work if necessary. They could call it her adjustment period. But they have already explained, twice, that they won't need her until the middle of May, when their regular physiotherapist is scheduled to give birth. A new person will come into the world, Ora thinks and swallows bitter saliva. How silly of her not to have made any plans until May. She'd been so preoccupied with planning the trip with Ofer that she'd thought of nothing else, but she'd had the feeling that there would be a turning point in the Galilee. The start of a real, full recovery for her and Ofer. So much for her feelings.

She tosses the eggplant into the trash can, scrubs the pan, wipes it devotedly, and gives a sideways glance at the treacherous phone. What now? Where was I? The door. The lower part of the door. Four short bars over thick frosted glass. She takes three sheets of A4 paper from the printer and tapes them over the glass. That way she won't see their military boots. And now what? The fridge is practically empty. In the pantry she finds a few potatoes and onions. Perhaps a quick soup? Tomorrow morning she'll go shopping and fill the house again. It occurs to her that they could arrive in the middle of all sorts of things. Like when she's unpacking the groceries and putting things in the fridge. Or when she sits down and watches television. Or when she sleeps, or when she's in the bathroom, or when she's chopping vegetables for soup.

Her breath pauses for a moment, and she quickly turns on the radio like someone opening a window. She finds the Voice of Music and listens for a couple of minutes to something from the Middle Ages. But no, she needs talk, a human voice. On the local station a young reporter is talking on the phone to an older women with a deep Mizrahi Jerusalem accent. Ora stops abusing the vegetables, leans against the cracked marble counter, wipes the sweat off her brow with the back of her hand, and listens to the woman talk about her older son who fought in the Gaza battle this week. "Seven soldiers were killed," she says. "All of them were his friends from the battalion." Yesterday they'd let him come home for a few hours, and this morning he was already back in the army.

"And while he was at home, did you give him your breast food?" the reporter asks, to Ora's astonishment.

"My breast food?!" repeats the woman, also surprised.

The reporter laughs. "No, I asked if you gave him the *best* food."

"Of course," the woman says, laughing softly. "I thought you asked . . . Of course I cooked all my best dishes for him, and I pampered him."

"Tell us how you pampered him," the reporter urges.

And the mother, with a generosity that envelops Ora in its warmth, recounts: "I pampered him just like he deserves, with his favorite treats, and a nice warm bath and a really soft towel, and the shampoo he likes, which I bought special for him." Then her voice turns grave. "But I want to say that, you know, I have two more sons, twins, and they also followed the way my oldest showed them, and they're in the same battalion, Tzabar, the three of them in the same battalion I have, and I want to make a request from our army over the radio, can I?"

"Certainly you may." Ora hears the slight derision in the reporter's voice. "What exactly would you like to say to the IDF?"

"What can I tell you?" The mother sighs, and Ora's heart goes out to her. "My sons, the two, when they were in basic training they signed a waiver, so they're allowed to serve together, and that was well and good when they were in basic training, I'm not saying it wasn't, but now they're going down to the border, and everyone knows that the border for Givati is Gaza, and Gaza, I don't have to tell you what that means, and I would really like to ask the army to think about it a bit more, and to think a little about me, too, I'm sorry for—"

What if they come in the middle of the potato? Ora thinks and stares at the large spud lying semi-peeled in her hand. Or in the middle of the onion? It gradually dawns on her that every movement she makes may be the last before the knock on the door. She reminds herself again that Ofer is unquestionably still at the Gilboa, and there's no reason to panic yet, but the thoughts crawl up and wrap themselves around her hands as they clutch the peeler, and for an instant the knock on the door becomes so inevitable, such an intolerable provocation of the capacity for disaster embodied in every human condition, that her mind confuses cause with effect and the dull, slow movements of her hands around the potato seem like the essential prelude to the knock.

During this eternal moment, she, and faraway Ofer, and everything that occurs in the vast space between them, are all deciphered in a flash of knowledge, like a densely woven fabric, so that the very act of her standing by the kitchen table, and the fact that she stupidly continues to peel the potato—her fingers on the knife whiten now—and all her trivial, routine household movements, and all the innocent, ostensibly random fragments of reality around her, become nothing less than vital steps in a mysterious dance, a slow and solemn dance, whose unwitting partners are Ofer, and his friends preparing for battle, and the senior officers scanning the map of future battles, and the rows of tanks she saw on the outskirts of the meeting point, and the dozens of smaller vehicles that moved among the tanks, and the people in the villages and towns over there, the other ones, who would watch through drawn blinds as soldiers and tanks drove down their streets and alleys, and the quick-as-lightning boy who might hit Ofer tomorrow or the day after, or perhaps even tonight, with a rock or a bullet or a rocket (strangely, the boy's movement is the only thing that violates and complicates the slow heaviness of the entire dance), and the notifiers, who might be refreshing their procedures at the Jerusalem army offices right now, and Sami too, who must be at home in his village at this late hour, telling Inaam about the day's events. Everyone, everyone is part of this massive, all-encompassing process, and the people killed in the last terrorist attack are part of it too, unaware of their role: they are the casualties whose death will be avenged by the soldiers now setting off on a new campaign. Even the potato she is holding, which is suddenly as heavy as an iron weight and she can no longer continue to slice it, it too might be a link, a tiny but irreplaceable link in the dark, calculated, formal course of the larger system, which comprises thousands of people, soldiers and civilians, vehicles and weapons and field kitchens and battle rations and ammunition stores and crates of equipment and night-vision instruments and signaling flares and stretchers and helicopters and canteens and computers and antennas and telephones and large, black, sealed plastic bags. And all these, Ora suddenly feels, as well as the visible and hidden threads that tie them to one another, are moving around her, above her, like a massive fishing net, tossed up high with a sweeping motion, spreading slowly to fill the night sky. Ora quickly drops the potato, and it rolls off the counter and onto the floor between the fridge and the wall, where it shines with a pale glow as she leans on the table with both hands and stares at it.

By nine p.m. she's climbing the walls. To her astonishment, she thinks she sees herself and Ofer on television, hugging goodbye at his battalion's gathering point. She remembers, horrified, that there were cameras there, just after he barked at her for bringing Sami. He had stopped his barking when he noticed her reddening face, and through his fury he had wrapped her in his arms and held her to his broad chest, and said warmly, "Mom, Mom, you're such a space cadet . . ." She jumps up, knocking a chair over, and practically glues her face to the screen, to Ofer—

Who holds her with a slightly authoritarian arrogance and turns her toward the camera—his move had caught her by surprise and she'd almost tripped, then held on to him with a nervous laugh, and it was all there, even the stupid purple handbag—to show the cameraman his worrying mother. Thinking back, she sees real treachery in the way he suddenly spun her around and exposed her to the camera. Her hand had flown up to make sure her hair wasn't too disheveled and her mouth had twisted into a sanctimoniously mollifying *Who, me?* smile. But the treachery had been smoldering between them since last night, when he had decided to volunteer for the operation and kept it from her. When he had given up, without much deliberation, on their trip. An even greater treachery, and an intolerable foreignness, resided in his ability to be such a soldier-going-to-war, so able to do his job, so insolent and joyful and thirsty for battle, thereby imposing her role upon her: to be wrinkled and gray, yet glowing with pride (a poor man's coat of arms: Mother of Soldier), and to be a total dimwit, blinking with ignorant charm at the men's stance in the face of death. There he is smiling at the camera, and her mouth—on television and at home—unwittingly mimics his shining grin, and there are the three little magic wrinkles around his eyes, and she pushes away a thought: When will they broadcast this picture of him again? She sees it clearly, right on the screen, the halo of a red circle around his head. Then someone shoves a boom pole between them. "What can a son tell his mother at a moment like this?" asks the reporter, all sparkling with amusement. "Keep the beer cold for me till I get back!" the son laughs, and hearty cheers come from every direction. "Wait!" Ofer stops the merriment and holds up one finger, effortlessly drawing the attention of the reporter, the cameraman, and everyone around them—such an Ilan movement, the gesture of someone who knows everyone will be silent whenever he holds up a finger like that. "I have something else to tell her," says her son on the television, and he smiles knowingly. He puts his lips to her ears and still looks at the camera with one twinkling eye, full of life and mischief, and she remembers his touch and his warm breath on her cheek, and she sees the camera quickly trying to invade the space between mouth and ear, and she sees the extremely attentive expression on her own face, her pathetic supplication exposed as she displays for all to see, for Ilan to see—do they get Channel 2 on the Galápagos?—what soft and natural intimacy flows between her and Ofer. The editor finally cuts away, and now the reporter is joking around with another solider and his girl-friend, who embraces him and his mother, both women with bare midriffs, and Ora feels two pinches. She drops heavily to the edge of the armchair and her hand grasps the skin of her neck, squeezing. It's a good thing they didn't show the way she had grimaced and pulled back when she heard what he whispered in her ear. The memory slaps her: Why did he have to tell me that? When did he rehearse that line, where did he get the idea?

She stands up quickly. She must not sit. Not be a sitting target for the beam already probing for her, for the huge fishing net slowly descending. She cocks her head to the door. Nothing. Through the window she sees a strip of road and sidewalk. She scans it but there is no unfamiliar car, no car with military plates, no nervous barks from the neighbors' dogs, and no band of evil angels. Besides, it's too early. Not for them, she replies. Those people come even at five in the morning, that's exactly when they come, they get you sleepy, dazed, defenseless, too weak to throw them down the steps before they can deliver their punch line. But right now it really is too early, and she honestly doesn't think anything has happened there in the few hours since they parted. She rubs the back of her neck. Relax, he's still with his friends in the Gilboa, there are procedures, paperwork, debriefing, lots of complicated processes. Before anything can happen they have to mix everyone's smells together, ignite the powerful lightning in their eyes and the beating pulse in their necks. She can feel Ofer renewing himself with them, with his friends, with their measured aggression, their battle thirst, their thick sap of warfare, their well-hidden fear; he receives and delivers these important things with a quick hug, half-chest pressed to half-chest, two pats on the back, slaps of identity, tickets punched. She distractedly drags herself into his room, where everything would freeze from this day onward, and she discovers that the room has beat her to it and already taken on the vacant expression of an abandoned place. The objects seem orphaned: his sandals with their splayed straps, the chair at his computer desk, the history textbooks he keeps by his bed because he liked history—likes, of course she means likes, and will continue to like—and all the Paul Auster books on the shelf, and the D & D books he liked as a kid, and the posters of Maccabi Haifa soccer players whom he worshipped at twelve and refused to take off the wall even when he was twenty-one, twenty-one, when he was twenty-one.

Perhaps she should not move around the room, not break the still-hanging threads of his motion, not silence the faint echo of his childhood vapors that still sometimes waft up from a pillow, a balding yellow tennis ball, a toy commando soldier equipped with endless miniature battle accessories, which she and Ilan used to bring him and Adam from their trips overseas, bought in toy shops they stopped visiting once the boys grew up, and hoped to return to in a few years, for the grandchildren. Their dreams were small and modest, yet they had quickly become so complicated and virtually unattainable. Ilan left, off to breathe in some bachelor air. Adam left with him. Ofer is away now. She steps sideways out of the room, careful not to turn her back on his belongings, and stands looking in with the yearning of the exiled. A crumpled Manchester United shirt, an army sock tossed in the corner, a letter peeking from an envelope, an old newspaper, a soccer magazine, a picture of him with Talia by some waterfall in the north, the small five-kilo iron weights on the rug, a book lying open, facedown—what was the last sentence he read? What would be the last picture he saw? A narrow alleyway, a stone block sailing through the air, and the masked face of a young man, eyes burning with fury and hatred. From there her mind skips quickly to an office at the army compound, where a soldier walks over to a filing cabinet full of personnel files—but that was how they did things in her day, in prehistoric times; these days it's a computer: one click, a flicker on the screen, the soldier's name, contact details for notification in case of a tragedy. Has he already let them know about the split in his parents' addresses?

The phone gives a wrenching ring. It's him. Overjoyed. "Did you see us on TV?" Friends had called to tell him.

"Listen," she whispers, "you haven't left yet, have you?"

"I wish! We'll still be here tomorrow night at this rate."

She hardly hears the words. Attentive only to the foreign deepness of his voice, the echo of his new treachery, the treachery of the one and only man who had always been loyal to her. Since yesterday, perhaps since he'd tasted the pleasure of betrayal, of betraying *her*, it seemed he wanted to savor the taste again and again, like a puppy eating meat for the first time.

"Hang on Mom, one sec." He laughs and calls out to someone standing near him: "Why are you making such a big deal? We'll go in, rattle our guns at them, and get out." Then he comes back to her fast and frantic, outflanking her and enjoying it. "Um, Mom, can you tape *The*

Sopranos for me tomorrow? There's an empty tape on the TV, you know how to work the VCR, right?" As they talk she rummages through the drawer of tapes looking for the scrap of paper on which she once wrote down the instructions he dictated. "You press the far left button, then the one with the picture of an apple . . ."

"But what are you doing there meanwhile?" she asks, mourning for these precious wasted hours that he could have spent at home, with her. On the other hand, what could she offer him here with her funereal face? Pretty soon, she thinks, he'll want to rent a room somewhere, or move in with Ilan like Adam did. And why not? With Ilan everything's such fun, good times, the three adolescents can party all they want without any annoying parents getting in the way. Meanwhile, Ofer is telling her something and she can't separate the words. She shuts her eyes. She'll find an excuse to phone Talia later that evening; Talia has to talk to him before he leaves.

He tries to drown out the chaos in the background. "Shut up already, it's my mom!" Then come roars of joy and admiration, and they howl like jackals in heat, sending warm regards to his awesome mom. "Tell her to send her *rugelach*!" Ofer walks to a quieter place. "Animals," he explains, "tank loaders, the lot of them."

She can hear his breath as he walks. At home he also walks when he's on the phone, and so does Adam. They learned that from Ilan—my genes are as soft as butter, she thinks. Sometimes the boys and Ilan would hold three simultaneous phone calls, each on his cell, all walking briskly around the large living room, crossing one another's paths in quick diagonals, never colliding.

Now it's suddenly quiet. Perhaps he's found a hiding place behind one of the tanks. The silence makes her nervous, and he seems to feel the same, facing her alone now without the entire Israel Defense Forces to protect him. He quickly tells her that 110 percent of the forces showed up, "all raring to go, jonesing to lay into them"—he militarizes himself as he talks. "The adjutant says he doesn't remember a call-up like this"—in that case they can do without you, Ora thinks, but manages to keep quiet—"and the problem is, there aren't enough ceramic vests for everyone, and some of the guys don't have vehicles to team up with, 'cause half the transporters are stuck in traffic in Afula." Whoever shoved this gravel into his mouth is probably the same person who makes her ask if he has any idea when it will be over. Ofer lets her question echo for a moment until its total pointlessness and stupidity is exhausted. That was also one of Ilan's little tricks against her. Kids pick up these things and use them without understanding what sort of multigenerational weapon they've activated. Ofer, at least, comes back to her quickly, but she's already wondering when that will end too, when he will jab her with one of Ilan's long needles and not come back to recover the casualty. "*Nu*, really, Mom." His voice is warm and healing like his embrace. "We won't stop until we eliminate the terrorism infrastructure"—here she can hear him start to smile, mimicking the prime minister's arrogant intonation—"and until we defeat the murderous gangs and sever the head of the snake and burn out the nests of—"

She quickly pushes her way into the crack of his laughter. "Oferiko, listen, I think I might go away for a few days after all, up north."

"Hang on, the reception here's lousy. Wait—what's that?"

"I'm thinking of going up north."

"You mean, to the Galilee?"

"Yes."

"Alone?"

"Alone, yes."

"But why go alone? Don't you have anyone who . . ." He immediately realizes his unfortunate phrasing. "Maybe you could go with a girl-friend or someone."

She chokes down his so-accurate tactlessness. "I don't have anyone who, and I don't feel like going with girlfriends or anything, and I don't feel like being at home now, either."

His voice wrinkles. "Wait, Mom, I'm not following. You're really going away alone?"

Suddenly the lid flips off her mouth. "Who have I got to go with, in your opinion? My partner bailed on me at the last minute, decided to volunteer for the Jewish brigades—"

He interrupts impatiently. "So you're going to go to our places, the ones we planned?"

She bravely overcomes the pilfered *our*: "I don't know, I only just now thought of it."

"Well, at least you have a backpack ready to go," he snickers.

"Two."

"Honestly, though, I really don't get it."

"What is there to get? I just can't be here now. I'm suffocating."

A huge engine turns on somewhere behind him. Someone shouts to hurry up. She hears his thoughts. He needs her at home now, that's the thing, and he's right, and she almost gives in, at that very moment, but she realizes just as quickly and urgently that she has no choice this time.

A gluey silence. Ora fights to make herself turn her back on him, and the map of memory with its countless little marks of blame spreads out inside her: Ofer at age three, undergoing complicated dental surgery. When the anesthesiologist placed the mask on his nose and mouth, she was told to leave the room. Ofer's terrified eyes pleaded, but she turned her back and left. When he was four, she left him screaming for her, clinging with all ten fingers to the preschool fence, and his shouts stayed with her for the rest of the day. There were many more of these little abandonments, escapes, eye-shuttings, face-hidings, and today, undoubtedly, is the hardest of them all. But every moment she spends at home is dangerous for her, she knows it, and dangerous for him too, and he can't understand that and there's no point hoping he will. He's too young. His desires are simple and crude: he needs her to wait for him at home without changing anything about home or about herself, preferably without moving at all for all these days—the way he pulled back from her and flailed in anger, she recalls, when he was five and she had her curls straightened!—so that if he comes home on leave, he will hug her and defrost her and he'll be able to use her, to impress her with the splinters of horror that he'll scatter around with affected indifference, revealing secrets he should not divulge. Ora hears his breath. She breathes with him. They both feel the unbearable stretching of tendons—the tendons of her back-turning.

"So how long d'you think you'll be gone for?" he asks in a voice touched by anger and weakness and a shred of defeat.

"Ofer, don't talk like that. You know how much I wanted this trip with you, you know how much I looked forward to it."

"Mom, it's not my fault there's an emergency call-up."

She heroically refrains from reminding him that he had volunteered. "I'm not blaming you, and you'll see, we'll take our trip when you're finished, I promise. I won't give up on that. But right now I have to get out of here, I can't stay here alone."

"Sure, no, sure, I'm not saying, but"—he hesitates—"you're not going to sleep in the field, like, alone?"

She laughs. "No, are you crazy? I won't sleep alone 'in the field.' "

"You'll have your phone, right?"

"I don't know, I haven't thought about it."

"But listen, Mom, what was I going to ask you . . . Does Dad know you're—"

"What about Dad? What does this have to do with Dad? D'you think he tells me where he is?"

Ofer retreats. "Okay, okay, Mom, I didn't say anything."

A thin sigh inadvertently leaves his lips, the sigh of a little boy whose parents have suddenly lost their minds and decided to separate. Ora can hear it, and she feels his battle spirit dissipate, and she thinks with alarm: What am I doing? How can I send him to battle when he's confused and dejected? A sourness fills her throat: Where did phrases like "sending him to battle" even come from? What do they have to do with her? She is not one of those mothers who sends her sons to battle, not part of one of those military dynasties like the communities of Um Juni or Beit Alpha or Negba, or Beit HaShita or Kfar Giladi. Yet she is now surprised to discover that that is exactly what she is: she escorted him to the battalion "meetery" and stood there hugging him with measured restraint, so as not to embarrass him in front of his friends, and she shook her head and shrugged her shoulders as required, with a proud grin of helplessness at the other parents who were making all the same moves—where did we learn this choreography? And how do I obey it all, obey them, those people who send him there? She was poisoned by the words Ofer whispered to her when the TV camera caught them. His final request. Her mouth had gaped in terrible pain, not only because of what he said but also because he had said it with a sort of matter-of-factness, completely lucid, as though he had rehearsed every word ahead of time, and as soon as he said it he hugged her again, but this time it was to hide her from the camera. She'd already embarrassed him once before, at the ceremony when he finished his training course, when she sat in the quad at Latrun and wept as the parade walked past the long wall inscribed with thousands of names of fallen soldiers. She had wept loudly, and the parents and commanders and soldiers looked at her, and the corps officer leaned over and whispered something to the division commander. But this time, well trained, Ofer threw himself on her like a blanket on a fire, almost strangling her with his arm, and probably glanced awkwardly over her head in all directions. "Stop, Mom, you're making a scene."

"Okay," he sighs now. "What's the story, Mom?"

He sounds defeated, and it shows and it pinches, and she says, "No story, there's no story."

"To tell you the truth, it's weird for me to hear you like this."

"What's weird? *What is so weird?* Going on a hike in the Galilee is weird, but going into the kasbah in Nablus you think is normal?!"

"But when I get home will you be there?"

"I don't know yet."

"What d'you mean you don't know?" He snorts. "You're not going to, like, disappear or something?" And now it's his familiar, worrying, almost fatherly voice, aimed squarely at her deepest thirst.

"Don't worry, Ofer'ke, I'm not going to do anything dumb. I just won't be here for a few days. I can't sit on my own and wait."

"Wait for what?"

She cannot say, of course, but he finally understands, and there is a long silence, and Ora makes up her mind with irrefutable simplicity: twenty-eight days exactly. Until his emergency call-up is over.

"But what if everything's over in a couple of days and I come home?" he asks with renewed annoyance. "Or let's say I get injured or something—where do they find you?"

She doesn't answer. They don't, she thinks, that's exactly the point. And something else flickers in her: if they don't find her, if they can't find her, he won't get hurt. She can't understand it herself. She tries to. She knows it makes no sense, but what does?

"And if there's a funeral?" Ofer inquires agreeably, changing tactics and unconsciously imitating Ilan, who uses death and its derivatives as punctuation in his sentences. She's never been immune to these remarks, least of all now, and his joke, if it can be called that, seems to shock them both, because she can hear him swallow.

The stray thought from this afternoon comes back to her: Why do I collaborate with all this instead of being loyal to—

His voice resurfaces. "Mom, I'm not joking. Maybe you should take a phone, so you can be contacted."

"No, no." From one moment to the next she feels a greater comprehension of her plan. "Just not that."

"Why not? You can leave it turned off, just use it for messages, for SMS."

In fact she has become a skilled text-messager, an expertise acquired recently thanks to her new friend, her maybe lover, the Character with a capital C, because that's her only way to communicate with him. She considers for a moment and shakes her head: "No, not even that." Then she gets carried away on a stray thought: "Ofer, d'you have any idea what SMS stands for?"

He stares at her through the phone. "What? What'd you ask?"

"Could it be 'Save my Soul'?"

Ofer sighs. "Honestly, Mom, I have no clue."

She quickly returns from her contemplations. "I'm not taking my cell. I don't want to be found."

"Not even by me?" he asks in a suddenly thin, stripped voice.

"Not even you. No one," Ora replies sadly. The vague notion gains clarity inside her. The whole time he's there, she cannot be found. That's the thing. That's the law. All or nothing, like a kid's oath, a crazy gamble on life itself.

"But what if something really does happen to me?" he yells, protesting this incomprehensible, shocking disruption of order.

"No, no, nothing will happen to you, I'm telling you, I know it. I just have to disappear for a while, please understand. Actually, you know what? I don't expect you to understand. Just pretend I took a trip abroad"—*like Dad did*, she manages not to say.

"Now? Now you're going abroad? At a time like this? At war?"

He is almost begging, and she moans, and her body and soul are transfixed on one point, on his mouth finding its way to her nipple.

She wrenches her gaze away from that mouth. It's for his own good. She's leaving him for his own good. But he won't understand. "I have to go." She repeats the words again and again like an oath, with a furrowed brow. She is denying him, she is doing this for him, she doesn't fully understand it either, but she's feels it strongly—

And how is it that I'm loyal to *them*, to the ones sending him there—she finally extricates something from the fog in her brain—more than to my motherhood?

"Listen, Ofer, listen to me, don't shout at me. Listen!" She cuts him off, and something in her voice must frighten him, introducing an unfamiliar coolness of authority. "Don't fight with me now. I have to leave for a while. I'll explain it, but not now. I'm doing this for you."

"For me? How is it for me?"

She almost says, *When you're older you'll understand*, but in fact she knows it's the opposite: When you're younger you'll understand, when you're a little boy again, making ridiculous bargains with frightening shadows and nightmares, then maybe you'll understand.

And now it's decided. She has to obey this thing that instructs her to get up and leave home, immediately, without waiting even one minute. She cannot stay here. And in some strange and confusing way, this thing seems to be her maternal instinct, which she thought had dulled, and upon which so many doubts had lately been cast.

"Promise me you'll take care of yourself," she says softly, trying to hide the rigid decisiveness emerging behind her eyes. "And don't do anything stupid, d'you hear me? Be careful, Ofer, don't hurt anyone there, and don't get hurt, and know that I'm doing this for you."

"Doing what for me?" He's exhausted by her capriciousness. He's never seen anything like this in her. Since when does she have whims? But then he has a small revelation: "What is this, some kind of vow you're making?"

Ora is happy that he has understood, has come very close. Who, if not he, could understand her? "Yes, you could say it's a vow, yes. And remember that we'll meet when your thing is over, your emergency call-up."

He sighs. "Whatever you say."

She feels him take one step back from the place where they just met—there are still moments, here and there, so rare, when his insides are exposed and revealed to her. And perhaps, she thinks, they are the reason that he prefers the kasbahs and the *mukataas* to a week in the Galilee with her. She guesses that what scares him is not her vow but the fact that she—*she*—is suddenly starting to flip out with all kinds of magical thinking.

Ofer is already pulling his voice together and taking another little step away from her. "Okay, Mom," he sums up, and now he is the grown-up shrugging at her girlish whims. "If that's what you need right now, then cool, go for it. I'm with you. Okay, gotta go now."

"See you soon, Oferiko. I love you."

"Just don't do anything stupid up there, Mom, promise me."

"You know I won't."

"No, promise me." He smiles, and the warmth seeps back into his voice, melting her away.

"I promise, don't worry, I'll be fine."

"Me, too."

"Promise me."

"I promise."

"I love you."

"Awesome."

"Take care of yourself there."

"You too, and don't worry, it'll be fine. Bye."

"Bye, Ofer, my sweet—"

She stands with the phone in her hand, spent and sweaty, and thinks with perfect lucidity: That might have been the last time I hear his voice. She is afraid she may forget it. And another thought: Who knows how many more times I will replay that trivial conversation of meaningless phrases? I told him to take care of himself, and he said don't worry it'll be fine. Perhaps in two or three days the campaign will end and that conversation will join with hundreds of others and settle down and be forgotten. But never before has she had such a clear feeling. All day, freezing cold shards have been digging into her lower abdomen, making every movement painful. Now she sucks the remainder of his voice out of the phone and remembers how, when he was a boy, they built up their goodbye kisses into a long and complicated ritual—but wait, was that with him or with Adam?—a ritual that began with hugs and loud, fervent kisses, growing subtler and gentler, until they finished with a butterfly kiss on his cheek, then on hers, on his forehead and hers, on his lips and hers, the tip of his nose and hers, until only the lightest echo of a touch remained, a fluttering breeze of flesh that was almost unreal.

The phone rings again. A gravelly, hesitant male voice asks if it's Ora. She sits down, short-winded, and listens to his heavy breathing. "It's me," he says, and she replies, "I know it's you." His breath keeps coming through in thin whistles and she thinks she can hear his heart beating. He must have seen Ofer on TV, she thinks, and something jolts her: Now he knows what Ofer looks like.

"Ora, it's over, isn't it?"

"What's over?" She is confused, and horrified by the shadow of the word.

"His army service," he whispers. "When we spoke before he enlisted, you said it would be over today, right?"

She realizes that in the general chaos of the day she has neglected to think about this, about him. She has managed to erase his part in the complication, this man who needs protection today even more than she does.

"Listen," she begins—again that tight-lipped, teacher's *listen*—and his tension reaches her like an electrical current, and she has to concentrate very hard to choose her words; she cannot make a mistake. "Yes, Ofer was supposed to be done today"—she speaks slowly, cautiously, but she can hear the panic in his soul, can almost see him shielding his head with his hands like a beaten child—"but you must know there's an emergency situation, I'm sure you heard it on the news, and there's that campaign, so they took Ofer. In fact they just showed him on TV." As she talks she remembers that he has no television, and she finally grasps the enormity of the shock she is giving him, the reversal from what he expected to what he is now finding out. "Avram, I'll explain everything and you'll see that it's not that bad, not the end of the world."

She tells him again that they took Ofer for the military campaign, and he listens to her, or doesn't, and when she finishes he says lifelessly, "But that's not good."

She sighs. "You're right, it's not good."

"No, I really mean it. It's not good. It's not a good time."

The phone is damp in Ora's hand and her whole arm aches from the effort of holding it, as if the man's entire weight has been poured into the receiver. "What's going on with you?" she whispers. "We haven't talked for ages."

"But you said he was getting out today. You said so!"

"You're right, today is his discharge date."

"Then why aren't they letting him out?!" He is yelling at her now. "You said today was his date! That's what you said!"

A breath of fire seems to come at her from the receiver. She holds the phone away from her face. She wants to scream with him: *He was supposed to get out today!*

They both fall silent. For a moment he seems to have calmed a little, and she whispers, "But how are you, tell me? You disappeared for three years."

He doesn't hear her, just repeats to himself, "This is not good. Keeping him on longer at the last minute is the worst."

Ora, who has rationed all her oaths and talismans to last exactly three years, to the second, and has now exhausted them and herself, feels that beyond Avram's words is a knowledge even keener than her own.

"How long will he be there?" he asks.

She explains that there's no way of knowing. "He was already on his discharge leave, and they suddenly phoned from the army"—she elides—"and asked him to come."

"But for how long?"

"It's an emergency call-up. It could be a few weeks."

"Weeks?"

"It's something like twenty-eight days," Ora says quickly, "but chances are it'll all be over long before that."

They are both exhausted. She collapses from the armchair onto the rug, her long legs folded beneath her, head bowed, her hair falling on her cheek, her body unknowingly reconstructing her adolescent pose. This is how she used to sit when they talked on the phone at seventeen, nineteen, twenty-two, long hours of pouring their souls out to each other. That was back when he still had a soul, Ilan comments from afar.

A quiet rustle passes through the line, interferences of time and memory. Her finger traces the curved pattern in the rug. Someone should research that one day, she thinks sourly: Why does running your finger over a woolly rug bring back memories and longings? She still cannot remove her wedding ring and may never be able to. The metal clings to her flesh and refuses to leave. *And if it came off easily, would you?* Her lips sag. Where is he now—Ecuador? Peru? He might be hiking with Adam among the turtles on the Galápagos, unaware that there's practically a war here. That she had to take Ofer on her own today.

"Ora," Avram says strenuously, as if hoisting himself out of a well, "I can't be alone now."

She stands up quickly. "Do you want me to . . . Wait, what do you want?"

"I don't know."

Her head is spinning and she leans against the wall. "Is there someone who can come and be with you?"

Long seconds go by. "No. Not now."

"Don't you have a friend, some guy from work?" Or some woman, she thinks. That girl he had once, the young one, what about her?

"I haven't been working for two months."

"What happened?"

"They're renovating the restaurant. Gave us all a vacation."

"Restaurant? You work at a restaurant? What about the pub?"

"What pub?"

"Where you worked . . ."

"Oh, that. I haven't been there for two years. They fired me."

I didn't tell him anything either, she thinks. About my dismissals, from work and from the family.

"I don't have the strength, I'm telling you. My strength lasted just until today."

"Listen," she says quietly, calculatedly, "I was planning to go up north tomorrow, so I could stop by your place for a few minutes . . ."

His breath turns rapid again, wheezing, but he doesn't rebuff her immediately. She stands at the window with her forehead touching the glass. The street looks ordinary. No unfamiliar vehicles. The neighbors' dogs aren't barking.

"Ora, I didn't understand what you said."

"Never mind, it was a silly idea." She pulls herself away from the window.

"Do you want to come?"

"Yes?" she answers in confusion.

"That's what you said, isn't it?"

"I guess so."

"But when?"

"Whenever you say. Tomorrow. Now. Preferably now. To tell you the truth, I'm a little afraid to be here on my own."

"So you were thinking of coming?"

"Just for a few minutes. I'm on my way anyway—"

"But don't expect anything. It's a dump."

She swallows, and her heart starts racing. "I'm not scared."

"I live in a dump."

"I don't care."

"Or maybe we could go out and walk around a little. What do you think?"

"Whatever you say."

"I'll wait for you downstairs, and we'll walk around a bit, okay?"

"On the street?"

"There's this pub down the road."

"I'll come and then we'll decide."

"Do you know my address?"

"Yes."

"But I have nothing to give you. The place is empty."

"I don't need anything."

"I've been on my own for almost a month."

"You have?"

"And I think the store's closed."

"I don't need food." As she talks she darts around the apartment, punted from one wall to the next. She has to organize, finish packing, leave notes. She'll go. She'll flee. And she'll take him with her.

"We can . . . there's a kiosk around here—"

"Avram, I couldn't eat a crumb. I just want to see you."

"Me?"

"Yes."

"And then you'll go back home?"

"Yes. No. Maybe I'll go on to the Galilee."

"The Galilee?"

"Never mind that now."

"How long will it take you?"

"To get there or to get out of there?"

No response. Perhaps he didn't get her little joke.

"It'll take me about an hour to close up everything here and get to Tel Aviv." A cab! she remembers and her heart sinks. I need a cab again. And how exactly was I planning to get to the Galilee? She shuts her eyes hard. A distant headache is signaling, probing. Ilan was right. With her, five-year plans last at most five seconds.

"It's a dump here, I'm telling you."

"I'm coming."

She hangs up before he can change his mind and proceeds to charge around in a frenzy. She writes a note for Ofer, sitting down at first, but soon finds herself standing up, hunched over. She explains to him again what she herself has trouble understanding and asks him to forgive her, and promises again that they'll go hiking together when he finishes and asks him to please not go looking for her, she'll be back in a month, mother's word. She puts the note in a sealed envelope on the table and leaves a sheet of instructions for Bronya, the maid, written in simple Hebrew with large letters. She says she is going on an unexpected vaca-tion, asks her to bring in the mail and take care of Ofer if he comes home on leave—laundry, ironing, cooking—and leaves her a check with a larger payment than usual for the month. Then she sends a few quick e-mails and makes some phone calls, mainly to girlfriends, to whom she explains the situation without exactly lying but without telling the whole truth—above all, without mentioning that Ofer went back today, of his own free will, to the army—and almost rudely intercepts puzzled questions. They all know about the planned trip with Ofer, and have been looking forward to it excitedly with her. They realize something has gone wrong and that a different idea, no less exciting and bold, a temptation that is hard to resist, has come up at the last minute. They think she sounds strange, dizzy, as if she has taken something. She keeps apologizing for being mysterious: "It's still a secret," she says with a smile and leaves a trail of worried friends behind her, who immediately call one another to analyze the situation and try to figure out what is going on with Ora. There are some colorful guesses and a few conjectures of passionate pleasure, probably abroad, and perhaps the occasional lick of jealousy at this newfound bird-of-freedom who is their friend.

She phones the Character—phones him at home, despite the time and the explicit prohibition. She does not ask if he can talk, ignores his huffs of anger and alarm, informs him that she'll be gone for a month and that they'll see what happens when she gets back. Then she hangs up, delighted with his muffled whispers. She records a message on the answering machine: "Hi, this is Ora. I'm going away probably until the end of April. Don't leave a message 'cause I won't be able to pick it up. Thanks and goodbye." Her voice sounds tense and too serious, not the voice of someone leaving on an exciting and mysterious vacation, so she records a new message, this time with the cheerful tone of a skier or a bungee-jumper, and hopes that Ilan will hear it when he finally gets wind of the situation in Israel and wants to find out how Ofer is, and that he will be filled with jealousy and amazement at the wild time she must be having. But then she realizes Ofer might call home too, and that sort of tone might rag him, so she records a third message, using the most toneless, formal pitch she can muster, although she is betrayed by her exposed and always slightly wondrous voice. She grows angry at herself for being preoccupied with such things, and in a state of distraction she dials Sami's number.

After leaving Ofer at the meeting point, she had sat down next to

Sami in the taxi and apologized for the shameful mistake she had made by calling him. With utter simplicity she explained what state she had been in that morning and, in fact, for the rest of the day as well. Sami drove while she spoke at length, until she had completely unburdened herself. He said nothing and did not turn to face her. She was a little surprised by his silence and said, "What I'd like most now is to just scream about the fact that you and I have even reached this point." Expressionless, Sami opened her window with the button on his side and said, "Go ahead, scream." She was embarrassed at first, but then she put her head out the window and screamed until she was dizzy. She leaned back against the headrest and started laughing with relief. She looked at him with eyes tearing from the wind and a flushed neck. "Don't you want to yell?" she asked. And he said, "Trust me, it's better if I don't."

The whole way back he sat hunched forward, focused on driving, and said nothing. She decided not to pester him anymore, and was so tired that she dozed off and slept until they got home. She has replayed their conversation countless times since then—if it could be called a conversation; he had barely spoken—and concluded that she did the right thing, because even though he didn't say anything, she was really talking on his behalf too, loyally representing his side in the little incident without letting herself off easy. When Sami finally pulled up in front of her building she had said, without looking at him, that now, after today, she owed him a favor beyond any of their ongoing scores. In her fluttering heart she thought: a Righteous Gentile's favor. He listened gravely, his lips slightly parted and moving, as if he were memorizing her words, and when he drove away and she walked slowly up the steps, she had the feeling that despite everything that had happened, despite his strange silence the whole way back, their friendship had actually deepened today, having been tempered by a more genuine fire: the fire of reality.

BUT WHEN SHE CALLS, even before explaining that she has to make a very urgent trip to Tel Aviv, Sami answers with crushing coldness that he isn't feeling well. He threw his back out right after getting home from their trip and he has to lie down for a few hours. Ora senses the lie in his voice and her heart sinks. The thing she has kept pushing away since they parted, which has tormented her with regular bites of mockery and doubt, now solidifies and slams her, revealing her own naïveté, her own stupidity. She wants to say that she understands and will call another taxi, but she hears herself trying to persuade him to come.

"Mrs. Ora, I need to rest now. I've had a rough day, and I can't do two big trips in one day."

She is deeply hurt by his "Mrs. Ora" and almost hangs up. But she doesn't, because she feels that until she clears up what happened between them today, she will have no peace. Patiently, without losing her temper, she says that she too, as he well knows, has had a difficult day, but Sami cuts her off and offers to send one of his drivers. At this point she pulls herself together and remembers that she has her dignity too, if only a little. She says haughtily that there is no need, thank you, she'll manage. The coldness in her voice must have alarmed him, and he asks her please not to take it personally, and then he pauses. Hearing the new acquiescence in his voice, she cracks and says, "But what can I do, Sami? I always take you personally." He sighs. She waits quietly. She can hear someone, a man, talking loudly and excitedly in Sami's house. Sami wearily tells the man to be quiet. And because of the fatigue in his voice, or perhaps because of a shadow of desperation that accompanies it, she suddenly feels a great urgency to see him again, immediately. She has the feeling that if she can just spend a little more time with him, even a few moments, she can straighten out everything that went wrong. What I did before wasn't really mending, she thinks. This time I'll talk with him about completely different things, things we've never talked about, the roots of my mistake today, the fears and the hatred we both drank with our mothers' milk. Maybe we haven't even started talking, she thinks oddly: maybe in all those hours that we drove and talked so much, and argued and jabbed each other and laughed, we never really started talking.

The yelling in Sami's house grows louder. There is a heated argument among three or four people, and a woman is shouting. It might be Inaam, Sami's wife, although Ora does not recognize the voice. She begins to wonder if it has something to do with her and what happened between them today, and if it is possible—a crazy thought, but on a day like this, in a country like this, anything is possible—that someone has informed on Sami for driving a soldier to the operation.

"Wait a minute," says Sami, and addresses the young man in sharp, quick Arabic. He shouts with a violence that Ora has never imagined in him, but instead of getting riled up, the man replies in an accusatory tone full of contempt, grunting his words in a way that sounds to Ora like a spray of poison. She hears the sobs of a small child, much smaller than Sami's youngest, and then there is a thud. Perhaps someone kicked a table or even threw a chair. She increasingly feels that the incident is connected to their trip and wants to end the call and disappear from his life without doing any more damage. He slams the receiver down on the table, and she hears his footsteps receding and almost hangs up, yet continues to listen, transfixed: the fabric of their privacy has been ripped open, providing a rare porthole, and she is drawn to it. This is what they're like when they're alone, she thinks, without us, if it really is without us, if they even have a without us. Then she hears a bitter, wild yell, and she cannot tell if it came from Sami or from the other man, and then there are two loud smacks, like hands clapping or cheeks being slapped, and then silence, broken only by the thin, desperate wail of the boy.

Ora leans weakly against the kitchen table. Why did I have to call him again? she thinks. How stupid. What was I even thinking— that after driving me to the Gilboa and back he'd be able to drive me to Tel Aviv? I just keep making mistakes. Whatever I touch goes wrong.

His voice comes back to her, frightened and cracked. Now he speaks rapidly, almost whispering. He wants to know where exactly she needs to go in Tel Aviv and asks if she minds making a stop in the south of the city, where he has to take care of something. Ora is confused. She was about to tell him to forget the whole thing, but she senses that he must need her very much, and his neediness presents an opening for mend-ing, and she swears to herself she will only go as far as Tel Aviv with him and then take a different cab to the Galilee, no matter the cost. He asks urgently, "Is that okay, Ora? Can I come? Are you ready to leave?" The commotion in the background has started up again, and now it is no longer an argument. The other man is shouting, but he seems to be shouting at himself, and a woman laments in a desperate sort of prayer—Ora now thinks it probably is Inaam—a prolonged, defeated wail. For a moment the sound is suffused with a distant moan that Ora has heard once before. It has been decades since she's recalled the sob-bing of the Arab nurse from the isolation ward, in the small Jerusalem hospital where she stayed with Avram and Ilan.

Ora asks Sami if they'll be delayed in South Tel Aviv for long. "Five minutes," Sami says, and when he senses her hesitation he implores her explicitly, which he seldom does: "I need this from you as a big favor." She remembers the promise she gave him only a few hours earlier and feels a twinge of poetic justice—Righteous of the Nations, my ass. "That's fine," she says.

She carries her backpack down to the sidewalk and with a sudden impulse goes back and picks up Ofer's, too, which is packed and ready for the trip and now sits forlorn. She ignores the ringing phone, because she thinks it must be Avram, alarmed at his boldness and calling to beg her not to come. But it might also be Sami, with a change of heart. And quickly, like a fugitive, she goes down the steps, those very same steps up which—in a day or a week, or maybe never, yet she knows they will, she has no doubt—the notifiers will climb, three of them usually, so they say, quietly they'll climb up those steps. It is impossible to believe that this will happen, but they will, they will climb up the steps, this one and the next, and that one that's slightly broken, and on their way they will silently recite the information they are bringing her. All those nights she has spent waiting for them, ever since Adam enlisted and through all his stints in the Territories, and then for the three years of Ofer's service. All those times she has walked to the door when the bell rings and told herself, This is it. But that door will remain shut a day from now, and two, and in a week or so, and that notification will never be given, because notifications always take two, Ora thinks—one to give and one to receive—and there will be no one to receive this notice, and so it will not be delivered, and this is the thing that is suddenly illuminated in her with a light that grows brighter by the minute, with needle-sharp flashes of furious cheer, now that the house is closed up and locked behind her and the phone inside is ringing incessantly and she herself is pacing the sidewalk, waiting for Sami.

The more she thinks about it, the more exciting she finds the strange notion that descends upon her unexpectedly but with a blaze of inspiration—and it's so unlike me, she laughs, it's much more like one of Avram's ideas, or even Ilan's, not at all mine—until she has no doubt that what she is about to do is right, that it is the right protest, and it delights her to roll that word over her tongue and bite into it: protest, my protest. She likes the way her mouth grips the fresh, squirming little prey, her protest, and the new muscularity spreading through her tired body feels good. It is a meager and pathetic sort of protest, she knows, and in an hour or two it will dissipate and leave an insipid taste, but what else can she do? Sit and wait for them to come and dig their notification into her? "I'm not staying here," she declaims, trying to embolden herself. "I'm not going to receive it from them." She lets out a dry, surprised laugh: That's it, it's decided, she'll refuse. She will be the first notification-refusenik. She stretches her arms over her head and fills her lungs with sharp, refreshing evening air. A deferment—she'll get a deferment, for her and, more important, for

Ofer. More than that she cannot hope for right now. Just a short protest deferment. Her mind is flooded with waves of warmth and she marches quickly around the backpacks. Undoubtedly there is a fundamental flaw in her plan, some obvious illogic that will soon be discovered and undo the whole thing and mock her and send her home with her two packs. But until then, she is free of herself, of the cowardice that has stuck to her for the past year, and she repeats softly to herself what she is about to do, and once again reaches the strange conclusion that if she runs away from home, then the deal—this is how she thinks of it now—will be postponed a little, at least for a short while. The deal that the army and the war and the state may try to impose upon her very soon, maybe even tonight. The arbitrary deal that dictates that she, Ora, agrees to receive notification of her son's death, thereby helping them bring the complicated and burdensome process of his death to its orderly, norma- tive conclusion, and in some way also giving them the pronounced and definitive confirmation of his death, which would make her, just slightly, an accessory to the crime.

With these thoughts her strength suddenly runs out and she col- lapses onto the sidewalk and sits between the two backpacks, which now seem to crowd in on her, protecting her like parents. She hugs the stubby, overflowing packs, pulls them to her, and silently explains that she might be a little insane at the moment, but in this wrestling match between her and the notifiers she must go all the way, head to head, for Ofer, so that she won't feel afterward that she gave in without even a flicker. And therefore, when they come to inform her, she will not be here. The parcel will be returned to sender, the wheel will stop for an instant, and it may even have to reverse a little, a centimeter or two, no more. Of course the notice will be dispatched again immediately—she has no illusions. They won't give up, they cannot lose this battle, because their surrender, even just to one woman, would mean the col- lapse of the entire system. Because where would we be if other families adopted the idea and also refused to receive notice of their loved ones' deaths? She has no chance against them, she knows. No chance at all. But at least for a few days she will fight. Not for long, just twenty-eight days, less than a month. This is possible, it is within her power, and in fact it is the only thing possible for her, the only thing within her power.

. . .

She sits down in the back of Sami's taxi again. Next to her sits a six- or seven-year-old boy—even Sami doesn't know his exact age—a thin Arab boy, burning with fever. "It's the kid of one of our guys," Sami says cryptically. "Just someone's," he replies when she presses. Sami was asked to take the boy to Tel Aviv, to a place on the south side of the city, to his family. Sami's family or the boy's? That, too, remains unclear, and Ora decides not to bother him with questions for now. Sami looks haggard and frightened, and one of his cheeks is swollen as if he has a toothache. He doesn't even ask why she's lugging two backpacks at this time of night. Without the spark of curiosity in his eyes he looks lifeless, almost like a different person, and she realizes there's no point bringing up the Gilboa trip again. Although the taxi is dark, she can see that the boy is wearing some familiar clothes: a pair of jeans that used to belong to her Adam, with a Bugs Bunny knee patch, and an ancient T-shirt of Ofer's bearing a Shimon Peres election slogan. The clothes are too big for him, and Ora suspects this is the first time he's worn them. She leans forward and asks what's wrong with him. Sami says the boy is sick. She asks his name, and Sami says quickly, "Rami. Call his name Rami." She asks, "Raami or Rami?" "Rami, Rami," he replies.

If he didn't need me for this trip, Ora thinks, he wouldn't have come. He's taking out on me whatever he has against those guys who were making a scene at his house. She consoles herself with the thought that as soon as she has the chance, she will tell Ilan about the way Sami has been treating her—let's see him act so tough with Ilan—and she knows Ilan will chew him out, for her sake, or maybe even fire him, to prove to her how committed he still is and how protective of her. Ora sits up a little straighter and pulls her shoulders back—why on earth is she enlisting Ilan to help her? This is between her and Sami, and as for that kind of protection from Ilan, that knightly patronage, she can do without it, thank you very much.

Her body sinks down again, and her face trembles uncontrollably, because she is pierced by his desertion. Not the loneliness or the insult, but the amputation itself, the phantom pain of the empty space Ilan left at her side. In the dark she sees her reflection in the window and feels the unfamiliar yet sharp sorrow of her skin, which has not been truly loved for a long time, and her face, which no one has looked at with the kind of love that has intensified over years. The Character, Eran, who got her the job with the museum in Nevada, is seventeen years younger than she, a meteoric computer genius full of entrepreneurial projects, and she doesn't even know how to define him: Friend? Lover? Fuck? And what is she to him? "Love" is undoubtedly a generous term for what they have, she thinks, laughing silently, but at least he is proof that even after Ilan her body still emits the particles that attract another person, another man. She sinks deeper and deeper into her thoughts, and all the while they drive in a long snarl of traffic that moves with unnatural silence through the valley of Sha'ar HaGay and becomes even thicker around the airport. "Checkpoints everywhere today," Sami suddenly throws out. Something in his voice seems to signal her. She waits for him to say something else, but he keeps quiet.

The boy has fallen asleep. His forehead glistens with sweat, and his head rocks with strange ease on his delicate neck. She notices that Sami has spread out a thin old blanket under him, probably so he won't soil the new upholstery with his sweat. His wafer-thin right hand suddenly rises and flutters in front of his face, then above his head, and Ora reaches out and hugs the boy to her. He freezes and opens his eyes, which look dark and almost blind, and stares at her uncomprehendingly. Ora does not move, hoping he will not reject her. He breathes quickly and his gaunt chest moves up and down, and then, as though having lost the power to understand or resist, he shuts his eyes and falls limply against her body, and his warmth spreads to her through their clothing. After a few moments she dares to readjust her arm around him and feels his birdlike shoulders tense up at her touch. She waits again, presses his head gently against her shoulder, and only then resumes breathing.

Sami straightens up and looks at them in the rearview mirror. His eyes are expressionless, and Ora has the peculiar sensation that he is comparing what he sees to some imagined scene. She grows uncomfortable under his gaze, and almost detaches herself from the boy, but she does not want to wake him. She finds the embrace pleasant, despite the intense heat he emits and the sweat pooling between his face and her shoulder and the thread of saliva smeared on her arm—or perhaps it is because of all these things, because of the heat and the dampness, like a forgotten stamp of childhood that now returns to imprint her. She glances at him sideways: his hair is cut crudely, and through the short bristle she can see a long sickle-shaped scar from a hurt that did not heal properly. His small face, crowded against her, is stubborn. He looks like a tiny, embittered old man, and she is happy to see that his fingers are long and thin and beautiful. He places them unconsciously on her hand, and after a few minutes he turns his hand over in his sleep, revealing a soft, cherubic palm.

Ora feels a pang: Ofer. She hasn't thought of him for almost an hour.

She will not have Ofer's hands today. Not the large, broad hands with the prominent veins and the black lines of gun grease under bitten fingernails that even three months after his release—she knows from Adam—will not completely disappear. Nor will the hard calluses covering every knuckle and joint, or the channels of healed cuts, and the scars, and the layers of skin that have been grazed, burned, scratched, cut, torn, stitched, grown and peeled, smeared and bandaged until they finally look like a brown, waxy coating. That military hand, still so expressive in its movements, in the generosity of its touch, in the fingers embracing one another, in the childlike habit of the thumb repeatedly smoothing over its brethren as if counting them, in the distracted gnawing of the skin around the little fingernail—*You're wrong, Mom*, he tells her as he gnaws, but she can't remember what they were talking about. Just a fragmentary image of his biting, furrowing his brow. *You're absolutely wrong about that, Mom.*

Now, as the boy leans on her with amazing trust and sows modest but unfounded pride in her, she seems to be getting confirmation of something she herself had begun to doubt. "You're an unnatural mother," Adam had explained not long ago, before he left home. Just like that, so simply and almost without any color in his voice, he had crushed and refuted her with an assertion that sounded scientific, objective. A lasso of distant memory floats over and tightens softly around her throat, and she sees Ofer's swollen little fist right after he was born. They placed him on her chest while someone did something to her down below, digging, stitching, talking to her, joking. "We'll be done in a minute," the man had said. "Time flies when you're having fun, huh?" She was too tired even to ask him to take pity on her and be quiet, and she tried to draw strength from the large blue eyes looking up at her with uncommon tranquillity. From the moment he was born he always searched for eyes. From the moment he was born she drew strength from him. And now she saw his tiny fist—*fistaloo*, Avram would have said had he been with her in the delivery room; even now she finds it hard to accept that he wasn't there with her and Ofer; how could he not have been there with them?—with the deep crease around the wrist, and the bold red of the tiny hand itself, which until moments ago had been an internal organ and still looked like it. The hand slowly opened and revealed to Ora for the first time its conch-like, enigmatic palm—What have you brought me, my child, from the deep, dark universe?—with the thicket of lines drawn all over it, covered with a white, fatty layer of web-bing, with its translucent pomegranate-seed fingernails, and its fingers that closed up again and gripped her finger tightly: You are hereby betrothed to me with the wisdom of thousands of years and ancient epochs.

The boy gurgles and his tongue explores his lips. Ora asks Sami if he has any water. In the glove compartment is her bottle from the previous trip. She holds it to the boy's lips and he drinks a little and splutters. Perhaps he doesn't like the taste. She pours some water into her palm and touches his forehead lightly, and his cheeks, and his dry lips. Sami looks at her again with that same tensely observing gaze. It is the gaze of a director, she realizes, examining a scene he has set up. The boy shivers and his body burrows more deeply into hers. He suddenly opens his eyes and looks at her without seeing, but his lips part in a strange, dreamy smile, and for a moment he contains both poise and childish-ness, and she leans forward again and asks Sami in a firm whisper what his real name is.

Sami takes a deep breath. "What for, Ora?"

"Tell me his name," she repeats, her lips white with anger.

"His name is called Yazdi. Yazdi, he's called."

The boy hears his name and trembles in his sleep and lets out frag-ments of Arabic words. His legs jerk sharply, as though he is dreaming of running, or fleeing.

"He needs to see a doctor urgently," Ora says.

"The people near Tel Aviv, the family, they have the most specialist doctor for his illness." Ora asks what his illness is, and Sami says, "Something with his stomach, he wasn't born right with the stomach, digestion, something about that. There's only three or four things he eats, everything else comes out." Then he adds, as if in a forced confes-sion, "And he's not right, here."

"Where?" The side of her body touching the boy tenses up.

"In the head. A retard. Around three years ago, all of a sudden, retarded."

"All of a sudden? That's not something that happens suddenly."

"With him it did." Sami purses his lips.

She turns to face the window. She can see her reflection with the boy leaning on her. They are driving very slowly. A sign alerts them to a roadblock three hundred meters ahead. Sami moves his lips quickly, as though arguing with someone in his mind. He raises his voice briefly: "What do I need this, everyone on me, *yechrabethom*, they think I'm some kind of . . ." Then his voice is swallowed up in incomprehensible mumblings.

Ora leans forward. "What's the story?" she asks quietly.

"No story."

"What's the story with this kid?" she demands.

"There's no story!" he suddenly shouts and hits the wheel with his hand. The boy grasps her and stops breathing. "Not everything always has to have a story, Ora!" She senses the contempt wrapped around her name in his voice. It seems to her that as he speaks, almost from one word to the next, he is shedding his Israeli, sabra accent, and a different sound, rough and foreign, is sneaking in. "You people," he hisses through the rearview mirror, "you're always looking for a story in everything. So you'll have it for your *telefision* show or a movie for your *bestivals*, not so? Ha? Not so?"

Ora pulls back as though she's been slapped. "You people," he called her. "Bestival," he said, brandishing the accent of Palestinians from the Territories, whom he's always derided. He was defying her with a put-on "dirty Arab" persona.

"And this kid, it's just a sick kid, just nothing. Sick. A *ree*-tard. You can't make a movie about him! There's no story here! We take him, we drop him at a house down there, with some doctor, we go to wherever you need, we drop you there, and *khalas*, everyone's happy."

Ora's cheeks are flushed. It was the way he shoved her into that "you people" that riled her up and, as though she really is not facing him alone—as though she is with *them*—she says slowly, almost spelling out each letter, "I want to know who this child belongs to. Now, before we reach the checkpoint, I want to know."

Sami does not reply. She senses that her voice, her authority, has restored his wits and reminded him of a thing or two, things she has never before wanted or needed to mention explicitly. There is a long silence. She feels her will and his arch their backs at each other. Then

Sami lets out a long breath and says, "He's the kid of a guy I know, an okay guy, there's nothing on him in the, you know, in the security. Don't worry. You got nothing to worry about." His shoulders droop and crumple. He runs his hand over his bald spot, touches his forehead, and shakes his head in dismay. "Ora, I don't know what's wrong with me. I'm tired, beat. You made me crazy today, the lot of you. I've had enough. I need some quiet. Just quiet, *ya rab*."

She leans her head back. Everyone's going out of their minds, she thinks. He's allowed. Through half-closed eyelids she can see him throwing nervous glances at the passengers in the cars on either side. The three lanes merge into two, then into one. Up ahead they can see blue flashing lights. A police jeep is parked diagonally on the side of the road. Without moving her lips Ora says, "If they ask me, what do I say?"

"If they ask, tell them he's your boy. But they won't ask." He stares ahead and tries not to meet her eyes in the mirror.

Ora nods quietly. So that's my role, she thinks. That's why he's wearing these clothes, the jeans and the Shimon Peres. She presses the boy to her and his head falls on her chest. She says his name quietly into his ear and he opens his eyes and looks at her. She smiles, and his eyelids shut again, but a moment later he smiles at her as if in a dream. "Turn the heat on, he's shivering."

Sami cranks the heat up. She is boiling, but the boy's shivering subsides a little. She wipes his sweat with a tissue and smoothes her hand over his hair. The fever speaks to her skin. About a year ago, an eccentric old man from the village of Dura was left in a meat locker in Hebron. He spent almost forty-eight hours there. He did not die and may even have fully recovered. But since that day her life, her family's life, had slowly begun to unravel. The blue lights are flashing everywhere now. There are six or seven police vehicles. Patrolmen and police officers and army officers dart on the shoulders of the road. Ora is dripping with sweat. She reaches into her blouse and pulls out a thin silver chain with a *shiviti* amulet, an enamel pendant bearing the inscription "I have set the Lord always before me." Gently, almost stealthily, she places the *shiviti* on the boy's forehead and holds it there for a moment. Her friend Ariela gave it to her years ago. "Everyone needs a little churchagogue," she said when Ora laughed and tried to reject the gift. But in the end she started wearing it every time Ilan went overseas, and when her father was hospitalized, and in other can't-do-any-harm situations—a superstitious belief in God, she explained to anyone who asked—and she kept wearing it throughout Adam's army service, and then Ofer's. Now, in order to do the right thing with everyone and not convert the little Muslim without his knowledge, she whispers to herself, *I have set Allah always before me.*

The police cars close in on their lane. Lengths of barbed wire zigzag all over the road. The cops are jumpy. They shine powerful flashlights into the cars and examine the passengers for a long time, constantly shouting to one another. A few officers stand along the side of the road talking on cell phones. This is worse than usual, Ora thinks. They're not usually this edgy. There is only one car in front of them, and Ora leans forward and says urgently, "Sami, I want to know now, who does this child belong to?"

Sami looks ahead and sighs. "He's no one, really, just the son of a guy who does plaster work for me, from the Territories. Honestly, he's an IR, you know. Illegal resident. And since yesterday night he got like this. Sick all night, and this morning, throwing up all the time, and with blood in . . . *ya'ani,* in the bathroom."

"Didn't you get him any help?"

"Sure we did. We brought a nurse from the village, *ya'ani,* and she said for his disease we have to go to a hospital urgent, but how can we go to a hospital with him illegal?" His voice dies down and he grunts and murmurs to himself, perhaps reconstructing some conversation or argument, and then he slams the wheel with his hand.

"Calm down," Ora says sharply. She runs a hand quickly to smooth over her disheveled face. "Calm down now, it'll be all right. And smile!"

A young policeman, almost a kid himself, comes up to them and vanishes from Ora's sight when the brilliance of his flashlight hits her. She blinks painfully; this sort of light is torture for her defective retinas. She smiles broadly in the general direction of the light. The officer makes quick circles with his other hand, and Sami rolls down his window. "All is good?" says the policeman in a Russian accent and thrusts his head into the car to scan their faces. Sami, in a pleasant, rich, masterly voice, replies, "Good evening, everything is excellent, *baruch hashem.*"

"Where are you coming from?"

"From Beit Zayit," Ora says, smiling.

"Beit Zayit? Where's that?"

"Near Jerusalem." Even without looking at Sami, Ora feels a spark of astonishment at the policeman's ignorance pass between them.

"Near Jerusalem," the officer repeats, perhaps to gain time for scanning them. "And where are you headed now?"

"Tel Aviv," Ora replies with a pleasant smile. "To visit family," she adds without being asked.

"Trunk," says the officer, backing away from the car window. He walks around to the trunk and they hear him rummage and shake the two backpacks. Ora sees Sami's shoulders tense up, and a thought flies through her mind: Who knows what he's carting back there? Possibilities flash in her mind like scenes from a deranged movie. Her eyes quickly scan Sami's body, gather information, sort, weigh, rule out. A completely impersonal mechanism has been activated in her, a complex array of acquired reflexes. She barely has time to realize what she is doing. A fraction of a second, no more. She flits around the whole world and back, and nothing on her face moves.

Sami might or might not have noticed what she went through. There is no way to know from his expression. He's had a lot of practice too, she thinks. He sits there, rigid and chunky, one finger drumming rapidly on the gearshift.

The policeman's face—sharp, fox-like, ears pulled back, the face of a boy whom life has chiseled too soon—reappears, this time in her window. "Whose are those two backpacks, missus?"

"Mine. I'm going to the Galilee tomorrow, on a hike." She smiles broadly again.

The policeman looks at her and the boy for a long time and turns back with half his body, apparently wanting to consult with someone. One of his fingers rests sloppily on the open window beside her. Ora looks at it and thinks: amazing how a thin finger can stop, prevent, decide a fate. How thin the fingers of arbitrariness are sometimes. The cop calls out to one of the officers, but he is busy on the phone. Deep down Ora knows that she is the one arousing suspicion. Something about her signaled to the policeman that there is guilt here. His face turns back to her. She thinks that if he looks at her that way for one more minute she will collapse.

The boy wakes up and blinks in confusion at the flashlight. Ora grins and grasps his shoulders tightly. The boy slowly moves his spindly arms in the ray of light, and for a moment he looks like a fetus swimming in amniotic fluid. Only then does he notice the face and the uniform behind the light and his eyes widen, and Ora feels a strong jerk through his body and she holds him tighter. The policeman leans in and examines the boy. A note of bitter abandonment stretches from his face to the boy's. The beam of light drops to the boy's body, lighting up the words *Shimon Peres, My Hope for Peace*. The cop pulls the corners of his mouth into a smirk. Ora feels a heavy weariness descend upon her, as though she has despaired of understanding what is going on. Only Yazdi's wild heartbeats against her arm keep her sitting up straight. She wonders how he knows that he must keep quiet now. How can he keep so wonderfully quiet? Like a baby partridge that freezes and camouflages itself when it hears its mother's warning chirp.

And how do I know how to be a mother partridge? she thinks. An utterly natural mother partridge.

A car honks behind them, and then another. The policeman sniffs. Something is bothering him. Something isn't right. He is about to ask another question, but Sami, with acrobatic swiftness, beats him to it. He laughs heartily, jerks his head back at Ora, and says to the cop, "Don't worry, buddy, she's one of ours."

The policeman curls his lip in slight revulsion, moves his flashlight around, and waves them through. The little interrogation had lasted for only a few minutes, but Ora's body is bathed in sweat—her own and the boy's.

"An IR?" she asks later, when she regains her voice and Sami starts accelerating toward the Ayalon freeway. "You employ workers from the Territories?"

Sami shrugs. "Everyone has workers from the Territories. Them ones are the cheapest, the *dafawim*. You think I can afford a plasterer from Abu Ghosh?"

She sits back more comfortably. The boy, too. Ora wipes off his sweat and her own. She keeps looking to her side, thinking she can still see the policeman's finger on her window ledge, pointing at her. She doesn't think she will ever be able to go through a roadblock experience like that one again. "And what you said to him about me being 'one of ours'?"

Sami smiles and licks his lower lip. Ora knows the gesture: he is savoring a good quip even before it comes out. She smiles to herself and massages her neck and stretches her toes. For a moment it feels as though they are putting the house back in order after a rampage.

" 'One of ours,' " says Sami, "means 'even though you look like a lefty.' "

The boy relaxes a little and falls asleep again. Ora puts his head on her lap. She leans back and breathes slowly. This may be her first quiet moment of the day.

Since Sami has always been a sort of distant extension of Ilan for her, and more recently a connecting thread to him, she begins to feel home-sick. Not for the house she rented in Beit Zayit after the separation, nor for the house in Tzur Hadassah that she and Ilan had bought from Avram. The home she misses achingly is the last home she and Ilan had in Ein Karem, an expansive old two-story house with thick, cool walls, surrounded by cypress trees. It had big arched windows with deep ledges, and decorative floor tiles, some of which wobbled. Ora had seen it for the first time as a student. It stood there, empty and closed up, and it was love at first sight. With Avram's encouragement she wrote a love letter. "My dear, despondent, lonesome house," she began, then pro-ceeded to tell the house about herself and explain how well suited they were for each other. She promised to make it happy. In the envelope she placed a photo of herself with long, curly, copper hair, wearing orange sweats and laughing as she leaned on a bike. She sent it with a note to the owners saying that if they ever decided to sell—and they did.

She and Ilan had become increasingly affluent, even becoming wealthy over the years—Ilan's office flourished: leaving his job twenty years ago to focus on the slightly esoteric field of intellectual property was a hugely successful gamble. Since the mid-eighties the world had filled with ideas, patents, and inventions that needed protection, requir-ing knowledge and swift action wherever legislation and legal loop-holes were concerned in various countries; new computer applications, inventions in communication and encoding, genetic medicine and engi-neering, all kinds of World Trade Organization treaties and agree-ments; Ilan was there one minute before everyone else—and although they could afford to renovate and beautify and build and design what-ever they wanted to, Ilan let her nurture and tame the house as she wished, and so she allowed it to be itself, to grow at its own pace, and happily mount into a plethora of disparate styles. For several years there was a huge glass-doored refrigerator in the kitchen, an extremely effi-cient eyesore that Ora had bought at a liquidation sale from a man who sold equipment to supermarkets. She got the dining-room chairs for a steal at the Jerusalem café Tmol Shilshom, because Adam once mentioned in conversation how comfortable they were. The shadowed living room was a lair of thick rugs, huge cushions, and pale bamboo furniture, with overflowing bookshelves covering three walls. The massive dining table, the hostess's pride and joy, which could seat fifteen guests without elbows touching, was carved and adorned by Ofer as a surprise for her forty-eighth birthday. Ofer made it round: "That way, no one ever has to sit at a corner." The house itself was finely attuned and responsive to Ora's moods. It carefully, hesitantly shed its age-old gloominess, stretched its limbs, and cracked its stiff joints, and when it realized that Ora was permitting it to retain the occasional pocket of charming abandon and even some healthy neglect, it grew into a comfortable unkemptness, until at times, when a certain light hit, it almost looked happy. Ora felt that Ilan was also content in the house, with the collegiate mess she created in it, and that her taste—meaning, her assortment of tastes—was to his liking. Even when things suddenly went bad between them, and their togetherness emptied out with alarming speed, she believed that his affection for the home she had made for them still pulsed inside him. And she remains convinced that beneath the layers in which he began to cloak himself—his impatience and grumbling and constant criticism of everything she did and said, of everything she was; beyond his back-turning, beyond his polite concern and insulting shell of decency toward her, beyond the small and large denials with which he tried to repudiate her and their love and their friendship, and despite his claim that he'd run his course with the relationship—that despite all this he still remembered and knew that he had no better wife or friend or lover than she, and that even now, as they both approach fifty and he has traveled to the far corners of the earth to get away from her, he knows deep in his heart that only together can they continue to bear everything that happened to them when they were young, practically children.

She remembers the way Ilan's face lit up—it was in the army, in Sinai, when they were nineteen and a half and Ilan still dreamed of making movies and music, and Avram was still Avram—when he told her how moved he was every time he read in the book of Kings of how the great woman of Shunem told her husband they should prepare a resting place for the Prophet Elisha. *Let us make, I pray thee, a little chamber on the roof,*

Ilan read to her from the little army-issue Bible. *And let us set for him there a bed, and a table, and a stool, and a candlestick; and it shall be, when he cometh to us, that he shall turn in thither.*

They were lying on a narrow cot in his room on the base. Avram must have been at home on leave. His empty cot faced them, and on the wall above it was a line handwritten in charcoal: *It is not good that man should be . . .* The quote trailed off without bothering to include the last word, *alone.* Her head rested in the depression of Ilan's shoulder. He read to her until the end of the chapter, slowly running his long musician's fingers through her hair.

As it turns out, they are not going to South Tel Aviv but to Jaffa, and not to a hospital but to an elementary school that Sami locates only after driving around for a long time. Yazdi, who has recovered slightly, sits with his face pressed to the window and laps up the streets and scenes. Every so often he turns to Ora with a look of disbelief that such things can truly exist. Behind Sami's back the two of them make up a game: he looks at her, she smiles, he looks back at the window and then peeks at her again over his shoulder. When they drive along the waterfront promenade, Sami says to Yazdi, *"Shuf el bahr"*—look at the sea. The boy puts his head and shoulders out of the window, but beyond the streetlamps the sea is just a dark mass with a few frothy mounds. He murmurs, *"Bahr, bahr,"* and spreads his fingers out. Ora asks, "Haven't you ever seen the sea?" He does not answer, and Sami laughs: "This one, where's he gonna see the sea? At the promenade of the refugee camp?" A breeze carries a whiff of saltwater, and Yazdi's nostrils widen as he sniffs and tastes. His face has a strange, almost tortured expression, as if its features cannot tolerate the happiness.

Then the illness bears down on him again. His arms and head begin to jerk, and he looks like someone trying to avoid things being thrown at him. Ora keeps mopping his sweat with tissues, and when they run out she uses a rag she finds under the front seat. There is a plastic bag there too, with his underwear, a pair of socks, a Ninja Turtles T-shirt that used to belong to Ofer and was passed on to Sami's kids, a screwdriver with spare blades, and a clear globe with a tiny dinosaur inside. Yazdi is thirsty and his tongue flicks around in his mouth. The water bottle is empty, but Sami is afraid to stop for water at a kiosk. "On a day like this, an Arab at one of these kiosks, it's not a good idea," he explains drily. Soon, perhaps because of Sami's nervous driving and the circuitous ambling around the maze of Jaffa's alleyways, Yazdi starts to vomit.

Ora feels his body seize up, his ribs spasmodically rise and fall, and tells Sami to stop the car. Sami gripes that he can't pull over here: a police van is parked on the opposite sidewalk. But when he hears another fitful gargle from the back, he speeds up as if he's lost his mind. He runs red lights, looking for a dark corner or an empty lot, and yells at Yazdi in Arabic to hold it in. He threatens the boy, and curses him and his father and his father's father. A projectile of vomit erupts from the boy's mouth. Sami yells at Ora to aim Yazdi's head at the floor, away from the upholstery, but the boy's head jerks in all directions like a balloon with its air let out, and Ora is sprayed all over her feet, pants, shoes, and hair.

Sami's right hand reaches back like lightning, feels around, touches something, and pulls back in disgust. "Gimme his hand!" he screeches in a thin, feminine voice. "Put his hand here!" Ora mechanically obeys the urgency in his voice, dimly hoping he might know some instant cure or Palestinian-Shamanic trick, and she holds Yazdi's limp hand on the fake-wood space between the two front seats. Sami, without even looking, slams down on the hand with his heavy sledgehammer of a fist. Ora screams as though she is the one who's been hit, and reaches to pull back Yazdi's hand, but Sami, who doesn't see what is happening, lands another blow on her arm.

A few minutes later they reach the school. They stop outside a locked gate and a young bearded man, who was waiting in the shadows inside, emerges and looks in all directions, then motions to Sami to follow him along the fence. They walk with the fence between them. At a dark corner the young man holds open a broken part of the fence and comes out to Sami, and the two men whisper quickly, glancing around. Ora gets out of the taxi and inhales the damp night air. Her left arm is burning, and she knows the pain will get worse. In the light of the streetlamp she sees that she is covered with vomit stains. She tries to shake herself off. The bearded man holds Sami's arm and walks him back to the taxi. They look at Yazdi lying inside, and Sami examines the upholstery with grieving eyes. They both ignore Ora. The young man gives some sort of signal over a cell phone, and three boys come running out of the dark school. Not a single word is uttered. The three pull Yazdi out of the taxi and carry him inside quickly, through a side gate. One of them holds Yazdi's shoulders, and the other two hold his legs. Ora looks at them and thinks, This is not the first time they've carried someone inside like that. Yazdi's head and arms droop, and his eyes are closed, and it is somehow clear to her that this is not his first time, either.

When she starts walking after them, the bearded man turns to her and then looks at Sami. Sami goes up to her: "Maybe it's better if you stay here."

Ora gives him a piercing look. He gives in, walks back to the bearded man, and whispers something to him. Ora assumes he is telling him it's all right; perhaps he even said, "She's one of us."

Inside, the school is completely silent and dark, illuminated only by the moon and the streetlamp. Sami and the bearded man disappear, swallowed up into one of the rooms. Ora stops and waits. When her eyes grow accustomed to the dark, she sees that she is in a fairly large auditorium, with a few corridors leading out of it. Empty window boxes are placed here and there, and posters promoting quiet, neatness, and cleanliness hang crookedly on the walls. She can smell children's sweat and a distant odor of locker rooms and above all the stench of vomit from her own clothes. She wonders how she will find Sami and Yazdi but is afraid to call out to them. She walks carefully through the darkness, taking small steps, with her arms out in front of her, until she reaches a round supporting column in the middle of the auditorium. Her gaze orbits the walls. She sees pictures of faces she cannot make out, possibly Herzl and Ben-Gurion, or perhaps the prime minister and the chief of staff. A small memorial made out of a heap of rocks sits in the corner opposite her, beneath a large picture that seems to be of Rabin, with black metal letters affixed to the wall above. Ora slowly walks around the column, touching it with one hand. The rotation awakens in her the sweet dizziness she used to summon as a child, with a slight sensation of burning in her fingertips.

As though gathering images while she circles, she begins to see shadowy figures of men, women, and children dressed in rags, silent, submissive, dusted with refugee ash. They are standing some distance away, along the walls, watching her. Ora freezes in terror. They're coming back, she thinks. For a brief deceptive moment she is convinced that her motion has made real the nightmare that always flickers in the distance.

A young woman walks up to Ora and whispers in broken Hebrew that Sami said she could wash her clothes in the bathroom.

Ora follows the woman. The hallways rustle with shadows and the sounds of quick steps. Dim shapes hurry past. She hears almost no voices. The woman silently points to the girls' bathroom and Ora goes in. She understands that she must not turn on the light, that the entire place must remain dark. In one of the doorless stalls she sits down and pees into the small toilet. Then she washes her face and hair in the sink, scrubs the vomit off her clothes as best she can, and runs cold water over her aching left arm. When she is done, she stands with both hands on the stainless-steel counter, shuts her eyes, and succumbs to an overwhelming weariness. But with weakness comes a sharp pang of fright, again, as though she has left her post.

What have I done.

I took Ofer to war.

I brought him to the war myself.

And if something happens to him.

And if that was the last time I touched him.

At the end, when I kissed him, I touched his cheek on the soft spot where there's no stubble.

I took him there.

I didn't stop him. I didn't even try.

I called a cab and we went.

Two and a half hours on the road, and I did not try.

I left him there.

I left him for them.

With my own hands, I did.

Her breath stops. She is afraid to move. Paralyzed. It's a feeling she has, a sharp, real knowledge.

Be careful, she thinks at him without moving her lips, and look behind you.

Then, of its own accord, her body begins to move very gently, almost imperceptibly. Shoulders, hips, a slight shift of the waist. She has no control over her limbs. She only feels that her body is communicating to Ofer how he should move to get out of some danger or trap over there. The peculiar involuntary motion continues for a long minute, and then her body quiets and returns to her, and Ora breathes and knows everything is all right, for now. *"Ahh,"* she sighs to her little abdomen reflected in the low mirror.

Sometimes I think I can remember almost every moment I had with him, from the second he was born. Yet at other times I find that entire phases are lost to me. "My friend Ariela gave birth prematurely, in her second trimester," she tells a heavyset older woman in a floral scarf who has come into the bathroom and stands quietly to the side. She watches Ora with kind eyes and seems to be waiting for her to recover from whatever is paining her.

"They gave her an injection," Ora says softly. "An injection that was supposed to kill the fetus in her womb. He wasn't right, he had Down syndrome, and she and her husband decided they couldn't raise a child like that. But the child was born alive, do you see? Do you understand me?" The woman nods and Ora continues. "There must have been a mistake in the amount of stuff they injected, and my friend asked them to let her hold the child for as long as he was alive. She sat up in bed, her husband walked out, he couldn't take it"—Ora flashes her eyes at the woman and thinks she sees a spark of understanding and comradeship— "and for fifteen minutes he was alive in her arms, and she kept talking to him, she hugged him and kissed him all over, it was a boy, and she kissed each of his fingers and fingernails. She always says he looked like a perfectly healthy child, except tiny, and translucent, and he moved around a little and had facial expressions, just like a baby. He moved his hands and his mouth, but he didn't make any sound." The woman listens with her arms folded over her chest. "And very slowly, he simply ended. He just went out like a candle, in total silence and without making any trouble about it, he twisted a little and folded in, and that was that. And my friend remembers those moments even more than the other three childbirths, before and after, and she always says that in the short time she had with him, she tried to give him as much life as she possibly could, and all her love, even though she was actually the one who killed him, or shared the decision to kill him." Ora murmurs and runs her hands stiffly over her head and temples and crushes her cheeks between her hands, and her mouth opens briefly in a silent scream.

The woman bows her head slightly and says nothing. Now Ora notices that she is very old, and that her face is furrowed with deep wrinkles and covered with tattoos.

"And what do I have to complain about?" Ora continues in a cracked voice. "I held my child for twenty-one years—*wakhad wa-ashrin sana*," she says in the tentative Arabic she remembers from high school. "But they went by so quickly, and I barely had time for anything with him, but now that his army is finished we could have really started." Her voice breaks but she pulls herself together. "Come on, ma'am, let's get out of here, please take me to Sami."

It isn't easy to find him. The old woman does not know Sami and seems not to understand what Ora wants. Still, she willingly leads her from room to room, pointing inside each one, and Ora peers into the dark classrooms. In some of them she sees people, not many, three here, five there, children and adults, huddled around a cluster of desks whispering, or sitting on the floor and warming up dinners on little gas cookers, or asleep in their clothes on desks and chairs joined together. In one room she sees someone lying on a long bench, with several people bustling around him quickly but silently. In another a man kneels down to bandage the foot of a man sitting on a chair. A young woman cleans the wound of a man with a bare chest and a grimace on his face. From other rooms she hears stifled moans of pain and murmurs of comfort. There is a sharp smell of iodine in the air.

"And in the morning, what happens?" Ora asks in the hallway.

"Morning," the old woman repeats in Hebrew and smiles broadly, "in the morning *kulhum mafish*—they're all gone!" She mimes a bubble bursting.

Ora finally finds Sami and Yazdi. There is no light but the moonlight and the room is utterly silent. She stands in the doorway and looks at the little chairs turned upside down on the desks. A huge cardboard cutout of a seal hangs on the wall, with the caption *Recon-seal-iation*. Each of its parts is a conflict that has to be reconciled: Ashkenazim and Sephardim, left wing and right wing, religious and secular. Sami and the bearded man stand a few steps away, next to the blackboard, talking quietly with an older man who is short, solid, and silver-haired. Sami nods slightly at Ora, but his face is impervious. Something in his posture and the way he cuts through the air as he makes hand gestures is new to her and very foreign. Three little children, two or three years old, discover Ora and start running around her, excitedly pulling her by the pants without any embarrassment. They also make almost no sound, to Ora's surprise: they too are well-trained partridge chicks. She follows them to the corner of the classroom, near the window. A little circle of women tightens around someone in the center. Ora glimpses between the women's heads and sees a large woman sitting on the floor, leaning against the wall with her bare feet stretched out in front of her. She is breast-feeding Yazdi. His mouth is attached to her nipple and his feet hang over her lap. He is wearing different clothes: a brown-and-white-checkered shirt with black pants. For the first time since Ora met him, his face looks serene. The breast-feeding woman watches him with deep concentration. She has a strong, wild face and bony, slightly masculine cheeks, and a full white breast. The women look hypnotized, all strung on one thread. Ora stands on her tiptoes, drawn inside the circle—after all, she has some part in Yazdi too, or perhaps she just wants to touch his hand one last time, to say goodbye. But when she tries to squeeze her way through, the women tighten up against her as one, and she withdraws and stands behind them.

A hand touches her shoulder. Sami. Pale and exhausted. "Come on, we're done here."

"What about him?" She motions at Yazdi with her eyes.

"It'll be okay. His uncle will come soon to get him."

"And who is that?" She looks at the wet nurse.

"A woman. The doctor told her to give him milk. Milk his body doesn't throw out."

"There's a doctor here?"

Sami arches his eyebrows at the short, silver-haired man.

"What is a doctor doing here? What is this place?"

Sami hesitates. "These, these people," he says halfheartedly, "from all over town they come here at night."

"Why?"

"At night it's the IRs' hospital."

"Hospital?"

"For all the ones that get hurt on the job, or the ones that get beat."

As though there's some permanent quota of beatings, Ora thinks.

"*Yalla,*" says Sami, "we're out of here."

"Why here?"

But Sami has left her in the room with the question echoing. She follows him down the corridor. She finds it difficult to leave the place and its secretive, beneficial murmur. And it is also Yazdi—why deny it—or whatever he aroused in her when he leaned against her, when she cleaned up his vomit, when they played peek-a-boo, when she comforted him in her arms after Sami hit them both. She feels that these small gestures have awakened in her a precious, obsolete trait, which she herself had almost forgotten. She thinks of turning back to sneak another look at the great woman breast-feeding him, to see once again the look of utter concentration on her face, and the slight tremor in her forehead. How gently she signaled to him not to bite, Ora thinks. Such natural maternity, and he isn't even her child.

Women and children are washing the floors of the auditorium, and she remembers that years ago Sami told her he could never understand the Jews' logic: "During the day you're always checking us and following us and going through our underwear, and at night you suddenly give us the keys to your restaurants and your gas stations and your bakeries and your supermarkets?"

"Wait," she calls out, chasing after Sami. "Don't the neighbors notice anything?"

He shrugs. "After a week or two, sure they do."

"And then what?"

"Then what? They go somewhere else. Always that way."

They stand outside and Ora looks back. She wonders if one can seek political asylum with refugees, because she feels completely willing to hide out here for the next month. To be the IRs' IR. At least she'd do some good for someone.

Ofer, Ofer, she thinks, where are you? What are you going through now?

For all you know he might be running into the younger brother of that woman, or the son of that guy.

When they reach the taxi, three cheerful little girls jump out holding rags and a little bucket and brushes. They stand aside, giggling and stealing looks at Ora. Sami checks the backseat and sighs deeply. Ora sits down next to him.

Instead of starting the engine, Sami jingles his heavy set of keys. Ora waits. He turns to her, struggling with his potbelly. "Even if you forgive me for before, for hitting, I don't forgive me. I would cut my own hand off for what I did to you."

"Drive," she says wearily. "Someone's waiting for me."

"Wait, I really need this from you."

"What do you want?"

Eyes dart opposite eyes, like dogs chained to either side of a fence. A friendly face, a loved one even, suddenly looks completely foreign. The kind you don't even want to make the effort to decipher, she thinks, to make it yours.

Sami holds his gaze and swallows. "Just that Mr. Ilan won't know anything about this."

A vague stench of vomit still lingers in the taxi, and it occurs to Ora that everything is meshing together, including the "Mr." he suddenly attached to Ilan. *Mister Ilan and Missus Ora.* She pauses. She'd been expecting this request, and had already decided what her price would be. Ilan would be proud of me, she thinks bitterly. "Drive," she tells Sami.

"But what . . . what do you say . . ."

"Drive," she commands, surprised by the trickling sensation of something she has never felt toward him before: the sweetness of power. A slight, tingling burn of her own arbitrary authority. "First drive, then we'll see."

DAYLIGHT BURGEONS as they lie on the edge of a field, bright shades of green unfurl as far as the eye can see, and they wake from a nap, still blanketed with a gossamer of dreams. They are the only two people in the world, there is no one else, and the earth steams with a primeval scent, and the air hums with the rustle of tiny creatures, and the mantle of dawn still hangs overhead, lucent and dewy, and their eyes light up with little smiles of not-yet-fear and not-yet-themselves.

Then Avram's eyes clear. He sees Ora sitting facing him with her back against a huge backpack, beyond which are a field, a grove, and a mountain. With surprising swiftness he jumps up: "What is this place?"

Ora shrugs. "Somewhere in the Galilee. Don't ask me."

"The Galilee?" His face rounds into infinite astonishment. "Where am I?" he whispers.

"Wherever he dumped us last night."

Avram runs a hand over his face. He rubs, scrubs, crushes, and rocks his head back and forth. "Who dumped us, the cabby? The Arab?"

"Yes, the Arab." She reaches out a hand for him to help her up, but he seems not to comprehend the gesture.

"You were yelling," he remembers. "I was asleep. You were shouting at him too, weren't you?"

"Forget about that, it doesn't matter now." She hoists herself up with a groan, encountering hostile joints. And rightly so, she thinks as she scans the list of her sins: lugging Avram's entire weight on her poor back down four flights of steps, then the nightmarish drive, and the two of them walking aimlessly through the fields. She'd fallen a few times on the way, and finally they'd collapsed on the edge of this field and spent a sleepless night on the ground. I'm too old for this, she thinks.

"Those pills knock me out," Avram mumbles. "Prodomol. I'm not used to them. I couldn't do anything."

You did plenty, Ora thinks to herself with a sigh. "What a day I had with him—don't ask."

"But why on earth did he bring us here?" Avram gets worked up again, as if he has only just grasped what has been done to him. "And what now? What do we do, Ora?" More and more fears crowd into him by the minute, and they no longer have space in his body.

Ora brushes her behind and shakes off some earth and dry leaves. Coffee would help, she thinks, and quietly mumbles, "Coffee, coffee," to silence the questions that dart wildly inside her. What do I do with him now? And what exactly was I thinking when I dragged him here? "We're leaving," she pronounces, without daring to look at him.

"What do you mean leaving? Where to? Ora! What do you mean leaving?"

"I suggest," she says, though she cannot believe the words are coming out of her own mouth, "that we pick up our backpacks and explore. Just walk. See where we are."

Avram stares at her. "I have to be at home," he says slowly, like someone explaining a simple fact of life to a mentally handicapped person.

Ora hoists the backpack over her shoulders, sways under its heft, and stands waiting. Avram does not move. The hems of his sleeves tremble. "That's yours," Ora says, pointing to the other backpack, the blue one.

"How could it be mine?" He stumbles away, as though the backpack is a sly beast about to pounce on him. "It's not mine, I don't recognize it," he murmurs.

"It's yours. Let's start walking, we'll talk on the way."

"No," Avram insists, and his unkempt beard bristles a little. "I'm not moving until you explain what—"

"On the way," she interrupts, and starts marching. Her shoulders are hunched and her whole body looks as though an unskilled puppeteer is pulling her strings. "I'll tell you everything on the way; we can't stay here anymore."

"Why not?"

"I mustn't," she replies simply, and as she utters the words she knows she is right, and that this is the law she must now obey: not to stay in one place for too long, not to be a sitting target—for people or thoughts.

Terrified, he watches her walking away toward a path. She'll be back soon, he thinks, she'll be right back. She won't leave me like this. She wouldn't dare. Ora keeps walking without looking back. His lips tremble with anger and insult. Then he stomps his feet and lets out a short, bitter screech that might be her name and might be fuck-you-you-bitch and who-the-hell-do-you-think-you-are and you-psycho and mommy-wait-for-me all in one breath. Ora walks on. Avram weakly lifts up the backpack, slings it over his left shoulder, and starts after her, dragging his feet on the ground.

The path winds through fields and groves. Poplars whiten, and wild mustard towers on both sides of the path in fragrant yellow clusters. It's lovely here, Ora thinks. She keeps walking. She has no idea where she is or where she is going. She can hear his stuttering steps behind her. She peeks over her shoulder: lost and frightened, he feels his way along the open space. She realizes that he moves in light the way she does in darkness, and she recalls the way he looked last night, a hunched, slow shadow in the depths of a dark apartment.

When he opened the door after she'd knocked and kicked for several minutes, she realized that he was in the habit of not turning any lights on. The bell had been yanked out of its casing. There wasn't a single bulb in the stairwell. She'd felt her way up the four flights of steps along crumbling walls and a greasy stone banister, through various stenches that lingered in the air. When he finally opened the door—she quickly removed her glasses, which were new to him—she saw a lump. In the darkness he looked hugely broad, so much so that she wasn't sure it was him at first, and she said his name dubiously. He did not answer, and she said, "I'm here," and searched for more words with which to fill the deepening chasm in her stomach. She was frightened by the darkness in the apartment behind him and by the sense that he was coming out to her like a bear from its den. She boldly reached a hand into the apartment, felt along the wall, and found a switch. They were both flooded with murky yellow light, and their eyes immediately exchanged unmerciful information.

She, ultimately, had been better preserved. Her short-cropped curly hair had turned almost entirely silver, but her expression was still open and innocent and it went out to him—he could feel it even in his dim state—and her large brown eyes still held a constant, serious question. Nevertheless, something in her was slightly dried up and dulled, he could see, and there were a few faint lines, footprints of a bird in the sand, around her lips. Something about her posture was diminished, that upright boldness she'd always had, like a foal. And the generous, laughing mouth, Ora's great mouth, now seemed limp and skeptical.

He had lost a lot of hair in the last three years, and his face had swelled and looked less open. Week-old stubble covered his cheeks and chin. His blue eyes, which used to make her feel parched, had darkened and seemed smaller and sunken. He still did not move, almost blocking the doorway with his body, his thick penguin arms held stiffly at his sides. He stood there in a faded T-shirt from which his body was bursting and grunted to himself and sucked his lips with such irritability that she had to demand: "Aren't you going to let me in?" He walked into the apartment, dragging his bare feet, grunting and growling to himself. She shut the door and followed him into a smell that was an entity unto itself, as if she were entering the folds of a thick blanket. It was the smell of the inside of suitcases and closed drawers and unaired linen and socks under beds and clumps of dust.

And there they were: the heavy breakfront with the peeling polyurethane lacquer, the bald fraying rug, and the awful red armchairs whose upholstery had been ripped and worn even thirty-five years ago. It was his mother's furniture, his only possessions, which he still moved around as he roamed from one apartment to the next.

"Where were you?" he grumbled. "You said you'd be here in an hour."

She hit him with the offer immediately, in a loud and anxious voice, with the defiance and awkwardness of someone who knows exactly how inappropriate her words are, but must somehow nail down her fancies and see what happens. He seemed not to hear her at all. He did not look at her, either. His head, bowed to his chest, moved right and left in delayed little jerks. "Wait, don't say no yet," she said. "Think about it for a minute."

He looked up at her. All his movements were very slow. In the light of the bare bulb she again saw what the last few years had done to him. He spoke heavily: "Regretably, I can't do it now. Maybe another time."

If it hadn't been so sad, she would have burst out laughing. *Regretably*, he said, like a beggar wallowing in trash and sticking his pinky up while drinking tea from a can.

"Avram, I—"

"Ora, no."

Even this monosyllabic speech was beyond his strength. Or maybe it was the taste of her name in his mouth. His eyes suddenly turned red and he looked as though he were sinking even deeper into his flesh.

"Listen to me." She berated him with a new aggression that drew on her confrontation with Sami. "I can't force you to do anything, but hear me out and then make up your mind. I've run away. Do you understand? I cannot sit there and wait for them to come."

"Who?"

"Them." She peered deep into his eyes and saw that he understood.

"But you can't sleep here," he mumbled angrily. "I don't have another bed."

"I don't want to sleep here. I'm going to keep traveling. I came to get you."

He nodded for a long time, even smiled slightly, with the politeness of a tourist in a land whose customs he did not understand. She could see: he wasn't taking in the words at all. "Where's Ilan?" he asked.

"I'm going up north for a few days. Come with me."

"I don't know her, what's the matter with her? Why is she even—"

To her amazement, he spoke his thoughts out loud. Once, years ago, this had been one of his tricks: "Ora doesn't want me anymore, thinks Avram forlorn and wishes he were dead," he would say to her, and grinningly deny that he'd said it, even accuse her of invading his private thoughts. But this was different, troubling, a private, internal conversation that hiccupped from him uncontrollably. He sought out the armchair and collapsed into it, leaning his head all the way back to reveal a thick, red, stubbly throat. "Where's Ilan?" he asked again, half pleadingly.

"There's a cab waiting for me downstairs. I want you to come with me."

"Where?"

"I don't know, we'll go up north. The main thing is not to be here."

One of his fingers moved weakly, as if conducting a tune that played in his mind. "What are you going to do there?"

"I don't know, don't ask me. I have a tent and a backpack and food for the first few days. I have everything for you, too. It's all packed, even a sleeping bag, so come with me."

"For me?" His face reappeared, moonlike and red. "She's mad," he muttered, "totally lost her mind."

Ora was horrified by this exposure of his deepest thoughts and hardened her heart. "I'm not going home until the whole business there is over. Come with me."

He sighed. "What does she think, that I can just pick up and—" He motioned ineffectually across the apartment and at himself, presenting her with evidence and extenuating circumstances.

"Help me," Ora said softly.

He sat silently. He did not, for example, say that they wouldn't come looking for him. That they had no reason to look for him. That he had nothing to do with them. He did not say that it was her problem. And that silence of his, with the traces of decency she imagined she saw in it, was a glimmer of hope. "But maybe they won't come at all," he tried halfheartedly.

"Avram," she said, almost warning.

He took a deep breath. "Maybe nothing will happen to him."

She leaned down right into his face, stared into his eyes, and the murkiest sliver of darkness darted between them, the covenant of their bitter knowledge, the worst of all possible worlds. "Give me two days. You know what? Give me one day, that's all, twenty-four hours, I promise, and tomorrow night I'll bring you back here." She believed what she was saying. She thought she needed to get through the first day and night, and then, who knows, maybe it would all be over and she and Avram could each go back to their lives. Or perhaps after one day and night she herself would wake up from the fantasy, pull herself together and go home and do what everyone else did—sit and wait for them. "So what do you say?" When he did not answer, she groaned, "Help me, Avram, just to get through the first few hours."

His head swayed, he furrowed his brow, and his face grew stern and focused. He thought about what she had done for him and what she had been to him. "What a piece of shit I am," he thought, "I can't even give her one day." She heard him. "I have to buy time. Just another few minutes and I won't be able to . . ." Ora kneeled in front of him and placed her hands on the armrests on either side of him. It was becoming intolerable. He turned his head away. "She's hysterical," he thought grumpily, "and there's something wrong with her mouth." Ora nodded and her eyes filled with tears. "I wish she would just leave," Avram thought out loud and squirmed in his seat. "Just go, leave me. What's she doing here anyway?"

Something prickled on the outskirts of her brain. She demanded to know what he meant when he said in another few minutes he wouldn't be able to . . .

He smiled crookedly, his heavy swollen eyelids barely open, exposing red crescents: "I took a pill. A minute from now I'll be knocked out. It'll be morning by the time—"

"But you knew I was coming!"

"If you'd come sooner . . ." His voice was thickening. "Why didn't you come sooner?"

She hurried into the little bathroom. The bulb over the mirror was burned out. She moved her fingers over the sink as if trying to pull in threads of light from the living room. There was rust on the taps and the drain and around the screws that held the shelves to the pink porcelain tiles. To her surprise there was virtually no medicine on the shelves. Confused, she thought back to the stash of medication he used to keep around. He liked to give her detailed accounts during their rare meetings, before Ofer enlisted: "Numbon, Zodorm, Bondormin, Hypnodorm," he would mumble, "they give them names that sound like notes on a toy xylophone." All she could find now were packets of antihistamines, probably for his hay fever, and a few Assivals and Stilnoxes scattered around, but it was mostly natural sleeping aids. That's good, she thought, he must have cleaned himself up. Finally one good thing. She crammed the tablets into a plastic bag she found in the laundry closet and left the room. But then she went back: on a separate shelf on one side were a large silver earring in the shape of a spur, a bottle of vanilla-scented deodorant, and a hairbrush covered with short, purple hairs.

Seeing the pantry full of cardboard boxes stuffed with empty beer bottles, she assumed he made part of his income by returning bottles for their deposits. When she went back to him, she found him in a deep slumber. His arms and legs were splayed out and his mouth was open. She put her hands on her hips. What now? Only then did she notice large charcoal drawings on the walls around her: godlike figures, or prophets, a woman breast-feeding a crane whose large human eyes had long eyelashes, and babies who looked like floating goats, their fine hair spread like halos around their heads. One of the prophets had Avram's face. The breast-feeding woman was actually a young girl with sweet, gentle features and a mohawk. Along one whole wall was an improvised desk—a wooden door on sawhorses—covered with heaps of junk of all sizes. There were tools, tubes of glue, nails, screws, rusty cans, ancient faucets, clocks in various stages of disrepair, old keys, and piles of tattered books. She opened an old photo album that was torn and moldy around the edges, and the odor of trash came at her in a wave. It was empty. All it contained were photo corners stuck on the pages, and slanted captions in unfamiliar handwriting: *Father and me, Odessa, Winter '36. Grandma and Mother and Abigail (in utero), 1949. Guess who's Queen Esther this year?*

Avram groaned and opened his eyes and saw her standing there. "You're here," he mumbled, and felt her fingernails digging into his forearms. He couldn't figure out how these things were connected. He shook his head. "Tomorrow, come tomorrow, it'll be fine."

She held her face very close to his again. He started sweating. She yelled into his ear, "Don't run away on me now!" The voice unraveled inside him into empty syllables and sounds. She saw his tongue move around his mouth and leaned over him again. "Come asleep, come unconscious, but come! Don't leave me on my own with this."

He gurgled with his mouth open. What about Ilan, he thought, why hadn't Ilan come with her—

Later, he wasn't sure if it was a minute or an hour later, he strained to open his eyes again, but she was gone. For a minute he thought she'd left, let him be, and wished he'd asked her to help him get into bed. His back would ache tomorrow. But then, terrifyingly, he heard her moving around in his bedroom. He tried to get up, to get her out of there, but his arms and legs were like water skins. He heard her feeling around the walls for a light switch, but there was no bulb in there. "I forgot to change it," he mumbled. "I'll put one in tomorrow." Then there were footsteps again. She's coming out, he thought with relief. Then the footsteps stopped and there was a long silence, and he froze in the armchair. He knew what she was looking at. "Get out of there," he groaned silently. She cleared her dry throat a couple of times, went to switch a light on in the hallway, and walked back to the bedroom, probably to get a better look. If he'd been capable, he would have got up and left the apartment.

"Avram, Avram, Avram," her voice again and her warm breath on his face. "You can't stay here alone," she whispered, and there was something new in her voice, even he could sense it. Not the panic from before, but some knowledge that worried him even more. "We have to run away together, you don't have a choice, I'm such an idiot, you don't have a choice." And he knew she was right, but warm threads were already tying themselves slowly around his ankles, he felt them crawling up, wrapping themselves with maternal devotion around his knees and thighs, enveloping him tightly in a soft cocoon where he could pupate for the night. He hadn't taken Prodomol for a few years now—Neta forbade it—and the effect was stunning. His legs were already melting away. Soon another exhausting shift of awakeness would be over, and he'd be rid of himself for five or six hours.

"You're wearing socks and shoes now," said Ora, straightening up. "Come on, give me your hand and try to stand."

He breathed slowly, heavily, with his eyes closed and his face strained. If only he could concentrate, if only she would be quiet for a minute. He was almost there, just a matter of seconds, and she must have known that too, because she wouldn't give in. She was chasing him all the way there—how could she be allowed in there? Calling his name over and over, shaking him, rocking his shoulders, such strength she had, she'd always been strong, thin and strong, she used to beat him at arm wrestling. But he mustn't think, mustn't remember, because beyond her shouting he could finally feel the blurry dizziness waiting, and there was an indentation in the shape of his body, as soft as a palm, and a cloud would cover everything.

Ora stood facing the man asleep in the armchair. Three years I haven't seen him, she thought, and I didn't even hug him. Sprawled out with his chin pressed to his chest, the patches of stubble protruded around his mouth and made him look like a drunken troll, and it was hard to decide if he was kindly or bitterly cruel. "Look at something weird," he'd said to her once, standing naked before her, when they were twenty-one. "I've just noticed that I have one good eye and one bad eye."

"Stop," she said now to the fallen heap of his flesh. "You have to come. It's not just for me, Avram, it's for you too, isn't it? You understand that, don't you?"

He snored softly, and his face grew calmer. In his bedroom she'd seen weird scribbles in black pencil all over the wall above his bed. At first she thought it was a childish sketch of train tracks or an infinitely long fence that twisted back and forth along the width of the wall and came down from the ceiling in rows, zigzagging all the way down to the bed. The fence poles were joined at their midpoints by short, crooked beams. She cocked her head to one side and examined it: the lines also looked like the long teeth of a comb or a rake, or some ancient beast. Then she discovered little numbers scattered here and there and realized they signified dates. The last one, right by the pillow, was the day that had just come to an end, and it had a little exclamation point next to it. Ora stood there and looked back and forth at the lines and could not stop until she had verified that each of the many vertical lines was crossed out with a horizontal one.

A shock of cold water slapped his face, and he opened a pair of stunned eyes. "Get up," she said. His temples started to pound. He licked the water off his lips and strained to lift a hand up to protect his face from her gaze. It scared him to be looked at by her eyes in this way. Her stare turned him into an object, a lump whose size and weight and center of gravity she was examining, planning how to move him from the armchair to a place he did not even dare to imagine. She put the toes of her shoes up against his, placed his limp hands on her shoulders, bent her knees, and pulled him toward her. She let out a moan of pain and astonishment when he fell on her with his full weight. "There goes my back," she announced to herself. She shuffled back with one foot, afraid she would tumble down with him at any moment. "Come on, let's go," she squeaked. He snorted into her neck. One of his arms hung down her hunched back. "Don't fall asleep," she croaked in a stifled voice. "Stay awake!" She felt her way across the room, rocking with him in a drunkard's dance. Then she pulled him through the doorway like a huge cork and slammed the door shut. In the dark stairwell she searched for the edge of the step with her heel. He mumbled again for her to leave him alone and expressed certain opinions about her sanity. Then he went back to snoring and a strand of his saliva dribbled down her arm. In her mouth she held the plastic bag with his sleeping tablets and toothbrush, which she'd grabbed from the top of a bureau, and she was already regretting not having taken some clothes for him. Through the plastic bag, with gritted teeth, she spoke and grunted at him, fighting to awaken him, to pull the edge of him out of the dark mouth that was swallowing him up. She panted like a dog, and her legs shook. She was trying to do it the right way, reciting to herself silently as she did during a particularly complicated treatment: the quadriceps extend, the gluteus contracts, the gastrocnemius and Achilles extend, you're doing it, you're in control of the situation—but nothing was working right, he was too heavy, he was crushing her, and her body could not take it. Finally she gave up and simply tried to hold him up as much as she could, so the two of them wouldn't roll down together. As she did so—and she had no control over this either—she began to emit fragments that had not passed her lips for years. She reminded him of long-forgotten things about him and herself and Ilan and told him a pulverized yet complete life story over sixty-four steps, all the way to the building entrance. From there she dragged him down a path of broken tiles and trash and shattered bottles, all the way to the taxi where Sami sat watching her through the windshield with impassive eyes, and did not come out to help her.

She stops and waits for him, and he comes over and stands one or two steps behind her. She waves her hand over the broad plain glowing in bright green, glistening with beads of dew, and over the distant, mauve mountains. There is a hum, and not just of insects: Ora thinks she can hear the air itself teeming with a vitality it can barely contain.

"Mount Hermon," she says, pointing to a pure white glow in the north. "And look here, did you see the water?"

"Do me a favor," Avram spits out, and walks on with his head hanging.

But there's a stream here, Ora thinks to herself. We're walking alongside a stream. She laughs quietly at his back as he recedes. "You and me by a stream, could you have imagined?"

For years she had tried to get him out of the house, to take him to places that would light up his soul and bathe him in beauty, but at most she'd managed to drag him to dull meetings in cafés he chose, a couple of times a year. It had to be one he chose, and she never argued, even though the places he picked were always noisy, crowded, mass-produced (his word, the old Avram's), as if he enjoyed seeing her aversion, and as if through these places he was confronting her, for the thousandth time, with his distance from her and from who he used to be. And now, in a completely unexpected way, it's just the two of them and the stream and trees and daylight.

On his body the backpack looks shrunken and smaller than hers, like a child clinging to his father's back. She stands looking at him for a moment longer, with Ofer's pack over his shoulders. Her eyes widen and brighten. She feels the first rays of sun slowly smoothing over her bruised wings.

Mist rises from the fragrant earth as it warms, and from the large, juicy rolls of excrement left by the cows that preceded them. Elongated puddles from the recent rains reply to the dawn sky, emitting modest signals, and frogs leap into the stream as they walk by, and there is not a human being in sight.

A moment later they come up against a barbed-wire fence blocking the path, and Avram waits for her. "I guess that's it, then?"

Ora can hear how relieved he is that the hike is over relatively quickly and painlessly. Her spirits fall—what is a fence doing in the middle of the path? Who would put a fence in a place like this? Her Moirae gather to determine her fate, to circle her in a dance of mockery and rebuke—for her *ungainliness*, her *appliance dyslexia*, and her *user-manual illiteracy*—but as she wallows in their juices, she notices some thin metal cylinders on the ground. She takes her glasses out and puts them on, ignoring Avram's look of amazement, and realizes that part of the fence is in fact a narrow gate. She looks for the tether that secures it and finds a twisted, rusty wire.

Avram stands next to her without lifting a finger, either because he hopes she will not be able to open it or because he is once again too weak to understand what is going on. But when she asks for his help he pitches in immediately, and after she explains what needs to be done— namely, to pick up two large stones and pound the wire on either side until it gradually gives way and breaks—he studies the tether for a long time, hoists the loop over the fence post in one swift motion, the barbed wire falls to the ground at their feet, and they walk through.

"We have to shut it behind us," she says, and Avram nods. "Will you do it?" He locks the gate, and she notes to herself that he needs to be constantly activated and have his engine started; he seems to have given up his volition and handed the keys to her. *Nu*, she thinks in her mother's voice, it's the blind leading the blind. After they go a little farther, something else occurs to her, and she asks if he knows why there was even a fence there. He shakes his head, and she explains about the cows and their pasture areas. Since she knows very little, she talks a lot, and is unable to determine how much of it he is taking in, or why he is listening with such stern concentration—whether he hears what she was saying or is simply lapping up the sounds of her voice.

She notices that he is becoming irritable again, throwing nervous glances behind him and jumping every time a crow caws. After losing focus on him for a moment, she turns to find that he has stopped walking and is standing a ways back, staring at the earth. She walks over and finds the rotting corpse of a little songbird at his feet. She cannot identify it, but it has black feathers, a white stomach, and brown glassy eyes. Ants, white maggots, and flies are swarming all over it. She calls Avram's name twice before he snaps awake and follows her. How much farther am I going to be able to drag him, she wonders, before he erupts or falls apart? What am I doing to him? What did I do to Sami? What's happening to me? All I do is cause trouble.

The path curves sharply and plunges into the stream. Ora stands close to the water and spots the path emerging on the opposite bank in a charming, innocent-looking zigzag. When she was planning the trip with Ofer, she had read something about how, in spring, "you'll need to wet your feet in the streams once in a while." But this is a torrent, and there is no other visible path. She cannot turn back—this is another new rule, a trick against her persecutors: *she must not reverse her tracks.* Avram stands next to her and stares at the glistening green water as though it were a huge mystery bustling with clues. His thick arms hang by his sides. His helplessness suddenly angers her, and she is angry at herself too, for not looking into what to do in such a situation before the hike. But before the hike she'd had Ofer. Ofer was supposed to navigate and lead, he would build bridges over the water for her, and now she is here alone with Avram. Alone.

She edges closer to the stream, careful not to slip. A large leafless tree is growing out of the water, and she leans in as far as she can and tries to break off a branch. Avram does not move. He stares hypnotically at the current, horrified when the dry branch snaps and Ora almost falls into the water. She angrily sticks the branch into the streambed, then pulls it out and measures it against her body. The ring of water reaches up to her waist. "Sit down and take off your shoes and socks," she says. She sits down on the path and takes off her own shoes, sticks her socks in a side pocket on the backpack, ties the shoelaces together after threading them through a loop on top of the pack, and rolls her pants up to her knees. When she looks up, Avram is standing over her, looking at her feet the way he stared at the stream.

"Hey," she says softly, a little surprised, and wiggles her pink toes at him. "Yoo-hoo!"

He sits down quickly to take off his shoes and socks. He rolls his pants up to the knees, exposing thick, pale legs that are slightly bent but look surprisingly powerful. She remembers those legs well—the legs of a horseman, and also, as he himself once said, the legs of a stretched-out dwarf. "Hey," he growls. "Yoo-hoo."

Ora looks away and laughs, excited by the flicker of old Avram from within his flatness, and perhaps also by his suddenly bared flesh.

They sit and watch the water. A translucent purple dragonfly flits by like an optical illusion. There was a time, Ora thinks, when I was at home in his body. And then there were years when I was in charge of it: I washed and cleaned and dried and clipped and shaved and bandaged and fed and drained and whatever else.

She shows him how to tie his shoes to the backpack, next to Ofer's pair, and suggests that he empty out his pockets so his money and other stuff won't get wet.

He shrugs.

"Not even an ID?"

Avram mumbles: "What do I need it for?"

She walks down to the water first, holding the branch, and lets out a yelp when she touches the cold torrent. She wonders what she will do if Avram gets swept away and thinks perhaps he shouldn't even walk into a current like this in his condition. But she decides, of her own accord, by unanimous proclamation, that it will be all right, because there is simply no choice. She puts one foot in front of the other, fighting the flow of water that reaches up to her stomach now and is so powerful that she is afraid to lift her feet off the bottom. But Avram will be fine, she determines again, frightened. He will walk into this water and nothing will happen. Are you sure? Yes. Why? Because. Because for the last hour, really the last day and night, she's had a continuous resolve, desperate yet determined, and she has used it countless times to force people and events to proceed exactly as she wished, because she needs them to, because she has no leeway for bargains or compromises, because she demands blind obedience to the new rules that her mind is constantly legislating—the regulations of this emergency state that has befallen her. And one of the rules, quite possibly the most important one, is that she has to keep moving, has to be constantly in motion. Besides, she must keep moving because the water is freezing her entire lower half.

Her feet grope pebbles and silt, and slippery weeds float around her ankles. Every so often her toes grasp a little stone or rock. They examine it, hypothesize, draw conclusions, and a primeval fishlike sensation flutters in her spine. A long thin branch floats by near the surface and suddenly whips into a twist and slithers away. Droplets of water spray her glasses, and she gives up wiping them off. Every so often she dips her swollen left arm into the water and delights in the cold relief. Avram wades in behind her, and she hears his gasp of pained surprise when the water envelops him with its coolness. She keeps going, already halfway across. Torrents of water flow and part around her body and lap against her thighs and waist. The sun warms her face, and a field of blue and green rays dances in her eyes and in the drops on her glasses, and it feels good to stand in this transparent bubble of the moment.

She climbs up the opposite bank through deep, doughy mud that enfolds her feet and sucks at them with its quivering lips, and clouds of gnats rise from the indentations left by her soles. Another few steps and she is on dry land, where she collapses against a rock with her backpack. She feels a new lightness; in the water, in the current that surged through her, she'd felt as though a stone had been rolled from the mouth of a well she thought was dry. And then she remembers: Avram. Stuck in the middle of the stream with half-closed eyes and a face distorted with fear.

She quickly walks back through the dark, rich mud, stepping in the dimples of her own footprints, and holds the branch out to him. He presses his head down between his shoulders and refuses to move. Over the rush of the water she shouts that he can't keep standing there—who knows what might be swimming in that water—and he instantly obeys her commanding tone, inches forward, and reaches for the branch. He moves slowly, and she takes tiny steps backward, then sits down on one rock and plants her feet against another, and pulls him out with all her strength. "Come on, sit down and dry off," she says, laughing. But he stands frozen in the mud, lost, his body reenacting his Tel Hashomer Hospital days, with the catatonic stares and the fossilized rigidity. With a panicked realization that he might fall back in, she rushes over to him. She fears that what she is doing to him might destabilize him. But he seems to be finding things easier now: after all, he did follow her for half an hour without collapsing. Perhaps over the years he has managed to acquire a certain strength, even a modicum of existential solidity (that was one of his idioms, the old Avram's), and she no longer needs to bend each joint to activate it—ankles, knees, and thighs—the way she did back in those days, like a sculptor of one body. She used to go to his physiotherapy sessions, in exercise rooms or in the pool, and sit watching and memorizing, jotting down notes on what she observed. She forced him to work with her, secretly, in between the professional sessions, during sleepless nights. Nine months passed before his body learned to mimic the positions she molded it into. He once introduced her to a doctor on the ward as his choreographer, a disclosure that let her know that there was still just a little bit of Avram inside the shell.

He lets out a long exhalation and begins to defrost his limbs. He stretches his arms, back, shoulders, elbows, wrists. Everything is working, Ora thinks as she watches surreptitiously: broad, diagonal movements, the large muscle groups. He looks at the stream without believing he really crossed it, and when he smiles awkwardly at Ora, a fraction of the old charm flashes through. She feels a pang as she looks at him: Oh, my old, suspended lover. She returns a measured smile, very careful not to flood him. This is another piece of wisdom she's learned in her long life among the tribe of men: the wisdom of not flooding them.

She shows him where to sit and how to put his feet on the rock so they'll dry faster, and from a side pocket in the backpack she takes some crackers, processed cheese, and two apples. She holds them out to him and he munches heavily and methodically, glancing around with his suspicious, studious look. He gets stuck again on her long, narrow feet, which have turned very pink from the cold water, and he quickly looks away. Then he slowly straightens his neck and spreads his arms out from his body, with cautious movements, like a huge dinosaur chick erupting from its egg. As he looks contemplatively at the opposite bank, Ora realizes that now, having crossed the stream, he is beginning to grasp that he has left behind what used to be, and that from here on there will be a new reality.

She starts talking, to distract him before he can get scared. She shows him how to peel off the large cakes of mud drying on his legs and slaps her own legs lightly to get the blood flowing. Then she puts her socks and shoes back on, ties her shoelaces the way Ofer taught her—she likes to feel that even from afar he is zipping and fastening her up with his embrace—and wonders whether she should try to tell Avram that Ofer, when he showed her the double knot, had said he was positive that no future invention could ever replace man's ingenuity when it came to the simple act of tying shoelaces. "No matter what they invent," he'd said, "we'll always have that, and that's how we'll remember every morning that we're human." Her heart had filled with pride, perhaps because he'd said "human" so naturally, with such humanness. She had quoted Nahum Gutman, who wrote in his *Path of the Orange Peels* that every morning when he put on his shoes, he whistled excitedly, "because I am glad of the new day breaking." And of course they both brought up Grandpa Moshe, her father, who had worn the same pair of shoes for seventeen years, explaining that he simply "walked lightly." Ora had not been able to resist telling Ofer—she thought he'd probably heard the story before, but she risked it anyway—that when he was about eighteen months old and she'd put his first pair of shoes on, she'd accidentally put the left shoe on the right foot and vice versa. "And to think that for half a day you walked around with your shoes on the wrong feet, just because I decided that was the right way. It's terrible how parents can determine their— Wait, have I already told you this story?" "Let's see," Ofer had said, laughing, and punched in a calculation on his phone. They had endless such conversations, full of laughter and mutual potshots. An awkward warmth flowed between them, with soul-penetrating glances. In recent years this was diminishing, much as everything between them was diminishing. It seemed that ever since the two of them started to mature, he and Adam, they'd moved more into Ilan's domain, and sometimes she thought they'd been transferred into a different magnetic field, with its own laws and sensibilities, and mainly its own impermeabilities, where she flailed in a tapestry of wires that tripped her up and made her falter ridiculously with each step. But it was still there, she convinced herself repeatedly. What existed between them must still exist somewhere, it's just that it was slightly subterranean now, especially while he was serving in the army, and it would come back after he finished, and it might even be richer and fuller. She sighs loudly and wonders how it happened that her expertise in recent years was to look for signs of life in people.

Avram gravely observes Ora's hands as she ties her laces, but he gets mixed up when he tries to follow, and she sits down next to him to show him. She notices that the water has washed the sharp smell of urine off him, and that she can now stand next to him without gagging. And then Avram himself suddenly says, "I wet myself yesterday, huh?"

"Don't ask."

"Where did it happen?"

"Never mind."

"I can't remember anything."

"It's better that way."

He examines her face and decides to let it go, and she wonders if she'll ever tell him about that night with Sami.

Only when she'd walked with Avram on her back right up to the taxi door had he deigned to get out of the cab, irate and begrudging, and the two of them together had managed to shove the sleeping Avram into the backseat. That was when it occurred to Ora that Sami hadn't even known up until this moment that they were picking up a man. For a few months now he'd lurked in his subtle, polite way, hoping to find out whether she had anyone new. This isn't really someone new, she'd thought. In fact he's someone very old. It's secondhand Avram, maybe even third. She stood by the taxi catching her breath, her shirt wrinkled and damp with sweat, her legs still shaking.

"Drive," she said when she sat down next to Sami.

"Where to?"

She thought for a moment. Without looking at him, she said, "To where the country ends."

"For me it ended a long time ago," he hissed.

Every so often, as they drove, she felt him throw her a questioning, hostile, and somewhat frightened look. She did not turn to face him, did not know what he saw, and felt that something about her was already different. They passed Ramat HaSharon, Herzliya, Netania, and Hadera, turned toward Wadi Ara, drove by the kibbutzim of Gan Shmuel and Ein Shemer, and the Arab villages of Kfar Kara, Ar'ara, and the city of Umm al'Fahm, crossed Megiddo Junction and HaSargel Junction, and took a wrong turn and got lost in Afula, which had presumptuously installed the new traffic patterns of a big city. They bounced from one traffic circle to the next, but finally they escaped Afula and drove past Kfar Tavor and Shibli, north on Route 65 all the way to Golani Junction, and farther north past Bu'eine and Eilabun to Kadarim Junction, which was also called Amud River Junction, and Ora thought to herself, It's been years since I hiked the Amud River. If I was with Ofer I would convince him to do it, but what am I doing here with Avram? They turned onto Route 85 and drove to Ami'ad Junction, and Ora, whose anger at Sami had imperceptibly faded away, just as it always did—she was quick to heat up and quick to cool down, and sometimes simply forgot she was angry—pointed out that there was a nice little café around here. "On a good day you could see the Kinneret, and on any day you can see the beautiful woman who owns the place." Ora smiled appeasingly, but Sami did not respond and refused the apple and squares of chocolate she offered. She stretched out and rubbed the body parts that ached and remembered that she hadn't even finished the story she'd started telling him—that afternoon? Was it only that afternoon?—about her father's glaucoma and the surgery he finally had to save his one seeing eye. It bothered her that the story had been truncated, although she knew that from their current positions there was probably no way back to the tone of voice that would allow the story to end. But it was good that she'd remembered it, she thought as she sat back comfortably and closed her eyes, because through it she could be with Ofer, who had insisted on staying with her father in the hospital the night after the operation and had taken him home with Ora, driving with a tenderness that had filled her with joy. She remembered how he walked the old man carefully from the car to the house, supporting him down the path through the apartment complex's garden, and her father had pointed wondrously at the lawn and the plants. After fifteen years of almost total blindness, his mind had confused the colors, and shadows looked like real things. Ofer realized immediately what was happening and translated the sights for him, and the different shades, reminding him gently: blue, yellow, green, purple. Her father had pointed at various things and recited the colors with Ofer. Ora had followed them and listened to Ofer and thought to herself, What a wonderful father he will make. He led her father up the stairs to the apartment with an arm around his shoulders, efficiently removing any obstacles in his way, and inside the apartment her mother had fled into the pantry. Ofer saw and understood and kept walking her father, holding his hand, to see the photograph of his grandchildren on the sideboard for the first time. Then he walked him through the rooms and showed him the various pieces of furniture purchased during his years of blindness. Still her mother did not show herself, and then Ofer had an idea. He took her father into the kitchen and they stood peering into the refrigerator together, and her father was amazed: "The fruits and vegetables are so colorful! In my day it wasn't like this!" He told Ofer with astonishment about every new thing he noticed, as if he wished to give him the gift of this primordial sight. And all that time her mother fussed around in the other rooms, and her father did not ask about her, and Ofer did not say anything, until finally, through the little window shared by the pantry and the bathroom, she presented her face to his eyes. Ofer gently smoothed his hand over his grandfather's back and signaled to his grandmother to smile.

Sami turned the radio on. Galei Tzahal, the military station, had a special news edition, and the prime minister was speaking. "The government of Israel is determined to shatter its enemies' cult of death, and in moments such as these we must remember that in the struggle against an enemy that has no moral reservations or considerations, we too are entitled, in order to protect our children—"

Sami quickly switched to an Arabic station and listened to a newscaster read an impassioned manifesto against a background of military music. Ora swallowed. She would not say anything. It was his right to listen to whatever he wanted. She should at least allow him that privilege. Avram was sprawled heavily in the back, snoring with his mouth open. Ora shut her eyes and imposed moderation and tolerance upon herself, trying to flood her sight with soft circles of color, which soon erupted into rows of dark, armed men, marching toward her with sparks flying from their eyes, humming a bloodthirsty tune that beat through all the spaces of her body. How can he not understand what I'm going through? she thought. How can he be incapable of thinking about what I'm going through now, with Ofer there? She sat motionless and riled herself up as she listened to the provocative music. Rapidly scanning the day's events, she could not grasp how she had gotten herself mixed up with this annoying and infuriating man, who had hung from her neck like a weight all afternoon and then, with unbelievable nerve, had mired her in his own private complications with Yazdi and his IR, creating in her a sense of unease and guilt, when all she wanted was to implement her extremely modest plans, to employ his services in the most decent and unsoiled way, and in the end he had taken control of her agenda and messed it all up!

"Please turn off the radio," she said with quiet restraint.

He did not respond. She could not believe this was happening. He was ignoring her explicit request. The men were thundering with their rhythmic calls and throaty breaths, and a vein in her neck started to throb painfully.

"I asked you to turn it off."

He drove on, his face impervious, his thick hands stretched across the wheel. Only a tiny muscle in the corner of his mouth quivered. She restrained herself with great effort. She tried to calm herself, to plan her next move . . .

And she knew, somewhere in the margins of her brain, she remembered, that if she only spoke to him candidly, if she only reminded him with a word, with a smile, of themselves, of the private little culture they had built up over the years, within the roaring and the drumming—

"Turn it off already!" she screamed as loudly as she could and pounded her lap with both hands.

He flinched, swallowed, and did not turn off the radio. She could see his fingers trembling, and she almost gave up. His weakness shocked her, and touched her, and awakened again a dim sense of guilt. She also had the feeling that his innate Eastern gentleness would not withstand this tension and would eventually melt away in face of the determination, the recklessness, even—both so Western—that was suddenly roused in her. And there were always, too, his fear of Ilan and his dependence on Ilan. She licked her burning lips. Her throat pounded and burned with dryness, and the thought that she would eventually win, that she would bend him to her will, was just as painful as the desire to subdue him. She wished she could stop here, right now, and erase it all, everything that had happened today. You're just going out of your mind, she thought. What has he done to make you torment him like this? What has he done to you, tell me, other than merely exist?

This was all true, Ora retorted to herself, but it made her crazy to see that he could not give in to her even an inch, not even out of basic human courtesy! It's just not in their culture, she thought. Them and their lousy honor, and their never-ending insults, and their revenge, and their settling of scores over every little word anyone ever said to them since Creation, and all the world always owes them something, and everyone's always guilty in their eyes!

The music grew louder and louder, waves that bubbled and surfaced and climbed up her throat, and the men with their thundering voices pounded deep inside her, and something in Ora cracked, a distillation of many forms of sorrow and anguish, and perhaps also the affront of their friendship, which had let them down, which had been let down, which had blown up in their faces. Her skin turned red, a blazing shawl wrapped itself around her neck, and she felt that she could murder him. Her hand flew out, hit the radio button, and turned it off.

They glanced sideways at each other, trembling.

"Sami," Ora sighed, "look what's become of us."

They kept on driving in silence, startled by themselves. To the left was Rosh Pina, deep in slumber, and then they passed Hatzor HaGlilit and Ayelet HaShachar and the Hula Reserve and Yesud HaMa'ala and Kiryat Shmonah, which blinked with orange lights, and then they turned onto Route 99 through HaGoshrim and Dafna and She'ar Yashuv. Every so often, when they reached an intersection, he slowed down and turned a cheek to her with a silent question: How much farther? And she jutted her chin out in response: Farther, keep going, until the country ends.

After Kibbutz Dan they heard a groan from the back. Avram woke up and wheezed. Ora turned to him. Lying on the seat, he opened a pair of waifish eyes and looked at her with a kind, dreamy smile. "I have to pee," he said in a deep, slow voice.

"Oh, we'll stop soon," Ora said.

"I need to go now."

"Stop!" she told Sami in a panic. "Stop as soon as you can."

He slowed down and drove off the road. Ora sat and stared straight ahead. Sami looked at her. She did not move. "Ora?" asked Avram imploringly, and she was terrified at the thought that in a moment he would be standing outside the car, leaning on her, and judging by his look she would probably have to unzip his pants and hold it for him.

She gave Sami a pleading, begging, almost ingratiating look, and when she encountered his eyes she was trapped in them for a long, bitter moment that quickly branched out into an endless maze, from Joseph Trumpeldor and the riots of 1929 and 1936 all the way to Avram's dick. She got out of the car and walked to the back door. Avram sat up with great effort. "It's that pill," he apologized.

"Give me your hand." She dug her heels into the ground and readied her back for the blow to come. Her hand hovered unmet. He nodded with his eyes closed. He wrinkled his face a little and smiled with relief, and she watched as a big, dark stain spread slowly over his pants and onto the new leopard-skin upholstery.

A few moments later the two of them were outside with their backpacks tossed nearby, and Sami was charging away madly. As he zigzagged across the white line, he shouted and bellowed bitterly into the night mist, cursing both the Jews and the Arabs, and mainly himself and his own fate. He beat his head and his chest and the wheel of the Mercedes.

NOW THEY ATE PRUNES and Ora buried the pits in the sludge and hoped two trees might grow there one day, trunks intertwined. Then they said goodbye to the lovely spot, loaded up their backpacks, his blue and hers orange, and everything Avram did took forever, and it seemed that each movement he made passed through every joint in his body. But when he finally stood up straight and glanced at the river, a slight vernal brightness ran over his forehead, as though a gleaming coin had shone its golden luster on him from afar, and she entertained a fleeting idea: What if Ofer were here with us? The notion was utterly unfounded. She had only been able to sneak Avram tiny crumbs of information about Ofer, as she'd been forbidden to talk about him or even mention his name all these years. But now, for a brief moment, she saw the two of them here, Ofer and Avram, helping each other cross the water, and her eyes shined at him.

"Come on, let's go."

After no more than a hundred steps, beyond a small hill, the path led them into the stream once again.

Avram stood defeated. This turn was too much for him. For me too, Ora thought and sat down angrily. She took off her shoes and socks, tied them and fastened them, rolled up her pants, and walked firmly into the freezing, snow-fed water, unable to stifle a tiny shriek. Avram was still stuck on the bank behind her, confused by the forces that both pulled and pushed him. Desperate as he was, he knew that the bank Ora was moving toward now was the side on which they had begun their trek, and there, it seemed, was some stability, perhaps because that was the side of home. He sat down and went through the motions, tied his shoes to the backpack almost without seeing Ofer's pair, and waded into the cold water with his lips pursed. This time he took resolute strides, kicking up a big commotion, and then came to sit down beside Ora on the bank. He slapped his feet dry and put his socks and shoes back on. Ora felt that he was at ease, not only because he was back on the familiar side but because he had seen that it was possible to cross over and back. And that is exactly what they did, three or four more times—they lost count—on that first morning of their Upper Galilee journey, which she was still calling a hike, if she was even calling it anything, if they even spoke more than a few words the whole day: "Come on," "Give me your hand," "Watch out here," "Damn cows." The path and the stream weaved and converged, and by the third crossing they no longer removed their shoes but simply walked through the mud and the water and climbed back up, sloshing around in their shoes until the water seeped out. Finally the path broke away from the Hatzbani River and became easier and earthier, an ordinary trail through the fields, dotted with big puddles of mud, pale cyclamens hovering on either side. Avram stopped glancing behind him every few minutes and did not ask whether Ora would know how to find the way back. He seemed to have realized that she had no intention of going back anywhere and that he was her hostage. He grew introverted, resigned to reducing his vitality to that of a plant, a lichen, or a spore. It must hurt less that way, Ora imagined. Why am I torturing him? she wondered as she watched him walk, frail and downtrodden, serving out a sentence he did not understand at all. He's no longer part of me or of my life and really hasn't been for years. She did not feel pained by this thought, merely baffled: How could it be that the person I thought was my own flesh and blood, the root of my soul, would not tug at my heartstrings when he is severed from me in this way? What am I doing with him now? Why did this fixation grab hold of me now, when I need all my strength to rescue one child—why burden myself with another?

"Ofer," she murmured, "I'm forgetting to think about him."

Avram turned around suddenly and walked back down the path, aiming himself at her with his faltering steps. "Tell me what you want, I don't have the strength for these games."

"I told you."

"I don't get it."

"I'm running away."

"From what?"

She looked into his eyes and said nothing.

He swallowed. "Where's Ilan?"

"Ilan and I separated a year ago. A bit less. Nine months."

He swayed a little, as though she had hit him.

"That's that," she said.

"What do you mean separated? From who?"

"From who? From us. From each other. That's it."

"Why?"

"People separate. It happens. Come on, let's go."

He raised a heavy hand and kept standing there like a dim-witted student. Under his stubble she saw his tortured expression. There were years when she and Ilan used to joke that if they ever split up, they'd have to keep pretending they were a couple, for his sake.

"What reason do you have to separate?" he growled. "I want to know what came over you all of a sudden. All these years you keep going and then you just get sick of it?"

He's scolding me, Ora realized with some surprise. He's complaining.

"Who wanted this?" Avram straightened up, suddenly full of power. "It was him, wasn't it? Did he have another woman?"

Ora almost choked. "Calm down. The two of us decided together. And maybe it's better this way." But then she seethed: "Anyway, why are you poking your nose into our lives? What do you even know about us? Where were you for three years? Where were you for thirty years?"

"I'm sorry." He huddled over, alarmed. "I . . . Where was I?" He furrowed his brow as though he truly did not know.

"Anyway, that's the situation." Ora spoke smoothly now, to compensate for her outburst.

"And you?"

"What about me?"

"You're alone?"

"I . . . I'm without him, yes. But I'm not alone." She looked straight into his eyes. "I really don't feel alone." Her attempt at a smile did not work.

Avram wrung his hands nervously. She could feel his body rallying to take in the news. Ora and Ilan are separated. Ilan alone. Ora alone. Ora without Ilan.

"But why? Why?!" He was riled up again, shouting into her face, all but stomping his feet.

"You're shouting. Don't shout at me."

"But how . . . you were always . . ." He let his backpack drop and looked up at her like a miserable puppy. "No, explain this to me from the beginning. What happened?"

"What happened?" She put down her backpack, too. "Lots of things happened since Ofer enlisted. Since you decided that you had to, I don't know, disappear on me."

His hands crushed each other. His eyes darted around.

"Our lives changed," Ora said softly, "and I changed. And Ilan, too. And the family. I don't know where to start telling you."

"Where is he now?"

"On a trip in South America. Took a vacation from the office and everything. I don't know how long he'll be gone. We haven't really had any contact recently." She hesitated. She did not tell him that Adam had gone along, too. That in fact she was separated from her older son as well. That from him, from Adam, she might even be divorced. "Give me some time, Avram. My life is a mess right now, it's not easy for me to talk about this."

"Okay, okay, we don't have to talk."

He stood up looking frightened and stricken, like an ant nest kicked by a crude foot. Once, Ora thought, these sorts of plot twists, new permutations, frenetic changes, used to excite him, stimulate his mind and body, *fermentize* him—his word. Oh, she sighed silently, all the endlessly possible. Remember? Remember? You invented that, you made those rules for us. Playing blindman's buff in lower Manhattan and opening our eyes in Harlem. And the way you said the lion *should* lie down with the lamb—let's see what happens, you said. Maybe for once in the history of the universe there'll be a surprise. Maybe this one particular lion and this one particular lamb will make a go of it together, this one time, and maybe they'll reach—she could not remember the word he'd used—"elevation"? "Salvation"? His words, an entire lexicon, a dictionary and a phrasebook and a glossary, at the age of sixteen and nineteen and twenty-two, but since then: silence, lights out.

They started walking again. Slowly, side by side, bowed under their weights. She could practically feel the news sinking into him, like a solution trickling into a substance and changing its composition. He was slowly grasping that for the first time in thirty-five years he was really with her alone, without Ilan, without even the shadow of Ilan.

Whether or not that was true, she had trouble deciding. For months now she hadn't been able to make up her mind. One minute she thought this way, and the next she thought the other.

"And the kids?" Avram blurted.

Ora slowed her steps. He wasn't even willing to say their names. *"The kids,"* she annunciated, "are grown now, the kids are independent. They can make up their own minds whom to be with and where."

He shot her a quick sideways glance, and for a moment a screen lifted and his eyes plunged into hers. He looked at her and knew her to the depths of her aggrievedness. Then the screen covered him over again. Within the sorrow and the pain, Ora felt a thrill: there was still someone inside there.

They kept on this way till the evening, walking a little then stopping to rest, avoiding roads and people, eating food from Ora's backpack, picking the odd grapefruit or orange and finding pecans and walnuts on the ground. They filled and refilled their water bottles from brooks and springs. Avram drank constantly, Ora hardly at all. They walked this way and that like a pendulum, and she wondered if he understood that they were intentionally disorienting themselves so they could not find their way back.

And they barely spoke. She tried to say something a few times about the separation, about Ilan, about herself, but he would put his hand up in supplication, almost pleading—he did not have the strength for it. Maybe later. Tonight or tomorrow. Preferably tomorrow.

He was growing weaker, and she too was unaccustomed to such exertion. Calluses developed on his heels, and jock itch set in. She offered him Band-Aids and talc, and he refused. In the afternoon they napped under the shade of a leafy carob tree, then meandered a little more and stopped to doze again. Her thoughts grew unfocused. She thought it might be because of him: just as he had once awakened her and turned her inside out, his presence was now extinguishing and uninspiring. At dusk, when they sprawled on the edge of a pecan grove on a bed of dry leaves and nutshells, she looked up at the sky—empty apart from two noisy, stationary helicopters that had been hovering for hours, probably watching the border—and thought that she really wouldn't mind meandering like this for the rest of the twenty-eight days, even a whole month. Just to stupefy herself. But what about Avram?

Perhaps he wouldn't care, either. Perhaps he also felt like roaming now. What do I know about what he's going through and what his life is like and who he's with? she thought. As for me, it's really not bad this way, it's less painful. She noted with surprise that even Ofer had somewhat quieted in her over the last few hours. Maybe Avram was right and you didn't have to talk about everything, or about anything. What was there to say, anyway? At most, if the right moment came along, she would tell him a bit about Ofer, carefully—maybe out here he wouldn't be so resistant—just a few little things, maybe the easy things, the funny things. So at least he'd know who Ofer was in general outlines, in chapter headings. So at least he would know this person he had brought into the world.

They pitched their tents in a small wooded area, among terebinth and oak trees. Ofer had drilled her at home on setting up the tent, and to her amazement she did it with almost no difficulty. First she set up her own, then she helped Avram, and the tents did not stealthily attack her or slyly wrap themselves around her and did not pull her inside them like a carnivorous plant, as Ofer had predicted they might. When she had finished there were two round little tents, hers orange and his blue, about three or four yards apart, two bubbles that looked like little spaceships, impervious to water and to each other, and both had tiny windows covered with long nylon foreskins.

Avram still avoided opening Ofer's backpack. Even the outside pockets. He said he didn't need to change his clothes, which had been washed several times on his body in the stream that day, and he could lie down just as he was, on the ground, he didn't need a pad, and anyway he wouldn't rest for long because Ora hadn't brought the sleeping pills he usually used, which were kept in a drawer next to his bed. The ones she'd brought, the homeopathic ones she'd found in the bathroom, were not his. "Whose are they, then?" Ora asked without moving her lips. "Um . . ." Avram dismissed the question. "They don't have any effect on me." Ora thought about the woman who used the vanilla-scented deodorant, who had purple hair, and who for a month, apparently, or so she thought he'd told her on the phone, had not lived with him.

At seven, when they could no longer bear the silence, they went to their tents and lay awake for hours, dozing off occasionally. Avram was exhausted from the day's efforts and almost managed to fall asleep with the help of the ludicrous pills, but eventually he overcame them.

They tossed and turned, sighed and coughed. Too much reality was bustling inside them: the fact that they were out in the open, lying on earth that felt uncomfortably knobby with stones and dimples, and frighteningly new, and the unseen but tense quivering of a large animal, and a nervousness instilled in them by the twinkling stars, and breezes—first warm, then cool, then damp—that kept moving in different directions like soft breaths from an invisible mouth. And the calls of nocturnal birds and the rustling all around and the buzz of mosquitoes. At every moment it seemed as if something was crawling on their cheeks or down their legs, and the sound of light steps came from the nearby thicket, and the jackals called, and once there was the yelp of a creature being preyed upon. Ora must have fallen asleep despite all this, because she was awoken early in the morning by three people in military uniform standing on the stoop outside her front door. They squeezed against the wall to allow the senior member to pass by and knock. The doctor felt in his bag for a tranquilizer, and the young officer readied her arms to catch Ora if she passed out.

Ora saw the three of them straighten up and clear their throats, and the senior one raised his hand and hesitated for an instant. She watched his fist, transfixed, and it occurred to her that this was a moment that would last a lifetime, but then he knocked on the door, knocked firmly three times, and looked at the tips of his shoes, and as he waited for the door to open he silently rehearsed the notification: *at such-and-such time in such-and-such place, your son Ofer, who was on an operational mission—*

Across the street a series of windows slammed shut and drapes were drawn closed, with only their corners pulled aside for someone to peek out. But her door would remain shut. Ora finally managed to move her feet and tried to pull herself into a seated position in the sleeping bag. She was bathed in cold sweat. Her eyes were closed and her hands felt rigid, unmovable. The senior officer knocked three times again and was so averse to doing it that he knocked too hard, and for a moment he seemed to want to break down the door and burst in with the news. But the door was closed and no one was opening it to receive his notification, and he looked awkwardly at the document in his hand, which stated explicitly that at such-and-such time in such-and-such place, your son Ofer, who was on an operational mission. The female officer walked backward on the stoop to check the house number, and it was the right house, and the doctor tried to peer through the window to see if there was a light on inside, but no light was on. Two more weaker knocks, and the door remained shut, and the senior officer leaned on it with his whole weight as if seriously considering breaking the door down and hurling his notification inside at any cost. He looked at his colleagues with a confused expression, because it was becoming clear to them that something had gone wrong with the rules of this ritual, that their businesslike and professional desire, their essentially logical desire, to deliver the notification, to rid themselves of it, to vomit it out, and above all to embed it quickly into the person it belonged to by law and by destiny, namely, that at such-and-such time in such-and-such place, your son Ofer, who was on an operational mission—this desire of theirs was now encountering a wholly unexpected yet equally powerful force, which was Ora's absolute unwillingness to receive the notification or accommodate it in any way, or even to acknowledge that it belonged to her at all.

Now the two other members of the team joined in the effort to push down the door, and with rhythmic grunts, wordlessly spurring each other on, they stormed the door again and again, ramming it with their bodies, and Ora still lay somewhere on the outskirts of her dream. Her head jerked from side to side and she wanted to shout but no sound came out. She knew they would never dare to do something so extraordinary unless they sensed the resistance projected onto the door from the inside, and this is what was enraging them, and the unfortunate door heaved and groaned between the willingness and the unwillingness, between their mature military logic and her childish obstinacy, and Ora fluttered and grew entangled in the folds of her sleeping bag until suddenly she froze, opened her eyes, and stared at the little window in her tent. She could see through the edges that it was getting light outside, and she ran her hand through her hair—so wet, as if she'd washed her hair in sweat—and lay down and reassured herself that her heart would stop racing soon, but she had to get out.

Much as she wanted to, she could not sit up. The sleeping bag was twisted and wrapped around her like a huge, tight, damp bandage, and her body was so weak that it did not have the power to resist this shroud, so full of life as it tightened around her. Perhaps she would just lie here a little longer, calm herself and gather strength, close her eyes and try to think about something more cheerful. But she soon felt a hushed grumble erupting from the team of notifiers, because they knew that they had to deliver their notice, if not now then in an hour or two, or in a day or two, and they would have to come all the way out here again and prepare themselves again for the difficult moment. People never think about the notifiers and the emotional burden they must bear; they pity only those receiving the news. But perhaps the notifiers are the ones who are angry, because as sad and sympathetic as they may be, they have, after all, begun to feel a certain tension—not to say excitement—and even a festive air, in anticipation of the moment of notification, which, even after they've experienced it dozens of times, is not and cannot be routine, just as there can be no routine execution.

With a stifled yell, Ora tore herself away from the damn sleeping bag and ran, fleeing from the tent. She stood outside with a horrified look in her wild eyes. Only after a few moments did she notice Avram sitting on the ground not far away, leaning against a tree, watching her.

They made coffee and drank silently, he wrapped in his sleeping bag, she in a thin coat. "You were shouting," he said.

"I had a nightmare."

He did not ask what it was about.

"What was I shouting?"

He got up and began to tell her about the stars. "This one's Venus, those are the Big and Little Dipper, and see how the Big Dipper points to the North Star?"

She listened, slightly hurt, slightly amazed at his new enthusiasm and unshackled voice.

"See?" He pointed. "There's Saturn. Sometimes, in summer, I can see it from my bed, with the rings. And that one's Sirius, the brightest—"

As he talked and talked, Ora remembered a line she and Ada had loved, from S. Yizhar's "Midnight Convoy": *You cannot point out a star to someone without putting your other hand on his shoulder.* But as it turned out, you could.

They folded up their little encampment and set off. She was happy to put some distance between her and the place where the nightmare had come, and the hint of sunrise in the sky—the light ascended as if from a slowly unclasping pair of hands—revived her a little. We've been on the road for a whole day and night, she thought, and we're still together. But her feet soon began to feel very heavy, and a dull pain coursed through her body.

She thought it was the exhaustion. She had barely slept for two days. Or perhaps it was sunstroke—she hadn't worn a hat the day before or had enough to drink. She hoped it wasn't an ill-timed bout of spring flu. But it didn't feel like flu or sunstroke. It was a different, unfamiliar sort of ache, stubborn and persistent and consuming, and at times she even thought it was a flesh-eating bacteria.

They sat down to rest near a ruin. Part of the structure was still standing; the rest had crumbled into a heap of chiseled stones. Ora closed her eyes and tried to calm herself by breathing deeply and massaging her temples, chest, and stomach. The pain and distress grew worse, her heartbeat pounded through her body, and then it occurred to her that her pain was Ofer.

She felt him in her stomach, beneath her heart, a dark and restless spot of emotion. He moved and shifted and turned inside her, and she moaned in surprise, frightened by his violence and desperation. She thought back to the attack of claustrophobia he'd suffered when he was about seven, when the two of them got stuck between floors in the elevator in Ilan's office building. When Ofer realized they were trapped, he started yelling at the top of his lungs for someone to help them, shouting that he had to get out, he didn't want to die. She tried to calm him and gather him in her arms, but he slipped away and thrashed against the walls and door, hitting and screaming until his voice cracked, and eventually he attacked her too, beating and kicking. Ora always remembered how his face had changed in those moments, and she remembered the twinge of disappointment when she realized, not for the first time, how thin and fragile his cheerful, vivacious surface was, this child who was the brighter and clearer of her two—that was how she had always thought of him: the brighter and clearer of her two—and she remembered that Ilan said at the time, half joking, that at least they knew Ofer wouldn't join the Armored Corps when he enlisted; he would never let himself be closed up inside a tank. But that prophecy was disproven, like so many others, and Ofer did join the Armored Corps, and he was closed up inside a tank, and there was never any problem with that—at least not for him. Ora was the one who felt suffocated almost to the point of passing out when she got inside a tank, at Ofer's request, after the military display that his battalion put on for the parents at Nebi Musa. And now she felt him, she felt Ofer, just as she had felt him that day in the elevator, terrified and wild with fear, sensing that something was closing in on him, trapping him, and that he had no way out and no air to breathe. Ora jumped up and stood over Avram. "Come on, let's go." Avram couldn't understand—they'd only just sat down—but he didn't ask anything, and it's a good thing he didn't, because what could she have told him?

She walked quickly, not feeling the weight of her backpack, and she kept forgetting about Avram, who had to call out for her to slow down and wait. But it was hard for her, it was intolerable, to walk at his pace. All morning she refused to stop even once, and when he rebelled and lay down in the middle of the path, or under a tree, she kept circling around him to dull herself more and more with continuous walking and sun exposure, and intentionally made herself thirsty. But Ofer would not let up, he raged inside her with rhythmic and painful spasms, and toward noon she started to hear him. It was not speech exactly, just the music of his voice carrying over all the sounds of the valley: the hums and the twitters and the chirping of crickets and her own breath and Avram's grunts and the hiss of the huge sprinklers in the fields and the distant tractor engines and the small planes that sometimes circled above. His voice came to her with strange clarity, as if he were right here walking beside her, talking to her without words—he had no words, only his voice, he was playing for her with his voice, and every so often she picked up the slight, endearing stammer in his *sh* sounds, especially when he was excited: *sh* . . . *sh* . . . She did not know whether to answer him and just start talking or ignore him as much as she could, because from the moment she had shut the door to her house in Beit

Zayit behind her, she had been tormented by a very familiar fear, the fear of what she might perceive and what her imagination might show her when she thought of him, and what might slip out of her head and wrap itself around Ofer's hands and over his eyes precisely at the moment when he needed all his vigilance and strength.

She felt it immediately when he changed his tactic, because he started to simply say *Mom*, time after time, a hundred times, *Mom*, *Mom*, in different tones, at different ages, nagging at her, smiling to her, telling her secrets, tugging at her dress, *Mom*, *Mom*, angry at her, ingratiating, flirting, impressed, clinging, jabbing, laughing with her, opening his eyes to her on an eternal morning of childhood: *Mom?*

Or lying in her arms, the baby he used to be, alert and tiny, his thin waist in a diaper, staring at her with that look he had even back then, embarrassingly tranquil and mature, with a constant speck of irony, almost from birth, perhaps because of the shape of his eyes, which leaned—*lean*—toward each other at a sharp and skeptical angle.

She tripped and pulled herself forward with outstretched arms, and looked as if she were feeling her way through an invisible swarm of hornets. There was something ominous in the vitality with which he had suddenly emerged inside her, rocking frantically. Why is he doing this? she asked herself feebly. Why is he feeding and sucking on me? Her entire body throbbed and exhaled his name like a bellows, and it was not that she missed him—there was no nostalgia. He was tearing her up from the inside, flailing around and beating his fists against the walls of her body. He claimed her for himself unconditionally, demanded that she vacate her own being and dedicate herself to him eternally, that she think about him all the time and talk about him incessantly, that she tell anyone she meets about him, even the trees and the rocks and the thistles, and that she say his name out loud and silently over and over again, so as not to forget him even for a moment, even for a second, and that she not abandon him, because he needed her now in order to *exist*—she suddenly knew that this was what his biting meant. How could she not have realized before that he needed her now, in order not to die? She stood with one hand on her aching waist and let out an astonished breath. Was that it? Just as he had once needed her to be born?

"What's the matter with you?" Avram asked breathlessly when he caught up. "What's gotten into you?"

She lowered her head and said softly, "Avram, I can't go on like this."

"Like what?"

"With you not even willing to . . . That I can't even say the name in front of you." And then a knot came untied in her. "Listen. This silence is killing me and it's killing him, so make up your mind."

"About what?"

"About whether you're really here with me."

He looked away. Ora waited quietly. Since Ofer's birth, she had hardly talked with Avram about him. Avram always made a hand gesture that was quick and repellant, like brushing away a bothersome fly, every time Ora couldn't resist talking about Ofer when they met, or even when she merely mentioned his name. She always had to protect him from Ofer, that was his stipulation, his condition for these pathetic meetings. She had to act as if there were no Ofer in the world and never had been. And Ora had grit her teeth and concluded that she was more or less over the insult and the anger and accepted his refusal and rejection and told herself that over the years she'd even grown a little accustomed to the total and arbitrary demarcation he demanded from her—after all, there was a certain relief in the clear boundaries, the total separation of authorities: Avram on this side, she on the other, and everything else over there. And in recent years she'd discovered, with a slight sense of shame, that the thought of any other option made her more nervous than the idea that this state of affairs would continue. Yet even so, with every rude push he gave, she was insulted to the depths of her soul and had to remind herself again that Avram's tenuous equilibrium seemed to be based on a total, hermetic self-defense against Ofer, against the fact of Ofer, against what, to him, was undoubtedly the mistake of his lifetime. This too always aroused a fresh wave of anger in her, the thought that Ofer was anyone's mistake of a lifetime, and worse, that Ofer was Avram's mistake of a lifetime. But on the other hand—and this is what had confused and maddened her these last two days—there were the etched lines on the wall above his bed, the countdown calendar of Ofer's army years, three years, more than a thousand lines, one line for every single day, and he must have crossed out the day every evening with a horizontal line, and how could she reconcile these two things— the mistake of a lifetime and the countdown—and which of the two should she believe?

"Listen, I was thinking—"

"Ora, not now."

"Then when? When?"

He turned away sharply and walked quickly ahead, and she hated him and disdained him and pitied him and realized she must have truly lost her mind to have believed he could help her or be with her in her time of trouble. The whole idea was fundamentally sick, sadistic even—to inflict this sort of trek on him, to expect that suddenly, after twenty-one years of erasure and separation, he would want to start hearing about Ofer. She swore she would put him on the first bus to Tel Aviv in the morning, and from now on she would not say a word about Ofer.

By evening the pain of him became so strong that she shut herself up in her tent and sobbed quietly, secretly, trying to muffle the noise. The contractions—that was how she felt: they were like labor contractions—came frequently and sharply and grew into a constant, blinding pain, and she thought that if this continued she would somehow have to get to an emergency room. But what would she say when she got there? And besides, a doctor might persuade her to go home immediately and wait for *them*.

Avram, in his tent, heard her and decided not to take a sleeping pill, not even his girlfriend Neta's pills, because Ora might need him during the night. But how could he help her? He lay awake, motionless, his arms crossed over his chest and his hands in his armpits. He could have lain that way for hours, almost without moving. He heard her sobbing to herself, a long, monotonous wail. In Egypt, in Abbasiya Prison, there was a short, thin reservist from Jerusalem who came from a family of Cochin Jews. He used to cry for hours every night, even if they hadn't been tortured that day. The guys almost lost their minds because of him, even the Egyptian wardens couldn't stand it, but the Cochin guy wouldn't stop. One day when he and Avram were standing in the corridor waiting to be taken to an interrogation, Avram managed to communicate with the man through the sacks over their faces, and the Cochin guy said he was crying out of jealousy for his girlfriend, because he could sense that she was being unfaithful. She had always loved his older brother, and his imaginings of what she was doing now were eating him alive. Avram had felt a strange reverence for this gaunt man, who within the hell of captivity could find such dedication to his own private pain, which had nothing to do with the Egyptians and their tortures.

Avram stepped quietly out of the tent and walked away until he could barely hear her, then sat down under a terebinth to try to focus. During the day, with Ora next to him, he could not think at all. Now he wrote the indictment of his pathetic and cowardly conduct. He dug his fingers into his face, his forehead and cheeks, and groaned softly: "Help her, you shit, you traitor." But he knew that he wouldn't, and his mouth twisted with loathing.

As he did whenever he thought about himself honestly, he simply found it difficult to comprehend why he was still alive. What made life hold on to him and preserve him? What was there in him, still, that justified such persistent effort on life's part, such stubbornness, or perhaps just vengefulness?

He closed his eyes and tried to conjure up the figure of a boy. Any boy. Recently, as Ofer's discharge date had grown closer, he would sometimes pick out a boy at the right age in the restaurant where he worked, or on the street, and observe him stealthily, even follow him for a block or two, and try to imagine how he saw things. He allowed himself more and more of these hallucinations, these Ofer-guesses, these shadows.

A thick nocturnal silence enveloped him. Soft breezes passed silently over him, plowing furrows through all of space. From time to time a large bird called out, sounding very close. Ora, in her tent, felt it, too. She listened as something seemed to flitter over her skin. Thousands of cranes made their way through the night sky heading north, and neither of them saw or knew. For a long time there was a huge invisible rustle, like the sighing of waves on a beach full of shells. Avram leaned against the tree with his eyes closed and saw the shadow of Ofer's back slip away in the image of young Ilan—for some reason it was Ilan who popped up, walking half a step in front of him and leading him through the paths of the despised army base where he'd had to live with his father, winking at the whitewashed graffiti on the walls of the stone huts. Then Avram tried to imagine a male version of the young Ora, but all he could see was Ora herself, long and fair, with red curls that bounced on her shoulders. He wondered if Ofer was also a redhead, like she used to be—she did not have even a drop of red left now—and he was surprised that this was the first time he'd ever entertained the utterly logical possibility that Ofer was a redhead. He was even more surprised that he was daring to indulge in such fantasies, more than he ever had before. Then, in a flash, he saw an image of Ofer that looked like him, like the twenty-one-year-old Avram, and the seventeen-year-old, and the fourteen-year-old. In a heartbeat he skipped among his various ages—for her, he thought feverishly, with prayer-like devotion; only for her—and saw the twinkle of a round, red-cheeked face that was always alert and eager. He felt a springy, agile dwarfishness that he hadn't felt for years, and the heat of a constant blaze coming from the tangled head of hair, and the glimmer of a sluttish wink, and then he was repelled, thrown from the spectacle, from his own self, as if tossed out by a rough bouncer. He sat panting, bathed in sweat, and for a few more moments his heart beat wildly and he was as excited as a young boy, a boy wallowing in forbidden fantasies.

He listened: total silence. Perhaps she'd finally fallen asleep, her torments lifted. He tried to understand what exactly had happened between her and Ilan. She hadn't explicitly said it was Ilan's fault. In fact she'd denied that. Perhaps she was the one who had fallen in love with someone else? Did she have another man? If so, why was she here alone, and why had she chosen to take him along?

She'd said that the children, the boys, were grown up now, and that they would decide who they wanted to live with. But he'd seen her lips tremble, and he knew that she was lying and could not figure out why. "Families are like calculus for me," he sometimes told Neta. Too many variables, too many parentheses and multiplications of products by powers, and just the whole complication of it—this is what he grumbled whenever she raised the topic—and the constant need to be *in a relationship* with every other member of the family, at every moment, day and night, even in dreams. When she turned gloomy and withdrew, he would try to appease her: "It's like being subjected to a permanent electrical shock, or like living in an eternal lightning storm. Is that what you want?"

For thirteen years he had not tired of telling Neta that she was wasting her youth, her future, and her beauty on him and that he was only holding her back, blocking her view. She was seventeen years younger than he. "My young girl," he called her, sometimes affectionately and sometimes sorrowfully. "When you were ten," he liked to remind her with strange glee, "I'd already been dead for five years." And she would say, "Let's bring the dead back to life, let's rebel against time."

He avoided her again and again with the age excuse. "You're much more mature than I am," he would say. She wanted children, and he laughed in terror: "Isn't one enough? You have to have multiple children?" Her narrow devilish eyes glimmered: "Then one child, okay, like Ibsen and Ionesco and Jean Cocteau were the same *child.*"

Lately it seemed he had gotten through to her, because she hadn't been around or even called for a few weeks. Where was she? he wondered half silently, and stood up.

Sometimes, when she made some money from her strange jobs, she just up and left. Avram could sense it approaching even before she could: a murky hunger started to surround her irises, a shadowy negotiation in which she apparently lost, and so had to travel. Even the names of the countries she chose scared him: Georgia, Mongolia, Tajikistan. She would call him from Marrakesh or Monrovia, nighttime for him, for her still day—"So now," he'd point out, "on top of everything else you're another three hours younger than me"—and with strange, dreamlike lightness she would recount experiences that made his hair stand on end.

He started walking around the tree. He tried to think, finally to ask himself when exactly he'd last heard from her, and found that it had been at least three weeks. Or more? Maybe it really had been a month since she'd disappeared. And what if she'd done something to herself? He froze and remembered her dancing with a ladder on the railing around the rooftop of her apartment building in Jaffa, and he knew that her potential in this area had been nagging at him for days now, and that his fear for her had existed alongside his profound confidence in her. He finally acknowledged how much the nerve-racking anticipation of Ofer's release must have scrambled the rest of his mind and even caused him to forget about her.

He sped up his circles around the tree and calculated again. The restaurant had been closed for renovations for a month now. And it was roughly since then that she hadn't been around. I haven't seen her or heard from her or looked for her since then. What was I doing all that time? He remembered long walks on the beach. Street benches. Beggars. Fishermen. Waves of longing for her that he forcefully repressed by beating his head against the wall. Alcohol in quantities he was not used to. Bad trips. Double doses of sleeping pills, starting at eight p.m. Bad headaches in the morning. Whole days of one album, Miles Davis, Mantovani, Django Reinhardt. Hours of digging through the garbage dumps of Jaffa looking for junk, work tools, rusty engines, old keys.

There were a few days of occasional work that had generated some decent income. Twice a week he shelved books in the library of a college in Rishon LeZion. Once in a while he served as an experiment subject for pharmaceutical and cosmetic companies. In the presence of friendly, polite scientists and lab technicians, who measured and weighed him and recorded every detail and gave him various forms to sign and finally handed him a voucher for coffee and a croissant, he swallowed brightly colored pills and slathered himself with creams that may or may not ever be used. In his reports, he invented physical and emotional side effects that the developers had never imagined.

For the past week, as Ofer's release date approached, he had not left the house. He stopped talking to people. Answering the phone. Eating. He felt that he needed to reduce the space he occupied in the world as much as possible. He hardly moved from his armchair. He sat waiting and diminishing himself. And when he got up and walked around the apartment, he tried not to make any fast movements, so as not to rip, not to disturb the gossamer thread from which Ofer now hung. And on the last day, when he thought Ofer was done, he sat motionless by the phone and waited for Ora to call and tell him it was over. But she didn't call, and he froze up more and more and knew that something bad had happened. The hours went by, evening fell, and he thought that if she did not call right now he would never be able to move again. With his last remaining strength he dialed her number and heard what had happened and felt himself turning to stone.

"But where was I for a whole month?" he moaned, and the sound of his own voice startled him.

He hurried over to Ora, almost running, just at the moment she called out to him.

She was sitting huddled in her coat. "When did you get up?"

"I don't know, a while ago."

"And where did you go?"

"Nowhere, I just walked around a bit."

"Did I disturb you when I cried?"

"No, it's okay. You can cry."

Dawn slowly opened its eyes. They sat quietly and watched the night bleed out its blackness.

"Listen," she said, "and let me finish saying this. I can't go on this way."

"What way?"

"With you not saying anything."

"I'm actually talking a lot." He forced a laugh.

"Yes, you'll get hoarse if you keep it up," she said drily. "But I just can't stand that you won't even let me talk about him."

Avram made a not-that-again gesture, and she slowly inhaled and then said, "Listen, I know it's difficult for you to be with me, but I'm losing my mind with this, too. It's worse than if I was on my own. Because then at least I could talk out loud to myself, about him, and now I can't even do that, because of you. I was thinking, what was I thinking"—she stopped and studied her fingertips; she had no choice—"that soon, when we reach the highway, we can try to get a ride to Kiryat Shmonah, and then we'll put you on a bus to Tel Aviv and I'll stay here and go on a bit farther. What do you say? Can you make the trip home on your own?"

"I can do anything. Don't make an invalid out of me."

"I didn't say that."

"I'm not an invalid."

"I know."

"There's nothing I can't do," he said angrily. "There are only things I don't *want* to do."

Like help me with Ofer, she thought.

"And how will you manage here?"

"Don't worry, I'll manage. I'll just walk. I don't even need to walk much. I'll be happy just crossing one field, back and forth, like yesterday or the day before. What's important to me is not where I am but where I'm not, do you understand?"

He snorted. "Do I understand?"

"It will be best for both of us," she said dubiously, sadly, and when he did not answer, she continued. "You may think I can stop it, that I can just not talk about him, I mean, but I can't. I'm incapable of holding back now, I have to give him strength, he needs me, I can feel it. I'm not criticizing you."

Avram lowered his head. Don't move, he thought, let her keep talking, don't interrupt.

"And it's not just because of your memory."

He gave her a puzzled look.

"You know, 'cause you'll remember everything, and my mind is like a sieve lately. That's not why I wanted you to come with me."

His head nestled against his chest and his whole body was hunched forward.

"I wanted you to come with me so I could talk about him with you, just tell you about him, so that if something happens to him—"

Avram crossed his arms and dug his hands deep into his sides. Don't move. Don't run away. Let her talk.

"And believe me, I wasn't thinking about all this before." Her nose was stuffed up. "You know me, I didn't plan anything. I wasn't even thinking about you when you called, and the truth is, you'd completely gone out of my thoughts that day, with everything that was going on. But when you phoned, when I heard you, I don't know, I suddenly felt that I had to be with you now, you see? With you, not with anyone else." The more she spoke, the straighter she sat and the sharper her eyes became, as though she had finally begun to decipher a secret code. "And I felt that we had to, both of us together, how can I put this, Avram—" She struggled to keep her voice steady and clean. She did not want her voice to shake. Not even a tremor. She constantly reminded herself of the allergy Ilan and the boys had to her frequent inundations. "Because really, we're his mother and father," she said softly. "And if we, together, I mean, if we don't do what parents—"

She stopped. He had stretched his arms out and up as far as he could, and his body was jerking as though ants were gnawing at his flesh. She scanned him and shook her head heavily a few times.

"All right." She sighed and started to stand up. "What more can I . . . I'm an idiot, how could I even think you—"

"No," he said quickly and put his hand on her arm, then pulled it away. "I was actually thinking . . . what do you say . . . maybe we could stay for another day, one day, no big deal, then we'll see."

"See what?"

"I don't know. Look, it's not like I'm all that, you know, it's not like I'm suffering, is it? It's not like you said"—he swallowed hard—"it's just that when you pressure me with it, with him . . ."

"With Ofer. At least say that."

He said nothing.

"You won't even say that?"

He dropped his arms to his sides.

Ora distractedly took off her glasses, folded them, and stuck them in a backpack pocket. She ran both hands firmly over her temples and kept them there for a moment, listening to a distant sound. Then suddenly she lunged at the ground and started to dig with her hands, pulling out clods of earth and stones, uprooting plants. Avram, with surprising quickness, jumped up and stood watching her tensely. She did not seem to notice him. She got up and started kicking the ground with her heel. Clods of earth flew, some of them hitting him. He did not move. His lips were pursed and his gaze was focused and stern. She knelt down, dislodged a sharp stone, and hit the ground with it. She pounded rapidly, biting her lower lip. Her thin-skinned face turned instantly red. Avram leaned over, knelt on one knee opposite her, and did not take his eyes off her. His hand rested on the earth with fingers spread, like someone about to run a race.

The pit grew deeper and wider. The white arm holding the stone rose and fell without pause. Avram cocked his head to one side in bemusement and looked somewhat canine. Ora stopped. She leaned on her arms and stared at the broken, unraveled earth as though not com-prehending what she saw, then stormed at it again with the stone. She moaned from the effort, from the fury. The back of her neck was flushed and sweaty, her thin shirt clung to her flesh.

"Ora," Avram whispered cautiously, "what are you doing?"

She stopped digging and looked around for a larger stone. She pushed a short tuft of hair off her forehead and wiped away the sweat. The pit she had dug was small and egg-shaped. She sat on her knees, grasped the stone with both hands, and struck down hard. Her head jerked forward with every strike, and each time she let out a groan. The skin on her hands began to tear. Avram watched, terrified, unable to look away from her scratched fingers. She did not seem to be weaken-ing. On the contrary: she picked up her pace, pounded and groaned, and after a moment she tossed the stone away and started to burrow with her hands. She dug up little stones and large ones and flung them away, and handfuls of damp earth flew through her legs and over her head. His face stretched and lengthened and his eyes bulged. She did not see. She seemed to have forgotten he was there. Dirt clung to her forehead and cheeks. Her beautiful eyebrows were covered with arches of earth, and sticky channels plowed their way around her mouth. With an outstretched hand she measured the little crater before her. She cleaned it out, smoothed the bottom with a gentle motion as though she were rolling dough into a baking pan. "Ora, no," Avram whispered into his palm, and even though he knew what she was about to do, he pulled back in fear. With three quick movements Ora lay down and buried her face in the gaping earth.

She spoke, but he could not make out her words. Her hands were palm-down on the sides of her head like grasshopper feet. Her short-cropped hair, speckled with earth and dust, trembled on the back of her neck. Her voice was a dim, crushed lament, like a person pleading before a judge. But it was a cruel and coldhearted judge, Avram thought, a cowardly judge, like me. From time to time she raised her head and opened her mouth wide for air, without looking at him, without seeing anything, then buried her face back in the ground. The morning flies were drawn to her sweat. Her legs, in dirty walking pants, moved and twitched every so often, and her entire body was tensed and bound up, and Avram, on the earth's surface, began to dart back and forth.

The Hula Valley turned golden at their feet, flooded with sunlight. The fish hatcheries glistened and the peach groves blossomed pink. Ora lay facedown and told a story to the belly of the earth and tasted the clods of soil and knew they would not sweeten, would be forever bland and gritty. Dirt ground between her teeth, dirt stuck to her tongue, to the roof of her mouth, and turned to mud. Snot ran from her nose, her eyes watered, and she choked and gargled dirt, and she beat her hands on the ground at either side of her head, and a thought drove like a nail, deeper and deeper into her mind—she had to, she had to know what it was like. Even when he was a baby she used to taste everything she made for him to make sure it wasn't too hot or too salty. Avram, above her, breathed rapidly, twitching, and absentmindedly bit the knuckles of his tightly clenched fists. He wanted to take hold of Ora and pull her out, but he did not dare touch her. He knew the taste of dirt in his eyes and suffocation in his nose and the sting of clods thrown from above—one of them, the bearded black man, had had a shovel, and the other one had used his hands to rake piles of earth dug from the pit. Avram himself had dug it, his hands covered with blisters. He had asked them to let him wear his socks on his hands. They'd laughed and said no. He'd been digging for over an hour and still couldn't believe they were going to do it. Three times already they'd made him dig his own grave, and at the last minute they'd laughed and sent him back to the cell. And this time, even when they tied his hands behind his back and shackled his feet and pushed him inside and told him to lie there without moving, he refused to believe it, perhaps because they were just two lowly soldiers, fellahin, and the *dhabet*, the officer, wasn't even there this time, and Avram still hoped they wouldn't go through with something like this on their own. He did not believe it even when they started throwing in handfuls of loose earth. First they covered his legs, very slowly and with strange carefulness, then they piled earth on his thighs and stomach and chest, and Avram squirmed and jerked his head back, searching for the *dhabet* who would order them to stop, and only when the first handful of dirt hit his face, on his forehead and eyelids—he can still remember the shocking slap of a clump landing straight on his face, the sting in his eyes, specks trickling quickly down behind his ears—only then did he realize that this time it might not be another show, another stage in the torture, but that they were actually doing it, burying him alive, and a ring of cold terror tightened around his heart, injecting paralyzing venom: time is running out, you're running out, one moment from now you'll be gone, you won't be anymore. Blood burst from his eyes and from his nose, and his body convulsed under layers of earth, heavy, heavy earth, who knew it was so heavy and burdensome on the chest, and his mouth shut to keep out the dirt, and his mouth ripped open to breathe in the dirt, and the throat is dirt and the lungs are dirt, and the toes stretch to inhale, and the eyes pop out of their sockets, and suddenly inside all this like a slowly crawling translucent worm, a sad little worm of thought about the fact that strangers, in a strange land, are pouring earth on his face, burying him alive, throwing dirt into his eyes and mouth and killing him, and it's wrong, he wants to yell, it's a mistake, you don't even know me, and he grunts and struggles to open his eyes to devour one more sight, light, sky, concrete wall, even cruelly mocking faces, but human faces—and then, above his head to the side, someone takes a photograph, a man stands with a camera, it's the *dhabet*, a short, thin Egyptian officer with a large black camera, and he takes meticulous pictures of Avram's death, perhaps as a souvenir, to show the wife and kids at home, and that is when Avram lets go of his life, right at that moment he truly lets go. He had never let go when he was left in the stronghold alone for three days and three nights, nor when the Egyptian soldier pulled him out of his hiding place, nor when the soldiers put him on a truck and beat him within an inch of his life with fists and boots and rifle butts, nor when Egyptian fellahin stormed the truck on the way and wanted to attack him, nor in all the days and nights of interrogations and torture, when they denied him food and water and withheld sleep and made him stand for hours in the sun and held him for days and nights in a cell just large enough to stand in, and one by one they pulled out his fingernails and toenails, and hung him by his hands from the ceiling and whipped the soles of his feet with rubber clubs, and hooked electrical wires to his testicles and nipples and tongue, and raped him—throughout all this he always had something to hold on to, half a potato that a merciful warden once snuck into his soup, or a bird's chirping he heard or imagined every day at dawn, or the cheerful voices of two little children, perhaps the prison commander's children, who once came to visit their father and chattered and played in the prison yard all morning; and above all, he had the sketch he wrote while he was on duty in Sinai, until the war started, with its complex plots and multiple characters, and he kept returning to a secondary plot that had never preoccupied him before he was taken hostage, but this was what saved him over and over again. It was the story of two neglected children who find an abandoned baby, and to his surprise Avram found that the imaginary characters did not fade while he was a prisoner the way the real people did, even Ora and Ilan, perhaps because the thought of the living people was intolerable, and quite simply crushed his remaining will to live, whereas thinking about his story almost always pumped a little more blood through his veins. But there, in the ugly yard next to the prison's concrete wall, with its hedges of barbed wire, and now, with the gaunt officer who took another step closer and leaned right over Avram to capture the last moment before all of Avram was covered with earth and swallowed up in it, Avram no longer wanted to live in a world where such a thing was possible, where a person stood photographing someone being buried alive, and Avram let go of his life and died.

Back and forth he walked wildly by Ora's body, grunting and shouting and tugging at his face and beard with both hands, yet at the same time a thin voice whispered inside him: Look at her, look, she can go all the way into the earth, she isn't afraid.

Ora had, in fact, quieted a little, as though she had learned how to breathe in the belly of the earth. She had stopped slamming her head and beating her hands. She lay still, and very quietly told the earth things that came to her, nonsense, little bits of it, things you'd tell a girl-friend or a good neighbor. "Even when he was little, a year or younger,

I tried to make sure that everything I gave him to eat, every dish I made for him, looked pretty, because I wanted things to be nice for him. I always tried to think not only of the flavors but also the colors, the color combinations, so it would be cheerful for him to look at." She stopped. What am I doing, she thought. I'm telling the earth about him. And she realized with horror: Maybe I'm preparing her for him, so she'll know how to take care of him. A great weakness filled her. She was on the verge of fainting, and she sighed into the belly of the earth and for a moment she was a tiny, miserable puppy snuggling into a large, warm lap. She thought she could feel the earth softening a little, because her scent grew sweeter, her deep exhalation came back to Ora. She took her in and told her how he liked to make figures out of his mashed potatoes and schnitzel, little people and animals, and then of course he would refuse to eat them because how could he, he would ask sweetly, eat a puppy or a goat? Or a person?

Suddenly two hands took hold of her, grasped her waist, rocked her, and pulled her out. She was in Avram's arms. It was good that he'd come with her, she knew. One minute longer and she would have been entirely swallowed up in the ground. Something nameless had pulled her down and she was willing to crumble into dirt. It was good that he'd come, and he was so strong, with one yank he uprooted her from the earth and charged away from the pit with her on his shoulder.

He stood there, confused, and let her slide off his body so she stood opposite him, face-to-face, until she collapsed in exhaustion. She sat cross-legged, her face covered with dirt. He brought a bottle of water and sat down in front of her, and she filled her mouth and spat out doughy globs of earth, and coughed, and her eyes streamed. She wet her mouth and spat again. "I don't know what happened to me," she mumbled, "it just came over me." Then she turned to look at him. "Avram? Avram? Did I scare you?" She poured water into her hand and wiped his forehead, and he did not pull back. Then she ran her wet hand over her own forehead and felt the cuts. "It's okay, it's okay," she blathered. "We're all right, everything will be all right."

Once in a while she checked his eyes and sensed a shadow slip away into a thicket of darkness, and she did not understand. She could not understand. He had never told her anything about that place. She kept smoothing over his forehead for several more minutes, reassuring, offering tenderness and promises of goodness, and he sat there accepting and absorbing and did not move, only his thumbs flicked back and forth over his fingertips.

"Stop, enough, don't torture yourself. We'll come to a road soon, we'll put you on a bus and you'll go home. I should never have brought you here."

But the softness in her voice—Avram felt it and the blood ran out of his heart—the softness and the compassion told him that something he had deeply feared, for years, had happened: Ora had despaired of him. Ora was giving up on him. Ora had accepted the failure that he was. He let out a bitter, toxic laugh.

"What is it, Avram?"

"Ora." He turned away from her and spoke in a dim, throaty voice, as if his own mouth were full of earth. "Do you remember what I told you when I got back?"

She shook her head firmly. "Don't say it. Don't even think it."

She took his hand and pressed it between her bleeding palms. It amazed her that for the last few minutes she had been touching him so often, with such ease, and that he had not resisted, and that he had grabbed her waist and lifted her out of the ground and run with her across the field. It amazed her that their bodies were acting like flesh and blood. "Don't say anything. I don't have the energy for anything now."

When he'd come back from captivity, she had managed to get on the ambulance that took him from the airport to the hospital. He lay on the stretcher, bleeding, his open wounds running with pus. Suddenly his eyes opened and, upon seeing her, appeared to focus. He recognized her. He signaled with his eyes for her to lean down. With his last remaining strength he whispered, "I wish they'd killed me."

From around the bend in the path came the sound of singing. A man was singing at the top of his lungs, and other voices dragged behind him without any charm or coordination. "Maybe we should duck between these trees until they pass," Avram grumbled. Only a few moments ago they had awoken from a slumber of total exhaustion, on the side of the path and in full daylight. But the walkers had already revealed themselves. Avram wanted to get up, but she put a hand on his knee: "Don't run away, they'll just walk by, we won't look at them and they won't look at us." He sat with his back to the path and hid his face.

At the head of the small procession walked a tall, skinny, bearded young man. Locks of black hair hung in his face, and a large colorful yarmulke covered his head. He danced and flung his limbs around in excitement as he sang and cheered, and ten or so men and women straggled behind him, hand in hand, zigzagging and daydreaming, mumbling his song or some feeble melody. Every so often they waved a tired foot, collapsed, bumped into one another. Wide-eyed, they stared at the couple sitting by the path, and the leader pulled his procession around the two and joined it in a loop and did not stop singing and hopping around. When he waved his arms up high, the others' arms were drawn up in spasmodic surprise, and the whole circle collapsed and then tied itself back up, and the man grinned, and as he sang and danced he leaned over to Ora and asked in a quiet and utterly businesslike tone if everything was all right. Ora shook her head, nothing was all right, and he examined her injured, dirty face, and looked to Avram and a crease deepened between his eyes. Then he looked back and forth as if searching for something—as if he knew exactly what he was looking for, Ora felt—and saw the pit in the earth, and Ora unwittingly tightened her legs together.

He quickly went back to his enthusiastic rocking. "A great trouble has befallen you, my friends," he said, and Ora replied in a small voice, "You could certainly say so." The man inquired: "Trouble from man or from the heavens?" Then he added quietly, "Or from the earth?" Ora replied, "I don't really believe in the heavens," and the man smiled and said, "And in man, you do?" Ora, slightly won over by his smile, said, "Less and less every day." The man straightened up and led the fumbling circle around them, and Ora tented her eyes from the sun to turn the dancing silhouettes into people. She noticed that one of them had odd-sized legs, another's head was strangely tilted to the sky and she thought he might be blind, and one woman's body was bent almost to the ground. Another woman's mouth was wide open and drooling, and she held the hand of a gaunt albino boy, who giggled with vacant eyes. The circle turned heavily on its axis, and the energetic young man leaned over again and said smilingly, "Guys, why don't you come with me for an hour or so?"

Ora looked at Avram, who sat with his head bowed and seemed not to see or hear anything, and she said to the man, "No thanks."

"Why not? Just an hour, what do you have to lose?"

"Avram?"

He shrugged as if to say, Your call, and Ora turned sharply to the man and said, "But don't talk to me about the news, you hear me? I don't want to hear a single word!"

The man seemed to lose his equilibrium for the first time. He was about to give a witty reply, but then he peered into her eyes and said nothing.

"And no proselytizing either," Ora added.

The man laughed. "I'll try, but don't come crying if you leave with a smile."

"I won't complain about a smile."

He held his hand out to Avram, but Avram got up without touching the hand, and the man, still dancing around her, helped Ora hoist her backpack up and announced that he was Akiva. He stood Avram in the middle of the line and Ora at the end and went back to shepherd his confused herd.

Avram held the hand of the hunchbacked old lady, and with his other he grabbed hold of the albino boy, and Ora took the hand of a bald woman with thick blue veins snaking up her legs. She kept asking Ora what was for lunch and demanded that she give her back the *cholent* pot. They all climbed up a little hill, and Avram kept turning his head back to check on Ora, and she would give him a shoulder-shrugging look: Beats me, I have no idea. Akiva looked back encouragingly, and sang a grating tune very loudly. They continued this way, up and down, and both Ora and Avram delved into themselves, blind to the abundant beauty around them, yellow beds of spurge, purple orchids, and terebinths blossoming in red. Nor did they notice the intoxicating nectar that the spiny-broom flowers had begun to emit in the heat of the day. But Ora knew that it was good and restorative for her to be led this way, led by the hand, without having to think about where to put down her foot for the next step. Avram knew he wouldn't mind going on like this all day, as long as he did not have to see Ora suffering because of him. Maybe later, when they were alone, he would tell her that he might be willing, perhaps, for her to tell him a little about Ofer, if she had to. But he would ask her not to start talking about him directly, not about Ofer himself, and that she talk about him carefully and slowly, so that he could gradually get used to the torture.

Ora looked up and a strange happiness began to gurgle inside her, perhaps because of how she had spoken into the earth—she could still taste it on her tongue—or perhaps because always, even at home, after she had these outbursts, when enough was enough, when her guys had really crossed the line, a physical sweetness always spread through her body. Ilan and the boys would still be looking at her in shock, frightened, full of peculiar awe and so eager to appease her, and she would spend several long minutes floating on a pall of satisfaction and deep pleasure. Or perhaps she was so happy because of the people in the procession, who imbued her with a dreamlike tranquillity despite their strangeness and forlornness and their broken bodies. *From dust we were taken.* She suddenly felt it down to the roots of her flesh. Just like that, from pure mud. She could hear the *pat-pat* sound of her own self being scooped out by the handful, back at the dawn of time, out of the muddy earth, to be sculpted—too bad they were stingy and did such a poor job with the boobs, and they made her thighs too thick, completely disproportionate, to say nothing of her ass, which this year, with all her desperate binge-eating, had really flourished. When she had finished denigrating her body—which was, incidentally, delightfully attractive to Akiva, judging by the glimmer in his eye, and this was not lost on her—Ora smiled to think of how Ilan had been sculpted: thin, strong, upright, and stretched out like a tendon. She longed for Ilan here and now, without thinking, without remembering or resenting, just his flesh boring into hers. She felt a sudden yearning in the sting. She roused herself quickly and thought of how Adam was sculpted, how delicately and meticulously they had worked on his face, his heavy eyes, his mouth with all its expressions. Her hand ran longingly over his thin body with the slightly hunched back that seemed almost defiant, and the cloudy shadows on his sunken cheeks, and the prominent Adam's apple that somehow gave him a scholarly look. She also thought about her Ada, making room for her, as always, and imagined what she would look like today if she were alive. Sometimes she saw women who resembled her on the street, and she had a patient who looked like her, a woman with a herniated disc whom she treated for a whole year, working miracles on her. And only then did Ora dare to think about Ofer: strong, solid, and tall he had emerged from the lump of mud—not immediately, not in his first years, when he was small and meager, little more than a huge pair of eyes and bony ribs and matchstick limbs, but later, when he grew up, how beautifully he had risen from the mud, with his thick neck and broad shoulders, and the surprisingly feminine ankles, such a delightful finish to the oversized, powerful limbs. She smiled to herself and looked quickly at Avram, ran her eyes over his body, examined, compared— similarities, dissimilarities—and was overcome with joy in the depths of her gut. It occurred to her, incidentally, that Avram fit in with this crowd quite well, and it seemed to her that he was also finding unexpected relief, because a new smile, the first smile, was spreading on his lips, almost a smile of exaltation. But then a shock wave ran through the hobbling procession, hands pulled back and disconnected, and Ora watched with alarm as Avram's mouth opened wide, his smile broadened, ripped open, and his eyes glimmered and his hands waved wildly, and he kicked and jumped like a horse and grunted.

After a moment he stopped himself, buried his head back down between his shoulders, and walked on, dragging his feet and swaying from side to side. Akiva looked at Ora questioningly, and she motioned for him to keep going. Then she forced herself to walk on too, shocked by what she had seen in Avram, by the sliver of secret revealed to her from inside him, as though for an instant he had allowed himself to try out a different possibility, a redemptive one. He had looked so distorted, she thought, like a boy playing with pieces of himself.

After a while they reached a small moshav hidden behind a hill and a few groves. Two rows of houses, most with tacked-on balconies and flimsy storehouses, were abutted by chicken coops and feed silos and separated by yards piled with crates, iron pipes, old fridges, and all sorts of junk. Avram's eyes lit up as he scanned the options. Concrete bomb shelters jutted out of the ground like snouts, covered with lettering in chalk and paint, and here and there a rusty tractor or a pickup truck with no wheels was propped up on blocks. Among the patchworked houses, the occasional sparkling new building stood out, towering castles of stone with turrets and gables and signs announcing luxurious guest rooms in a charming Galilee atmosphere, including Jacuzzis and shiatsu massage. Adults and children started to pour out of the houses as they arrived, shouting, "Akiva's here! Akiva's here!" Akiva's face lit up, and he stopped at various houses to deliver a member of the gang to a woman or a child. At every house they asked him to come in just for a moment, for something to drink or nibble, and lunch would be ready soon, but he refused: *"The day is short and there is much work to be done."*

He walked the length of the main street—it was the only street—in this fashion, until he had dispersed his flock and was left only with Avram and Ora, whom no one came to claim. Children and young boys walked beside them and asked who they were and where they came from, and whether they were tourists or Jews. They agreed among themselves that they were Jews, albeit Ashkenazim, and wondered about their backpacks and sleeping bags and about Ora's scratched, dirty face. Mangy, malcontented dogs ran after them and barked. They both longed to get back to their path and their solitude, and Ora could barely hold back the talk about Ofer, but Akiva was somehow unwilling to let them go. As he talked and jumped around he seemed to be searching for a place where he could help them, and between waving to an old man and giving a quick blessing to a baby, he told them that for him this was both a mitzvah and a living. The local council had arranged a special job for him as "gladdener of the dejected"—that was what his pay stub actually stated—and he did this every day, six days a week. Even when they cut his salary in half this year, he did not cut down on his work; on the contrary, he added two hours a day, *"For one must multiply acts of holiness, not diminish them."* Besides, he said, he remembered Avram from the pub on HaYarkon Street. Back then, neither of them had a beard, and Akiva's name was Aviv, and Avram sometimes used to belt out "Otchi Tchorniya" and Paul Robeson songs from behind the bar. If he remembered correctly, Avram had developed a fairly interesting theory about the memories that old objects had, whereby if you put together all sorts of junk, you could make them play out their memories. "Did I remember correctly?" "You did," Avram grunted, and glanced at Ora evasively. Ora pricked up her ears, and Akiva walked quickly and told them that he had found religion five years ago. Before that, he was getting his doctorate in philosophy in Jerusalem. Schopenhauer was half God for him, the love of his life—or actually, the hatred of his life. He let out a green-eyed laugh. "Do you know Schopenhauer? Such a masking of the divine face! Such total blackness! And you, what about you guys? What's with the gloom and doom?"

"Forget it," Ora laughed. "You won't cheer us up with a blessing or a dance, we're a really complicated case."

Akiva stopped in the middle of the street and turned to face her with his vivacious eyes and his strong high cheekbones, and Ora thought, What a waste.

"Don't be condescending," he said. "Everything here is really complicated too, what did you think? These are things that can break the strongest faith. In this place you'll hear stories that only the most misanthropic author could write, maybe Bukowski on a really bad day, or Burroughs jonesing for a fix. And if you're a believer, where does that leave you, hey?" There was no jocularity on his face. His lips trembled for a brief moment, in anger, or from heartbreak. Then he said quietly, "Once, when I was like you, maybe even a lot more cynical than you—a Schopenhauer freak, you know?—once I would say about these kinds of things: God is cracking up with laughter."

Ora pursed her lips and did not reply. She thought to herself, Shut up and listen, what harm could it do to gain a little strength, even with his help? Do you have such reserves of strength that you can pass up even a drop of reinforcement? For a moment she considered offhandedly pulling out her *shiviti* from her blouse, so he'd see that she too had an elated Jewish soul. Oh, you miserable woman, she rebuked herself. You beggar. Or maybe it was just that this Akiva was arousing something in her, despite his tzitzit and all his jumping around and his religious nonsense.

Akiva wiped the anger off his face with both hands, smiled at her, and said, "Now, ladies and gentlemen, we shall go to Ya'ish and Yakut's house to cheer them up, and maybe we'll cheer ourselves up as well."

Even before they arrived, a small, round, laughing woman came out to them, wiping her hands on her apron and calling, "Oh my, we've been waiting so long, we could've died! Hello, Akiva! Hello mister and missus, such an honor, really. What happened to you, lady, did you fall, God forbid?" She kissed Akiva's hand, and he put his palm on her head and blessed her with his eyes closed. The house was dark, despite the midday hour, and two young boys were dragging a table with a chair on it across the room to replace a burned-out lightbulb, and there was great rejoicing when they walked in. "Akiva brought the light! Akiva brought the light!" When the family members saw Ora and Avram, they fell silent and looked at Akiva for guidance. He waved both arms and sang, *"Hineh ma tov! Behold, how good and how pleasant it is for brethren to dwell together in unity!"* Avram was quickly seated in an armchair with much fanfare, and Ora was taken by a big-boned woman to the bathroom, where she washed her face and hair for a long time, flushing out streams of mud. The woman stood watching her with kind eyes, then handed her a towel and some cotton wool and gently applied yellow iodine to her cuts and scrapes. She said it was good that it stung, that meant all the germs were burning off, and then she took Ora back to the living room, washed and placated.

Meanwhile, from the bustling kitchen, there had emerged a silver platter adorned with little silver fish around the edges, bearing sunflower seeds, almonds, peanuts, pistachios, and dates. Then came a round copper platter with glasses of tea in delicate silver holders, and the lady of the house urged Ora and Avram to snack, saying lunch would be served soon. With some horror, Ora noticed a muscular young man with both legs amputated, darting around on his arms with amazing speed. Akiva explained that the three boys in the family were born deaf-mute, and it was from God: "The girls came out all right, praise God, but not the boys. Something hereditary. And that one you see there, Rachamim, the youngest, he decided in childhood that the handicap wouldn't get in his way. He went to high school in Kiryat Shmonah, got all Bs on his finals, and had a profession as a bookkeeper in a metal factory. Then one day he got sick of it and decided he wanted to see the world." Akiva turned to the young man and announced: "Isn't that true, Rachamim? You were a real jet-setter, hey? Monaco?" Rachamim smiled and gestured with one hand at his no-legs and made a warmhearted yet terrifying cutting motion, and Akiva explained that two years ago, in Buenos Aires, Rachamim was working in a quarry when a heavy machine flipped over and crushed him. "But even that didn't stop him," Akiva said as he leaned over and put his arm around Rachamim's shoulders. "Last week he was back at work in the moshav, doing night shifts as a guard in the egg storeroom, and God willing"— he gave Ora a look that denied his grin—"next year we'll marry him off to a kosher Jewish girl."

They were urged to have lunch at this house too, and this time Akiva did not immediately reject the offer. He hesitated, closed his eyes, and consulted with himself, using broad hand gestures, and murmured, "*Let thy foot be seldom in thy neighbor's house; lest he be sated with thee, and hate thee.*" The others crowded around him and yelled out, "No! They won't be sated with thee and they won't hate thee!" Akiva's eyes lit up, and he raised his right hand and called out musically to the housewife: "*Make ready quickly three measures of fine meal, knead it, and make cakes.*" The swarm of women dispersed and hurried to the kitchen, and Ora guessed from his look that he had accepted the invitation because this house was slightly less poor than the others and could withstand the burden.

Akiva himself went into the kitchen to make sure they didn't go overboard, and Ora and Avram were left in the room with a few of the family members, mostly girls and young children. There was utter silence until one boy plucked up the courage to ask where they were from. Ora told him she was from Jerusalem and Avram was from Tel Aviv, but originally he was also from Jerusalem, and when he was a little boy he lived in a neighborhood near the *shuk*. But they were not impressed with her folkloric image of Jerusalem, and a thin young girl who was very pale and bundled up asked with some alarm, "You're not married?" The others giggled and shushed the impudent girl, but Ora said softly, "We've been friends for over thirty years." Another boy, with thin side locks tucked behind his ears and long black eyes like a young goat's, jumped up and protested: "Then why didn't you get married?" Ora said it just hadn't worked out that way and resisted saying, It seems we weren't meant to be together. Another girl giggled and held her hand over her mouth as she asked, "So did you marry someone else?" Ora nodded, and an excited whisper frothed up the room. All eyes were drawn to the kitchen to seek help from Akiva, who would certainly know how to behave in such a situation. Ora said, "But I don't live with him anymore," and the girl asked, "Why? Did he divorce you?" Ora ignored the painful blow, although it was like a punch in her stomach, and said, "Yes," and without being asked, she added, "I'm alone now, and Avram, this guy, is my friend, and we're hiking around the country together." Something a little unctious, the same thing that had tempted her to specify "Jerusalem" and "a neighborhood near the *shuk*," now compelled her to add, "Our beautiful country."

The thin pale girl persisted with a stern expression. "And this man, does he have a wife?"

Ora looked at Avram, waiting for an answer, and he hunched over and stared at his fingers. Ora thought about the earring that looked like a horseman's spur, and the purple hairs in the brush in his bathroom, and when his silence persisted, she answered for him, "No, he's alone now." Avram gave an imperceptible nod, and a shadow of worry passed over his face.

Other men and women came into the house, placed dishes on the table, and brought chairs. The thin boy with the goat eyes jumped up and asked, "But what's the matter with him? Why is he like that? Is he sick?" Ora said, "No, he's sad," and everyone looked at Avram and nodded understandingly, as if all at once he had been deciphered and was now clear and simple. Ora said boldly, "His son is in the army, in that campaign that's going on now." A coo of understanding and sympathy spread through the room, and blessings rolled off tongues, for this particular soldier and for our Defense Forces in general, and there were declarations, and God curse the Arabs, with everything we gave them they still want more, all they think about is killing us, *for Esau hated Yaakov,* and Ora, with a very broad smile, suggested that today they not talk about politics. The difficult girl furrowed her brow in surprise: "That's politics? That's the truth! It's from the Torah!" Ora said, "Yes. *But we don't want to talk about the news today!"* An unpleasant silence congealed in the room, and at that moment, fortunately, Akiva came back from the kitchen and announced that the food would be ready soon, and meanwhile they should rejoice, *"For he who eats without rejoicing in Hashem, it is as if he eats sacrifices of the dead."*

His arms and legs were already flying, and he started to sing and dance around the whole room, clapping his giant hands over his head and sweeping up one boy after the other. He snatched an eight- or nine-month-old baby out of a girl's lap and proceeded to wave him in the air. The brave baby was brown and chubby: he was not scared at all, and he laughed out loud, and his laughter infected everyone. Even Avram smiled, and Akiva's eye picked it up, and in a graceful wave he danced over to Avram and placed the baby in his lap.

Within the joyful commotion Ora felt a thin frosty line stretch instantly around Avram as his body hardened and fossilized. His hands enveloped the outline of the baby's body without touching him. From her side of the room she could feel Avram's limbs retreat into the shell of their skin, far from the baby's touch.

The baby was completely absorbed in the revelry around him and in Akiva's wild dancing, and did not pay the slightest attention to the distress of the person in whose lap he had been dropped. His curvy brown body rocked cheerfully to the rhythm of the song and the clapping, his arms moved around as though he were conducting the tumult, and his fleshy mouth, a perfect little red heart, opened wide in a bright smile, and immeasurable sweetness poured forth.

Ora did not move. Avram stared straight ahead and seemed not to see anything. His heavy head with its stubbly beard was suddenly dark and foreign behind the baby's illuminating face. There was something almost intolerable in the scene. Ora imagined that this was the first time since his captivity that Avram had held a baby, and then it occurred to her that it might be the first time in his life. If only I had brought Ofer to him when he was a baby, she thought. If only I had come to him, unannounced, and placed Ofer in his arms, just like that, naturally, with utter confidence, as Akiva did. But it was now, with the actual picture before her, that Ora could not imagine Avram holding Ofer in his arms, and she wondered how he had caused her to erect a total barrier within herself between him and Ofer.

The baby must have been incredibly even-tempered; he reached out and grabbed hold of Avram's hand, which was lying lifelessly next to his hip, and he tried to hold it up to his head. When he found it too heavy, he twisted his face angrily and reached his other hand out. With great effort he pulled Avram's hand up and moved it this way and that like a conductor's baton, and it seemed to Ora that the baby had not grasped that he was holding a person's hand, and moreover, that he was sitting on a living human being. His distress grew when he noticed the hand's fingers and began to study then, and then play with them, but he still did not look back to see who the hand belonged to and in whose lap he was sitting so intimately. He simply folded and bent the unfamiliar fingers at their joints, wagged them in his hands as though they were a soft hand-shaped toy or a glove, and every so often he smiled at Akiva dancing before him and at the women and the girls who came and went from the kitchen. After he had carefully examined the gentle fingers and wondered about their fingernails and a fresh scratch he found—Ora remembered the way Avram used to torture himself with endless hand flexes, struggling to tone his muscles—the baby turned over Avram's hand and explored its soft palm with his finger.

Everyone was now busy setting the table and distributing bowls of food, and no one apart from Ora was watching. The baby put his lips to Avram's palm and made a soft, truncated bleating sound: *"Ba-ba-ba."* He utterly delighted in the sound and the tickling sensation on his lips. Ora herself felt a teasing hum in her throat and mouth. Inside her, a voiceless murmur also bleated, *Ba-ba.*

With both hands the baby held the limb and played with it on his rosy mouth, wrapped his cheeks and chin in it, gave himself over to the apparently pleasurable touch of the hand—Ora remembered, she remembered Avram's amazingly thin skin, astoundingly soft, all over his body—and the baby's dark eyes focused somewhere in the space of the room, and he was consumed with pure wonder at his own voice echoing through the shell he had made. Within the hubbub around him he listened only to his voice coming from outside and inside at the same time, as if hearing the first story he had ever told himself. He seemed to sense that with Avram it was good to tell stories, Ora thought. Avram did not move, and hardly breathed, so as not to disturb the baby, but after a while he shifted and straightened up a little in the chair, releasing his body, and Ora saw his shoulders soften and open and his lower lip tremble slightly in a movement that only she noticed because she knew to anticipate it—how she had once loved these reflections of his subcutaneous turmoils, and the way every emotion left its mark on him, and the way he used to blush like a girl. She wondered if she should get up and rescue him by taking the baby, but she could not move. From the corner of her eye she could see that Akiva had also noticed what was going on, and that as he danced to and from the kitchen he constantly monitored the situation. He did not look worried or fearful for the baby, and her heart told her to trust his calmness.

She leaned back and allowed herself to sink into Avram, who finally turned to her and gave her a complete, lingering look, the look of a living person, and Ora felt then, right in the palm of her hand, the baby's breath, and how without even touching her the baby was imprinting her with the stamp of his warm, damp vivacity. Her hand closed over the burning secret, the kiss of another human's inner being, a tiny human in a diaper. Avram gave her a very slight nod of recognition, of acknowledgment. She replied with a similar nod, and for the first time since leaving home, and in contradiction to the despair that had consumed her only a few hours ago, when she had buried her face in the earth, she now had the thought that things might be good, and that perhaps she and Avram, together, were doing the right thing after all. But it was then that the baby started crying. He spread his chubby arms and cried at the top of his lungs, his face lit up in bright purple insult, and Ora dashed over and took him. As she did so, Avram let a few quick words escape, but she did not hear them properly because of the crying baby, or because of a slight shock that hit her when she touched the place where the baby's body had sprung from Avram's—and what she thought he said was, "But start from a distance."

She smiled awkwardly, confused by his words. Start what? And why from a distance? The baby's mother hurried in from the kitchen, her face red from the stove, and apologized for leaving the baby with Avram. "We turned you into a baggage claim! Any minute now he'd be calling you daddy." She laughed at how the little one had already been passed around, keeping everyone busy. "Not one minute of quiet from this one," she complained affectionately. "Hungry, Daddy?" she asked, and Ora noticed that Avram was nodding distractedly, but he quickly pulled himself together and looked away from the mother, who sat down nearby and deftly pushed the baby under her blouse, where his head disappeared.

Ora thought about Ofer, and the terrible pain from last night subsided. Akiva walked through the room with a large bowl, humming a tune, and looked at her out of the corner of his eye as if he knew now why he had dragged them all this way. Her gaze was drawn to the baby, whose tiny fist kept opening and closing as he sucked eagerly, and she knew that Ofer, wherever he was, was safe and protected now. She repeatedly played through her mind what Avram had whispered, and then she understood.

Start from a distance?

He nodded once and looked away.

She sat down, crushing her fingers together, suddenly feeling flustered and a little frightened. He sat down opposite her. The room bustled and hummed around them, and for a long time they both watched something out there, in a time that had no time.

Should we stay for lunch? Ora asked Avram soundlessly, with only her lips moving.

"Whatever you want," he whispered, salivating at the dishes.

"I don't know, we just fell on them out of nowhere—"

"Of course you'll stay for lunch!" The housewife laughed—an unfortunately expert lip-reader. "What did you think, that we'd just let you go? It's an honor for us to have you eat here. All of Akiva's friends are our guests."

But start from a distance, he warned her, and she doesn't know what kind of distance he needs, whether he meant distance in time or space, and besides—what is distant for him now, where he is? She walks behind him, looks at the worn heels of his ancient Converse sneakers, so unsuited for this nature walk, and resists asking when he's planning on finally switching to Ofer's heavy hiking boots, which dangle from his backpack. But perhaps they would be too big for him, she thinks, and perhaps that's what worries him. He had, and still has, small hands and feet—*footlets*, he used to call them, *my footlets and handlets*—which always embarrassed him, and of course that was the reason he called himself Caligula, "little boot." She remembers how he marveled at the way her breasts fit perfectly in his cupped hands, although today they probably would not, having been suckled by two children and the mouths of many men—but not that many, in fact. Let's see. What is there to see? You know exactly how many, but some wicked little creature inside her has already started to count them off on its fingers as she walks: Ilan is one, Avram is two, and Eran, the Character, makes three— no, wait, four, with that Motti guy she brought home one night to the house in Tzur Hadassah, years ago, who sang in the shower at the top of his lungs. So that makes four men. Fewer than one per decade, on average. Not a monumental achievement, considering there were girls who by the age of sixteen—but forget about that now!

The air bustles and hums. Flies, bees, gnats, grasshoppers, butterflies, and beetles hover and crawl and leap from the foliage. There is so much life inside every particle of the world, Ora thinks, and this profusion suddenly seems threatening, because why should the abundant, wasteful world care if the life of one fly, or one leaf, or one person, were to end at this very moment? The sorrow of it makes her start talking.

In a soft, flat voice she tells him that until recently Ofer had a girlfriend, his first one, and she left him, and he still hasn't gotten over it. "I really liked her. You could say I adopted her a bit, and she adopted me, too. We became very close, which was probably a mistake on my part, because it's not good to get so close to your boys' girlfriends"—well, this is really useful information for him, she thinks. "Everyone warned me, but Talia, that was her name, I just fell in love with her as soon as I saw her. And by the way, she wasn't all that beautiful, although to me she was, she had—she *has*, I have to stop thinking about her in the past tense, I mean she's still around, she's still alive, right? So why do I . . ."

For a few seconds the only sounds are their footsteps, the path crunching under their feet, and the buzzing hum. I'm talking to him, Ora thinks with astonishment. I'm telling him these things, I don't even know if this counts as starting from a distance, but it's the farthest from Ofer that I can be now, and Avram's not running away.

"And Talia's face . . . how can I describe it to you"—descriptions were always your thing, she thinks at him—"a face with strength, and character. A strong nose, full of personality, and big lips, which I love, and a large, feminine bust. And she had wonderful fingers." Ora giggles and waves her own fingers before her eyes. They used to be lovely too, until recently, when their joints grew thick and crooked.

In her wallet, secretly, behind a little picture of Ofer and Adam with their arms around each other—it was taken the morning Adam enlisted; they both had long hair, Adam's dark and straight, Ofer's still golden, curly at the edges—she keeps a picture of Talia. She can't bring herself to remove it, and she's always afraid Ofer might find it and get angry. Sometimes she pulls it out of its hiding place and looks at it. She tries to guess what sort of children might have been born from a combination of Talia and Ofer. Occasionally she slides the photo into the empty clear plastic slot that, until six months ago, had contained a picture of Ilan, and looks from the boys to Talia and back again, imagining Talia as her daughter, and then it dawns on her: it looks so possible and natural.

"She's a totally levelheaded girl. She even has a bit of an old person's bitterness. You would have liked her"—she smiles at his back—"but don't think she was so . . . how should I put this? She wasn't the easiest person. Well, what do you expect, that Ofer would choose someone easy?"

She thinks the back of his neck grows denser between his shoulders.

They are walking down a riverbed on a worrisome rocky slope—a double-X trail, the boys would have called it: Extra Extreme. When they started their way down and she saw Avram slip and grab on to a jutting rock, she mumbled that she hoped this was just a little deviation from the path and immediately winced at the echo of her words in his mind and wondered if someone inside him would say, in that clownish nasal voice and with a wicked trollish smile: *Avram is actually quite fond of little deviations*. But she felt no voice or echo of a smile in him, and his eyes did not glimmer, and perhaps there really was nothing there, no one. Get that through your head already, she told herself, and just accept it.

Now they're on an escarpment of slippery rocks, which pulls them deep down into a gorge, and that too is a word that once would have tickled him and prompted him to say something *gorgey, gorgeous, gorging,* to delight in the way his tongue touched the roof of his mouth . . . Stop— She cuts herself off. Let him be, he's really not inside there anymore. But on the other hand, he clearly has been listening to her for the last several minutes as she talked about Ofer. He isn't brushing her off the way he usually does, so maybe he really is giving her an opening, a crack. And for her, these sorts of cracks have recently become a familiar nesting spot. She is now a creature of the cracks. After living with two well-armored adolescent boys, and lately, seeing Eran, who allocates at most ninety minutes a week to her, this seems easy.

"She became part of the family immediately," Ora continues as they descend, and she holds back a little sigh, because something changed at home when Talia came, when she started having meals with them and staying over and even going on vacations abroad with them (all of a sudden I had someone to go to the bathroom with when we were on trips, she remembers). But how can she tell him this? How can she describe to a man like him—that apartment of his, the darkness, the solitariness— the slight shift that occurred in the balance between men and women at home, and her feeling that womanhood itself had been given, for the first time perhaps, its rightful place in the family? How can she recount something like that, and what could he, in his state, understand? And what business is it of his anyway? Truth be told, she does not yet feel ready to admit to him, to an almost stranger, how amazed she was, and how it taunted her even to see how this young woman effortlessly attained something she herself had never even tried to demand from her three men: their full recognition of the fact that she was a woman, her discrete self-definition as a woman in a house of three men, and the fact that being a woman was not just another of her annoying whims, nor a pathetic defiance of the real thing, which was how the three of them often made her feel. Ora quickens her steps, her lips move soundlessly, and a slight headache starts to hum, as in her high school days when she faced a page full of equations. What Talia had brought about, God only knows how, through the very light motions of her being! Ora snickers to herself, because even Nicotine, the family dog, of blessed memory, experienced a slightly embarrassing change when Talia was around.

"I was very hurt when she left. And you know, I felt something just before it happened. I felt it before anyone else did, because she stopped coming over whenever she had a spare moment. She avoided me, and suddenly she didn't have time to sit with me over morning coffee, or just chat on the balcony. Then she came up with the idea that maybe she wouldn't do her army service and would go to London for a year instead, to sell sunglasses and make some money and study art and experience things. And when she said 'experience things,' I immediately told Ilan that something was going on. Ilan said, 'No way, she's just dreaming a little, she loves him, and she's a girl with a good head on her shoulders. Where else would she find a guy like him?' But I was nervous, I had the feeling that all of a sudden her plans did not include Ofer, or that she was getting a little tired of him, or I don't know what"—that she'd *run her course* with him—"and Ofer was totally surprised when it came, he was really in shock, and I'm not sure he's out of it yet."

Ora purses her lips. You saw it all, you with your eagle eye—she stabs herself and twists the knife around—the only thing you missed were the signs in Ilan. He *ran his course* with you.

How happy she used to be, Avram thinks and glances at her face. She used to be such a giggler. He remembers how he came to visit her when she was in basic training, at Bahad 12. He walked along the edge of the parade ground, suddenly finding it difficult to stand proudly upright in front of all these hundreds of girls—in his fantasies, the legendary city of girls had a constant soundtrack of sighs and damp moans and longing gazes, but this one buzzed like a hornet's nest of giggles and sneers, sideways Cleopatra eyes—and suddenly, from afar, a tall, crumpled soldier draped in a sack-like uniform, with red bouncy curls cascading under a crooked cap and cherry lips, ran toward him with open arms, legs slightly askew, laughing joyfully and calling from one end of the camp to the other, "So very very much Avram!"

"Because I was so insulted by her," Ora continues a sentence whose beginning Avram has missed—she ran to him so happily on the base, he remembers, and she wasn't ashamed of him in front of all the girls— "she didn't even call me to explain, to say goodbye, nothing. From one day to the next she was out of our lives. And the truth is that other than the insult, what hurt were the thoughts about why they broke up, why she left him. Because the whole time she was with us, I learned to rely on her judgment so much, and on her perception, and I'm trying to understand if it was something about Ofer that made her leave, something that I myself can't see.

"Maybe it's because he shuts himself off," she murmurs, thinking of the slight whiff of anger that has emanated from Ofer recently, repelling and belittling, especially toward anything and anyone who was not connected to the army. "But even before the army he was pretty closed off. *Very* closed off, even. And Talia made him open up, to us too; he really blossomed with her."

I'm talking, she marvels again, and he's not stopping me.

There's this guy, a person, who is Ofer, Avram thinks strenuously, as if struggling with both hands to stick a label that says "Ofer" onto a vague and elusive picture that constantly squirms in his soul as Ora speaks. And she is telling me a story about him now. I'm hearing Ora's story about Ofer. All I have to do is hear it. No more. She will tell the story, and then it will be over. A story can't go on forever. I can think about all sorts of things in the meantime. She will talk. It's only a story. One word followed by another.

Ora tries to pick and choose what to tell Avram. She wonders why she even slammed him with this stuff about Talia—why start with that? Why did she depict Ofer in his weakest state? She has to take him quickly to more uplifting places. Maybe she'll tell him about the birth, everyone likes hearing about births. But on the other hand—she gives him a sideways glance—what interest could he have in births? A birth would terrify him, push him even farther away, and to be honest, it's too early for her to lie naked and unraveled before him. And she certainly won't tell him about what preceded the birth, that dawn, the one she erased from her book of life, and every time she thinks about it she can't believe the way she and Ilan were seized by some kind of madness, and for years that memory was mingled with fear and bitter guilt—how could she have been tempted? How could she not have protected Ofer in her belly? How could she not have had the instinct that must exist— is supposed to exist—in every normal, natural mother? For all she knows it might have caused some damage to Ofer. Maybe his childhood asthma started with that? Maybe the attack of claustrophobia in the elevator was because of that? Her mind pulls back from the memory, but the pictures maddeningly resurface, the strange fire in Ilan's eyes, the grip that locked them into each other, the growls that escaped from them, and her belly, her earth-belly that trembled and bumped as two skinned beasts struggled and mated over it.

"Let's sit down, I'm a little dizzy." She leans her head back on the rock face and takes quick sips of water, then passes him the canteen. She has to find something light and amusing, quickly, something that will make him laugh and fill him with affection and warmth for Ofer. And here it is, she's found it: Ofer, at age three, used to insist on going to day care in his cowboy costume, which included twenty-one items of clothing and weaponry (they counted them once), and for one entire year they were not allowed to forgo even a single accessory. Her eyes brighten and the commotion in her head quiets down a little. This is exactly the sort of thing she should tell him: sweet slices of life, trivial Ofer episodes, nothing complicated or heavy, just calmly describe the mornings of that year, when Ilan and she darted around Ofer with guns and ammunition belts, and Ilan crawled under the bed to look for a sheriff's star or a red bandana. The meticulous daily construction of a brave fighter, erected on the fragile scaffolding of little Ofer.

But that won't really interest him, she retorts, all the minutiae, the thousands of moments and acts from which you raise a child, gather him into a person. He won't have the patience for it, and ultimately these details are fairly boring and dreary, especially for men, but really for anyone who doesn't know the child in question, although there are of course some stories that are, one might say, unusual, that might draw Avram to Ofer—

But why, for God's sake, do I need to draw him in at all? she wonders angrily, and the headache that had subsided lunges back boldly and digs its claws into the familiar spot behind her left ear. Am I supposed to be marketing Ofer to him now? Tempting him with Ofer? She sighs, stands up at once, and starts walking briskly, almost running. How do you tell an entire life? A whole decade would not be enough. Where do you start? Especially she, who is incapable of telling one story from beginning to end without scattering in every direction and ruining the punch line—how will she be able to tell his story the right way? And what if she discovers that she doesn't have that much to tell?

There are an infinite number of things she can say about him, yet she suddenly panics at the thought that if she talks about him for two or three hours straight, or five hours or ten, she might cover most of the important things she has to say about him, about his life. She might sum him up—*exhaust* him. And perhaps this is the fear that is pressuring her brain, the discomfort that has been eating away at her for some time: she doesn't really know him. She doesn't really know her son, Ofer.

The pulse in her neck beats to the point of pain. How quickly her tiny joy has faded. And what, really, will she say about him? How can you even describe and revive a whole person, flesh and blood, with only words—oh God, *with only words*?

She roots around inside herself, as though if she continues to be silent for even one more minute Avram may think she really has nothing to tell. But everything she feverishly digs up seems banal and marginal—agreeable anecdotes, like the time when Ofer rehabilitated a small well that had dried up near Har Adar. He opened the aqueduct and renewed the spring and planted an orchard nearby. Or perhaps she will tell him about the amazing bed that Ofer built with his own hands for her and Ilan. All right, so she'll tell him that, so what? A well, a bed, stories that ultimately fit a thousand boys just like him, no less clever and sweet and lovely. It occurs to her that although there are lots of things about Ofer that are good and special, there may not be one truly extraordinary thing, something unique that puts him head and shoulders above everyone else. And with all her might Ora resists this loathsome thought that clings to her, this thought that is so foreign to her—how did she even arrive at such an idea? But wait, what about the movie he made for his cinema class in the tenth grade? There was definitely something there, Avram would like the idea. She glances at his head thrust deep between his slouching shoulders and thinks: Maybe not.

There was something troubling about that film, and to this day, five years later, it nags at her. Eleven minutes shot on their home video camera, documenting an ordinary day in the life of an ordinary young boy: family, school, friends, girlfriend, basketball, parties. But the film did not show a single flesh-and-blood figure, only the shadows of the characters—shadows walking, alone or in pairs, even in groups, shadows sitting in class, shadows eating lunch, kissing, making out, drumming, drinking beer. When she asked Ofer what the idea behind the film was, or what his intention was when he made it (just as she had asked him about the empty plaster molds he cast in his own image, which he displayed at the school's year-end exhibition, or the menacing series of photographs of his own face with a vulture's beak sketched in charcoal over each photo), he shrugged his shoulders and said, "I don't know, I just thought it would be nice to do." Or, "I just wanted to photograph someone, and I was the only person in the room." And if she insisted— "You overwhelmed him again," Ilan told her afterward—he would impatiently shrug her off: "Does there have to be an explanation? Can't something just happen? Does every little thing have to be analyzed to the bone?"

Ora accompanied the film shoots for three weeks as driver, caterer, and water girl, and not infrequently as the furious sheepdog who ran around after the unruly actors, Ofer's peers, who constantly ditched rehearsals and shoots. And when they finally deigned to appear, they would argue with Ofer with an arrogance and rudeness that drove her mad. She would leave as soon as an argument broke out. He was still smaller and shorter than most of his classmates and slightly excluded and hesitant, and Ora could not stand the sight of his bowed head and his downcast look and the tremble in his lower lip. Still, he stood his ground: making his presence known, his shoulders stretched almost to his ears, his face an uncontrollable assemblage of pain and insult, but not giving an inch.

She also acted in the film, cast in the role of an annoying and nosy teacher. Ilan passed by in the background, too, on a motorcycle, waving hello and disappearing. There was a nice credit at the end: "And thanks to Mom and Dad, who contributed their shadows." Now she wonders if Avram might think the film had a uniqueness, or a spark, or a "one-off"-ness—all his words—and she heard the old tune of those words, as when she and he and Ilan used to come out of a movie or a play that had moved him, and he would caress the word that electrified him most of all, "greatness," with a hoarse, excited whisper full of awe: *Greatnesssss!* accompanied by a broad, kingly sweep of the arm. He was around twenty then. Or twenty-one? The same age Ofer is today, which is hard to believe. And it's even harder to believe how arrogant and pretentious he was, how she could even stand him, with the silly goatee he cultivated . . .

She walks on, trapped in a poisonous dialogue with herself, because she finally recognizes how important it is to her that Avram should love Ofer—yes, love him, fall in love with him right then and there without any reservations or criticism, fall in love with him despite himself, just the way he once fell in love with *her*, in whom there was not even a single drop of greatness, and when he fell in love with her she was nothing but a broken vessel—ill and bedraggled, drugged up and bleeding all day and night, and Avram was in that state, too. It was the optimal state for falling in love with me, she thinks, and weakly slows her pace. And perhaps it is true, as he himself joked years later, that it was the only way a *yiddeneh*'s id could meet a *yid*'s id. Her strength is sapped, and she stands panting in pain, pressing her fingers between her eyes. All these thoughts—where have all these thoughts come from? And who needs them now?

Avram sees her swaying and quickly skips over to catch her a moment before she falls. How strong he is, she thinks again, surprised, as her knees buckle. He gently lays her on the ground, quickly takes off her backpack and places it under her head. He removes a sharp stone from under her back, takes off her glasses, pours some water into his palm, and softly caresses her face. She lies with her eyes closed, her chest rising and falling heavily, her skin covered with cold sweat. "See how the mind works," she murmurs. "Don't speak now," he says, and she does as she is told. She finds his concern pleasing, and his hand on her face, and the quiet command in his voice.

"I remembered," she says later, her hand holding his wrist limply, "that you once told me about a radio play, or a story. It was about a woman whose lover leaves her, and you hear her talking with him on the phone but you can't hear him."

"Cocteau. *La Voix Humaine.*"

"Yes, Cocteau," she whispers, "how do you remember . . ." She feels the water slowly drying on her face. She can see a mountainside covered with bushes and a very blue sheet of sky. A sharp scent of sage enters her nostrils. His hand is as soft as it was then—how can the gentleness and softness still be there? She closes her eyes and wonders if it is possible to reconstruct him from so little. "You were in your French period back then, and your radio play–writing period. Remember? You had a whole theory about the human voice. You were convinced that radio would beat out television. You built a little recording studio at home."

Avram smiles. "Not at home. In the shed outside. It was a real studio. Days and nights I sat there recording, cutting, splicing, mixing."

"And I thought," Ora whispers, "after Ilan left me, the first time, after Adam was born, I used to talk with him on the phone sometimes, and I must have sounded like her, like the woman from your Cocteau play, pathetic like her, and so forgiving and understanding about his difficulties, his difficulties with *me*, the son of a bitch . . ."

Avram's hand moves away from her forehead. She opens her eyes and sees his face withdrawn, closed off.

"He left me right after Adam was born, didn't you know?"

"You didn't say."

Ora sighs. "You really don't know anything. You're an ignoramus when it comes to my life."

Avram stands up and looks out into the distance. A falcon glides in circles high up in the sky above his head.

"It's terrible how much of a stranger you are," she murmurs. "What am I even doing here with you?" She lets out a bitter laugh. "If I weren't so afraid to go home, I would get up this minute and leave."

Perhaps because he is standing above her, she remembers: Ofer was a year old. She was lying on her bed, rocking him on her upturned feet and arms in a game of airplane. He laughed and his whole body quivered, and his fine halo of hair softly fell and rose as he sailed. The sunlight coming through the window shone through his ears, and they were orange and translucent. They stuck out from his head, just as they do today. She moved him into the light and saw a delicate braid of veins and soft twists and bumps. She became quiet and focused, as if someone were about to tell her an indescribable secret. Her face must have changed, because Ofer stopped laughing and looked at her gravely, and his lips lengthened and protruded in a wise, even ironic old man's expression. She marveled at the precision in each of his limbs. A sweetness filled her. She spun him slowly on the soles of her feet, moved him this way and that, catching the entire wheel of the sun in one of his ears.

The wound was as deep as a fist, and it discharged an endless stream of thick pus. It was very close to the spine, and the doctors were unable to heal it for months. There was something terrifying and hypnotizing about the never-ending flow, as though the body itself were ridiculing the abundance that had always streamed from Avram. For many months, almost a year, the wound was the focal point of concern for Ora and Ilan, and for a succession of doctors. The word "wound" was uttered so often that it sometimes seemed Avram himself was fading away, leaving only the wound as his primary being, while his body became merely the platform from which the wound produced the fluids it needed to survive.

For the hundredth time that day, Ilan dipped a gauze bandage in the pus, carefully twisted it in the crater of flesh, soaked up the fluids, and threw it away. Ora, sprawled on a chair near Avram's bed, looked at the precise movements of Ilan's hand, and wondered how he was able to dig into the wound without causing pain. Later, when Avram fell asleep, she suggested they take a short walk for some fresh air. They meandered through the paths among the little buildings and talked, as usual, about Avram's condition, his upcoming surgery, and his complicated financial dealings with the Ministry of Defense. They sat on a bench near the X-ray center, with some distance between them, and Ora talked about Avram's balance problem, whose cause the doctors had not yet determined. Ilan murmured, "We need to look into his ingrown toenail, that could drive him crazy. And I think the Novalgin is giving him diarrhea"—and she thought, Stop, stop with that now, and turned to him and jumped over the void and kissed him on the mouth. It had been such a long time since they'd touched each other that Ilan froze, then hesitantly took her in his arms. For a moment they moved cautiously against each other, as if they were covered in shattered glass, amazed at the force with which their bodies ignited as though they had only been waiting for someone to come to them for comfort. That night they drove to Avram's empty house in Tzur Hadassah, where they had been living since he was released from the POW prison, and which they had turned into a sort of private headquarters for all matters concerning his treatment. There, in his boyhood room, with the sign on the door from when he was fifteen, saying *Only the Mad May Enter*, on a straw mattress on the floor, they conceived Adam.

She doesn't know how much Avram remembers of the period when he was hospitalized, operated on, rehabilitated and treated, and periodically investigated by agents of the Shabak and Field Security and Military Intelligence, who tormented him relentlessly with their suspicions about information he might or might not have given away as a POW. He was indifferent to it all and devoid of any volition, yet still, from the depths of his absence, he consumed her and Ilan like a baby, and not just because of the many complications, medical and bureaucratic, that resulted from his situation and that only they could handle for him. It was his actual existence—empty, hollow—that devoured them constantly, so she felt at the time, and sucked the life out of them. Almost without moving, he turned them into shells, like he himself was.

Adam's birth, she says. They are sitting side by side in a rocky hiding place above the valley, surrounded by a yellow sea of acacia and spiny broom whose blossoms make the bees frantic. The lichen-covered rocks glisten red and bright purple in the sun, and she knows that she can talk with greater ease about Adam. She can even tell him about Adam's birth and ostensibly *start from a distance*.

"I had a difficult labor with him. It was long and hard. I was in Hadassah Mount Scopus for three days. Women came and gave birth and left, and I lay there like a rock. Ilan and I joked that some women who were barren had already come in and had babies, and I was still lying there waiting. Every doctor and resident had checked me and looked at me and measured me, and there were regular medical staff meetings around me, and they kept arguing over my head about whether or not to induce labor, and how I would respond to this or that. They told me I should walk around. They said the movement would induce labor. So we walked together, me and Ilan, two or three times a day. Me with the Hadassah robe and a belly like a whale, walking arm in arm and hardly talking. It was nice. There was a pleasantness between us, or so I thought."

Start from a distance. She smiles to herself and remembers that on the night she and Avram first met, as teenagers, he sailed in large circles around the room where she lay in the dark, in the isolation ward, coming closer and then receding, as if he were secretly practicing routes for getting nearer and farther away from her.

"After the birth, Ilan drove us home in the Mini Minor—you remember it, my parents bought it for me when I started going to university. When you were in rehab, I sometimes used to drive you around Tel Aviv."

She gives him a sideways glance and waits, but if he does remember he gives no sign, and it's as if all those endless, dreamlike drives never existed. He needed them in order to "believe," he had explained laconically. Hours of driving in circles to look at streets, alleyways, squares, people, people. And the suspicion and doubt that were constantly in his eyes, in his furrowed brow. And the city, which seemed to be going out of its way to convince Avram of its existence, its reality.

"We put Adam in a car seat with padding all around, and Ilan drove all the way home on eggshells and did not say a word. I didn't stop talking. I was in seventh heaven. I remember how happy I was, and proud, and positive that from now on everything would start to fall in place for us. And he drove silently. At first I thought it was because he was so focused on the road. You see, I felt that the whole world had completely changed from the moment Adam was born. Everything may have looked the same, but I knew everything was different, that some new dimension had been added—don't laugh—to everything and everyone in the world."

I didn't laugh, Avram thinks, and leans his head back. He tries as hard as he can to see them in the little car. He tries to remember where he was back then, when Ora and Ilan had Adam. Don't laugh, she'd said. Nothing could be further from him now than laughter.

"And I remember that I looked at the street and thought, Silly people, blind, you don't even know how different everything is going to be now. But I couldn't tell Ilan that, because I'd already started to feel his silence, and then I fell silent, too. All of a sudden I was incapable of uttering a word. Even when I wanted to talk, I couldn't. I felt completely smothered, like something was grabbing my throat. And it was you."

He glances at her, his forehead upturned.

"You were with us in the car. We felt you sitting there in the back next to Adam's seat." She pulls her knees into her stomach. "And it was impossible to bear. It was intolerable in the car, and all my happiness burst like a balloon and splattered over me. I remember that Ilan sighed loudly, and I asked, 'What?' And he wouldn't say and wouldn't say, and finally he said he hadn't imagined it would be so difficult. And I thought about how this wasn't the drive I'd pictured when I dreamed about the trumpets that would sound when I went home with my first child.

"Look," she says a moment later in surprise, "I haven't thought about that for years."

Avram says nothing.

"Should I go on?"

I'll take that as a yes, she tells herself, that jerk of the head.

The closer they got to home, to Tzur Hadassah, the more tense and nervous Ilan grew. She noticed that from a certain angle his chin looked weak, evasive. She saw the damp marks his fingers were leaving on the wheel—Ilan, who almost never sweated. He parked the car opposite the rusty gate, took Adam out, and handed him to her without looking in her eyes. Ora asked if he wanted to carry Adam into the house himself, for the first time, but he said, "You, you," and pushed the baby into her arms.

She remembers the short walk down the paving stones through the garden, the lopsided little house with its sharp textured walls dotted with cement spots. It was a "Jewish Agency house" that Avram's mother had inherited from a childless uncle and lived in with Avram since he was ten. She remembers the neglected garden, which became overgrown with weeds and tall thistles during the years when Ora and Ilan could only tend to Avram. She even remembers thinking that as soon as she recovered she would go into the garden and introduce Adam to her beloved fig and grevillea trees. And she remembers the feel of her crooked steps as she duck-walked painfully around her stitches. She talks softly. Avram listens. She sees that he's listening, but for some reason she feels as though it is mostly herself she is talking to now.

Ilan walked quickly ahead of her up the three uneven steps, opened the door, and stood aside to let her go in with Adam. There was something chilling and hurtful in his courtesy. She made a point of taking the first step in on her right foot, and said out loud, "Welcome home, Adam"—she felt, as she did every time she said or thought his name, a secret caress of Ada inside her—and carried him to his room, where his crib was already set up. Although he was sleeping, she turned him around in all directions to show his translucent eyelids the bureau, the chest of drawers with a changing pad, the box of toys, and the bookshelves.

Then she discovered a piece of paper taped to the door: *Hello Baby-o*, it said. *Welcome. Here are a few instructions from the hotel management.*

She placed the baby in his crib. He looked tiny and lost. She covered him with a thin blanket and stood gazing at him. Something prickled at her back, causing unease. The paper taped to the door seemed full of words, too many words. She leaned over and stroked Adam's warm head, sighed, and walked back to the door to read it:

The hotel management asks that you respect the peace and quiet of the other lodgers.

Remember: the proprietress belongs solely to the hotel owner, and your use of her is limited to her upper portion only!

The hotel management expects guests to leave when they reach the age of 18!

And so on and so forth.

She crossed her arms over her chest. She suddenly felt tired of Ilan and his wisecracks. She reached out and ripped the paper off and crumpled it tightly.

"You didn't like that?" Ilan piped up, sounding annoyed. "I just thought . . . Never mind. It didn't work. Want to drink something?"

"I want to sleep."

"And him?"

"Adam? What about him?"

"Should we leave him here?"

"I don't know . . . Should we take him into our room?"

"I don't know. Because if we're asleep and he wakes up here, alone . . ."

They looked at each other awkwardly.

She tried to listen to her instincts and couldn't hear anything. She had no desire, no knowledge or opinion. She was confused. Deep in her heart she had hoped that when the baby was born she would immediately know everything she needed to know. That the baby would infuse her with a primal, natural, and unimpeachable knowledge. Now she realized how much she had looked forward to that throughout the pregnancy, almost as much as to the baby itself—to the acuteness of knowing the right thing to do, which she had lost completely in recent years, since Avram's tragedy.

"Come on," she said to Ilan, "we'll leave him here."

She felt the pain of unraveling again, as she had whenever she'd had to part with Adam in the hospital. "Yes, he doesn't need to sleep with us."

"But what if he cries?" Ilan asked hesitantly.

"If he cries we'll hear him. Don't worry, I'll hear him."

They went to their room and slept for two whole hours, and Ora woke a minute or two before Adam made a sound and immediately felt the fullness in her breasts. She woke Ilan to go and bring the baby to her. She arranged the pillows on the bed and leaned back heavily, and Ilan came in from the other room holding Adam, his face glowing.

She breast-fed him and was once again amazed at how small his head looked against her breast. He sucked strongly, firmly, almost without looking at her, and she felt blades of unfamiliar pleasure and pain turn over clods of body and soul. Ilan stood looking at them the whole time, mesmerized, all corporeality stripped from his face. Every so often he asked if she was comfortable, if she was thirsty, if she felt the milk coming out. She pulled the child away from one nipple and moved him to the other breast and wiped her nipple with a cloth. Ilan stared at her breast, which she thought looked huge, moonlike, and webbed with bluish veins, and there was a new awe in his expression. He suddenly looked like a little boy, and she asked, "Don't you want to take pictures of him?"

He blinked as though awakening from a dream. "No, I don't feel like taking pictures now. The light in here isn't good."

"What were you thinking about?"

"Nothing, no one."

She could see what looked like a dark spider settle down over his face. "Maybe you'll take some later," she said weakly.

"Yes, of course, later."

But he hardly took any pictures later, either. Sometimes he would bring the camera, take off the lens cover, aim and focus, but somehow he didn't like the lighting, or didn't think the angle would work. "Maybe later," he'd say, "when Adam is more alert."

Avram clears his throat to remind her of his existence. She smiles at him in surprise: "I got carried away. I suddenly remembered all sorts of . . . Do you want to keep walking?"

"No, it's okay here." He leans back on his elbows, even though his entire body is bubbling with a desire to leave this place.

They sit looking down at the verdant valley. Behind Avram, in his shadow, is a silent commotion. Ants bustle along a dry stem of fennel plant, gnawing at the wood and the crumbs of congealed honey left by last year's bees. A tiny scepter of orchid stands tall, purple and light as a butterfly, its pair of tuberous roots in the earth—one slowly emptying out, the other filling up. A little farther away, in the shade of Avram's right upper back, a small white deadnettle, engaged in its complicated affairs, sends out olfactory signals to insects that constantly flit between it and other plants, and it grows fertile sepals, for self-pollination, in case the insects fail it.

"And one night, when Adam was about a month old, he woke up hungry. Ilan got up to bring him to me, but when I fed him Ilan didn't stay with us in the room. It was strange. I called him, he was in the living room, and he said he would be right with us. I couldn't understand what he was doing there, in the dark. I didn't hear any noise or movement. I had the feeling he was standing by the window looking out, and I got nervous."

Scenes she hasn't thought of for many years rise up before her eyes, and they are sharp and alive, more lucid than ever. She realizes that perhaps she is no less afraid to tell these things than he is to hear them.

"When I finished feeding, I took Adam back to his crib, and then I saw Ilan standing in the middle of the living room. He was just standing there, as if he'd forgotten where he was going. I saw him from behind, and I knew straightaway that something was wrong. His face was awful. He looked at me as if he was afraid of me, or wanted to hit me. Or both. He said he couldn't do it anymore, he couldn't take it. That you—" She swallows. "Look, are you sure you want to hear this?"

Avram grunts something, pulls himself up into a seated position, and rests his head on his arms. She waits. His back heaves. He does not get up and walk away.

"Ilan said his thoughts about you were destroying him. That he felt like a murderer—'*I have killed and also taken possession,*' he said—and that he couldn't look at Adam without seeing you and thinking about you at the stronghold, or in prison camp, or in the hospital."

The back of Avram's neck contracts.

She asked him, "What do you want us to do?" Ilan did not answer. The house was heated, but she was still cold. She stood barefoot in her robe and shivered and leaked milk. She asked again what he proposed doing, and Ilan said he didn't know, but he couldn't go on this way. He was starting to scare himself. "Before, when I brought him to you—" He stopped.

"It's not our fault," she mumbled—that was their mantra during those years. "We didn't want it to happen, and we didn't invite it. It just happened, Ilan, it's just a terrible thing that happened to us."

"I know."

"And if it hadn't been him there, in the stronghold, it would have been you."

He snorted. "That's just it, isn't it?"

"It was you or him, there was no other option." She walked over to hug him.

"Stop it, Ora." He raised a hand to keep her away. "We've heard it, we've said it, we've talked about it. I'm not to blame and you're not to blame, and Avram is certainly not to blame, and we didn't want it to happen, but it did happen, and if I wasn't such a nothing I would kill myself right this minute."

She stood silently. Everything he said she had thought of countless times before, in his voice and hers. She couldn't gather up the strength to tell him not to talk such nonsense.

As she tells these things to Avram now, she feels cold in the day's intensifying heat, and her voice trembles a little from the tension. She cannot see his face. His face is hidden in his arms, and his arms embrace his knees. She has the feeling that he's listening to her from within the depths of his flesh, like an animal in its lair.

"And the fact that we're living here," Ilan said.

"It's just until he gets back," she murmured. "We're just looking after his house."

"I keep telling him that when I'm with him," Ilan whispered, "and I don't know if he even understands that we're actually living here."

"But as soon as he gets back, we'll leave."

Ilan sneered. "And now our kid is going to grow up here."

Ora thought that if Ilan didn't come over and hold her immediately, her body would fall to the ground and shatter.

"And I can't see any way out of it, or any chance that anything will ever work out for us"—he was shouting now—"and just think about it, we'll live out our lives here, and we'll have another child and maybe another, we once talked about four, including one we'd adopt, right? To repay a kindness to humanity, didn't we say? And every time we look into each other's eyes we'll see *him*. And all that time, through all our lives, and his; twenty, thirty, fifty years, he'll sit there in his darkness, do you understand?" Ilan seized his head with both hands and hammered with his voice, and Ora was suddenly afraid of him. He bellowed: "There will be a child here who'll grow up and be an entire world, and over there he'll be a living dead, and this child could have been his, and you could have been his too, if only—"

"And then maybe you would have been a living dead somewhere."

"You know what?"

And she did.

"Is this hard for you?" Ora asks Avram in a muffled voice.

"I'm listening," he answers, his jaws breaking the words up into tight syllables.

"Because if it's too difficult—"

He lifts his head and his face looks as though a firm hand is crushing it. "Ora, it's my finally hearing from the outside something I've been hearing inside my head for years."

She wants to touch his hand, to absorb some of what's overflowing from him, but she doesn't dare. "You know, it's strange, but it's the same way for me."

. . .

She had no strength left. She collapsed on the couch. Ilan came and stood facing her and said he had to leave.

"Where to?"

"I don't know, I can't stay here."

"Now?"

He was suddenly very tall. It was as though he stretched out more and more from above and looked all stiff and his eyes glistened.

"You mean you're going to walk out and leave me alone with him?"

"I'm no good here, I'm poisoning the air, I hate myself here. I even hate you. When I see you like that, so full, I just can't stand you." Then he added, "And I can't love Adam. I can't manage to love him. There's a glass wall between him and me. I don't feel him, I don't smell him. Let me go."

She said nothing.

"Maybe if I think quietly a bit, for a few days, maybe I'll be able to come back. Right now I have to be alone, Ora, give me one week alone."

"And how am I supposed to manage here?"

"I'll help you, you won't have to worry about anything. We'll talk on the phone every day, I'll find help for you, a nanny, a babysitter, you can be totally free, you can go back to school, find a job, do anything you want, just let me go now, it's not good for me to stay here even for ten minutes."

"But when did you think about all this?" Ora murmured dully. "We were together the whole time."

Ilan spoke rapidly, organizing her bright future in a blink. "I could actually see," she tells Avram, "how in a second that mechanism of his was turned on, you know? The cogwheels in his eyes?"

She looked at Ilan and thought that as smart as he was, he didn't understand anything, and that she had made a terrible mistake with him. She tried to imagine what her parents would say and how devastated they would be.

"And I thought about how they always warned me about you," she tells Avram, "and how they admired *him*, mainly my mother, who in my opinion always wondered what a guy like him saw in me."

Avram smiles, his face hidden in his arms. *Hochstapler*, her mother used to call him, and Ora had translated: a guy with holes in his pockets who thinks he's a Rothschild.

"And I lay on the couch and tried to figure out how I would manage alone with Adam. And think about it, I was still barely able to move, to go out of the house, to keep my eyes open. And I thought this couldn't be happening, it was just a nightmare and I would wake up any minute. And all the time I also felt that in fact I understood him so well, and I wished I could do that too, run away from myself, and from Adam and from you and from everything, from the whole mess. And I felt sorry for Adam, sleeping calmly without knowing that his life was being screwed up.

"I lay there with my robe open, just the way I was, I didn't care about anything. I heard Ilan moving around the bedroom quickly. You know how he moves when he's decisive"—they smile at each other, a glimmer between them, a tiny thread—"I heard closets opening, doors, drawers. He was packing, and I lay there thinking that for the rest of our lives we would keep on paying for one minute, for a stupid coincidence, for nothing."

She and Avram both look away quickly.

"Take a hat," Ilan and Avram had told her cheerfully over the military phone from the base in Sinai, "and put two slips of paper in it, but identical ones." Then they'd both laughed: "No, no, you don't have to know what you're drawing lots for." That laughter still rings in her ears. They haven't laughed that way since. They were twenty-two, in the last month of their regular army service, and she was already in Jerusalem, a first-year student, studying social work, which was opening up a whole new world for her, and she thought how lucky she was to have found her calling at such a young age. "No, no," Ilan repeated, "it's better if you don't know what the lottery is for, that way you'll be more objective." When she insisted, they softened: "Okay, you're allowed to guess, but do it silently. And quickly. Ora, they're waiting for us, there's a command car outside." (And then she got it: A command car? One of them is going to be allowed home. Who? She quickly ran to get a hat, one of her old military caps, and found a piece of paper and tore it into two equal halves, and inside she was bubbling: Which of the two did she want to come home?) "Two identical slips," Ilan repeated impatiently. "One with my name and one with fatso's name." Then she heard Avram: "Write 'Ilan' on one, and 'Jehovah' on the other. Wait, on second thought, just write 'His armies.' " Ilan interrupted: "Okay. Desist all chatter. Now pick one out. Did you do it? Which one? Are you sure?"

Ora weighs a pointy little stone in her hand, and slowly, methodically cleans the dirt off it. Avram sits hunched over, his hands grasping each other, his knuckles turning white.

"Should I go on?"

"What? Yes, all right."

"Then he stood over me. I couldn't even get up, I was so weak. I felt like an avalanche. I didn't even have the strength to cover myself. He didn't look at me. I felt that I was disgusting him. I was disgusting myself, too." She speaks in a narrow, contracted voice, as if forced to report everything, down to the last detail. "And he said he'd hang around outside for a while that night, go to some all-night café, there was one on Queen Helena Street back then, and he'd call the next morning. I asked if he wasn't going to say goodbye to Adam. He said it was better if he didn't. I felt that I had to get up and fight, if not for me, for Adam, because if I didn't do something right then, it would no longer be possible to change anything. Because with Ilan these kinds of decisions spread like lightning, you know him, within seconds there's already a new reality, a fancy settlement with red rooftops and paving stones, and you cannot uproot it.

"And look how wrong I was," she mumbles in astonishment, and for a moment, in her eyes, Ilan and Adam row a little wooden boat up a green river, making perfectly coordinated strokes, through a jungle thicket. "Look how in the end everything turned out differently than I thought. It came out the exact opposite."

"He called in the morning to say he was staying at a hotel and was planning to rent a small apartment. 'Not far from you two,' he said. Do you understand? 'From you two'! It had only been a few hours and already he was not one of us. Not even one of me.

"He rented a studio apartment in Talpiot, as far away as he could get, on the other side of town. He called twice a day, morning and evening, decent, responsible, you know him. Killing me softly. And I would cry to him over the phone to come home. I was so stupid, I really humiliated myself, and I probably made him hate me even more with all that sobbing, but I didn't have a drop of energy to put on heroic shows for him. I was a wreck, body and soul. I don't even know how I made enough milk to breast-feed or how I managed to take care of Adam. My mom came to stay with me, a bundle of good intentions, but after about two days I realized what was going on and what she was doing to me, how she was starting in with the comparisons between Adam and other babies, and he always lost, of course. I asked my dad to come and take her home. I didn't even say why, and the worst thing was that he understood immediately.

"And there were the girlfriends, who came right away, an emergency call-up. They helped and cooked and cleaned, and of course it was all done gently and tactfully, but all of a sudden I was once again surrounded by this cluster of girls, like when I was fourteen, and they all knew exactly what was best for me, and what I really needed, and they reminded me of how much I always, always, except for Ada, got along much better with boys.

"It was mainly their venom toward Ilan that I couldn't stand, because I'm telling you that despite everything, I understood him, and I knew that I was the only one who could understand what was really going on. In all the world, only he and I could understand, and maybe you too, if you even had any understanding at all back then."

Avram nods to himself.

"*Ugh.*" She stretches and rubs her stiff neck. "It's not easy, all this."

"Yes," he says, and distractedly massages his own neck.

She checks in to make sure she can abandon Ofer for this long. An internal ray beams out, probes, touches lightly: womb, heart, nipples, the sensitive spot above the navel, the curve in the neck, upper lip, left eye, right eye. Quickly she weaves the feeling of Ofer inside her like a game of connect the dots, and she finds that things are all right, that in some dim way Ofer is even growing a little stronger while she talks, while Avram listens.

"Adam was on me most of the time," she tells him as they get up and continue walking on the narrow path down the mountainside. "From the minute Ilan left, he simply refused to be alone. He clung to me like a little monkey, day and night, and I didn't have the strength to resist. I would put him down to sleep in our bed—I mean, in mine. I mean ours—mine and Adam's.

"I slept with him for almost two years, and I know, it was against the instructions, but I'm telling you, I didn't have the strength to fight him when he was screaming, and I didn't always have the strength to put him back in his crib after feedings. And the truth is that I kind of liked it when he fell asleep with me after feeding, the two of us melting away together, and it was nice to have another living, warm body in the bed."

She smiles. "It was as though after a short period of separation we went back to our natural state, one body, one organism that more or less supplies all of its own requirements and doesn't need any favors from anyone."

Mom and I were a little bit like that, Avram thinks. In the beginning, for the first few years after he left us.

You and your mom might have been like that, she says with her eyes. I always remembered what you told me. I thought about the two of you a lot then.

"Ilan kept calling every day like clockwork, and I would talk to him, or actually I would mostly listen. Sometimes—I told you, like that Cocteau woman of yours, that lamebrain, except in Hebrew—I would even give him advice about things, like how to get out an ink stain, or whether he could iron this shirt or that one. I would remind him to get his teeth cleaned and listen to him grumble about how difficult it was without me. If someone had listened in on one of our phone calls, they would have thought it was an ordinary conversation between a little wifey and her husband away on a short business trip.

"And sometimes I would just stare with my ears while he told me what he was doing, how his studies were going, how the criminal justice professor already had his eye on him, and the contract law tutor told him that with grades like his he could get a clerkship at the supreme court. I would hear him and think about how I was focused on Adam's poop and problems with the diaper service and my cracked nipples, and there he was, floating in a sky of diamonds—"

"But he gave up the filmmaking," Avram says softly.

"As soon as the war was over."

"Yeah?"

"You know, after you came back."

"But he wanted it so badly."

"That's exactly why."

"I was always sure he'd be—"

"No, he cut it off, like only Ilan knows how to cut things off." She slices the air with her hand and feels herself falling on the other side of the knife.

"Because of me? Because of what happened to me?"

"Well, not just that. There were other things." She stops walking and looks at him in despair. "Tell me, Avram, how will we have time for everything?"

The mountain towers above them in a bed of forest, and Avram sees her brown eyes colored green, sees how those eyes still sparkle, still, still.

"And don't forget," she continues after a while, "that during the first months after Adam was born he also took care of you on his own. He would drive to the hospital every single day, and to all the convalescent homes where they sent you, and every day he gave me a detailed report. We had long telephone conferences every evening about your treatments, the medications, the side effects. And those interrogations, don't forget that."

"Aha," Avram says and looks out into the distance.

"And you, you never even once asked him about me. How I was doing. Where I'd suddenly disappeared to."

He breathes deeply, straightens up, widens his steps. She has to work hard to keep up.

"You didn't even know that I'd had Adam. Or at least that's what I thought at the time."

"Ora?"

"What?"

"Did he take any interest in Adam?"

"In Adam?" She lets out a thin laugh.

"I was just asking."

"Well," she stretches, preparing to massage an old insult. "At first he definitely asked about Adam. Or rather, made a point of asking. Then he asked a little less, and I could tell that he found it difficult even to say his name. And then one day he started talking about 'the boy.' How does the boy sleep at night, how is his digestion, that sort of thing. And that was when I lost it. Even a sucker like me has some kind of limit, I guess.

"I think it was then, when he started calling him 'the boy,' that I began to feel like myself again. I told him to stop calling me. To get out of my life. I was finally able to tell him what I should have said months before. I'm stupid, you know, what can I say. For maybe three months I kept dragging out that twisted arrangement. Just imagine. When I think about it now—"

They stop in a patch of shade on a vista that looks out onto the entire Hula Valley. All the muscles in their bodies are aching now, and not just from walking. Avram collapses to the ground and doesn't even have the strength to take his backpack off. Ora notices that every time he stops walking and moving, he takes on a sort of heavy, rock-like lumpiness. Secretly, through her teenage girl's eyes, she watches him: he avoids looking fully at the broad valley spread out at the foot of the mountain, at the mountain itself as they walk down it, at the expanse of sky. She remembers that Ilan once said about Avram, "He just turned himself off and he's sitting inside himself in the dark." And here too, on the path, in the sun, his skin is fair and reddens easily, but his body seems impervious to light.

And to beauty. And to Ofer.

She briskly wipes her glasses off and breathes on them. She wipes them again. Calms herself.

"But as soon as I hung up on him, he called back. He said he could definitely understand me throwing him out of my life. He totally deserves that. But I can't remove him from the joint responsibility we share for our second child."

"What? Oh."

"Yes, well."

So that's how they thought of me, Avram muses. Very soon, in a minute or two, he will ask her to stop talking. There's no room left in him for all this.

"And then we had another conversation. One of the most outlandish ones we've ever had. We figured out how we'd keep taking care of you, and how we'd hide what was happening to us from you, because it was obvious that the last thing you needed was this sort of crisis with us, with the parents, you know." She laughs feebly.

Avram remembers for some reason that when he was about thirteen, years after his father got up one morning and disappeared, he convinced himself to believe that his real father, the secret one, was the poet Alexander Penn. For weeks, every night before bed, he would read Penn's poem "The Abandoned Son" in a whispered voice.

"And we talked like total strangers, Ilan and me. No, like the lawyers of total strangers. With a matter-of-factness that I could not believe I was capable of, with him or at all. We opened our calendars and settled exactly how long Ilan would keep caring for you alone, and when I would start doing shifts again, and we agreed that we'd keep pretending that everything was okay when we were with you, at least until you recovered a little. We knew it wouldn't be much of an effort, because you didn't show any interest in anything anyway. You barely knew what was happening around you—or is that what you wanted everyone to think, so they'd leave you alone? Hey? So they'd give up on you?"

His eyes move sideways under his half-closed lids.

"In the end you got what you wanted," she says drily.

And then, in mid-breath, she freezes, because she is suddenly unable to recall Ofer's face. She jumps up quickly and starts walking, and Avram groans and gets up to follow her. She stares straight ahead without seeing anything, her eyes burning like black chimneys in the daylight, but they cannot see Ofer. As she walks, his face breaks up inside her head into a whirlwind of fragmentary expressions and features. At times they swell and burst, as though someone has shoved a huge fist behind his skin and cleaved him from the inside. She knows she is being punished for something, but she does not know what. Perhaps for continuing her journey instead of going home right away to receive the bad news? Or for not being willing to accept any compromise (a minor injury? A moderate one? One leg? From the knee down? From the ankle? A hand? An eye? Both eyes? The penis?). Almost every single hour of the day, behind all the things and the words and the acts, these propositions have hummed inside her, dispatched from far away: You can live a pretty good life with one kidney, even with one lung. Think about it, don't be quick to say no, it's not every day you get these kinds of offers, and you'll be sorry one day that you rejected them. Other families took them and now they're happy, relatively speaking. Think about it again, think good and hard: if it's a phosphorus burn, for example, they can do skin grafting. They can even rehabilitate the brain these days. And even if he's a vegetable, he'll still be alive, and you can take care of him yourself, you can use all the experience you gained after Avram was injured. So please, reconsider. He'll have a life, sensations, emotions. It's not the worst bargain you could make in your condition.

And for all those days and nights she has pushed away these buzzing communications. Now too she holds her head up and walks between them, careful to look away from Avram, to protect him from the gorgon face she feels she has taken on. She won't be cutting any deals. And she will not be accepting any bad news of any kind, *of any kind whatsoever.* Go on, keep going. Talk, tell him about his son.

. . .

"A different life started for me then. I didn't have the strength for it at all, but I had a baby who simply forced me to live and came into my life with the determination of a . . . well, of a baby, who is convinced that everything was created for his benefit, especially me. We were together all the time, he and I, almost twenty-four hours a day. For the first year I didn't have a nanny or much help, just a few girlfriends who came on shifts, twice a week, when I started going to see you again in Tel Aviv. But the rest of the time, days and nights, he and I were alone."

Her look hovers somewhere in the distance. There are some things that are futile to try to explain to him: the murmured conversations between her and Adam while he nursed, before bed, half asleep in the middle of the night, when the whole world was asleep and it was just the two of them, eyes to eyes, learning each other. And the peals of laughter they shared when he got the hiccups. And the way their gazes grasped each other when evening fell and shadows grew long in the room. And his quiet expression of bewilderment when he saw tears in her eyes, and his lips that curled and trembled around questions he did not know how to ask.

Avram walks beside her, nodding to himself, hunched inward like a question mark.

"It was also a wonderful time. Our age of wonders. Mine and Adam's."

And to herself she thinks: The happiest years we had.

"I slowly got to know him." She smiles, remembering his grumpiness when she dared to pull him off one nipple, until his mouth locked in on the other. He would scream bloody murder, with furious eyes, and his entire head would turn red with insult. "And the lovely humor in his looks and his games and the way he played around with me. I never knew babies had a sense of humor, no one told me."

Avram keeps nodding to himself, as though reciting an important lesson. Ora realizes: We're practicing together, Avram and I. Practicing on Adam, before we get to Ofer. Exercising vocabulary, boundaries, endurance.

"And with me, there was always turmoil inside. It was like all my systems had gone awry, body and soul. I was very sick too, with endless infections and bleeding, and I was terribly weak. But I also felt a crazy sense of power, lots of power, don't ask me why. I had attacks of sobbing and joy and desperation and euphoria, all within three minutes. I used to wonder how I would get through another hour with him when he was running a high fever and screaming in my ear, and it was two o'clock in the morning and the doctor wouldn't pick up the phone, but at the same time—I could do anything! I could carry him by my teeth to the farthest corners of the earth. *Terrible as an army with banners*."

Avram lights up for an instant and smiles to himself. He seems to be tasting the words silently with his lips: *Terrible as an army with banners*. Her shoulders relax, opening up to him like a freshly sliced challah—he sometimes used to call her that, but he also called her "malted spirits," or "wool gabardine." These names had no meaning, apart from the endearment with which he enveloped her in the words, the sweet exotic sounds, as though covering her shoulders with a shawl so fine that only she and he could see it. He loved to pepper his speech, sometimes expediently and sometimes not, with dudgeon wood and jasper stones, curtilages and sippets, pedicels and ovules. "That's Avram's," she and Ilan used to say to each other in the years after Avram, when somewhere in the conversation, or on the radio, or in a book, a word that had simply been born for him would pop up—a word that bore his seal.

"And one day he calls to tell me his address and phone number have changed, like I'm his reserve duty office. The apartment in Talpiot is too cold, he says, so he's renting a different one, on Herzl Boulevard in Beit HaKerem. 'Good for you,' I say, and cross out his old number on the note on the fridge.

"Two months later, in the middle of a regular conversation about you, about your condition, he gives me a new number. What happened? Did you get a different phone? No, but they've been doing roadwork outside his place for three months now, digging up the street and paving it over day and night, and there's a terrible racket, and you know how noise makes him crazy. 'So where does your new number live?' 'In Evan Sapir, near Hadassah Hospital. I found a nice little apartment in someone's backyard.' 'Is it quiet there?' I ask. 'Like a graveyard,' he assures me, and I change the number on the fridge.

"A few weeks later, another call. His landlord's son bought a drum set. He holds the phone out the window, so I can enjoy it, too. Huge drums, apparently. A tom-tom, at the very least. A person can't live this way. I agree with him and walk to the fridge with pen in hand. 'I've already settled on a little place in Bar Giora,' he says in a nasal voice. Bar Giora? That's pretty close, I think, it's right across the valley. I feel my stomach contracting, and I can't tell if it's excitement or alarm at his sudden proximity. But a week goes by, and another week, and I see no change in our relationship. He's over there, we're over here, and there starts to be more and more of an 'us.'

"After a while, another phone call. 'Listen, I had a slight falling-out with the landlord, he has two dogs, murderous rottweilers. I'm moving again, and I thought you'd want to know: it's quite close to you.' He giggles. 'It's more or less in Tzur Hadassah itself, I mean, if that won't bother you.' 'Hey, Ilan, are you playing hot and cold with me?' "

Ilan had laughed. Ora knew him and his systems of laughs, and in this laughter there was something weak and pathetic, and she felt once again how strong she was. "I'm telling you," she says to Avram, "I didn't even know up to then that I was such a lioness. But I'm also a dishrag, as you know, and a doormat, and I missed him almost all the time and everything reminded me of him—Adam's suckling used to make me so horny for Ilan." She laughs quietly to herself as she remembers. "I would pick up Ilan's smell from Adam at night and it woke me. And all that time I felt as though he were just a couple of meters away."

When she says that, she can hear the music in which Ilan spoke to her on the phone all the years they were together, with a firm sort of sharpness and a rousing "Ora!" Sometimes, when he said her name that way, she had a vague sense of guilt—like a soldier asleep on guard duty whose officer calls him out—but there was almost always something daring in the way he addressed her too, and teasing, and arousing and inviting: Ora! She smiles to herself: Ora! As though he were establishing a decisive, solid fact that she herself often doubted.

"So I pretend to be strong and ask softly, 'What's going on, Ilan? Is this like some kind of Monopoly game for you, renting and selling houses in all sorts of streets around town? Or is my learned friend a little homesick?' And without even blinking, he says yes, that he's had no life since he left home, that he's going crazy. And then I hear myself say, 'Then come back,' and straightaway I think, No! I don't need him and I don't want him here. I don't want any man getting under my feet around here."

She smiles broadly when Avram briefly lifts his heavy eyelids and an ancient spark glimmers slyly in his eyes. "There you are," she says.

"Sometimes at night," Ilan told her back then, "I drive to the house. It's some kind of force . . . It just gets hold of me, wakes me up at one o'clock in the morning, or two, throws me out of bed, and I get up like a zombie and get on my motorbike and drive to you, and I know I'll be with you in one minute, in your bed, begging you to forgive me, to forget, to erase my madness. And then, when I'm twenty meters from the place, the counter-force kicks in, always at the same point, as if that's where the magnet's poles get reversed. I can actually feel something physically pushing me, and it says: Move away, get out of here, it's no good to be here—"

"Is that really what happens?"

"I'm going crazy, Ora, I have a child and I can't see him?! Am I sane? And I have you, and I'm one thousand percent sure that you're the only person I'm able and willing to live with, the only person who can stand me, and so what? What am I doing? I thought maybe I just needed to escape this place, to get out of Israel, maybe go to England, finish my studies there, get a change of air, but I can't do that either! Because of Avram I can't leave this place! I don't know what to do, tell me what to do."

"And then," Ora tells Avram, "when he said that to me, it occurred to me for the first time that you were definitely the reason for his running away from us, but you may also have been the excuse."

"Excuse for what?"

"For what?" She lets out a thin, unpleasant snicker. "For example, his fear of living with us, with me and Adam. Or of just living."

"I don't understand."

"*Oof,*" she grunts, shaking her head firmly a few times. "You. The two of you."

"He rented a house next to the children's park, you know, the one that all the parents in Tzur Hadassah built, a hundred meters from our house as the crow flies. And he didn't call for maybe three weeks. I turned into a bundle of nerves again, and of course Adam picked up on it immediately. I would push him around the neighborhood for hours in his stroller, that's the only way he would calm down at all, and no matter which direction I set off in, I always ended up at Ilan's house."

Avram walks next to her with his head bowed, not looking at her or at the view. He sees the young woman, lonely and restless, pacing about with the stroller. He leads her along the paths of the village he grew up in, down the loop road and the side street that splits off past houses and yards he knows.

"Once we met face-to-face. He was just coming out, and we happened to run into each other at the gate. We said cautious hellos and both got stuck. He looked at me as if he was about to bed me right there on the sidewalk—I knew that hunger of his so well. But I wanted him to look at Adam, too. Adam was a mess that day—he had a cold and he was kvetchy, with sleep and gunk in his eyes, but Ilan threw him such a fleeting glance that I thought he'd barely noticed a thing.

"But as usual I was wrong. He said, 'It's him,' and got on his bike, hit the gas, and sped away, waking up Adam. Only after he was gone did it occur to me that he'd meant something completely different. I pulled back all the blankets covering Adam to look closely at his face, and for the first time, I saw that he looked like *you*."

Avram perks up and turns to her in surprise.

"Something in his eyes, something in the general expression. Don't ask me how it's possible." She chuckles. "Maybe I was thinking about you a bit when we made him, I don't know. And by the way, to this day I can sometimes see a certain similarity to you in him."

"How?" Avram laughs awkwardly and his feet almost trip over each other.

"There is such a thing as inspiration in nature, isn't there?"

"That's in electricity," he replies quickly. "There's a phenomenon where a magnet creates an electrical current."

"Hey, Avram," she says softly.

"What?"

"Just . . . Aren't you hungry?"

"No, not yet."

"Do you want some coffee?"

"Let's keep going for a while. This is a good path."

"Yes, it's a good path."

She walks in front of him, spreads her arms out, and inhales the clear air.

"A week later, Ilan called at eleven-thirty at night. I was asleep, and without any introductions he asked if it would be all right with me if he came to live in the hut in the yard."

"In the hut?" Avram splutters.

"That shed, you know, where all the junk is, where you had your studio."

"Yes, but what—"

"Without even thinking about it, I told him to come. I remember that I put the phone down and sat up in bed, and I thought about how this game we'd been playing for two years was just like us, this push-pull force that was working on him, and that gravitational force of Adam's."

"And yours," Avram says without looking at her.

"You think so? I don't know . . ."

The only sound now is their footsteps on the dirt. Ora tastes the idea: my gravitational force. She giggles. It's nice to remember. She had never felt it as strongly as she did in those days, when it drove Ilan frantically all over town.

"Oh well." She sighs. (Now he's gone all the way to Bolivia and Chile, all light and airy, a traveler without cargo, a bachelor.)

"The next morning I went to the shed and started emptying it out. I threw out piles of two-thousand-year-old junk and crap, I mean it was the scrapyard of everyone who ever lived in that house of yours, from the beginning of the century, it seems. I found crates full of your sketches, texts, and reels of tape. I kept that, I kept all your stuff, I have it, if you ever want—"

"You can throw it out."

"No no, I'm not throwing it away. If you want, throw it out yourself."

"But what's in there?"

"Thousands and thousands of pages full of your handwriting. Maybe ten crates full." She laughs. "It's unbelievable, it's as if your whole life, from the moment you were born, all you did was sit and write."

Later, after a silence that goes on for an entire hill and half a valley, Avram says, "So you cleared out the shed—"

"I worked there for a good few hours while Adam crawled around near me on the lawn, naked and happy as can be. Maybe he sensed that something was happening. I didn't explain anything to him, because I couldn't exactly explain it to myself. And when there was a huge pile on the path outside the shed, I stood and looked at it with a matronly sort of satisfaction, and then I got this zap in my heart—what was the name of that woman in the Cocteau story?"

"I don't think she had a name."

"Serves her right."

Avram laughs deeply, tickling something inside her.

"And I started putting everything back inside. Adam probably thought I'd lost my mind. I shoved it all in and could barely push the door shut with my shoulder, and I locked it, and I felt that I had saved myself from glorious humiliation.

"A few days later, on Sukkoth, when I was at my parents' in Haifa with Adam, Ilan turned up and cleared out the shed himself. He put his stuff in, brought someone in to build him a little kitchenette and bathroom and hooked up to my power and water. When I got back, it was night and Adam was asleep on me, and from a distance I could see the piles of trash and junk around the Dumpster. I walked down the path through the garden and saw a light on in the shed. I didn't look right or left. What can I tell you, Avram.

"Then came the days. I don't even know how to tell you about them. It was like torture. Me here and him there. Maybe ten meters between us. The light goes on his place and I jump into position by the window, behind the curtain, thinking maybe I'll catch a glimpse of him. His phone rings, and I swear to you, I embodied the expression 'I'm all ears.'

"Sometimes, in the morning, I would see him slip away just after sunrise, so—God forbid—he wouldn't run into me with Adam. And he usually came home very late, almost running down the path, in such a hurry, with a student's satchel under one arm, fleeing for his life. I had no idea what he did all day, if he had a girlfriend, where he hung out after school so as not to be here while Adam and I were awake. All I knew is that he went to see you three or four times a week. That was the only sure thing: he took care of you on the days I didn't.

"You probably don't remember, but I used to try anything to get you to talk about him, to steal a little information about him from you. Do you remember that?"

Avram nods.

"You really do?"

"Go on. Afterward I'll . . ."

"I told Adam that there was a man living in the shed. He asked if the man was our friend, and I said it was too soon to tell. He asked if he was a good man, and I said yes, although he had his own ways of showing it. Of course Adam wanted us to go and visit him, but I explained that he was a very busy man and we couldn't visit him because he was never home. Adam was enchanted by this new thing, and perhaps by the idea that there was a man who was never home. Every time we went out or came home, he would pull me to the shed. He drew pictures and wanted to bring them as gifts to the man in the shed. He kept kicking his ball at the shed. He would stand there and stroke Ilan's motorbike with both hands, and the chain that tied it to the gate.

"Sometimes I played with him in the garden, near the shed, or gave him a bath in a big tub outside, or we would picnic on a blanket on the lawn. About once every minute he would say, 'Can the man see us?' 'Maybe we should invite him?' 'What's the man's name?'

"When I finally broke down and told him the name, he started calling him. 'Ilan, Ilan!'" She cups her hands over her mouth to illustrate: "Ilan, Ilan." Avram looks at her.

"You see, up until then he'd had some instinct not to even learn the word 'daddy.' But now he started to say 'Ilan' with such dedication. He would open his eyes in the morning and ask if Ilan was still there. Come back from day care and check with me whether Ilan was back from work. In the afternoons he would stand on the porch facing the garden, hold on to the railing, rock it as hard as he could, and shout 'Ilan!' a hundred times, a thousand times, never giving up, until I took him inside. Sometimes I really had to drag him into the house.

"You know, telling you this, I realize what I did to him.

"I wasn't thinking about anything then, do you understand?

"Ilan and I were—

"You have to understand.

"There was a kind of circle of madness around us both.

"And all my natural instincts just seemed to—

"Listen, I don't know where I was.

"It was as though I didn't exist."

She picks up only after a long break, during which she wipes her eyes and nose and swallows down the toxic thought that perhaps it is this too that Adam is now punishing her for. "It wasn't his usual attraction to men. Not the attraction to every man who happened to come through the house, every postman delivering a package, whom he would flirt with and ask to stay and cling to his leg. There was something in Ilan—

you know, his absent presence, and the fact that he was capable of ignoring Adam so completely, when everyone else made such a big deal about how cute he was—something that just drove him mad. And to this day it's like that." She sighs. She can see Adam performing on a stage, his eyes rolling back in a very private ecstasy, a mixture of torment and pleading.

"Like what?"

"Like he's always wanting Ilan to see him.

"And just so you know, at least twice a day I would decide that was it, Ilan had to leave, get out of the shed, just to stop torturing Adam. But on the other hand, I wasn't able to give up that one-thousandth of a chance that he might still come home. I kept trying to understand what Ilan was going through when he heard Adam wailing on the porch, and how it could not make him crazy. What sort of a person was he, tell me this, that he could withstand that kind of thing?"

"Yes," Avram says, his voice hardening.

"I also thought maybe that was exactly what he was looking for."

"What?" Avram grunts.

"Exactly that torture."

"Which was what? I don't get it."

"That right-across-the-way," she says rhythmically. "*For thou shalt see us afar off, but thou shalt not go thither.* That sort of thing. And believe me, that kind of torture I don't—"

His face tenses up and his eyes dart around. His entire expression alters. She stops. Puts a hand on his arm.

"I'm sorry, Avram, I didn't . . . Don't go there now, be with me."

"I'm with you," he says after a minute. His voice is thick and strained. He wipes the sweat off his upper lip. "I'm here."

"I need you."

"I'm here, Ora."

They walk silently. A road runs by not too far away, and they can already hear the vehicles. Avram senses them the way a dreamer starts to be aware of sounds in the household that has awoken before he has.

"I looked down on him, and sometimes I pitied him the way you pity a handicapped person. And I hated him, and I missed him, and I knew I had to do something to extract him from it, from the curse he had put on himself and on us. But I didn't have the strength to do anything. Not to take a single step.

"And all that time, just so you understand, Ilan and I talked on the phone at least twice a week, because we also had you. About once a month you had another little operation, the final touches, cosmetic stuff, and all the never-ending coordination with the Ministry of Defense, and finding you an apartment in Tel Aviv. Twice a week I drove to see you, to be with you, and Ilan did it the other days. And you didn't know anything about us, or so we thought. You didn't know that we had a son, or that we'd separated, or about all of Ilan's roaming back and forth across Jerusalem. Tell me—"

"What?"

"Do you even remember anything from then?"

"Do I remember? Yes."

"Really?" She is astonished. Stops still.

"Almost everything."

"But what exactly? The treatments, the operations, the interrogations?" She runs after him.

"Ora, I remember that period almost day by day."

"I used to sit with you," she continues immediately—the new information is too much to contain, too frightening: she cannot take it in now; later, later—"sit and tell you stories about me and Ilan, as if nothing had changed. As if we were still twenty-two-year-old kids, like on the day you left. As if we had stayed in exactly the same spot, waiting for you to get back. Freeze tag."

They walk quickly, almost running for some reason.

"Not that you showed much of an interest. You would sit there in your room, or in the garden, saying almost nothing. You made no contact with the other wounded soldiers, or with the nurses. You didn't ask anything. I never knew how much of all my chatter you were taking in. I told you about my social work program, which I had stopped right after you got back, because who could be bothered with that. I would babble on about the great campus life, and describe my project with the underprivileged kids, which I had dropped after you came back, of course, but I kept retelling you how I was setting it up, who was helping me and who wasn't. I described the negotiations with the kibbutzim as though they were really going on right then. Ma'agan Michael agreed to host the kids but wouldn't let them swim in their pool, and Beit HaShita put them in buildings with holes in the walls, and don't ask what happened yesterday, all the kibbutzim were demanding that I remove the kids immediately because they had head lice. I would sit with you and just continue my life from where it left off. It was a bit of therapy for me too, what's wrong with that?"

Yet she remembers: One day, while she was chattering at him, he had suddenly turned to her and grunted: "How is your boy?"

When she stammered, he pressed on: "How old is your boy? What's your boy's name?"

She was paralyzed for a moment. Then she pulled her wallet from her purse and took out a picture.

His face trembled. His lips twitched uncontrollably. When she was about to put the picture back in her wallet, he reached out and grasped her wrist, bending it hard, and shivered as he looked at the picture.

"He looks like both of you," he finally said.

"Avram, I'm so sorry," she said, trying not to cry. "I didn't know that you knew."

"When you look at him you can see how alike you are."

"Me and him? Really?" Ora had felt happy for a moment. She saw almost no similarity between herself and Adam.

"You and Ilan."

"Oh." She released her hand from his grip. "How long have you known?"

He shrugged his shoulders and said nothing. Ora quickly calculated: she'd stopped coming to see him as soon as she'd started showing, and Ilan had taken care of him alone. She suddenly became furious. "Just answer me this—when did he tell you?"

"Ilan? He didn't tell me."

"Then how?"

Avram stared at her with expressionless eyes. "I knew. I knew from the start."

She had a crazy thought: He knew as soon as I found out.

"And Ilan doesn't . . . doesn't know that you know?"

A conspiratorial flicker ran over his face. His old cunning, his love of plot twists.

They've been walking for several minutes on a narrow side road, but the surprising amount of traffic makes them both unquiet. It's been at least two days since they've walked on a road, and the cars seem to be zooming by far too close. They see their own reflection in the drivers' looks: two weathered refugees. For a few hours they forgot that's what they are—escapees, persecuted. Avram drags his feet again and grumbles incessantly. Ora is troubled by a vague, silly, yet stubborn suspicion that this remote road is ultimately connected, through infinite streets and intersections, to its brothers in faraway Beit Zayit, and that some bad news may trickle back through the asphalt network's nervous system. They both calm down at once when they spot an orange-blue-and-white marker, which they have started seeing and learned to trust. It directs them to turn left after a small concrete bridge and depart from the road to an inviting field. It does her good, Avram too, to feel the live earth beneath their feet again, and the easily trampled weeds and bushes that respond to their footfalls and add a spring to their steps, and the little pebbles that fly up like sparks from the labor of walking.

Their backs straighten, their senses awake. She can feel her body rousing, like a wild animal. Even the steep incline—a narrow goats' path through what seems like a massive rockslide—does not frighten them now. Giant oaks erupt from the rocks, their branches slope down to the escarpment, and Ora and Avram walk in silence, concentrating on the difficult descent. They help each other, careful not to slide on the rocks made slippery by a flow of spring water.

Later—neither of them has a watch, and for days they have had neither minutes nor hours, their time measured only by the light's refraction on the prism of each day—Avram leans his back and backpack against a tree trunk and slowly sits down with his legs sprawled out in front of him. His head droops a little, and for a moment it looks as though he's asleep. Ora rests her head on a cool rock and listens to the gently flowing stream somewhere nearby. Without opening his eyes, Avram says, "We've walked a lot these past days."

"I can barely move my feet."

"It must be thirty years since I've walked this much."

It's his voice, she thinks. He's talking to me. When she opens her eyes, he is looking at her. Straight and clear into her.

"What?" she asks.

"Nothing."

"What are you looking at?"

"At you."

"What do you see?"

He does not reply. His eyes avoid her. She is certain that her face is no longer beautiful to him. She thinks he sees her face as another broken promise.

"Ora."

"What?"

"I was thinking today while we were walking. I was thinking—what does he . . . look like?"

"What does he look like?"

"Yes."

"What does Ofer look like?"

Avram pouts worriedly. "Isn't that a good question?"

"No, it is, it's an excellent question."

She turns her face this way and that, to dry her eyes.

"I have a little picture of him in my wallet, together with Adam, if you—"

"No, no." He sounds alarmed. "Tell me."

"Just with words?" She smiles.

"Yes."

A bold, joyous chirping sound suddenly fills the crevice. An invisible bird sings from within the thicket, and Ora and Avram lower their heads to absorb the tiny gaiety, a soul full of life and stories. A whole plot is narrated, perhaps the events of the passing day, praise for food, the tale of a wonderful and convoluted rescue from the claws of a predator, and in between, a chorus made entirely of claims and responses, a bitter settling of scores with a petty adversary.

"When I saw you walking," Ora says after the singing dies down a little and turns to secular chirping, "even today, just a few minutes ago, I thought about how Ofer's walk has changed over the years."

Avram leans forward, attentive.

"Because up until he was about four, he walked exactly like you do, with the . . . you know, rocking to the sides, arms like a penguin, just like you walk."

"You mean that's how I walk?" Avram seems hurt.

"You didn't know?"

"Still today?"

"Listen, why don't you try those shoes? Try them on, what do you care?"

"No, no, I'm comfortable in these."

"So you're just going to carry them the whole time?"

"So you say he walks like me?"

"That's when he was little. Four or five. Afterward he went through all kinds of periods. You know that kids mimic what they see, too."

"They do?" He thinks about Ilan's supple, battle-ready stride.

"And in adolescence—do you really want to hear?"

"I'm hearing," Avram murmurs.

"He was terribly thin up to then, and small. If you saw him now, you'd never believe it was the same person. But he made this giant leap, at around sixteen and a half, in breadth and height. Until then he was"—she draws a figure in the air, a thin reed or a twig—"he had matchstick legs, it broke your heart to see them. And he always used to walk around—I just remembered this—in huge, heavy hiking boots, a bit like the ones tied to your backpack now. From morning to night he never took them off."

"But why?"

"Why? Do you really not know why?"

Of course he does, she thinks immediately. Don't you understand? He just needs to hear it from you, word for word.

"Because they gave him some height, and they probably also gave him the feeling that he was stronger, more solid, masculine."

"Yes," Avram murmurs.

"I'm telling you, he was really small."

"How small?" Avram scoffs in disbelief. "How small?"

She signals to him with her eyes: Very small. Tiny. Avram slowly nods, for the first time digesting with his eyes the Ofer reflected in her gaze. A wee boy. Like Thumbelino. She wonders who he's been seeing in his mind's eye all these years.

"Didn't you think he—"

"I didn't think anything." He cuts her off, his face closing up.

"And you never tried to imagine how—"

"No!"

They sit quietly. The bird has also stopped singing. A very small child, Avram muses, and something in him moves, crushed. A weak boy, a passing shadow. I wouldn't be able to take it, the sorrow of such a child, his envy of other boys. How can he survive at school, on the street. How do you let him out of the house. Cross the street alone. I would never be able to take it.

Love him, Ora asks silently.

"I really didn't think," he mumbles, "I just didn't think anything."

How could you? she asks with her eyes.

Don't ask me, he responds in silence and lowers his gaze. His thumbs dart over his fingertips. The tightening muscle in his jaw says, Don't ask me those kinds of questions.

"But I told you," she goes on, consoling. "He sprang up all at once after that, in height and in breadth. Today he's a real . . ."

But back then, thinks Avram, somehow refusing to part with a strange new pain, like a cruel pinch of the heart that ends with a light caress.

Avram himself, she remembers, was always short, but broad and solid. "Today I look like a dwarf," he'd explained once, very matter-of-factly, to the boys and girls in his class. And then he'd continued with his boldfaced lie: "And that's how it is with all the men in my family. But at nineteen, we suddenly start growing and growing and growing, and you can't stop us, and then we get even!" He'd laughed. At recess, in the locker room, he once stopped Meir'ke Blutreich and announced in front of everyone that from now on Meir'ke's appointment as the class fatty was annulled, and that he, Avram, now bore the official title and had no intention of sharing it with amateur fatties, posers whose arms and bellies were not sufficiently flabby and flaccid.

"I was thinking," Avram whispers, "I don't know if he . . ."

"What? Ask."

"Is he also, um, a redhead?"

Ora laughs with relief. "His hair was actually pretty red when he was born, and I was really happy about that, and so was Ilan. But it changed to yellow very quickly in the sun. And now it's a little darker. Like your beard, more or less."

"Mine?" Avram said excitedly, smoothing the rough ends of his beard.

"He has wonderful hair, full, abundant, thick, with curls at the ends. It's a pity he shaves it all off now. He says it's more comfortable that way in the army, but maybe after his release he'll start growing it—"

She stops.

Adam is surprised by her onslaught with the camera and flash but cooperates with suspicious enthusiasm. She takes pictures of him playing, drawing, watching television, lying in bed under his blanket. Ora is worried he might get celluloid poisoning. One day, in the middle of a photo shoot, he looks up with a supposedly innocent gaze and asks: "This is for the man in the shed, right?"

Ora splutters, "No, why would you think that? It's for my friend who's sick in the hospital in Tel Aviv."

"Oh," says Adam, disappointed, "the one you always go to see?"

"Yes, the one I go to see. He very much wants to know what you look like."

But Adam never wants to know anything about that friend.

Avram recovers from another operation. Ora brings him a little photo album. The pictures have been screened for anything that may cause him pain, like his childhood home in the background, his rooms, his garden. He flips through the album, barely stopping on any photo. He does not smile. His face shows no expression. After a few pages he shuts it.

"Do you want me to leave it with you?"

"No."

"I'll just leave it here, why not."

"Good-looking kid," he says, and she can feel how heavy his tongue is in his mouth.

"He's wonderful, you'll meet him."

"No, no."

"Not now. One day. When you want to."

"No!" He starts shaking his head wildly. "No, no, no!" His whole body sways, the wheelchair starts to rock, and Ora holds him with both hands and shouts, "Calm down, calm down." A nurse comes running, and then another one, and they take her out of the room. She watches him struggle, all his strength suddenly restored, and he seems to finally comprehend what has really happened to him. She sees them jab him with a needle, and the limpness, and the dazed senses that dull his face again.

She calls Ilan and tells him. He is furious at her for bringing the pictures. For not realizing what that would do to Avram. "It's like torturing a dead man!" he yells. "You're going to a cemetery and standing over a grave and showing off your life."

But when Ilan visits him the next day, Avram asks him to bring the album. Ora puts it outside the shed that night, knocks on the door, and slowly walks back to the house. A few minutes later she watches through the window as Ilan walks out, looks around him, picks up the album, and takes it inside. From her place by the window she leafs through the album with Ilan. Later, through his drawn curtain, she sees him pace back and forth, back and forth.

Avram finishes his rehabilitation and refuses to go back to the house in Tzur Hadassah. Ilan rents a nice apartment for him in Tel Aviv, and they take turns cleaning it and getting it ready for him. On a stormy day in early winter, Ilan brings Avram to the apartment and Avram begins his new life. For the first few weeks he has a live-in caregiver paid for by the Ministry of Defense, but he doesn't want him. The rehab department tries to interest him in various jobs, but they wear him out and he can't hold any of them down. Ora talks with the case managers repeatedly. She bargains, argues, tries to find a job that will suit his personality and skills. The case managers claim he simply doesn't want to work, isn't interested in anything. Ora detects a tone of impatience. They intimate that her expectations for him are unrealistic.

Avram starts to go out on his own. Sometimes she phones him for hours and he doesn't answer, and then she panics and calls Ilan, who says, "Let him breathe."

"What if he's done something to himself?"

"Can you blame him?"

Avram walks on the beach. He goes to the movies. He sits in parks and befriends strangers. He adopts certain mannerisms and a sort of immediate friendliness that is both welcoming and hollow. Ilan is impressed by his pace of recovery. Ora feels that much of it is show. When she comes to see him, twice a week, he looks fresh and clean-shaven; "well maintained," she reports to Ilan. He smiles often, even when there's no reason to, and chatters quite a bit. His vocabulary grows rich again, and every time he says something Avram-like, Ora turns pink with joy. But she quickly discovers that the topics of conversation are well defined and delimited: no talk of the distant past, none of the recent past, and certainly none of the future. Only the present exists. The moment itself.

At around the same time, Ilan and Ora meet with the Ministry of Defense psychologist who has treated Avram since he came back from the POW prison. They learn, to their surprise, that Avram is not defined as shell-shocked. The doctors cannot precisely determine the type of damage or the outlook for recovery, but they all agree that he does not have the distinct symptoms of shell shock. "If he's not shell-shocked, then what is he?" Ilan asks in astonishment, his forehead tipped forward, ready to butt.

The psychologist sighs. "It's hard to say. His characteristics are on the margin. It's certainly possible that he'll be better in a few weeks or months, but it might take longer. Our estimate—our guess, to be more accurate—is that he is somehow controlling it, his rate of recovery, not consciously of course—"

"I don't understand! Are you telling me he's pulling our leg? That he's acting?"

"God forbid." The psychologist holds his hands up. "I—we, meaning, the system—just think that he probably prefers to return to life with small steps. Very, very small. I would suggest trusting that he probably knows better than all of us what's best for him."

"Let me ask you something," Ora says, placing a restraining hand on Ilan's arm. "Is it possible that the fact that we had a child, Ilan and I, is somehow connected to . . . how can I put it . . ."

"To his unwillingness to live," Ilan hisses.

"That is a question only he can answer," says the psychologist without looking at them.

Ilan keeps on living in the shed, and his presence, like his absence, gradually fades. Ora stops believing he'll ever be able to cross the ocean between the shed and the house. He himself tells her on the phone one night that this seems to be the distance he can tolerate from her and Adam. She no longer asks what he means. Deep inside, she's already given up on him. He asks again, as he does occasionally, if she wants him to leave. She just has to say the word and he'll be gone tomorrow. Ora says, "Leave, stay, what difference does it make."

For a short while she has a new boyfriend, a guy called Motti, a divorced accordion player who leads public sing-alongs, whom her friend Ariela set her up with. She usually meets him out of the house, more because of Adam than Ilan. When Adam goes to stay with her parents in Haifa for three days, she invites Motti to sleep over. She knows that Ilan in his shed can see, or at least hear. She doesn't try to hide it. Motti sleeps with her ungracefully. He probes his way inside her and keeps asking insistently if he's "already there." Ora doesn't want to be his *there*. She remembers the times when she was entirely *here*. Afterward, Motti sings "Where Are You, Beloved?" in the shower, in a ringing tenor voice, and Ora sees Ilan's shadow in the shed, darting back and forth. She doesn't invite Motti back again.

One evening, in Avram's apartment in Tel Aviv, she and Avram are making a salad, and she watches out of the corner of her eye to make sure he's using the knife properly and not throwing out half the cucumber with its peel. He tells her about a nurse from Tel Hashomer who's asked him out twice, and he's said no.

"Why did you say no?"

"Because."

"Because what?"

"Because, you know."

"No, I don't, what am I supposed to know?" But she suddenly feels cold.

"Because after the movie she'll invite me up to her place."

"And what's wrong with that?"

"Don't you get it?"

"No, I don't get it," she almost shouts.

He keeps chopping vegetables silently.

"Is she nice?" Ora asks casually, as she crushes a tomato.

"She's fine."

"Is she attractive?" she asks with trembling disinterest.

"She's pretty good-looking, nice body, barely nineteen years old."

"Oh. So what's wrong with going up to her place?"

"I can't," he says emphatically, and Ora quickly switches to an onion, to have an excuse for the tears that will come.

"Ever since I got back I'm this way. Can't do it." He snickers: "A broken reed."

She feels chilly and hollow in her stomach. As if only now, after several years of delay, has the final and terrible shock wave of his tragedy settled over him. "Have you even tried?" she whispers, and thinks, How did I not know about this? How did it not occur to me to find out about this? I took care of his whole body, and I forgot about that? About *that*, with *him*, I forgot?

"I tried four times. Four times is a representative sample, isn't it?"

"With who?" she asks, amazed. "Who did you try with?"

He doesn't seem embarrassed. "Once with the cousin of a soldier who was in the bed next to mine, and once with a Dutch volunteer who works there. Once with a soldier from rehab, once with someone I met on the beach a while ago." He sees the expression on her face. "What are you looking at me like that for? I didn't even initiate it! It's them . . ." Then he adds helplessly, "Turns out the prisoner fantasy works with POWs too, otherwise I can't explain it."

"Has it occurred to you that they like you?" she bursts out, upset by the tinge of jealousy that jabs her. "Maybe your charm wasn't damaged? Maybe even the Egyptians couldn't hurt the . . ."

"I can't get it up, Ora. The minute I go to bed with them, each one of them. I'm actually not bad at jerking off, but how long can I spend stuck with myself? And anyway, lately I'm having problems masturbating, too. When I'm on Largactyl, I can't come."

"But did you really want them?" she asks, and something in her voice seems to split into several directions. "Maybe you didn't really want it?"

"I wanted it, I wanted it," he grunts angrily. "I wanted to fuck, what's the big deal? I'm not talking about immortal love here, I wanted a fuck, Ora, why are you so—"

"But maybe they weren't right for you," she whispers and thinks painfully that a woman who is going to be with Avram has to be just right for him, for his subtleties.

"They were fine, don't look for excuses, they were just right for what . . ."

"And with me?" she asks with a glazed look. "Could you sleep with me?"

There is a long pause.

"With you?"

She swallows. "Yes, with me."

"I don't know," he mumbles. "Wait, are you serious?"

"It's not something to joke about." Her voice trembles.

"But how—"

"We were so good together."

"I don't know, I don't think I'll ever, with you—"

"Why not?" She jumps into her pain immediately. "Because of the lots we cast? Because I drew you?"

"No, no."

"Then because of Ilan?"

"No."

She grabs another tomato and dices it in tiny pieces. "Then why not?"

"No. I can't do it with you anymore."

"You're so sure."

They stand by the sink without touching, looking at the wall. Their temples throb.

"And Adam?" Avram asks now.

"What about him?"

Avram hesitates. He isn't sure what he meant to ask.

"Adam? You want to know about Adam now?" she says.

"Yes, is there something wrong with that, too?"

"There's nothing wrong with it," she says, laughing. "Ask anything you want. That's what we're here for."

"Well, just if he was also a kid who . . . You know what? Tell me whatever you want."

Here we go, she thinks and stretches her limbs.

They are walking through a thicket of prickly burnet and sage. The oaks are as low as bushes here. Lizards dart under their feet in a panic. Side by side they walk, looking for the path, which has been swallowed up in the abundant growth, and Ora steals a glance at their elastic shadows that hover on the shrubbery. When Avram waves his arms as he walks, it briefly looks as though he is placing his hand on her shoulder, and when she plays with her body in the sun a little, she can make the shadow of his arm hug the shadow of her waist.

"Adam was also a thin boy, just like Ofer, but he stayed thin. A beanpole."

"Oh." Avram looks around as if randomly, indifferently, but Ora, as it turns out, still knows all the cards in his deck.

"As a child, he was always taller than Ofer—well, don't forget he's three years older. But when Ofer started getting older and growing, it changed and the order was reversed."

"So now—"

"Yes."

"What?"

"Ofer is taller. Much."

Avram is amazed. "Really? Much taller?"

"I told you, he had a growth spurt and just overtook him all at once, almost by a whole head."

"You don't say . . ."

"Yes."

"So in fact," Avram says, speeding up and thoughtfully sucking on his cheek, "he's taller than Ilan, too?"

"Yes, he's taller than Ilan."

Silence. It almost embarrasses her to witness this.

"But how tall is Ilan? One meter eighty?"

"Even taller."

"You don't say . . ." The flash of a well-played ploy glimmers in his eye. He mumbles wonderingly, "I never thought he'd be like that one day."

"What did you think?"

"I didn't think anything," he repeats, this time so feebly that his voice is barely audible. "I hardly thought, Ora. Every time I tried . . ." He spreads both hands out in a gesture that might indicate a wish, or perhaps an explosion cracking open.

She resists asking, Then what were you so afraid of, if you didn't think anything? Who were you protecting from afar, just so long as you didn't know anything about him?

"And how old is Adam now?"

"Twenty-four and a bit."

"Wow, a big boy."

"Almost my age," she says, attempting one of Ilan's jokes. Avram looks at her, finally gets it, and smiles politely.

"And what's going on with him?"

"Adam? I told you."

"I didn't . . . I must not have been paying attention."

"Adam is with Ilan now, touring the world. South America. Ilan took a year off. They're having the time of their life, those two, it seems. They don't want to come home."

"But Adam," Avram probes, and Ora thinks his tongue is straining to learn the music of the questions. "What does he do normally? I mean, does he work? Is he studying?"

"He's still searching, you know. These days they spend a lot of time searching. And he has a band, did I tell you?"

"I don't remember. Maybe." He shrugs helplessly. "I don't know where I was, Ora. Tell me again, from the beginning."

"He's an artist. Adam is really an artist in his soul." Ora's face brightens as she talks.

A silence thickens, rustles, and one question goes unasked. Ora feels that if she could tell Avram that Ofer was also an artist, an artist in his soul, things might be a little easier.

"A band? What band?"

"Some kind of hip-hop thing, don't ask me too many questions." She waves her hand. "They've been together for ages, he and his guys. They're working on their first CD. They even have a company that wants to produce them. It's a kind of hip-hop opera, I really don't understand it, it's very long, three and a half hours, something about exile, a kind of voyage of exiles, lots of exiles."

"Oh."

"Yes."

Ora and Avram's shoes scratch through the bushes as they walk.

Ora remembers something that caught her ear by chance, when Adam was on the phone with a friend. "And there's a woman in it. She walks along with a length of string, unraveling it behind her."

"A string?"

"Yes, a red one. She unravels it behind her on the ground."

"Why?"

"I don't know."

"What an idea," he murmurs, and the skin around his eyes reddens.

"Adam and his ideas," she giggles, somewhat repelled by Avram's sudden excitement.

"You mean, it's like the land was ripped apart? Unraveled?"

"Maybe."

"And this woman is giving the earth a string . . ." Avram latches on to the idea.

"Yes, something symbolic like that."

"That's powerful. But exiles from where?"

"They're a very serious bunch, his band. They did their research, read about places around Israel, about early Zionism, dug through kibbutz archives, and on the web, and they asked people what they would take with them if they had to flee suddenly." This is the sum of what she knows about the topic, but she doesn't feel comfortable with Avram knowing that, at least not yet, and so she chatters on. "It's him and a group of guys, and they write everything together, lyrics and music, and they do gigs all over the place." She smiles with visible effort. "By the way, Ofer played music once, too. Drums, bongos. But he stopped pretty quickly, and at the end of the tenth grade, for his final project—this is actually interesting—he made a movie."

"Who are the exiles?"

"And Ofer was in a little band too, when he was eleven."

"Exiled from where, Ora?"

"From here." She gestures with a suddenly feeble hand over the brown mountain cliffs that encircle them, the oak, carob, and olive trees, the thickets of shrubbery that curl around their feet. "From here," she repeats quietly. In her ears she can hear the words Ofer whispered to her in front of the TV cameras.

"Exiled from Israel?" Avram seems upset.

Ora takes a deep breath, straightens up, and puts on a weary smile. "You know how they are at that age. They want to astound people at any cost, to shock them."

"Have you heard it?"

"The opera? No, I haven't had the chance."

Avram gives her a questioning look.

"He hasn't played it for me," she says, giving in, emptying out. "Look, Adam and I—forget it, he doesn't tell me anything."

"The Hornies," thinks Ora, her lips pursed, as she walks on, turning her back on Avram and his sudden, irritating eagerness. Why is he so hung up on Adam? Ofer started his band with three guys from school. They had four drum sets and no guitar or piano. They wrote wild songs, with most rhymes involving "schmuck" and "fuck," she recalls as she rubs her arms to pump some blood into them. They put on a show for the families once, in one of the boys' basements. Ofer was frozen and reserved for most of the show—at that age, he almost always shrank away in the presence of strangers—but every so often, especially after the band sang a rude word, he would peek at her with the defiant boldness of a young chick, and her insides would flutter.

Toward the end of the gig he finally let loose and suddenly started banging on his bongos with a strange, violent glee, bursting out of his own skin. His three band mates were at first amazed by the outburst, and then, exchanging glances, hurried to keep up with his pace on their own drums, and the whole thing became a noisy commotion, a jungle of beating drums and screaming and groaning, the three of them against Ofer. Ilan shifted in his seat, about to get up and put an end to it, but it was she—who usually did not read situations well at first, and had real dyslexia when it came to comprehending basic human interactions— Wasn't that what he'd said? Weren't those the central tenets of his *I've run my course* speech?—who'd placed a hand on his arm and stopped him, because she noticed something, a very slight change in Ofer's rhythm, a new channeling of the streams of violence and competitive-ness that flowed between him and the three others, and she had the feel-ing (unless she was wrong as usual) that Ofer was infiltrating the other three without them realizing it. At first he mimicked them, doing a per-fect impersonation of their apish rowdiness, and then he started to echo them with his own gentler drumming, just a hairsbreadth behind them, and she thought he was letting them hear themselves in a softer, more ironic version. He had that seemingly perplexed look on his face, the eyes drawn diagonally upward in an innocent slant, an expression that was entirely Avram, and then she knew she was right: he was seducing them with a subtlety and cunning that she did not know he had, with a whispered rhythm that was new to them. They responded immediately, unable to resist the temptation, and they too whispered and murmured, and suddenly they were engaged in a conversation of hints and secrets that only eleven-year-old boys could understand.

A breeze of enjoyment blew through the basement. The parents exchanged looks. The four boys' eyes shone, beads of sweat glistened on their faces, and they wiped them away with a sleeve or a tongue dart-ing over lips, and kept on chattering and mumbling in drum-speak, in a thick whisper she had never heard before, which circled around her, approaching and retreating.

A minute went by, and another, until the four of them could no longer continue whispering, and all at once they burst out in a storm of thunder and lightning, and sang the opening song again at the top of their lungs, and the audience sang with them and went wild. Ofer retreated to his usual position, gathered up his forces, and shut the door, looking serious and somewhat gloomy, but his forehead still bore the occasional wrinkle, in which she could read something of his tempestu-ous thoughts. A flush of pride burned on his cheeks, and she thought: Avram, you are so much with us. Ilan put his hand on her thigh. Ilan, who almost never touched her in public.

. . .

"You can't sleep with me," she said ponderously.

"I can't sleep with you," he echoed in a hollow voice.

"You're incapable," she said and put down the knife and stood motionless at the sink.

"I'm incapable," said he, curiously probing for the meaning of the strange tone in her voice.

She reached out sideways without looking at him, found his hand, and pulled it to her.

"Ora." His voice was hesitant, cautionary.

She took the knife out of his hand. He did not resist. She lingered for a moment, her head bowed, as though seeking advice from someone invisible. Maybe even from the old Avram. Then she led him to the bedroom. He walked with her as though he had no volition. As though all his vitality had leaked out. She lay him on his back and placed a pillow under his head. Her face was close to his. She kissed him lightly on his lips for the first time since he had come back and sat next to him on the edge of the bed and waited to understand.

"You can't sleep with me," she said after a moment in a slightly firmer voice.

"I can't sleep with you," he repeated, astonished at her intention, and very hesitant.

"You simply cannot sleep with me now," she said decisively, and started to take her blouse off.

"I simply cannot," he repeated suspiciously.

"Even if I take my shirt off, it won't make any difference to you."

"Even then." He looked at her blouse without any expression as it fell to the floor.

"Or even if I take off, let's say . . . this," she added with total matter-of-factness and hoped Avram could not sense her embarrassment as she took off her bra—he had once suggested calling bras "booby-traps"—"it wouldn't interest you at all." Without looking at him, she felt for his hand and placed it on her right breast, the smaller and more sensitive one, which the old Avram had always turned to first. She softly caressed herself with his hand.

"Nothing at all," he murmured and watched his hand stroke the pure, delightful breast, and those words, "pure, delightful breast," pierced him from a great distance, through a thick coat of dullness.

"And not even when I . . ." She stood up and slowly took off her pants, her hips moving softly, still asking herself what she was really doing, knowing that only when she did it would she understand.

"Nothing," he said carefully, and looked at her long, pale legs.

"Or even this," she murmured, and took off her underwear and stood facing him naked, tall, thin, and downy. "Take off your clothes," she whispered. "No, let me undress you, you have no idea how long I haven't been waiting for this moment." She took off his shirt and pants. He lay in his underwear looking forlorn. "You can't sleep with me," she said as though to herself and ran her hand down his body, from his chest to his toes, and lingered on his many scars, stitches, scabs. He said nothing. "Say it," she said, "say, I can't sleep with you, say it after me, say it with me."

"I can't sleep with you." His chest rose and expanded slightly.

"You're simply incapable."

"I'm incapable."

"And even if you really want to, you won't be able to fuck me."

"Even if I . . ." He swallowed.

"Even if you're dying to feel my legs around you, hugging you and tightening against you." She knelt on the floor by his side and rolled down his underwear, and her hand hovered over his penis, and he let out a soft moan. "And even if my tongue rolls and glides on it," she said with complete nonchalance, almost indifference, and felt that she had finally found the right voice, and that only thanks to the old Avram did she know how to do what she was doing. She dotted him with quick spots of wetness and rounded her lips around him. "Even if your tongue—" Avram murmured and choked up, and his hand lifted up of its own accord and came to rest on his forehead. "And even if, say," she whispered in between licking and lightly sucking. "Even if," he sighed and propped himself up on his elbows to see her body crouched on all fours next to his, and he stared at the way her beautiful long white back arched, and at the curve of her ass, and at the impertinent little breast hidden under her arm. "And even if maybe it roused a little, completely against its will, of course," Ora added and ran her damp fingers over his glans, and tightened her grip, and sucked and bit lightly. "Even if it—" Avram murmured and licked his dry lips and his Adam's apple bobbed up and down. "And even if I kiss and lick at it and feel it warm and throbbing in my hand." "Even if you feel it warm," Avram groaned, and a thread of passion suddenly glowed red inside him. "And even if, for example, I take it all deep inside my mouth," she said with a calmness that surprised her, and did not take him into her mouth, and Avram moaned and moved his hips up toward her, longing to be gathered in. "And even if it stays asleep and keeps on dreaming inside my mouth," she said, and enveloped him with her mouth. "Even if it—" Avram's head fell back and his eyes rolled up, and he deeply inhaled the fullness that whispered in his thighs.

Ora dozes. Lying on her back, her head turned to one side, her face is tranquil and beautiful. Next to her ear, alongside a stem of onion weed, three fire bugs crawl in single file, gleaming like tiny red shields. In the shadow of her feet, hidden beneath some fringed rue, swallowtail caterpillars swell in black and yellow, batting their feelers against enemies, real and imagined. Avram looks at her. His eyes scan and caress her face.

"I was thinking," his voice suddenly pipes up.

"What?" Ora awakes immediately.

"I woke you . . ."

"Never mind. What were you saying?"

"When you told me about his shoes, the big ones, I wondered if you remember all kinds of things."

"Like what?"

He laughs awkwardly. "You know. Like, how he started to walk, or how—"

"How he started to *walk*?"

"Yes, the beginning . . ."

"Ofer? As a baby?"

"Because we talked about how he walked, and I was thinking—"

She laughs too, but there is something unpleasant in her giggle, exposing how completely she has accepted the fact that he never thought about Ofer as flesh and blood, as a human being who once, at some moment in time, had stood up on a pair of tiny legs and started to walk.

"It was when we still lived in Tzur Hadassah," she says quickly, before he can take it back. "He was thirteen months old, and I remember it really well." She pulls herself up into a seated position, rubs her eyes, and yawns. "Sorry," she says with a strained jaw and clumsily covers her mouth. She has a pleasant sensation in her limbs. She's had a good nap, but she hopes it won't keep her awake at night. "Should I tell you?"

He nods.

"Ilan and Adam and I were in the kitchen. I remember how crowded it always was in there, before we did the renovations." She gives him a sideways glance. "Do you really want me to?"

"Yes, yes, why are you—"

She folds her legs beneath her. Every sentence she utters seems to contain firecrackers of memory and new information that could hurt him. For example, the slightly dark kitchen, and its smallness, and its crowded aromas, and the damp stains on the ceiling, and how she'd made love with him there once when they were young, standing up with her back against the pantry door. She felt bad telling him that they'd renovated the kitchen, as though by doing so they had removed all traces of him.

"The three of us were in the kitchen, us and Adam, and Ofer was playing on the rug in the living room. We were talking, chattering, it was in the evening. I was probably cooking something, maybe frying an omelet, and Ilan was probably making spaghetti. I'm just guessing now. And Adam . . . I think he was already sitting on a proper chair by then. Yes, of course, he was four and a half or so, right? So we'd already switched the high chair to Ofer." She speaks slowly. Her hands move, furnishing the picture in her mind, positioning the actors and props in their places. "And I suddenly noticed that it was very quiet in the living room. And you know, when you have a baby—" Avram blinks to indicate, to warn her, that he doesn't know, and Ora, without thinking, blinks twice: *Now you do know*—"when you have a baby, you always have one ear tuned to him, especially when he's not right next to you. And somehow you're always picking up little signals, every few seconds. A cough or a sniffle or a mumble, and then you—I—can relax for a few seconds." She examines his face. "Should I go on?"

"Yes."

"Are you interested?"

He shrugs. "I don't know."

"You don't know?"

"No."

She sighs. "Where was I?"

"It was quiet in the living room."

"Yes." She takes a deep breath and chooses not to respond to the insult. At least he's honest, she says to herself. At least he says exactly what he feels.

"I realized immediately that I wasn't getting the signal. And so did Ilan. Ilan had the instincts of an I-don't-know-what. Of an animal," she says, and Avram picks up what she isn't saying: Ilan took good care of your boy. Ilan was a good choice. For both of us. She can barely resist describing what she now remembers, a series of scenes in which Ilan uses his teeth to remove a tiny splinter from Ofer's foot; Ilan licks a speck out of Ofer's eye; Ofer lies on Ilan, who lies in the dentist's chair and strokes and hypnotizes Ofer with soft purring breaths—"Ofer got the injection and my whole mouth went numb," he tells her later.

"So I rush to the living room and I see Ofer standing in the middle of the room with his back to me, and it was obvious that he'd already taken a few steps."

"On his own?"

"Yes. From the round table, you remember that low wooden table we found in a field once, when the three of us were hiking, a kind of round thing that was used to store cable?"

"Something from the electrical company . . ."

"You and Ilan rolled it all the way home."

"Yes, sure." He smiles. "That thing still exists?"

"Of course it does. When we moved to Ein Karem we took it with us." They both laugh in astonishment.

"And Ofer," she continues, and draws a thin line in the dirt with her finger, "must have moved from that table to the big brown couch—"

I remember, Avram's face says.

"And from there he walked to the floral armchair—"

"I still have its sister to this day," Avram murmurs.

"Yes, I saw that," Ora notes with a grimace. "And from there, I guess, he went toward the bookcase, the brick bookcase—"

"The red bricks—"

"That you and Ilan used to pick up all over the place—"

"Ahh, my bookcase."

Ora wipes the dirt off her hand. "This is all guesses, you see, 'cause I don't really know exactly how he walked, what his route was. By the time I got to the living room he was already standing a few steps beyond the bookcase, and then he didn't have anything more to hold on to, nothing, so he was walking in an open space."

It takes off inside her now, the greatness and the wonder of the act, the bravery of her little astronaut.

"And I actually stopped breathing. So did Ilan. We were afraid to startle him. He stood with his back to us." She smiles, her gaze lost in that room, and Avram steals a look and draws his face in the same direction. And Ilan, she remembers, came up and hugged her from behind. He steadied her and crossed his arms over her belly, and they stood together quietly, swaying in a sort of muted coo.

A feathery quiver in her back climbs up and spreads around her neck and takes hold of the roots of her hair. She silently allows Avram to look at the scene: the room he knows so well, with its jumble of furniture, and Ofer standing there, a crumb of life in an orange Winnie-the-Pooh T-shirt.

"And of course I couldn't help it, and I laughed, and the sound startled him and he tried to turn around and fell over."

The soft, padded bump as his diaper hit the rug. The heavy head rocking back and forth. The insult at being surprised in this way, and then the wonderment on his face as he turned to her, only to her, as though asking her to interpret what he had just done.

"And where was Adam?" Avram asks from somewhere in the distance.

"Adam? He was still in the kitchen, I suppose, probably kept on eating—" She stops: How did he realize so quickly that Adam was left on his own, abandoned? Why did he rush to take his side? "But when he heard my laughter and Ilan's cheers, he jumped up and came running."

Alive and lucid she sees it: Adam grabs Ilan's pants with his fist, head cocked to one side to examine his little brother's achievement. His lips curl into a grimace that gradually, over the years, through the slow process of sculpting the soul in the flesh, would become a permanent feature.

"Listen, the whole thing lasted three or four seconds, it wasn't some kind of saga. And the three of us quickly ran over to Ofer and hugged him, and of course he wanted to get up again. From the minute he learned how to stand up, you couldn't stop him."

She tells him how hard it was to put Ofer down at night. He kept standing up, holding on to the wooden bars and pulling himself up, and he would stand there, then collapse with exhaustion, then stand up again. In the middle of the night, confused, crying, longing to sleep, he'd get up and just stand there. And when she changed his diaper, or tried to sit him in his chair to eat, or when she strapped him into the car seat, he constantly squirmed and pushed his way up, as if a big spring were launching him, as if gravity were reversed in him.

She sighs. "Do you really want to hear all this, or is it just to make me feel good?"

He produces a slightly diagonal nod, which she has trouble interpreting. Perhaps he means both things? And why not, in fact? This is something, too. Take what there is.

"Where was I?"

"He fell."

"Oh," she groans in painful surprise, the air slashed out of her in one sweep. "Don't say that."

"I wasn't thinking. I'm sorry, Ora."

"No, it's okay. You should know that when I talk about him with you, he's all right, he's protected."

"How?"

"I don't know. That's what I feel. He's preserved."

"Yes."

"Does that sound crazy?"

"No."

"Should I tell you more?"

"Yes."

"Say it with words."

"Tell me more. About him."

"About Ofer."

"About Ofer, tell me about Ofer."

"So we helped him up"—her eyes flutter for a moment, having seen an ungraspable picture: he said "Ofer"; he touched Ofer—"and we stood him on his feet and held out our arms and called him to us, and he walked again, very slowly, wobbling—"

"To who?"

"What?"

"To which one of you?"

"Oh." She strains her memory, surprised by his new sharpness, the dim flash of determination in his face. Just like long ago, she thinks, when he was intent on understanding something new, an idea, a situation, a person, and he would circle around and around in a slow gallop, very lightly, with that predatory glint in his eye.

Then she remembers. "To Adam. Yes, of course. That's who he walked to."

How could she have forgotten? Tiny Ofer, very serious and focused, looking intently ahead with his mouth open and his arms straight in front of him. His body rocked back and forth and one hand dropped and grasped the wrist of the other, declaring himself a closed, independent, self-sufficient system. She can see it alive and sharp: she and Ilan and Adam stand across from him, some distance from one another, holding their hands out, calling, "Ofer, Ofer," laughing, tempting him, "Come to me."

As she recounts the story, she realizes something she missed at the time: the moment of Ofer's first choice between them, and his distress when they forced him to choose. She shuts her eyes and tries to guess his thoughts. He had no words, after all, just the inner push-and-pull, and she and Ilan and Adam cheered and danced around him, and Ofer was torn as only a baby can be torn. She rushes away from his distress, and her face is already lighting up with Adam's astonished glee when Ofer finally turned to him. His amazement and happiness and pride momentarily erased the grimace and turned it into an excited smile of disbelief at being chosen, at being wanted. A stream of pictures, sounds, and smells churns inside her, everything coming back now—how Adam had welcomed Ofer when she and Ilan brought him home from the hospital, just over a year before that day. She has to tell Avram about that, but maybe not now, not yet, she mustn't flood him, but she tells him anyway: "Adam jumped up and down and went wild, and his eyes burned with electric fear, and he hit his own cheeks with both hands, slapping himself hard and shouting wildly, 'I'm happy! I'm so happy!' "

Then Adam made the same high squeaks that used to erupt from the depths of his body every time he went near Ofer's crib for the first few months, a series of small uncontrollable shrieks, an almost animalistic mixture of affection and jealousy and uncontainable excitement. That was exactly how he chirped that day, when Ofer wobbled over to him at the first moment of choice. Or perhaps they were different chirps. "What do I know? Maybe he was guiding and encouraging Ofer in a language only the two of them knew."

Ofer took another step, then another. He walked without falling, and perhaps thanks to his brother's chirps, to which he had tied his willpower, he managed to maintain some stability. Like a tiny airplane in a storm, homing in on a beam of light from a control tower, he walked over and collapsed into his brother's arms, and the two of them rolled on the rug, embraced and squirmed and shrieked with laughter. She suddenly feels like writing down this little memory so it won't slip away for another twenty years. She just wants to describe the seriousness of Ofer as he walked, and Adam's screeching excitement, and his huge relief, and above all, their puppy-like embrace of each other. That was the moment they truly became brothers, the moment Ofer chose Adam, the moment Adam, perhaps for the first time in his life, truly believed he had been chosen. Ora smiles, bewitched by the heap of her children on the rug, and thinks how clever Ofer was, because he knew how to give himself to Adam, and because he carefully avoided getting trapped in the thicket of secrets and silences that lurked between her and Ilan's open arms.

"So that was how he walked for the first time," she sums up hastily, exhausted, and gives Avram a strained smile.

"The second time."

"What do you mean?"

"You said so."

"What?"

"That you didn't see the first time, the real first steps."

She shrugs. "Oh, yes, that's true. But really what does it—"

"No, nothing."

She wonders whether this is some strange insistence on historical accuracy, or perhaps a hint of haggling with her and with Ilan, a sort of "I didn't and you didn't, either."

"Yes," she says, "you're absolutely right."

They look at each other for a moment, and she knows: it's haggling. And perhaps even more than that, it's the settling of accounts. The discovery is frightening, but also exciting, like the first sign of an uprising, the rousing of someone who has been depressed and silenced and dormant for too long. Then it occurs to her that when Ofer rolled over onto his back for the first time, no one was there, either. Is that true? She checks quickly with herself. True. I swear: Ilan went over to his crib one afternoon and found him lying quietly on his back, looking at his blue elephant mobile—she even remembers the mobile, in its every detail, with utter clarity now. It's as though someone has come along and removed a cataract that had covered her eye for years. And when he sat up for the first time he was alone too, she thinks with increasing bewilderment. And when he stood up for the first time.

For one moment, no longer, she hesitates, and then she gives Avram a simple reportage of facts, the facts that now belong to him too, because he has finally come to demand them. His eyes narrow: she can almost see the wheels in his mind straining.

"Somehow the first time he did all these things—turning over, sitting up, standing, walking—he really was alone."

"So," Avram murmurs, staring at his fingertips, "is that something, you know, unusual?"

"Honestly, I've never thought about it before. I never made a list of all the first things he did. But for instance, when Adam sat up for the first time, or stood up or walked, I was with him. Well, I told you that for the first three years of his life we were never apart. And I remember how he glowed every time he accomplished something like that, and Ofer, yes, Ofer is—"

"Alone," Avram quietly finishes, his features suddenly softening.

Ora gets up and hurries to her backpack, digs through it urgently, and pulls out a thick notebook with dark blue binding. From a side pocket she takes out a pen. Without introductions, still standing with her head slightly tilted, she writes on the first page: *Ofer walked funny. I mean, his walk, at first, was strange. Almost from the moment he started walking he used to veer around all sorts of obstacles that no one else could see, and it was really funny to watch. He would avoid something nonexistent, or draw back from some monster that must have been lurking for him in the middle of the room, and you could absolutely not convince him to step on that tile! It's a bit like watching a drunk walk (but a drunk with a method!). Ilan and I agree that he has a private map in his head, and he always follows it.*

She cautiously walks back to her spot, puts the open notebook on the ground, and sits down next to it, very straight, then looks at Avram.

"I wrote about him."

"About who?"

"Him."

"What for?"

"I don't know. I just—"

"But the notebook—"

"What about it?"

"Why did you bring it?"

She stares at the lines she wrote. The words seem to scurry about on the page, wagging their fingers at her, calling her to go on, not to stop now. "What did you ask?"

"What did you drag a notebook along for?"

She stretches, tired suddenly, as though she'd written whole pages. "I don't know, I was just thinking I'd write down all sorts of things we saw on the way, Ofer and I. A kind of travel diary. When we used to go on vacations abroad with the boys, we always wrote our experiences together."

She was the one who used to write. Every evening in the hotel, or on rest stops, or during long drives. They refused to cooperate—Ora hesitates, and decides not to tell Avram this—and the three of them affectionately mocked her endeavor, which they thought was unnecessary and childish. She insisted: "If we don't write things down, we'll forget them." They said, "But what is there to remember? That the old man in the boat threw up on Dad's foot? That they brought Adam eel, instead of the schnitzel he ordered?" She wouldn't answer, thinking, You'll see how one day you'll want to remember how we had fun, how we laughed—how we were a family, she thinks now. She always tried to be as detailed as possible in those diaries. Whenever she didn't feel like writing, when her hand was lazy, or her eyelids drooped with exhaustion, she would imagine the years to come when she might sit with Ilan, preferably on long winter evenings, with a mug of mulled wine, the two of them wrapped in plaid blankets, reading each other passages from the scrapbooks, which were decorated with postcards and menus and tickets from tourist sites, plays, trains, and museums. Ilan guessed it all, of course, including the plaid. She was always so transparent to him. "Just promise you'll shoot me before that happens to me," he told her. But he said that about so many things . . .

How did it happen, she wonders, that while I only softened with the years, the three of them grew tougher? Maybe Ilan's right, maybe it's because of me that they hardened. They hardened against me. A good cry would do me some good now, she notes to herself.

When she opens her eyes, Avram is sitting across from her, leaning with his backpack against a rock, delving into her.

Once, when he used to look at her like that, she would immediately open herself to him, allowing him to see into her inner depths unhindered. She did not let anyone else see inside her like that. Not even Ilan.

But she was easy with Avram—such a horrible word, "easy"; she was always easy with Avram, letting him see all of her, almost from the first moment she met him, because she had a feeling, a conviction that there was something inside her, or someone, perhaps an Ora more loyal to her own essence, more precise and less vague, and Avram seemed to have a way to reach her. He was the only one who could truly know her and could pollinate her with his look, with his very existence, and without him she simply did not exist, she had no life, and so she was his, she was his prerogative.

That's how it was when she was sixteen, and nineteen, and twenty-two, but now she pulls her gaze sharply away from him, fearing he might hurt her there, punish her for something, take his revenge on her there. Or perhaps he will discover that there's nothing inside her anymore, that his old Ora has dried up and died along with what dried up and died inside him.

They sit quietly, digesting. Ora hugs her knees, rationalizing that she isn't all that accessible and permeable even to herself anymore, and that even she herself doesn't go near that place inside her. It must be that she's growing old, she decides—for some time now she's had a strange eagerness to pronounce her aging, impatient for the relief that comes with a declaration of total bankruptcy. That's how it goes. You say goodbye to yourself even before other people start to, softening the blow of what will inevitably come.

Later, much later, Avram gets up, stretches, gathers some firewood in a pile, and surrounds it with a circle of stones. Ora senses new purpose in his movement, but she knows herself and remains cautious: she might simply be convincing herself that she's seeing things—seeing Avram in Avram's shadow.

She takes out an old towel and spreads it on the ground. She lays out plastic plates and cutlery and hands Avram two overripe tomatoes and a cucumber to chop. She has crackers too, and canned corn and tuna fish and a small bottle of olive oil that Ofer loves, from the Dir Rafat monastery, which she was planning to surprise him with. She had other little surprises that were supposed to make him happy on their trip. Where is Ofer now? She isn't sure whether she should think about him or let him be. What does he need from her now? Her eyes are drawn to the open notebook. Maybe the answer is there. She wants to close it, but cannot. It's all exposed there, yet to close it would be to stifle it, even to stamp it out. She gets down on one knee, straightens the corner of the towel, and weighs it down with a stone. As she does so she pulls the notebook to her and reads what she has written. She is surprised to find that in just a few lines she skipped from past to present: *Ofer walked funny . . . It's a bit like watching a drunk . . . Ilan and I agree that . . .*

Ilan would have something to say about that.

Avram lights a piece of newspaper and coaxes the fire to the twigs. Ora stares at the paper, wondering what day it's from, and looks away from the headlines. Who knows how far things have gone there? She quickly shuts the notebook and waits for the paper to be consumed. Avram sits down opposite her and they eat silently. Actually, Avram eats. He boils water for a Cup-a-Soup and gobbles down two of them, one after the other, claiming he's addicted to MSG. She asks casually about his nutritional habits. Does he cook? Does someone cook for him?

"Sometimes. Depends," he says.

She watches his appetite in astonishment. She herself can't put a bite in her mouth. In fact, she realizes that her stomach has locked up since she left home. Even at the feast in the house of the laughing woman, the baby's mother, she could hardly swallow the food. Maybe one good thing has come of this trip after all. Then, as quick as she can, like someone pickpocketing herself, she reaches out to the notebook and opens it.

I'm afraid to forget him. His childhood, I mean. I often get confused between the two boys. Before they were born I thought a mother remembers every child separately. Well that's not exactly how it is. Or maybe with me it's especially not that way. And stupidly, I didn't keep a notebook for each boy, with their development and all the clever things they did since they were born. When Adam was born I didn't have the mind for that with everything that was going on, when Ilan left us. And when Ofer was born I didn't either (again because of all the complications back then—apparently every time I give birth there's something going on). And I thought that maybe now, on this hike, I would write down a few things I still remember. Just so they'll finally be written down somewhere.

The stream runs in the distance. Evening gnats hum, and crickets chirp madly. A branch cracks in the fire, flicking charred specks over the notebook. Avram gets up and moves the backpacks away from the fire. She is surprised: his movements really are more confident, lighter.

"Coffee, Ofra?"

"What did you call me?"

He laughs, very embarrassed.

She laughs too, her heart pounding.

"So, coffee?"

"Can you wait? I'll just be a minute."

He shrugs his shoulders, finishes eating, and arranges Ofer's sleeping bag like a pillow. He sprawls out, crosses his arms behind his neck, and looks up at the sheltering branches and hints of dark sky. He thinks about the woman with the crimson thread walking all the way down the country. He sees the procession of exiles. Long lines of people with bowed heads come out from every populated area, from the cities and the kibbutzim, to join the main line, the long one, which moves slowly down the spine of the land. When he was in solitary confinement in Abbasiya Prison and thought Israel no longer existed, he saw the picture in detail—the babies on shoulders, the heavy suitcases, the empty, extinguished eyes. But the woman walking with the crimson thread gives some comfort. You could imagine, for example, he thinks, sucking on a piece of straw, that in every town and village and kibbutz there was someone stealthily tying his own thread to hers. And that way, secretly, a tapestry was being woven all over the country.

Ora bites the tip of her pen and clicks it against her teeth. His slip of the tongue a moment ago confused her, and she has to make an effort to get back to where she was.

Ofer was born in a routine delivery, nothing difficult, and very quick. Maybe twenty minutes from when Ilan got me to the hospital. It was Hadassah Mount Scopus. We got there at around seven a.m., after my water had broken at six or so, in my sleep.

Not exactly sleep, she writes, and gives Avram a sideways glance, but he's still pondering the sky, lost in a thought that jerks the length of straw in his mouth this way and that. *There was something going on and my water broke in bed. And when I realized that's what it was, I mean, that nothing else made sense under the circumstances, we got organized quickly. Ilan had already prepared bags for me and for him, it was all arranged, written instructions, phone numbers, phone tokens, etc., Ilan being Ilan. We phoned Ariela to come and stay with Adam and take him to day care later. He slept all night and never knew a thing.*

Ofer was born at seven twenty-five a.m. It was a very easy, quick delivery. I got there and gave birth. They hardly had time to prepare me. Gave me an enema and sent me to the bathroom. I felt strong pressure in my stomach, and as soon as I sat down on the toilet, I could feel him coming out! I yelled for Ilan, and he came in and just picked me up the way I was, and put me down on a bed in the corridor, and shouted for a nurse. Together they pushed me, running, to the large delivery room, which by the way was where I had Adam (in the same room!), and three more pushes, he was out!

Her face glows, and she smiles generously at Avram. He responds with a questioning smile.

Ofer weighed three kilos six hundred. Pretty large, based on my limited sample. Adam was barely two kilos (minus three grams!). They've come along nicely since then, the two of them.

That's it. That is exactly what she wanted to write down. She takes a deep breath. Just for that it was worth lugging the notebook all this way. Now she's ready to eat. A sudden hunger gnaws at her. But she sucks on the pen for a moment longer, wondering if there's anything else to add about the birth. She shakes out her strained wrist. A high school kind of pain, she thinks: How often do I find myself writing by hand?

The midwife was called Fadwa, I think, or Nadwa? From Kfar Raami anyway. I met her another few times during the two days I spent there, and we chatted a little. I was interested to know who this girl was, whose hands were the first to touch Ofer when he came into the world. A single woman. Strong, a feminist, really sharp, and very funny, she always made me laugh.

Ofer's feet were slightly blue. When he was born he hardly cried, just made one short sound and that was it. He had huge eyes. Exactly Avram's eyes.

She turns on a flashlight and reads what she's written. Maybe she should be more detailed? She reads it again and finds she likes the style. She knows what Ilan would say about it, and how he would erase her exclamation marks, but Ilan will probably never read it.

But maybe there is room for a little more detail? Facts, not embellishments. What else happened there? For some reason she goes back to Adam's birth again, a long and difficult delivery, and to how she kept trying to make the midwife and the nurses like her, wanting them so badly to admire her endurance and to praise her when they talked in the nurses' room and compare her to the other mothers, who screamed and wailed and sometimes cursed. How much effort she put into ingratiating herself at the most important moments in her life, Ora thinks sadly. Her legs are starting to lose their feeling. She tries sitting on a different rock, then another, and eventually goes back to the ground. These are no conditions for writing an autobiography, she thinks.

And after a few minutes they laid Ofer on me. It bothered me that he was wrapped in a hospital blanket. I wanted to be naked with him. Everyone else in that room except the two of us was completely unnecessary for me. And Avram wasn't there.

She gives him a cautious glance. Maybe she should erase the last few words. Maybe she'll want Ofer to read this one day? Maybe she and Ilan will—

In her gut she begins to feel disquiet. Who is she writing this for? And why? There are almost two pages now. How has she produced two pages? Avram lies on his back on the other side of the fire, which by now is only a heap of glowing embers. He faces the sky. His beard looks disheveled. Someone should tidy up his beard. She studies his face: at twenty he started going bald, from the forehead back, the first in his age group, but by that time he'd grown an impressive head of strong, wild hair, and he had thick sideburns down to the middle of his cheek, which made him look even older than he already did, and gave him—as he once wrote to her in a letter—*the face of a moist-lipped, avaricious, Dickensian landlord.* As usual, his description was right, and there was no point arguing with him. He always had picturesque depictions, so cruel and captivating—particularly the way he described his own appearance and personality. It was thanks to these descriptions—she only now realizes—that he was able to seduce everyone else into seeing him through his own eyes, and perhaps that was how he protected himself from any overly autonomous gazes that might have caused real pain. Ora smiles at him furtively, with amused appreciation, as though discovering after the fact that someone had played a clever and incredibly successful trick on her.

And perhaps also from gazes that are too loving, she adds in the notebook without thinking, and looks at the words with some surprise. She quickly crosses them out with one sharp line.

Later, when all the doctors and midwives and nurses and the guy who stitched me up had left, I unwrapped Ofer and held him to my bosom.

That last word sends a warm tremor through her body. What does that tremor remind her of? What is it bringing back to her now? *To my bosom*, she whispers inside, and her body replies sweetly: Avram. He used to lick the tiny hairs on her cheeks, beneath her temples, and murmur, "the segment of thy temples," or "feathery down." As he held her and dreamily whispered, "the curvature of your hips," or "the silk behind your knees," she would smile to herself and think: Look at him working up his heart with words. She quickly learned that when she overcame her shyness and repeated into his ear, "feathery down," "you against my bosom," and other such phrases, he hardened inside her.

The way Ofer touched me, right from the first moments, from the minute he was born, was the most comforting, simple, smooth touch anyone had ever given me. Ilan once said that Ofer seemed, from the beginning, like a person who was at peace with his position. A person perfectly adapted to his life. And it was so true, at least when he was a child, not so much later. We went through all sorts of periods with him. Difficult things, too. In fact recently, in the army, we had a complicated situation with him. For me, mainly. Because they, the three of them, got over it very nicely.

Maybe I shouldn't write this, but because of that tranquillity Ofer had at first, I always had the illusion, or some sort of faith, that with him I could guess the future with some certainty (and by the way, Ilan admitted it too, so it's not just my notorious naïveté). I mean, I thought that with him we could guess, more or less, what kind of person he would grow up to be, and how he would act in all sorts of situations and that we could know there would be no surprises along the way. (Talking about surprises, I forgot to mention that I'm in the Galilee now, in some valley, and his father Avram (!) is lying not far from me (!!), dozing, or watching the stars.)

She takes a deep breath, only now truly grasping that she is here, far away from her life. Her heart surges with gratitude for the darkness full of whistling and chirping crickets, for the night itself, which for the first time since she left is taking her in with a tender generosity, agreeing to hide her away from everything at the bottom of this remote ravine, and even giving her the trees and the bushes, whose scents waft sweetly but sharply toward the nocturnal butterflies.

I'm going back a little, to just after the birth: Ilan stood next to us and watched. He had a strange look on his face. There were tears in his eyes. I remember that, because when Adam was born Ilan was completely cool and functional (and I didn't realize that those were actually the signs of what was starting to bubble up inside him). But with Ofer he cried. And I thought that was a good sign, because throughout the pregnancy I was afraid he was going to leave me again after the birth, and those tears reassured me a little.

Her lips are slightly open and her nostrils widen. She stays with the momentum: *With Ilan, it's when he laughs that he looks sad, even a little cruel sometimes (because his eyes somehow stay distant), and when he cries he always looks as if he's laughing.*

And I suddenly realized that Ilan and I were completely alone with the baby.

I remember that it got very quiet suddenly, and I was afraid he would try to crack a joke. Because Ilan, when he's tense, he has to force a joke out, and that was so wrong for me. I didn't want anything to grate on our first moments together.

But Ilan was clever this time, and he didn't say anything.

He sat down next to us and didn't know what to do with his hands, and I saw that he wasn't touching Ofer. Then he said, "He has an observant look." I was glad that those were the first words he said about him—or that anyone in the world said about him. I never forget those words.

I took Ilan's hand and placed it on Ofer's. I could tell it was hard for him, and I felt Ofer respond immediately. His whole body tensed up. I interlaced my fingers with Ilan's, and together I stroked Ofer with him, back and forth along his body. I had already decided to call him Ofer. I'd considered other names while I was pregnant, but as soon as I saw him, I knew they weren't right. Not Gil or Amir or Aviv. They had too many I's, and he looked more like an O, calm and even a little grave (but with a drop of thoughtful distance, sort of observing, like an E). I said to Ilan: "Ofer." And he agreed. I realized I could have named him Melchizedek or Chedorlaomer and Ilan would agree, and I didn't like that, because I know Ilan, and obedience is not his strong suit, and besides, I was suspicious.

So I said, "Call him." Ilan murmured a slightly faded "Ofer." I said to Ofer: "That's your dad." I felt Ilan's fingers freeze in my hand. I thought it was all coming back. Now he'll get up and leave, it's some sort of reflex with him, to leave me when I give birth. Ofer fluttered his eyelids a few times, as though he was goading Ilan to talk already! And Ilan had no choice at that point, so he smiled crookedly and said, "Listen, pal, I'm your dad and that's that, no arguments."

She looks up at Avram and smiles distractedly, though with a glimmer of distant happiness, and sighs.

"What?" asks Avram.

"It's good."

Avram props himself up slightly. "What's good?"

"To write."

"So I hear," he says dismissively and turns away.

He, who wrote all his life, right up to the last minute, until the Egyptians came and more or less took the pen out of his hand. From six in the morning until ten at night, every day. And he wrote more than ever after he met Ilan and their bond was forged. She knows that that was when his engine was really started, because there was finally someone who truly understood him and competed with him and stimulated him. She thinks about everything that poured out of Avram in the six years after he met Ilan in the hospital—well, Ilan and her. Plays, poems, stories, comedy sketches, and mostly radio plays, which he and Ilan wrote and recorded on the clunky Akai reel-to-reel in the shed in Tzur Hadassah. She remembers one series—it had at least twenty episodes; Avram liked horribly long epics—about a world in which all human beings are children in the morning, adults at noon, elderly in the evening, and back again. And there was a serial play that described a world where humans only communicate honestly and openly in their sleep, through dreams, and know nothing about it when they awake. One of their more successful series, in her opinion, was about a jazz fan who is swept into the ocean and reaches an island inhabited by a tribe that has no music at all, not even whistling or humming, and he gradually teaches them about what they lack. Avram and Ilan created a world in almost everything they did. Avram usually came up with the ideas, and Ilan would try to anchor him to reality as much as he could. Ilan collaborated on the writing and added "musical embellishments" on his saxophone, or with the help of his many albums. A Sambatyon River of ideas and inventions burst out of Avram—"My Golden Age," he called it once, after he had dried up.

For his twentieth birthday, she bought him his first idea book. She was sick of watching him turn the house upside down and his pockets— and hers—inside out as he desperately searched for his scraps of paper. A constant foliage of notes whirled around his head wherever he went. She scribbled a limerick on the first page of the notebook: "There was a young man who could write / Like a spring he gushed out, day and night. / All day long he would wander / Imagine and ponder / This notebook will be his delight." Within two months he'd filled up the entire thing and asked her to buy him a second one. "You inspire me," he said, and she laughed, as usual: "*Moi?* A bear of little brain like me?" She honestly could not understand how she could inspire anyone, and he looked at her warmly and said that now he knew what Sarah's laugh had sounded like, when she was told at the age of ninety that she would give birth to Isaac. He added that she didn't understand anything, about him or about inspiration. After that, Ora always bought his idea books. They had to be small enough to fit in the back pocket of his jeans, and he took them everywhere. He slept with them too, and kept at least one pen in every bed he slept in, so he could jot down nocturnal ideas. He wanted the notebooks to be very simple, no bells and whistles, although he did like the fact that she varied the colors and styles. The most important thing to him was that they came from her. They had to come from her, he stressed, and looked at her with such gratitude that it churned her insides. She felt ceremonious whenever she went to buy a new notebook. She browsed in different stationery shops, first in Haifa and then, after her army service, in Jerusalem, her new city, looking for a notebook that would be just right for the particular period, for the specific idea he was writing about, for his mood. She moans distractedly, tightens her legs together, and her stomach excites at the open pleasure with which he used to hold her notebooks: she liked to see him weigh the new notebook in his hand, feel it, smell it, flip through the pages quickly and greedily, like a card player, to see how many pages it had—how much pleasure was in store for him. A titillating, exposed, shameless pleasure. Once he told her—she never forgot it—that every time he wrote a new character he had to understand its body, that's where he started. He had to wallow in the character's flesh and saliva and semen and milk, feel the makeup of its muscles and tendons, whether its legs were long or short, how many steps it took to cross this or that room, how it ran for a bus, how tight its ass was when it stood facing a mirror, and how it walked, and ate, and how exactly it looked when it took a shit or danced, and if it climaxed with a shout or with modest, prudish moans. Everything he wrote had to be tangible and physical—"Like this!" he yelled, and held up one cupped hand, fingers spread, in a gesture that from anyone else would look rude and cheap, but from him, at least at that moment, was an overflowing basin of fervor and passion, as though he were palming a large, heavy breast.

Regretting the pain she has caused him, she quickly explains that she was just writing down a few lines about how Ofer was born. Just straight facts. "For posterity," she snorts.

Avram, in a more appeased voice, says, "Oh, well, that's good."

"Do you really think so?"

He straightens up on one elbow and prods the embers with a branch. "It's good to have it written down somewhere."

Ora, very carefully, asks, "Hey, have you written anything since then, over the years?"

Avram shakes his head briskly. "I'm done with words."

"I didn't make a baby book for Ofer. I didn't have the patience to sit down and write back then, and I always felt bad for not doing anything"—but what he just said diffuses inside her like poison. If he's done with words, how can she even dare to write anything?—"because if you don't write it down immediately, you don't remember. That's the way I am, and also so many things happen in the first few months. The child changes by the minute."

She's blathering, and they both know it. She is trying to dilute his avowal. Avram stares at the embers. All she can see is one cheek and one glimmering eye. This was exactly the cadence he used when he told Ilan he didn't want anything to do with life.

"For example," she says after a long silence, "I remember that he never gave himself over easily, Ofer. He wouldn't let you hug him. You could only hug him if he really wanted it. And he's still like that today," she adds, thinking about how lately he envelops her gingerly, carefully holding his body away from her breasts, bending over in a ridiculous arch as if God knows what! But when she was a girl, and her awkward father hugged her on rare family occasions, she would also arch her body so that he wouldn't really touch her. She longs so badly for one full, simple hug with her father now, but it's too late. Maybe she'll write about that too, in a few words, just so that one memory remains of that physical motion between her and her father.

Oh well, she thinks, and slams the notebook closed. This could go on forever. It's like walking around with a bucket of whitewash.

"When Ofer was a baby, he used to make this strong, sudden movement with his body"—she stops and sucks the tip of the pen—"or if I tried to breast-feed him when he was full, then he'd arch his whole body back and throw his head to one side." She demonstrates Ofer's stance, and unwittingly, her own embrace of him, linking her hands together away from her chest, and Avram stares at the empty space between her arms.

"He had such sharp movements. Full of character and willpower." Then she laughs. "You know, most of the time I completely idolized him. The way he knew exactly what he needed to know. The way he was perfect as a baby, while I"—she hesitates, her lip curling—"was a lousy mother."

"*You?*"

"Forget it. I don't want to get into that now. We're talking about Ofer. Listen to something else"—but she keeps it in her heart: *"You?"* A real outcry. What should she take from that? "He was a climbing baby. Ilan used to call him 'Ivy.' " She remembers with delight as it all comes back, wave upon wave, filling up with life, filling Ofer with life too, somewhere out there.

"I would hold him on me, and within a second he would start to climb up, slithering through my hands like a fish. He couldn't stay where I wanted him for one second. And always up, climbing, higher up, and it annoyed me sometimes, that motion of his, and the determination, like he was using me to get to something else, or someone else, someone more interesting." She laughs. "A bit like you, when you wanted something. When you had some new idea."

He says nothing.

"The way you would hunt, you know, when I told you about someone interesting I'd met, or a conversation I'd overhead on the bus. I'd see your wheels start to spin, so you could find out if it was right for a story, or a sketch, and in your mind you'd be trying out the different characters you could give the line to, or my laughter, or my breasts." Why torture him with this talk? she thinks. Yet she cannot stop. It's as though her nostalgia for him has become a strange, infectious aggression. "Or when you asked me to pose for you naked so you could write me, with words, not draw. I remember how I sat—I swear, I can't believe I did that—on the veranda facing the wadi, because it had to be outside, you insisted, remember? You said the light was better there. And I agreed of course, I did everything you asked back then, and I let you draw me with words, on the veranda, and of course God forbid Ilan should know about it. That was what we played at back then, or that was how you played me, and Ilan, with your parallel dimensions. So there I was, facing the wadi, naked, with the shepherds from Hussan and Wadi Fukin who may have been out there, you didn't care, you didn't care about anything when you needed something for your writing, when you were on fire"—Shut up, she thinks. Why are you attacking him? What's gotten into you? There's a statute of limitations on these things, isn't there?—"and me, I swear, I had chills all over from the way you broke me down into words. I wanted it so badly—you must have felt that—but at the same time I felt so exploited, as though you were looting my most private things, my skin and my flesh, and I didn't dare tell you, I mean it was impossible to talk to you when you were in that state." She shakes her head in bewilderment. "I was even a little afraid of you. You looked like a cannibal in those moments, but I loved that about you, the fact that you had no control over yourself, that you had no choice. I loved that so much about you."

"I wanted to write you like that every year," Avram suddenly grunts, and Ora stops, breathless. "I thought it was something I would do with you over the years, many years. Fifty years like that is what I wanted." His voice is dull and weary and seems to be coming from a great distance. "I thought . . . my plan was, once a year I would describe your body and face, every part of you, every change in you, word by word, throughout our lives together, and even if we weren't together, even if you kept being his. That you'd be my model, but for words."

She folds her legs beneath her body, agitated by the long, surprising monologue.

"I really only had time to do it twice: Ora at twenty, and Ora at twenty-one."

She doesn't remember that being his plan. Maybe she hadn't even known about it. He wasn't always capable of talking about his ideas. Sometimes he didn't want to. And usually, when he was in heat with creativity—that's how he referred to it—he could only let out slivers of thoughts, sentence fragments that did not always cohere outside his mind. When she didn't understand, he would start to dance around her in circles, whether they were in his room, on the street, in bed, in an open field, or on a bus. He would grimace with impatience and anger and gesticulate wildly, like someone gasping for air. She would feel her eyes glaze over: "Explain it again, but slower." Desperation darkened his look, and the loneliness—the exile—into which he felt pushed by her doubts, her caution, her clipped wings. He had such hostility toward her in those moments, perhaps because of his being doomed to fall deeply in love with a woman who could not understand him instantly—"with a hint and a wrinkle," he said, quoting Brenner, but she hadn't read Brenner: "All that breakdown and bereavement stuff is too depressing for me," she said. He loved her anyway, despite Brenner, despite Melville and Camus and Faulkner and Hawthorne. He loved her and lusted and longed for her and held on to her as though his life depended on it. And that was another thing she wanted to talk to him about on this journey, tomorrow or the next day. She wanted him to explain finally what he'd seen in her, to remind her of what she had possessed back then, so that perhaps she could take a little of it for herself now.

She grows irritable. Sparks of thought fly through her. She unfolds herself and gets up: "Is there a ladies' room around here?"

He points with his forehead into the darkness. She takes a roll of paper and walks away. She crouches down next to a thick shrub and pees. Drops splash on her shoes and pants. First thing tomorrow I have to take a shower and do some laundry, she thinks. For a moment she dares to contemplate what she lost: the ability to sit facing him, nude, another twenty-eight times, to look into his eyes and see the way he saw her. To see how, year after year, the words that described her slowly changed, different shadows cast on a familiar landscape. Perhaps it would have hurt less to grow old in his words. But no, she has no doubt. It would have hurt more.

After she finishes, she leans against a thin tree trunk in the dark and hugs herself, suddenly lonely. Pictures of herself over the years flutter by. Ora the teenager, Ora the soldier, pregnant Ora, Ora and Ilan, Ora with Ilan and Adam and Ofer, Ora with Ofer, Ora alone. Ora alone with all the years to come. What does he see in her today? Vicious words appear before her eyes: dry, shriveled, veins, moles, fat, lips, that lip of hers, breasts, limpness, stains, wrinkles, flesh, flesh.

From the darkness she sees him dissolve in the embers' red glow. He gets up and takes out two mugs from her backpack. He wipes them with his shirt. He pours water into the sooty *finjan*. He's making coffee for her. He pushes the notebook away so it doesn't get wet. His fingers hover on the blue binding, touching its texture. She thinks she can see him secretly assessing its thickness with his thumb.

Over the days and weeks after she slept with him in his apartment in Tel Aviv, Avram began to decline again, spending hours staring at the window or the wall, neglecting his body, not bathing or shaving, not answering the phone. And he withdrew from Ora. At first he made up excuses, then asked her explicitly not to come. When she came anyway, he tried to get her to leave. He was wary of being alone with her at home. She was frightened. Her thoughts constantly dwelled on him and what had happened that night. For weeks she could barely do anything.

The more he fled, the more she felt compelled to chase him. Time after time she tried to reassure him, to explain that all she wanted was for them to go back to the way they were. He pushed away, shook her off, and firmly refused to talk about that evening.

Then she discovered she was pregnant. After a month she finally managed to tell Avram. At first he froze. His face fossilized and his little remaining vitality vanished in an instant. Then he asked if she knew where to get an abortion. He would pay for it, he'd get a loan from the Ministry of Defense, no one would have to know. She refused even to hear about it. "It's too late for that anyway," she murmured, hurt and heartbroken, and he said that in that case he wanted nothing to do with her. She argued, tried to remind him of everything they meant to each other. He stood with a face of stone and stared somewhere above her head, so as not to risk looking at her stomach. Her head spun. She could barely stand up. She felt that if he kept this up a moment longer her body would simply spit out the fetus. She tried to grab his hand and put it on her stomach, but he let out a horrible shout. His eyes were mad with fury and raw hatred. Then he opened the door and practically kicked her out and left her standing there—so she felt—for thirteen years. And then, just before Ofer's bar mitzvah, but ostensibly unrelated to that date, he called her one evening without any explanations or apologies and suggested in his gruff voice that they meet in Tel Aviv.

When they met, he adamantly refused to hear about Ofer, or about Adam and Ilan. The photo album she'd spent weeks preparing, with carefully selected pictures of Ofer and the family, spanning thirteen years, remained in her bag. Avram told her at length about fishermen and vagrants he met on the beach in Tel Aviv, about the pub where he'd started working, about an action flick he'd seen four times, and the sleeping-pill habit he was trying to kick. He lectured her about the social ramifications and Catholic allusions in various computer games. She sat staring at his mouth, which did not stop gushing with words that seemed to have lost their content long ago. At times she thought he was making a great effort to prove that she could no longer expect anything of him. They sat for almost two hours on either side of a table in a noisy, ugly café. She kept drifting outside of herself to observe the two of them. They looked like Winston and Julia in *Nineteen-Eighty-Four*, when they met after being brainwashed and forced to betray each other. At a certain moment, for no apparent reason, Avram got up, said a formal goodbye, and walked away. She assumed she would not see him for another thirteen years, but roughly every six months he would invite her for another insipid, depressing meeting, until Ofer was drafted. That was when he informed her that he could not be in touch with her until Ofer's discharge.

But the day after she told him she was pregnant, the day after he threw her out of his home and his life, Ora put on a flowing white linen dress and went onto the porch outside the house in Tzur Hadassah. She stood there displaying her full glory, of which no one else was aware yet—even her mother hadn't noticed. She didn't know if Ilan was in the shed, but she had the feeling she was being watched from there.

At nine in the evening, after putting Adam to bed, she knocked on the shed door and Ilan opened straightaway. He was wearing the green T-shirt she liked and a pair of faded jeans she had once bought him. His bare, sinewy feet sent sparks through her. Behind his back she saw a remarkably monastic room. A cot, a desk, a chair, and a lamp. Bookshelves lined the walls. Ilan looked into her eyes and down to her still innocent-looking stomach, and the skin on his scalp stretched taut.

"It's from Avram," she said. She thought she sounded as if she were handing him a gift and declaring who had sent it. Then she realized perhaps that was the case. He stood there amazed and confused, and she, by the force of her new power, pushed him aside and walked in.

"When did this happen?" He flopped onto the bed.

"This is how you live?" She ran a finger over the books on a shelf. "*Tort Law and General Tort Theory, Collateral Law,*" she accentuated, stealing a look at the large spiral-bound notebooks on his table: property law, family law. "Ilan the student," she said, slightly pained, because she had always dreamed they would be students together—well, the three of them—and had hoped to spend hours and days with them on the Givat Ram campus, in lecture halls, in the library, on the lawn, in the cafeteria. But she had quit her studies as soon as Avram came home, and she wondered if she'd ever go back—what would she study now? Not back to social work, she didn't have the strength to spend months or years battling state authorities and officials. She could not tolerate any contact with rigidity, arbitrariness, and cruelty—not now, after the war, after Avram—and she knew from her one-year project how all these would echo through every meeting with the deputy coordinator of welfare in the Katamonim neighborhood. On the other hand, she wasn't drawn to anything academic or abstract. Something with her hands. That's what she wanted to do. Or with her body. Something simple and touching and unequivocal, and without a lot of words—most important, without words. Perhaps she could revive her childhood athletic career, this time as a teacher. Or maybe she could treat people, ease their pain—yes, why not, just as she had done for Avram during his years of hospitalization. But all that would probably be postponed for a while now. "To answer your question," she finally told Ilan with strange cheer, "it's been almost three months."

"Are you sure it's from him?"

"Ilan!"

Ilan buried his face in his hands, digesting. She suddenly felt important. Critical. She could even relax. She studied him, and for the first time she almost thanked him for what he had done to her by leaving. Amused, she observed the deliberations darting around beneath the smooth skin on his forehead. Ilan always had considerations and counter-considerations, she thought. Mainly counter-considerations.

"What does he say?"

"He doesn't want to see me." She pulled over the only chair in the room and sat down, her mind settled, her body settling. Her legs knew just how far apart to spread for a woman in her state. "And he wants me to have an abortion."

"No!" Ilan yelled and jumped off the bed. He held her hand in both of his.

"Hey, Ilan," she said softly, looking into his eyes, alarmed by the cyclone she saw in them: there were no considerations or reasonings, only naked, tortured darkness.

"Keep this child," he whispered urgently. "Please, Ora, don't do anything, don't hurt him."

"I'll have him in April." The simple sentence filled her with unimaginable strength, the seal of a secret partnership forged through those words between her body and the baby and time itself. But maybe it will be a girl, she thinks, daring to entertain the idea for the first time. Of course it will be a girl, she realizes with amazement. She feels a sudden clarity, the pressing intuition of a tiny girl splashing around inside her.

"Ora," Ilan said to his feet, "how would you feel about—"

"What?"

"I was thinking, don't jump up now, hear me out."

"I'm listening."

Ilan says nothing.

"What did you want to say?"

"I want to come home."

"Come home? Now?" She is utterly confused.

"I want us to get back together," he said, though his hardened expression seemed to contradict his words.

"But now?"

"I know it's—"

"With his child—"

"Would you be willing?"

And everything she had somehow held in and held back all those years burst out. She cried and bellowed, and Ilan held her and steadied her with his strong hands, his supple, rapacious body, and she pulled him to her, and they made love on the sagging cot, careful as they writhed not to hurt the little fingerling inside her. And Ilan, with his sweet smell, his large hands, and his unequivocal body: wanting, wanting, wanting her, how she had missed that protruding desire, and she answered him with torrents she did not know a pregnant woman was capable of.

At dawn, they walked arm in arm down the path to the house, and Ora saw the fig tree and the bougainvillea bow to them, and together they walked up the crooked concrete steps, and Ilan went inside. He let go of her arm and walked quietly through the rooms with his quick feline movements, and he peeked into Adam's room and came out, too quickly, and Ora knew there was still a long way to go. Together they made an early breakfast and went out onto the porch wrapped in a blanket to watch the sunrise. The sun lit up the garden and the wadi, shadows and all, and Ora thought that no one in the world could understand what had happened to them, only the two of them could understand, and that in itself was proof that they were right.

In the morning Adam got up and saw Ilan there and asked Ora, "Is that the man from the shed?"

Ilan said, "Yes, and you're Adam," and he held out his hand.

Adam clung to Ora, hid his face in her dressing gown, and from behind her leg he said, "I'm mad at you."

"Why?"

" 'Cause you didn't come."

"I was very silly, but now I'm here."

"Will you leave again?"

"No, I'll stay here forever."

Adam thought for a long while and looked at Ora for help. She smiled encouragingly, and he said, "And you'll be my daddy?"

"Yes."

Adam thought some more, his face turning red with the effort to understand, and finally he let out a sigh that tugged at Ora's heart, the sigh of a hopeless old man, and said, "Well, make me some cocoa, then."

That afternoon Ilan went to see Avram in Tel Aviv and came back a whole year later—that's how it felt to Ora—dejected and gray. He hugged her with all his body and mumbled that everything would be all right, maybe, or maybe not. She asked what happened, and he said, "Never mind, everything happened, we went through all possible situations. Bottom line, he doesn't want us in his life. You or me. Our story with him is over."

She asked if there was any chance Avram might be willing to meet with her, even for a few minutes, at least to say goodbye properly. "No chance," Ilan said, with an impatience that she did not like. "He doesn't want anything to do with life, that's what he said."

"What?" Ora whispered. "Is he talking about suicide?"

"I don't think so, he just doesn't want anything to do with life."

"But how can that be?" she shouted. "How can he turn his back like that and erase everything?"

"Do you really not understand him? Because I do. I so understand him." He grunted at Ora as though she were to blame for something or as though he envied Avram for now having an unshakable excuse to cut off his ties with human beings.

"Then why did you come back? Why do you even want to come back?"

He shrugged his shoulders and looked at her belly, and she exploded inside but said nothing, because what could she say?

That night they got into bed, he on his side and she on hers, as though years had not gone by without this routine and their familiar gestures, the shower, the brushing of teeth together, his sounds in the bathroom, the way he sat on the bed with his back to her, naked and glorious, and quickly put on his sweatpants, then lay down and stretched his body out with a pleasure she found jarring. Ora waited for him to quiet down and asked in the calmest voice she could produce whether he was only coming back to her for Avram—she motioned with her chin at her stomach—or because he loved her, too.

"I never stopped loving you even for one day. How is it possible not to love you?" he replied.

"Well, obviously it's possible. Avram doesn't love me anymore, and I don't really love myself."

Ilan wanted to ask, what about him—how did she feel about him? But he said nothing, and she understood, and said she didn't know. She didn't know what she felt. He nodded to himself, as though he enjoyed hurting himself with her words. She saw the color drain from his bronzed temple and from the cheek that faced her, and again, as always, she was amazed to discover how precious and important she was to him, yet how he constantly withheld the simple security of that knowledge from her.

"It's one hell of a job, this life," he said.

As if from within a dark mine, she said, "That's how I've felt for years. Since the war, since Avram, I've felt like I was crawling through the dark, digging. But tell me more, what happened with him, what did you talk about?"

"Listen, he literally begged us to leave him alone. To forget that he even existed."

Ora laughed. "Forget Avram. Yeah, sure. Did you talk about *this*?" She hinted at her belly.

"He almost hit me when I tried to say something. He just goes berserk, physically, it drives him mad to think that he will have a child in the world."

And Ora thought: That he'll have something to hold him here.

Ilan murmured, "It's like he was on his way out, and his sleeve caught on a nail in the door."

Ora briefly felt as though there really was a nail in her womb.

She turned the light off and they lay there quietly, feeling the vapors of the previous night's untamed happiness dissipate. Their mouths filled with the metallic taste of what was and always would be irredeemable.

"I actually thought it would make things easier for him," Ora said, "rescue him even, you know, connect him with life again."

"He doesn't want to hear about it." He was quoting Avram and the hardness in his voice again. "He doesn't want to hear or see or know anything about this kid. Nothing."

"But what do *you* want?"

"You."

She had many more questions that she did not dare ask, and she did not know if he understood what he was getting himself into, and whether he might not regret it the next day. But there was something unfamiliar in his determination, a molten thread that suddenly glowed in him, and it occurred to her that perhaps Ilan could tolerate it better this way, with the complications. Perhaps he could only tolerate it this way.

"And I promised him," Ilan said, hinting. "He really begged me—"

"What?" Ora lifted up on one elbow and examined his face in the dark.

"Never to say anything."

"To who?"

"Anyone."

"You mean, not even—"

"No one."

A secret? The thought of raising a child with a secret weighed on her. She lay back, feeling as though someone were trying to erect a transparent, cold partition between her and the little creature in her stomach. She wanted to cry, and she had no tears. She saw images of those close to her, the people she would have to hide the secret from, the people she would lie to for the rest of her life. With each of them, the lie and the concealment had a different painful taste. She felt the mine branching out into more and more tunnels and caves, and she was suffocating.

"I won't be able to keep a secret like that for even one day, you know what I'm like."

Ilan shut his eyes tight and saw Avram, the pleading in his face, and said, "We owe him this." And Ora heard: *Take a hat, put two identical slips of paper in it.*

Ilan reached out and put his arm around her shoulders, but they did not move closer to each other. They lay on their backs and looked at the ceiling. His arm was under the back of her neck, lifeless, and they both knew that what had happened the night before in the shed would not happen again until after the baby was born. Perhaps not then, either. Adam, in his room, delivered a tempestuous monologue in his sleep, and they listened. Ora felt how much coldness had built up behind her eyes. She could feel that the secret and the hiding were already starting to distort her.

Then Ilan fell asleep and breathed very quietly, leaving not a scratch in the air. She felt some relief. She got up quietly and went into Adam's room and sat down on the floor, leaning against the chest of drawers opposite his bed. As she listened to his restless sleep, she thought about the three years of raising him on her own and about what they had meant to each other in those years. She hugged her body and felt the blood coursing through her veins again. She would have time to figure out everything that was happening, she thought. She didn't have to solve it all tonight. She got up and fixed Adam's blanket and stroked his forehead until he calmed down and slept peacefully. Then she went back to bed, lay there, and thought about the little creature and how she would change everyone's life, would maybe even manage to change Avram's life, just by existing. She felt sleepy. Her last thought was that now Adam and Ilan would have to learn to be father and son again. A moment before she fell asleep, she smiled: Ilan's toes were poking out from the bottom of the blanket.

She comes back from the dark bushes in a hurry, pebbles flying under her feet. Avram looks at her, and she goes straight for the notebook, signaling to him that she's remembered something.

She writes.

A minute after he came out of me, even before they cut the umbilical cord, I closed my eyes and told you in my heart that you had a son. I said, "Mazel tov, Avram, you and I have a son."

I've often wondered where you were at that moment. What exactly were you doing? Did you feel something? Because how could you not feel anything, or not even know, with some seventh or eighth sense, that this *was happening to you?*

She bites the pen. Hesitates, then spurts out onto the page: *I want to know if it's possible to feel nothing, or know nothing, when your son is, say, getting hurt somewhere?*

A cold wave hits the bottom of her gut.

Stop, stop, what am I even doing here? What is this writing? It's better not to think about it.

Automatic writing they call it, I think. Like automatic fire. In all directions. T-t-t-t-t-t.

I feel that I haven't told you enough about what happened after the birth.

About two hours after the delivery, when the whole team was gone and everyone had really finally left us alone, and Ilan had gone to tell Adam, I talked with Ofer. I just said everything. I told him who Avram was, and what he meant to me and to Ilan.

The pen flies over the page now as though she's chopping a salad. Her teeth bite her lower lip.

It surprised me how simple the story was when I told it to him. That was the first time (and probably the last) that I was able to think about us that way. The whole complication that was us, Avram and Ilan and me, all of a sudden became one little unequivocal child, and the story was simple.

Avram pours coffee into the mugs and hands her one. She stops writing and smiles a thank-you. He nods, You're welcome. They briefly emit the calm, kettlish hum of a couple. She looks up with distracted confusion, then back to the notebook.

I was alone with him in the room, and I talked into his ear. I didn't want a single word to escape into the open air. I gave him an infusion of his history. He lay in total silence and listened. He already had huge eyes. He listened to me with his eyes open and I spoke into his ear.

She feels the warmth of that virginal touch with her lips. Her mouth on the delicate oyster.

If you had been there, if you had only seen us there, everything would have been different. I'm certain. For you, too. It's silly to think that way, I know, but there was something in that room—

I don't even know how to put it. There was such health *there. Within all the complication there was health, and I felt that if you would only come and stand with us for a moment, or sit next to us on the edge of the bed and touch Ofer, even just his toes, you would instantly be healed and finally come back to us.*

They flow and flow, the words flow out of her. The sensation is sharp, sturdy, focused: when she writes, Ofer is safe.

If you had come and sat on the edge of my bed in the hospital, you could have told Ofer exactly what Ilan said to him: "I'm your dad and that's that. No arguments." It wouldn't have confused him. He would simply have been born into it like a child is born into two different languages and doesn't even know he's supposed to adapt to something.

She tastes the coffee, and it's lukewarm. Gone cold. She smiles at Avram with encouragement, with thanks, but he notices the tiny quiver of her mouth, and he takes the mug away and empties it and pours her a new one from the boiling *finjan*. She drinks. It's good, now it's very good. Her eyes, above the lip of the mug, run over the lines she has written.

And I told him all the things it was important for him to know, everything he had to hear once in his lifetime—even when he dozed I talked to him. I told him how I met Ilan and Avram, and that I was more or less a girlfriend to both of them since we met, Ilan's girlfriend and Avram's friend (although I occasionally got confused with that division). And I told him how I finished my army service while they stayed on for one more year in regular service and another year in the standing army, and I was already living in Jerusalem, on Tiberias Street in Nachlaot, and I was in my first year studying social work, and I really loved my studies and my life. He lay on me and listened with his eyes open.

I also told him about the lots they asked me to draw, forced me to, and what happened afterward in the war, and how Avram came back from there, and about the treatments and the hospitalizations and the interrogations, because for some reason the Shabak was convinced he'd given the Egyptians the most vital state secrets. Of all the people, they picked him to harass, and maybe they really did know something, you could never tell with Avram, after all, with his parallel-dimension games and plot twists, and the way he had to be loved by everyone, everywhere, and everyone had to know that he was special, that he was the best. So maybe they did know something.

I told him how we took care of Avram, we were the only ones there to take care of him, because his mother had died when he was in basic training and he had no one in the world except the two of us. And I told him how Ilan and I made Adam when Avram was still in the hospital, almost by accident we made him, almost unconsciously, I swear, we were so I-don't-know-what that we clung to each other and made him, we were just two frightened children, and Ilan left me right after the birth, he said it was because of Avram, but I think he was also afraid to be with me and Adam, he was simply afraid of what we could give him, it had nothing to do with Avram.

And I talked a bit about his brother, Adam, so he'd get to know him, so he'd know how to behave with him, because you needed an instruction manual for Adam. And in the end I told him that about two and a half years after Adam, I had made him with Avram, and I even told him it was "the negative of a fuck," just like Avram had whispered in my ear while we were doing it. So he'd know his father-language right from the start.

She's warming up now. Really, who knew it was so good to write! Tiring, even more exhausting than walking, but when she writes she doesn't have to keep walking and moving. Her whole body knows it: When she writes, when she writes about Ofer, she and Avram don't need to run away from anything.

When I finished telling him everything, I gave him a little tap with my fingertip under the nose, in the indentation of his lip, so he'd forget everything he'd heard and start over fresh and innocent.

And then he burst out crying, for the first time since he was born.

She lets go of the notebook, which falls between her legs, propped open like a little tent on the ground. Ora has the feeling that the words will hurry away from the lines and slip into the cracks of the earth. She turns the notebook up. She cannot believe that all those words came out of her. Almost four pages! And Ilan says she needs a few drafts just to write a grocery list.

"Avram?"

"Hmmmm . . ."

"Let's sleep a bit."

"Now? Isn't it early?"

"I'm beat."

"Okay. Whatever you want."

They cover the embers with dirt and stones. Avram rinses the utensils in the stream. Ora gathers up the leftovers and packs them in her backpack. Her motions are slow, contemplative. She thinks she detected some forgotten breeze in his voice, but when she replays his last few lines, she assumes she was wrong. The night is warm and there's no need to set up the tents. They spread their sleeping bags out on either side of the extinguished fire. Ora is so tired that she falls asleep immediately. Avram stays awake for a long time. He lies on his side looking at the notebook with Ora's hand resting on it. Her beautiful hand, he thinks, her long-fingered hand.

Shortly after midnight she awakes, and her fear for Ofer leaps up inside her like an evil jack-in-the-box. It is a frantic, noisy fear that rattles its limbs, flashes a crazy look, and cackles loudly: Ofer will die! Ofer is already dead! She sits up, stung, and looks with wild eyes at Avram snoring heavily beyond the ashes.

How can he not feel what's happening?

The same way he didn't feel it when Ofer was born.

She can't trust him. She's alone with this.

Their gloom as a pair falls upon her again, and the sadness of their lonely presence here, at the end of the world. What was she really thinking when she dragged him here? What is this foolishness? These sorts of sweeping, dramatic gestures are unlike her. They were right for the old Avram, not for her. She's only an imposter, pretending to be tempestuous and daring. Just go sit at home, bake your pies, wait for the news about your son, and start getting used to life without him.

She jumps up out of the sleeping bag, grabs the notebook, and in the dark writes *Ofer Ofer Ofer,* line after line, dozens of times, in large, crooked letters, and mumbles his name half out loud and aims and transmits his name in the darkness straight to Avram. So what if he's asleep? This is what needs to be done now, this is the most effective antidote she has to the poison that might be consuming Ofer at this very minute. She shuts her eyes and imagines him, note for note, and wraps him in protective layers of light. She swaddles him in the warmth of her love and plants him, plants him over and over again in the sleeping consciousness beside her. Then, in the dark, guessing her way, without seeing the lines, she writes:

I think, for example, about how he discovered his feet when he was a baby. How he enjoyed chewing and sucking them. I just think of the way he must have felt—that he was chewing something that existed in the world, that he could see it right in front of his eyes, but that it was also somehow arousing sensations within him. And maybe while he was sucking his toes, he started to grasp the very very edge of what is "me" and what is "mine."

And that sensation started flowing around the circle he'd drawn between his mouth and his feet.

Me-mine-me-mine-me-mine-me

It's such a huge moment, and I hadn't thought about it until now. How? Where was I? I'm trying to imagine where in his body he felt most "me" at that moment, and I think it's exactly in his center, his pee-pee.

I can feel it too now, when I write. Only with me it's also very painful.

So much of mine is no longer me.

I wish I knew how to write more about that moment. There should be a whole story about that moment, when Ofer sucked his toes.

Once, when he was about eighteen months old, he had a fever, maybe after a vaccination (What did they vaccinate against? Was it the triple one? Who can remember? I only remember that the nurse couldn't find a fleshy enough spot on his bottom, and Ilan laughed and said Ofer needed an anti-triple vaccine). Anyway, he woke up in the middle of the night and was burning up, and he was talking to himself and singing in a high-pitched voice. Ilan and I stood there, two o'clock in the morning, dead tired, and we started to laugh. Because all of a sudden we didn't recognize him. He was like a drunk, and we just cracked up, I think because now we saw him from a certain distance, and we both felt (together, I think) that he was still a bit foreign, like every baby that arrives from somewhere out there, from the unknown.

But he really was a little foreign. He was Avram's. He was at greater risk of foreignness than any other baby.

She stops and tries to read what she's written. She can barely see her writing on the page.

I was so relieved when Ilan picked him up and said, "It's not nice to laugh at you, you poor sick thing, and you're a little inebriated, too." I was so grateful to him for saying "It's not nice to laugh at you," rather than "at him." All at once he cut through that foreignness, which had almost reared its head between us. And it was Ilan who did that.

And just so you know—she looks at the sleeping Avram—so you don't have any doubts, he was a wonderful father, to both boys. I really think fatherhood is the best thing about him.

Then she turns to a new page and writes over its entire width, pressing hard so the pen almost tears through the page: *Fatherhood? Not couplehood?*

She stares at the three words. She turns to the next page.

But Ofer didn't calm down. On the contrary—he started singing at the top of his lungs, really yodeling, and we got the giggles again, but now it was something completely different between us and there was a feeling that we were allowing ourselves to let loose a little, perhaps for the first time since the pregnancy, and also because it was suddenly clear to both of us that this time Ilan was staying. This was it, we were finally starting our life, and from now on we were a regular family.

She breathes deeply, stilling her mind.

You're sleeping, snoring.

What would you do if I came over and lay down next to you?

I've been gone from home for almost a week.

How did I do such a thing? How did I run away at a time like this? I'm insane.

Maybe Adam's right. Unnatural.

No, you know what? I really don't feel that way.

Listen: so many feelings and nuances came to me with the children. I don't know how much of it I understood at the time. If I even had a minute to stop and think. All those years now seem like one big tempest.

That evening, with the fever and the yodeling, we gave Ofer a cold bath to bring his fever down. Ilan didn't have the heart to do it. I put him in the bath. A diabolical invention, but an effective one. You just have to overcome the fear of stopping his breath in the first second. And I was convinced that he was turning blue in front of my eyes. His lips were shaking, and he screamed, and I told him it was for his own good. His fingers were around his tiny chest, and his heart beat almost without any gaps, and he shivered from the shock and probably also from my betrayal.

Another time when I did that, Adam saw it and screamed at me that I was torturing Ofer. "You get into that water yourself!" he shouted. I said, "You know what? You're right!" And I really did get in with him, and then the whole thing instantly turned into a funny game. Adam was the wisest of children.

She holds her head in her hands. Cut by the pain of the wheel that cannot turn back. She sits and rocks herself. A uniform, persistent rustle comes from the bushes behind her, and a few seconds later two hedgehogs, perhaps a couple, march past in single file. The smaller one sniffs at Ora's bare feet as she sits motionless. The hedgehogs pad away and disappear down the channel, and Ora whispers thank you.

Look, Avram, about Ofer. I don't know if I was a good mother to him. But he grew up pretty okay, I think. He is without a doubt the most stable and solid of my children.

I lacked self-confidence when they were little. I made mistakes left and right. What did I know?

Earlier you shouted at me, "You?" when I said I may not have been the best mother in the world. When I dared to destroy your—your what? Your illusion of the ideal family? Of the perfect mother? Is that how you thought about us?

When it comes to the most important things, you're such an illiterate.

She looks up. Avram sleeps peacefully. Curled up in himself, maybe smiling in his sleep.

The bottom line is that I think we were actually a pretty good family. Most of the time we were even, excuse the expression, pretty happy together. Of course we had our problems, the usual miserable troubles, the unavoidable ones.

(What did you write to me once when you were in the army? "All happy fam-
ilies are miserable in their own way." How did you know?) But still, I can say
without reservation that since Ofer was born and up until the whole episode in
the army, in Hebron, about a year ago, we were very happy together.

And in a very uncharacteristic way for us, Ilan and I knew that even at the
time. Not just in retrospect.

She looks over at him. A lost and irrelevant leaf of joy hovers in her
eyes.

We had twenty good years. In our country, that's almost chutzpah, isn't it?
"Something the ancient Greeks would be punished for." (You said that once, but
I don't remember the context.)

Twenty years we had. A long time. And don't forget that six of those years
covered the two boys' army service (there was a five-day gap between Adam's
discharge and Ofer's enlistment). And they both served in the Territories, in
the lousiest places. The fact that we somehow managed to walk between the
raindrops without really getting splattered even once, from any war or terror-
ist attack, from any rocket, grenade, bullet, shell, explosive device, sniper, sui-
cide bomber, metal marbles, slingstone, knife, nails. The fact that we just lived
out a quiet, private life.

Do you get it? A small, unheroic life, one that deals as little as possible with
the situation, God damn it, because as you know, we already paid our price.

Sometimes, once every few weeks—

Once a week or so, I would wake up with a panic attack and say quietly into
Ilan's ear: "Look at us. Aren't we like a little underground cell in the heart of
the 'situation'?"

And that really is what we were.

For twenty years.

Twenty good years.

Until we got trapped.

AT THE TOP of Keren Naphtali mountain, on a bed of poppies and cyclamens, they lie sweaty and breathless from the steep incline. They agree that this was the hardest climb so far, and gobble down some wafers and biscuits. "We have to get some food soon," they remind each other, and Avram gets up to show her how much weight he's lost over the past few days. He's impressed at having slept through the night for the first time, four hours straight without a sleeping pill—"Do you know what that means?" "This trip is good for you," she says, "dieting and walking and fresh air." Avram agrees, although he sounds surprised: "I really do feel pretty good." Then he says it again, like someone taunting a sleepy predator from a place of safety.

Chiseled stone ruins sprawl behind them, remnants of an Arab village or perhaps an ancient temple. Avram—who happened to flip through an article not long ago—believes the stone is from the Roman era, and Ora welcomes his theory. "I can't deal with Arab village ruins now," she says. But a momentary illusion in her mind, composed instantaneously from the ruins, projects a tank roaring down a narrow alleyway, and before it can trample a parked car or ram the wall of a house, she moves her hands in front of her face and moans, "Enough, enough, my hard drive is overloaded with this stuff."

Broad Atlantic terebinths spread their branches and sway meditatively in the breeze. Not far away, antennas protrude from a small fenced-in military post, and a handsomely chiseled Ethiopian-born soldier stands motionless at the top of an observation tower, surveying the Hula Valley below, perhaps stealing a glance at them to spice up his guard duty. Ora stretches her whole body out and lets the breeze cool her skin. Avram sprawls in front of her, leans on one arm, and sifts dirt through his fingers.

"It happened just before he turned four," Ora tells him now. "Two or three months before, while I was making him lunch one day. I was already studying physiotherapy at the time, it was my last year, and Ilan had just opened his law firm, so it was a really crazy period. But at least I had two days a week when I finished school early and I could pick him up from day care and make him lunch. Is this really interesting to you, all this—"

Avram chuckles and his eyelids blush. "I'm . . . it lets me—"

"What? Tell me."

"I'm peeking into your lives."

"Yeah? Well, don't peek: look. It's all open. Ofer asked me what was for lunch. So I told him this and that, rice, let's say, and meatballs."

Avram's mouth moves distractedly, as though chewing the words. Ora remembers how he loved to eat, and to talk about food, *man's best friend*, and how she had longed to cook for him all these years. At big family meals, at dinner parties, on holidays, every year at Seder night, she would set aside a big, full plate for him in her heart. Now she has the urge to tempt him with a dish of eggplant in tomato sauce, or lamb with couscous, or maybe one of her rich, comforting soups—he doesn't even know what a good cook she is! Probably all he remembers are burned pots in her student apartment in Nachlaot.

"Ofer asked me what meatballs are made of, and I mumbled something. I told him they were round balls, made of meat, and he thought about it and asked, 'Then what's meat?' "

Avram pulls himself up into a seated position and hugs his legs.

"To tell you the truth, Ilan always said he was just waiting for Ofer to ask that question, from the minute he started talking. From the minute we saw what kind of boy he was, really."

"What do you mean, 'what kind of boy he was'?"

"Wait, I'll get there."

Something has been gnawing at her for several minutes, trying to get her attention. Something that was left on—a faucet in the house? A light? Her computer? Or maybe it's Ofer? *Is something happening to Ofer now?* She listens in, clearing a path through her whispers and conjectures, but no, it's not Ofer.

"Ora?"

"Where was I?"

"You saw what kind of boy he was."

"So I said to Ofer that it was nothing, you know, just meat. I said it in the most casual voice: It's nothing special, it's just meat. You know, like we eat almost every day. Meat."

She sees it: thin little Ofer, her lovely child, starts padding from one foot to the other, like he always did when he was troubled or frightened—she gets up and demonstrates for Avram. "And he used to tug his left earlobe over and over again. Like this. Or he'd walk sideways, back and forth, quickly."

Avram doesn't take his eyes off her. She comes back and sits down with a sigh. Her soul longs for that Ofer.

"I stuck my head in the fridge and tried to avoid him, that look on his face, but he wouldn't let it go. He asked who they took that meat from. And you should know that he really loved meat back then, beef and chicken. He hardly ate anything else, but he loved meatballs and schnitzel and hamburgers. He was a real carnivore, which made Ilan very happy. And me, for some reason."

"What?"

"That he loved meat. I don't know, some kind of primal satisfaction. You can understand that, can't you?"

"But I'm a vegetarian now."

"So that's it!" she cries out. "I noticed the other day, on the moshav, that you didn't touch—"

"Three years already."

"But why?"

"I just felt like cleansing myself." He stares intently at his fingertips.

"Well, you remember, there was a time when I didn't eat meat for a few years."

When he came back from the POW prison. Of course she remembers: he used to gag every time he walked by a steak house or a *shawarma* stand. Even a fly burning in an electric bug trap nauseated him. And she suddenly remembers how her own stomach turned, many years later, when Adam and Ofer jokingly explained—it was a Shabbat dinner on a white tablecloth, with braided challah and chicken soup— what they thought "MBT" really stood for. Adam drove an MBT in the army, and then Ofer was a gunner, and later a commander, in the same tank. They rolled around laughing: "No, it's not main battle tank! Where did you come up with that? It's mutilated body transporter."

Avram continues. "But after a few years, five or six, I got my appetite back, and then I ate everything, and you know how much I love meat."

She smiles. "I know."

"But about three years ago, I gave it up again."

Now she gets it. "Three years ago exactly?"

"Plus a few days, yes."

"A sort of vow?"

He throws her a sly sideways glance. "Let's say, a bargain." And after a minute—her neck is flushed now—he adds, "You think you're the only one who can make them?"

"Make those bargains with fate, you mean?"

Silence. She draws short lines in the dirt with a twig and puts a triangle over them—a roof. Three years of abstinence from meat, she thinks, and every evening he crossed off one line on the wall. What does that say? What is he saying to me?

She went on. "Ofer thought about it some more, and asked if the cow that you take the meat from grows out new meat."

"Grows out," Avram repeats with a smile.

"I squirmed, and I said, 'Not really, that's not exactly how it works.' Ofer paced around the kitchen again, faster and faster, and I could see that something was starting up inside him, and then he faced me and asked if the cow got a boo-boo when you took its meat. I had no choice, so I said yes."

Avram listens, every cord of his soul suddenly fascinated by the picture. By Ora talking with her child in the kitchen, and the little boy, thin and serious and troubled, darting around the narrow room, tugging on his earlobe, looking helplessly at his mother. Avram unwittingly holds his hand up in front of his face to ward off the domestic particles being hurled at him with intolerable abundance. The kitchen, the open fridge, a table set for two, steaming pots on the stove, the mother, the little boy, his distress.

"Then he asked if they take the meat from a cow that's already dead so it doesn't hurt her. He was really trying to find some dignified way out of the mess, you see, for me, but somehow also for all of humanity. I knew I had to make up a white lie, and that later, with time, once he grew stronger and bigger and had enough animal protein, the time would come to tell him what you once called 'the facts of life and death.' Ilan was so furious with me afterward for not being able to come up with something, and he was right, he really was!" Her eyes grow fiery. "Because with kids you have to cut corners here and there, you have to hide things, soften the facts for them, there's just no other way, and I wasn't . . . I was never able to, I couldn't lie."

Then she hears what she is saying.

"Well, apart from . . . you know."

Avram does not dare to ask with words, but his eyes practically spell out the question.

"Because we promised you," she says simply. "Ofer doesn't know anything."

There is a hush. She wants to add something, but finds that after years of silence, of contracting the large muscle of consciousness, she cannot talk about it even with Avram.

"But how can you?" he asks with a wonderment that confuses her. She thinks she hears a tone of condemnation.

"You just can," she whispers. "Ilan and I together. You can."

She is flooded by the warmth of the covenant they made together, which had only deepened around the large open pit of secretive silence, through the tenderness that emanated from the two of them on its brink, the cautious way they held on to each other so as not to fall in but not get too far away either, and the bitter knowledge, which also held a hint of special sweetness, that their life story was always being written in inverted letters too, and that no one else in the world—not even Avram—could read it. Even now, she thinks, even apart, we have that, that definitive thing of ours.

She clenches her jaw and pushes deep back inside her what had dared to peer out into the light for a moment, and then, through the force of almost twenty-two years of practice, she transposes herself back onto the straight track, the simple one, from which she was displaced a moment ago, and she wipes the last few minutes off her slate—the memory of the vast and ungraspable anomaly of her life.

"Where was I?"

"In the kitchen. With Ofer."

"Yes, and Ofer of course got even more stressed out by my silence, and he was flying around the kitchen like a spinning top, back and forth, talking to himself, and I could see that he wasn't even capable of putting into words what he suspected. Finally, I'll never forget it, he bowed his head and stood there all tense and crooked"—with the subtlest of gestures, she becomes him in her body, in her face, in his torn look that peers out of her eyes, and Avram sees it, he sees Ofer: Look, you're seeing him, you'll never forget now, you won't be able to live without him—"and then he asked me if there are people who kill the cow so they can take her meat. What could I say? I said yes.

"So then he started running around the whole house in a frenzy, and he yelled"—she remembers a thin wail, not his voice, not a human voice at all, but it came from him—"and he touched things, the furniture, pairs of shoes on the floor, he ran and screamed and touched, the keys on the table, door handles. It was scary, to be honest, it looked like some kind of ritual, I don't know, like he was saying goodbye to everything that . . ."

She looks at Avram softly, saddened by what she is telling him, and by what he has yet to hear from her. She feels that she is infecting him with the sorrows of raising children.

"Ofer ran to the edge of the hallway, by the bathroom door, you know, where the coatrack was? And he stood there and yelled: 'You kill her? You kill a cow to take her meat? Tell me! Yes? Yes? You do that to her on purpose?' And at that moment I got it. Maybe for the first time in my life I got what it means that we eat living creatures, that we kill them to eat them, and how we train ourselves not to realize that the severed leg of a chicken is sitting on our plate. And Ofer couldn't cheat himself that way, do you see?" Her voice lowers to a whisper. "He was totally exposed. Do you know what it is to be that kind of child, like that, in this shitty world?"

Avram pulls back. Deep in his gut he senses a flutter of the terror that had gripped him once, when Ora told him she was pregnant.

She drinks water from a bottle and washes her face. She holds the bottle out to him, and without thinking, he empties it over his head.

"And all at once his face sealed up, locked, like this"—she shows him, tightly clenching her fist—"and then he ran all the way down the hallway, from the bathroom to the kitchen, and kicked me. Just imagine, he'd never done that before! He kicked my leg as hard as he could and screamed: 'You're like wolves! People like wolves! I don't want to be with you!' "

"What?"

"He screamed, and he ran—"

"That's what he said? *Like wolves?*"

And this is a kid who one year earlier was hardly talking, she thinks, he couldn't string three words together.

"But where did that come from? How did he get that—"

"He ran to the door, he wanted to run away, but it was locked, and he threw himself against it, kicking and pounding, he was totally crazed. You know, I've always felt that that's when something started in him that was irredeemable, something lifelong, a first scratch, you know, the first sorrow."

"No. I don't get it, explain to me," Avram murmurs and thrusts his suddenly sweaty palms into his lap.

How can she explain? Maybe she can tell him about himself. About him and his father, who got up one day when Avram was five and disappeared, and was never seen again. His father, who once grabbed little Avram's face in his hands and held it up for Avram's mother to study, and asked with a grin if she thought the child looked anything like him, and whether it was really possible that a creature like that had come from a man like him, and if she was sure she'd given birth to him or if maybe she'd just crapped him out.

She speaks quietly. "I always have the feeling that there, in the kitchen, he found out something about us."

"About who?"

"About us, about humans. About this thing we have in us."

"Yes."

Avram looks at the earth, at the dust. *You're like wolves.* He rolls the words around in his mind. *I don't want to be with you.* He is profoundly unsettled by these simple words, which he has sought for almost thirty years and were yelled out by his son.

Ora asks herself, for the first time, what really happened in the kitchen that day. Exactly what melody did she use, and which tone, to teach Ofer the facts of life and death? Was it really as she had described it to Avram? Not exactly a lie, but an attempt to soften for Ofer, as much as she could, the matter of the slaughter itself, to save him from the true horror? For some reason she remembers how her own mother had told her, when she was six, in great detail and with a trace of defiance and even a peculiar reproach, about the abominations committed by inmates in the concentration camp where she spent the war.

"I don't really know whether, by telling him those kinds of things . . . I don't know when it was really an essential part of his education, preparing him for life and all that, and when, at what moment, there was a tiny bit of, how to put it, cruelty?"

"But why? Why would you say cruelty?"

"Or even a bit of gloating."

"I don't understand, Ora, what are you . . ."

"I mean, wasn't I really hinting, in an oblique sort of way, that what I was telling him was also, somehow, his punishment for having joined my screwed-up team in the first place? Or the whole game itself, you know, the game of the human race."

"Oh, that."

"Yes, that."

They sit quietly.

Avram nods, his eyes very heavy.

"And when I tried to hug him, to calm him, he writhed in my arms and scratched me so hard it drew blood. He kept crying at night too, in his sleep, it was burning so hard in him. The next morning he woke up with a high fever, and he wouldn't let us comfort him, wouldn't let us touch him, touch him with our meat hands, you see, and from that day, for twelve years, he didn't touch meat or anything that had been near meat. Until he was sixteen or so, until he started growing up, maturing, that kid did not touch meat."

"So why did he start at sixteen?"

"Wait, I'm not there yet." We still have a long way to go, she thinks; we'll understand it slowly, together. "At first, during meals, he wouldn't talk to me if I happened to point at him with a fork that had touched chicken. Do you understand how far it . . . Just like Ilan said at the time: Ofer belonged to the Shiite wing of vegetarianism." She laughs.

That's it, she has to write it down, that whole period. Ilan's struggles with Ofer, the unbelievable stubbornness and determination that came out of Ofer, and the slightly confusing weakness that beset her and Ilan in the face of this four-year-old child who had such solid principles. And the feeling they both had that he was drawing strength from some hidden source that was both beyond his age and beyond them, his parents. "Where's my notebook?" She stands up. The unresolved distress from moments ago grows denser inside her and finally erupts: "Where's the notebook, Avram? Did you see where I put the notebook?" She storms the backpack and digs through it, but the notebook isn't there. Not there! She looks in a panic at the other backpack, Avram's, and Avram tenses up. She asks cautiously: "Could it be with your stuff?"

"No, I didn't put it there. I didn't even open it."

"Do you mind if I look?"

He shrugs his shoulders indifferently: It's not mine and it's not my business, his shoulders say. He gets up and walks away from the backpack.

She opens hooks, zippers, knots. Scans the contents from above. Everything still looks more or less as it did when she packed the bag with Ofer at home. Avram had somehow managed not to unsettle anything, through all these days of carrying the thing on his back.

It sits wide open between them. At the top of the pile of clothes is the red "Milano" T-shirt, just the way Ofer packed it, and she can tell immediately that the notebook isn't there, but she cannot close it up again.

"There are lots of clean clothes here," she says drily, delivering useful information. "Socks, shirts, toiletries."

"I don't smell so good, do I?"

"Let's just say I always know where you are."

"Oh." He lifts up an arm and takes a sniff. "Don't worry, we'll find a spring or a faucet, it'll be okay." His voice is unconvincing. He has the craftiness of a boy fibbing to his camp counselor about why, to his regret, he cannot shower with the other kids.

"Well, whatever you say." She breathes deeply. Her fingers hover over Ofer's backpack with a life of their own.

"Anyway, his clothes probably won't fit me."

"Some may. The pants definitely will. He's pretty broad. And by the way, it's not just *his* clothes in here." She scans the backpack, eyebrow raised, still not touching. "There are some of Adam's and Ilan's shirts, too. And there's a pair of *sharwals* he always wears when he goes to Sinai. You could definitely wear those, they're so baggy." And silently she adds: They won't infect you with Ofer.

"But why Adam's and Ilan's clothes?"

"That's what he wanted. To be enveloped in the two of them while he hiked."

She resists telling him that they share underwear too, her three men.

She finally reaches in, hesitant at first, afraid to disturb Ofer's order, but then she plunges deep down, penetrating, and now both hands are tunneling in, grabbing handfuls of sun-warmed clothes that have been baking for a week now, and her hands encounter paired socks, and they thrust into crevices with pickpocket speed, and here a towel, and there a flashlight, and sandals and underwear and T-shirts. Her fingers dig wildly in the depths, beyond her field of vision, looting whatever they can. A strange feeling spreads through her: his clothes, his shells, and somehow his insides, warm and damp.

She leans down and buries her face in the backpack. The smell of clean clothes, crammed in and unaired. They had packed together the night before, recalling the solemn preparations on the eve of the great battle in *The Wind in the Willows*, which Ora had read to him three consecutive times in his childhood: *a shirt for Mole, and a pair of socks for Toad*. And it turns out that through the whole cheerful ceremony, while Ora could not stop rolling around with laughter, Ofer was planning and scheming, perhaps even already knew with complete confidence that he wasn't going on the trip with her, that it was all a big charade. How could he trick her? And why, in fact, did he do it? Maybe he was afraid he'd be bored spending a whole week with her. That they wouldn't have anything to talk about, or that she'd interrogate him about Talia and the breakup again, or whine about Adam, or try to recruit him to her side—which would never have occurred to her!—against Ilan, or ask him about Hebron again. Yes, it might have been mainly that.

The entire state of particulars revolts her. A sour taste crawls up her throat. Her face is buried in the backpack and her hands clutch it on either side. She looks like someone drinking thirstily from a well, but Avram notices that the lovely, slender vertebrae on the back of her neck are twitching beneath her skin.

Inside, she sobs uncontrollably, flooded with self-pity over the ruination of her life, her family, her love, Ilan, Adam, and now Ofer out there, and God forbid, and what is left of her, and who is she now that all these have vanished or simply ripped themselves away from her, and what was all her brilliant motherhood worth? Nothing but cowardice—that's what her motherhood was. A skilled sponge. Most of what she'd done for twenty-five years was mop up everything that poured out of the three of them, each in his own way, everything they spat out constantly over the years into the family space, namely into her, because she herself, more than any of them, and more than the three of them together, *was* the family space. She'd mopped up all the good and all the bad that came out of them—mainly the bad, she thinks bitterly, prolonging her self-castigation, though she knows in the depths of her heart that she's distorting things, wronging them and herself, yet still she refuses to give up the bitter spew that flies out of her in all directions: so many toxins and acids she's absorbed, all the excrements of body and soul, all the excess baggage of their childhood and their adolescence and adulthood. But someone had to absorb all that, didn't they? she sobs into the shirts and socks that cling to her face like little consolation puppies—soft, how soft the touch, soft the scent of laundry, despite its gently mocking derision: two-bit feminist, an insult to women's lib, a stain on the neon glow that emanates from the books her friend Ariela insists on buying her, books she's never managed to read more than a few pages of, written by decisive, witty, opinionated women who use expressions like "the duality of the clitoris as signifier and signified," or "the vagina as male-encoded deterministic space," which immediately activate in her feeble, characterless mind an interfering hum of machines and home appliances, blenders and vacuum cleaners and dishwashers—women who perceive her limp existence itself as a crude insult to them and their just struggle. Fuck feminism, Ora thinks and laughs a little through her tears. But it's so obvious, she argues into a T-shirt that insists on cramming itself into her face, that without the mechanisms of drainage and irrigation and purification and desalination that she has created and constantly refined, and without her never-ending concessions and her continuous swallowing of self-respect and her occasional kowtowing—without all these, her family would have crumbled long ago, years ago, for sure, though maybe not, who knows? Yet still, always, through all the years, the question had hovered in her mind: What really would have happened had she not volunteered to be their cesspit, or rather—this sounded slightly less humiliating, slightly more sophisticated and polished—their lightning rod? And which of them would have volunteered to replace her in that exhausting, thankless job? The satisfactions of which, incidentally, are incredibly deep and well hidden, right down to the depths of her innards, down to the top of her womb, which arches at the very thought, and the three of them know nothing about that—how could they know, really? What do they know about the sweetness that flows through the clefts of her soul after she manages to quell and ground another lightning storm of anger or frustration or vengefulness or insult, or just the momentary misery of each and every one of the three of them, at each and every age? She weeps a little more into the laundered fabrics, but the sorrow has subsided in her tears, and she wipes her face on the T-shirt that Ofer's battalion gave all the soldiers when they finished serving on the base near Jericho, which read *Nebi Musa—Because Hell Is Under Construction.* She feels comforted now, even refreshed, as she always does after a short, sharp cry, just like after sex, ten or twenty strokes and then the explosion, always, without any delay or complication, and now that the cloud has passed she has the urge to dive down into the backpack again and grab his clothes by the handful, spread them out here in front of Avram, on the bushes and on the rocks, and conjure him from the clothes—his height, his breadth, his size. Excitement flutters down her body: if she really tries hard—and for a moment she almost believes that anything is possible on this journey strung along on a thin web of oaths and wishes—she can pull him out, deliver Ofer himself from the depths of the backpack, tiny and delightful and twitching his arms and legs. She settles for an army hat, a pair of sweatpants, and the *sharwals,* and these make her happy, with her arms entirely immersed, kneading her child out of the fabric like a village baker shoulder deep in a basin full of dough. But it's also like picking through his estate—the thought pecks at her and intercepts her pleasure, and only then, with her chin over the edge of the backpack and her face buried in pairs of warm walking socks, she remembers, and stares at Avram with frightened eyes: "Listen, I'm such an idiot, I left the notebook there."

"Where?"

"Down there. Where we slept."

"How?"

"I was writing a bit this morning, before you woke up, and I somehow forgot it."

"So we'll go back."

"What do you mean go back?"

"We'll go back," Avram says and straightens up.

"It's a serious hike."

"So what?"

She snivels. "I'm such an idiot."

"It doesn't matter, Ora, it really doesn't matter." He smiles. "We've been going around in circles most of the time for a week anyway."

He's right, and a warm ripple gurgles in her at the realization that only she and he can understand how little it matters, to go on or go back, turn around, lose their way. The point is to be in motion, the point is to talk about Ofer. They zip up and buckle up and tie down. They stop at the small military base to fill their water bottles, and the soldier from the lookout tower gives them two slightly stale loaves of sliced bread, three cans of tuna and corn, and two handfuls of apples. They walk back down the steep incline, holding on to pine trees, and Ora thinks feverishly about the man they met on the trail that morning, about his long, dark, wise face. Who knows what he thought about her and Avram? What story did he tell himself in his mind? She stops abruptly, horrified, and Avram almost walks into her: "What if that guy finds the notebook and reads it?"

Between two rocks, she remembers. I put it down for a minute, this morning, while I rolled up my sleeping bag, and I left it there. How could I leave it there?

"With any luck," she says out loud, perhaps too loud, "no one will find it before we get there."

It happened very early that morning. She and Avram were hiking up the riverbed when they saw a figure walking down the hillside in their direction. Perhaps that was why he had at first seemed taller and thinner than he was. And the strange light coming through the terebinth branches—a dusty, yellowish dawn light—made him look dark and blurry. Ora stood watching the figure for a moment, pondering the way sometimes, in the morning, when someone comes at you from the opposite direction and the sunlight is behind them, in your eyes, all you can see is the outline of a spindly Giacometti body that disintegrates and re-forms itself with every step, and it's hard to know if the figure is a man or a woman, and whether it's coming toward you or moving far-ther away. And then she heard stones skidding behind her, and Avram jumped ahead in a flash to stand between her and the stranger, who gave them a slightly bewildered smile.

Avram's move also confused her, and she did not respond. Having planted himself in front of her, Avram stood breathing deeply, his chest puffed out, and stared intently not at the man in front of him but at the pebbles on the ground. He looked like a guard dog: loyal, stubborn, dense, protecting his lady.

The men faced each other as Avram blocked the path. The stranger cleared his throat, said a cautious good morning, and Ora answered fee-bly, "Good morning." "You're coming from down there?" asked the man redundantly, and Ora nodded. She didn't look at him, either. She felt that she did not have the strength to make even the slightest trivial connection. She only wanted to keep walking with Avram and talking with Avram about Ofer, and anything else was a distraction and a waste of energy. "So long," she said, and waited for Avram to keep going. But he did not move, and the man cleared his throat again and said, "When you get to the top, you'll see some lovely flowers. Carpets of spiny broom, and the redbuds are in bloom, too." Ora glanced at him wearily: What was he talking about? All this nonsense about blossoms. She noticed that he was around her age, a little older, fifty-something, bronzed and solid and relaxed. In his eyes she saw herself and Avram. They gave off a forlorn whiff of the persecuted, and disaster hovered over them. The man grasped the straps on his backpack with two remarkably long, arched thumbs, and seemed to be considering taking the bag off.

"So you're hiking the trail?"

"What?" she murmured. "What trail?"

"The Israel Trail." He pointed to an orange-blue-and-white marker on one of the rocks.

"What's that," she said. She did not have the strength to round her voice into a question mark.

"Oh," the man said, smiling, "I thought you were—"

"Where does the trail go?" Ora asked urgently. Too many things were suddenly demanding her comprehension at once. The smile that cleaved his long, serious face into two. And the warm olive tone of his skin. And the way Avram was still standing between them, a lump, a human wall. And maybe also the *Yedioth* newspaper rolled up in the pocket of the stranger's backpack, and a pair of large feminine glasses, like hers, but blue—hers were red—that hung on a string around his neck and looked completely wrong for him, and somehow also indescribably annoying. And on top of all that, now he was saying that this modest, intimate path that she and Avram had been walking for a week, had a name. Someone had given it a name. All at once, she had been robbed of something.

"It goes all the way to Eilat. All the way to Taba. Goes down the entire country."

"From where?"

"From the north. Around Tel-Dan. I've been hiking it for a week. I hike a bit, then I go back a bit. Around in circles. It's hard for me to leave this area, with the blossoms and everything, but you have to keep going, right?" He smiled at her again. She had the feeling that his face was gradually revealing itself to her, being painted in front of her eyes to adapt to her pace of perception, which was suddenly very slow.

"Did you sleep down there?"

He wouldn't give up. Why wouldn't he leave her alone? Just let her keep walking. She smiled helplessly, unsure whether to lose her temper at him—those affected glasses, like some private, irritating joke that he waved around for all to see—or to respond to a certain natural, comfortable softness that she felt in him.

"Yes, down there, but we're only . . . How far does it go, you said?"

"Eilat." Thick eyebrows and short, solid, silver hair were now added to his face.

"What about Jerusalem?"

"That's more or less on the way, but you still have a long way to go." He smiled again, as he did after every sentence. Bright white teeth, she saw, and full, dark lips, with a deep crack in the middle of the lower one. She sensed a hushed anger from Avram's body. The man threw him a cautious glance. "Do you need anything?" he asked, and Ora realized he was worried about her, that he suspected she was in some sort of trouble, maybe even taken captive by Avram.

"No." She straightened up and smiled as charmingly as she could. "We're fine. The truth is, we're still waking up."

And she started smoothing down her wild hair with both hands—she hadn't even combed it that morning before leaving; there was a tinge of remorse at her principled decision this past year not to dye her hair. She quickly wiped the corners of her eyes and made sure there were no crumbs on the edge of her lip.

"Listen, I'm making some coffee. Will you join me?"

Avram grunted no. Ora did not say anything. She could have used some coffee. She had a feeling he made good coffee.

"Can I ask you something?" she said.

"What?"

"What is this place?"

"Here? It's the Kedesh River." He smiled again. "Don't you know where you are?"

"The Kedesh River," she murmured, as though there were magic encoded in the words.

"It's good to be in nature," he said encouragingly.

"Yes, it is." She gave up on her hair. What difference did it make anyway? She'd never see him again.

"And it's good to get away from the news a bit," he added, "especially after yesterday."

Avram let out something that sounded like a warning bark. The man took a step back and his eyes darkened.

Ora put a hand on Avram's back, calming him with her touch.

"No news," Avram pronounced.

"Okay," said the man carefully, "you're right. There's no need for news here."

"We have to get going," Ora said without looking at him.

"Are you sure you don't need anything?" His eyes moved across her face. Ora could feel how one of his fingers, the one still holding the backpack strap, was drawn to glide over her lip.

"We're absolutely fine," she repeated. It was all she could do to resist asking what was on the news yesterday. And if they'd released the names yet.

"Anyway," the man said.

Avram uprooted himself and walked past the man. Ora passed him too, with her head bowed.

"I'm a doctor," the man said quietly, for her ears only. "If you need anything."

"A doctor?" She lingered. She thought he was trying to give her a secret message. Maybe he was hinting that Ofer needed a medic?

"A pediatrician," he said. He had a soft, pleasant baritone voice. His eyes were focused and dark when he looked at her. She felt that he was concerned for her, and her skin responded. She had to tear herself away from this tenderness immediately.

"I'm sorry," she whispered, "it's just not the right time."

They kept going up the riverbed, Avram at the head and she behind, feeling the man's gaze plowing through her back. She kept trying to guess what was on the news and how bad it was. At least it was clear now that things weren't over there yet, that it was probably going to be a long affair this time, which only confirmed what she'd sensed all along, that things were getting worse and worse, things were deteriorating. In the same breath she thought how annoying it was that he'd been looking at her all this time from behind—not exactly her strong side, the behind, and no one could convince her otherwise. She was even more annoyed that she was capable of being annoyed by such stupid things while the situation over there was probably intensifying. She marched angrily up the riverbed, replaying the short meeting in her mind, and she felt as though something of Avram's obtuse lumpiness was sticking to her, in her movements and her appearance, and it was encumbering her natural talent for coquettish small talk with friendly strangers. Before the next bend in the path she could not resist turning around, with a hint of reproach, with pride in her remote self. She saw him standing just where they had left him, looking attentive and grave. He seemed so worried that her stern face broke into a soft, surprised smile, and she thought she could see him nod at her once.

After leaving the shaded riverbed, they found themselves suddenly on a path flooded with strong morning light and walked along it silently. Ora is constantly amazed to think of Avram's lightning jump in front of the man, as though he had sworn to protect her at any cost from the outside world and its representatives, from any sliver of information about what was happening *there*. She considers that he might also be protecting himself, but cannot entirely understand that. She thinks again of his vegetarianism, the dates he crossed off on the wall above his bed, and the hope in his voice when he called her on Ofer's scheduled release date: "Is it over?" he asked. "Is his army over?" At that moment she hadn't had the capacity to comprehend how much he must have been waiting for the release and how he had anxiously anticipated it for the three years preceding the date, day after day, crossing out line after line.

She quickens her steps. The path narrows, and bushes of spiny broom—she remembers the name; that's what that guy was talking about—as tall as she is blossom in yellow on either side, giving off a delicate perfume. And there are those little flowers, yellow and white chamomile blossoms that look like they were drawn by children, and cistus shrubs, and hyacinths, and pale blue stork's bill, and the beloved Judean viper's bugloss, which she had barely noticed all these days—but what had she noticed? "And look," she says, pointing happily, expanding her lungs and her eyes: "That pink over there is gorgeous—a flowering redbud tree."

The mountain is padded with round yellow cushions of flowering spurge and pink blankets of Egyptian honesty. Ora snaps off a branch of spiny broom, crushes the flowers, and holds it out for Avram to smell. With his face almost in the palm of her hand—his large, lost face—she remembers him yelling at Ilan that he didn't want anything to do with it, anything to do with life. It occurs to her that perhaps it was during these past years, with Ofer in the army, and even more so now, with Ofer being *there*, that Avram suddenly realizes that if, God forbid, this one thread of connection he has with them is torn, he will find himself suddenly tied to life with the thickest of ropes, with a bond of affliction that can be ended only by ending life. Avram, in a confirmation of sorts, sneezes loudly on her.

"Sorry," he mumbles, and wipes slivers of saliva and flower stamen off her forehead and the tip of her nose.

She grasps his wrist and says into his face, "You're practiced at this, aren't you?"

"At what?" he grumbles and scans her face suspiciously.

"At running away from bad news. You're a thousand times more practiced at it than I am, right? You've spent your whole life running from bad news." She looks straight into his eyes and knows without a doubt that she is right. She clutches his hand and rhythmically folds in finger after finger: "Running away from the bad news that is life itself, one. Running from the bad news that is Ofer, two. Running from the bad news that is me, three."

He sucks awkwardly on his lip. "This is bull, Ora. What's with the roadside psychology?"

But she has a newfound strength now. "Just remember that sometimes bad news is actually good news that you didn't understand. Remember that what might have been bad news can turn into good news over time, perhaps the best news you need." She gives him back his hand and folds it over the branch of sunny yellow buds. "Come on, Avram, let's go."

To the right of the path is a tall antenna, and a long chain-link fence in front of an ugly fortress. It looks like a police stronghold from the British Mandate, with gloomy concrete structures, guard towers, and narrow viewing slits. "Yesha Fortress," Ora reads from a small sign. "Let's get out of here, I'm not in the mood for fortresses."

Avram hesitates. "But the path . . . Look, the path goes through here."

"Isn't there another one?"

They look this way and that, and there isn't another. Except for one marked with red, but the man at the river said if they followed the orange-blue-and-white markers, they'd get to Jerusalem, home. Momentarily confused, she checks in with herself: You wanted to run away from home, didn't you? So why are you now—

She turns to Avram and puts a finger on his chest and decrees, "We'll go through, but quickly, no stopping, and tell me something on the way."

"What?"

"Doesn't matter, talk to me, tell me, I don't know, tell me about your restaurant."

And so, as they walk quickly, she learns that for the past two years, since being fired from the pub, he's been working in an Indian restaurant in South Tel Aviv. They were looking for a dishwasher. He wouldn't wash dishes because that left too much time to think, but he was willing to wash the floors and do general cleaning work. He and dirt have been *like this* for years—he presses two fingers together and smiles, trying unsuccessfully to distract her from the sparse grove of cypress trees—twenty-eight of them, each with a wooden name plaque, a cypress for each of the men killed here in April and May of 1948 while trying to capture the fortress from the Arab fighters.

"Vacuuming is also okay for me," Avram prattles on, "and small hauling jobs, why not? I'm an odd-job man, and it's good there."

"Good?" She glances at him from the side. She hasn't heard that word from him for a long time.

"Young people. *Shanti.*"

"Go on, go on," she murmurs, heroically passing a plaque with a poem by Moshe Tabenkin, where a moustached tour guide stands reading it out loud to a group of tourists. They must all be deaf, Ora thinks angrily and speeds up; he's practically yelling. The mountains echo back to her:

> *Our boy was— like a pine in the woodlands.*
> *Was— a fig tree putting forth its figs.*
> *Our boy was— a myrtle of dense roots.*
> *Was the most fiery of poppies—*

"Well, go on," she gripes. "Why did you stop?"

Avram, rapidly: "The whole restaurant is really one big room, like a very wide hall, with no interior walls, just support pillars. It's a pretty run-down building." He describes the place with a furrowed brow, like someone delivering extremely important testimony that has to be exhaustive and precise. She is grateful for the meticulous details, which take her away from here—from the marble square. The twenty-eight names are carved in stone, she remembers, and there's a mass grave, too. She was on a school trip here once, when she was thirteen. The teacher stood facing them, wearing shorts, and read with a booming voice from a page: "Nebi Yusha was but a fortress on the road, and now it is a symbol for all times!" Ora had surreptitiously peeled a clementine on the marble square, and a teacher had yelled at her: "Show some respect for the fallen soldiers!" If only she could be that stupid and ignorant of sorrow today, to stand eating a clementine on the marble square. It's good to get away from the news a bit, that man had said. Especially after yesterday. A scream kicks around inside her body, searching for a way out, and Avram, continuing his mission, takes her to a district of auto-repair shops, trucking companies, and massage parlors in South Tel Aviv. He walks her up a crooked, dirty staircase. Starting on the second floor, there are rugs on the stairs and pictures on the walls, and the smell of incense. "And you walk in," he says, and she suddenly remembers: Dudu was killed here. Dudu from the song: *In the Palmach, none could outdo / Our hero, our lost soldier, Dudu.* She racks her brain for a word that rhymes with Ofer.

"And inside"—Avram's voice hovers somewhere out there in his little India—"the whole big room is covered with rugs, and there are lots of low tables, and you sit on big cushions. As soon as you walk in, at the far end opposite you, you see gas ranges with huge, charred pots. Mighty pots."

They leave the fortress and Ora lets her breath out. She looks at Avram gratefully, and he shrugs his shoulders.

The words, she thinks dimly, they're coming back to him.

"You'll laugh, but I'm the oldest one there," he says.

"No kidding," she mumbles, stealing a look back at the fortress. "Come on, let's cross the road here."

"I swear," he chuckles, shrugging one shoulder as if apologizing for some trick played on him long ago, in the years when she was absent from his life. "The owner is all of twenty-nine, and the cook is maybe twenty-five. All the others, too. Sweet kids."

Ora feels somehow robbed—why is he so excited about a few kids he barely knows?

"They're all graduates of India. I'm the only one who hasn't been. But I already know everything as if I've been there. And they don't fire anyone at this place. There's no such thing as firing."

They walk among hedgerows of fleshy prickly pears, past a large tomb with domes on its roof and trees growing out of its walls. Blankets and mats are scattered around the large chambers that look out onto the Hula Valley, and there are a few empty dishes, left from offerings brought by the faithful to Nebi Yusha—Yehoshua Ben Nun.

"Some of the people who work there couldn't get a job anywhere else."

People like him, she thinks. She tries to picture him there. The oldest one, he'd said with real surprise, as if that were utterly improbable. As though they were still twenty-two years old, and everything else was a mistake. She sees him among those sweet young people, with his heaviness and his bulky slowness, with his big head and long, thinning hair hanging down on either side. Like some exiled, downfallen professor, forlorn and ridiculous at the same time. But the fact that they never fire anyone reassures her.

"And they don't give you a check at the end of your meal."

"So how do you know how much to pay?"

"You go up to the register and tell them what you ate."

"And they believe you?"

"Yes."

"What if I cheated?"

"Then you probably had no choice."

"Are you serious?" A little light goes on inside her. "Is there really such a place?"

"I'm telling you."

"Take me there, now!"

He laughs. She laughs.

"The walls are covered with big photos that someone took in India or Nepal. They change them every so often. And on the side, near the bathroom, there are three washing machines running constantly. Free, for whoever needs them. While people eat, some guys and girls go around offering treatments, Reiki and acupressure and shiatsu and reflexology. And soon, when the renovations are done, I'll start working in the sweets."

"Working in the sweets . . ." she echoes.

The picture suddenly picks up speed. She sees him darting around, clearing tables, taking out the trash, vacuuming, lighting candles and incense sticks. She is fascinated by his movements, his swiftness, his lightness. "Avram FSF," as he used to introduce himself to new girls, with a flourish and a bow: fat, speedy, and flexible.

"And whoever wants to can smoke. Anything, no problem."

"You, too?" She laughs nervously—she can't see the fortress any-more, but she suddenly feels as if they're running, as if the path is pulling them too quickly to Jerusalem, to home, to the notice that might be waiting there for her with the calm patience of an assassin. I'll go back—it flickers in her—and there'll be death notices up on the street. On the utility poles. Next to the grocery store. I'll know from a distance.

"Go on, tell me." She turns to Avram in a panic. "I want to hear!"

"Well, nothing heavy, mostly joints." His hand habitually pats the non-pocket on his chest. "Sometimes a hash blunt, some E, acid, if there's any going around, nothing serious." He looks at her and smiles. "Do you still uphold the Scouts' commands?"

"I was in the Machanot Olim, not the Scouts," she reminds him drily. "Forget it, I'm afraid of those things."

"Ora, you're running again."

"Me? It's you."

He laughs. "You suddenly get these . . . You start running ahead as if God knows what is chasing you."

To their left, the Hula Valley grows steamier as the heat increases. Their faces are red, burning with effort and warmth, they drip with sweat, and even speech is tiring. On the side of the road, at the foot of an old olive tree, lies a huge, fancy chandelier. Avram counts twenty-one crystals, all intact, connected with stylish thin glass pipes. "Who threw this here?" he wonders. "Who throws out something like that? It's too bad we can't take it." He crouches down and examines the chandelier. "Good stuff." He tilts his head and laughs softly, and Ora questions him with her eyebrows. Avram says: "Look at it. What does it remind you of?" She stares and doesn't see anything. "Doesn't it look like some sort of ballerina? Like an insulted prima donna?" Ora smiles. "It does." Avram stands up. "It's shimmering with insult, hey? Look at it from here, wallowing in its tutu, I swear." Ora laughs deeply. A forgotten pleasure gurgles into the corners of her eyes.

"And Ofer?" he asks later. "Does he take anything?"

"I don't know. How can you know anything about them at this age? Adam, I think so. Here and there."

Or most of the time, or all of it, she thinks. How could he not? With those guys he hangs out with, with his eyes, always bloodshot, and that bashed-up, bashing-up music. Oh God, what do I sound like? When did old age creep up on me like this?

"It's too bad you didn't take some weed from my place when you kidnapped me. You'd have seen what good stuff is."

"So you keep it around at home?" She struggles to maintain a measured, enlightened voice and feels like a social worker interviewing a homeless guy.

"For personal use, what do you think? I grow it in a flower box. With the petunias."

"Do you miss it now?"

"Let's just say, it would have set me right, especially in the first few days."

"And now?"

"Now I'm okay." He sounds astonished. "Don't need anything."

"Really?" Her face lights up, her glasses glisten with happiness.

"But if there were any"—he quickly cools her excitement and puts her in her place; for a moment she looked as though she'd pulled off a rapid intervention plan straight out of a kids' comic book—"if there were any, I wouldn't say no."

How far apart we've grown, she thinks. A whole life separates us. She imagines him in his restaurant again, circling among the low tables, clearing leftovers, joking with the customers, taking their banter with good spirits. She hopes they don't mock him. She hopes he doesn't seem pathetic to those young people. She tries to picture herself there.

"You take your shoes off before you go in," he notes, as though guiding her.

She sits down on a cushion. She's uncomfortable. Too upright, doesn't know what to do with her hands. She smiles in all directions. Her fakery rustles all around her. She wonders if she could have lived with Avram, in his apartment, in the meager neglect of his life. For some reason her thoughts adopt the guttural Mizrahi speech of the man they met in the riverbed. She thinks about his red checkered shirt. He looked like someone had dressed him up nicely this morning and sent him off on a hike. She sees the colorful woman's glasses that dangled on his chest. Maybe they were not tasteless foppishness or a defiant pose, as she had thought, but a small private gesture? A gesture to a woman? She sighs softly and wonders if Avram had picked up on anything back there.

And without even noticing it, they're having a conversation. Two people conversing as they walk on one path.

"On the army base in Sinai, there was an Ofer," Avram muses. "Ofer Havkin. He was a special guy. Used to wander around the desert on his own, playing the violin for the birds, sleeping in caves. He wasn't afraid of anything. A free spirit. And so all these years I thought Ilan had that Ofer in mind when you chose the name."

Ora delights in the words that came out of his lips—"free spirit"—then says, "No, I was the one who chose it, because of the verse in Song of Songs: *'My love is like a young hart'—Domeh dodi le'Ofer ayalim.* And I liked the way it sounds, too: *o-fer.* It's soft."

Avram silently repeats the name in Ora's music, and then says quietly, reverently, "I could never give someone a name."

"When it's your own child, you'll be able to," she says—it just slips out, and they both fall silent.

The path is wide and comfortable. So many colors, she thinks, when all I saw at first was black and white and gray.

"I'm just curious, did you think of any names other than Ofer?"

"We thought of girls' names too, because we didn't know what we were having. I was convinced halfway through the pregnancy that it was a girl."

A flock of birds alights inside Avram, noisily beating their wings: He had never thought of that possibility—a daughter!

"And what . . . Which names did you think of for a girl?"

"We thought of Dafna, and Ya'ara, or Ruti."

"Just imagine . . ." He turns to face her. The bags under his eyes glow, and now he is entirely here, shining with life, and the pillar of fire he used to be is visible through his skin. Ofer is protected now, she senses, protected in the palms of two hands.

"A girl," she says softly. "That would have made everything simpler, wouldn't it?"

Avram expands his chest and takes a deep breath. "A girl" rocks him even more than "a daughter."

They walk, each lost in thought, the path crunching beneath their feet. She thinks: Even the path suddenly has voices. How did I not hear anything all those days? Where was I?

"Didn't you want to try again?" he asks bravely.

Ora replies simply that Ilan didn't want to, because as it was, he said, with all the complications, we already had an excess of kids.

And parents, Avram thinks. "And you? Did you want to?"

Ora lets out a little bray of pain. "Me? Are you asking seriously? My whole life I've felt that I missed out terribly by not having a daughter." After a moment's hesitation she adds, "Because I always think a girl would have made us into a family."

"But you . . . I mean, you already are . . ."

"Yes," she says, "we were, absolutely, but still, that's how I felt all these years. That if I had a daughter, if Adam and Ofer had a sister, it would give them so much, it would change them"—she outlines a circle with both hands—"and also, if I'd had a daughter, I think it would have strengthened me against them, the three of them, and maybe it would also have softened them a little toward me."

Avram hears the words and does not understand their meaning. What is she giving him here?

"Because I'm alone," she explains. "I wasn't enough to soften them, and they turned so hard over time, especially toward me, and even more so recently. Hard and tough, the three of them. Ofer, too," she adds with some effort. "Listen, it's really difficult to explain."

"Difficult to explain to *me*, or in general?"

"In general, but especially to you."

"Try."

The insult in his voice is good, it's a sign of life, but she can't explain it, not yet. She'll bring him in slowly. It's painful to admit to him that even Ofer wasn't tender with her. Instead of answering, she says, "I always thought that if I'd had a daughter, maybe I would have remembered what it was like to be me. The me from before everything that happened."

Avram turns to face her. "I remember how you were."

Every time he touches the thought of a daughter, he feels a caress of light on his face. "Listen," he probes, "if it had been a girl, I mean—"

"I know."

"What do you know?"

"I know."

"Go on, say it."

"If it had been a girl, you would have come to see her, right?"

"I don't know."

"But I do." Ora sighs. "You think I never thought about that? You think I didn't pray for a girl the whole pregnancy? That I didn't go to a seer—like Saul, who *came to the woman by night*—in the Bukharian neighborhood, so she could give me a blessing for a girl?"

"You did?"

"Of course I did."

"But you were already pregnant! What could she have—"

"So what? You can always barter. And by the way, Ilan also wanted a girl."

"Ilan, too?"

"Yes, I'm sure of it."

"But he didn't tell you?"

"You wouldn't believe how quiet we kept around that pregnancy. We only talked when Adam asked us something. Through Adam we talked about what was in my belly, and what would happen when the new baby was born."

Avram swallows and recalls how that whole time he lay in bed, paralyzed by the terror of the growing pregnancy.

And praying it would fail.

And planning in great detail how he would nullify his life as soon as he heard the baby was born.

And counting the days he had left.

And in the end he did nothing.

Because even when he was a POW, and increasingly after he came home, he always latched on, at the last minute, to Thales, the Greek philosopher he had admired as a youth, who said there was no difference between life and death. When asked why, in that case, he did not choose death, Thales replied, Precisely because there is no difference.

Ora laughs. "We called him Zoot. Adam made up the name."

"You called who Zoot?"

"Ofer."

"I don't understand."

"When he was still in my belly. A sort of pregnancy name, you know."

"No," Avram murmurs, defeated, "I don't know. I don't know anything. I know nothing."

She puts a hand on his arm. "Don't."

"Don't what," he grumbles.

"Don't torture yourself more than you have to."

"Still, Ofer is a good name," he says after a while.

"A very Israeli name. And I like that it has 'o' and 'e' in it. Like *khoref*, winter, and *boker*, morning."

Avram sees her lovely forehead enveloped in brightness now. Like *osher*, happiness, he thinks, but does not say it.

"It's good for nicknames, too," she adds.

"You thought about that?"

"And also it's like the English word 'offer,' which is soft and open, sort of giving."

He laughs. "You're amazing."

She resists telling him that she also thought about how the name would sound in bed, coming from the lips of the women who would love him. She had even tried it out, whispering breathlessly to herself, *Ofer, Ofer*, which had made her giggle at the confusion that flooded her.

"Nicknames, of course," he murmurs. "I never thought of that. And insults, too. You wouldn't want it to rhyme with any curses."

"Like 'Ora Gomorrah.' "

"No-Fair Ofer," he laughs.

Is he still smiling, like we do, Ora sadly hums to herself, *Our hero, our lost soldier, Dudu.*

The green, sedate pasture, dotted with black-and-white cows, curves abruptly into a steep mountain. They groan and sigh as they walk and grab at tree trunks that lean into the incline. If I'd had a daughter, she thinks, if I'd had a daughter there are a few things I could have repaired in myself. She tries to explain this to Avram, but he doesn't really understand, not the way she needs him to understand her, not the way he once knew her instantly, *with a hint and a wrinkle.* There were things she'd once hoped to change in herself through the boys, and it had never happened. "What things?" Avram asks. She has trouble explaining it and thinks again about Ofer's Talia, and the way all the men in the household responded to her, happily and simply giving her what they'd held back from Ora. She tells Avram that it was only recently, once Adam and Ofer were grown up, that she realized it would probably never happen to her through them, this change, this repair. It became clear to her, late in the day, that it would not be through them that she would solve anything—"Perhaps because they're boys, perhaps because they're them, I don't know." She stops talking and breathlessly climbs up the mountain, and thinks, They weren't really attentive to me, and they weren't really generous, not in the way I needed.

"I didn't write it properly," she says now, as they go back down the mountain to find the lost notebook. "I just don't feel that I'm getting the main point across. Not when I write, and not when I'm talking to you. I want to tell all the minutiae about him, the fullness of his life, his life story, and I know I can't, it's impossible, but still, that's what I need to do for him now." Her speech ebbs and turns to mumbles as she pictures the man with his long, sinewy hands, and those thumbs. They were the hands of a worker, not a doctor, and she sees them opening her notebook and leafing through the pages as he tries to understand what he's reading, what story it contains. Her heart leaps: Maybe at this minute he's sitting on a rock, maybe even the same rock she herself sat on the night before, the only comfortable rock around, with her notebook on his lap, and he knows without a doubt that the person who wrote these pages was the woman he met coming up from the riverbed, the one with the wild hair and the slightly paralyzed lip.

"At first it was hard"—she resumes what was interrupted long ago on the way up the mountain—"his vegetarianism, and the way Ilan fought to get him to taste some meat, or at least fish, and the fighting and yelling at mealtimes, and Ilan's personal insult at Ofer's decision to stop being a carnivore."

"Why was it an insult? Why personal?"

"I don't know, that's how he took it, Ilan."

"You mean, like it was something against him?"

"Like it was, you know, against masculinity. That it was somehow feminine to be disgusted by meat. Can't you understand that?"

"Yes," Avram says, surprised at her rebuke, "but I wouldn't take it as a personal affront. I don't know, maybe I would. What do I know, Ora?" He spreads both hands out in a slightly flamboyant gesture of acquiescence, and an image-fragment of the old Avram flashes. "I don't understand anything about families."

"Come on, you?"

"What do you mean, me?"

"Well, I mean, really!" Ora blinks and the tip of her nose turns red. "Weren't you ever born? Didn't you have parents? A father?"

Avram says nothing.

"Let's sit down for a minute, all my muscles are spasming." She rubs her thighs. "Look, they're actually shaking. It really is harder to go downhill than up!

"I'll never forget the expression on his face the day after he found out that we kill cows, and the way he looked at me for having made him eat meat since he was born. For four years. And his astonishment at the fact that I ate meat, too. Ilan was one thing—that's maybe how he felt, I'm trying to get into his head at the time—you could believe it about Ilan, but me? To think I was capable of murdering for food? I don't know, maybe he was afraid that under certain circumstances I might be capable of eating *him*, too?"

Avram's thumbs run back and forth over his fingertips. His lips move soundlessly.

"Maybe he felt like everything he'd thought about us was completely wrong, or worse—that it was all our conspiracy against him."

"To wolferize him," Avram murmurs.

She looks at him with tense pleading. "Explain to me how I never asked myself what a four-year-old boy feels when he finds out that he belongs to a carnivorous breed?"

Avram can see that she is torn apart and does not know how to comfort her.

"I have to think about it some more," she whispers. "I mustn't stop here. I always stop here, because there was something there, you see, in that whole vegetarianism thing. It's not for nothing that I'm so . . . Look, for example, the way he was depressed afterward, for weeks, really depressed, a four-year-old boy who doesn't want to get up in the morning for preschool because he doesn't want some kid to touch him with 'meat hands,' or he's just afraid of the children and the teacher and recoils from everyone and suspects everyone, do you understand?"

"Do I understand?" Avram snorts.

"Of course you understand. I think you could have understood him perfectly," she says quietly.

"Really?"

"You could understand children in general. Understand them from inside."

"Me? What do I—"

"Who better than you, Avram?"

He lets out a snicker and turns red. The skin of his face glows suddenly. Ora thinks she can see all the pores of his soul opening up.

"When he finally agreed to go back to preschool, he started inciting all the children not to eat meat. He kicked up an intifada at every snack break, dug through their sandwiches, mothers called me to complain, and when he found out that the girl who gave them music lessons was also vegetarian, he simply fell head over heels in love with her. You should have seen it, he was like some alien living among humans who suddenly finds a female alien. He used to draw pictures for her and bring her gifts and all day long all he talked about was Nina, Nina, Nina. He used to call me Nina by mistake. Or maybe it wasn't such a mistake."

They stand up and linger. Avram thinks about the story he wrote when he was serving in Sinai and up until he was taken hostage. It had a subplot whose power he discovered only when he was a POW, and he used to dive into it over and over again to revive himself a little. It was about two seven-year-old orphans who find an abandoned baby in a junkyard. Lots of people were getting rid of their children and babies at the time, and the two kids, a boy and a girl, find the baby, crying and hungry, and decide that he is a God-baby, the afterthought child born to an elderly God, who also apparently wanted to get rid of his child and so he threw the baby into this world. The two children vow to raise the baby themselves and bring him up to be completely different from his cruel, bitter father, so that he will fundamentally change what Avram called simply, long before he was taken hostage, *the ill fate.* And so in between tortures and interrogations, every time he found a drop of energy within himself, Avram delved into the lives of the two children and the baby. Sometimes, mostly at night, he would manage for several minutes to merge completely with the little baby. His broken, tortured body would melt into the innocent, whole creature, and he would remember, or imagine, how he himself was once a baby, and then a little boy, and how the world was one clear circle, until his father got up one evening from the dinner table, overturned the pot of soup on the stove top, and started beating Avram's mother and Avram himself with an outpouring of fury, almost tearing them to shreds, and then walked out and vanished as though he'd never existed.

Avram touches her arm gently. "Come on, Ora. Let's keep going, so we'll find it before—"

"Find what?"

"The notebook, no?"

"Before what?"

"I don't know, before people get there, you don't want anyone—"

She follows him, weak and parched. That whole era pushes its way up inside her. The nightmarish mornings, the decontaminated, censored sandwiches she made—only after, of course, dressing him meticulously as an armed cowboy—the vegetarianism on the one hand, and that murderousness on the other, she now realizes in astonishment. And the suspicious way he checked his sandwich several times, the sour expression of a customs official that came over his little face, the haggling over what time she would pick him up from the preschool of carnivores, and his desperate clinging to her back—she rode him there on a bike—as they got closer to the preschool and heard the children shouting happily. And his wild delusions—that's how she had preferred to think of them at the time—that the children kept touching him on purpose, spitting hot-dog spit on him.

Day after day she abandoned him, left him stuck to the chain-link fence with iron diamonds imprinted on his cheeks, his face smeared with tears and snot as he sobbed loudly. She would turn her back on him, slip away and keep hearing him bawl for many more hours, and as she got farther away from the preschool, she heard him shout louder and louder. And if when he was four she did not know how to help him—powerless against what she felt raging inside him—what good can she do for him now, on this silly, pathetic journey? What good are her chattering with Avram and her baseless bargain with fate? She walks on, and her heavy feet barely obey her. It's good to get away from the news, that man said, especially after yesterday. What happened yesterday. How many. Who. Have they informed the families yet. Run home, run, they're on their way.

She walks almost without looking. Falls through the expanses of an infinite space. She is one human crumb. Ofer is also one human crumb. She can't slow his fall by even one second. And though she gave birth to him, though she is his mother and he came out of her body, now, at this moment, they are merely two specks floating, falling, through infinite, massive, empty space. What it all comes down to, Ora senses, is randomness in everything.

Something makes her zigzag, a slight arrhythmia of the feet, and then comes a painful spasm where her thigh meets her groin.

"Wait, don't run."

Avram seems to be enjoying the quick descent down the hill, the wind slapping his face, cooling it down, but she stops to lean against a pine tree and holds on to the trunk.

"What's up, Ora'leh?"

Ora'leh, he called her. It just slipped out. They both glance quickly at each other.

"I don't know, maybe we should slow down."

She takes small, cautious steps, avoiding as best she can the tormented iliacus muscle. Avram walks beside her, as *Ora'leh* skips between them like a cheerful kid goat.

"Sometimes I used to fantasize that you came in disguise, or sat in a cab by the playground when I was there with him, and watched us. Did you ever do anything like that?"

"No."

"Not even once?"

"No."

"No temptation to know what he looked like, what he was?"

"No."

"You just cut him out of your life."

"Stop, Ora. We've run our course with this."

She swallows a double dose of bile over the "run our course" that somehow rolled from Ilan to him. "Sometimes I would get this feeling in my back, something between a tickle and a prick, here"—she points—"and I wouldn't turn around, I would force myself not to turn around. I would just say to myself quietly, with an insane sort of calmness, that you were there, around me, looking at us, watching us. Come on, let's stop for a minute."

"Again?"

"I don't know. Look, it's not right. To go back down, to go back, it's not good for me."

"The downhill is hard for you?"

"*Going back* is hard for me, retracing our steps—in my body. I feel all crooked, I don't know."

His arms hang by his sides. He stands waiting for her instructions. At such moments, she feels, he annuls his own volition. In the blink of an eye he steps out of his own being and covers himself with an impenetrable coating: *nothing to do with life*.

"Listen, I think—I can't go back."

"I don't get it."

"Me neither."

"But the notebook—"

"Avram, going back is not good for me."

As soon as she says it, the knowledge is as strong and clear as a compulsion. She reverses direction and starts going up the mountain, and it's the right thing, she has no doubt. Avram stands there for a moment, sighs, then uproots himself and follows her, grumbling to himself, "What difference does it make?"

She walks, suddenly light-footed against the incline and against the weight of the man who is probably sitting on her rock right now, at the bottom of the valley, reading her notebook. The man she will probably never see again, who begged her with his eyes to let him help her—his lips like a ripe, cleaved plum—and from whom she now parts with a slight twinge of sorrow. She could do with his cup of coffee, but she has felt the bite of home, and she cannot go backward.

"Even before Ofer was born, ever since the war, since you came back, I've lived with the feeling that I'm always being watched by you."

There. She'd told him what for years had embittered and sweetened her life at the same time.

"Watched how?"

"In your thoughts, in your eyes, I don't know. Watched."

There were days—but of course she will not tell him this, not now—when she felt that at each and every moment, from the second she opened her eyes in the morning, through every motion she made, every laugh she laughed, when she walked and when she lay in bed with Ilan, she was acting a part in his play, in some mad sketch he was writing. And that she was acting for him perhaps more than for herself.

"What is there to understand here?" She stops and suddenly turns around and unwillingly hurls at him: "It's something Ilan and I felt all the time, all those years—that we were acting out a play on your stage."

"I never asked you to be my play," Avram mutters angrily.

"But how could we feel otherwise?"

They both get sucked back, absorbed into one moment, two boys and a girl, almost children: Take a hat, put two pieces of paper in it. But what am I drawing for? You'll find out only afterward.

"And don't get me wrong. Our lives were completely real and full, with the kids and our work, and the hiking and nights out and trips abroad and our friends"—the fullness of life, she thinks again in Ilan's voice—"and there were long periods of time, years, when that look of yours in our back, we hardly felt it. Well, maybe not years. Weeks. Okay, maybe a day here and there. Overseas, for example, when we went on vacation, it was easier to be free of you. Although that's not accurate either, because in the most beautiful places, the most tranquil spots, I would suddenly feel the jab in my back—no, in my stomach, here, and Ilan would feel it too, at the same second, always. Well, it wasn't that hard to feel, because the minute we said anything that sounded like you, or one of your jokes, or just a sentence that begged to be said in your voice, you know. Or when Ofer folded his shirt collar with your exact movement, or when he made the spaghetti sauce you taught me how to make, or a thousand and one other things. And then we'd look each other in the eye and wonder where you were at that moment, how you were doing."

"Ora, don't run," Avram groans behind her, but she doesn't hear.

And that was part of life too, she thinks with some surprise. Part of the fullness of our lives: the void of you, which filled us.

For one moment her entire being is the look she used to give Ofer sometimes, when she gazed deep inside him as if through a one-way mirror, into the place where she saw in him what he himself did not know.

And maybe that's exactly why he stopped looking you in the eye? Maybe that's why he didn't come to the Galilee with you?

She can no longer contain what wells up inside her. She has reached some sort of peak, and something inside her crumbles and melts and relaxes and loosens with an internal surprise mingled with warm sweetness. Tall, strong, and Amazonian she stands on a rock above Avram, hands on her hips, and scans him with a penetrating look. Then she laughs. "Isn't this nuts? Isn't it crazy?"

"What?" he asks breathlessly. "What, out of all that?"

"That first I run away to the edge of the world, and now I suddenly can't take half a step farther from home?"

"So that's what this is? You're running home?"

"I was aching before, my whole body, when I started getting farther away."

"Oh." He massages his hip, which hurts from the last few minutes' sprint.

"You must be thinking, This madwoman has kidnapped me."

He looks up at her with a large, sweaty face and smiles. "I'm still waiting to hear what to offer as ransom."

"That's easy." She leans down to him with her hands on her knees, and her breasts round into the opening of her shirt. "The ransom is Ofer."

They set off—she likes feeling the words pulse: setting off, two friends set off on their way, off we go—and the path is effortless, and they are too, and for the first time since starting the walk, their heads seem less bowed and their eyes are not simply staring at the path and the tips of their shoes. They go uphill and downhill with the path, which becomes a broad gravel road, then they climb over a security fence and lose the markers in a thicket of growth. A field of tall green thistles covers everything, so they decide to trust their nascent travelers' intuition and walk bravely and quietly for another few hundred meters through the thistles, without a clue which way to go, without a grasp—like a baby's first steps, Ora thinks—and her anxiety for Ofer rouses in her, and she feels that she is not helping him now, that the thread she is tying around him is suddenly loosening. Still there is no sign of the path, and their steps grow heavy, and they stop every so often to look around while other pairs of eyes watch them: a lizard pauses to scan them suspiciously, another darts by with a grasshopper in its mouth, and a swallowtail hesitates briefly before laying a pale yellow egg on a fennel stalk. All these creatures seem to sense that something in the general rhythm has gone awry, someone has lost his way. But then they spot an orange-blue-and-white marker glimmering on a rock, and they both point at it, delighting in the sweetness of their small victory. Avram runs over and scuffs his sole on the rock, a male marking his territory, and they both confess to their worry and praise themselves for having managed to keep it to themselves and not burden each other. The markers become frequent again now, as though the path is seeking to compensate its walkers for having tested them.

"I remembered something," Ora says. "When Ofer was born, when we brought him home from the hospital, I stood over his crib and looked at him. He was sleeping, tiny, but with that big head, and the scrunched-up red face with capillaries visible on his cheeks, from the effort of being born, and his fist was clenched next to his face. He looked like a little boxer, tiny and furious, as if he was focused on an anger he had somehow dragged into this world. But mainly, he looked lonely. As though he had fallen from a planet and the only thing he knew was that he had to defend himself.

"And then Ilan came and stood next to me and hugged my shoulders and looked at him with me, and it was so different from when we brought Adam home."

Avram watches the three of them, then quickly looks away and quotes the sign Ilan had stuck on the door to Adam's room: *"The hotel management expects guests to leave when they reach the age of 18!"*

"And Ilan said that when he was in the army and they used to send him to a new base where he didn't know anyone and didn't want to, the first thing he would do was find himself a bed in the farthest corner, and spend his first few hours napping, just to allow himself to adjust to the place unconsciously, in his sleep."

Avram smiles distractedly. "That's right. Once they spent half a day looking for him on the base at Tassa. They thought he'd flipped out on the way."

Ora remembers how she'd elbowed Ilan next to Ofer's crib as he slept with his fist clenched and said emphatically, "Here you are, my darling, I've made another solider for the IDF." Ilan had quickly given the requisite reply that by the time Ofer grew up there would be peace.

So, she thinks, which one of us was right?

They walk side by side, each within himself, yet woven together. Capillary channels burst through Avram constantly as Ora speaks. Where was I when they stood over Ofer's crib? What was I doing at that moment? Sometimes, when he tries out a new medication, he wakes up with an unfamiliar pain and lies awake, his face flushed with cold sweat, listening inside as a stream of infected blood makes its way into an internal organ whose existence he has never been aware of. That's how he feels now, except the fear is completely different, both concealed and alarming, and the channels seem to be drawing a new map as they emerge.

Ora's backpack suddenly feels almost weightless, as though someone has quietly come up to support her from behind. She feels like singing, shouting in joy, dancing through the field. The things she is telling him! The things they're saying to each other!

"Ora, you're running."

She's not sure if he's referring only to how fast she's walking.

She starts to squeak out a laugh. "And do you know what Ofer always says he wants to do when he grows up?"

Avram molds his face into a question mark, holds his breath, amazed at her reckless incursion into the future.

"He wants"—she doubles over, snorting, unable to speak—"he wants a job where they'll do experiments on him while he sleeps."

There you go again smiling, she thinks at Avram. Be careful, otherwise it might stick. Incidentally, I do appreciate your smiles, don't hold back. At home I didn't see much of them from my three wiseacres. Because mostly what those three are good at is making jokes. They're not nearly as good at laughing, especially not at my jokes. They have some sort of screwed-up team spirit, which makes them refuse to laugh at my cracks. "But how do you expect anyone to laugh at your jokes when you hog all the laughter from the get-go?" Ilan had once wondered.

She wants to tell him: You know, Ofer has a laugh exactly like yours. Like a kookaburra in rewind. She hesitates. Your laugh? That one you used to have? She doesn't even know how to phrase it. She almost asks: Do you still laugh that way sometimes, until tears run from your eyes? Until you lie down on your back and twitch your hands and legs? Do you laugh at all? Is there anything that can make you laugh?

The girl, the one he used to mention, the young one. Does she make him laugh?

They come across a tiny lake, and after some hesitation they take a dip, Ora in her underwear—a compromise between several convoluted, conflicting wishes and fears—and Avram fully clothed, then after a few minutes, wearing only his pants. And there is his body, glisteningly pale, dotted with scars and wounds, fleshier than she remembered, but also more solid than she imagined, and it is when he is nude that he emits a surprisingly brawny power. And he of course, as always, chooses to see only the "fleshy" that passes before her eyes, and apologetically pinches a fold of flesh, presenting it for her to study, and shrugs his shoulders with a this-is-all-I've-got sort of grief. But what she remembers is how he used to whisper when he saw her naked body, "Oh God, Ora'leh, such resplendence." Apart from Ada, no one she knew had ever used that word, which had existed only in poetry. Or he would swing his heavy head over her and neigh like a horse, or roar like a lion, or, like old Captain Cat in *Under Milk Wood*, bellow: "*Let me shipwreck in your thighs!*"

She goes under the shallow water and can dimly sees his froggish body faltering nearby, and an old pain resurfaces, the memory of the moments when that thick, creased, careless body would light up and stretch into a blazing thread, and she would hold his face with both hands and force him to look in her eyes, to stay as open as he could, and she would study his eyes and see a gaze with a distant edge that was entirely open, endless, and she would know that there was one place where she was entirely, unconditionally loved, where all of her was gratefully, happily accepted.

Ora was the center, the focal point, and this too was something new he gave her. Ora—not Avram, and not Ora-Avram—was the place where their lovemaking occurred. Her body, far more than his, was the intersection of their passion, and her pleasure was always more desired by him than his own. This astonished her and sometimes troubled her—"Let me do it to *you* now," she would urge, "I want you to enjoy it, too." And he'd laugh: "But when you enjoy it, that's when I enjoy it most, can't you feel that? Can't you see that?" And she did feel it, and she did see it, but could not truly understand it. "What's with the altruism?" she would ask angrily. "What altruism?" he'd say with a sly grin. "It's pure egoism." And she would smile, as if at an incomprehensible joke, and would once again respond to his caresses and licks and feel that she was picking up on something complicated and warped about him, something she might have to work harder to understand if she really wanted to know Avram. But the kisses were sweet, and the licking shook the earth, and she gave in every time, and the moment was never right, and eventually that thing remained unspoken.

But if it had been the other way around, she knew—she hears Avram step out of the water with a splash, which is a pity, she wanted to play around with him a little (but he didn't seem interested), and now she'll have to walk out naked in front of him—if it had been the other way around he would not have given in, he would have investigated and wondered at every answer she gave, and remembered and treasured it and turned it over again and again. She hurries out of the water, hopping from one foot to the other and covering her cold breasts, which are even more shriveled now of course—where's the towel, damn it, why didn't she lay it out before?

Avram throws her a towel, almost without looking, and her teeth chatter a thanks. She turns her back to him and dries herself and remembers what he told her when she was nineteen: that they were perfect because they fit right in his palms. He insisted on referring to her breasts in the feminine, even though the Hebrew word was puzzlingly masculine. "How could it be any other way?" he claimed, and she gladly adopted his view. And how he marveled at them, and never had his fill of them. "Your *resplendencies*," he called them, and "Your *res-plenties*," which confirmed to her again that he honestly did not see her as she was, that he was blind to her shortcomings, that he apparently loved her. And she loved him so much for giving her breasts a place in the world, even before anyone had noticed them, and for believing so passionately that she was a woman, when she herself still doubted it. In the years that followed, when she breast-fed the boys, she often wished Avram could enjoy her too, wished he could know her when she was large and milky and abundant. "Your cup runneth over," he used to delight in telling her when they were together.

She dries herself vigorously, as she always does, scrubbing her skin until it turns pink and steamy, amusing herself with her thoughts, and she stares at Avram with a strange, eager look. He gives her a sideways glance and says, "What?" She pulls herself together and straightens up and flutters her eyelids as if to clean up quickly after the unruly, damp gaze that had slipped out.

When Avram stands up to put his shirt on, Ora announces that enough is enough. "This shirt has to be washed right here, and we'll dry it on the backpack while you walk. And please, open up your backpack right now and find something clean to wear."

They walk past a string of natural springs: Ein Garger, Ein Pu'ah, and Ein Khalav. Pale orange lichen upholsters the branches of almond trees alongside the path. Tadpoles dart away when the shadow of Avram's head falls on the springs. Ora talks. At times she glances at Avram and sees his lips moving, as though he is trying to engrave her words inside him. She talks about long nights sitting with Ofer in the rocking chair when he was burning with fever, sweaty, occasionally shaking and whimpering. She used to fall in and out of sleep with him, talk to him softly, and wipe the sweat off his tortured face. "I never knew you could feel someone else's pain like that," she says, and throws Avram a quick glance, because who more than he had once had the capacity to overflow with another person's pain?

She talks about breast-feeding. How for months Ofer consumed nothing but her milk, and how he held entire conversations with her just by gurgling and looking. "A whole language, so rich that no words can describe it."

She wants him to see her there too, not just Ofer. With her stained nursing bra and her wild hair. With her potbelly that refused for months to deflate, and her desperate helplessness when faced with Ofer's mysterious pains, as he cried and screamed. With her mother's stinging advice, and the far more experienced neighbors', and the nurses' at the lactation clinic. With the joy of knowing that she herself, with her own body, was sustaining a living creature.

And the moments—the chasms—between Ofer's cries of hunger and the second her nipple disappeared into his lips. When he screamed, his body seemed to utterly collapse, like a body that knows it will die. The fear of death flowed into him quickly, and she filled the spaces that were void of food. He screamed and wailed until the rhythmic stream of her life stuff slowly filled him up, and a glow of relief illuminated his little face: he was saved, she had saved him, she had the power to.

She, who every single time she shifted from fourth to third gear had a morbid fear that she was shifting into reverse—she was giving life to a person!

Sometimes, when he was in her arms, she would run her hand quickly over his face and body, and when she did so, she always thought of the transparent threads, a web that tied Ofer to Avram, wherever he was. She knew it made no sense, but she could not stop her hand from making that motion.

Nighttime. The two of them alone in the world, darkness all around, and warm milk gurgles secretly from her innards to his. His tiny hand on her breast, the pinky finger extended like an antenna, the others moving rhythmically with his sucking, and his other hand crushing the fabric of her robe, or a tuft of his hair, or his ear. He opens his eyes and looks at her, and she dives in, imprinted in his gaze. That is how she feels: her face is now being imprinted on his tender, still foggy brain. She experiences a thrilling moment of eternity. In his eyes she sees her own image, and she is more beautiful than she has ever been. She vows to make him a good person, at least better than she is. She will repair everything her own mother ruined in her. Her zeal gushes into a milky spurt that spills on Ofer's mouth and nose: surprised, he chokes and bursts into tears.

As she walks now, she hugs her body while a storm washes over it in waves. Forgotten sensations: fullness and hardness, dribbles that leaked through her shirt in the middle of the street, at work, or in a café, at the mere thought of Ofer—"Just thinking of him made me drip," she laughs, and Avram, his face bathed in her light, wonders if she let Ilan taste her milk.

. . .

A shadow falls on them at midday. They are walking through the Tsivon streambed, a deep, strange channel that silences them. The path meanders among large, broken rocks, and they must climb and take calculated steps. The oak trees around them are forced to grow tall, stretch higher and higher to reach the sunlight. Pale ivy and long ferns cascade down from the treetops. They walk over a bed of crumbling dry leaves among bloodless cyclamens and albino fungi. It's almost dark here. Touch, she says, and puts his hand on a rock covered with green moss. It feels soft and furry. They are surrounded by silence. Not a single bird chirps. "Like a fairy-tale forest," Ora whispers. Avram looks around him. His shoulders are slightly hunched. His fingers dart, counting each other constantly. "Don't worry," she says, "I'll find the way out." Avram points: "Look over there." A single ray of light has penetrated the foliage and shines on a rock.

When we get back, he thinks, I'm going to read a book about the Galilee, or even just look at a map. I want to see where I've been. What would it be like for her to be hiking here with Ofer instead of me? he wonders. What would she talk about with him? What is it like to be completely alone with your child in a place like this? Must be terribly awkward. Then again, Ora wouldn't let him keep quiet. He smiles. They wouldn't stop talking and laughing at the people they met on the way. Maybe they'd laugh at me if they happened to run into me.

They climb up a narrow path where thick tree roots crawl all over the earth. The backpacks weigh them down. She thinks: What would it be like if Avram and Ofer were walking here in the forest, alone? A journey of men.

Suddenly, as if a hand has passed in front of their faces, they walk out of the shade into the sunlight. Another few moments and a meadow is revealed, and a hillside, and orchards blossoming in white. "So beautiful," she whispers so as not to shock the silence.

The path flows softly. A broad, well-trodden walking path, with an avenue of weeds down the center. Like a horse's mane, Avram thinks.

She tells him about Ofer's journeys of discovery through the house, his insistent examinations of every single book on the bottom shelves, the plant leaves, the pots and lids in the lower kitchen drawers. She gives him every memory chip of his babyhood that pops into her mind. When he fell off a chair and had to get seven stitches in his chin at Magen David; when a cat scratched his face at the playground—"there's no scar," she says reassuringly, and Avram snatches a fluttering touch of some of his own scars, on his arms, shoulder, chest, and back, and a surprising ripple of joy runs through him because Ofer is whole; his body is whole.

Avram seems to be growing more and more awake: he wants to know when Ofer started talking and what his first word was. *"Abba,"* Ora says. Daddy. But Avram mishears and responds incredulously: *"Avram?"* Then he realizes his error, and they both laugh. And of course he asks immediately what Adam's first word was. (*"Or,"* she replies. Light. She feels him swallow back the obvious question: Not *ima?* But instead Avram says, *"Or* is almost 'Ora,' " and she hadn't even thought of that; she remembers that Ofer always claimed his first words were: "Take me to your leader.") She reminds Avram of his mother's heavy bureau, which became a changing table for the boys, and the black bookshelf, which held all their childhood books. She manages to remember quite a lot from the books she used to read to them and recites by heart: "Pluto was a dog from Kibbutz Megiddo . . ." Then she explains to the ignorant Avram about the charms of every child's favorite rabbit, Mitz Petel, and his animal friends. She smiles to herself: the two of us are a bit like the giraffe and the lion in the book.

She tries to imagine little Ofer, bathed and clean and ready for bed, resting his head on Avram's shoulder while he tells a story. Ofer is wearing his green pajamas with the half-moons, but she can't see what Avram is wearing. She can't even see Avram himself, but she feels his broad physical presence and the way Ofer leans on it. She thinks Avram would have probably made up a new story for Ofer every night and put on plays and shows for him. She has no doubt he would have been bored reading the same story every evening for weeks, as Ofer used to insist. She can hear the special, mysterious, soft, stomach-trembling voice that Ilan used when he read bedtime stories to the boys. She does not tell Avram, but remembers for herself and for Ofer how much Ilan loved bedtime. Even when the office was terribly busy, he would come home to help put the boys to bed, and she loved to cuddle with them in bed, and listen to him read.

The path is easy and fluid. Avram spreads his arms out, surprised at how comfortable the *sharwals* feel on his body—Ora had folded the cuffs up three times until they fit his "peanut stature," as he'd joked. She tells him about Ofer's day care and his first friend, Yoel, who moved to the States with his parents and broke Ofer's heart. "Such little stories," she apologizes, but from one story to the next, from one word to the next, baby Ofer becomes clearer in her own mind, slowly sculpted into a boy: the tiny baby draws out into the toddler, his clothes change, his toys, his haircut, his eyes. She shows him Ofer playing alone, concentrating, absorbed in a game. She tells him about Ofer's affection for minuscule toys with lots of detailed accessories. She was amazed at his ability to collect them with infinite patience, match them up, put them together, and take them apart again.

"That's not something he got from *me*." Avram laughs, and Ora is moved: In what he negates, she hears what he is affirming.

When he was eighteen months old, they went on vacation to Dor Beach. Early in the morning he woke up while Ora, Ilan, and Adam were still asleep, climbed down from his bed, and walked out of the cabin alone. Barefoot, wearing a T-shirt and a diaper, he padded onto the big lawn adjacent to the beach and saw, probably for the first time in his life, a huge sprinkler spraying water. He stood watching in amazement, giggling and murmuring to himself, and then he started playing with the sprinkler. He crept up to the giant spurts of water and ran away before they could lick his feet. Ora, now awake and watching from behind the cabin wall, could see his happiness right before her eyes: she could see happiness itself, sunny and golden, refracted in the sprays of water.

Then the sprinkler caught Ofer and doused his body and head. Shocked, he stood paralyzed in the stream, trembling all over, his face scrunched up and turned to the sky, shaking his tight fists. She shows him to Avram, standing with her eyes closed and her lips in a trembling pout. A tiny, lonely human among the lashes of water that spun all around him, accepting a sentence he did not understand. She hurried over to rescue him, but something stopped her and sent her back to her hiding place. Perhaps, she tells Avram, it was a desire to see Ofer all alone like that just once. To see him as a person out in the world.

Ofer finally uprooted his feet and went to stand at a safe distance from the sprinkler, which he now watched with wounded pride, soundlessly whimpering and trembling through all his limbs. But he quickly forgot his insult when he spotted a wonderful new creature: a limping old horse with a straw hat on its head and its ears sticking through holes torn out of the hat. The horse was drawing a cart on which sat a man, also elderly, also wearing a straw hat. The old man came every day at dawn to pick up the garbage from the beach, and now he was taking it to the dump. Ofer stood in a state of excitement, still dripping with water, and a circular sense of wonder lit up his eyes. As the horse and cart drove by, the man noticed the baby, gave him a toothless smile, and charmingly removed his fraying straw hat with a flourish that stretched from his old age to Ofer's childhood.

Ora was afraid Ofer would be scared of the man, but he only patted his little stomach, laughed a rolling laugh, and slapped his head a few times with both hands, perhaps mimicking the doff of the hat.

Then he followed the horse.

He walked without looking back, and Ora followed him. "He was full of power and without a hint of fear. Just a little thing of eighteen months."

A tiny leaf ripples inside Avram's soul and floats on ahead of him. Behind his tightly shut eyelids, a small boy walks on an empty beach, his body leaning forward, wearing nothing but a diaper and a T-shirt, all of him moving toward and onward and ahead.

The cart bore piles of garbage, cardboard boxes, torn fishing nets, and large trash bags. Flies hovered above it, and a trail of stench lingered behind it. Every so often the old man wearily yelled at the horse and waved a long whip. Ofer walked behind them, along the water's edge, and Ora behind him, seeing through his eyes the wonder of the large, emaciated beast, and perhaps—she is guessing now, as she recounts the story for Avram—perhaps he even thought that everything moving up there in front of him was one single wonderfully complex creature, with two heads and four legs, large wheels, leather harnesses and straw hats, and a buzzing cloud above. As she talks, she distractedly quickens her pace, pulled along by the living memory—Ofer on the beach, a bold puppy bristling with the future, she behind him, hiding at times, although there was no need because he never turned to look back. She wondered how far he would go, and he answered her with his steps: forever. She saw—and this she does not have to say, even Avram understands—how the day would come when he would leave her, just get up and go, as they always do, and she guessed a little of what she would feel on that day, a little of what now, without any warning, digs its predatory teeth into her.

When he could no longer keep up with the horse and the old man,

Ofer stopped, waved at them for a moment longer, his fist opening and closing, then turned around with a sweet, mischievous smile, and spread his arms out to her happily, as if he'd known all along that she was there, as if anything else were not possible. He ran to her arms shouting: "Nommy, Nommy, bunny!"

"You see, in his books, in the pictures, a creature with a long head and long ears was a bunny."

"That's a horse," she told him and hugged him tightly to her chest. "Say 'horse.' "

"That was one of Ilan's things," she tells him on their next coffee break, in a purple field of clover dotted with the occasional unruly stalk of yellow asphodel humming with honeybees. "Every time he taught Ofer or Adam a new word, he would ask them to repeat it out loud. To tell you the truth, it got on my nerves sometimes, because I thought, Why does he have to do it that way—he's not their trainer. But now I think he was right, and I even envy him, retroactively, because that way he was always the first one to hear every new word they said."

"That *is* from me," Avram says with awkward hesitation. "You know that, right? That's me."

"What is?"

He stammers, blushing. "I was the one who told Ilan in the army that if I ever had a kid, I would hand him every new word, present it to him, and it would be like, you know, like a covenant between us."

"So it's from you?"

"He . . . he didn't tell you?"

"Not that I remember."

"He probably forgot."

"Yeah, maybe. Or maybe he didn't want to tell me, not to pour salt on your wound with me. I don't know. We both had all sorts of rituals about you, and moments to be with you, but it was mainly the words, and the way they spoke, the boys." She sighs, and her droopy upper lip seems to droop a little more. "Well, you know, I mean he had that whole thing with you—"

"With me?" Avram sounds alarmed.

"Come on, it's obvious. The two of you were so *verbal*, such chatterboxes, I swear, and with Ilan . . . Hey, what's that sound?"

Something disturbs the thistles nearby. They hear short, rapid thrashings coming from several directions, and then the rustle of a living creature, something that runs and stops, with panting breaths. Avram jumps up and pokes around, and then comes the barking, in different voices, and Avram shouts at her to get up, and she spills her coffee and tries to stand up and trips on something and falls, and Avram stands over her, frozen, his eyes and mouth gaping in a transparent shout, and dogs—dogs come from all around them.

When Ora finally manages to get up, she counts three, four, five. He jerks his head to the left, and there are at least four more there, of different breeds, large and small, dirty and wild, standing there barking furiously at them. Avram pulls Ora to him, grabs her wrist, but she still doesn't get it. How painfully slowly her brain processes the joints and connectors of every new situation, always. And on top of that, instead of kicking into self-defense mode, she has a foolish tendency—a completely un-survivor-like tendency, as Ilan once pointed out—to linger on the minor details (beads of sweat are spreading quickly under Avram's armpits; one of the dog's legs is broken and folded beneath its body; Ilan's eyelid had jerked wildly when he told her, nine months ago, that he was leaving her; the man they met at the Kedesh River had been wearing, on top of everything else, two identical wedding rings on two fingers).

The dogs crowd into a sort of triangle, with a large, black, broad-chested hound at its vertex, and slightly behind him, a strapping golden mutt. The black one barks wildly, almost without stopping for breath, and the golden one makes a deep, prolonged, ominous rumble.

Avram spins around and breathes asthmatically. "You here, me there!" he says quickly. "Kick, and yell!"

She tries to shout but finds she cannot. Some kind of shame in front of Avram, idiotic embarrassment, and perhaps in front of the dogs, too. And herself? When has she really shouted? When has she yelled throat-rending howls? And when will she?

The dogs bark madly, their bodies rocking, their snarls and wailing charged with stubborn, raw fury. She stares at them. She is fascinated by the gaping mouths, the strands of saliva between the teeth. The dogs slowly approach, closing in on them. Avram hisses at her to find a stick, a branch, something, and Ora tries to remember things she's picked up here and there from Adam, or in chance conversations with his friends.

There was one sweet boy, Idan, a gifted musician, who had joined the army's K-9 special forces unit. Once, when she drove him and Adam to a concert in Caesarea, he told them how they train dogs to attack the "dominant part" of a wanted suspect, a hand or a foot, which the suspect might use to try to protect himself from the dog. He explained to Ora that a regular dog will "click" its teeth when it bites someone's arm, but a dog in their unit—Idan himself had a Belgian shepherd, which he said had the strongest instincts: you could condition them any way you wanted—could lock in on an arm or a leg or a face. Amazing how she can pull out this useful information. But Idan was the one who sicced dogs on people, and now she was on the receiving end.

"The black one," Avram exhorts, "keep looking for him." The large male, undoubtedly the leader, stands nearby, watching her with blood-shot eyes. A huge, dense lump that seems to be shedding its canine shell and reincarnating itself as a primeval beast. And right then another dog, a smaller, bolder one, cuts through the bushes in Avram's direction, and Ora jumps up and grabs hold of Avram, almost pulling him down with her. He turns to her furiously and his own face is like an animal's for a second—a peace-loving, vegetarian, and generally fearful animal. A gnu or a llama or a camel that has suddenly found itself in the midst of a massacre. Then he hurls one sharp kick at the dog, who sails through the air with terrifying silence, spread out like a rag, with its head bent backward unnaturally, and he is closely followed by one of Avram's sneakers.

"I killed him," Avram whispers in astonishment.

Silence hangs in the air. The dogs sniff nervously. It occurs to Ora that if she and Avram don't attack, the dogs will settle down. She thinks about her own dog, Nicotine, and tries to draw his softness to this place, coaxing his domestic scent to waft out of her toward them. She looks around. The whole field is dotted with dogs. Almost all of them look like pets gone feral. Here and there a colorful collar peeks out, sub-merged in thick, filthy fur. A few glorious tails still wag, hinting at pam-pering and devotion. All their eyes are infected, covered with layers of yellow crud, and flies hover around them. Nicotine, who was her gift to Ilan when he stopped smoking, was as plain to her as a sister soul, but what is happening here is almost outside the realm of nature. It is rebel-lion. Betrayal. The big black one stands quietly, examining the situa-tion, and the others—including Ora and Avram—tensely await his expressions. Slightly behind him stands the golden dog. When Ora looks at it closely, it turns away in embarrassment and runs its tongue over its upper lip, and Ora knows it's a bitch.

"Stones, pick up stones," Avram whispers out of the corner of his mouth. "We'll throw them."

"No, wait." She touches his arm.

"Just don't show them we're afraid—"

"Wait, don't do anything, they'll leave."

The dogs cock their heads as though following the conversation.

"And don't look them in the eye, not in the eye."

Avram looks down.

He and Ora face each other silently. A pair of falcons hovers above in a mating dance, cackling with laughter.

A shudder runs through the big black dog's chest. He takes a few steps and circles them broadly. The other dogs stand tense, their fur on end.

"Fuckit," Avram whispers, "we've lost our chance."

The black one keeps pacing slowly, drawing an invisible line around them, without taking his eyes off them. The dogs follow along, completing a circle. Ora seeks out the golden bitch, who looks wild and bold as she stands beside the black dog. A handsome couple, Ora thinks with a strange twinge of jealousy—the forgotten longing, to be a handsome couple.

Suddenly it all sparks up again, as though the circular motion has fanned a primordial urge in the dogs. At once their faces and bodies sharpen. Wolves and hyenas and jackals now encircle Ora and Avram, and they too turn around in a circle. Avram's back touches hers. He is wet. They move together, forward, backward, to either side. They are one body. She can dimly hear a deep, hoarse growl. But perhaps it's hers.

The dogs break into a slow trot around them. Ora feverishly searches for the golden one. She must find her. She scans dog after dog like beads on a necklace. There she is, running with them. Ora's spirits fall: the bitch's face is also sharp and gaping now, and her cheeks are drawn up in a grimace that exposes her canines.

Gray lightning flashes, something seizes Ora's pants from behind, at her calf, and she jumps in horror and kicks out without seeing. She hits something, her foot almost dismantled by the powerful pain, and a dirty, bedraggled mutt screeches, runs away, and sits licking its wound at some distance. Avram emits twisted, high-pitched sounds, not words but crushed syllables. She can almost feel the shaky scaffolding of his soul, which he has worked so hard to erect, collapsing because of this foolishness. Right at that moment he thrashes a stick, very close to her thigh, and a gaping hole opens up in the circle. Then comes another whistling blow, followed by a nauseating sound: something broken escapes with a whimper, pulling its rear body with its two front legs, and again she sees Nicotine, old and sick, dragging himself to his basket with a befuddled look in his eyes.

She starts to whistle. Not a tune. Something meaningless and monotonous and mechanical that sounds like the hum of a broken appliance. Her lips are pursed and she whistles. The dogs prick up their ears. Avram throws her a suspicious glance. His beard is wild, his face alarmingly sharp.

She keeps on. Sensitive ears vibrate as they decipher a signal broadcast from another world. Her eyes dart in every direction. She tries to produce a low, soft whistle, as full and rich as her lungs can muster, then sticks with the loose whistle, guarding it like an ancient fire.

An emaciated brown mutt stops moving, sits on its hind legs, and scratches behind its ears. In so doing, it breaks the circle. The other dogs spread out a little. The golden bitch walks hesitantly to one side, panting heavily. A large Canaan with an ugly open wound on its thigh limps away, then stops in the middle of the field and looks up at the sky as though he's forgotten what he meant to do. Ora thinks she sees him yawn.

The black dog shakes his head a few times and tediously scans the other dogs. Now Ora whistles her Nicotine whistle, the first few notes of "My Beloved with Her Pure White Neck," a song she and Ilan used to whistle to each other, too. The black dog barks vacantly at the sky and walks away. The others straggle behind him. He pricks up his tail and starts to run, and they follow. The golden bitch trails behind them. The pack looks smaller to Ora now. She gives Avram a sideways glance. His stick—now she sees it's a branch, from a eucalyptus or a pine tree— is still held high in his hand. His chest rises and falls like a bellows.

She whistles. Ilan always distractedly whistled their song in the shower, and she, lying in bed, would put down her book to listen. Once he whistled it in a low key, standing at one end of the bustling lobby of the Jerusalem Theater. She, at the other end, picked it up and started walking toward him, whistling softly until they met and embraced.

Avram looks at her questioningly. She whistles after the pack of dogs as they recede into the distance. She rounds her lips and whistles to the golden bitch, who grudgingly turns her head and slows down. Ora leans forward with her hands on her knees. "Come," she whispers.

The other dogs sprint away, barking, chasing one another, engaging in momentary fights, galloping across the field with floppy or perked-up ears, re-forming themselves into a pack. The golden one looks at them and back at Ora. Then, hesitantly, with a trembling paw, she starts to walk in Ora's direction. Without moving, Ora whistles softly, almost imperceptibly, guiding the bitch. Avram lets the branch drop. The bitch walks through a patch of stubbly growth that clings to her broad chest.

Ora slowly crouches down on one knee. The bitch stops abruptly, one paw suspended, her black nostrils open wide. Ora finds a slice of bread on their cloth, and carefully tosses it near the dog. She pulls back and growls.

"Eat it, it's good."

The bitch cocks her head. Her eyes are large and dirty. Ora talks to her: "You lived in a house once, you had a home, people took care of you and loved you. You had a bowl for food and a bowl for water."

With cautious, hunched steps, the bitch walks over to the bread. Growling, her brows arched, she does not take her eyes off Avram and Ora.

"Don't look at her," Ora whispers.

"I was looking at *you*," Avram says awkwardly, and turns away.

The bitch grabs the bread and devours it. Ora throws her a piece of cheese. She sniffs it and eats. Then a few pieces of salami. Some biscuits. "Come here, you're a good dog, good, good dog." The dog sits down and licks her chops. Ora pours water from a bottle into a plastic dish and sets it down on the ground between her and the dog, then goes back to her place. The dog sniffs at it from a distance. Reluctant to approach, attracted yet repelled. A slight whimper escapes her lips. "Drink, you're thirsty." The bitch approaches the dish without taking her eyes off Ora and Avram. Her leg muscles shake and she looks as though she might collapse. She laps up the water quickly and retreats. Ora moves closer and the bitch bares her teeth and her fur stands on end. Ora talks to her and pours some more water. She does this two more times, until the bottle is empty. The bitch sits next to the dish. Then she sprawls out and starts gnawing at a ball of fur and thistles stuck to her paw.

And now they can no longer avoid looking at each other.

Ora and Avram stand there, spent, their sweat heavy with the stench of fear, ashamed. A flicker of embarrassment crosses their faces. They have not yet had time to robe themselves in their former skins. Avram stares at her and shakes his head slowly, wonderingly, gratefully, and his blue eyes fill with an undulating stir, and her body suddenly remembers his embrace, and for a moment she wonders stupidly if she should whistle for *him* to come. But he comes anyway, a mere three steps, and hugs her, grasps her tightly, as he used to, and whispers, "Ora, Ora'leh." The bitch looks up at them.

A moment later Ora pulls away and stands staring at him as though she has not seen him for years. Then she falls on him again and starts to pound him with both hands and hit his face and scratch it, without saying anything, panting drily. Taken aback, he shields his face, then tries to hold her, to encircle her in his arms so that she cannot hurt him or harm herself, because she has started to scratch herself too and hit her own face with her hands. "Ora, stop, stop," he shouts, he begs, until he is able to trap her in his arms and hold her tightly to his body to stop her wildness. She struggles and grunts and kicks him, and every time she feels a space of nothing between them she tries to fill it with a punch or a kick or an angry breath, and the wilder she gets, the closer he has to hold her, until they are practically molded into one, intertwined, and she grits her teeth and yells, "You piece of shit, all these years . . . punishing us . . . who is to blame here . . ." Her voice grows weaker and weaker until she flops against his chest, her head in the round of his shoulder, amazed at herself, at what came out of her—why now, why, this was not at all what she wanted to say to him. He does not move, only holds her to him and runs his hand up and down her back, over her sweat-soaked shirt, and she breathes deeply and whispers into his body just as she spoke a few days earlier into the pit she dug in the earth. Avram somehow senses that she is praying, but not to him, rather to someone inside him, asking him to open up and let her in. His hands and body constantly knead her body, and she kneads his, fingers tightening over limbs, wondering, remembering. For one moment—no more—there is a sudden abandonment, like a fleeting moment of disorderly conduct, and Ora's legs almost fail her, but she remains standing with the last of her strength. What is this? she wonders. What's happening here? She holds her head back, wanting to look in his eyes and ask, but he pulls her to him with new-old fervor, imprinting himself on her again. That's exactly how he used to be, and she suddenly remembers how the whole time they were screwing—*nut-and-bolting*, he called it—it was as though he were hallucinating inside her, growing intermittently harder and softer, moving in a slow somnambulism, a sort of continuous sleepwalking in which his mind and body were unshackled, so different from his usual rhythm when he was outside of her, different from his huntsman-like alertness. He once told her that from the moment he entered her, it was though a circle closed inside him and he immediately sank into a dream. "It's like an underwater maze," he said, when she asked him to try to describe it. "No, no, forget that. It's like a dream that you can't tell anyone or re-create when you wake up. That's what's fun about it: that I can't find the words. That *I* can't find the words."

Of course she felt, in those distant years, the other women and girls he saw through the canopy of his closed eyelids. She felt the rhythmic, salacious alternating of his passions and fantasies as he made love to her. And every time she felt a twinge of jealousy, she told herself that you could not love Avram without loving his imagination, his parallel dimensions, his thousands of hallucinatory women. But she would quickly search for his mouth so that she could give it *her* kiss—deep, demanding, vigorous—or even just touch the tip of his tongue with hers, to bring him back to the source that gave rise to all that in him, and he would instantly realize what she was doing and smile with his swollen eyelids and make a movement with his body that said: Here, I'm back.

All that time, in all those years, with all the talk and the chatter, intrigues lodged between his foot and her ankle, between his eyelashes and her navel. And she was so young, she didn't even know you were allowed to laugh like that in the midst of lovemaking. She hadn't realized that her body was so lighthearted and mischievous and cheerful. And it all somehow comes back to her now, barely able to stand, almost falling into his body. It's been years since she's allowed herself to remember how interwoven they used to be, and how all of his limbs climbed over all of her limbs—"Is that why they call it *clim*axing?" he joked once. "We mustn't waste even one-thousandth of a touch," he would murmur, "not a finger or a hip or an eyelid, certainly not two thighs or an earlobe." And when she was with him she was inexhaustible, climaxing and laughing, laughing and climaxing in short, quick spurts, while he held back like a Tibetan yogi, gathering it in from all the corners of himself, as he explained with a conspiratorial smile. From the farthest regions, from the tips of his toes, his elbows, eyelashes, neck, *starting from a distance*, until she felt his signals, and she would smile in her heart, here it is, here, the sharpening of all his flesh, the filling up, the high tide, and the quick departure of humor from his body—suddenly serious, determined, fateful, with his muscles weaving around her, and the grasping, like a giant clamp, and then his essence, the beat of his imprint deep inside her. She remembers.

Then, with his head heavy on her chest, she would feel him resurface to his senses. Slow, suspended, with fetal movements, he would moan, "Ora'leh, did I hurt you?"

Here too, in the open field, he hugs her, steadies her, then gently holds her away. A pity. She was ready, if he'd only wanted to. They may have struggled that way for a minute, no longer, yet she crossed an ocean of time. And where is he? What does he want? What does she know? Only that he is grasping her, holding her in his arms, softly caressing her hair, asking, "Did I hurt you?"

Then he lets go, pushes himself away from her as though he has realized what almost happened, the ghost that was almost conjured up. Ora rocks dizzily and takes hold of his arm again. "Wait, don't run away, why are you running away from me?" She looks at him weakly, touches a long bloody scratch on his nose, which she has given him, and says quietly, "Avram, do you remember us?"

"ILAN CAME HOME. After he ran away from me and Adam and tried out houses all over Jerusalem, he came back to us, to the house in Tzur Hadassah. As soon as he did, he was shocked at Adam, I mean at me, at the way I'd neglected Adam and his education and his speech, and any order and discipline, and he started improving him." Ora laughs. "Do you understand? For almost three years, Adam and I were more or less on our own, two wild beasts in the jungle, no laws, no commandments, and then the missionary landed. And we suddenly discovered that nothing we did was right, that we didn't have an agenda or a routine, we ate when we were hungry and slept when we were tired, and the house was pretty much a dump.

"Wait," she says, holding up a finger, "there's more. That Adam walked around the neighborhood naked and scarfed down massive amounts of chocolate and watched TV indiscriminately and got to day care at eleven a.m. And at his advanced age he still didn't know how to go potty properly. And he called me Ora, not Mom!

"Ilan, being Ilan, took matters into his own hands right then and there. He did everything very nicely of course, with lots of smiles—he knew he was on probation with me—but all of a sudden, for example, clocks turned up around the house. One in the kitchen, a little one in the living room, and a Mickey Mouse clock in Adam's room. And there were cleaning days, and we had to clear out the mess and get rid of the junk. The fun was over! 'This Saturday we're sorting through Adam's toys, next Saturday your paperwork, and what about that pharmacy spilling out of the bathroom cabinet?' "

She laughs joylessly.

"I liked it, don't get me wrong. It was nice to have a man in the house and to feel that someone was starting to eliminate the chaos. A sort of purification. The rescue forces had arrived. And don't forget that I was pregnant with Ofer, so I didn't have a lot of strength to resist, and all his enthusiasm signaled that he was pretty serious about his nesting and that maybe this time he would stay."

Avram walks beside her, wriggling his toes in Ofer's shoes. When he first stepped into the shoes, he immediately announced that he was swimming in them, and that it wouldn't work. "It will, it will," Ora mumbled and took out a pair of thick walking socks from his backpack. "Put these on." He did, and still the shoes were a little big, but they were more comfortable than his old pair, whose soles were so worn out that he could feel the ground through them. "Just let your feet sail, and think about what a nice feeling that is," Ora advised.

He spreads out in Ofer's space, measuring his toes. The soles of his feet study his son's footprints. Tiny dips and mounds, secret messages. Things even Ora doesn't know about Ofer.

"But most of all, he fixed up Adam. Cleanliness and neatness and discipline, like I said, and then came the reeducation. How can I explain it? Adam was a fairly quiet boy. I wasn't much of a chatterbox either, back then. I didn't really have that many people to talk to. Adam and I were alone at home most of the time, and we had our little life, and it was pretty good, considering, and talking really wasn't the most important part of it. We got along just fine without a lot of words. We understood each other perfectly. And I also think—although maybe not—"

"What?"

"Maybe I'd had a little too many words out of the two of you, all those years, you and Ilan together. Maybe I wanted a bit of quiet."

He sighs.

"All that talk of yours, the brilliant, witty yada yada yada that never stopped for a second, that constant effort the two of you made."

Ilan and me, Avram thinks. Two arrogant peacocks.

"And I always felt a bit left out."

"You? Really?" Troubled, he does not know how to tell her that he always felt she was the center, their focal point. That she, in her own way, created them.

"Well, I never really got into that thing of yours."

"But it was all because of you, for you."

"Too much, too much."

They walk silently. The dog trails them at a fixed distance, her ears cocked in their direction.

"And Ilan"—she returns from her contemplations—"was really amazed at Adam, at his underdeveloped speech, as he put it, and he started teaching him how to talk. Do you get it? At the age of two and three-quarters he put him through talking boot camp."

"How?"

"He just talked to him all the time. He would take him to day care in the morning and talk about everything they saw on the way. Bring him home from day care and talk to him about what happened at day care. He asked questions and demanded answers. He wouldn't let him off the hook. It was like a one-man protest movement: Fathers Against Silence."

Avram laughs softly and Ora turns red: her joke worked.

"He talked to Ofer while he dressed him and while he put him to bed and while he fed him. I heard him all the time. There was a constant hubbub of speech at home, and Adam and I weren't used to that kind of noise, and it wasn't easy for me. I'm sure it wasn't for Adam, either.

"There was no more pointing and saying 'that.' Now there was 'doorframe,' 'lock,' 'shelves,' 'saltshaker.' I heard it in the background the whole time, like a broken record. 'Say "shelf." ' 'Shelf.' 'Say "grasshopper." ' 'Grasshopper.' And he was right, I'm not saying he wasn't. I felt he was doing the right thing, and I could really see Adam's world growing richer and fuller because he suddenly had names for things. I'm just not . . . I don't . . . You see, I don't really know how to say it exactly." She laughs and points sharply to the spot between her eyes: "This."

Her heart pounded when she saw the immense thirst coming from Adam, which she previously hadn't detected at all. Because after the initial shock, he seemed to get what Ilan was offering him, and she suddenly had a prattling child.

Ilan—she explains to Avram—talked to Adam like you talk to a grown-up, both in vocabulary and in tone. It stung her to hear the businesslike, egalitarian way Ilan addressed the boy, using a voice that did not contain a hint of the childish, slightly playful tone that she herself used. There was almost no word he considered too sophisticated for a conversation with Adam. "Say 'association.' " "Association." "Say 'philosophy,' 'Kilimanjaro,' 'crème brûlée.' "

Ilan explained to him about synonyms, drawing pictures of words as identical twins. At three, Adam learned that the moon was also a crescent, or Luna. That at night it could be dark, dim, or even dusky. That a person could jump, but also leap and hop. (As Avram listens, a strange smile curls inside him, slightly proud, slightly embarrassed.) Ilan used nursery rhymes to teach him grammar and spent hours practicing "my child," "his rabbit," "her fingers."

Every so often Ora would find the courage to protest. "You're training him to do tricks, you're turning him into your toy."

"For him it's just like LEGO, but with words," Ilan replied.

She wanted to object—You're just marking him as your territory—but all she said was, "He's too young for that, a boy of his age doesn't have to know all about possessive pronouns."

"But look how much he enjoys it!"

"Of course. He can tell you're enjoying it and he wants you to like him. He'll do anything to make you like him."

"And listen to this"—she tells Avram parenthetically—"about six months after Ilan came home, Adam asked where the man in the hut had gone."

"What did you say?"

"I just couldn't talk, and all Ilan said was, 'He left, he's never coming back.' I only just remembered that. What were we talking about?"

She was weak. Her second pregnancy, which had begun with ease and a sense of health, grew burdensome and sickly toward the end. Most of the time she felt elephantine and drained and ugly. "In the last trimester, Ofer was pressing on a nerve that gave me horrible pain every time I stood up." For the last two months she had to spend most of the time lying in one position, in bed or in the big armchair in the living room, and her breathing was labored, cautious—it hurt to breathe sometimes. She would stare at Ilan and Adam as they buzzed around her with intellectual fervor while she grew weaker and weaker, squeezing into the old familiar niche she had carved out years ago with a dull sort of self-deprecation.

She had no way to prevent Ilan and Adam from constantly amusing themselves with synonyms, rhymes, and association games, and of course she was flattered when the day-care teacher talked about Adam's huge leap, and how within such a short time he seemed to have matured by at least two years. His status at day care greatly improved, although his wetting problem grew worse for some reason. But at least he was able to report the little accidents, so it was hard to get angry. " 'My pee-pee escaped,' " Ora quotes with a crooked smile. "What are you smiling about?" she asks irritably.

"I was thinking," Avram says without looking at her, "that I would have definitely done that, too."

"With your child? What Ilan did?"

"Yes."

"I can't say the thought never crossed my mind," she notes, and vows not to expand on this point, ever.

"What?"

"Never mind."

"Come on, what?"

"That that was really what he was looking for. A partner like you. So that he'd have someone to be witty and clever with."

Avram silently twirls a strand of his beard.

"Because I wasn't a good enough substitute," she continues drily. "At least not in that regard. I couldn't do it and I didn't try, either."

"But why did you even have to?"

"Ilan needed it. Oh, how he needed you and what you had together. And how withered he felt without you."

Avram's face burns, and Ora has the sudden gnawing thought that she may not have understood what Ilan was going through at all, and that perhaps he had not been looking for a substitute for Avram, but trying to *be* Avram. Excited, she hastens her steps: Maybe he was trying as hard as he could to be a father the way he imagined Avram would be.

They are so lost in their thoughts that the sudden appearance of a road startles them. What's more, the path markings have disappeared. Ora walks back to look but returns disappointed. We were happy with our path, she thinks, and now what? How will we get to Jerusalem?

The road is not especially wide, but vehicles zoom past frequently, and they both feel slow and dull in comparison. They would happily retreat to the quiet, light-filled meadow, or even back to the shadowy forest. But they can't go back. Ora cannot, and Avram seems to have been infected by her onward-and-forward purposefulness. They stand there confused, looking left and right, pulling their heads back with every passing car.

"We're like those Japanese soldiers who emerged from the forests thirty years after the war was over," she says.

"I really am like that," he reminds her.

She can see that the road and the violence that emanates from it are scaring Avram. His face and body have locked up. She looks for the bitch. She was walking behind them just a few moments ago, keeping her distance, but now she's gone. What to do? Should she go back and look for her? And how will she get her across the road? How will she get the dog and Avram across?

"Come on," she says, swinging into action, knowing that if she doesn't do something now, his enervation will seep into her and paralyze them. "Come on, we're crossing."

She holds his hand, feeling how defeated and stalked he is by the road.

"When I give the word, run."

He nods feebly. His eyes are on the tips of his shoes.

"You can run, right?"

His face suddenly changes. "Tell me something, wait a minute—"

"Later, later."

"No, wait. What you said before—"

"Pay attention, after the truck. Now!"

She takes some steps into the road but is pulled back—his mass, his weight. She quickly looks to both sides. A bright purple jeep roars around the bend at them, flashing its headlights. They are stuck almost in the middle of the lane—can't swallow and can't throw up—and Avram is frozen. She calls to him and tugs at his hands. She thinks he's talking to her, his lips are moving. The jeep whips past them with an angry honk and Ora prays no one comes from the other side. "Tell me," he mumbles again and again, "tell me."

"What?" she groans in his ear. "What's so urgent right this minute?"

"I . . . I . . . What did I want to ask . . . What did I want to ask . . ."

A truck rolls in their direction, bellowing with what sounds like a foghorn. They're standing in its lane. Ora pulls Avram toward her and out of the truck's path, then they freeze on the white stripe in the middle of the road. They will die here. Run over like two jackals.

"Nobody else, either?"

"Nobody else *what*? What are you talking about, Avram?"

"About what you said, the substitute, that Ilan . . . that Ilan didn't have."

Through the din of a passing horn she hears a thin whisper slip away in his voice like the sleeve of a child playing hide-and-seek behind the drapes. She stares at him: his large, round, sun-scalded head, the wild tufts of hair sprouting on both sides, his blue eyes with their gaze refracting like a teaspoon in a glass. She finally understands what he's asking.

She slowly smoothes both hands over his face, his disheveled beard, his broken eyes, erasing the road around them with one stroke. The road will wait. Very quietly she says, "Do you really not know? Can't you guess? Ilan never had another friend like you."

"I didn't, either," he says, and bows his head.

"Me neither. Now come on, give me your hand, we're crossing."

"I'm in hell!" he announced in a letter from a pre-military training camp, at age seventeen. "I'm at the Be'er Ora base, which is undoubtedly named after you. You would like it here, because we get to eat sand and gun grease, and jump off twelve-foot-high platforms like hunted fowl, to land on canvas sheets. All your favorite pastimes. Me? I make do with fantasies about you, and failed attempts to deflower your stand-ins. Last night, for example, I invited a young lady named Atarah to my room. I have no love for her in my heart, as you well know, but (a) I had the impression that she was available, and (b) biology calls . . . The excuse (a lowly trick!) was that we'd listen to *Paul Temple* (it was the Vandyke Affair episode) on the radio together, but then they announced that the girls weren't allowed in the boys' rooms, and I would therefore be left on my lonesome to shrivel away in my hole. Meanwhile, Ilan disappeared with the guys—who included, if you ask me, a number of girls (FYI), and there was undoubtedly some fooling around going on there."

"This morning, my dear," he wrote the next day, "we got up at five-thirty and went to work on a mountain, clearing stones, weeding, and building terraces (Can you imagine me there? Without an undershirt?). I devised a plot whereby I was the only boy working with seven members of your gender, but they turned out to be cold-buttocksed females with no fondness for the common Avram wherever he may grow. Next to me was Ruchama Levitov (I wrote to you about her, we once had a hasty and cheerless affair), so I had the opportunity to examine our relationship more profoundly. But in the end, as usual, we just engaged in small talk (I've made up a new word for it: 'chat-air.' Do you approve?), and she had the audacity to tease me about how we always argue and fight and break up and then start over again, like a double diagram. I gave her a perfect Jean-Paul Belmondo look and said nothing, but afterward it occurred to me that this has always been my fate with girls, that something never quite works out, and even when I have the occasional success, there's always a moment when she suddenly gets scared of me and runs away, or claims I'm too much for her (Did I tell you about Tova G.? About how when we finally horitzontalized, she declared that I was 'too intimate' [??!!] and literally fled from the bed?!). Honestly, Ora, I don't know what my problem is with girls, and I'd be happy to discuss it with you one day, candidly and uncensored.

"Yours, blister-footed Caligula, as he rushes to dinner."

Ora rummaged through the brimming shoe box and fished out another letter from the same period. She glanced at Avram as he lay there covered in bandages and casts, and read out loud.

"My *Shaina-Shaindle*. Chemistry class yet again, with promising talk of endodermic and exothermic activation reactions. I had a huge argument with the teacher. It was fantastic! She tried to get out of it, so I had to smite her hip and thigh. She crawled out of the jubilated classroom with her tail between her legs, and I made my triumphant victory laps around the classssss!"

She glanced at him. No response. Two days earlier, the doctors had gradually started to bring him out of the induced coma, but even when he was half awake he did not open his eyes or speak. He was snoring now. His mouth was open, his face and exposed shoulder covered with open, pussy wounds. His left arm was in a cast, as were both his legs. His right leg was raised and suspended in a Thomas splint, and tubes emerged from every part of his body. For several nights she had read to him from letters he'd sent her when they were young. Ilan did not believe in this therapeutic approach, but she hoped Avram's own words would be able to penetrate him and rouse him to speech.

Perhaps there really was no point. She leafed through the letters and notes. Every so often she pulled one out and read from it. Usually her voice died down after a few lines, and then she read to herself and laughed again, struck by how Avram, at the age of sixteen and a half, used to describe his dates with other girls—"Don't worry, they're only pale imitations of you, and this is only until you decide to lift the passion embargo you've imposed on me and give yourself to me wholly, including the holy sites"—and his failed courtships, and the mishaps. Above all, he described the ridiculous, humiliating mishaps. Ora had never met anyone who reported with such glee on his own failures and shortcomings. One evening, after seeing a movie with Chayuta H., he had walked her to Peterson Street, where she lived. He pulled her into a yard and they started making out. When he reached into her pants, Chayuta stopped him and said, "No, I've got the curse," and Avram, who didn't realize what she meant, was overcome with compassion. He consoled her and encouraged her and tried to rescue her from this surprising, exciting self-loathing, which he would never have imagined existed in lighthearted Chayuta. Chayuta listened silently as he prattled on, and since she was so quiet, for the first time that evening, Avram felt that he was finally reaching a pure spot in her cynical, socialite soul, and when he went so far in his eager consolations as to rival Gregor Samsa and the Brothers Karamazov, Chayuta cut him off and grinningly explained to him what exactly she had meant.

He described the episode to Ora with merciless precision, and she laughed from the bottom of her heart and wrote how much she hated that ugly euphemism for menstruation. With rare courage, she added that when she gets her period—I had a medical problem for a few years after Ada, but now it's all right, she explained—she actually feels extremely feminine. He replied immediately that the fact that she had chosen to tell him something like that meant she had already made up her mind to be only his *friend*, and that he must be like some sort of male girlfriend to her, and in his opinion that's what she had really decided about him right from the start, when they met in the hospital, and it killed him, but that seemed to be his permanent fate, to suffice with the leftovers of her love, or of any love.

Hundreds of notes and letters were stuffed into that shoe box, written in his crowded, frenetic handwriting, which shuddered sometimes with a tension that could not be released even in words. The pages were covered with doodles, charming illustrations, arrows, asterisks, and footnotes. He overflowed with inventions and puns and tricks and little traps, meant to test her attention to all his details and minutiae. On the backs of the envelopes she read: "Hilik and Bilik, Ltd., Accessories and Auxiliary Equipment for Dreams and Nightmares." Or, "S. Bubari, Pharmacological Consultant for Cuckoldry Troubles." On each envelope, next to the official stamp, he stuck his own private stamps, on which he drew himself and her, and, of course, her with Ilan, and with their three, five, seven future children. He cut out funny or rude newspaper clippings for her, and copied engravings from tombstones in Jerusalem ("This one reads, 'Dispirited by Torments'—it's like they were thinking of me!"). He sent detailed knitting patterns for an elf's hat made of thick wool with red tassels, and his own recipes for hamantaschen, quiches, and cakes, which she never dared to bake because simply reading the recipes made it clear that too many conflicting flavors were doing battle.

Avram groaned in his sleep and his lips moved. Ora held her breath. He mumbled something incoherent, squirmed with pain, and sighed. She wet his lips with a washcloth and wiped the sweat from his face. He relaxed.

He had started writing to her the morning after their last night together in isolation. "I feel as though we've been surgically separated," he wrote. "I am wounded, bruised, and desolate, now that you're uprooted from me." Another wave of wounded soldiers had arrived, and Ora, Ilan, and Avram had been moved to different hospitals. He wrote to her daily for three weeks, even before he got hold of her address, and then he sent the first twenty-one letters in a decorated shoe box. After that, for six years, he never ceased producing missives of five, ten, or twenty pages, covered with limericks and poems and quotations and excerpts from radio plays. He sent telegrams too—he called them yellegrams—and sketches of stories he would one day write and swirling footnotes and erasures that intentionally revealed more than they concealed. He gave her his whole heart, and she always read his letters with a voyeuristic lust, slight suspense, raw nerves, an almost physical longing for Ada, and a vague sense of guilt at betraying her. In the first months of their correspondence, she had a half-formed snicker ready

and waiting at the corner of her mouth each time she opened a letter—
a snicker that sometimes, as she read, turned into a sort of pre-crying
spasm.

And in each letter he interjected something about Ilan. To pique her
curiosity or to torture himself—she wasn't sure.

"Today, Ora," she read to him in a whisper and leaned in closer to his
face, which was cut to the bone, "I am mired in lonesome sorrow, and I
walk by myself, like Rudyard Kipling's cat (do you know him?). The
only character I commune with is Ilan, he that is maimed in his privy
parts. As you know, we habitually discuss the female species, or rather, I
discuss it, particularly you, of course, and Ilan does not respond. But it
is his silence that makes me think he is not completely indifferent to
you, although it's obvious to me that he has yet to make what I have
termed, in consultation with my friend Søren Kierkegaard, 'the leap of
love.' On the other hand, he does insist on maintaining total indifference to the herds of fair girls—and some unfair ones too—who inun-
date him and seek his favors (!?). For the most part, I am the one who
advises him, due to his lack of experience and utter numskullery in his
relations with women. I do this, of course, with complete neutrality, as a
person now observing exclusively from the margins, without any personal stake in the subject—a.k.a., *you*. You wouldn't believe the enthusiasm with which I attempt to convince him that you are his intended
one. You must be asking yourself why I do this. It is because integrity
dictates that I do so, and because I can plainly see that even though I am
intended for you, you are, unfortunately, *not intended for me*. That is the
bitter truth, Ora, and that is the law of my love for you: I shall bring you
only heartache and complications, and so, precisely because I care so
deeply about you, and precisely because of my total and un-egotistical
love, I must fan the flames of Ilan in your direction, open his bedaubed
eyes, and remove the foreskin of his heart—isn't it nuts of me?"

"Get cracking and write quick, lest I sprain my heart with longings!"

But in the P.S. of that same letter he cheerfully reported his intricate
and unfortunate affairs with other girls, who were, as always, only a
cheap and available substitute, and only because she, in the depths of
her heart, insisted—he was convinced—on loving the forlorn Ilan, he of
the Kafkaesque joie de vivre, who was utterly unwilling to acknowledge
her existence, and because she refused to wed Avram and move into a
chamber (preferably one with maid service) with him.

During the first few weeks she replied with short, cautious letters whose timidity embarrassed her. He did not complain. He never kept score with her over the number of pages or the meagerness of their content. On the contrary: he was always enthusiastic and grateful for every sign she sent. Then she grew bolder. She told him, for example, about her older brother, the rebellious Marxist who was making her parents' lives miserable, doing only what he felt like, which made her angry but also jealous. She wrote about her loneliness among her friends, and her anxiety before competitions—she had almost abandoned other athletics and was focusing on swimming; the transition from dry to wet made her feel instantly better; there were days when she felt like a burning torch hitting the water. And she wrote to him about Ada, missing her in writing as only he could understand. Every so often—actually, in every letter—she could not resist asking him, in a P.S., to send Ilan her warm regards. Although she knew it pained him, she could not help it, and in the next letter she would be unable to hold back from asking if he'd given the regards.

Of this correspondence, of this new friendship, and of the maddening heartache caused by thinking about Ilan, she told none of her friends. Since coming home from her hospitalization in Jerusalem, Ora knew that what had happened to her there all those nights was too precious and rare to be handed over to strangers, and this was all the more true of what was happening to her with them now, with both of them; the duality presented a mystery she did not even try to decipher. It had snuck up on her secretly and struck her, like lightning or an accident, and all she could do was adapt to the consequences of the strike. But from day to day it grew more obvious, until she knew with unimpeachable certainty: they were both necessary to her. They were essential, like two angels who ultimately fulfill the same mission: Avram, whose presence was inescapable down to the very last thread, and Ilan, who was entirely absent.

Almost without her noticing it, writing to Avram became a sort of diary she kept. But since she could not write to him about how much she missed Ilan, day and night, and about the physical longing that burned in her, she wrote about other things. More and more she wrote about her parents, mainly her mother. She filled pages upon pages about her and had never imagined she could have so much to say. At first, when she read her own words, she would be shocked at the treachery, yet unable to keep from saying these things, and in any case she had the peculiar feeling that Avram knew everything about her, even what she might try to hide. She told him about the constant, exhausting efforts to guess the reasons for her mother's anger and for the implied accusations that were concealed in the space of the house like dense, inescapable netting. She revealed the well-kept family secret of her mother's attacks: every few days she would shut herself up in her room and beat herself cruelly. Ora found out by accident, when she was ten and hiding, as she often did, in the linen chest in her parents' closet. She saw her mother come into the room quickly and lock the door, and then she started to hit herself silently, scratch her own stomach and chest, then scream in a whispered voice: "Garbage, garbage, even Hitler didn't want you." At that moment Ora made up her mind that she would have a wonderful family of her own. It was a determined, crystalline decision, not the kind of fantasies little girls often entertain. For Ora, it was a life decision. She would have her own family, with a husband and children—two, no more—and their house would always be full of light, even in its farthest corners. She could see it vividly in her mind's eye: a house flooded with light and free of shadows, in which she and her husband and her two small children sailed happily, transparent and open, so that there would never be any surprises in it *like this one*. She still pictured it when she was fifteen, and twenty. She would have at least one person, or two, or three, of all the people in the world, of all the mysterious and unexpected strangers, whom she could really know.

As she wrote the letters, she gradually found that dim and burdensome things became clear when she laid them out on paper. She was somewhat surprised to discover that she could write with such clarity and precision—she had always thought she was best as a reader of the really good writers—and then she started to feel that she wanted, *needed*, to write, and that, no less than that, she wanted Avram to read what she had to say and to tell her more and more of what he saw in her.

And warm regards to Ilan.

Once he wrote: "You are my first love."

She was dumbstruck for two weeks. Then she wrote that she was not ready to talk about love yet. That she felt they were both too young and immature and that she wanted to wait a few years before discussing matters of love. He said that now, after having written it explicitly, and after having told Ilan, he was completely certain of his love for her, and that she held his fate in her hands. He enclosed a stamped envelope for her reply. She asked him vehemently to stop talking about his love for her, because it introduced anxiety and unhealthy feelings to their beautiful, pure relationship. He replied: "A: In my opinion love is the healthiest, loveliest, purest feeling there is. And B: I can no longer stop talking about my love for you, my love for you, my love for you . . ." He filled the whole page.

"It was not love at first sight," he wrote in a telegram he sent a few hours after the letter—but which reached her one week sooner—"because I loved you long before that stop before I met you stop I love you backwards too stop even before I existed stop because I only became me when I met you stop." She sent a short letter saying it was difficult for her to keep corresponding with him now, she had a lot of exams and competitions coming up and she was very busy. As evidence, she enclosed an article from *Maariv Youth* that described a high-jump meet at the Wingate Institute in which she had participated. He sent back the letter with the article's ashes and did not write for three weeks. She almost lost her mind with anticipation, and then he started writing again as if nothing had happened:

"Last night I was at a jazz show with Ilan, RIP (who, amazingly, sends his regards this time and keeps trying to peek over my arm at what I'm writing, even though he continues to insist that he's not interested in you!). Anyway, last night we were at Foos-Foos. It was extremely wonderful, and I had full-on experiences with all sorts of lovely women who exchanged looks with me, but unfortunately not phone numbers. With the music in the background, I was able to pull together some of the opinions I've been gathering about girls lately, and I came up with some well-founded and interesting theories about them, and mainly about you. I believe that, ultimately, you will not tie your fate with mine but with some other dude, Ilan or someone of his ilk, the point is, a guy who will definitely not tickle your navel with giggles like I do, and won't drive your mind wild with sharp observations like I do, and make every organ of your body tremble with pleasure like I do. But the thing is, he'll be hunkier, much hunkier, and calmer and more solid, and mainly more *understandable* to you than I am (and your mother will love him at first sight, I'm positive!). Yes, yes, treacherous Ora, such are the thoughts that came to me as I sat in that damp little grotto that was aromatic of *hashish* (!!!), surrounded by the angels climbing up and down the harmonic scales of Mel Keller, and I lost my train of thought . . .

"Yes: that in the end you'll mate for life with some gorgeous, grave-looking, silver-haired alpha male, a guy who may not know to ask if your viscera pullulate at the sight of a beautiful sunset, or upon reading a lipless poem by David Avidan, but your future by his side will be secure and solid forever and ever. For I suspect, my duplicitous Ora, that deep in the depths of your light-filled and beautiful soul (which, I do not need to tell you, I love very much) lies a minuscule recess (like the ones in some corner stores, where they keep the old preserves?) that is, forgive me, slightly narrow-minded in matters of love. Of true love, I mean. And that is why you will probably make the choice you will make and doom me to misery for the rest of my life, and of this (the misery) I have no doubt, and I treat it now, in a purely philosophical mode, as a permanent state, like a chronic illness from which I will suffer for the rest of my life, and therefore you can stop reacting so hysterically every time I talk about it!

"On the way back from the jazz club I discussed it with Ilan-long-legs (and they're not the only thing that's long . . .), and I expounded upon my theory about him and you, and of course I lamented my bitter fate at being destined to be indentured to a woman who scorns the gifts of my love, and having to suffice with cheap substitutes for the rest of my life. Ilan, as usual, said maybe you'd change your mind and grow up and offered other foolish consolations, and I explained to him again why I thought he was much more suitable for you than I am, being an alpha male etc., and that it is only for his sake that I am willing to vacate the space in your heart to which I still cling tooth and nail in the most pathetic manner, and he reiterated that you're not his type at all, and that he doesn't really know you anyway, and then he repeated that on that night when the three of us talked in the hospital he was completely blurry, but that didn't reassure me, because I do feel that something powerful happened between the two of you that night, precisely because of his blurriness, and yours, something happened there, and it kills me that you won't confirm or deny that for me, and it's like the two of you were together in some place I couldn't get into (and probably never will), and I can only eat my heart out over the fact that it didn't happen to you with me, that revelation of love (because love is a revelation!!), because I was so close (fuckit, hissed the defeated Avram as he poured out his wrath), and that's also something I feel quite a lot in my life, the almost-happened, and I only hope it won't be the guiding principle of my life, the main tenet of all the guiding principles of my life.

"Yours, Dispirited by Torments."

She was then finally able to overcome her cowardice and the paralyzing confusion that had seized her and told him with simple words that grew increasingly complicated that she really thought she was in love, but unfortunately not with him, and she hoped he could forgive her, it wasn't something she could control, and she liked and loved him like a brother, and would always like and love him, but in her opinion he didn't really need her—and here her hand shook wildly, to her amazement; the pen jumped around on the page like a horse trying to throw off its rider—because he was, after all, such a brimming person, a thousand times wiser and more profound than she was, and she was positive that once he got used to this idea he would have many other beloveds, she was really convinced, and they would be much more suitable for him than she was, whereas she believed that the boy she loved needed her "like air to breathe, and I'm sorry, but in this case it's not a cliché at all. That's really the way I feel." She added that it was a love that had troubled her and crazed her for months, almost a year, in fact, because it was very clear to her that it was senseless and hopeless, and she wished she understood why this had happened to her, and so on and so forth. Avram sent a rushed telegram: "Do I know him question mark is it Ilan question mark just say his name and I will murder him exclamation point."

When she confirmed, after weeks of interrogations and pleading, that she was in love with Ilan, he almost went mad. For a week he was unable to eat a thing. He did not change his clothes, and he walked the streets for nights on end, crying. He told everyone he met about Ora and explained in a measured, considered way why what had happened was inevitable, even essential and desirable, in terms of evolution, aesthetics, and in many other regards. Of course he told Ilan the secret immediately, and Ilan repeated that he had no interest in Ora, and made fun of her crazy notion that he needed her "like air to breathe." "Is that what she said?" he asked Avram with slightly alarmed amazement. "That's what she wrote about me?" He promised Avram he would never have a relationship with her.

"Not on my initiative, at least," he mumbled afterward in an obligatory sort of tone.

The next day, during morning recess, Avram climbed the giant pine tree in the school yard, cupped his hands over his mouth, and announced to the dozens of onlooking students and teachers that he'd decided to divorce his body, and that he would henceforth create a total separation between body and soul. To prove his indifference to his newly divorced fate, he jumped off the tree and plummeted to the asphalt.

"I love you even more now," he wrote the next day from his hospital bed with his left hand. "The second I jumped, I understood that my love for you is a law of nature for me. It is an axiom, a truism, or as our Arabian cousins would say, *min albadhiyat*. It doesn't matter what your objective state is. It doesn't even matter if you hate me or if you live on the moon or if, God forbid, you have a sex-change operation. I will always love you. It will always be irredeemable and I can do nothing to stop it, unless I am killed/hanged/burned/drowned, or any other thing that brings about the conclusion of the curious episode known as 'the life of Avram.' "

She wrote to him that it was awful that they were both suffering so much from unrequited love and promised again that even if she didn't love him the way he wanted, she still felt that she would always be his soul mate and that she could not imagine life without him. As in all of her recent letters, she could not resist asking about Ilan: How had Ilan responded to his jumping off the tree? Had Ilan come to visit him in the hospital? She then, completely against her will, in contrast to her character and her basic decency, in contrast to everything she wanted to think about herself, launched into long pages of conjectures regarding Ilan's secret desires, his inhibitions and hesitations, and repeatedly asked Avram why he thought this had happened, why she had fallen in love with Ilan. Because, after all, she didn't even know Ilan, and everything she had experienced with him for the past year (minus one month and twenty-one days) was as if a stranger had taken control of her soul and was dictating to her what to feel. "It's actually very simple," Avram replied venomously. "It's like an equation with three factors: fire, survivor, and fireman. Which one do you think the survivor will choose?"

Avram now gave Ilan a detailed account of each of her letters, as he listened and shrugged his shoulders. "Write something to her," Avram begged. "I can't take her torturing me with this anymore." Ilan said for the thousandth time that he had no interest in Ora and any girl who pursued him like that made him sick. The problem was that Ilan had no interest in any girl. Girls buzzed and hummed around him, but he didn't really get excited about any of them. From date to date, from experience to experience, he became more and more sad and subdued. "Maybe I should just be a homosexual," he said to Avram one evening as they sprawled on the big soft cushions in Jan's Tea House, in Ein Karem. They both froze at the explicit word, which had somehow hovered between them for a long time. "Don't worry," Ilan added forlornly, "you're not my type." In Avram's pocket was Ora's latest letter, which he had not dared tell Ilan about: "Sometimes I think that he is now in the state I was in up until about a year ago, until I met you (and him) in the hospital. Because I was really sleepwalking, afraid to open my eyes. And now, with all the terrible pain of his ignoring me, I still feel that I've come back to life, and that's also in large part thanks to you (really it's mainly thanks to you). I can also reveal to you that sometimes I deeply wish he would fall in love with some (other) girl already, even though I know it will cause me great pain. Or even with some other *guy* (don't laugh, sometimes I really do think that might be what he needs and that he doesn't dare to even comprehend it, and sometimes I even think *you* are the one he's a little bit in love with, yes, yes . . .), and even that is something I could accept from him, as long as he found some happiness and woke up from his slumber, which scares me to death. Oh, Avram, what would I do without you?

"Yours, the corner-store lady . . ."

She woke up with a start. The room was dark (perhaps the nurse had come in and found her sleeping and turned off the light), except for the glowing red coils of the space heater. The last letter she'd read to him was still in her lap. Ilan was probably right. Not a single expression passed Avram's face when she read to him. All she was doing was breaking her own heart. She put the letter back in the shoe box, stretched out, and stopped: his eyes were open. He was awake. She thought he was looking at her.

"Avram?"

He blinked.

"Should I turn on the light?"

"No."

Her heart began to pound. "Should I fix your covers?" She stood up. "Do you want me to call the nurse to change your IV? Is the heater okay for you?"

"Ora—"

"What? What?"

He breathed heavily. "What happened to me?"

She blinked. "You're going to be fine."

"What happened?"

"Wait a minute," she mumbled and retreated to the door, her body strangely tilting. "I'm going to get—"

"Ora," he whispered with such profound distress that she stopped herself, walked back, and quickly wiped her eyes.

"Avram, Avram," she said, taking pleasure in the way her mouth pronounced the name.

"Why am I like this?"

She sat down by his side and moved her hand through the air above his bandaged arm. "Do you remember that there was a war?"

His chest dropped and a drenched, heavy sigh escaped his lips. "Was I injured?"

"Yes, you could say so. You should rest now. Don't speak."

"A land mine?"

"No, it wasn't—"

"I was *with them*," he said slowly. Then his head drooped and he dived into sleep.

She thought of running for a doctor to report that Avram had regained his speech, or calling Ilan to let him know, but she was afraid to leave him even for a minute. Something in his face told her not to move but to sit by his side and wait, to protect him from what he would understand when he awoke.

His voice cracked. "Is there anyone else here?"

"Just you. And me." She crushed out a smile. "You have a private room."

He digested the information.

"Should I get the doctor? Or a nurse? There's a bell above the—"

"Ora."

"Yes."

"How long have I . . . ?"

"Here? About two weeks. A little longer."

He shut his eyes and tried to move his right arm but could not. He craned his neck to look at the mess of tubes and wires growing out of his body.

"They gave you a few . . . treatments," she murmured, "some small operations, you'll be fine. Another few weeks and you'll run—"

"Ora." He stopped her with a heavy voice, exempting them both from her pretenses.

"Should I get you something to drink?"

"I . . . There are things I don't remember." His voice was frightening, throaty and clumsy, as though being squeezed out of a bent tube.

"You'll remember gradually. The doctors say you'll remember everything." She spoke quickly, in a high-pitched voice that was too cheerful. He slowly ran one hand over his face, then touched his broken teeth with a surprised finger. "They'll fix that for you, don't worry." She heard herself sounding like a rental agent eager to convince a hesitant tenant to keep on renting the dump. "They'll take care of your elbow too, and the fractures here, in your fingers, and your ankles."

She thought about his adolescent jump from the pine tree and wondered if that divorce from his body had helped him at all recently when they tortured him *there*. Not for the first time, she contemplated the fact that with Avram everything ended up being connected to the depths, everything became the fundamental law of Avram, and she remembered how she used to say he was a magnet for unbelievable occurrences and amazing coincidences. But perhaps he had lost that too, now. And who knew what else he had lost? Things that did not even have names, which would only gradually become apparent to her, and to him.

"Everything's going to be okay," she said. "They want to finish with the big, urgent things first"—she pulled out a crooked, apologetic smile—"and then they'll do the cosmetic stuff, and they'll take care of your mouth. That's nothing, easy as pie."

She thought he wasn't hearing her at all. That he no longer cared what they did with him. She kept chattering, unable to stop herself, because the thoughts of what he might have lost and what might have been lost with him—things she had not dared to contemplate while she sat by his side these past weeks—now erupted from within her. And to think that Avram himself may still not understand, that comprehension itself was still ahead of him.

"What month is it?"

"It's January."

"January . . ."

"Seventy-four."

"Winter."

"Yes, winter."

He sank down into himself. Thinking or sleeping, she wasn't sure. From one of the rooms, perhaps the burn ward, came whimpers of pain.

"Ora, how did I get back?"

"In an airplane. You don't remember?"

"Yeah?"

"You flew back from there." I can't take this, she thought, this talk is tearing me apart.

"Ora—"

"Yes, what?" She noticed that he was opening his eyes wide. A cold, strange spark shone out of them.

"Is there . . . Is there an Israel?"

"Is there a what?"

"Never mind."

She didn't understand. Then she felt the saliva drying in her mouth. "Yes. There is. Of course. Everything. Everything's just as it was, Avram. Did you think we were—"

His chest rose and fell quickly under the blankets. The heater that had turned off kicked on again. She stared at his fingertips, their flesh devoid of fingernails, and thought that from the place he had come from now, they would never really meet again. He was lost to her forever.

He fell asleep, and rocked and shouted in pain. It was hard to tolerate. He was fighting someone invisible, then he started to cry softly and plead. She jumped up and snatched a piece of paper from the box and read out loud, persistently, like a prayer: "Yesterday I went with my mother to buy her a dress. I always give her advice about these things, and I saw a beautiful dress for you at Schwartz Department Store. It was green, sleeveless, really slim, the kind that would hug your slender figure. Most importantly, it had a large gold zipper from top to . . . bottom!" Avram moaned and writhed on the bed, and Ora quickly, almost without breathing, read the silly, wonderful lines that came from so far away, like the light of a dying planet. "At the top there's a big ring that you pull the zipper open with, and even more thought-provoking is that it opens in the front (!!!) like in this movie I saw with Elke Sommer, where she opens her dress slowly, all the way down to her belly button, and there's a lovely full-frontal (the audience moaned and groaned!). Anyway, 49.75 liras and the dress is yours."

. . .

Hours went by.

"The war," Avram murmured during one of those hours.

"Yes, it's okay," said Ora, waking from an elusive dream. She drank some water and ran her hands over her face.

"What?" Avram's breath was shallow.

"The war is over." She somehow felt that in saying these words she had joined an ancient dynasty of women. Climbed up a rung. But then she felt foolish: perhaps he had wanted to ask *how* the war had ended and who had won. But when she looked at him she could not bring herself to say that they had.

"How long was I—"

"There? Six weeks. A bit longer."

He groaned in bewilderment.

"Did you think it was less?"

"More."

"You slept a lot when you got back. And they had you sedated for part of the time."

"Sedated . . ."

"You're on all kinds of medications now. They'll taper them off later."

"Medications?"

The effort of conversing overcame him and he fell asleep again, sometimes coughing and moving restlessly. He looked as though he were fighting someone who kept trying to strangle him.

The hostages had come down the ramp from the plane. Some walked on their own, others needed help. The airport was chaos. Soldiers, journalists, and photographers from all over the world, airport workers who gathered to cheer the returning hostages, ministers and Knesset members who tried to reach them and shake their hands in front of the cameras. Only the families were explicitly told not to come to the airport but to wait for their loved ones at home. Since Ora and Ilan were not Avram's relatives, they didn't know they were not supposed to come. And they didn't know Avram was wounded. They waited, but he did not come off the plane. The hostages walked past with their shaved heads, wearing rubber shoes without socks, and looked at them with dim surprise. A field-security officer walked a hostage whose eye was bandaged and read to him out loud from a piece of paper: "Anyone delivering information to the enemy is subject to penalty . . ." A tall hostage who limped with a crutch asked one of the journalists loudly whether it was true there'd been a war with Syria, too. Ilan suddenly discovered that soldiers were carrying stretchers down the back of the plane. He grabbed Ora's hand and they ran over there. No one stopped them. They rushed around among the wounded soldiers but could not find Avram, and they stood looking at each other, terrified. One last stretcher was carried off the plane. A team of doctors and medics walked down with it, carrying a pole swinging with an IV and other tubes. Ora took one look and her mind grew weak. She saw a large, round head, undoubtedly Avram's, rocking this way and that, covered with an oxygen mask. He was bald, and the top of his head was shaved and partly bandaged, but the bandage had come loose, exposing glistening wounds like gaping mouths. She noticed that the men rolling the stretcher had turned their heads aside and were breathing through their mouths. Ilan was already running alongside the stretcher, glancing at its occupant every so often. Ora followed his expression and knew it was bad. Ilan helped lift the stretcher into an ambulance and tried to get in, but he was pushed away. He shouted and protested and waved his arms, but the soldiers removed him. Ora walked up and, quietly but firmly, told an elderly medical officer: "I'm the girlfriend." She climbed into the ambulance and sat by the stretcher with the doctor and nurse. The doctor suggested that she sit next to the driver, but she refused. The ambulance driver turned on the siren and Ora watched the highway, the cars, and the people sitting in them, alone or in pairs, sometimes whole families, and she knew that her previous life was ending. And she still hadn't looked straight at Avram.

The nurse handed her a fabric face mask to protect her from the smell. The doctor and nurse started to undress Avram. His chest, stomach, and shoulders were covered with open, infected ulcers, deep gashes, bruises, and strange, thin-lipped cuts. The right nipple was misplaced. The doctor touched a gloved finger to each wound and dictated to the nurse in a toneless voice: "Open fracture, dry blow, cut, edema, whipping, electrical, compression, burn, rope, infection. Check for malaria, check for schistosomiasis. Look at this—the plastic surgeons will have a field day."

He and the nurse turned Avram over and exposed his back. Ora stole a look and saw a lump of raw flesh bubbling in red, yellow, and purple. She felt her stomach turn. The stench from his body was unbearable. The doctor held his breath and his glasses fogged over. He bared Avram's buttocks and took a deep breath: "Animals," he murmured. Ora looked out the window and wept silently and tearlessly. The doctor covered Avram's behind and cut open his pants. His legs were broken in three places. Around the ankles were bloody bracelets of puffy, raw flesh that looked as though it was seething with live creatures. The doctor mimed a noose to the nurse, and Ora saw Avram in some dark cell, hanging by his feet with his head rocking, and she suddenly grasped that the entire time he had been a POW, she had hardly dared to imagine what they were really doing to him. He was in the Intelligence Corps and knew so much. She had pushed away every scene or thought—at the moments right before she fell asleep they would lunge at her, but the sleeping pills were effective against nightmares—and now she wondered how it was possible that she and Ilan had not discussed the torture and what happens to people who are tortured, even once.

She thought of how little they had spoken of Avram at all, despite the fact that all those days and weeks they had had little else of interest to talk about. Almost every day they drove to the Contact Center for Families of POWs and MIAs, to hear what little news and whatever rumors they could. Over and over again they examined blurry photographs of hostages published in Israel and abroad and talked to the commanders and clerks who were willing to listen. When they didn't go to the center, they would call to find out if there was any word. They were already starting to feel that they were being avoided, shunted around, but they did not give up—how could they? They were both distraught, and when they ate anything they thought, he's not eating this, and when a song he liked came on the radio they thought, he's not hearing this, and when they saw something beautiful they thought, he's not seeing this. And that way—Ora now realized—they wouldn't have to think about what was really happening to him; they'd turned Avram into everything he wasn't.

The doctor said, "Don't worry, you'll get him back as good as new." Ora stared at him. She knew that if the ambulance stopped for a second, she would open the door and flee. It was almost beyond her control. The doctor started writing things on a thick notepad. Then he paused and said: "Your boyfriend?"

She nodded.

He scanned her closely. "It'll be all right," he said finally. "They've done a real number on him, those shits, but we're better than them. I'm telling you, a year from now you won't recognize him."

"And what about his . . ." She stammered and her hand dropped. The very question was a sort of betrayal.

"His mind? That's not really my department," the doctor mumbled. He sealed up his face and went back to his notepad. Ora looked pleadingly at the nurse, but she also avoided her. Ora forced herself to look at Avram. With the fervor of a vow, she decided that she could not leave him even for a moment without a loving gaze and that from now on she would always look at him lovingly and would always be with him to look at him lovingly, because perhaps only a lifetime of love could mend what they had done to him there. But she could not overcome the nausea and her aversion to his nearly eyebrowless face, and she could not put any love in her gaze, and a metallic voice hissed inside her, just as it had after Ada: Life goes on, doesn't it?

The ambulance careened down the road, kicking up a commotion. Avram's face suddenly tensed; he slammed his head from side to side as if trying to evade a slap and whimpered in a young boy's voice. She watched him, hypnotized, never having seen these expressions on him. She'd thought her Avram wasn't afraid of anything or anyone. He simply did not know fear. She'd always felt he was protected from evil, and that it was utterly inconceivable that anyone would want to hurt this man who roamed the world with open arms, and feet turned out, with his curious-interrogative head tilt, with his donkey's bray laughter and sharp gaze. Avram.

Perhaps that was precisely why they had done this to him, she thought. Crushed him this way, shattered him. Not just because he's in Intelligence.

Avram gaped. He gurgled and choked. She could not guess what was being done to him in his imagination at that moment. She thought he was trying to raise his hands and protect his face, but only a few fingers moved slightly. The thought flew through her that she would never have a child. That she would not bring a child into a world where such things happened. Just then Avram's eyes opened, and they were red and dirty. She leaned down to him, struck by the stench that came from his raw flesh. He saw her and his gaze focused. Even the blue of his eyes looked bloodshot.

"Avram, it's me, Ora." Her fingers hovered over his shoulder; she was afraid to hurt him, afraid to touch him.

"Pity," he whispered.

"What's a pity? What is? What's a pity?"

He gargled as the words seeped into the fluids filling his lungs. "Pity they didn't kill me."

Then the ambulance doors swung open and there was a sea of faces, tugging hands, and shouts that hit her ears. Ilan was there, somehow having managed to arrive before the ambulance. Fast Ilan, she thought with a touch of resentment, as if his speed were an advantage gained illegally over Avram. They both ran behind the stretcher into a hut that had been converted into an ER. Dozens of doctors and nurses gathered around the wounded soldiers, drew blood, collected urine, took mucus samples, and grew cultures from the wounds. A Medical Corps major noticed Ora and Ilan and shouted them out of the building. They staggered to a bench outside and wrapped themselves around each other. Ilan made sounds she did not recognize, like dry, hoarse barks. With tight fists she clutched his hair until he groaned in pain. "Ilan, Ilan, what's going to happen?" she whispered loudly.

"I'm staying with him here until he comes back," he said. "Until he's back to being what he was, I don't care how long it takes, even years, I'm not moving."

She let go of his hair and looked at him. He looked older and heavier in his sorrow and terror. "You'll stay with him," she repeated, dumbstruck.

"What did you think, that I'd leave him here alone like that?"

Yes, she thought to herself. The truth is, that is what I thought. I thought I'd be alone with him in this.

Then she came back to her senses. "No, no, of course you're staying, I don't know what I was . . . Listen, I can't go through this alone."

He looked angry and hurt. "But why alone?"

And she thought, Because there's always a little bit of you that's not there, even when you're there. "Come on, let's go back to him. We'll wait by the door until they let us in."

They walked side by side among the bustling huts. For some time, since the war, they had not been able to touch each other. But now, to her surprise, she was filled with desire for him, and her longing was a primary, naked hunger to bite into his flesh, into his healthy, whole body. She stopped and grabbed his arm and pressed it to her, and he responded immediately, turned her to him, and held her tight against his body, and suddenly he leaned down and kissed her lustfully. His mouth filled her mouth, and she felt all of him, his entire body, pene-trating her, turning her inside out, and she even forgot to be amazed at how he, normally so shy, was kissing her like that in front of everyone. She felt that he was stronger now, bonier and more steadfast. There was something in his grasp, in his kiss—he literally picked her up off the ground and held her against his mouth, and then she grew blurry and felt that he was suspending her in midair with just the force of his mouth, and it vaguely occurred to her that whoever was watching them might think Ilan was the one who had come back to his girl from a POW prison. She pulled away from him, almost shoved herself back-ward, and they stood facing each other breathlessly.

"Tell me," she heard him say suddenly and was horrified: that voice of his, the shattered breaths. "Ora . . ." He looked at the ceiling. "I have to know."

"What, ask me."

"Something . . . I can't remember."

"Ask me."

He was silent. He kept trying to move his suspended leg and scratch an itch under the cast.

"Things aren't right in my head."

"What things?"

"You and me."

"Yes?"

"It's like I have a hole in the middle of—"

"Ask."

"What . . . What are we?"

She was not expecting that. "Do you mean . . . ?" She must have leaned toward him too sharply. His head pulled back and his face shrank in terror. Perhaps in the dark he thought something—a hand or an implement—was about to hit him. She murmured, "What are we now?"

"Don't be angry, I'm not quite . . ."

"We're good friends, and we'll always be good friends." She suddenly felt compelled to add with a grating sort of cheer: "And you'll see, we'll make a new life for you!"

Afterward, for months, she tormented herself over that stupid line. And then there were times when she thought perhaps it had been pre-scient. *We'll make a new life.* But at that moment she could almost hear his bitter ridicule. His heavy head moved slowly on the pillow as he tried to examine her face. She was glad the room was dark.

"Ora."

"What?"

"Isn't there anyone else in this room?"

"Just us."

"The cast is driving me crazy," he said thickly. Everything he did was so slow. She realized how much the old Avram was, for her, perhaps more than anything else, his rhythm, the sharpness of the way he moved through the world. "I'm cold."

She covered him with a third blanket. He dripped with sweat and shivered with cold.

"Scratch it for me."

She reached out and scratched his leg where the cast met the skin. She felt as if her finger was dipping in an open wound. He moaned and grunted with a mixture of pain and pleasure.

"Stop. It hurts."

She sat back. "What, what do you want to know?"

"What were we?"

"What were we? We were all sorts of things. We were lots of things to each other, and we still will be, you'll see, we still will be!"

With one hand, in an infinite motion, he pulled the blankets up over his chest, as if to protect himself from the deceit in her voice. He lay silently for a few minutes. Then she heard his dry lips part, and she knew what was coming.

"And Ilan?"

"Ilan . . . I don't know where to start, I don't know what you remember and what you don't. Ask me."

"I can't remember. There are parts. In the middle it's all erased."

"Do you remember that you were on the base in Sinai with Ilan?"

"In Bavel, yes."

"You were at the end of your army stint. I was already in Jerusalem, studying." As she spoke, she thought: Stick to the facts. Only answer what he asks. Let him decide what he can hear.

There was silence again. The space heater sparked.

And wait for him, she warned herself. Go at his pace. Maybe he doesn't even want to talk about it, maybe it's too soon for him.

Avram lay still. His eyes were open. He had only one eyebrow, half of which was missing.

"You used to come home every other week in rotation from Sinai. You and Ilan."

He gave her a questioning look.

"One week you, the next week him. One of you always had to stay on the base."

He thought it over. "And the other?"

"The other would go on leave, to Jerusalem."

"And you were in Jerusalem?"

"Yes"—stick to the facts—"do you remember where I lived?"

"There was a geranium," Avram said after some thought.

"That's right! You see, you do remember! I had a little room in Nachlaot."

"You did?"

"Don't you remember?"

"It comes and goes."

"With an outhouse? And a tiny kitchen in the courtyard? We used to cook late at night. Once you made me chicken soup on a cooker."

"And where was my mom?"

"Your mom?"

"Yes."

"You . . . You don't remember?"

"Isn't she—"

"When you were in basic training, she—"

"Yes, you walked with me at the funeral, that's right. Ilan was there, too. He walked next to me, on the other side. Yes."

She stood up, unable to tolerate any more. "Are you hungry? Should I get you something?"

"Ora."

She sat down obediently, as if ordered by a stern teacher.

"I don't understand."

"Ask me."

"My mouth."

She soaked a washcloth in water and dabbed his lips.

"But in the war—"

"Yes."

"Why was I—"

He stopped himself, and Ora thought: Now he's going to ask about the lots.

"I went down to the Canal, and Ilan didn't."

He remembered, she knew. He was remembering and did not have the courage to ask. She looked miserably at the window, searching for a hint of dawn, a sliver of light.

"You and me, what did we have?"

"I told you, we were friends. We were—listen, we were lovers," she said finally, simply, and the words tore her heart.

"And I came back in an airplane?"

"What?" She was confused. "Yes, in an airplane. With the others."

"There were others?"

"Many."

"For a long time?"

"You were there for about—"

"No, me and you."

"A year."

She heard him repeat the words to himself. She resisted asking whether he thought it had been longer, so as not to hear him say shorter. Then he fell asleep again and snored. He seemed capable of digesting only one crumb of his previous life at a time.

"But we really did love," she said, even though he was asleep. "You and me, we were really . . ." It's horrible, she thought, the way I'm already talking about it in the past tense.

He moved, entangled in the covers, and swore at the cast that pressed on his leg. She heard the large plate screw in his arm clicking against the bedrail.

"Ora—"

"What?"

"I'm not."

"Not what?"

"You need to know."

"What?"

"I can't . . ." He moaned, searching for the words. "I don't love anything. Nothing."

She sat silently.

"Ora?"

"Yes."

"That's it."

"Yes."

"And no one."

"Yes."

"I don't have it . . . Love."

"Yes."

"For anything." He groaned. A remnant of his old compassionate, chivalrous self made him wish to protect her, she could sense it, but he did not have the strength. "I wanted to tell you earlier."

"Yes."

"Everything died in me."

She bowed her head. How could there be an Avram without love? What was Avram without love? And who, she thought, am I without his love?

But since the war, since he was taken hostage, she'd had no love for anyone, either. Just like after Ada—her blood had dried up in her again. It was comfortable. She lived precisely within her means. But why did it seem so much more terrible in Avram?

"Tell me."

"Yes."

"How long were we?"

"Almost a year."

"And you and Ilan?"

"Five years. From age seventeen or so. She laughed joylessly. "You hooked us up, remember?" We were in a hospital then too, she thought. There was a war then, too.

"That, I remember," he murmured. "And I remember that you were a couple. I didn't remember us."

She swallowed the insult heavily.

Then he mumbled in surprise, "Of course we were, how could I forget."

"You'll remember everything, there's no rush."

"I think they did things to me there."

"It will come back to you," she said, and her stomach felt desiccated. "It'll take a while, but you'll—"

A tall, strong nurse opened the door, switched the light on, and peered inside: "Are we all right?"

"We're all right," Ora said and jumped up with a panic that turned into a sort of feverish, habitual happiness: "I'm glad you came, I was about to call you."

To her astonishment, Avram was snoring loudly, and this time she had trouble believing he was asleep, but she stopped herself and did not tell the nurse he had regained consciousness. The nurse changed his infusion and urine bags and spread some cream on his fingertips and above his eyes, where the brows had been pulled out. Then she turned him over and cleaned the pus oozing from the wound in his back, bandaged him up again, and gave him a massive injection of antibiotics.

"Sweetie, you need some sleep," she told Ora while she worked.

Ora smiled with great effort. "I'll go home in the morning."

"So tell me, what are you to him? You and the tall guy. Family?"

"Sort of. Well, yes, we're his family."

It occurred to Ora that Ilan had been changing from day to day since Avram's return. It was as though a new energy had filled him and was somehow enlarging his volume, the space he occupied. His gait was more vibrant, stronger. There was something confusing and a little bothersome about it. Sometimes she looked at him in surprise: it was like someone had traced over his pencil-drawn features with black ink.

The nurse laughed. "It's just that I keep seeing just the two of you here. Doesn't he have anyone else?"

"No, just the two of us."

"But how are you related to him? You don't look anything like him." Having finished her business, she stood in the doorway, refusing to leave them. "You actually look more like each other, you and that other guy. Like brother and sister. So how are you related to him?"

"It's a long story," Ora murmured.

"Door," Avram whispered when the nurse left. Ora got up and shut the door.

"And you were Ilan's," he said, probing for solid ground to put his foot down on.

"Yes, you could say. That, too. But you really shouldn't make such an effort now."

"And Ilan . . . You loved him, right?"

Ora nodded. She pondered how it was possible to use the very same word to describe such different feelings.

"So how . . . I mean, how did you also . . ."

Either he's testing me—a strange idea flashed in her mind—or else he's playing one of his games with me. "How what?"

"How were we also."

She thought she could finally see a very thin strip of pale light in the window. Why are you torturing him with your stammerings? she thought. What are you afraid of? Just tell him. Give him back his past. That may be all he has left. "Listen, Avram, there was one year, up until not long ago, until the war, when I was with you and with him."

He let out a heavy, hoarse breath of surprise. "Remember, I have to remember," he mumbled to himself. "Why is all the time erased? She was with me and with him? Together? How did he let me . . ."

He sank back into himself again and melted away for several minutes. Ora thought: He cannot understand what was once the spirit of his life.

"I don't understand anymore, Ora, help me."

His body twitched and jerked as if a battle was raging within him. She squirmed too, suffocating in her own skin. What is this strange interrogation? He must remember. How could you forget a year like that, and everything we went through?

"But with both of us?"

"Yes."

"Together? At the same time?"

She held her head up straight and said, "Yes."

"And did we know?"

Ora could not do this anymore. These questions, this diminution of him, as though something was becoming irredeemably polluted in her own mind, too.

"He—Ilan—and I, we knew?"

"What?" she shouted in a whisper. "Knew what?"

"That both of us . . . that we were with you together?"

"What do you want from me? What do you want to hear?"

His voice climbed into an agitated whisper: "We didn't know?"

She no longer had a choice. "But *you* knew."

"And he didn't?"

"Apparently not. I don't know."

"You didn't tell him?"

She shook her head.

"And he didn't ask?"

"No."

"And he didn't ask me, either?"

"You never told me he did."

"But did he know?"

"Ilan's a smart guy," Ora spat out. She had a lot more than that to say.

The word "smart" explained nothing. There was something broad and deep, wonderful in its own way, in what the three of them had been given in that silenced year. She looked at Avram's strained face, at his narrow, haggling apprehension, and realized he was incapable of comprehending even the tip of the iceberg now.

"But we were friends," he murmured with dim amazement. "Ilan and I. We were friends, he's my best . . . so how could I . . ."

Had she been able to, she would have put him to sleep again, so he wouldn't understand so much, so he wouldn't encounter himself so unprotected.

It was too late. With a stare suspended in infinity, his eyes glazed over. Ora felt as though a slow explosion of comprehension was detonating inside him.

Beyond the shoulder of the road they've just crossed lies a fertile stretch of pasture. A barbed-wire fence is partially trampled to the ground, and the clover blooms abundantly. "Hey!" Avram smiles and points happily to a round rock, where the orange-blue-and-white path marker winks at them in the sunlight. "We've found it!" He plants one foot on the rock and sweeps his arm out in the direction of the path. "That's quite a mountain," he exclaims as his eyes follow his arm all the way up the path, and he tentatively moves his foot off the rock.

"Are mountains also an issue for you?"

"Roads aren't an issue either," he says, "I don't know what got into me."

"I was really scared. We could have got run over back there."

"So it turns out I owe you my life."

"Let's say another few times like that and we'll be even?" She sees the shadow of a bitter smile pass over his lips like a sly animal caught stealing something delectable—perhaps a heart pang.

"And your dog, where is she?"

"*My* dog? Now she's mine?"

"Ours, okay, ours."

They walk back to the roadside and whistle to the dog. Over the rush of traffic, they shout out, "Hey! Whoa! Doggy! Dog! Come here!" They hear the interweaving sounds of their own voices. If she had the courage, Ora would yell, just once, *Ofer, Oh-Fer, come home!*

But the dog is gone, and perhaps it's for the best, Ora thinks. I don't want to get attached to her, I can't take another separation. Still, it's a pity, we could have been good friends.

The mountain is steep and meandering, entangled with olive trees and terebinths and spiny hawthorn. The path strains their calf muscles painfully and wears out their lungs. "I wonder which mountain this is," says Avram breathlessly. "I don't even know where we are."

Ora stops and takes gulps of air. "All of a sudden you care where we are?"

"Well, it's just weird to walk without knowing where you are."

"The map is in your backpack."

"Should we look at it?"

They sit down and suck on hard lemon candy. Avram hesitates briefly, then opens the right pocket of the backpack. For the first time since they left, he reaches inside. He pulls out a Leatherman penknife, a matchbox, and candles. A ball of twine. Mosquito repellant. Flashlight. Another flashlight. Sewing kit. Deodorant, aftershave. A small pair of binoculars. He spreads his loot on the ground and looks at it. For a moment she thinks he's trying to form a mental image of Ofer from these items.

"Ofer's always prepared, but you know he didn't get that from me or from you," Ora says, laughing.

On a bed of poterium they spread out a large, plastic-covered 1:50,000-scale map and pore over it, heads almost touching.

"Where are we?"

"Maybe here?"

"No, that's not even the right direction."

They strain their eyes. Two fingers dart around, run into and cross over each other.

"Here's our path."

"Yes, it's marked."

"That's what that guy said, the Israel Trail."

"Which guy?" she asks.

"The one we met."

"Oh, him."

"Yes, him."

Her finger runs back along the path until it hits the border. "Oops." She stops and folds in her finger. "Lebanon."

"If you ask me, that's more or less where we started."

"Maybe it was here? Because that's right where we waded into the stream, remember?"

"Could I forget?"

"And we followed it along here in a zigzag, like this." She leads her finger down the winding path. Avram's finger is next to hers, just behind. "This is where we climbed up, and here there was a wooden bridge, and here we saw the flour mill, and maybe this is where we slept the first night? No? Maybe here, next to Kfar Yuval? How can anyone remember? What did we even see those first few days? Who could see anything at all?"

He laughs. "I was a total zombie."

"Here's the Kfar Giladi quarry, and here's the Tel Chai Forest, and the sculpture path, and here's where we ate, at Ein Ro'im."

"I wasn't seeing anything back then."

"No, you weren't. You just walked and cursed me for dragging you along."

"And 'round about here, I think, we met Akiva, and then we went down into the wadi."

"This whole stretch was a real hike, see?"

"Yes, and that must be the Arab village."

"What's left of it."

"I wanted to see it, but you ran on."

"I've had enough ruins in my life."

"And that's the Kedesh River."

"So here's where we slept."

"And then we walked up the riverbed and met that guy of yours."

"Since when is he mine?" Her fingers press into the map, leaving a brief indentation in the plastic. "And here's Yesha Fortress, and that's the Sheik's tomb, Nebi Yusha."

"And here, you see, here's where we walked up all the way to Keren Naphtali, and then down again because you left the notebook at the Kedesh River."

"And here was another stream, Dishon."

"It looks so innocent on the map. And look here, it's those turbines we couldn't figure out. Apparently that was the Ein Aviv Regional Pumping Station. So we've learned something."

"And I think this is the pool where we bathed."

"And here we walked along that big pipe to cross the water."

"I was shaking."

"Seriously? I didn't know, you didn't say anything."

"That's me."

"And here, look, it's your fairy-tale forest, Tsivon Stream."

"And here's the meadow we walked through earlier. Definitely."

"And here's the road we crossed."

"Yes, it said 'Highway 89.' "

"So if we crossed here," Avram says musically, "then now we must be—"

"On Meron," she determines.

"*Mount* Meron?"

"See for yourself."

Their fingers point reverently.

"Avram," she whispers, "look how far we've walked."

He gets up, hugs his chest, and paces among the trees.

They fold up the map, hoist their backpacks, and start making their way up the steep incline again through the thistles. Avram leads now, and Ora has a hard time keeping up. These shoes are really good for me, he decides. Excellent socks, too. He finds a long, supple branch of an arbutus tree, breaks it into the right size with one stomp, and uses it to help with the climb. He suggests that Ora use one, too. He comments on the excellent path markings in this section. "Frequent and consecutive, just like they should be," he pronounces. She thinks she can hear him humming a tune to himself.

It's a good thing the path is so long, she thinks, watching him from behind. This way, there's time to get accustomed to all the changes.

"Black-Maned Horse. That was one of Ilan's nicknames for Adam, when he was maybe three and a half. There was also Giant-Trunked Elephant. Get it?"

Avram mumbles the words, hearing them in Ilan's voice.

"Or Lovely-Braying Donkey. Or Angry-Browed Cat. That kind of thing."

"Angry-Browed Cat?"

"I'm telling you, it was like he was conducting human experiments."

She saw Adam changing in front of her very eyes, twisting and turning himself to adapt to Ilan's desires. He painted an orange cat: "I oranged it," he told her, "and now I'm trickling some yellow with my paintbrush." She smiled crookedly. Of course she was proud of him, but with every accomplishment she felt him grow farther away from her. She looked at him as he wagged his tail for Ilan and was alarmed at what she felt toward him. She could not understand how all that time he had hidden from her the eagerness that now overflowed, bursting from every pore in his skin. The exposed—and so masculine—fervor with which he turned his back on the years he had spent with her, in their little paradise for two. Bambi and his mother, RIP.

"My stomach is butterflying!" he'd shout joyously after Ilan spun him over his head. "Yes," she'd say, straining to smile, "lucky you."

It seems to her that shortly after he mastered speech, speech mastered him. He started to voice his thoughts out loud. She didn't notice it immediately, but at some point she realized that another channel had been added to the already bustling soundtrack of their domestic life. He vocalized all his thoughts, wishes, and fears. And since he still talked about himself in the third person, it made for entertainment sometimes: "Adam is hungry, hungry, hungry! Just wait a bit! No, he's sick of waiting for Mom to come out of the bathroom. Adam is going into the kitchen now, and he's going to make himself a snack. What should he put in his sandwich? And which should he put in his sand-what?"

He would lie in his bed after the bedtime rituals and mumble his thoughts. Ora and Ilan would stand behind the door eavesdropping halfheartedly. "Adam has to go to sleep. Maybe a dream will come? Teddy, here's what we have to do now. You have to go to sleep, and if a dream comes, shout 'Adam!' Dreams aren't real, it's just a drawing in your brain, Teddy."

"It was strange," Ora says now, "and a little embarrassing, as though his subconscious was completely exposed to us." She looks away from Avram so as not to remind him of his own narcotic-induced ramblings the night she kidnapped him. She wonders if she should tell him what he said about her that night: "She's totally nuts, she's gone off her rocker."

Adam knew all the letters and vowel marks by the time he was four. He picked them up with incredible ease, and you just couldn't stop him. He read, he wrote. He saw characters in the cracks of a soap bar, in a crust of bread, in the whitewash on the walls. He insisted on reading words in the folds in his sheet and the lines of his palm.

"Remind me what kind of pie you are?" Ilan said, tickling Adam while he bathed him.

"I'm a *pi*rate," Adam answered, laughing.

"And what else?"

"A pied piper!"

"And?"

"A grieving magpie!"

"*Thieving*," Ilan corrected him with a smile. "And what else?"

"A pile of cow pie!"

Bubbles of rolling laughter foamed up in the bathroom and burst in front of her as she lay in bed.

But now, walking up Mount Meron, she tries to remember why she was so angry at the time. What I wouldn't give to lie in that bed again, pregnant, with the aching back and the exhaustion, with Ofer in my belly, hearing that laughter of theirs. "Let's sit down for a minute. This is no mountain; this is a ladder."

She plunges to the ground. The incline, and the longings—her old heart can't take it. Adam is here with her, four years old at most, running around in the field. His childish movements, his curious, fragile, slightly suspicious looks. And the light that shines when he allows himself to be happy, when he excels at something, when Ilan praises him. "I keep talking about Adam, but Ofer is never Ofer alone. You understand that, don't you? Ofer is always also Adam, and Ilan, and me. That's the way it is. That's a family." She giggles. "You have no choice, you'll have to get to know us all."

Pictures and more pictures: Adam and baby Ofer napping together in a sleeping bag on the living-room rug—an Indian camp—naked, cuddling, their sweaty hair clinging to their foreheads, and Adam's right arm hugs Ofer's belly with its protruding navel. Adam and Ofer, five and a half and two, setting up house in an empty cardboard box, their two faces peeking from a little round window she'd cut out for them. Ofer and Adam, one and four and a half, very early in the morning, sleeping naked in Adam's bed; while they slept, Ofer had pooped and smeared Adam thoroughly, diligently, and undoubtedly with generosity and love. Ofer puffing his cheeks to blow out three candles on his birthday cake, and Adam running up from behind to finish them off with one breath. Ofer reaching up on his matchstick legs after Adam has snatched his beloved stuffed elephant, and shrieking: "Ofer e'phant!

Ofer e'phant!" He stands his ground so firmly that Adam panics and gives it back to him, then stares at him with a new tinge of reverence, as Ora watches from the kitchen.

A big family picnic. The scene is as vivid as though it is happening right here on the mountain. Adults and children sit in a circle watching Ofer, who stands in the middle. A fair, thin, tiny child with huge light-blue laughing eyes and a golden mass of hair. He is about to tell the funniest joke in the world, which Mom—he assures his audience—has already heard seven times and rolled around with laughter every time. Then he launches into a long, incomprehensible yarn about two friends, one called Whaddayacare, the other named Whatsupwithyou. He gets it all wrong and forgets things, then remembers, and sparks of laughter dart around his eyes. The audience flutters with delight, and Ofer keeps stopping to remind his listeners: "Soon comes the end of the joke, and that's when you laugh!"

All that time, Adam—Eight years old? Seven?—looking thin, secretive, and shadowy, slinks from one person to the next, following a hidden code known only to him. He never lingers, never allows anyone to hug or caress him, only watches ravenously as they all focus on Ofer. He loots them, a little predator, preyed upon.

Avram listens to Ora and a titmouse chirps joyously in the thicket. Nearby on the mountainside, in a patch that must have recently burned, mustard plants are starting to bloom again in a wild, joyous rabble of fauna. Ora laughs. The flowers have clearly decided to just get on with it, and the scorched spot now buzzes with mustard plants and bees.

"And Ofer kept quiet until he was almost three. Well, not quiet, but he didn't make much of an effort to learn how to talk."

Avram asks hesitantly, "And that . . . that's old, three, right?"

"It's pretty late to start talking."

Avram furrows his brow, considering the new information.

"I mean, he had a few basic words, and some very short phrases, and lots of fragments. A syllable here, a syllable there. Other than that he simply refused to learn how to talk. But he got by very well with his smiles and his charm, and those eyes of his. Which you gave him," she adds, unable to resist.

To Ora's surprise, Ofer had even convinced Ilan that you could live a full life without saying almost a single word correctly. "And this is Ilan, you know?" she notes with a raised eyebrow. "Ilan who told me, even before Adam was born, that he already knew he wouldn't be capable of loving a baby—not even his own son—until the baby started talking. And then comes Ofer, and he went on like that for almost three years, quiet as a monk, and look how it turned out."

Ilan and Ofer dug beds in the garden together and planted vegetables and flowers. They built a fancy ant farm and cared for it meticulously, and they built multisectioned LEGO castles, and spent hours making things out of plasticine and Play-Doh, and they played with Ofer's huge eraser collection, and baked cakes together. "Ilan!" She laughs. "Imagine! And Ofer, just so you know, was crazy about taking things apart. As soon as he could do anything, he liked to take things apart and put them back together, over and over again, a thousand times. The automatic sprinkler in the garden, an old tape recorder, a transistor, a fan, and of course watches. Ilan taught him some basic technical skills, and carpentry, and electrical engineering, and all that happened almost without words. You should have heard the gargles and squeaks that came out of those two. You should have seen Ilan. It was like he took a vacation from himself."

Avram smiles. Near happiness distorts his unaccustomed face for a moment. He really wants to hear, Ora observes once again, and her heart replies simply what she has always known about Avram: that he may never be able to or dare to connect himself to Ofer, but he certainly can and will connect to the story of Ofer.

A lighthearted, laughing Ilan emerged in Ofer's life. An Ilan whom she loved very much. He rolled around and wrestled on the floor with him, and played soccer and tag in the living room and in the yard, and ran around the house with Ofer on his shoulders, shouting and yelling, and walked Ofer up and down the hallway perched on his own feet, and sang silly songs with him.

They stood at the mirror and made funny or scary faces. Ilan would hold his face close to Ofer's, nose almost touching nose, and whoever laughed first lost. Then he'd disappear into the kitchen and emerge with his face covered in flour and ketchup. And the way those two horsed around in the bathtub, water fights and splashing. "You should have seen the bathroom when they were done. It looked like the scene of a water terrorist attack."

"And what about Adam?"

"Adam, yes"—she thinks of how he keeps coming back to Adam—"of

course Adam was also welcome in these games, it's not that he wasn't."
She tightens her arms over her chest. "It's just so complicated . . ."

Because when Adam was with them, she always had the feeling that
Ofer and Ilan held back a little, toned down their wildness and cheerfulness to tolerate Adam's incessant chatter, his flood of speech, which
often turned into a frightening display of physical rowdiness, a tempest
of hitting and kicking, aimed at them both, over some silly little excuse
or an imaginary insult. Sometimes he would throw himself down in a
tantrum and pound the floor with his hands and feet, and even his
head—Ora remembers the thuds with horror—and then Ilan and Ofer
would try as hard as they could to calm him, to appease him, to flatter
him. "It was really touching to see Ofer, all of two years old, caressing
Adam, sitting next to him, leaning over him and making wordless murmurs of comfort.

"It was such a difficult period, because Adam couldn't understand
what was going on, and the more he tried to get close to them, the more
they seemed to pull back. And then he'd get even more anxious and turn
up his volume, because what could he do? He only had one tool to
express everything he wanted, he only had what Ilan had taught him."
She shakes her head angrily. Why hadn't she intervened more? She'd
been so weak, so green. "In fact, now I think he was simply begging Ilan
to come back to him, to reaffirm their covenant. I also think about Ilan,
about how he just let Ofer be himself and loved everything about him.
He even gave up his damned judgmentalism, just so he could absolutely
love everything Ofer was, without any inhibitions."

And when he did that—she knows this, though she cannot say it out
loud—he turned his back on Adam. There's no other way to describe it.
She knows that Avram also understands exactly what happened. That
Avram can hear the half sounds and the silences.

Ilan didn't do it on purpose. She knows that. He probably never
wanted it to happen. He loved Adam very much. But that's what happened. That's what he did. Ora felt it, Adam felt it, maybe even tiny
Ofer felt something. It had no name, this act of Ilan's, the surreptitious,
subtle, terrible shift, but during that period, the air in their home was
thick with it—with a breach of trust so profound, so convoluted, that
even now, twenty years later, when she tells Avram about it, she cannot
call it by its explicit name.

. . .

One morning when Adam was about five, Ilan was feeding him eggs and toast, and Adam licked his lips in between bites and said, "Toast is what I like most."

This had been their favorite game for a while, before Ofer was born, and Ilan responded immediately: "Better than pot roast."

Adam laughed gleefully, thought for a minute, and said, "Scarier than a ghost!"

They both laughed. Ilan said, "You're good at this, but now you have to get dressed so we won't be late."

"For a very important date."

As Ilan was dressing him in a shirt, Adam said, "Into the sleeves, like green leaves."

Ilan smiled. "You're the greatest, Adamon."

When Ilan tied his shoes, Adam said, "Put my shoes on my feet, like a blanket on a sheet."

"I see you're full of rhymes."

"Go eat some limes."

On their way to kindergarten, they passed the Tzur Hadassah playground, and Adam observed that there was a bride on the slide and a king on the swing. Ilan, whose mind was preoccupied with other matters, mumbled something about how Adam was becoming a poet, and Adam replied, "You know it."

When Ora came to pick Adam up later that day, the teacher grinned and told her that Adam was having a very special day: he was talking to the class and the teacher only in rhymes, and had even infected a few of the other children, although not all of them were as good at rhyming as Adam was. "The kindergarten was full of rhymes today! We had a school full of little poets today, didn't we, children?"

Adam furrowed his smooth brow and said in a slightly angry voice, "Girls and boys, make some noise. And play with toys."

As they rode home on Ora's bike, he squeezed her waist tightly with an unfamiliar strength and answered all her questions in rhyme. Her patience for these games of his and Ilan's was limited to begin with, so she asked him to stop. He said: "With a skip and a hop." Ora decided he was just doing it to aggravate her, so she said nothing.

He kept it up at home. Ora threatened that she'd stop talking to him until he could behave, and he shouted, "Brave, save, wave!" He sat watching *Pretty Butterfly* on TV, and when Ora looked, she found him hunched forward, his hands in fists on his lap, and his lips moving after each sentence uttered by the characters on the show. She realized he was answering them in rhyme.

She took him for a drive, thinking the excursion would refresh him and make him forget the strange rhyming compulsion. They drove to nearby Mevo Beitar, and she showed him roofers fixing tiles on a roof, and he said, "Miles, piles, woof, hoof." When they drove past the store, he shouted out, after some moments of distress: "Snore." She stopped to let an old dog cross the road and heard a heavy silence from the backseat. When she looked in the mirror she saw his lips moving quickly and his eyes brimming with tears because he could not find a rhyme for "dog." "Fog," she said softly, and he breathed a sigh of relief. "And log," he quickly added.

"Now tell me how your day was at school?" she asked when they sat in a hiding place they both liked, on the way to the Ma'ayanot River. "Cool, fool," he blurted. She put her finger on his lips and said, "Now don't talk, just listen to what I have to say." He looked at her fearfully and mumbled, "Way, hay." Ora suddenly grew concerned at the sadness and desperation in his eyes. He seemed to be begging her to be quiet, for the whole world to be quiet, not to make a single sound ever again. She gathered him in her arms and held him close, and he buried his head in her neck, his body taut and rigid. She tried to calm him, but every time she forgot herself and said even one word, he was compelled to answer with a rhyme. She took him home, fed him and bathed him, and noticed that even when she was completely silent, he made rhymes for the sounds of the water in the bath, and a distant door slamming, and the beeping of the hourly news update on the neighbors' radio.

The next day, when she woke him up—in fact she asked Ilan to wake him, but he suggested that she go, and she went into the room with fictitious merriment and said to Ofer and Adam cheerfully: "Good morning, my dears!"—she heard Adam mumble into his pillow, "Fears, tears." His eyes quickly sharpened out of sleepiness, and his face turned dark with terror.

"What's wrong with me?" He sat up and asked her with a distant voice, and even before she could answer, he said, "Be strong with me, sing a song with me." He reached out for her to hug him. "I don't even want to speak," he shouted. "Leak, weak, sneak."

Ilan stood in the doorway. There was shaving cream on his face, and Adam pointed to him feebly and whispered, "Saving, waving."

"*Je ne sais quoi faire*," Ora whispered to Ilan.

"Bench, wrench," Adam murmured, and Ora was relieved for a moment, but her heart sank when she realized he was finding rhymes for "French."

"What's the matter, honey?" Ilan said severely.

"Money, funny," Adam sighed and buried his face in Ora's neck, seeking shelter from Ilan.

"This went on for maybe three months," Ora tells Avram. "Every sentence, every word, whatever anyone said to him and whatever sounds he heard. A rhyming machine. A robot."

"What did you do?"

"What could we do? We tried not to say anything. Not to make him nervous. We tried to just ignore it."

"There was that movie," Avram says, "we saw it once at the Jerusalem Cinema, the three of us."

"Yes, *David and Lisa*. 'What do you see when you look at me?' "

Avram replies: " 'I see a girl who looks like a pearl.' "

"Three months," she repeats, astounded. "Every sound in the home had a rhyme."

With all her strength she pushes down a moan of sorrow over what is now awakening in her—the desire, the urge, the passion to go back and talk about it with Ilan, to try to understand what Adam was going through, to chew it over with him again and again in one of their kitchen conversations, or sitting on the living-room sofa hand in hand in the dark, facing a muted television, or on one of their evening walks along the village paths.

There's no Ilan, she reminds herself sternly.

But for a moment, as it does every morning when she opens her eyes and reaches a probing hand to her side, it hits her with all its initial force: She has no partner. There's no rhyme for her.

"From morning to night it went on this way, day after day, and at night, too. And then it somehow stopped, almost without us noticing. Like with all sorts of other crazy phases they had, he and Ofer. That's how it goes." She struggles to laugh. "You're convinced that's it, they're stuck on some crazy notion forever. That Adam will talk in rhymes forever, or that Ofer will spend the rest of his life sleeping with a monkey wrench in his bed so he can beat up the Arabs when they come, or that he'll wear his cowboy costume until he's seventy, and then one day you notice that for some time now, that thing that was making the whole household crazy, that was depressing us for months on end, has just—*poof*—vanished into thin air."

"Beat up the Arabs?"

"Well, that's another story," she says, laughing. "Your kid had an overactive imagination."

"Ofer?"

"Yes."

"But why . . . why Arabs? Did something happen to him with—"

"No, no." She waves her hand dismissively. "It was all in his head."

They walk past the Mount Meron Field School, and Avram runs to fill their water bottles at a tap. Ora sees the water overflowing from the bottle and gushing down and discovers that he is looking out at the grove they've just emerged from and is smiling gently. When she follows the thread of his smile, she sees the golden bitch standing by the trees, panting. Ora fills a dish with water and puts it down not far from the dog. "It's your dish," she reminds her and fills it for her again and again until she is sated. At a nearby snack stand—only after the owner agrees to turn off his radio—they buy three hot dogs for the bitch and some food and candy for themselves. Then they continue their ascent up the mountain. The loudspeaker on the nearby army base emits constant calls for technicians, drivers, antenna operators. This human presence thickens and fills them with nervousness. They avoid encountering or conversing with other couples hiking on their trail—who look pretty much like us, Ora thinks with a moment's jealousy: people around our age, friendly yuppies who've taken off work for a nature day, a little escape from the job and the kids; they probably think the same thing about me and Avram. He was really alarmed when I mentioned Ofer's fear of the Arabs. What button did I press?

On the peak of Mount Meron they stand at a lookout point: "Restored by the family and friends of First Lieutenant Uriel Peretz, of blessed memory, born in Ofira on the 2nd of Kislev, 5737 (1977), fell in Lebanon on the 7th of Kislev 5758 (1998). Scout, soldier, devoted to Torah and to his country," Avram reads—and they look north, to the purple-misted Hermon, and to the Hula Valley and the green Naphtali mountain range. They once again pat themselves on the back with proud modesty, trying to estimate how many kilometers they have traversed. A new and unfamiliar power diffuses their bodies. Knots of strength have amassed in their calves, and when they take off their backpacks, they feel as though they are floating on air.

"So, should we sleep up here?"

"It'll be cold. Maybe we should go a bit farther down. Let's follow the path downhill?"

"I'd like to go all the way around the peak first"—Avram stretches and shakes out his arms—"even though it's not on the path."

"Then let's do it," she says happily. "We don't have to stick to the path."

They circle the peak on a loop, and the dog runs ahead for the first time. Every so often she pauses to look at them, waiting and urging them on with her gaze, then runs on. The air is soaked with the scents of loose earth and blossoms. Ivy climbs up tree trunks, and sudden flames of colorful redbuds ignite among the oak and hawthorn trees. Thin branches erupt from the roots of a massive arbutus tree, like fingers from a huge open palm, and its body is bare of bark, almost embarrassing in its colors and textures, like human nudity, like a woman's body.

Ora stops suddenly. "Listen, I have to tell you something. It's been eating at me the whole time, but I couldn't do it. Do you want to hear?"

"Ora," he says, scolding.

"Look, when I said goodbye to him, to Ofer, when I took him to the army meeting place, there was a TV crew there. They filmed us."

"Yes?"

"The reporter asked him what he wanted to tell me before he left, and Ofer sort of smiled and asked me to make him all kinds of dishes, I don't remember exactly what, and then he whispered something in my ear, right in front of the cameras and everything."

Avram stops and waits.

"And what he said was"—she takes a deep breath, pursing her lips—"that if, if he . . ."

"Yes?" Avram whispers. He wants to give her strength, but his body unwittingly responds as though a blow is about to land on it.

"That if something happens to him—do you hear me?—if something happens to him, he wants us to leave the country."

"What?"

" 'Promise me you'll leave the country.' "

"That's what he said?"

"Word for word."

"All of you?"

"I guess so. I didn't even have time to—"

"And did you promise?"

"I don't think so, I can't remember, I was so stunned."

They keep walking, their bodies hunched now. "If I'm killed," Ofer had whispered, "leave the country. Just get out of here, there's nothing here for you."

"And what's most depressing is that it's obvious to me that it wasn't something he just said on the spur of the moment. He'd thought about it ahead of time. He'd planned it."

Avram tramples the ground heavily as he walks.

"Wait, slow down."

He rubs his face and head roughly. A cold sweat breaks out. Those three words that had come out of her mouth: *If I'm killed.* How could she say them? How could they get through her throat?

"When Adam was in the army, he once said that if anything happened to him he wanted us to erect a bench in his memory opposite the Submarine."

"What submarine?"

"The Yellow Submarine. It's a music club, in Talpiot, where he plays sometimes with his band."

They walk on in silence, without noticing the other hikers they occasionally pass. Near an ancient winepress carved out of rock, they sit down. The first of the salamanders swim in the pool of rainwater in the press. Clumps of green weeds chewed by wild boars are strewn around. They both sit silently, gathering strength.

"And somehow, in all these days . . . what can I say . . . in the moments I cannot repress, I feel that the whole time I'm walking, I'm also saying goodbye to the country."

"You won't leave," he says firmly, almost panicking. "You can't."

"I can't?"

"Come on. Let's go."

His jaw is tightly clenched, crushing thoughts and words. He wants to tell her that only here, in this landscape, in the rocks, the cyclamens, in Hebrew, in this sun, does she have any meaning. But it sounds sentimental and ungrounded, and he says nothing.

Ora straightens up. It suddenly occurs to her that Ofer guessed something about Avram. That he was almost saying: If it happens to me too, if it passes down to the next generation, you have nothing to keep you here. "But in any case," she says quietly, "if I do, it won't be just the country."

"Ora—"

"Forget it. Forget that now, why ruin the view?" Her mouth trembles. She bites her lip hard.

Avram, by her side, drags his feet and a terrible, leaden heaviness fills him with every step. Perhaps that's why she's telling me about him, he thinks, so there'll be someone here to remember him.

"Avram." With her last remaining strength she pulls herself out of the muddy silence.

"What, Ora'leh?"

"Do you know what I feel like?"

"What do you feel like?" He smiles distractedly through his gloom. All you have to do is ask, he thinks, his feelings rushing at her.

"Tomorrow or the next day, I want to give you a haircut."

"What's wrong with the way it is?"

"Nothing's wrong. It's just an urge I get in high mountains."

"I don't know. We'll see. Let me think about it."

The air is clear and sharp. Cistus bushes abound in pink and white on both sides of the path. He thinks: She's always jumping from one thing to another. She's always in everything.

"Who usually cuts your hair?" She throws out the question with measured lightness.

"Once, a long time ago, I had a barber friend on Ben Yehuda, and he'd do me a favor."

"Oh."

"But in the last few years it's usually Neta, about once every six months." He fingers his long, sparse hair, which flaps in the wind. "Maybe you really should straighten it out a bit."

"You won't feel it, it won't hurt."

Empty acorn caps crunch under their feet. A cool breeze laps around them. The grove is dotted with red, blue, and purple anemones. A new intimacy shakily hovers between them.

"You know," Ora says, "since the day before yesterday, since we both came out of our shock a bit, when I felt that you were doing better too—that was around the day before yesterday, wasn't it?"

"Yes?"

"Yes, after I wrote in my notebook that night. Since then, I've suddenly noticed that almost everything I see, the view, the flowers, the rocks, the color of the earth, the light at different times"—she makes a sweeping, circular motion—"everything, you know, even you, and the stories I'm telling you, and both of us, and this hyacinth here"—she greets it with a nod—"I'm trying to engrave all of this in my memory now, because you never know"—she mischievously gives Avram a clown face that does not make him laugh—"this may be my last time with them."

"Nothing's going to happen to him, Ora, you'll see, he'll be fine."

"You promise?"

He raises his eyebrows.

"Promise me." She bumps her shoulder against his. "What do you care—make an old lady happy."

They pass by another lookout point, dedicated to Yosef Bukish, of blessed memory, who fell in service on July 25, 1997:

> So many things in the world are pretty,
> Flowers and animals, nature and city,
> And if you open your eyes and explore,
> You'll see hundreds of wonders each day—maybe more!
>
> LEAH GOLDBERG

Remember, Avram thinks as he rushes around in his own mind, slamming against its walls. This head that you emptied, that you erased, that you sullied, that you filled with trash, with shit, will now store every word she says, everything she's telling you about Ofer. Give her at least that, what else do you have to give? All you can give her is your damn, sick memory.

"What he said to you," Avram suggests cautiously after a while, "I was thinking, maybe he was a little influenced by Adam's opera?"

"About exile? Where everyone leaves in a convoy?"

"Maybe."

She blushes from chest to neck. She had entertained that same thought herself. And now he is. It is amazing how he is learning to weave his threads into her tapestry. They stand swaying lightly. At their feet are the green expanses, forests, and rocky mountains of the Mount Meron Nature Reserve. Avram thinks again about the woman unraveling the crimson thread behind her. Perhaps it is an umbilical cord that comes out of her and keeps going forever. He imagines more and more men, women, and children streaming out of the towns and villages, the kibbutzim and moshavim, to tie their own threads to hers. For a moment he sees a red tapestry spreading out over the expanses below him, clinging to them like a fishing net, a thin, bleeding mesh that glistens in the sun.

"There's something special about this kind of walk, isn't there?" he says later.

Ora, lost in thought, laughs. "There's a lot, yes, you could definitely say so."

"No, I mean the walking itself, where you have to go from point to point, you can't skip anything. It's like the trail is teaching us to walk at its pace."

"It's so different from my normal life, with the cars and the microwave and the computers, where you can defrost a whole chicken with the click of a button, or send a message to New York. Oh, Avram"—she stretches her arms and inhales the sharp mountain air—"this heel-to-toe is much more suited to me. Maybe we can spend our whole lives just walking and walking without ever getting there."

They leave the path and find a lovely pillow of green, where they sprawl on their backs on the warm earth, facing the sun. It's afternoon, and near Ora's head is a heron's bill flower that has finished its pollination work and now sheds its blue petals before dying. An earthy, rocky, primeval strength seeps into her body from the mountain beneath her. The bitch sprawls some distance away, licking and cleaning herself thoroughly. Avram takes Ofer's hat out of his backpack—*Shelach Battalion, Company C, The Guys*—and covers his face. She also shelters her face with a hat. The warm sun makes her sleepy. A deep silence plunges all around them. A tiny beetle burrows through fallen poppy leaves by her fingers. Next to her knee, an iris hurries to seduce the followers of the deceased heron's bill by displaying its blue blossoms.

"Before, when we were standing at that lookout point," Ora says softly under her hat, "when we looked down on the Hula Valley and it was so beautiful, with the fields in all those colors, I realized that it's always like this for me with this land."

"Like what?"

"Every encounter I have with it is also a bit of a farewell."

Hidden under his hat, Avram fleetingly sees the shred of an Arabic newspaper he had found in a bucket in the latrine at Abbasiya Prison. Through the smeared excrement he had managed to decipher a brief report about the executions of deputy ministers and fifteen mayors from Haifa and the surrounding suburbs, held the previous night in the central square in Tel Aviv. For a few days and nights he was convinced that Israel no longer existed. Then he realized the fraud, but something had been damaged in him.

His eyes are wide open now. He remembers the interminable drives around the streets of Tel Aviv with Ora and with Ilan, after he got out of the hospital. Everything had seemed real and alive, but also like a big act. During one of those drives he'd said to Ora: "Okay, it's all very well to say, *If you will it, it is no dream,* as Herzl said, but what if you stop willing it? What if you can't be bothered to have the will anymore?"

"The will for what?"

"To stop being a dream."

A flock of partridges alights with beating wings from within the nearby thicket, and the bitch emerges, disappointed.

"And in those moments," Ora says through her hat, "I always think: This is my country, and I really don't have anywhere else to go. Where would I go? Tell me, where else could I get so annoyed about everything, and who would want me anyway? But at the same time I also know that it doesn't really have a chance, this country. It just doesn't. Do you understand?" She plucks the hat off her face and sits up, surprised to find him sitting there watching her. "If you think about it logically, if you just think numbers and facts and history, with no illusions, it doesn't have a chance."

All of a sudden, as if in a clumsy theater performance, a few dozen soldiers burst onto the green meadow, running in two lines, and split off on either side of Ora and Avram. *Ordinance Corps Officers' Course,* their sweaty shirts read. Thirty or forty young men, strong but exhausted, with a delicate-looking blond soldier jogging in front of them. She sings an irritating tune:

"*Tem-em-em-em-em!*"

And they answer with a hoarse roar: "All for lovely Rotem!"

"*Tem-em-em-em-em!*"

"All to war for Rotem!"

. . .

What do you tell a six-year-old boy, a pip-squeak Ofer, who one morning, while you're taking him to school, holds you close on the bike and asks in a cautious voice, "Mommy, who's against us?" And you try to find out exactly what he means, and he answers impatiently, "Who hates us in the world? Which countries are against us?" And of course you want to keep his world innocent and free of hatred, and you tell him that those who are against us don't always hate us, and that we just have a long argument with some of the countries around us about all sorts of things, just like children in school sometimes have arguments and even fights. But his little hands tighten around your stomach, and he demands the names of the countries that are against us, and there is an urgency in his voice and in his sharp chin that digs into your back, and so you start to name them: "Syria, Jordan, Iraq, Lebanon. But not Egypt—we have peace with them!" you say cheerfully. "We had lots of wars with them, but now we've made up." And you think to yourself: if only he knew that it was because of Egypt that he himself had come into being. But he demands precision, a very practical, detail-oriented child: "Is Egypt really our friend?" "Not really," you admit, "they still don't completely want to be our friends." "So they're against us," he solemnly decrees, and immediately asks if there are other "countries of Arabs," and he doesn't let up until you name them all: "Saudi Arabia, Libya, Sudan, Kuwait, and Yemen." You can feel his mouth learning the names behind your back, and you add Iran—not exactly Arabs, but not exactly our friends, either. After a pause he asks softly if there are any more, and you mumble, "Morocco, Tunisia, Algeria," and then you remember Indonesia and Malaysia, Pakistan and Afghanistan, and probably Uzbekistan and Kazakhstan too—none of those *stans* sounds so great to you—and here we are at school, sweetie! When you help him get off the bike seat, he feels heavier than usual.

Over the following days Ofer started to listen closely to the news. Even if he was in the middle of a game, he would perk up just before the hour and again at the half-hour bulletin. Secretly, with spy-like movements, he would move toward the kitchen and stand, as if by chance, near the door, listening to the radio that was always on. She watched his little face twist into a mixture of anger and fear every time there was a report of an Israeli killed in an act of hostility. "Are you sad?" she asked him when he sobbed after another bomb went off in the market in Jerusalem, and he stomped his feet: "I'm not sad, I'm angry! They're killing all our people! Soon we'll run out of people!" She tried to reassure him: "We have a strong army, and there are some very big and strong countries that will protect us." Ofer treated this information with skepticism. He wanted to know where exactly these friendly countries were. Ora opened an atlas: "Here's the United States of America, for example, and here's England, and here are another few good friends of ours." She quickly waved an overgeneralizing hand near a few European countries that she herself did not particularly trust. He looked at her in astonishment. "But they're all the way over there!" he shouted, in disbelief at her stupidity. "Look how many pages there are between here and there!"

A few days later he asked her to show him the countries that were "against us." She opened up the atlas again and pointed to each country, one after the other. "Wait, but where are we?" A glimmer of hope shone in his eyes: Maybe they weren't on that page. She pointed with her pinky finger at Israel. A strange whimper escaped his lips, and he suddenly clung to her as hard as he could, fought and plowed his way to her with his whole body, as though trying to be swallowed up in it again. She hugged him and stroked him and murmured words of comfort. Sharp sweat, almost an old man's sweat, broke out all over his skin. When she managed to hold up his face, she saw in his eyes something that knotted her gut in one pull.

Over the next days he grew uncharacteristically quiet. Even Adam could not cheer him up. Ilan and Ora tried. They plied him with promises of a trip to Holland over summer vacation, or even a Kenyan safari, all in vain. He was depressed and lifeless, lost in himself. Ora realized then how much her own happiness depended on the light of this child's face.

"His gaze," said Ilan. "I don't like the look in his eyes. It's not a child's look."

"At us?"

"At everything. Haven't you noticed?"

She may have noticed, of course she'd noticed, but as usual—"You know me," she sighs as she and Avram walk down the Meron. "You know how I am with these things"—she simply preferred not to think about what she saw, to turn a blind eye to all the signs, and certainly not to say anything about them out loud, hoping they would fade away. But now Ilan would say it, he would define it, he would soberly and crudely put words to it, and then it would become real, and it would grow and multiply.

"It's like he knows something we don't yet have the courage to—"

"Don't worry about it, it's just a phase. These are normal fears at that age."

"I'm telling you Ora, they're not."

She giggled joylessly. "You remember how when Adam was three, he was really preoccupied with the question of whether there were Arabs at night, too?"

"But this is something different, Ora. My feeling is that—"

"Listen, let's take him to spend a day on the horse ranch he once—"

"Sometimes I have the feeling he's looking at us like—"

"A parrot!" Ora fluttered desperately. "Remember he asked us to buy him a—"

"Like we've been given death sentences."

And then Ofer demanded numbers. When he heard there were four and a half million people in Israel, he was impressed, even reassured. The number seemed enormous to him. But after two days a new thought came—"He was always a terribly logical child," she tells Avram, "and that's not from you or from me either, that analytical, purposeful mind"—and he wanted to know "how many are against us." He wouldn't stop until Ilan found out for him exactly the number of citizens in each Muslim country in the world. Ofer enlisted Adam, who helped him with the calculations, and they shut themselves up in their room. "What do you do with a child like that, who suddenly learns the facts of life and death?" Ora asks Avram as they pass a rocky monument for a Druze soldier. *Sergeant Salah Kassem Tafesh, May God Avenge His Blood,* Avram reads out of the corner of his eye—Ora hurries ahead— *Fell in Southern Lebanon in an Encounter with Terrorists, on the 16th of Nissan 5752, at Age 21. Your Memory Is Engraved in Our Hearts.*

"What do you do with a child like that?" she repeats with pursed lips. A child who goes out and uses his pocket money to buy a little orange spiral notebook and every day writes in it, in pencil, how many Israelis are left after the last terrorist attack. Or who at Passover Seder, with

Ilan's family, suddenly starts crying that he doesn't want to be Jewish anymore, because they always kill us and always hate us, and he knows this because all the holidays are about it. And the adults look at one another, and a brother-in-law mumbles that it is kind of difficult to argue with that, and his wife says, "Don't be paranoid," and he quotes, *"That in every generation, they rise up against us to destroy us,"* and she replies that it's not exactly scientific fact, and that maybe we should examine our own role in the whole *rising up against us* business, and the familiar argument ensues, and Ora, as usual, flees to the kitchen to help with the dishes, but she suddenly stops: she sees Ofer looking at the adults as they argue, horrified at their doubts, at their naïveté, and his eyes fill with fervent, prophetic tears.

"Look at them," Avram had said to her once, in one of their drives around the streets of Tel Aviv after he got back. "Look at them. They walk down the street, they talk, they shout, read newspapers, go to the grocery store, sit in cafés"—he went on for several minutes describing everything they saw through the car window—"but why do I keep thinking it's all one big act? That it's all to convince themselves that this place is truly real?"

"You're exaggerating," Ora had said.

"I don't know, maybe I'm wrong, but I don't think the Americans or the French have to believe so hard all the time just to make America exist. Or France, or England."

"I don't understand what you mean."

"Those are countries that exist even without having to always *want* them to exist. And here—"

"I'm looking around," she said, her voice slightly hoarse and high-pitched, "and everything looks completely natural and normal to me. A little crazy, that's true, but in a normal way."

Because I've looked at it from a different place, Avram thought, and sank silently into himself.

The next day, Ora told him now, Ofer woke up with a conclusion and a solution: from now on he would be English, and everyone had to call him John, and he would not answer to the name Ofer. " 'Cause no one kills *them*," he explained simply, "and they don't have any enemies. I asked in class, and Adam says so too, everyone's friends with the English." He started speaking English, or rather, what he thought was English, a gibberish version of Hebrew with an English accent. And just to be on the safe side, he buttressed his bed with protective layers of books and toys, trenches of furry stuffed animals. And every night he insisted on sleeping with a heavy monkey wrench next to his head.

"I happened to look in his notebook one day, and I saw that he kept writing 'Arobs.' When I told him it was spelled with an 'a' he was amazed: 'I thought it was A-robs, 'cause they keep robbing us.'

"Then one day he found out that some Israelis were Arabs. Well, by that time I didn't know whether to laugh or cry, you know? He discovered that all his calculations were wrong, and he had to deduct the Israeli Arabs from the number of Israelis."

She remembers how furious he was when he found out. He stomped his feet and shouted and turned red and hurled himself on the floor and screamed: "Make them go away! Back to their own homes! Why did they even come here? Don't they have their own places?"

"And then he had an attack, a bit like the one he had at age four, with the vegetarianism. He ran a high fever, and for almost a week I was in total despair. And there was one night when he was convinced there was an Arab with him."

"In his body?" Avram asks in horror, and his eyes dart to the sides. She has the feeling that he has lied to her about something.

"In his room," she corrects him softly. "It was just feverish nonsense, hallucinations."

The hair on her skin stands on end, telling her she has to be careful, but she's not sure of what. Avram seems to have ossified right in front of her. His eyes harden with the look of a captive.

"Are you okay?"

There is shame and terror and guilt in his eyes. For a moment Ora thinks she knows exactly what she is seeing, and the next moment she flings herself away. An Arab in his body, she thinks. What did they do to him there? Why doesn't he ever talk?

"I'll never forget that night," she says, trying to abate the horror on Avram's face. "Ilan was on reserve duty in Lebanon, in the eastern sector. He was gone for four weeks. I put Adam to sleep in our bed so Ofer wouldn't disturb him. Adam didn't have a lot of patience for Ofer through that whole episode. It was like he couldn't see that Ofer was afraid of something. And just imagine: Ofer was—I don't know, six? And Adam was already nine and a half, and it was like he couldn't forgive Ofer for breaking down like that.

"I sat with Ofer all night, and he was burning up and confused, and he kept seeing the Arab in the room, sitting on Adam's bed, on the closet, under the bed, peering at him from the window. Madness.

"I tried to calm him, and I turned on the light, and I brought a flash-light to prove to him there was no one there. I also tried to explain some of the facts to him, to put things in perspective—me, the big expert, right? There I was in the middle of the night, giving him a seminar on the history of the conflict."

"And then what?" Avram asks very quietly, his face fallen.

"Nothing. You couldn't even talk to him. He was so miserable—you'll laugh—that I almost thought of calling Sami, our driver, you know, the one who—"

"Yes."

"To explain to him, or something like that. To show him that he was an Arab too, and that he wasn't Ofer's enemy and didn't hate him and didn't want his room." She falls quiet and swallows a bitter lump: the memory of her last drive with Sami.

"At nine the next morning, Ofer had an appointment with our family doctor. At eight, after I sent Adam to school, I bundled up Ofer in a coat, sat him in the car, and drove to Latrun."

"Latrun?"

"I'm a practical girl."

With a stern and determined look, she had climbed up the steps, walked down the gravel path, put Ofer down in the center of the huge courtyard at the Armored Corps site, and told him to look.

He had blinked hazily, blinded by the winter sun. Around him were dozens of tanks, both ancient and new. Tank barrels and machine guns were aimed at him. She held his hand and walked him to one of the larger ones, a Soviet T-55. Ofer stood facing the tank, excited. She asked if he was strong enough to climb on it. He replied in amazement: "Am I allowed?" She helped him climb up the turret, then clambered up after him. He stood there, swaying, looked fearfully around, and asked, "Is this ours?"

"Yes."

"You mean, all this?"

"Yes, and there's lots more, we have loads of these."

Ofer waved his arm in the air over the semicircle of tanks in front of him. Some of them had been discontinued as long ago as the Second

World War, metal toads and iron tortoises, antiquated booty tanks from at least three wars. He asked to climb on another tank, and another, and another. He ran his fingers in awe over tracks, firing platforms, equipment chambers, and transmissions and rode like a cavalier on the barrels. At ten-thirty they both sat down in the restaurant at the Latrun gas station, where Ofer devoured a huge Greek salad and a three-egg omelet.

"Maybe it was a little primitive, my instant treatment, but it was definitely effective." Then she adds drily, "Besides, at the time I thought that what was good enough for a whole country was good enough for my child."

In the heart of a pasture, at the foot of a giant lone oak tree, a man is lying on the ground. His head rests on a large rock, a backpack sits beside him, and Ora's blue notebook peeks out of one of its pockets.

They stand awkwardly by his side, afraid to wake him, yet drawn to the notebook. Ora snatches her glasses off her face and hides them in her fanny pack. She quickly runs her fingers through her disheveled hair to tidy it. She and Avram try to understand—exchanging looks and furrowed brows—how the man has managed to get here ahead of them. Ora, slightly envious, admires the tranquillity and confidence with which he has abandoned himself in this open, invadable space. His dark, masculine face is so exposed. Those glasses lie on his chest like a large butterfly, tied to a string around his neck.

Avram signals to her that if she has no objection, he will take the notebook. She hesitates. The notebook is nestled comfortably in his backpack pocket.

But Avram is already approaching, and with a pickpocket's expertise he fishes the notebook out of the bag and signals to Ora that they should move away quickly if they don't want to get embroiled in explanations, especially with someone who, at their first encounter, had made the mistake of mentioning the news.

She hugs the notebook to her heart, soaking up its warmth. The man goes on sleeping. With his mouth half open, he snores, making soft, woolly sounds. His arms and legs are clumsily splayed out. A rug of silver hair rises out of his shirt collar and awakens in Ora a vague longing to put her head there, to give herself over to a deep, infectious slumber, like his own. In a moment's impulse, she tears out the last page of the notebook and writes, "I took back my notebook. Bye, Ora." She hesitates, and quickly adds her phone number, in case he wants a more detailed explanation. When she leans over to put the note in his backpack, she notices them again: two identical wedding rings, one on his ring finger, the other on his pinky.

They slip away quickly, bubbling sweetly with the success of their plot, their eyes glimmering with childlike mischief. As they walk, she leafs through the notebook, amazed to see how much she had written that night by the river. She scans her lines with his eyes.

The path appears again, bending and twisting cheerfully, and the dog circles around them, sometimes runs alongside them and at other times sprints ahead quickly, then suddenly stops for no reason. She sits on her behind, turns her head back to Ora, the black arches above her eyes slightly raised, and Ora makes a similar gesture.

"She's a happy dog, see? She's smiling at us."

But as they walk down the mountain, over heaps of shattered fallen rocks, a bothersome thought nags at her. She could not have written so many pages in one night. A few steps later, next to a huge rock with a mysterious oblong shape, she has to stop. She pulls the notebook out of her backpack, puts her glasses back on, and quickly leafs through the pages. She lets out a little shriek: "Look!" She shows Avram. "Look, it's his handwriting!"

Avram studies the pages and his face wrinkles. "Are you sure? Because it looks like—"

She holds the page close to her face. It looks like her handwriting, or a masculine version of it: straight, neat characters, all at the same angle. "It really does look like mine," she mumbles awkwardly, feeling naked. "Even I was confused."

She turns the pages back, looking for the place where the writers switched. Twice, then three times, she flips past the right point before recognizing her final lines: *Aren't we like a little underground cell in the heart of the 'situation'? And that really is what we were. For twenty years. Twenty good years. Until we got trapped.* Immediately after those words— even without turning the page: such chutzpah! Even without a separating line!—she reads: *Next to Dishon River I meet Gilead, 34, an electrician and djembe drummer, who used to be from a moshav in the north. Now lives in Haifa. What does he miss: "Dad was a farmer (pecans), and in slow years he did all kinds of jobs. There was a time when he gathered construction planks from dumps and sold them to an Arab in the village nearby."*

"What is this?" She thrusts the notebook at Avram's chest. "What is this supposed to be?" She pulls it back and reads with a choked-up voice:

"Wood, you see—you have to know how to treat it. You can't just throw it in the basement. You have to carefully stack big ones on big ones, and small ones on small ones, and put bricks on top of it all, otherwise it warps. But first of all you have to take out the nails. So I would stand with Dad at night in the sheltered area where he kept the wood—

"What on earth is this? What is all this stuff?" She raises her eyebrows at Avram, but his eyes are closed, and he signals: Keep reading.

"Dad had a blue undershirt, with holes here. And we had a crowbar that we connected to an extension handle, and we would take an iron chisel and separate, say, two planks nailed together. Dad on this end, me on that end, bracing, and after we separated them, we'd work together on the plank, pulling out nails with the other end of the hammer. It went on for hours, with a little bulb hanging above from a string, and that's something I still miss to this day, the way I worked with him like that, together.

"There's more. Listen, that's not all. There's more.

"Now about the regret. Well, that's a harder one. I regret lots of things (laughs). I mean, do people just come out and tell you? Look, at some point I had a ticket to Australia, to work on a cotton farm. I had a visa and everything, and then I met a girl here and I canceled my trip. But she was worth it, so it's just a partial regret."

Ora frantically turns the page and her eyes run over the lines. She reads silently: *Tamar, my darling, someone lost a notebook with her life story. I'm almost positive I met her earlier, when I walked down to the river. She looked like she was in a bad state. In danger even (she wasn't alone). Ever since I saw her, I've been asking you what to do but you haven't answered. I'm not used to not getting answers from you, Tammi. It's all a little confusing. But I am asking the questions you posed at the end: What do we miss most? What do we regret?*

Ora slaps the notebook shut. "What is he? Who is this?"

Avram's face is gloomy and distant.

"Maybe a journalist, interviewing people along his way? But he doesn't look like one at all." A doctor, she remembers. He said he was a pediatrician.

She glances at the pages again: *Near Moshav Alma I meet Edna, 39, divorced, a kindergarten teacher, Haifa: "What I miss most is my childhood days in Zichron Yaakov. Originally I'm a Zamarin, that was my maiden name, and I miss the days of innocence, the simplicity we had then. Everything was less complicated. Less, kind of, 'psychological.' You wouldn't believe it to look at me, but I have three grown sons (laughs). It doesn't show, does it? I married early and divorced even earlier . . ."*

Ora is sucked in. She turns the pages rapidly and sees, on every page, longings and regrets. "I don't understand," she murmurs, feeling deceived. "He looked like such a"—she searches for the right word—"solid man? Simple? Private? Not a man who . . . who would just walk around asking people these kinds of questions."

Avram says nothing. He digs the tip of his shoe into the gravel.

"And why in *my* notebook?" Ora asks loudly. "Aren't there any other notebooks?"

She spins around and starts to walk away, head held high, pressing the notebook close to her. Avram shrugs his shoulders, looks back for a moment—there's no one there, the guy must still be asleep—and follows her. He does not see the thin smile of surprise on her lips.

"Ora—"

"What?"

"Didn't Ofer want to go on a big trip somewhere, after the army?"

"Let him finish the army first," she says curtly.

"Actually, he did talk about that," she picks up later. "Maybe to India."

"India?" Avram bites back a smile and buries an unruly thought: He should come see me at the restaurant. I can tell him all about India.

"He hasn't decided yet. They were thinking of traveling together, he and Adam."

"The two of them? Are they really that—"

"Close. Those two are each other's best friend." A seedling of pride grows inside her: At least in that realm she'd been successful. Her two sons were soul mates.

"And is that—is that normal?"

"What?"

"For two brothers, at that age . . ."

"They were always like that. Almost from the beginning."

"But didn't you say that . . . Weren't you telling me that Ilan and Ofer—"

"That changed, too. Things kept changing in that period. I just don't know how I'm going to have time to tell you everything."

It's a bit like describing how a river flows, she realizes. Like painting a whirlwind, or flames. It's an *occurrence*, she thinks, happily recalling one of his old words: A family is a perpetual occurrence.

And she shows him: Adam at six and a bit, Ofer almost three. Adam lies on the lawn at the house in Tzur Hadassah. His arms are spread-eagled and his eyes are closed. He is dead. Ofer goes in and out of the screen door, and the slamming wakes Ora from a rare afternoon nap. She looks out the window and sees Ofer bringing presents to Adam, sacrificial offerings to bring him back to life. He takes out his stuffed animals, toy cars, a kaleidoscope, board games, and marbles. He piles his favorite books and a few choice videotapes around Adam. He is serious and worried, almost frightened. Again and again he toddles up the four concrete steps into the house and back to Adam to place precious objects around him. Adam does not move. Only when Ofer is inside the house does he raise his head a little and open one eye to examine the latest offering. She hears heavy panting. Ofer pulls out his favorite blanket and places it tenderly on Adam's legs. Then he looks at Adam pleadingly and says something she cannot hear. Adam lies motionless. Ofer makes fists, looks around, and runs back into the house again. Adam wriggles his toes under Ofer's blanket. How cruel he can be, she thinks. Yet his cruelty is so hypnotic that she cannot put an end to Ofer's torture. Outside her closed door she hears sounds of effort and struggle. Something heavy is being dragged. Chairs are pushed aside, and Ofer breathes rhythmically, grunting a little. A moment later his mattress appears at the top of the stairs, towering over his head. Ofer feels for the top step with his foot. Ora freezes, careful not to laugh so as not to frighten him and make him fall. Adam opens a slit in one eye and an admixture of amazement and awe emerges on his face as he watches his little brother carrying almost his own body's weight on his head. Ofer walks down the steps, rocking back and forth under the clumsy mattress. He groans, pants, and propels himself forward with trembling legs. He reaches Adam and collapses beside him on the mattress. Adam props himself up on his elbows and looks at Ofer with deep, grateful, open eyes.

It seemed to Ora, as she watched from the window, that in fact Adam was not being cruel but rather testing Ofer, to find out if he could sustain a far greater mission, which Ora could not identify at the time; she still thought it was merely the usual, sufficiently complicated mission of being Adam's little brother.

"What do you mean?" Avram asks hesitantly.

"Wait, I'll get there."

"So you're not dead anymore?" Ofer asked. "I'm alive," said Adam, and he got up and started to run around the yard with his arms outstretched, declaring that he was alive and kicking. Ofer pranced along behind him, smiling, exhausted.

"Ilan may have betrayed Adam, but Ofer never did," she explains.

Small, thin, and stuttering, enchanting everyone with his gaze, his large blue eyes, his golden hair, his wondrous smile. He had certainly sensed that he could capture hearts effortlessly, simply with his sweetness and the light that shone from his face. And obviously, she thinks, he'd already noticed that every time he went anywhere with Adam, everyone's eyes immediately skipped over his older, restless, slippery, bothersome brother and were drawn to him. "Just think about what a temptation that is for a boy—to rake in the whole pot at his brother's expense. But he never did. Never. Always, in any situation, he chose Adam."

"From his first step," Avram reminds her generously.

"That's right, you remember," she says happily.

"I remember everything." He reaches out to embrace her shoulders. They walk on that way, side by side, his parents.

They are nine and six, one tall and thin, the other still small, walking and talking feverishly, gesticulating, climbing on top of each other's ideas. Weird, complicated conversations about orcs and gnomes, vampires and zombies. "But, Adam," Ofer squeaks, "I don't get it. A wolfman is a boy born from a family of wolves?"

"It could be that way," Adam replies gravely, "but it could be that he's just got lycanthropy."

Ofer is stunned for a moment, then tries out the word and stumbles. Adam explains at length about the disease that turns humans, or quasi-humans, into human-animals. "Say 'lycanthropy,' " Adam says, his voice hardening, and Ofer repeats the word.

Before going to sleep, in the dark, in their beds they talk: "Is the green dragon, who breathes clouds of chlorine gas and whose chances of knowing how to talk are thirty percent, is he more dangerous than the black one, who lives in swamps and salt flats and breathes pure acid?"

Their door is open just a crack, and Ora, with a pile of laundry in her arms, stops to listen.

"Crazy Death is a creature that has completely lost its sanity."

"Really?" Ofer whispers reverentially.

"And listen what else I made up. He can turn into a crazy undead, whose whole purpose is to kill, and anyone who gets killed by him turns into a crazy zombie in one week and walks around with Crazy Death everywhere."

Ofer's voice is hoarse: "But are they real?"

"Let me finish! Once a day, all of Crazy Death's crazy zombies unite into a huge ball of death-craziness."

"But it's not real, is it?"

Adam replies sweetly, "I made it up, and that's why it obeys only me."

"So make something up for me, too," Ofer asks urgently. "Make something up against it for me."

"Maybe tomorrow," Adam murmurs.

"Now, now! I won't sleep all night if you don't make up something for me!"

"Tomorrow, tomorrow."

Ora hears the thin wires that twist through both voices and interweave them: wires of fear, of bared cruelty and submissive pleading, the power to save and the refusal to save, which is also, perhaps, the fear of being saved. And all these also come from her, even Adam's cruelty, which angers her, which is so foreign to her, yet at that moment it strangely excites her, animates her wildly and seems to reveal something about herself that she had not dared to know. The two of them, Adam and Ofer, unraveling from the root of her soul in a double reel.

"Good night," Adam says and starts to snore loudly.

Ofer whines, "Adam, don't sleep, don't sleep, I'm scared of Crazy Death! Can I get in your bed?"

Eventually Adam stops snoring and invents a Skort for him, or a Stark, or a hawk-man, and describes his characteristics and heroic properties in detail. As he talks, a new tenderness enters his voice, and with a rustle in her back Ora can feel how much he enjoys buttressing Ofer, enveloping him in the protective pillows of his imagination, his one and only source of power. And that padding, the kindness and compassion and protection that now emanate from Adam, are also a little bit hers, until suddenly, in the midst of Adam's speech, she hears Ofer's soft hums of sleep.

They are constantly scheming. In every corner of the yard and garden they set traps for androids, which Ora usually falls into, and they create fantastical creatures from painted cardboard rolls and thin wooden rods and nails. They build futuristic vehicles out of cardboard boxes and develop satanic weapons meant to annihilate the bad guys, or all of humanity, depending on Adam's mood. In a special lab they grow plastic soldiers inside sealed glass jars full of water, with faded flower petals floating around. Every soldier in this sad phantom army has a name and a rank, a detailed biography that they can recite by heart, and a deadly mission that he will be required to carry out when the order is given. For days on end they busy themselves building cardboard fortresses for dragons and Ninja Turtles, designing battlefields of dinosaurs, drawing knightly seals in venomous black, yellow, and red. Here too Adam is usually the inventor, the fantasizer, the Dungeon Master, while Ofer is the elf—the enchanted, obedient imp, the implementer. In his slow, deliberate way, he explains to Adam the limitations of feasibility and wisely constructs the solid bricks from which his brother's air castles will be built.

"But it wasn't just that," says Ora, who eavesdropped and looked in on them whenever she could. "Because Ofer learned *from* Adam, but he also learned *him*."

"What do you mean?" asks Avram.

"I don't know how to explain it, but I could see it happening." Ora gives an embarrassed laugh. "I could see Ofer realize that he could figure out how Adam's mind worked, how Adam could leap from A to M in one thought, and how he flipped ideas over midway, playing with absurdities and paradoxes. At first Ofer mimicked Adam, simply parroting his brilliant ideas. But then he learned the principle, and when Adam talked about a step walking down a staircase, Ofer would come up with an apartment moving a house, coins buying money, a path going on a hike. Or he would invent a paradox: a king who orders his subjects not to obey him. It was so lovely to see how Adam molded Ofer, but also taught him how to act with someone like him, someone special and sensitive and vulnerable. He gave Ofer the secret key that opened him, and to this day Ofer is the only one who has that key." Her face softens and glows: she doesn't know if there's even any point in telling all this to desolate Avram, or whether he can understand her that far, all the way to that bend in her soul. After all, Avram was an only child, and from a very young age he didn't even have a father. But he had Ilan, she realizes. Ilan was a brother to him. "And you should have heard those two talking. Their endless, hallucinatory conversations. If I happened to be around, I could have—"

But the pair of little faces look up at her gravely, with exactly the same resentment: "Mom, stop it! Go away, you're bothering us!"

The blades of insult and delight dig inside her simultaneously: She's in their way, but they already have an "us." She feels both cut in two and multiplied.

"And there were lots of other things, but there's one thing I really have to tell you, which happened to us with Adam and with Ofer. Just tell me when you get tired."

"Tired?" He laughs. "I've slept enough."

"We had this episode, just before Adam's bar mitzvah, something I still can't really explain."

The dog turns around and grunts, her fur stranding on end. Ora and Avram quickly look back, and Ora has time to think: It's *him*, the notebook man, he's chasing me. But a few yards away, near a raspberry bush, stand two heavy, bloated wild boars, watching them with beady eyes. The bitch howls, lowers her body to the ground, and takes a step back, almost touching Ora's leg. The boars sniff and flare their nostrils. For a moment or two there is no movement. A songbird on a nearby tree screeches. Ora feels her body respond to the wildness in the boars. Her skin quivers, and whatever flows through her is sharper and more animalistic than what she had felt when the dogs attacked them. Suddenly the boars take off, grunt angrily, and run away with victorious glee, their thick bodies dancing lightly.

"Did you notice his twitches?" Ilan had asked one night in bed.

"Adam's? With his mouth?" She murmured and nestled her head in the round of his shoulder. (Later, when she fell asleep, Ilan would gently turn her over and snuggle against her back; every night she sleepily returned to the sweet journey, in her father's arms, from the living room couch to her bed.)

"And did you see the way he touches his fingertip to the spot between his eyes?"

She opened her eyes. "Now that you mention it."

"Should we ask him? Say something?"

"No, no, let's not. What good would it do?"

"Yeah, it'll pass. I'm sure it will."

Two days later she noticed that Adam was breathing into his cupped hand every few minutes, like someone smelling his breath. He turned around and let out quick, short exhalations, as though trying to banish an invisible creature. She decided not to tell Ilan, for the time being. Why worry him needlessly? The whole thing would pass in a few days anyway. But the next day there was more: every time Adam touched an object, he blew on his fingertips, and then on his arms, up to the elbows. He rounded his lips like a fish before he said anything. She started to find his overflowing creativity a little worrying and was reminded of something her mother used to say: There's no end to trouble's ideas. Finally, after he got up from lunch three times with various excuses, sneaked into the bathroom, and came back with wet hands, she phoned Ilan at the office and described the latest symptoms. Ilan listened quietly. "If we make a big deal out of it," he eventually said, "it'll only make it worse. Let's just try to ignore it, and you'll see, he'll calm down." She had known this was what he would say. That was exactly why she had called him.

The next day she found that if Adam happened to touch any part of his body, he quickly blew on it. The new rule, which he apparently had to obey categorically, was rapidly turning him into a tight knot of gestures and counter-gestures, which he tried very hard to hide, but Ora saw. And Ilan saw.

Strange, thinks Avram, why didn't they take him to see someone?

"Maybe we should take him to someone," she told Ilan at night, in bed.

"Who?" Ilan asked tensely.

"I don't know. Someone. A professional, to have a look."

"A psychologist?"

"Maybe. Just to have a glance."

"No, no, it'll only make it worse. It will be like we're telling him he's—"

"What?"

"Not right."

But he isn't, she thought.

"Let's wait a bit. Give him some time."

She tried to nestle into his shoulder, but her head could not find its place. She felt hot and sweaty. There was no peace in her body, or in his. For some reason she remembered something Avram had once said: if you look at someone for a long time, at anyone, you can see the most terrible place they might reach in their lifetime. She didn't sleep that night.

The next weekend they went to the beach at Beit Yannai. From the moment they arrived, Adam was constantly busy cleaning. He washed his hands over and over again and scrubbed his inflatable beach mattress with damp cloths. He even turned it over every few minutes to clean "the bit that touched the sea."

At sunset, Ora and Ilan sat in deck chairs, Ofer played and dug in the sand, and Adam stood waist-high in the water, turning in circles, blowing in every direction, touching every joint and knuckle in his hands and feet. A tall, tan elderly couple walked arm in arm on the beach and stopped to look at Adam. From a distance, with the sunset's blush on his back, he looked enmeshed in a poetic fairy dance, one movement following the other, each born from its predecessor.

"They think it's Tai Chi," Ilan hissed, and Ora whispered that it was starting to drive her mad. He put a hand on her arm. "Wait. He'll get sick of it. How long can he keep this up?"

"Look at how totally indifferent he is to people watching him."

"Yes, that's what worries me a little."

"A little? Adam? In front of everyone?"

She thought about Ilan's father, who during his final days in the hospital had lost all shame and would undress in front of everyone to show yet another place on his body where the growth had spread.

"And look how Ofer keeps peeking at him, all the time," Ilan said.

"Think about what it must do to him, to see Adam like that."

"Has he talked to you about it?"

"Ofer? Nothing. I tried to ask him this morning, when we were alone on the beach. Nothing." She forced a smile. "Well, he's not going to collaborate against Adam."

Adam kissed his fingertips and showered light touches on his waist, thighs, knees, and ankles in the water. He straightened up, spun around in a circle, and blew in all four directions.

"What's going to happen when school starts in September, I want to know."

"Wait. There are almost two months to go. It'll pass by then."

"And if it doesn't?"

"It will, it will."

"And if it doesn't?"

"How could it not?"

Now she pulls her knees in to her chest, holds her breath, and looks at Avram for a long time. Avram feels that he can't sit still for much longer. Ants are crawling all through his body.

Adam seemed to grow more distant day by day. Bad thoughts congregated, and Ora sensed that they had been lying in wait for some time. During the day they hovered like shadows in her head. At night, she sleepily banished them until she was exhausted, and then they descended. Ilan woke her and caressed her face and held her close to him and told her to breathe with him, slowly, until she calmed down.

"I had a nightmare," she said. Her face was buried in his chest. She would not let him turn on the light, afraid he might read in her eyes what she had seen: Avram walked past her on the street, dressed in white and looking very pale, and when he came close he murmured that she should buy the newspaper today. She tried to stop him, to ask how he was and why he insisted on being estranged from her, but he pulled his arm away from her grip in disgust and left. The newspaper headline said that Avram was planning to go on a hunger strike outside her house until she gave in and delivered one of her sons to him.

Adam needed new gym shoes for the school year, and she kept putting off the shopping expedition. He asked her repeatedly to take him to the mall so he could choose a gift for Ofer, and while only two weeks earlier she would have been filled with excitement by such a request—"And after we finish shopping, can I take you out to a café?"—she now avoided him with such feeble excuses that he seemed to understand, and he stopped asking.

Every day brought new symptoms. He quickly pulled his arms away from his shoulders and to the sides before talking. He pulsed his fists open and closed before he said "me." The washing and rinsing became more and more frequent. In the course of a single meal he was capable of getting up to wash his hands and mouth five or ten times.

After a Shabbat spent at home, during which Ilan saw Adam for a whole day, including three meals, he told Ora, "Let's call someone."

As predicted, Adam refused even to hear about it. He hurled himself on the floor and screamed that he wasn't crazy and they should leave him alone. When they tried to persuade him, he locked himself in his room and pounded on the door for a long time.

"We'll wait a bit," said Ilan, as they both tossed and turned in bed. "Let him get used to the idea."

"How long? How long can you wait with this?"

"Let's say, a week?"

"No, that's too long. A day. Maybe two, but no more."

There was something paralyzing about watching Adam in the days that followed. Her child was turning into a process. During the hours she spent at home with him—when she could not find an excuse to go out for some fresh air, to absorb the smooth, harmonious movements of other people like an elixir, and to suck up some bitter jealousy at the sight of Adam's peers having fun on their summer vacations—in those hours with him she witnessed his entire existence being chopped up into separate parts, whose connection was growing more and more tenuous. At times it seemed that the gestures—the "phenomena," as she and Ilan called them—were themselves the tendons and nerves that now sustained the affinity between the parts of the child he used to be.

"It all happened so close," she says, whether to Avram or to herself. "It happened inside our home. You could reach out and touch it, but there was nothing to hold on to. Your hand closed in on emptiness."

"Aha," says Avram faintly.

"Tell me if you don't feel like hearing this."

He gives her another look that says, Stop talking nonsense.

She shrugs as if to say, How am I supposed to know? I've spent so many years getting used to being silent with you.

They set up their little camp at the spring of Ein Yakim in the Amud River wadi, next to a Mandate-era pumping station. Ora spreads the cloth on the ground and lays out food and dinnerware. Avram gathers wood, makes a circle of stones, and builds a fire. The dog crosses the skinny river back and forth, shaking her wet fur off in thousands of sprays, and looks at them playfully. Before sitting down to eat, they wash socks, underwear, and shirts in the spring water and lay them on bushes to dry when the sun rises. Avram digs through his backpack and finds a large, white Indian shirt and fresh *sharwal* pants. He changes his clothes behind a shrub.

The next day, when she was alone at home with Adam, he told her about something in his favorite computer game, and he seemed happy and full of excitement. She tried to focus on what he was saying and share his happiness, but it was hard: now he marked the ends of his sentences with exhalations, too. And after certain letters—she thought it was the sibilant consonants, but this rule may have had exceptions that demanded their own penalties—he sucked in his cheeks. Sentences that ended with question marks incurred a new tic: he folded back his upper lip toward his nose.

She stood in the kitchen with him and fought a malicious urge to stick her lips out at him in a crude imitation. So at least he'd know how he looked. So he'd understand what people saw when they looked at him, and how hard it was to tolerate. She managed to stop herself only when she realized that was exactly what her mother had done to her after Ada. She'd had her own little physical quirks, though far less severe than these.

But when she saw Adam's piercing, knowing look, she had a sudden impulse to wrap her arms around him. It had been weeks since she'd hugged him. He wouldn't let anyone touch him, and she'd stopped trying, averse to touching his alien body. Perhaps she had the vague feeling that her touch would not find warm skin but a hardened shell. Now she kissed his cheek and forehead. She'd been so foolish to avoid it, to collaborate with his aversion, when perhaps all he needed was a simple, strong hug. And indeed, in one large wave, he suddenly emerged from captivity, leaned his whole body into her, and put his little head on her chest. She responded fervently and felt her own power again, her vivacity. How could she have agreed to give up on all that? How had she even considered letting her child be treated by a stranger before she herself had given him this simple, natural thing? She swore that from this moment on she would give him everything she had, empty her healing powers into him, her vast experience of treating bodies and giving calm-ing massages. How had she withheld all this from him?

She shut her eyes and gritted her teeth above his head so as not to fal-ter on the trip wire of tears gathering inside her and remembered what Ilan had once explained: he always hugged the boys a little less than he wanted to, because that was always a little more than they needed. Oh well, Ilan and his calculations. She kissed Adam's forehead again, and he looked up at her with a sweet can-I-have-a-special face, which made her incredibly happy. The "special" was an old childhood tradition between her and the boys. It had been years since either of them had agreed to it, but now Adam puckered his lips, and she laughed with embarrassed delight—after all, he was almost thirteen, with the dark shadow of a moustache. But he seemed to need it so much that nothing embarrassed him, and he kissed her warmly, first on her right cheek, then on her left, and on the tip of her nose, and on her forehead, and Ora rejoiced: she would show him the way home with kisses. He smiled and lowered his gaze, indicated that he wanted another round, and kissed her on her right cheek again, then her left, then the tip of her nose and her fore-head. Ora said, "Now my turn," and Adam grunted, "Just one more time." He tightened his hands around her face and the back of her neck stiffened. He showered sharp pecks on her right cheek and left cheek, the tip of her nose and her forehead. She struggled to pull her face away and he grasped her with sharp fingers until she shouted: "Stop it, what's the matter with you?" He grimaced, at first with a lack of comprehen-sion, then with deep insult, and they faced each other for a moment, standing between the kitchen table and the sink, and Adam quickly touched the corners of his mouth and the spot between his eyes, then blew on his hands, first right then left, and his eyes kept filling with murky, thick liquid, and then he walked backward away from her, mon-itoring her suspiciously, as if fearing she would pounce on him, and she remembered: this was exactly the look Ofer had given her when he found out that she ate meat. That same flash of recognition—the possi-bility of rapaciousness—which had passed between them then, which had flickered across his cerebral cortex like an ancient drawing. How could she explain this to Avram? This moment between a mother and her child. Yet she does explain it, right down to the last detail, so he'll know, so he'll hurt, so he'll live, so he'll remember. Adam's eyes widened and almost filled his entire face, and he kept backing away from her, still watching, and before leaving the kitchen he gave her one last sober, awful look, and she thought he was wordlessly saying, You had the chance to save me, and now I'm leaving.

Finally, after pressure and threats—taking away his computer privileges was the most effective method—they overcame Adam's resistance and took him to see a psychologist.

After three meetings the man summoned Ora and Ilan. "Adam seems like an intelligent boy with a lot of potential. A boy with strong character. Very strong." His voice sounded weak. "The truth is, he sat here on this chair for three hours and didn't say a word."

Ora was amazed. "He didn't speak? What about the gestures?"

"No gestures. He just sat here like a statue. He looked at me and barely blinked."

Ora suddenly remembered that when Ilan was a boy, he had blackballed his whole class.

"Not an easy experience," the man said. "Three whole sessions. I tried this, I tried that, but there's some kind of resistance in him." He tightened his hand into a fist. "A bunker, a sphinx."

"So what do you suggest?" Ilan asked rancorously.

"Of course we can try another few sessions," the man replied without looking in their eyes. "I'm certainly willing, but I have to say there's something in the interaction—"

"Tell us what we should do," Ilan interrupted. The vein in his temple was turning blue. "I want you tell me in simple words, what—do—we—do—now!"

Ora looked in despair at the iron layer descending over Ilan's face.

The man blinked as he spoke. "I'm not certain there's an immediate solution here. I'm just trying to think out loud with you. Perhaps it would be more successful with someone else? Perhaps a woman therapist?"

"Why a woman?" Ora sat back in her chair, feeling accused. "Why does it have to be a woman?"

One evening, Ora sat poring over receipts for her income-tax return— every two months she had to report her income from the physiotherapy clinic ("But patients I see at home, I don't report on principle," she tells Avram with a proud sense of conspiracy between two mutineers; he doesn't even carry an identity card!)—when Adam came up to her and asked her to help him tidy his room. This was an unusual request, especially in those days, and the mess in his room was intolerable, but she had to finish her taxes. "Does it have to be now?" she asked irritably. "Why didn't you ask me an hour ago, when I wasn't busy? Why is it that only my time is expendable in this household?"

Adam danced and fidgeted away in his complex of tics. Ora tried to keep sorting through her receipts, but she could not concentrate. More than anything, it depressed her to think that he had walked away without arguing. Without saying a word. As though he knew he could not waste even one drop of energy now.

As she calculated her mileage and per diem expenses, she could sense that Adam was in his room crumbling into shards of despair and loneliness. She knew his disintegration was sucking her in too, and that soon it might dissolve her and Ilan as a couple, and the entire family. We're so weak, she thought, staring at the neat little piles of paper. How can the two of us be so paralyzed, instead of really fighting for him? It's like—the thought punctured her—it's like we can feel that it's . . . what? Our punishment? For what?

"For *you* we fought a lot harder," she says to Avram.

Avram tightens his hands around the hot cup of coffee. His body is tense, his eyes enthralled by the last glimmers of light on the stream.

Ora got up and almost ran to Adam's room with a foreboding heart. But he was just standing there in the middle of the room he shared with Ofer, surrounded by incredible heaps of clothes, toy parts, notebooks, towels, and balls, leaning slightly forward, frozen.

"What's going on, Adam?"

"I don't know, I'm stuck."

"Is it your back?"

"Everything."

In mid-motion, while trying to erect barriers between one fragmentary movement and the next, he must have been trapped into cessation. Ora hurried over and hugged him, and rubbed his neck and back. His body was rigid. For several moments she unfroze him, just as she used to do for Avram in rehab, and miraculously did for her patients, restoring the body's memory, replaying the music of its movement. Adam finally loosened a little, and she lowered him into a chair and sat on the rug at his feet.

"Does it still hurt?"

"No, it's okay now."

"Come on, let's do it together."

She picked up objects and clothes off the floor and handed them to him so he could put them away. He obeyed, moving robotically to the closets and shelves, then back to her. She did not say a thing about his movements and gestures. She could not stop looking.

Then Ofer arrived home from a weeklong vacation at his grandparents' in Haifa and eagerly joined in the operation. It seemed as if a bright light had been turned on in the room, and the bad thoughts retreated. Even Adam's face lit up. Ora, who knew how much Ofer hated untidiness and dirtiness, was amazed at how he had let Adam turn their room into a dump. He'd never complained even once that whole month. Perhaps it was time to give them separate rooms. They had talked about it a year ago. But she knew what that would mean to Adam, and she had no doubt that Ofer would refuse now, too.

With Ofer's help, she turned the chore into a game. She asked questions about each item she fished out of the pile, and Adam and Ofer answered. They all laughed. Adam laughed tightly, with pursed lips, and every titter obligated him to perform a series of acts that probably canceled out the effect of the laughter. For two whole hours Ora sat on the floor and sorted through the material culture of their childhood. Games they no longer played, drawing papers and work papers, crumpled notebooks, depleted batteries, old election ballots Ora had once stolen for them from the polling booth, books about soccer players and TV stars, worn-out gym shoes, LEGOs, various amulets, Boglins and ugly monsters that had once filled their world, weapons and fossils, torn posters, towels, and socks with holes in them. Some toys and games they refused to give up, and they were truly hurt when she suggested giving them away to children who were smaller and had less. Ora learned for the first time about a complicated emotional relationship between her sons and a bald stuffed bear made of wool. There was also a particularly disgusting rubber snake and a small broken flashlight that reminded them of nighttime adventures she never imagined had occurred behind their closed door when she thought they were asleep.

Gradually, despite the struggles and the haggling over every old toy or moth-eaten shirt from some Spanish soccer team, the room emptied out. They filled up huge trash bags and stacked them by the door, to give away or throw away. She sensed some relief in Adam: his movements became rounder, almost at ease. He walked this way and that in the room without interrupting his steps or speech to make any gestures. No commas or periods with an elbow or a knee. Finally, when the tidying was done and Ora got up to order a pizza, he went up to her and hugged her gently. A simple hug.

But the reprieve lasted only a few moments. "You know what Ilan says: 'Happiness is always premature.' "

"That's not Ilan's, that's mine!"

"Yours?"

"Of course! Don't you remember how I always used to . . ."

The dog lifts her head off her paws and looks up at Avram in surprise. Ora watches the little tempest brewing inside him and thinks: *This* is what you get angry about, of all the things he took from you?

She went on: after the lull, Adam was compelled to wash his mouth and fingers at the sink again, and you could practically see the tightropes he walked on. This time Ora's despair was intolerable, and just as she was about to burst out and scream at him with everything that had built up inside her, she put down her slice of pizza, left the boys, who were now chattering in their usual way, and walked into Ilan's study, where she sat by the table and let her head collapse on the receipts and invoices.

A heavy shadow settled in her mind. She wanted to call Ilan and ask him to come home from work. She wanted him to come home and hold her, because she was falling. What was he doing out and about when everything here was coming apart? Lately he'd hardly been at home. He left early in the morning, before the boys got up, and came home at midnight, when they were already asleep. Where are you? How can we both be this paralyzed? How can we disintegrate so quickly? Why does all this look like a curse that has waited patiently for years—the revenge of the wicked witch who wasn't invited to the birthday party—to hurt us precisely when things are good? But she didn't have the energy to reach for the phone.

"We're not treating it," she told him that night in the living room as she lay on the rug, exhausted. Ilan was sprawled on the couch, his long legs dangling over the arm. He looked weak and tired. "What's happening to us? Tell me, explain to me, why can't we do anything?"

"Like what?"

"Force him to get treatment, drag him to a doctor, a psychiatrist, I don't know. I feel that the fear is paralyzing me, and you're not helping. Where are you?"

"Make an appointment for him with someone else." He seemed frightened. Something in his face, his chin, suddenly reminded her of the days after Adam's birth, right before he left.

Tomorrow, she swore, first thing in the morning. She reached out and squeezed Ilan's arm. "We don't even know what he feels. I try to talk with him and he runs away. Just think how frightening this is for him."

"And for Ofer. We're so focused on Adam that Ofer is being neglected."

"I just think that if it was some kind of normal danger, like a fire, or even a terrorist, something familiar, logical, wouldn't I jump up to rescue him? Wouldn't I give my own life for him? But this . . ."

Adam came out of his room to get a drink in the kitchen. From the dark living room, Ora and Ilan followed his progress to the fridge. When he finally managed to bring the water bottle up to his lips, Ilan cleared his throat and Adam turned to them in surprise.

"Hey, what-are-you-do-ing-there?" His voice was monotonous, angular, bionic.

"Nothing," said Ilan. "Just resting. How are you doing, sweetie?"

"Do-ing-great," he said dismissively. He turned and fidgeted his way back to his room, lifting his knees as he walked in a mechanical imitation of human motion, subsiding into a stutter of Adam.

And then she knew. A membrane inside her tore open all at once and she knew that something completely new had been revealed to Adam— some new knowledge or power. It suddenly seemed so clear. You only had to look at him to see it: the force of negation, of collapse, of absence, had pulled him inside and was consuming him from within. "That is what Adam was discovering, and it must have been a huge force, don't you think?" she asks Avram in a hoarse voice. "The force of *no*, the force of not-being?"

Avram does not move. His hands almost crush the empty coffee mug. In the first few months after he came home—after his hospitalization and rehab—he used to walk the streets of Tel Aviv and imagine himself as one single bee amid a huge swarm. It was good for him to know that he could not understand the actions of the entire swarm.

He had one mission: to be. He needed only to move, eat, shit, and sleep. Other parts of the swarm might be experiencing emotions, or gaining knowledge or an entire consciousness, or perhaps they were not. Perhaps that wasn't happening anywhere. That was not his business. He was just one insignificant cell, easily replaced, unflinchingly destructible.

Sometimes, though rarely, he did different things, opposite things: he would talk to himself out loud as he walked, intentionally, as though he were alone in the world, or as though the whole world were occurring only inside his mind, a figment of his imagination, which also created those boys making fun of him, the old men pointing at him, the car that screeched to a halt only inches away from him.

When Adam shut his door behind him, Ora got up and went into the kitchen. She opened the fridge with Adam's motions, held up the water bottle to her mouth as he had done—elbow, wrist, fingers—closed her lips over the opening of the family bottle, drank, and navigated her soul to Adam. And then she knew, for one instant—enough for a lifetime— what it is like when you cannot see the line but only the dots that create it, the darkness in the blink of an eye, the chasm between one moment and the next.

"Yes," Avram says softly, and she thinks he has not been breathing for several minutes.

She put the bottle back in the fridge, reenacting her son's fragmentary movements, and forgot about Ilan, who lay watching her from the dark. Here was the fall between two steps. Here was the whisper of the dismantling. Here was how her Adam watched with wide eyes and, perhaps, saw what no one was allowed to see: how he himself could crumble into nothing. Into the dust from which he had come. He saw how tenuously it was all held together.

She sat down in the dark next to Ilan, who quickly wrapped her in his arms and clung to her with strange fervor and, she thought, a hint of awe.

"What?" Ilan asked in a whisper. "What did you feel?"

She did not answer. Afraid to wake up, afraid it would disappear, afraid that the place in which she had known Adam would melt away like a dream.

. . .

Ora yawns and enjoys seeing Avram unwittingly repeat her yawn. "Let's continue tomorrow," she says. Although he would like to hear more, Avram gets up and clears away their dinner, picks up the trash, and rinses the dishes, then rolls out his sleeping bag near hers. He does all this in silence, and she sees the thoughts and the questions darting around his forehead and tells herself: Tomorrow, tomorrow. She goes behind some bushes to do her business and thinks of Scheherazade, and then they both undress, back to back, and zip themselves up in their sleeping bags, and lie with their eyes open by the glowing embers of the fire. Avram, restless, gets up and fills two bottles at the river, douses the embers, and lies down again.

As soon as the fire goes out, all the creatures around the river awake and a chorus of toads, night birds, jackals, foxes, and crickets erupts into a deafening commotion. They wail, screech, snort, caw, yowl, and chirp. Ora and Avram lie there feeling the entire riverbed rustle and stir around them. Small and large animals pass next to them and over them, running or flying, and Ora whispers, "What's going on?" Avram whispers back, "They've all gone mad." The dog stands up restlessly, her eyes aglimmer in the dark. Ora needs Avram to come and lie next to her, even just hold her hand and calm her with a caress, with long, quiet breaths, the way Ilan does—did—but she doesn't say a word. She won't push him, and he does not offer, but the dog moves closer, step by cautious step, until finally she is standing beside her. Ora reaches out and strokes her fur in the dark, and the fur trembles with tension because of the sounds all around, or because of the human touch, her first contact in such a long time. Ora strokes and strokes, rubbing delightedly, feeling the warmth of this new body, but the dog suddenly recoils, unable to bear it any longer, and goes off to lounge not far away and watches Ora.

The three of them lie quiet and slightly afraid, and the commotion gradually dies down and gives way to the hum of mosquitoes. Meaty and impudent, they hack at every exposed inch of flesh. Ora hears Avram slap himself and curse, and she curls up in her sleeping bag and zips it around her head, leaving only a tiny opening for air, and she sinks down into herself, sleepily arranges her head so it nestles in her favorite place, in the round of Ilan's shoulder, and then, subtly, like the gushing of a small spring, a longing awakens in her for the house in Ein Karem. She yearns for their house, for the scents embedded in it and the textures woven through the window lattices at different times of day, and for Ilan's and the boys' voices rolling through the hallways. She walks through the house, room by room.

When Ofer surfaces in her, she gently moves him away, tells him it's okay, not to worry, she's doing what needs to be done. He shouldn't think about her right now. He should look after himself there, and she'll look after him here.

A few months after she and Ilan separated, she had gone back for one last time to the empty house. She opened the blinds and the windows in all the rooms, turned on all the faucets, watered the neglected garden, rolled up the rugs, dusted, swept the floor, and washed it thoroughly. She spent almost a whole morning there, without sitting down or drinking a glass of water. When she was finished cleaning, she drew the blinds and closed the windows and turned off the power and walked out.

It should at least be clean, she thought. It's not the house's fault we broke up.

Avram's voice came through: "Ora, are they similar?"

She has almost fallen asleep, and his question shocks her awake. "Who?"

"The boys. Today. Are they similar?"

"To who?"

"No, I mean . . . to each other. Their personalities."

She sits up and rubs her eyes. He is sitting up bundled in his sleeping bag.

"Sorry, I woke you up," he mumbles.

"It's okay, I was barely asleep. But what's the sudden . . ." Her tongue steals a circle of delight around his "boys." As though he has finally accepted her own vision of them, even her tone of voice when she thinks about them. She watches him affectionately. For a moment it seems possible: Uncle Avram. "Maybe we should make some tea?"

"Do you want some?" He jumps up and runs to gather branches in the dark. She hears him walk into a bush, curse, slip on the wet stones, grow farther away and then closer. She holds in her laughter.

"Yes and no," she says afterward, with a cup of tea warming her hands and face. "They're completely different in the way they look, I told you. On the other hand, you couldn't have any doubt about them being brothers. Although Adam is more—"

"More what?"

She stops. Afraid that now, in her state, in the state of her relationship with Adam, she may get carried away into all sorts of unnecessary and unfair comparisons between Adam and Ofer. How could *she*—

She sighs deeply, and the dog looks up and comes to sit next to her.

"What?" Avram asks tenderly. "What did you remember?"

"Wait."

She, whose mother always had compared her to others, even in front of total strangers, and almost always to her detriment. *She*, who had sworn at a very young age that when she had her own children she would never, ever . . .

"Ora?" Avram asks carefully. "Listen, we don't have to . . ."

"No, it's okay. Just give me a minute."

Of course she and Ilan had often compared the boys to each other. How could they not?

"At first, what was difficult in the first few years with Ilan, what I found really intolerable, was the way he looked at the boys. You know how he is, with his exact, objective definitions."

"Oh yeah, I know that. I know all about Ilan and his onslaughts of rationalism."

"Yes, that's exactly it." She laughs and scratches the dog's head.

Ilan's definitions, in which he summarized Adam's and Ofer's personalities, their virtues and their shortcomings, seemed to determine their fate for all eternity without any possibility of appeal or even the change and development that come with age. Only years later—she finds that she can talk about this now with Avram; she thinks he understands— only years later had she learned that she could contradict those definitions of his with statements that were no less thoughtful and lucid, with a sober and different perspective that always illuminated the boys in a brighter, more generous light. When she did so, she found how relieved and even happy Ilan was to agree and adopt her position. It sometimes even appeared as though she had redeemed him from something in himself.

"Why is he like that, can you tell me?" she asks Avram. "You knew him so well"—she almost says, You knew him better than I did—"so you tell me, why does he always fight himself? His softness, his gentleness. Why must he always be such a clenched fist?"

Avram shrugs his shoulders. "With me, he wasn't like that."

"I know. He really wasn't."

They sit quietly as the cicadas around them go berserk. Ora wonders if she is doomed to keep trying to understand Ilan and his illusions for the rest of her life, or whether the day will come when she can simply be herself, with none of his echoes inside her. But the idea offers no relief or gladness, and her yearnings descend in full force.

She thinks back to the way she and Ilan used to talk about the boys. The talking was such an enjoyable part of the labor of family, and they did so much of it. And she often thought it might be thanks to Avram that she and Ilan had been able to talk like that. Had they not met him, had he not tutored them when they were still teenagers, they might have remained far quieter and more shy. So thank you, she tells him silently. Thank you for that, too.

More than anything, they liked to talk about the boys on their evening walks, after the bedtime ritual. Without asking Avram whether he wants her to, she takes him straight there, to the boys' messy bedroom, roiling with the tumultuous preparations for the difficult, complicated sail into the night, with its shadows and foreignness, and the exile it imposes upon every child in his little, separate bed. After giving them one last hug, another cup of water, pee-pee again, and one more nightlight, and another kiss for the teddy bear or the monkey, and after Adam and Ofer had finished chattering and finally fallen asleep . . .

At first, when they still lived in Tzur Hadassah, they would walk the path to Ein Yoel. They passed by the plum and peach orchards of Mevo Beitar, and the remnants of quince, walnut, lemon, almond, and olive groves in the Arab villages that had ceased to exist—every so often Ora told herself she had to at least find out their names—and sometimes they walked to the Ma'ayanot River, down in a wadi full of gushing water and little gardens where the villagers of Hussan and Battir planted eggplants, peppers, beans, and zucchini. When the first intifada started and they were afraid to walk in that part, they chose a wooded area near a fork in the road—"in autumn, there are crisscrossing meadows of crocuses and cyclamens; maybe I'll take you there one day; remind me"—and when they moved to Ein Karem, even before locating the nearest grocery store, they sought out a walking path that was not too capricious but not boring either, not remote but not too popular, a path where a couple could walk and talk calmly and sometimes hold hands or kiss. Over the years they found other paths, less open ones, in wadis and among olive groves, near sheikhs' tombs and the ruins of houses and ancient watchmen's huts. They walked these paths whenever they had time, which was sometimes early in the morning, but that was only when the kids were older and more independent, and Ofer could make fancy omelets and sandwiches for school, for both himself and Adam. Even during Ilan's busiest times, he never gave up their daily walk: "Our walk."

Avram listens and sees Ora and Ilan. A couple. Ilan's sideburns might be gray by now, and Ora is almost entirely silver-haired, wearing glasses. Perhaps Ilan has glasses, too. They walk along their hidden path, at the same pace, very close to each other. Every so often her head turns to him. Sometimes their hands find each other and link. They talk in soft voices. Ora laughs. Ilan smiles his three-wrinkled smile. Suddenly Avram misses Ilan. Suddenly he is horrified to realize that he has not seen Ilan for twenty-one years.

"We have this way of talking, where I almost always know what he's going to tell me. From the way he breathes before he starts a sentence, I know the direction he'll take and which words he'll use. And I'm so happy it's that way, that we can guess what the other is thinking."

But apparently Ilan found it annoying, she tells Avram. "It bored him that he could guess my mind by the way I breathed before I spoke or laughed or before I told a joke. Or maybe he just needed a break from me. That's what he said. I guess I'm hard work." She shrugs her shoulders. "But I started telling you something else—what was it? I'm so scattered. It's wrong, and it's not true either, it's really not the whole truth, he doesn't deserve it."

She and Ilan on the path, in the evening, breaking the day into pieces and then tasting them together, holding them in their mouths, comparing impressions, adding more and more details to the big picture of their life, laughing at this and that, embracing, separating, arguing, consulting each other about work. Ilan didn't understand much about her business, she tells Avram, and she didn't expect him to. After all, how exciting can it be to hear about rubbing a sprained ankle or resetting a dislocated shoulder? But she was disappointed that he didn't get as excited as she did over the little dramas she heard while releasing a bad back or a face whose musculature had gone wrong. She, on the other hand, had become his confidential advisor over the years, his secret jury, his final adjudicator. In his office it was an open joke: "Ora hasn't confirmed it yet"; "Ilan is waiting for the supreme court decision." She blushes—it's a good thing it's dark—and notes that he really did have complete confidence in her, utterly amazing confidence in her instincts, her intuitions, her wise heart ("Ilan said that," she adds apologetically), even though she wasn't really interested in the convoluted legal aspects of intellectual property, confidentiality agreements, noncompete contracts, trademarks for an irrigation system or a generic drug, or the question of when exactly an idea contained that slippery, mysterious thing that Ilan liked to call, with glimmering eyes, *the inventional spark*. And truth be told, she had never been attracted to the complex process of patent registration in Israel, or in the United States or Europe, nor in all of Ilan's persuasive tricks that were meant to cause wealthy people to invest in a young doctor from Karmiel who had developed a medical camera that disintegrated in the bloodstream after use, or in a biochemist from Kiryat Gat who had discovered a cheap way to produce diesel from oil. "And Ilan, being Ilan . . ." She laughs. "That man, I'm telling you, he should have been a chess champion, or a politician, or a Mafia consigliere. You never knew that side of him, it only started developing after you."

On their path, in the evening, Ora and Ilan easily and generously divvied up the next day's chores. "We never fought over who would do what, you know? We were such a good team." They quickly settled household affairs, bills, repairs, shuttling the kids, finances, and a few burning foreign and domestic topics, like finding an old-age home for her mother, or what to do about their lazy, lying, manipulative cleaning lady, whom neither of them had the courage to fire for years—even Ilan was afraid. Only their separation had put an end to her regime.

And more than anything else, they would circle above and around their children, constantly amazed at the two joyous young people sprouting up between them day by day. They quoted to each other things Adam had said and replayed things Ofer had done, and watched in astonishment, and compared them to who they had been years ago, or even weeks ago, amazed at how much they could change in such a short time—"Oh God, they're growing up so fast!" They delighted in fragments of memories and inconsequential moments that grew between him and her, to be mighty and shining, because only to the two of them were they so precious, the riches of their lives.

"Ofer, too?" Avram asks softly. "Was Ofer also . . . I mean, for Ilan—Ofer, too?"

She smiles at him, her eyes full of light. Avram can see it even in the dark, and he takes a big sip of his boiling tea, burning his tongue and the roof of his mouth, and he holds the burn in his mouth with strange pleasure.

When she and Ilan walked and talked, they could feel the flowing force of life itself, the glory of life that lifted up their two little boys and carried them to their futures. Time after time they marveled at the strong bond between the boys—"they have some kind of secret; to this day there's a secret between them"—and without ever saying it out loud, they both sensed that this connection between Adam and Ofer might be the central axis of their home and was probably the strongest and most solid and alive of all the currents—hidden and visible—that held the four of them together.

Avram listens and recites: remember, remember it all. Sometimes Ilan and Ora tilt their heads toward each other as they walk. They lean on each other and dare to guess—cautiously, keenly aware of how fragile things are—what the future will bring for the boys and where their lives will lead them. They wonder if Adam and Ofer will continue to sustain their precious enigmatic couplehood.

She sits alone one evening in Ilan's study, staring at the legal books on the shelves, unable to do a thing. Adam has had two therapy sessions in the past week with a very experienced elderly female therapist who seems pleasant and tranquil. He said nothing to her either, and he hid the "phenomena" from her, too. But she was not worried. She told Ora and Ilan that these sorts of symptoms were not unusual at Adam's age, just before physical maturation began, and added that something in Adam's eyes told her he was a fundamentally strong young man. Just in case, and to reassure them, she referred him to a prominent specialist for neurological tests. He cannot see them for another three weeks, and while Ilan has tried to pull strings and get an earlier appointment, Ora feels that she is losing her mind.

Adam and Ofer are in the kitchen, engaged in a deep conversation about rhinos. She sends her usual maternal sonar waves out to them every few seconds and processes the returns almost unconsciously. Only after several minutes does she vaguely realize that she hasn't heard this sort of talk between them for a long time. Adam's tone of voice sounds lighter this evening. He is even helping Ofer with a project for his summer "creativity day camp." He invents a water rhinoceros with two big fins and a curly rhino and then a pearly rhino—"he's an unendangered animal," he dictates to Ofer, "who sits looking at himself in the water for hours. And there's also a girly rhino." They both roll around laughing. "But the girly one is invisible," Adam warns. "Then I'll just draw his footprint!" Ofer says. He cheers. "Give it to me, I'll draw it for you." Their chatter flows on, and Adam heartily goes through all his rituals. Ora can hear the rhythmic breaths, the lip-sucking, the faucet turned on for quick rinses. She sinks back into herself, but perks up when she hears Ofer's thin voice asking very calmly, "Why do you do that?"

She doesn't know what Ofer is referring to, but a subterranean wave rolls through the kitchen and all the way to her chair, wraps itself around her, and squeezes.

"What?" Adam asks suspiciously.

"Wash your hands and all that."

"No reason. I just feel like it."

"Are you dirty?"

"Yes. No. Stop it, you're bugging me."

"But what from?" Ofer asks in that same calm, lucid voice, the balanced and matter-of-fact tone she wishes she could have, especially in these moments.

"What from what?"

"What d'you get dirty from?"

"I don't know, okay?"

"Just tell me one more thing."

"What now?"

"When you . . . when you wash like that, then do you get clean?"

"Kind of. I don't know. Now shut up!"

Silence. Ora does not dare move. She thinks of how Ofer has held it in all these weeks and not asked Adam anything. Something in his voice, in his persistence, hints that he has planned in advance what to ask, chosen the circumstances well, and perhaps carefully primed Adam's mood for this moment.

"Adam—"

"What now?"

"Will you let me, too?"

"Let you what?"

"Do one instead."

"One what?"

Ora can feel Ofer's arc of boldness and audacity grating on her nerves. She does not twitch an eyelid. She wonders what risky, daring game he is playing.

"One of these."

"Hey!" Adam makes an effort to laugh, but Ora can hear his embarrassment. "Are you crazy?"

"Just one, what do you care?"

"But why?"

"So you'll have to do one less."

"*What?*"

"Stop it, you're getting water on my drawing!"

"What did you say?"

"That if I do one, then you'll have one less to do."

"You're crazy, you know that? Totally nuts. Anyway, this doesn't have anything to do with you."

"Whaddayacare? Just one. A loaner."

"Which one?"

"Whatever you say. This one, or like that, or—"

She hears a chair flung aside and quick steps. She guesses Adam's little steps around himself on his way to the faucet, his eyes now scurrying in panic.

"Adam—"

"I'm gonna beat the crap out of you. Shut up!"

A long silence.

"Come on, Adam, just one."

She hears steps and a thud. Panting and bodies falling to the floor. A chair turned over. Stifled grunts. She realizes that Ofer is holding back his shouts so she won't come in to separate them and ruin his plan. She stands up.

"Give in?"

"Just let me do it once."

"You're such an annoying kid!" Adam screeches. "Don't you have any friends, you midget? Pest!"

"Just once and that's it, I swear."

She hears the slaps, one and two, and Ofer's deep, stifled yelp. Without realizing it, she is biting her fists.

"Now d'you understand?"

"Whaddayacare, just once each time."

Adam lets out a high-pitched giggle of amazement.

"I'll do it so you won't even know," Ofer groans.

Adam sucks his lips, blows on the backs of his hands, and spins around. Finally, he says quietly, "No. I think I have to do them all. The whole thing."

"Then I'll just do them next to you."

The faucet is turned on. A quick rinse. Blows. Silence. Then the faucet again, a little longer this time, and different blowing, stronger and slower.

"Did you do it? Okay, now get lost."

"Let me do one every time," Ofer says with an assertiveness that amazes Ora. Then she sees him run out of the kitchen with a serious, focused look on his face.

Over the next few days, Ofer and Adam spend all their free time together. They seldom leave their room, and it's hard to know what's going on. When she listens behind the door, she hears them playing and blathering the way they used to when they were seven and four. They seem to be returning, together, to an earlier era, as if drawn instinctively to some moment in time when they were both little children.

One morning, after she wakes them up and lets them lie chattering in bed for a while, she walks by and hears Adam ask: "How many today?"

"Three for me, three for you."

"But which three?" Adam's voice sounds so submissive and soft that she hardly recognizes him.

"You do the water and the feet and the turning, and I'll do all the rest."

"Can I do the mouth, too?" Adam whispers.

"No, I'm doing the mouth."

"But I have to . . ."

"I already have dibs on the mouth. That's it."

She places both hands on her temples. Ofer must have dropped an anchor inside Adam. She has no other words to describe it. He's already there, working in the depths of Adam with that same calm determination with which he builds giant LEGO castles or dismantles old televisions.

"Aren't I allowed any today?" Adam asks at the breakfast table, out in the open, in her presence.

Ofer thinks about it and decrees, "None. Today I'm doing them all." Then he comes around: "You know what? You can do the one with the lip. When you fold it."

"And everything else is you?" Adam asks. His voice is childish and obedient, and it horrifies her.

"Yes."

"But d'you remember to do it?"

"All the time."

"Are you sure, Ofer?"

"I never missed any till now. Come on, let's go to the room."

She practically runs to her post behind the closed door. Her body, she notes to Avram, remembers that station very well from childhood, when she used to eavesdrop on her parents from behind the closed door of her own room, trying to pick up hints, voices, giggles. Human traces. Forty years have gone by—declares the tight-lipped judge in her mind—and what has madam done in those four decades? I've changed sides at the door, your honor.

"The cop's name will be Speed," Ofer says.

"And the thief?"

"Let's call him Typhoon."

"Okay."

"Speed rides a motorbike and he has a hovercraft."

"And the thief?" Adam asks weakly.

"The thief will have long hair, and on his shirt there's a black star, and he has a bazooka and a laser drill."

"Okay," Adam says.

Ora puts her hand to her neck. This is an ancient game. They used to play it—how long ago? Two years? Three? They would lie on the rug and make up pairs of cops and robbers, or orcs and halflings. Except that back then Adam was the creator and Ofer the nodding pupil.

"Don't," Ofer says casually. "I'm doing the fingers today."

"Did I do the fingers?"

"You didn't notice."

"Then do it already."

"Wait. You have to pay a fine, 'cause you did mine."

"What's the fine?"

"The fine," Ofer answers thoughtfully, "is that I'm taking the eye thing from you too, where you blink hard and open them."

"But I have to do that one," Adam whispers.

"Well, I took it."

"I don't have anything left."

"You have the hands and feet left, and the one where you blow."

There is a long silence. Then Ofer picks up as if nothing has happened. "Now I'm bringing in a cop with an iron fist. He's called Mac Boom Boom, and he can open his shirt—"

"How many days are you taking mine for?"

"Three days not counting today."

"So today I can still do it?"

"No, today neither of us can."

"Neither of us? Then who's going to do it?"

"No one. It doesn't get done today."

"Is that allowed?" Adam whispers sadly.

"Whatever we decide," says Ofer in a Dungeon Master's voice.

Ora tells Avram she will probably never know what really went on behind Adam and Ofer's closed door during that whole period. Because what, in fact, did happen? Two kids, one almost thirteen, the other just over nine, spent every day together, usually just the two of them, for three or four weeks during summer vacation. They played computer games and foosball, chattered for hours, made up characters, and every so often they cooked *shakshuka* or pasta together. "And while they did all that—don't ask me exactly how it happened—one of them saved the other."

"You were asking if they're alike?" His question from the night before suddenly pops into her head.

"Yes, that's what I asked."

"Ofer, I think, is a little more . . . Actually, a little less, um . . ."

"What?"

"Oh, it's complicated. Look, let me put it this way: Adam is kind of . . . Kind of what? What am I trying to say?" She pouts. "It's funny how hard it suddenly is to describe them. Almost everything I want to say about them sounds so inaccurate." She shakes herself off and gathers her thoughts. "Adam—I'm only talking about outward appearances now, right? Well, he's less, say, he draws less attention at first glance. You know? But on the other hand, when you really get to know him, he's a very charismatic young man. The most charismatic. He's the kind of guy who can—"

"What does he look like?"

"You mean, you want me to describe him?"

"You know me—I like details."

The detaileater: a distant relative of the anteater, a virtually extinct sub-species of the order Pilosa, survives exclusively on details. That was how Avram had defined himself in a booklet he put together in his senior year at high school, "The Class of '69 Encyclopedia of Human Fauna." It contained his descriptions of the students and teachers, with precise illustrations, arranged by their zoological categorizations.

"He's a little bit short, relatively speaking. I told you that. And he has very black hair, like Ilan's, but he parts it in the middle and it comes down in a kind of wave over his left ear." Ora illustrates. Her face sparkles at Avram.

"What?"

"Nothing at all," she answers and shrugs one shoulder provocatively. But the more Avram comes back to life—quiet and heavy and lacking as he is—the more he magnetizes her to an internal precision, a private nuance that spreads the kind of warm ripples through her body she hasn't felt in years.

Two young couples pass by. The women nod hello and look at them curiously. The men are immersed in a loud conversation. "We're mostly into biometric identification smart cards," the taller one says. "We're working on a card called BDA, and what it does is that a Palestinian who wants to get in just has to hold his hand and face under the biometric reader. Get it? No contact with soldiers, no talking, no nothing. Clean as a whistle. CWC—communication without contact."

"So what's 'BDA' stand for?" asks the second man.

The first one snickers. "Actually, it's an acronym for biometric access device, but we realized that that came out BAD, so we changed it."

"And his left ear," Ora says when the people have gone, "is always exposed. It's cute, like a little pearl."

She shuts her eyes: Adam. His cheeks still look a little red beneath his shadow of stubble, a childhood souvenir. And he has long sideburns. And big, bitter eyes.

"His eyes are what stand out most. They're big, like Ofer's, but completely different, more sunken and black. All in all we're a family of eyes. And his lips—" She stops suddenly.

"What about them?"

"No, I think they're beautiful." She concentrates on her hands. "Yes."

"But?"

"But . . . but here, on the top one, he has a sort of tic, a permanent one. Not a tic, but an expression—"

"What sort of expression?"

"Well . . ." She takes a deep breath, girding her face. The time has come.

"You see what I have here?"

He nods without looking.

"So it's this. Except his is turned upward."

"Yes."

They skip from stone to stone across a shallow creek, holding on to each other every so often.

"Tons of flies today," Avram says.

"It must be the heat."

"Yes. This evening it will be more—"

"Can I ask you something?"

"What?"

"Does it really stand out?"

"No, no."

"Because you didn't say anything about it."

"I hardly noticed."

"I had this thing, it was nothing, something in the nerves on my face, about a month after Ilan left. It happened in the middle of the night. I was alone at home. I was terrified. Does it look awful?"

"I'm telling you, you can hardly see it."

"But I can feel it." She touches the right corner of her upper lip, pushes it slightly up. "I keep thinking my face is falling to one side."

"But you really can't see anything, Ora'leh."

"It's just a couple of millimeters that I can't feel. The sensation in the rest of my lips is totally normal."

"Yes."

"It should go away at some point. It won't always be like this."

"Of course."

They walk down a narrow path among orchards of strawberry and walnut trees.

"Avram, tell me something."

"What?"

"Stop for a minute."

He stands waiting. His shoulders hunch up.

"Would you mind giving me a little kiss?"

He comes up close to her, rigid and bearish. Without looking at her, he hugs her, and plants a decisive kiss on her lips.

And lingers, and lingers.

"Ahhh." She breathes softly.

"A-ah." He sighs in surprise.

"Avram."

"What?"

"Did you feel anything?"

"No, everything's normal."

She laughs. " 'Normal'!"

"I mean, like you used to be."

"You still remember?"

"I remember everything."

"Remember how I get dazed from kissing?"

"I remember."

"And that sometimes I almost pass out from kissing?"

"Yes."

"You be careful when you kiss me."

"Yes."

"How you loved me, Avram."

He kisses her again. His lips are as soft as she remembered. She smiles as they kiss, and his lips move with hers.

"One more thing—"

"Hmmmmm . . ."

"Do you think we'll ever sleep together?"

He presses her against his body and she feels his force. She thinks again of how much good this journey is doing him, and her.

They walk on, at first hand in hand, then they let go. Threads of new awkwardness stretch out between them, and nature itself winks behind their backs and plays nasty tricks on them, scattering yellow clods of asters and groundsel, blanketing purple clover and pink flax, erecting stalks of huge—but smelly—purple arum flowers, sprinkling red butter-cups, and hanging baby oranges and lemons on the trees around them.

"Very arousing," Ora says. "This walk, and the air. Isn't it? Don't you feel it?"

He laughs, embarrassed, and Ora—even her eyebrows suddenly feel warm.

He's known Neta for thirteen years. She claims that she sat several evenings in the pub where he worked, on HaYarkon Street, and he did not take his eyes off her. He says he didn't even notice her until she threw up and passed out on the bar one night. She was nineteen and weighed eighty-two pounds, and he carried her in his arms, against her will, on a stormy winter night—not a single cabdriver would take them—to a doctor friend in Jaffa. She squirmed in his arms the whole way, her gaunt limbs swirled around him and hit him mercilessly, and she hurled vile curses at him. When she ran out of those, she worked her way through the insults showered upon Sholem Aleichem by his stepmother, in the alphabetical order in which he had recorded them, calling him "carbuncle," "forefather of all impurities," "leper," and "purloiner." Avram himself mumbled the occasional choice curse to fill in what she omitted. When these ran out too, she started to pinch him painfully, and as she did so she laid out in detail the various uses one could make of his flesh, his fat, and his bones. Here Avram raised an eyebrow, and when she told him about the strips of wax she would be glad to produce from him, Avram—who never forgot a line he read—mumbled into her ear, *"It was the idea also, that this same spermaceti was that quickening humor of the Greenland Whale."* This was a sentence he and Ilan had loved to quote in their youth, when *Moby-Dick* served as a particularly fertile ground for quotations. The tangle of vipers in his arms fell silent at once, gave a cross-eyed glance at the heavy monster exhaling condensation into the downpour, and noted, "There are some similarities between you and the book."

"She was nineteen?" Ora asks. And thinks: I was sixteen when we met.

Avram shrugs. "She left home at sixteen and wandered around Israel and the whole world. The gypsy from next door. About two months ago was the first time she ever rented a real apartment. It was in Jaffa. Yup-pified, you know."

Ora doesn't feel like talking about Neta now.

Reluctantly, she learns that Neta always looks starved—"not necessarily for food, but a general, existential starvation," Avram explains with a laugh—and that her fingers almost always shake, maybe from drugs or maybe because, Avram quotes with a smile, "life zaps her at high voltage." For years, she spent every summer living in an ancient Simca that a friend had left her. She also had a small tent, which she pitched whenever she found a place she wasn't asked to leave. As he talks, the name "Neta" begins to etch a circle of frost in Ora's gut, even though the sun is shining. What is this flood of speech suddenly coming out of him? What is he doing sticking Neta between us now?

"How does she make a living?" (Be generous, she commands.)

"This and that. It's not really clear. She needs very little. You wouldn't believe how little she needs. And she paints."

Ora's heart sinks a little lower. Of course she paints.

"Maybe you saw in my apartment, on the walls? That's her."

The huge, stirring charcoal drawings—how had she not asked him about them before? Perhaps because she had guessed the answer—prophets breast-feeding goats and lambs, an old man bending over a girl turning into a crane, a maiden being born from a wound in the chest of a godlike deer. She thinks about the drawing of a woman with a mohawk, and asks if that's how Neta looks.

Avram chuckles. "Once, a long time ago. I didn't like it, and now she has long hair, all the way down to here."

"Yes. And the empty albums I saw at your place, the ones without any photos—are those hers, too?"

"No, those are mine."

"Do you collect them?"

"I collect, I search, I aggregate. Things people throw out."

"Aggregate?"

"You know, I put together all sorts of *alte zachen.*"

They are walking down the side of a cliff. The river, far below, is invisible. The dog leads, Ora walks behind her, and Avram brings up the rear as he tells her about his little projects. "It's nothing, just something to pass the time. Like photo albums that people throw away, or albums that belonged to people who died." He takes the photos out and puts in ones of other people, other families. He copies some of the photos onto tin boxes, right on the rust, or on the sides of ancient, rusty engines. "I'm very interested in rust lately. That place, or that moment, when iron turns to rust."

It's a good thing you found me, then, Ora thinks.

The path descends into the channel again, and suddenly Avram is alert and bright. He excitedly describes an atlas he found in the trash, printed in England in 1943. "If you looked at it, you wouldn't understand anything about what happened in the world back then, because all the countries are still in their old borders, there's no annihilation of the Jews, no occupation of Europe, no war, and I can sit looking at it for hours. So on the corners of the maps, I stuck pieces of a Russian newspaper I found in the dump, *The Stalinist*, also from 'forty-three, and there the war is described in detail, with battle maps and vast numbers of casualties. When I put those two objects together, I can really— Ora . . . I can feel electricity going through my body."

She discovers that he and Neta do joint projects sometimes, too. "It's this thing we have going together," he says, blushing. They look for old objects and junk on the street, then they fantasize about what they could do with the things. "I'm always a little more practical," he says with an apologetic snort, "and she's much bolder." He inadvertently drops himself from the story and describes some of what Neta has done in her brief life, her trials and tribulations, the skills she's learned, her hospitalizations and adventures, and the men who have passed through her life. Ora thinks he is describing the life of a seventy-year-old. "She's so brave," he says admiringly, "much braver than I am. She may be the bravest person I've ever met." He laughs softly when he remembers that Neta says she's composed mainly of fears. Fears and cellulite.

Ora sees the crossed-out black lines over his bed, and a thick streak runs from them to the charcoal drawings in his living room. A spark lights up in her: "Avram, does she know?"

"About Ofer?"

Ora nods quickly. Her heart starts to pound.

"Yes, I told her."

She walks ahead in confusion, with her hands held out. She steps into the stream, balancing on the slippery stones. This is the Amud River, she thinks. I hiked here in high school, on a sea-to-sea trip. It seems like it was yesterday. As if just yesterday I was still a young girl. She rubs her eyes. The hillside across the way is covered with thick growth, and a family of hyrax dots the rocks. The scene blurs, and she finds it's best to look only to the next steps: pay attention, you're going up again, walking on the rock ledge, and the river below plunges into a waterfall, and just don't fall, hold on to this railing, and Neta knows.

The dog comes over and rubs against Ora's leg as if to encourage her. Ora leans down and strokes her head distractedly. Neta knows. The secret bubble has been burst. The sealed, stifling bubble that Ora has taught herself to breathe in. Avram himself has punctured it. A stream of outside air bursts in. Such relief: a new, deep breath.

"What did she say?" Ora asks as her legs almost fail her.

"What did she say? She said I should go and see him."

"Oh." She lets out a thin, involuntary coo. "That's what she said?"

"And I thought, when I called you, that evening, before you came. That's what I wanted to tell you."

"What?"

"That."

"What?" She is almost suffocating. Her entire body hunches over the dog, burying ten trembling fingers in her fur.

"That if he's finished with the army," Avram says, hewing word by word, "I would like to, but only if you and Ilan didn't have any objection . . ."

"What? Say it already."

"Maybe see him one day."

"Ofer."

"Just once."

"You would like to see him."

"Even from a distance."

"Yeah?"

"Without him . . . Look, I don't want to interfere with your—"

"And you're telling me this now?"

He shrugs his shoulders and plants his feet firmly on the rock.

"And when you phoned"—she finally gets it—"I told you he was . . ."

"Going back there, yes. And then I no longer—"

"Oh." She moans, holds her head in both hands and presses hard and curses this war from the depths of her heart—this eternal war that has once again managed to shove its way into her soul. She opens her mouth wide and her lips roll back to expose her gums, and the cord of a sharp scream leaves her throat and shocks all the birds into silence. The dog looks up and her wise eyes expand until she can bear it no longer, and she too erupts into a heart-rending howl.

. . .

The last time he'd seen her was when he went to help paint her new apartment in Jaffa. A one-bedroom fourth-floor walk-up with a kitchenette and a rooftop. She was standing on a tall painter's ladder with a joint in one hand and a brush in the other, and he was on an aluminum stepladder. Her three cats slunk around between the ladders. One had a kidney disease, one was retarded, and one was a reincarnation of her mother, who in this form continued to make Neta's life a misery. Before she moved in, the apartment had housed foreign workers from China, and one whole wall was still studded with little nails hammered in a pattern whose meaning she and Avram were trying to discern. She insisted on wearing a man's gray undershirt full of holes, which she'd found in a pile of trash left behind in the apartment. "This is how I honor the memory of the one billion," she said, and he was just happy to see her in an undershirt.

"Every so often she stocks up my fridge," he tells Ora, "and cleans my apartment. Gives me a makeover. Does this even interest you?"

"Yes, of course, I'm listening."

With money she didn't have, Neta bought him a first-rate stereo system, and they listened to music together. Sometimes she read entire books to him out loud. "And she doesn't say no to any drug. She even does coke and heroin, but somehow she doesn't get addicted to anything."

"Except you," Neta laughed when he suggested she quit her Avram addiction and go into rehab.

"Nothing good will come of me for you," he'd said.

"And what are illusions, chopped liver?"

"You're young, you could have children, a family."

"You're the only person I'm willing to familiate with."

But maybe she's fallen in love with someone else? The thought pains him far more than he had imagined it would. Maybe she finally changed her mind?

"What?" Ora asks. "What is it?"

"I don't know." Avram hastens his steps. He suddenly realizes that if Neta is not in his life, or he in hers, he may not have a reason to go home after this trip. "I'm a little worried about her. She's disappeared on me lately."

"Is that unusual for her?"

"It's happened before. That's how she is, she comes and goes."

"When we reach a phone, try calling her."

"Yes."

"Maybe she left you a message at home."

He walks quickly. Tries to remember her cell-phone number, but cannot. He, who remembers everything, every bit of nonsense, every stupid sentence anyone said to him thirty years ago, every random combination of numbers his eyes fall upon. In the army he could recite all the serial numbers of all the soldiers and officers in the listening bunker; and the unlisted phone numbers of all the unit commanders; and of course the names and serial numbers of all the Egyptian units and divisions and armies, and of the commanders of all the military airfields in Egypt; and their private addresses and home phone numbers, and sometimes the names of their wives and children and mistresses; and the lists of monthly code names of all the intelligence units under the Southern Command. But now, with Neta, he can't get the numbers straight!

"She's very young," he murmurs. "I'm old, and she's so young." He laughs glumly. "It's a bit like raising a dog who you know will die before you do. But I'm the dog, in this case."

Ora distractedly covers the bitch's ears with her hands.

Through Neta he has met a whole gang of people. People like her. Kind and hardworking. "Chipped mugs," she calls them. They roam in packs. The beaches of Sinai, Nitzanim, the Judean Desert, ashrams in India, music festivals with drugs and free love in France, Spain, and the Negev.

"Do you know what an Angel Walk is?"

"Something in sports?"

He takes Ora to a "rainbow gathering" in the Netherlands or Belgium. "Everyone shares everything," he explains enthusiastically, as if he himself has been there. "Everyone helps out with meals and pays for food with whatever they have. The only thing that costs money is drugs."

"I see."

"One evening she took part in an Angel Walk." Avram gives Ora a smile that is not intended for her, the likes of which she has not seen on him since he was a boy. Like the flicker of a candle in an old, dusty lantern. The smile is irresistible. "Two rows of people stand opposite each other, very close"—he demonstrates with his hands—"and usually they don't know each other. Total strangers. And one person goes in with his or her eyes shut, and walks all the way down between the rows."

The two rows of hitters, Ora suddenly remembers. So many times he'd talked about them, in a thousand different contexts and digressions, until sometimes it seemed that the entire world was those two rows, into which a person is thrown when he is born, and he gets pummeled around between them as they hit and kick, until finally he is spat out, bruised and crushed.

"And they lead this one person slowly, gently, between the rows, and everyone strokes him, touches him, hugs him, whispers in his ear: 'You are so beautiful, you are perfect, you are an angel.' It goes on that way right to the end, and then someone is waiting for him with a big, pampering hug, and then he steps back into the rows of givers."

"Did she get hugged like that?"

"Wait. First she was in the rows, and for a few hours she stroked and hugged and whispered all those lines, which usually make her giggle. Those kinds of words really don't work for her." He perks up. "Listen, you have to meet her."

"Okay, when we have a chance. And then what happened?"

"When her turn came to receive, to walk through the lines, she didn't go in."

Ora nods. Even before he said it, she knew.

"She ran away to the forest and sat there until morning. She couldn't do it. She felt that it wasn't her time to receive yet."

Ora suddenly knows what Avram and Neta share: they have both found that those who stroke can also hit. She hugs herself tightly as she walks. This girl Neta arouses conflicting emotions in her, because suddenly, in the last few moments, she feels affection toward her, and a maternal tenderness. And Neta knows about Ofer. Avram told her about Ofer. "Does she know anything about me?"

"She knows you exist."

Ora swallows heavily, then finally manages to cough the pit out of her throat. "And do you love her?"

"Love? What do I know? I like being with her. She knows how to be with me. She gives me space."

Not like me. Ora thinks about the boys and their complaints.

Too much space, Avram thinks fearfully. Where are you, Nettush?

After they'd finished painting her little apartment, they took the ladders out onto the roof and she taught him how to ladder-walk. "In her wanderings, when she travels sometimes, she makes a living as a street performer. She swallows fire and swords, she juggles, and joins street circuses." Like two drunken grasshoppers, they'd walked toward each other under the evening sky, between the water tank and the antenna. Then she leaped up off the ladder onto the roof ledge and Avram's blood froze.

"So what do you say?" she asked with her sweet, sad smile. "It's not going to get any better than this. Should we get it over with now?"

He leaned over and gripped his ladder. Neta crab-walked along the edge of the roof. Behind her he could see rooftops and a bloodred sunset and a mosque dome. "You're a tough nut, Avram," said Neta, almost to herself. "You've never, for example, told me that you love me. Not that I ever asked you, as far as I can remember, but still, a girl needs to hear it from her man once in her life, or something like it, even a paraphrase. But you're cheap. At most you'll give me an 'I love your body' or 'I love being with you' or 'I love your ass.' That kind of witty sidestep. So maybe I should get the message already?"

The ladder's legs clicked against the stone lip of the roof. Avram decided in a flash that if something happened to her, he would, without thinking, throw himself after her.

"Go into my room," she murmured. "On the table, next to the ashtray, there's a small brown book. Go and get it."

Avram shook his head.

"Go, I won't do anything until you get back. Scout's honor."

He got off his ladder and went into the room. He was there for a second or two, and every vein in his body yelled out that she was jumping. He grabbed the book and went back to the roof.

"Now read where I marked it."

His fingers trembled. He opened the book and read: " '. . . for I had *my life support* in Vienna. I use this expression to describe the one person who has meant more to me than any other since the death of my grandfather, the woman who shares my life and to whom I have owed not just a great deal but, frankly, more or less everything, since the moment when she first appeared at my side over thirty years ago.' " He turned over the book: *Wittgenstein's Nephew* by Thomas Bernhard.

"Keep going, but with more feeling."

" 'Without her I would not be alive at all, or at any rate I would certainly not be the person I am today, so mad and so unhappy, yet at the same time happy.' "

"Yes," she said to herself, her eyes closed in deep concentration.

" 'The initiated will understand what I mean when I use this expression to describe the person from whom I draw all my strength—for I truly have no other source of strength—and to whom I have repeatedly owed my survival.' "

"Thank you," said Neta, still swaying on the ladder as if in a dream.

Avram said nothing. He seemed loathsome and despicable in his own eyes.

"Do you understand what the problem is?"

He moved his head to indicate something between yes and no.

"It's very simple. You are my *life support*, but I'm not your *life support*."

"Neta, you're—"

"Your life support is her, that woman who had a child with you, whose name you won't even tell me."

He buried his head between his shoulders and did not answer.

"But look." She smiled and brushed the hair away from her eyes. "It's not such an original tragedy, what we have here. And not such a big problem, either. The world is just a very unfocused picture. I can live with that—how about you?"

He did not answer. She asked for so little, but he could not give her even that. "Come on, Neta." He held out his hand.

"But think about it?" Her soft eyes lingered on him, full of hope.

"Okay. Now come on."

A flock of starlings soared by with a flutter of wings. Avram and Neta stood there, both immersed in themselves.

"Not yet?" she murmured to herself after a while, as though responding to an unheard voice. "It's not time yet?"

With two swift strokes she landed the ladder on the rooftop floor. "Look at you," she said, sounding surprised. "You're shaking all over. Are you cold inside? In your no-heart?"

Ora tells him more about Adam the next day. She would prefer to talk again about the old Adam, baby Adam, about the three years when he was hers alone. But he asks about today's Adam, and without holding anything back, she describes her older son, whose eyes are always red and bloodshot, whose body is slender and a little stooped, hunched forward with troubling languor, his hands and fingers drooping to the ground, his lip pulled up with a slightly contemptuous expression of subtle, nihilistic scorn.

She is struck by the things she says about him and by the fact that she is capable of looking at Adam this way. Ilan's objective view of the boys is now hers, too. She is learning to speak a foreign language.

Note by note, she depicts a young man of twenty-four who looks both weak and tough at the same time, conveying a quiet strength beyond his age. "I don't quite understand it," she says hesitantly, "this strength he has. It's something elusive, even a bit"—she swallows—"dark." There, I've said it.

"His face isn't anything special, at least not at first sight—he's pale, with cheeks darkened by stubble, sunken black eyes, and a very prominent Adam's apple—still, to me he looks exceptional. I find him really beautiful from certain angles. And he has this combination of features that looks as though several of his ages are all there at the same time. I find it so interesting sometimes just to look at him."

"But what is that strength? What do you mean?"

"How can I explain it?" She knows she must be precise now. "It's like you can't surprise him with anything. Yes, that's it. Not with anything happy or anything sad, and not with something really painful or really terrible, either. You'll never surprise him." Having said it, she realizes for the first time how accurate her perception of him is. She also understands how different he is from her—the opposite. "He has such power," she says in a fading voice. "The power of contempt."

She's seen two of his shows. One he invited her to, and the other she snuck into after he'd dropped her. There were dozens of young boys and girls there, and their faces leaned toward him in the blinding lashes of light whipped from every direction, all drawn, with their eyes closed, to his indifferent, slightly sick frailty, which sucked them out of themselves. "You should have seen them. They looked like . . . I don't know what. I don't have the words to describe it."

Avram sees a field of albino sunflowers. Albino sunflowers in a solar eclipse.

They rest at the peak of Mount Arbel, above the thirst-quenching Kinneret Valley. The area is full of hikers. A school group of screeching girls and boys arrives. They take one another's pictures and scurry around. Buses spit out groups of tourists, and their guides compete against one another in a shouting match. But Ora and Avram are immersed in their own affairs. A soft breeze refreshes them after the exhausting ascent. On the way up they hardly spoke—it was an especially steep climb. Carved steps and iron posts in the rock helped them, but every few steps they had to stop for a breather. From the Bedouin village at the foot of the hill came roosters' crowing, a school bell, and the commotion of children. Above them, in the cliff side, a chain of gaping mouths: the caves where the Galilean rebels hid from Herod ("I read about it somewhere," Avram murmured). Herod's soldiers had cleverly propelled themselves down the mountain in cages and used rods fitted with iron hooks to hunt down the cave dwellers and hurl them into the valley.

Above the mountain, above the human tumult, a large eagle glides against the blue sky, floating on a warm, transparent air column that rises up from the valley. In broad circles, with spectacular ease, the eagle hovers above the air column until its towering warmth evaporates, then glides away in search of a new breeze. Avram and Ora take pleasure in its flight, and in the mountains of the Galilee and the Golan, glowing purple in the warm vapors, and the blue eye of Lake Kinneret, until Ora notices a plaque in memory of Sergeant Roi Dror, of blessed memory, who was killed below this cliff on June 18, 2002, during a training operation of the Duvdevan special forces unit. *He fell as gently as a tree falls. There was not even the slightest sound, because of the sand* (The Little Prince). Without a word, they get up and flee to the opposite end of the mountaintop, but there is another monument in their new place of refuge, in memory of Staff Sergeant Zohar Mintz, killed in '96 in Southern Lebanon. Ora reads with tears in her eyes: *He loved the country and died for it, he loved us and we loved him.* Avram pulls her hand but she does not move, so he forcefully tugs her away. "You started telling me about Adam," he reminds her.

"Oh, Avram, where will this end? Tell me, where will this end? There's no more room for all the dead."

"Now tell me about Adam."

"But listen, I remembered that I wanted to tell you something about Ofer." She could feel it again. The slight push she gives Ofer to the front of the stage every time she thinks Avram is too drawn to Adam.

"What about Ofer?" he asks, but she can feel that his heart is still caught in the riddle of Adam.

They walk down the mountain heading south, toward Karnei Hittin.

On either side of the path are fields of wheat ears turning golden in the sun. They find an isolated patch, like a little nest on the ground, surrounded by a meadow of purple lupines. Avram sprawls out, Ora lies down opposite him, and the dog nuzzles under Ora's head. Ora feels the warm, breathing body, which needs her, and thinks she might break the vow she'd made after Nicotine died and adopt this dog.

"When Talia left Ofer—I guess my boys always get deserted; so they did inherit something from me after all. But wait, I have to explain that Adam never had a serious girlfriend, I mean a true love, before Ofer had Talia. And think about that. Two boys like them, they're not that bad, are they? They're definitely a catch, but neither of them had a girlfriend until a pretty late age. Think about us at their age. Think about you."

Of course he already has. She sees in his face that he is instantly there, at seventeen and nineteen and twenty-two. Buzzing around her like mad, but at the same time pursuing every other girl he laid eyes on. She could never understand his taste in girls, and he found every one of them worthy of his undying love. Each grew greater and more beautiful in his eyes, even the stupidest and ugliest ones, and especially the ones who scorned and tormented him. "Remember how . . . ," she starts, and he shrugs his shoulders in embarrassment. Of course he remembers. She thinks about his efforts to enchant, to seduce, and how he would hollow out his soul for them, humiliate himself, stammer, blush, and then poke fun at himself: "What am I? Nothing more than a hormonal fermentation bacterium." And now, thirty years later, he still has the nerve to argue with her: "It was all because you didn't want me. If you'd said yes right away, if you hadn't tortured me for five years before giving in, I wouldn't have needed that whole march of folly."

She hoists herself up on her elbows. "I didn't want you?"

"Not the way I wanted you. You wanted Ilan more; I was just the zest."

"That's not true. That's really inaccurate, it's a lot more complicated than that."

"You didn't want me, you were afraid."

"What did I have to be afraid of?"

"You were afraid, Ora, because the fact is you gave up on me in the end. You gave up. Admit it."

They both sit quietly. Her face is flushed. What can she tell him? She couldn't even explain it to herself back then. When she was with him for that one year, she sometimes had the feeling that he was flushing through her en masse, like a whole army. What can she tell him? After all, she wasn't even always convinced it was *her* he loved so much, that *she* was the one creating that love storm. Perhaps it was someone he had once fantasized about, and he just kept on daydreaming her with all his creative powers. She also suspected that simply because he had fallen in love with her once, in a hasty, crazy moment, in the isolation ward, he would never admit, not even to himself, that she wasn't right for him. With his peculiar, Quixotic chivalry, he would never go back on his resolution. (But how could she have told him that at the time? She hadn't even had the courage to say it to herself, as she was doing now.) Sometimes she felt like a mannequin on which he constantly piled more and more colorful outfits that only underscored her dryness, her diminution, her narrowness. But every time she told him, full of sorrow and a broken heart, a little of what she felt, he was deeply insulted, amazed at how little she knew herself and him, at how she could hurt the most beautiful thing he had ever had in his life.

Why does everything have to be so exaggerated with him? Why does everything have to have such force? she used to wonder. And then she'd feel ashamed, and she'd think of the girl who jumped out of his bed because he was *too intimate* for her. She also often felt that he had so much love and passion that he was invading her, raging inside her body and soul like an oversized carnivorous puppy, without even imagining how much it pained her and ripped her apart. At times he would look into her eyes so intently. There were no words to describe what was in his eyes at those moments. And it didn't necessarily occur in times of passion. Usually it came *after* the passion. He would look at her with such exposed, piercing, almost mad love, and she would teasingly touch his nose, or giggle, or make a funny face, but it was as if he did not sense her embarrassment. His face would take on a strange expression, imploring her for something she did not understand, and for one long moment he would sink into her eyes without taking his look off hers, and he was like a massive, shadowy body drowning in dark liquid, and he would gradually disappear as he looked at her, and her eyes would slowly close and cover him inside them, sheltering from herself, too. She could no longer look, and yet she did, and she saw his gaze emptying to reveal something else, something skeletal and terrible, with no end. He would dive deep inside her, hold her tight against his body, clutch her until she almost choked in his grip, and every so often he shuddered powerfully as though he had absorbed something from her that he could not tolerate. She did not know what was there, what she'd given him, what she'd received.

"I couldn't be with you," she says simply.

The sun sets slowly, and the earth gives off a fresh, steaming scent of insides. Ora and Avram lie motionless in their nest on the field. Above them the sky mingles with the various evening blues. *Take a hat and put two slips of paper in it. No, you don't have to know what you're drawing lots for. You're allowed to guess, but do it silently. And quickly. Ora, they're waiting for us, there's a command car outside. Now pick one out. Did you do it? Which one? Are you sure?*

Her face grows long in the shadows. She shuts her eyes. *Which one did you pick? And which one did you want to pick? And which one did you really pick? Are you sure? Are you really sure?*

"Listen, I just couldn't breathe. You were too much for me."

"How could it be too much?" Avram asks quietly. "What is too much when you love someone?"

"Adam and Ofer were so lazy, it took them forever to find girlfriends," she tells Avram the next day, walking through Switzerland Forest. "They spent almost all their time with each other, always shared a room. They refused to be separated until finally, when Adam was about sixteen, we gave them separate rooms. We thought it was time."

"Where did you put the rooms?"

Ora hears the flicker in his voice and tenses. "In . . . you know, down-stairs, where the storage room was. That basement? Where your mother's Singer sewing machine was?"

"So you partitioned the basement?"

"With drywall, yes. Nothing major."

"Wasn't it too crowded?"

"No, it came out nicely. Two rooms, kind of nooks. It was great for teenagers."

"And a bathroom?"

"A small one, you know, with a tiny sink."

"What about air?"

"We put two windows in. More like peepholes. Symbolic."

"Yes," he says thoughtfully. "Sure."

When he'd finished all his treatments and surgeries and hospitalizations, Avram had decided he didn't want to go back to his mother's house in Tzur Hadassah. Not even to visit. Ilan and Ora, with help from Ora's parents, and loans and a mortgage, bought the house from Avram. They made a point of buying it at a higher price than its real value—much higher, Ilan liked to stress whenever the topic came up—and they followed all the rules and carried out the transaction through a lawyer who had been a friend of Avram's from before. But Ora—and perhaps Ilan too, although he always denied it—never forgave herself for that heartless act, for their *prolonged torment of him* (there, she's finally said it to herself), which ended only when she and Ilan moved to Ein Karem. Now, faced with his pained look, as though blinded by the attempt to follow the innovations and changes in the home that was once his, she can hardly resist giving him the list of rationales that are always on the tip of her tongue, ready for use: everything was done with the best of intentions, thinking only of his needs; they wanted to save him from having to deal with buyers and agents; they really thought he'd feel better if he knew that in some way the house was staying in the family. But they purchased his house from him (at full price, yes, at an excellent price), and they lived their lives in it, she and Ilan and Adam and Ofer.

Sometimes, when no one was looking, she would touch a wall as she walked by, in the rooms or in the hallway, slowly sliding her fingers over it. Sometimes she would sit and read, as he had, at the top of the steps to the yard, or on the windowsill facing the wadi. There were the window handles, which she would linger on every time she opened them, as if in a secret handshake. There were the bath and the toilet, the cracked ceilings, the cabinets with their dense smell. There were the sunken tiles and the ones that stuck out. There were the rays of sun that came from the east in the morning, and she would stand and bathe in them for long moments, sometimes with little Ofer in her arms, quietly watching her. There was the evening breeze, which came from the wadi, which she would sway in, letting it float over her skin and breathing it deep inside.

"Surprisingly, Ofer had a girlfriend before Adam did." Ora hopes this information will make Avram happy. But he darkens a little and asks what she means by "surprisingly." She explains: "After all, he's younger. But I guess Adam needed Ofer to pave the way in that realm, too. Even when they were grown up, they were both at home with us all the time until Adam's military service, until the army separated them, and then everything changed. Suddenly Adam had friends, lots of friends, and so did Ofer, and then Ofer found Talia. All at once they both opened up and went out into the world—so the army did them some good after all. But until Adam turned eighteen, until his enlistment, most of the time it was just him and Ofer. I mean, him and Ofer and us, the four of us together"—she mimes stuffing something tightly into a suitcase or backpack. "Even though they always had lots of things going on, school, and Adam's band, we still felt, Ilan and I, that they were mostly directed inward, to the house, and even more, to their own relationship. I told you, they had this secret." Her hands grip the backpack straps and her head tilts slightly. She hardly sees what is in front of her: cliffs, raspberry hedges, blinding sunlight. It suddenly occurs to her that within the longer, cumbersome secret, Ofer and Adam had made their own little secret, a kind of igloo in the ice.

"It was fun, that togetherness. They were always with us, they went everywhere with us—'like bodyguards,' Ilan used to joke, or maybe complain—and we went on trips together, and sometimes to movies, and they even came with us to our friends' sometimes, which is really hard to believe." She gives a meager laugh. "They would come with us and sit on the side and talk as if they hadn't seen each other in a year. It was wonderful, I'm telling you, it was such a rare thing. But still, Ilan and I always have—always *had*—the feeling that it was a bit, how can I put it—"

For an instant, in the wandering beam of her gaze, Avram sees the four of them moving through the rooms of the familiar house. Four bright, elongated human spots, with a dim light around their edges, like figures seen through night goggles, foggy shadows surrounded by a greenish, downy halo, stuck to one another, moving clumsily together. And when they briefly come apart, they each leave in the other strands of sticky, glowing fibers. To his surprise, he senses a constant effort emanating from them. There is tension and caution. He is even more astounded to discover that there is no ease or pleasure in the four of them. They do not evince the joy of living together, which he had always pictured when he thought of them, when he had given in to thoughts of them, when he had drizzled into his veins, drop by drop, the poison of thinking about them.

"And when Ofer had a girlfriend," he asks hesitantly, "wasn't Adam jealous?"

"At first it wasn't easy. Yes, Adam had a hard time with Ofer finding a new soul mate, and with the fact that he had no part in this very close connection they shared. Just think—it was the first time that had happened since Ofer was born. But they were a nice couple, Ofer and Talia. There was a tenderness between them." She finds it hard to talk. "Later, later."

She picks up after a while. "When Talia left Ofer, he crawled into his bed and barely left for a week. He stopped eating, completely lost his appetite. He just drank, mostly beer, and friends came to see him. All of a sudden we saw how many friends he had, and even though it wasn't planned, they basically began to sit shiva in our house."

"Shiva?!"

"Because they sat around his bed and consoled him, and when they left others came, and the door was open all week long, morning, noon, and night, and he kept asking his friends to tell him about Talia, to tell him everything they remembered about her, in great detail. And by the way, he wouldn't let them say anything bad about her, only good things. He's such a kind soul." She giggles. "I haven't even told you anything about him, you haven't begun to know him . . ." Suddenly she is flooded with nostalgia. Simple, hungry, incautious longing. She hasn't seen him for a long time, or talked to him. This may be the longest she has gone without speaking to him since he was born. "And the guys played him songs Talia liked, and watched one of her favorite movies, *My Dinner with André*, in an endless loop. And they gobbled down bags and bags of Bamba and Tuv Taam, which she was addicted to. And this went on for a whole week. And of course I had to feed and water the whole tribe. You wouldn't believe the quantities of beer those guys could down in one evening. Well, you probably could, because of the pub."

Maybe, she thinks, Ofer or Adam, or even both of them together, on one of their pub crawls in Tel Aviv one evening, when they were on leave from the army, had turned up at his pub. Could he have somehow recognized them? Known without knowing?

"Ora?"

"Yes." She smiles to herself. "Look, I guess it turned into this thing around town"—like everything Ofer touched, she intimates—"and people started turning up who didn't really know Ofer but had heard that something was going on, this kind of love shiva. They came and sat there telling stories about their own soured loves, and about affairs that had ended, and all sorts of heartbreaks they'd experienced."

An afternoon ray of sun smooths her forehead, and Ora distractedly turns her cheek to pamper herself in the warmth. Her face is young and lovely now, as though nothing bad has ever happened to her. She can get up now and go out into life, whole and innocent and pure.

"And by the way, that's how Adam met Libby, who became *his* girl-friend. She's like an overgrown puppy, a homeless puppy, a bear cub, although she's a head taller than he is. During the first days of the shiva she just sat in a corner and cried nonstop, and then she pulled herself together and started to help me with the food and the drinks and the dishes, emptying ashtrays and taking out empty bottles. But she was so exhausted from something that she would fall asleep in any available bed around the house. Just collapse into a slumber. And somehow, without us noticing, in our sleep, she came into our lives, and now they're together, she and Adam. I think they're happy, because even though Libby is a puppy, she's also very maternal toward him." A tinge of sorrow trails behind Ora's voice. "I think he's really happy with her. At least I hope so."

She surrenders to a deep, pent-up sigh, a sigh of total bankruptcy. "Look, I wasn't exaggerating when I told you a few days ago that I know nothing about his life now."

The dog stops and comes up to Ora when she hears her sigh. Ora leans down to the damp, sharp snout nuzzling between her thighs. She speaks to Avram over the dog's head. "Sometimes, when I say a certain word, or if I say something in a slightly different tune—"

"Or when you laugh suddenly—"

"Or cry—"

"She responds immediately."

"Yesterday, when you were chasing the flies around with a towel and shouting, did you see how upset she was? What did that remind you of, sweetie?" Ora tenderly rubs the dog's head as she leans into her. "Where did you come to us from?" She kneels on one knee, holds the dog's face between her hands, and rubs noses with her. "What happened to you? What did they do to you?"

Avram watches them. The light turns Ora's hair even more silver and glows in the dog's fur.

"So you don't have any contact with him, with Adam?" he asks when they start walking again.

"He totally cut me off."

Avram does not reply.

"There was this thing," she mutters. "Not with him. It was with Ofer, actually, in the army. We had this whole story with him, some screwup that happened in his unit in Hebron. No one died, and Ofer wasn't to blame—he certainly wasn't the only one. There were twenty soldiers there, so why would it be his fault? Never mind, not now. I made a mistake, I know that, and Adam was very angry at me for not supporting Ofer"—she takes a deep breath and portions out, one by one, the words that have been tormenting her ever since—"for not being able to support Ofer wholeheartedly. Do you understand? Do you understand the absurdity? Because with Ofer I've already made up long ago. Everything's fine between us"—but her eyes shift a little, this way and that—"but Adam, because of his lousy principles, won't forgive me to this day."

Avram doesn't ask anything. Her heart pounds in her throat. Did she do the right thing by telling him? She should have told him long ago. She's afraid of his judgment. Maybe he'll also think, like Adam, that she's an unnatural mother.

"Do they hug?" Avram asks.

"What did you say?" Ora jolts out of a fleeting daydream.

"No, nothing." He sounds startled.

"No, you asked if they—"

"Hug. Sometimes, yes. Ofer and Adam."

She looks at him gratefully. "Why do you ask?"

"I don't know, I'm just trying to imagine them together, that's all."

That's all? She rejoices inside: *That's all?*

They've walked far. At the village of Kinneret they had stocked up on food and visited the nearby cemetery, where they leafed through the book of Rahel's poems chained to the ground next to her grave. They crossed the Tiberias-Tzemach highway, strolled through orchards of date trees, and paid their respects to a mule named Booba, buried near the Jordan River, who had *Loyally Plowed, Tilled, and Furrowed the Kinneret Soil in the 1920s and 1930s.* They saw pilgrims from Peru and Japan sing and dance as they dipped in the river. They walked a ways between the clear river and a foul-smelling sewage channel, until the path led them away from the Jordan and toward the Yavne'el. At Ein Petel they enjoyed a feast fit for kings in the shade of eucalyptus and oleander trees. They could see Mount Tabor and knew without a doubt that they would reach it.

The day is extremely hot and, feeling toasted, they dip in the occasional spring or run through giant sprinklers on the fields. They get scratched by raspberry bushes, and every so often they doze in a spot of shade, then get up and walk for a while longer. They slather themselves repeatedly with sunscreen; he spreads it on the back of her neck and she does his nose, and they sigh at how unsuitable their skin is for this climate. As he walks, Avram carves "the stick of the day" for Ora with Ofer's penknife, and today it's a thin oak branch, slightly crooked and partially gnawed, perhaps by a goat. "Not the most convenient thing," she announces after trying it, "but it's full of personality, so it can stay."

"When they were boys they almost never hugged," she tells him when they sit down on a heap of stones in the shade of a large Atlantic terebinth on the heights of the Yavne'el mountains. The spot has a rare view of the Kinneret, the Golan, the Gilead, Mount Meron, the Gilboa mountains, Mount Tabor, the Shomron, and the Carmel. She even sensed that the boys were a little embarrassed by each other's bodies. She found this awkwardness strange: they shared a room, and when they were little they always showered together, but to touch each other, body to body . . . They wouldn't even hit each other, she thinks now. They only fought when they were little, but not much. And when they grew older, almost never.

What she wouldn't give to know whether they talked about puberty, about the changes in their bodies, or about girls, and about masturbation and making out. She guesses they didn't. Puberty seemed to embarrass them both, as though it were some alien force that had invaded their intimate twosome and expropriated parts they preferred to keep silent about. She often wondered, and asked Ilan repeatedly, where they'd gone wrong in bringing up the boys. Maybe we didn't hug enough in front of them? We didn't show them what it's like when a man and a woman love each other?

"I find it very strange," she says, trying to sound amused, "how modest and shy my boys are about that kind of stuff. I used to try to get them to be crude, to curse here and there, what's the big deal? When Ofer was little he gleefully joined in. He'd say rude words and giggle and blush terribly. But when they grew up, especially when they were with the two of us, it almost never happened."

It's Ilan with his lousy puritanism, she thinks. Always on guard, making sure not a hint of lining sticks out, God forbid. "Sometimes I had the feeling—you'll laugh—that they thought they had to preserve our innocence, as if *we* didn't know which end was up. Come on, let's walk, this is getting on my nerves."

The trail is now a path of cracked, dry clods of earth. Bare stones and narrow cracks, spindly weeds trampled yet resprouting. Here and there some humble white and yellow chamomile earn the pity of their feet, which avoid them. Dry leaves from last spring, crumbled and perforated, translucent, only their spines remaining. A rocky path, yellowing brown, dusty and warty, *no form nor comeliness*, exactly like a thousand others, scattered with withered twigs and orange-brown pine needles. A line of black ants carries crumbs and shelled sunflower seeds. Here a deep ant-lion pit, there a pattern of gray-green lichen on fractured rocks, a shriveled pinecone, and the occasional glistening black mound of deer droppings or crumbly brown mound of a queen ant returned from her nuptial flight.

"Listen," Ora says and holds his hand.

"To what?"

"To the path. I'm telling you, paths in Israel have a sound I haven't heard anywhere else."

They walk and listen: *rrrrsh-rrrsh* when their shoes drag in the dirt; *rrrhh-rrrhh* when their toes hit the path; *hhhhs-hhhhs* when they stroll; *hwassh-hwassh* when they trot; a rapidly drumming *rrish-chrsh* when little stones fly up and hit each other; *hrappp-hrappp* when their feet step through bushes of poterium. Ora laughs. "It's a good thing they all have the right sounds in Hebrew. How would you possibly describe these sounds in English or Italian? Maybe they can only be accurately pronounced in Hebrew."

"Do you mean these paths speak Hebrew? Are you saying *language springeth out of the earth*?" And he runs with the idea that words had sprouted up from this dirt, crawled out of cracks in the arid, furrowed earth, burst from the wrath of *hamsin* winds with briars and brambles and thorns, leaped up like locusts and grasshoppers.

Ora listens to his flow of speech. Deep inside, a fossilized minnow stirs its tail and a wavelet tickles at her waist.

"I wonder what it's like in Arabic," she says. "After all, it's their landscape too, and they have rhonchial consonants too, that sound like your throat is choking on the dryness." She illustrates, and the dog pricks up her ears. "Do you still remember the Arabic words you learned for all those thistles and nettles, or didn't they teach you that in Intelligence?

Avram laughs. "Mostly they taught us about tanks and planes and munitions; for some reason they didn't get around to nettles."

"A grave mistake," Ora decrees.

He'd asked whether they hug. She remembers going out to a restaurant on Adam's birthday, not long ago. It was a new place, "a little too froufrou for my taste," she says, on one of the moshavim in the Jerusalem hills, surrounded by fields and empty chicken coops—it occurs to her that although Avram has worked in a pub and a restaurant and God knows where else, he may not know what it's like to go out for a family meal, being as socially illiterate as he is. So she explains, before anything else, how they choose a restaurant in her family. Adam has refined, picky taste, so first they have to call and find out if there's anything for him to eat, course by course. Once they choose a place and get there and sit down—"You can't imagine what an operation it is just to sit down! We have a whole settlement policy. For a simple family we're pretty complicated."

She talks on and on, and Avram can see it.

"First of all, Ilan has to find the perfect table: far from the bathroom and the kitchen, with the right lighting—not too bright, not too dim— and as quiet as possible, and a spot where he can sit facing the door, to be aware of any danger that might threaten his little family—and the evening I'm talking about was at the height of the terrorist attacks."

"When isn't it?" Avram grumbles.

"And Adam has to sit as close as possible to a wall, almost hidden, with his back to everyone, but he also has to be able to embarrass his parents with his torn pants, dirty shirts, and the quantities of alcohol he pours down his throat. And Ofer is like me: he doesn't care about anything, he'll happily sit anywhere as long as the food is good and there's lots of it." Ora herself wants privacy, of course, but also to be able to show off her family a little.

"So after we sit down comes the ordering, with Adam's performances. The waitress always marks him straightaway as problematic, an obstacle in the rhythmic flow of her execution, because of his pedantic instructions—nothing with cream in it; can it be fried in butter? Do any of the dips, God forbid, contain eggplant or avocado, in any form? And Ilan's usual wisecracks with the waitress." Ora is always amazed and amused to see how utterly blind he is to the fact that the poor girl—any poor girl, at any age—goes weak when he floods her with the arctic green of his glowing eyes. And then there's Ora's heroic struggle with her own eye, which keeps veering to the prices. Every time anyone orders anything, she conducts a secret negotiation between gluttony and frugality—okay, let's get all the embarrassing facts out. With her, it's cheapness, quite explicitly. There, she's admitted it. Somehow she finds it easy to confess to Avram what she has held back from Ilan all these years. She sighs. "Where was I?"

"Cheapness," Avram comments with slightly malicious glee.

"Yes, use it against me, go ahead." A spark flies between her eyes and his.

She is always the one who feebly suggests: "Why don't we just order three entrées? We never finish everything anyway." And they argue with her, always, as though her proposal contains a veiled slight of their appetites, perhaps even their masculinity. In the end they order four entrées and never finish even three of them. Adam orders a horribly extravagant aperitif—why does he need to drink so much? She and Ilan exchange glances—leave him alone, let him enjoy it this evening, on me! And when the waitress heads to the kitchen with their orders a sudden silence—freezing, obviating—falls on them all. The three men stare at their fingertips, study a fork, or ponder a philosophical conundrum—"an abstract, even cosmic problem," Ora hisses.

She knows everything will be fine soon, even good. They always enjoy themselves at restaurants, and the boys like going out with her and Ilan. All in all the four of them are a great team. Soon the jokes will come, and the giggles and the waves of affection. In just a short while she'll be able to splash around in the warm, sweet latency that commingles—"for such rare moments; far rarer than you might imagine"—complete happiness and family. But there's always that lousy, unavoidable moment before, a sort of transit toll they charge her, the three of them, on her way to that sweetness. It is a regular torture ritual that she perceives as cunningly, conspiratorially, aimed solely at her, which she alone provokes in them, and it is precisely because they sense how much she yearns for that sweetness that they tighten ranks to withhold it from her and make her path to it a little harder. "Why? Don't ask me, ask them." They sit there in front of her, the three of them and their fingertips, the three of them in their eagerness for a little scheming against her, unable to resist the temptation, not even Ilan. "He didn't used to be like that," she says, letting out what she never meant to tell. She and Ilan used to be . . . well, of one mind—she almost said "of one flesh"—and when they had to, they presented a united front against the boys. He was a full partner. But the last few years—"I really don't understand it," she says, seething with overdue anger—since the boys started growing up, something went wrong, as though he had decided it was time for him to be an adolescent, too.

When she thinks about it now, it seems to her that recently, particularly since the time of their separation, around a year ago, she keeps finding herself faced with three rebellious adolescents who act angrily and impudently—the toilet seats were always left up in bold defiance—and she wishes she knew what it was about her that aroused this idiotic, infantile compulsion, and what turned them instantly into three ravenous kittens when a ball of conspiracy against her rolled at their feet, and why on earth it was her responsibility to rescue them from the silence at a restaurant. What if one day she partook in the grave pondering of the fingertips? What if she hummed an intricate song to herself all the way to the end, until one of them broke down—and it would probably be Ofer; his sense of justice would step up, his natural compassion, his urge to protect her would eventually overcome even the pleasure of belonging to the other two. But her heart quickly fills with tenderness for him—why would she trip him up on their men's games? It was better for *her* to break down rather than him.

Again the same old thought: if only she'd had a girl. A girl would have stitched everyone back together with her cheerfulness, her simplicity, her ease. With everything Ora used to have and lost. Because Ora was a girl once, let that be clear. Maybe not as happy and light-hearted as she would have liked to be, but she certainly had wanted and tried to be that kind of girl, a joyful, carefree girl just like the daughter she never had was supposed to have been. And she remembers only too well, she tells Avram, the sudden hostile silences that often came between her parents. Silences with which her mother punished her father for sins he could not even conceive of. Back then, Ora was the magic needle that quickly scurried between her father and mother to stitch up the unraveled moment through which the three of them had almost plunged to the depths.

That silence in the restaurant lasts no more than a minute, Avram understands from Ora's stammered description and her lowered eyes, but it feels like a cursed eternity. Everyone knows that someone has to talk and melt away the silence, but who will start? Who will step up? Who will proclaim that he is the most spineless, the doormat, the softy? Who will break down first and say something, even something silly? Hey, silly is what we do best, Ora knows. Even a snide remark will play well. Like her story about the plump Russian lady who had shared Ora's umbrella earlier that week in a rainstorm. She hadn't asked, hadn't apologized, just said to Ora with a smile, "We walk together now awhile." Or she could tell them about the elderly spinster who came to her clinic with a sprained ankle and laughingly told Ora her trick for making dough rise: she takes it into bed, lies down for forty winks with the dough under the blanket, and that's how it gets its first rise! Yes, Ora would prattle on, and they'd all laugh warmly and wonder how the Russian woman had picked out Ora as a sucker even in the middle of a storm. They'd make fun of the old lady with the dough and tease her about her other patients and her job in general, which they found slightly odd: "You just come up to a total stranger and start prodding them?" And the little flame she lit would start curling and burning, and they would be warm and happy. "Do you understand what I'm getting at? Do you see the picture, or am I just . . ."

He nods, fascinated. Maybe he did see a thing or two in his pub after all, she thinks, or at the Indian restaurant. Or just walking the streets, or on the beach. Maybe he didn't give up those eyes of his after all. Maybe he noticed and watched, and peeked and eavesdropped, and collected it all inside. Yes, that's just like him, a detective gathering evidence for a crime of extraordinary scale—the human race.

"And after that everything's all right, we're all totally there, and we laugh and jab and talk. The three of them are sharp, witty, cynical, and horribly macabre, just like you and Ilan were." This fills Avram with sadness, perhaps because he can also sense what she is not disclosing: she always has the feeling that something in the conversation is beyond her grasp, that a subliminal lightning bolt has flashed between them but she hears only the thunder that follows. When the food arrives, the buzz of commerce begins, and that's what she likes most. Plates and bowls and spoonfuls are passed from hand to hand, forks peck at one another's dishes, the four of them compare, savor tastes, criticize, and offer to share. A canopy of generosity and delight spreads above them, and this, finally, is the quiet, honeyed moment, her portion of happiness. She follows the conversation only superficially now. The conversation is not the main point—it's even a distraction. She thinks they're poking fun at themselves, at the dishes soaring back and forth like flying saucers, and at what the people at the other tables must think of them. Or else they're discussing the army, or some new CD. What difference does it make? The point is this moment: embraced.

"That sucks," she heard Ofer say to Adam. "We spent the whole summer killing flies in Nebi Musa, and it turns out we killed the weak ones, so we created a generation of resistant flies, and now their genetics are much stronger." They laughed. They both have lovely teeth, Ora thought. Adam described the rats that run freely around the kitchen at his reserve duty unit. Ofer struck back with a winning card: a fox, maybe even a rabid one, had infiltrated his crew's room while people were dozing and stolen a whole cake out of someone's backpack. They spoke in loud, deep voices, as they always do when they talk about the army. "But that might also be because Ofer's ears are always full of dust and grease," she explains to Avram. Ora and Ilan laughed and laughed, delighted, and gobbled down pieces of herb bread. Their role here was clear: they represented the sufficiently blurry background, the sounding board against which their children repeatedly declared their maturity and independence, and from which their declaration echoed back to the children themselves, at every age, so that they could finally believe in it. The boys changed the topic to accidents, big and small. There was practically a permanent order to these conversations, Ora realizes now, an organized, gradual escalation. Adam told them about how when he started his service in the Armored Corps, one of the commanders had demonstrated what could happen to a tank driver who got stuck in the gun's side traverse. He set a wooden crate on the hull, rotated the gun sideways, and showed how the barrel shattered the crate, "which is exactly what could happen to anyone who steps out of a tank without coordinating," Adam cautioned his younger brother, and Ora felt a chill.

"We have this soldier," Ofer said, "poor guy, a real screwup, he's the company's punching bag—everyone who walks past him gives him a punch. About a month ago, in a camouflage drill, he fell off the tank and his arm swelled up. So they sent him to rest in the DT"—the "discipline tent," he begrudgingly translated when he saw Ora's look—"and there an antenna fell on his head and cracked it open." Ilan and Ora exchanged quick glances of horror, but they knew they must not respond to the story with a single word. Anything they said, any concerned expression, would be met with mockery ("skirt on the left," Adam liked to warn Ofer against Ora), but Adam and Ofer of course picked up on their glances, and everyone got what they wanted, and now, once the foundations were laid, once the parents had been duly enlightened about the many and varied dangers from which they could no longer protect their sons, Ofer told them casually that the suicide bomber who had blown himself up two weeks earlier at the central bus station in Tel Aviv, killing four civilians, had probably passed through his roadblock—meaning, the roadblock his battalion was responsible for.

Ilan asked guardedly if they knew when exactly the terrorist had gone through, and whether anyone was holding Ofer's battalion responsible. Ofer explained that there was no way to tell who was on shift when he'd gone through, and that he could have been carrying a new kind of explosive that was impossible to detect at the roadblock. Ora was dumbstruck, unable to speak. Ilan swallowed and said, "You know what? I'm glad he blew himself up in Tel Aviv and not on you at the roadblock." Ofer was outraged: "But, Dad, that's my job! I stand there precisely so they'll blow themselves up on me and not in Tel Aviv."

And Ora—what was she doing at that moment? Her memory is hazy, she cannot reconstruct it. All she remembers is that she suddenly felt hollow, a shell of herself. There was something stuck in her mouth, probably pine nut–studded rye bread dipped in walnut pesto. Ofer and Adam were already deep in conversation about a soldier they both knew, who on parents' day at the end of training had come up to a strange couple with his arms outstretched and shouted, "Mom, Dad, don't you recognize me?" Ofer and Adam, and probably Ilan too, rolled around laughing, and Ora sat with her mouth half open while nymphlike waitresses hovered around the tables and whispered: "How is everything?" And two weeks ago a terrorist packed with explosives had walked right past Ofer, and that was Ofer's job: he stood there precisely so that terrorists would blow themselves up on him and not in Tel Aviv.

Then Ofer turned very serious, and he told Adam and Ilan about his stint in Hebron during the past week. He wasn't allowed to talk about it, but he could give them the gist. The battalion was sent there to wage a campaign to eliminate wanted men in the kasbah—Ora was no longer really listening to him; she'd been transported—something they hadn't done before and which had never been one of their duties. They commandeered a whole building to use as a lookout post, and locked up the residents in one apartment. "We actually treated them really well," he said and gave her a sideways glance, but she was no longer there. Had she been listening, perhaps she could have changed something. Or perhaps not. And then—how did the conversation end up there? Only in retrospect, through a supreme effort that lasted weeks and months, was she able to piece together the fragments of that conversation into an approximate tapestry of the entire evening. Ofer asked Adam to explain something about the procedure for arresting a suspect, but here too she heard only fragments. You yell three times, in Hebrew and in Arabic, "Stop! Who's there?" And then three times, "Stop or I'll shoot" (Adam). *"Wakef wa'la batukhak"* (Ofer). And then you cock your weapon and aim at sixty degrees through the sight (Ofer again?). And then you shoot (Adam). The music of their voices, Ora dimly noticed, sounded exactly like it did when they used to study for Adam's grammar exams together, when Adam was the teacher and Ofer the student. "You aim for the legs, yeah, knees-down, static, through the sight, and if he doesn't stop, you go for the center of the body mass and you shoot to kill." Ofer sheepishly admits that he doesn't remember what that "mass" is, exactly. Adam scolds: "Didn't you learn any physics at school?" Ofer says, "Yes, but where is it on a person?" Adam scoffs: "When I was in the Territories they told us, 'Shoot between their nipples.' " Ofer said, "At my last target practice, I shot the dummy in the stomach, and the P.C. goes, 'I told you to aim for the knees!' So I say, 'But, sir, won't he go down this way, too?' " They both laughed, and Ofer threw Ora a cautious glance. He knew she didn't like that kind of joke. Adam, who also knew, grinned and said, "Some soldiers are convinced that the Arabs walk around with bull's-eyes on their faces, just like in practice."

And now here she is with them again. She's back. The temporary fault in her brain has been fixed. She had experienced some sort of electrical short when Ofer said, "But, Dad, that's my job! I stand there precisely so they'll blow themselves up on me and not in Tel Aviv." She laughs with them, laughs despite herself, laughs because the three of them are laughing and she can't afford to stay outside their circle of laughter. But something is not right. She looks helplessly from Ilan to Ofer to Adam and back. Something smells funny, and she laughs nervously and tries to figure out whether they can detect it, too. At the moment of the electrical short, she saw something: a picture, a real one, completely tangible, of someone who came running in from outside, from the fields, jumped up on the table, pulled down his pants, crouched down between them, and dumped a huge stinking pile of shit among the dishes and glasses. And they kept on talking as if nothing had happened, her guys, and everyone at the other tables was behaving normally too, and the nymphs fluttered and chirped, "How is everything? Is everything okay?" Yet something did not make sense to her, and everyone else seemed to have passed a course on how to act in this situation, when your son tells you something like, "But, Dad, that's my job! I stand there precisely so they'll blow themselves up on me and not in Tel Aviv," and it turns out that she's missed a lot of classes, and the air in the restaurant suddenly becomes unbearably hot, and now she realizes what happened, she feels the signs coming closer, and she starts to drip with sweat. She's had these kinds of attacks before. It's purely physical, it's nothing, just hot flashes, the rampages of menopause. It's completely beyond her control, a little intifada of the body. It happened at the ceremony after the advanced training course, in the parade courtyard at Latrun, when the formation passed by a huge wall covered with thousands of names of fallen soldiers; and at a fire demonstration in Nebi Musa to which the parents were invited; and on two or three other occasions. Once her nose bled, another time she threw up, and once she cried hysterically. And now—she laughs nervously—now she thinks she's going to have diarrhea, and it's entirely possible that she won't even make it to the bathroom, it's that bad, and she clenches and constricts her body, even her face is strained. How can they not notice what's happening to her? She looks weakly from one to the other as they talk. It's good for them to laugh: Go ahead, laugh, she thinks, let out the week's tension. But inside her body the systems are collapsing. She is a shell containing only fluids. She is a coconut. Maybe they are actors? Maybe her family has been switched? Her heart pounds. How can they not hear it? How can they not hear her heart? Loneliness closes in on her. The basement loneliness of childhood. It's so hot in here, I swear, it's like they turned on all the ovens and shut all the windows. And it stinks. Horribly. She practically gags. She has to pull herself together, and most important, she must not show them anything, not ruin this wonderful, happy evening. They're having such a good time, it's so fun here, and she's not going to ruin it for them with the stupid nonsense coming from her body, which has suddenly turned bleeding heart on her. One more minute and she'll have everything under control, it's just a matter of willpower. She just has to not think about the severity and the responsibility and the gravity with which he said, "But, Dad, that's my job!" And now, right in front of Ilan and Adam and Ofer's laughing faces, oh God, it's coming back, he's here again, in this soft lighting, among the dainty dragonflies—"How is everything? Is everything cool?"—there he is, jumping right up on the table with both feet and dumping a huge pile of shit, and a terrifying wave rises inside her, one second from now she'll have no more room in her body, it will burst out of her mouth, her eyes, her nostrils, and she desperately closes every-thing off, scurries among the treacherous orifices, and all she can think about is the relief of that guy, the immense, scandalous relief of the lowlife who jumped onto the table with two solid legs, and just like that, among the little white dishes and the delicate wineglasses and the nap-kins and the dark bottles of wine and the asparagus spears, simply crouched down and shat out a huge, steaming pile of radioactive stench. And Ora struggles with all her might to uproot her gaze from the cen-ter of the table, from the huge naked fiend smiling at her with excre-mental seduction—he isn't, he isn't here, but he's about to split her open—wait for me! she chirps with charming sweetness and pursed lips, and flits away.

A long time ago, at the beginning of Ofer's service in the Territories ("This is parenthetical," she tells Avram. "It has nothing to do with that evening in the restaurant"), they were living in Ein Karem, and she heard a strange sound from the steps that led from the back of the house down to the garden. She followed the sound to the edge of the garden and saw Ofer sitting there, wearing shorts and an army shirt—he was on leave—carving a beautiful stick with his penknife. She asked what it was, and he looked up at her with his ironic, arched eyebrows and said, "What does it look like?"

"Like a rounded stick."

He smiled. "It's a club. Club, meet Mom. Mom, meet club."

"What do you need a club for?"

Ofer laughed and said, "To beat up little foxes." Ora asked if the army didn't give him weapons to protect himself with, and he said, "Not clubs, and clubs are what we need most, they're the most efficient weapon in our situation." She said that scared her, and he said, "But what's wrong with a club, Mom? It's minimal use of force."

Ora, with uncharacteristic cynicism, asked if they had an acronym for that, "MUF, or something."

"But clubs prevent violence, Mom! They don't create it."

"Even so, allow me to feel bad when I see my son sitting here making himself a club."

Ofer said nothing. "He usually avoids getting into these arguments with me," she tells Avram. "He could never be bothered with that kind of talk, always said politics just didn't interest him." He was doing his job and that's that, and when he got out, when everything was done, he promised her he would think over exactly what had happened.

He kept on smoothing the stick until it was completely round. Ora stood over him, at the top of the steps, and hypnotically watched his skilled hands at work. "He had wonderful hands. You should see some of the things he's made. A round dining table. And the bed he made for us."

Ofer wrapped elastic webbing around the head of the stick. Ora went down and asked to touch it. For some reason it was important to her to touch it, to feel what it's like when it strikes you—"a black, rigid, unpleasant sort of fabric," she reports to Avram, and he swallows and looks out into the distance—and Ofer added more brown binding around the stick itself, and then the club was ready, and that's when he made the *move*. She shows Avram how Ofer hit his open palm with the club three times to assess its strength, to appraise its hidden force. And he played around with it, like someone would with a dangerous animal whose training has only just begun. "That was a bad moment, when I saw Ofer sitting there whittling a club. And it was important to me that you know about that."

Avram nods to confirm that he has accepted this too from her.

"Where was I?"

"Hugs," he reminds her, "and that restaurant." He likes the way she asks "Where was I?" every so often. A sloppy, dreamy, distracted young girl peers out of her face when she does.

Ora sighs. "Yes. We were celebrating Adam's birthday, and the truth is we didn't even think they'd both be home that Shabbat until the last minute. Adam was on reserve duty in the Bik'ah, and Ofer was in Hebron and wasn't supposed to get out for the weekend, but they let him go at the last minute, there was a vehicle leaving for Jerusalem, and he got home late and was exhausted. He even nodded off during dinner a couple of times. He'd had a hard week, we later learned, and he was so tired he barely knew where he was."

Avram looks at her expectantly.

"It was a lovely evening," she says, skipping tactfully over the sudden indigestion that meant she ate almost nothing the whole meal. "And then I wanted us all to toast Adam," she continues in the same tense voice, hoping she has managed to establish for Avram the fact of Ofer's abysmal exhaustion, his main line of defense in the inquiries and questionings held afterward, and in his endless arguments with her. "We always have a little toasting ritual when we're celebrating something . . ."

She hesitates again: All these family affairs of ours, all our little rituals, do they pain you? His eyes signal back to her: Go on, go on already.

"Normally, Adam never let us toast him. We weren't allowed to do that in public, where strangers could hear. He's so much like Ilan that way."

Avram smiles. "God forbid you might be overheard by all those people who booked tables months in advance so they could eavesdrop on you?"

"Exactly. But that evening Adam said yes, though only if Ofer would do it. Ilan and I quickly said, 'Fine,' we were so surprised he'd agreed at all. And I thought I'd give him my toast later, when I was alone with him, or I'd write it for him. I always used to write birthday wishes for him, to all of them actually, because I think, I thought, that these occasions were an opportunity to sum things up, or to summarize a period, and I knew he kept my cards— Hey, have you noticed we're really talking now?"

"So I hear."

"We'll have to hike the whole country three times to fit everything in."

"That's not a bad idea."

She says nothing.

"Where was I?" Avram says a while later instead of her, and replies, "The restaurant. Ofer's toast."

"Oh, the birthday."

She sinks back into her thoughts. That weekend, those final moments of the careful, fragile happiness. And she realizes what she's been doing here all these days: reciting a eulogy for the family that once was, that will never be again.

"So Ofer leaned his head between his hands and thought quietly for a few minutes. He wasn't in any hurry. He's always a little slower than Adam. In general, there's something heavier, more solid about him, his movements, his speech, even his appearance. Usually strangers who see them both think he's older than Adam. And it was so nice, the way he treated Adam's request so seriously.

"Then he said that first of all he wanted to say how happy he was to be Adam's little brother, and how in the last few years, since he'd started going to Adam's high school, and even more once he joined the battalion where Adam had served, he was getting to know Adam through all the other people who knew him—teachers, soldiers, officers. At first it got on his nerves the way everyone kept calling him Adam by mistake, and treating him as just Adam's little brother, but now . . ."

"Seriously," Ofer said in his slow, raspy, deep voice, "people are always coming up to me and talking about you—what a great guy you are, what a good friend, and how you always took the initiative. Everyone knows your jokes, and everyone in the battalion has a story about how you helped him, how you cheered him up when he was bummed out—"

"This is Adam?" Avram asks carefully. "You're talking about Adam, right?"

"Yes, we were also intrigued by this new side of him. Ilan even joked that Ofer was recklessly destroying the reputation Adam had spent years building up at home."

"Or like the bingo you invented," Ofer told Adam with a giggle, "which is still named after you at school."

"What's that?" Ilan interrupted.

"You pick seven words that are totally unlikely for a teacher to say in class. Like 'pizza,' or 'belly dancer,' or 'Eskimo.' And when class starts, everyone has the words written down in front of them, and they have to ask the teacher questions that sound all innocent, like they have something to do with the material, so that the teacher himself, without knowing it, says all the words."

Ilan leaned forward with a glimmer in his eye and slowly interlaced his fingers. "And the teacher doesn't know anything about it, of course."

"Not a thing." Adam smiled. "He's just happy to see the students suddenly so interested in his boring class."

"Ha!" Ilan said and looked admiringly at Adam. "I've raised a real snake."

Adam bowed his head modestly, and Ofer said, smiling at Ilan, "An 'inventional spark,' don't you think?" Ilan confirmed this, and bumped his shoulder against Ofer's. Ora still didn't get the rules of the game, and she didn't like what she did understand. She was impatient to get back to what Ofer had started saying to Adam.

"And who wins?" asked Ilan.

"Whoever makes the teacher say the most words from the list."

Ilan nodded. "Okay. Give me an example of how you get him to say a word."

"But Ofer was in the middle of telling Adam something," Ora reminded them.

"Hang on, Mom," Ofer said cheerfully, "this is super cool. Go on, gimme a word."

"You pick one," said Adam.

"But don't let me hear it, I'm the teacher!" Ilan laughed.

The boys leaned in, whispered, laughed, and nodded.

"But it's a history lesson," Adam said, adding a twist.

"Then we'll do the Dreyfus affair," Ilan decided. "I still remember that one a bit."

Ilan launched into an account of the French Jewish officer accused of treason, and Ofer and Adam bombarded him with questions. He talked about the trial, about the silencing of Dreyfus's defenders, about the conviction. They were more interested in Dreyfus's family, its customs, its dress and food. Ilan stuck to his lecture and avoided all the traps. Theodor Herzl showed up in the audience at Dreyfus's public humiliation. The boys' questions grew more frequent. Ora leaned back and watched, and the three of them felt her watching them and picked up the speed. Dreyfus was imprisoned and exiled to Devil's Island, Emile Zola wrote his *J'accuse!*, Esterhazy was captured and convicted, Dreyfus was released, but the boys were more interested in Herzl. *Der Judenstaat* was published, and then came Herzl's meetings with the Turkish Sultan and the German Kaiser. Ilan leaned forward and licked his lips. His eyes sparkled. The boys salivated on either side of him like two young wolves closing in on a buffalo. Ora found herself swept up in the excitement, though she was entirely unsure whom she wanted to win. Her heart was with the boys, but something about the wild enthusiasm on their faces made her crumple, and she felt compassion for the new, scant grayness gradually emerging on Ilan's temples. The First Zionist Congress convened in Basel, *Altneuland* was published, Britain offered the Zionists a state on a large piece of land in Uganda—" 'a land that will be beneficial for the health of whites,' " Ilan quoted, recalling his high school days—and Adam wondered what things would have been like had the offer been accepted: all of Africa would have been stricken with frenetic zeal had the Jews gone there and started stirring things up with their hyperactive nervousness. Ilan added, "And you can be sure that within sixty seconds there would already be deep-seated anti-Semitism."

Ofer laughed. "And then we'd have had to occupy Tanzania."

"And Kenya and Zambia!"

"Of course, just to protect ourselves from their hatred."

"And teach them to love Israel and give them a little *Yiddishkeit* with chicken soup!" Adam rolled around laughing.

"Not to mention gefilte fish," Ilan snickered, and the boys jumped up and cheered: "Bingo!"

The main courses arrived. Ora remembers every dish. Adam had steak tenderloin, Ilan ordered the goose leg, and Ofer got steak tartare. She remembers her gaze being drawn to Ofer's raw meat; she missed the vegetarian Ofer. In the weeks and months that followed, during the sleepless nights and nightmarish days when she replayed the events of that evening, minute by minute, she often wondered what really went through Ofer's mind when he ate the steak, or during that game of bingo, and whether he honestly did not remember anything—after all, they had talked about occupation and hatred and had even mentioned locking up people and releasing them, and there was even something about silencing. How could it be that not a single alarm bell had sounded in him? How had he not picked up even the vaguest association between all of that and, say, an old man with his mouth gagged, trapped in a meat locker in the cellar of a house in Hebron?

"He was just really tired," she states apropos of nothing. "His eyes were half closed and he could barely hold his head up. He hadn't slept for two whole days, and he'd had three beers, too. But somehow the game and the joking around kept him up."

There was a moment, she thinks, when it seemed as if he remembered. He suddenly asked for Adam's phone and wanted to call the army. She can see it: he held the phone in his hand. His eyebrows moved. His forehead was strained. He was trying to gather something in through the tiredness. But then he saw the screen and got excited about some new function he'd never seen before, and Adam demonstrated it for him.

"Ofer, you didn't finish toasting Adam," Ora said.

"You're off the hook," said Adam and started to devour his steak.

"No fair!" Ora pleaded. "He hasn't said anything yet!"

"Only if he wants to," Adam said. "And no violins!"

Ofer turned serious again. His face softened and hardened intermittently. His chiseled, generous lips, Avram's lips, moved unconsciously. He put down his fork. Ora noticed the exchange of amused glances between Adam and Ilan: Watch out, their eyes said, get your handkerchiefs ready.

Then Ofer spoke. "The truth is, I don't even know how I would get along in life without your help, and without the way you took care of me in all kinds of bad situations that Mom and Dad don't even know about."

That was surprising. Ora perked up, and so did Ilan. "Because we only knew the opposite situation, where Ofer took care of Adam. And he suddenly opened up a whole world we'd never known, but which I'd always somehow hoped did exist, you know? Do you understand?"

Avram nods vigorously. His lower lip surrounds his whole mouth.

"And I saw Adam lower his gaze, and he got this kind of flush on his neck, and I knew that it was true."

"And I think," Ofer continued, "that there's no one else in the world who knows me like you do, knows all my most private stuff, and who always, from the minute I was born, did only good things for me."

Adam did not comment or crack a joke. Ora felt that he really wanted her and Ilan to hear these things.

"And there's no one in the world I trust like you, and value and love like you. No one."

Ora and Ilan bowed their heads so the boys wouldn't see their eyes.

"Even though I always used to get mad at you, especially when you got preachy, or made fun of my taste in music."

"Guns N' Roses is not music," Adam put in, "and Axl Rose is not a singer."

"But I didn't know that back then, and I was so mad at you for ruining my enjoyment of them, and in the end I realized you were right. See, you improved me in every way. And you protected me from all kinds of crap, and even though you weren't exactly a bruiser, and I couldn't threaten the kids who hit me and tell them my brother would come and beat the crap out of them, I still felt that you always had my back, and you wouldn't let anyone do anything to me." Then he blushed, as though only now comprehending the candor he'd permitted himself.

There was a long silence. Everyone's heads were bowed. They had touched on the root of the matter. Ora held her breath and prayed that Ilan wouldn't try to make them laugh. That none of them would give in to their stand-up-comic reflex.

"*Lechayim,*" Ilan said softly. "Here's to our family." There were tears in his eyes, and he looked at her gratefully and held his glass up to her.

"*Lechayim,*" Adam and Ofer repeated, and to her surprise they also looked straight at her and raised their glasses. "To our family," Ofer added quietly, and his eyes met hers on a new frequency, and for one brief moment she thought—he knows.

"After that he seemed a bit stiff, stunned by his own speech, and then he leaned his head on his hands again, like this, and Adam turned to him and hugged him. He really hugged him, with both arms"—Avram sees, he sees them—"and small as Adam is compared to him, he still enveloped him, and Ofer's head leaned in, like this."

She remembers his handsome, shapely head. Back then he wasn't shaving it yet, and it was very fair after his haircut. For a minute it looked like Adam was smelling Ofer's hair, the way he used to do when Ofer was a baby and he'd just had it washed.

Her head unconsciously reconstructs the gesture and nestles into her own shoulder.

"Ilan and I watched them, and I had a feeling, maybe Ilan did too, I never asked him—"

"What feeling?"

"When they hugged, I suddenly knew, body and soul, that even when Ilan and I were gone they would stay together, they wouldn't grow apart, they wouldn't be cut off, they wouldn't be alienated, and they'd help each other out if there was a need. They would be *family*, you see?"

Avram's mouth stretches out in a tortured grimace.

"What's going to happen, Avram?" She looks up at him with tear-filled eyes. "What will happen if he—"

Avram almost shouts: "Tell me, tell me about him!"

On the drive home from the restaurant, everyone was full and soft and pliable. The boys sang a silly Monty Python song about a sexed-up lumberjack who likes to wear women's clothing, and Ora noted the heartwarming deviation from their usual puritanism, as though they were confirming that they now viewed their parents as grown-ups. In the backseat they slapped their knees, stomachs, and chests while they sang—Ofer's broad chest produced a dense, drum-like echo that excited her—and then they discussed which pub to go to. Ora and Ilan were amazed that they still had the energy to go out drinking so late, when Ofer had barely been able to keep his eyes open. Ilan asked only that they not go together into the same place and reminded them that a month ago a terrorist strapped with explosives had been caught trying to enter a Jerusalem bar. The boys put their hands to their hearts and promised gravely that they would split up: Ofer would go to the "*Shahid* Hope" pub, and Adam to the "Hezbollah Martyrs" nightclub. "Then we'll meet up in "Seventy Virgins" square and hang around downtown for a while, mostly in crowded places, and we'll get right up close to people with Middle Eastern features and piercing looks."

The next day, at eight a.m., Adam and Ofer were still asleep—they'd probably come home around dawn—and she and Ilan sat in the kitchen, still basking in the ambience of the night before, getting ready for their morning walk. Before leaving, they made a big salad for the boys, and *jachnun* and hard-boiled eggs and crushed tomatoes, to be ready when they got up. They peeled and chopped and spoke in quiet voices about the dinner, the things Ofer had said to Adam, and the rare hug. Suddenly there was a cautious knock on the door, and then a firm, foreign-sounding ring.

Ilan and Ora glanced at each other. It made no sense, but still, that kind of ring, at that time on a Saturday morning, could only mean one thing. Ora put her knife down and looked at Ilan, and his eyes grew wide. A lightning flash of insane, almost inhuman terror clotted between them. Everything slowed down until it finally froze. Even the definite knowledge that Adam and Ofer were at home iced over—because in fact, maybe they weren't. "We hadn't seen them for a whole night, and one night is a long time in Israel. Maybe something had happened, maybe they'd been called back to the army urgently. We hadn't even heard the news, how could we not have turned on the news?"

Ora's eyes sought out the car keys that Adam had taken the night before. She thought she could see them hanging on the hook, but maybe it was a different bunch. Another impatient ring. "They're at home, they're both at home now," Ora insisted adamantly, "they're asleep, there's no way this has anything to do with them." Maybe they'd left the lights on in the car and a neighbor had come to let them know. Maybe someone had broken into the car—she could accept that, she would welcome it. Another sharp knock, and neither of them moved, as though hoping to hide their existence here.

Everything suddenly had the strange quality of a dress rehearsal, as though they were practicing for something that had always been lurking, but they still could not play their parts. Ilan leaned one hand on the countertop. She saw how old he'd grown in recent years, since the boys' army service. His face was drawn, almost defeated, and she could read his thoughts: the sweet illusion in which they'd existed had been shattered. Their private underground cell had been breached. For twenty years they'd walked on air above an abyss, always knowing it was there below, and now they were falling, and they would fall forever, and life was over. Their previous lives were over.

She wanted to go to him so he could hold her, gather her in, as he always did, but she couldn't move. Another jarring ring came, and for a moment Ora experienced a peculiar sensation, the merging of two utterly different dimensions of reality: in the one, Adam and Ofer were sleeping soundly in their beds, and in the other the army had come to notify her about one of them. The two dimensions were concrete yet somehow did not contradict each other. She heard Ilan murmur, "Open the door, why aren't you opening the door?" Ora said in a foreign voice, "But they're both home, right?" He shrugged his shoulders with submissive misery, as if to say, And even if they're at home now, how long will we be able to protect them? And then Ora thought: But which one of them? Her fog was pierced with the memory of the lots. *Take a hat, take two pieces of paper . . .*

Ora opened the door and found, to her horror, a pair of awkward-looking men in uniform. They were two very young MPs, and her gaze skipped beyond them to look for the doctor who always comes with the notification team, but it was just the two of them. One had very long eyelashes, crowded like a soft brush. The fact that she noticed such trivial details was completely un-survivor-like; in this country you need sharper instincts. The other, whose face was still pocked with acne, held a printed document signed with a large stamp. He asked if Ofer was home.

In the notebook they swiped back from the man at the Kedesh River, there are still some blank pages and lines, and Ora covers one of them with tiny handwriting:

Thousands of moments and hours and days, millions of deeds, countless actions and attempts and mistakes and words and thoughts, all to make one person in the world.

She reads it to Avram.

"He'll be fine, you'll see. We're making it so he'll be fine."

"You really think so?" she asks.

"I think you know exactly what to do, always." After a pause, he says, "Show it to me for a minute." She hands him the notebook. He holds it carefully and reads to himself in a whisper: "Thousands of moments and hours . . . countless actions . . . mistakes . . . all to make one person in the world." He puts the notebook in his lap and looks at Ora, and a cloud of slight fear darkens in his eyes.

"Add another sentence," she says without looking at him, and hands him the pen. "*One person, who is so easy to destroy.* Write that."

He writes.

She remembers:

"Let's work on nested parentheses. Do you know how to do that?"

"You start with the square brackets and then do regular parentheses?"

"Let's do it like the example. They give you an example here."

"But it's tons of numbers . . . Can't you just do it for me?"

"How will you learn if I do it for you?"

"Have you no mercy on a poor child?"

"Enough, stop being a wiseass. And sit up straight, Ofer, you're practically on the floor."

"I don't even know how to read this!"

"Stop whining."

"I stopped."

"Believe me, I have plenty of things to do other than teach you about nested parentheses."

"Is the artichoke ready?"

"Wait, it takes time."

"The smell is driving me crazy."

"At least clean the table if you're going to do your homework in the kitchen. You'll stain your notebook. What page are you on?"

"A hundred and fifty. It's a huge test. I'll never pass."

"Calm down. Let's do these equations first. Read this one. Go on, stop staring."

"*Maaaan* . . ."

"I'm not a man. Now read it already!"

" 'What—separates—the—2x—and—the—3?' "

"Well, what separates them? Leave the cake alone!"

"How should I know? I don't understand what this says. Is it even in Hebrew?"

"Come on, start with the internals."

"But what do I do with this lousy 2x?"

"You multiply that by 3. Every term gets multiplied by 3! Try it."

"*Merde*, I got 2x again."

"Let's try it again, but without getting annoyed, okay? And stop eating the cake! You've already polished off half of it!"

"What can I do? I need energy."

"Now solve your 3 minus 2x."

"Mine? It's mine now?"

"Yours, yours, I'm done with school."

"I just want you to know that my brain is rotting, and it's your fault."

"Ofer, listen to me. There's no reason why you can't do this exercise."

"Yes there is."

"Well?"

"I'm stupid."

"No you're not."

"I just don't have the part of the brain that solves equations."

"Come on now, shut up, honestly, talking with you is like talking with a lawyer! It's only a few exercises in—"

"A *few*? All the way to page one sixty-one . . ."

"You've done far more complicated ones before. Remember what we had last week?"

"But in the end I did it!"

"Of course you did. When you want to, you can do anything. Now come on, let's finish this up nicely, and then we'll do the problems."

"Oh, we'll do the problems, great!"

They laugh together. His head rubs against her shoulder and he purrs like a cat, and she responds.

"By the way, has anyone fed Nicotine and rinsed out his bowl today?"

"Yes, I did. Scratch!"

She scratches his head again. "Now do the exercise."

"That's my thanks?"

"Pay attention. You're going too fast again, you're not checking it."

"Stop, Mom, I can't do it anymore! Where's the phone?"

"What do you need the phone for now?"

"I'm calling Child Protective Services—"

"Very funny. Now concentrate: once you get the principle of coefficients and simplifying terms—what are you laughing at?"

"I don't know, it's just that I don't see anything efficient or simple about this!"

They both crack up. Ofer lies down on the floor and waves his legs around.

"Come on, pull yourself together. We're not making any progress."

"Have pity on me, Mom, I'm a poor, innocent, wretched waif."

"Will you shut up already?"

"Okay, okay, what did I say?"

"Now work quietly. I don't want to hear another word out of you. Follow the sequence."

"And then you'll make me an artichoke?"

"I'd love to. It's done now, I think."

"With mayonnaise dipping sauce?"

"Yes."

"And also— Oops, sorry, I let one out. I made a mistake, a horrible mistake . . ."

"A fart isn't a mistake."

"So x equals a fart?"

They roll around laughing.

"I think we're both losing it. Come on, let's move on to the problems."

"I don't want problems! I want an easy life!"

"Is that you whistling?"

"It's not me, it's Dad from the living room."

"Ilan, do me a favor, stop whistling. As it is I'm—"

"Yes, it's breaking our concentration, Dad."

"Go on, do your work."

"I bet you now he'll come in here and do a dance to make us laugh . . ."

"*You wish!*"

"He has the ears of a wildcat. You married a wildcat."

"Enough, stop babbling. How do you approach this problem?"

"With the face of a murderer."

"Be careful, it's still hot. Dip it in this, and don't get your book dirty."

" 'If we multiply a number by 4, and add 2 to the result, we get 30.' How am I supposed to know how to do this?"

"Think: x times 4 plus 2 is 30."

"Then I know! 4x plus 2 equals 30."

"Meaning?"

"Meaning 4x equals 28. Meaning x equals 7! Hallelujah! Genius, genius!"

"Excellent. Always remember to carry. You always want x on one side and the numbers on the other."

"I'm starting to enjoy this."

"Now let's go on to this exercise. This also has one variable."

"Why is this guy so variable, I'd like to know."

"Will you be quiet and do the work?"

"Do you want some of the heart?"

"Don't you want the heart? It's the best part."

"Take it. A good, warm Jewish heart."

"Okay, now concentrate. You're almost done."

"Will you help me with Bible Studies, too?"

"Bible is Dad."

"Yeah, that's what he thinks, too."

A few days later Ilan told her that while he was lying on the couch reading the paper and their voices drifted in from the kitchen, he stopped paying attention to his article and listened to them. At first, he said, he could hardly resist getting up and going into the kitchen to put an end to Ofer's whining and acting up. He was angry at Ora's indulgence and lenience, and her excessive collaboration with Ofer's spoiled ways. With me, he thought, the whole thing would last for ten minutes, tops, and Ofer would have had all his equations solved long ago. But he felt that if he interfered he would make both of them angry at him, and he also sensed that they might not want to be stopped at all, even though they were arguing and teasing each other. So he just lay there and listened, and felt—in body and soul—the thousands of actions and words and thoughts and moments and mistakes and deeds, the slow, patient, stalactite accumulation of Ofer's being in her hands. And he knew that he could never do that. He could not sit with Ofer for so long, absorbing his frustration and defeatism, and his jabs, nor would he know how to divert them and lead him slowly to the solution.

Ora listened. It was late in the evening, the boys were in their room, and she and Ilan were lying together on the couch. His fingers played with the fine hair on the back of her neck, and her face cuddled against his. She said, "But you're so much a part of bringing them up. I don't know many fathers who are so involved in their kids' lives."

"Yes, but when I heard you in the kitchen, I don't know—"

"I mean, the whole way they think, their sense of humor, all the things they know, and their sharp wit, it's so you."

"Maybe so, I don't know, I'm sure it's both of us. I guess it's the combination of us." He felt for her hand and his fingers grasped hers. "Because I always feel that whatever I give them, they would have somehow gotten it anyway, from life, from other people. But what you give them"—the fingers of his other hand made an uncharacteristic movement, like the kneading of dough.

Avram looks at her fingers as they replay Ilan's kneading motion, and he is grateful to her for allowing him to be with them there, and to touch the soft, maternal dough of their day to day.

Ora wrapped Ilan in her arms and thrust her knee between his legs to make him feel good, and they lay entwined for several minutes. Then Ilan smiled over her head. "Still, I would have stopped his acting up a lot sooner."

Ora laughed into his neck. "I'm sure you would have, my love."

HE SIGHED DEEPLY, and she reached her foot out and touched his, to encourage and comfort him. They'd been lying in bed, awake and silent, almost the whole night. Every so often one of them would sigh, and the other's gut would tighten. This time he repaid her with a touch, his toes in the concave of her foot. She moaned softly, he sniffled, she voiced a thin syllable, he softly cleared his throat, and she began the clumsy operation of turning herself over and moving her giant hump of a stomach to the other side. Then she pushed herself closer to him, edging forward like a sea lion on the sand, until she placed her head in the round of his shoulder and asked, "Why aren't you asleep?"

"I can't," Ilan replied.

"You're anxious."

"Yes, a little. Aren't you?"

She did not move from her nest in his body, but she was no longer there. "Just tell me, you're not by any chance planning another little escape, are you?"

"No, of course not!"

"I just want you to know that if you leave this time, you won't have anywhere to come back to. It won't be like last time."

Adam mumbled in his sleep from the next room, and Ilan thought about how her voice always used to be cheerful with him; no one rejoiced at his arrival like that anymore, with the happiness and innocence and trust of a child. When he used to bask in her welcoming expression, he had felt that he was almost the person he wanted to be, and moreover, he'd believed that he could be that person, simply because Ora believed he already was. He murmured, "I'm staying, Ora, I'm not going anywhere. Why would you even think that?"

As if she hadn't heard him, she went on in the same knotted voice. "Because you can pull that same trick on me again, I can take it, but Adam will fall apart. It will finish him, and I won't let you."

Ilan repeated that he was staying, but he stopped caressing her shoulder, and Ora lay still and measured the distance between her skin and his hand, which hung limply above her. Ilan thought: Caress her, touch her. Ora waited some more, then heavily gathered her body and turned over.

Later, in the next wave of fear, they found themselves embracing again, his stomach against her back, his head buried in the back of her neck.

"I'm afraid of him," he murmured into her hair. "Do you understand? I'm afraid of an unborn baby."

"What, tell me, talk to me."

"I don't know, I feel like he already has a fully formed personality. A mature one."

"Yes." Ora smiled inside. "I feel that way, too."

"And that he knows everything."

"About what?"

"About me. About us. About what happened."

Her fingers tightened on his forearm. "You haven't done anything bad to him. All you ever did for Avram was good."

"I'm afraid of him," he whispered and hugged her more tightly. "I'm afraid of what I'll feel when I see him for the first time, and I'm afraid he'll look like him." Or worse—that he'd somehow look like both of them. A mixture of her and him. And that every time he'd look at him, he'd see how alike they actually are.

She thought about little Adam, who didn't resemble her or Ilan. Oddly, there was something of Avram in his face and expressions sometimes.

"Ora," he whispered into her neck, "don't you think we should tell him a bit about his dad? So he'll know where he came from?"

"I tell him all the time."

"How?"

"When I can't fall asleep."

"You talk to him?"

"I think to him."

"About what?"

"About Avram, about us. So he'll know."

His fingers dug through her hair, and she arched her head into the palm of his hand. The sharp smell of her scalp had intensified during the pregnancy. Ilan loved the smell, even though it was slightly unpleasant, or perhaps because of that, because it was unprocessed, peasant-like, the simple aroma of her body. This is home, he thought, with a slight flutter at his root.

She smiled quietly and pressed her buttocks against him. "In the eleventh grade, I think, I wrote to him that even if we weren't boyfriend and girlfriend, a couple, like he wanted, I felt we'd still be together forever, no matter how, but we would be. And he sent me a telegram, you know those yellegrams of his"—Ilan laughed into her nape—"saying that ever since he got my letter he was walking around with a rose in his lapel, and when people asked him what the occasion was, he said, 'Yesterday I got married.' "

"I remember, a red rose."

They said nothing. She stroked his fingers gently. Since Avram's return, even fingernails were not something to be taken for granted.

"I want us to live, Ilan."

"Yes."

"Our lives, I mean. Yours and mine."

"Of course, yes."

"I want to get out of this coffin already."

"Yes."

"Both of us."

"Yes."

"You and me, I mean."

"Yes, obviously."

"And for us to start living."

"Ora—"

"You can't spend your whole life paying for one moment."

"Yes."

"And for a crime we didn't commit."

"Yes."

"We didn't commit any crime, Ilan."

"That's right."

"You know we didn't."

"Yes, of course."

"Why don't I believe you?"

"Slowly. It will come, slowly."

"Hold me hard, carefully . . ."

She took his hand and placed it on her belly. His hand pulled back at first, but then climbed up the belly and reached higher than it had meant to. Ora lay motionless. She felt that she had sprouted giant breasts in the last few months, tremendous fruits, hippopotamus-like. She felt uncomfortable with him touching them. Her skin was stretched painfully. If he pressed, the breast would crack open. She moved his hand back to her stomach: "Feel here."

"That?"

"Yes."

"Is that really him?"

His long fingers roamed carefully over her stomach. Since they had slept together in the shed, since he had come back to live with her and Adam, he couldn't make love with her. She hadn't pushed him; she found it comfortable that way, too.

"What's this?"

"A knee, maybe an elbow."

How will I be able to love him? he thought desperately.

"Sometimes I don't know whether I'll have enough love for him," she said. "Adam fills me up so much, I don't know how I'll have room in my heart for another child."

"He's moving . . ."

"He always does that. Won't let me sleep."

"He's tough, eh? Full of strength."

"He's full of life."

They talked carefully. Through all the months of the pregnancy they had not said these simple things to each other. Sometimes, through Adam, they talked about the "baby in the belly," and guessed things about him. Privately they said almost nothing, and the due date had come and gone nine days ago.

In fact, Ilan thought—this notion had come to him every night in recent months—there's a concentrated, condensed little Avram in bed with us, and from now on he'll be with us forever. Not just like a shadow, the way we're more or less used to, but a real little Avram, alive, with Avram's moves and his walk, maybe his face, too.

Your father, Ora thought at the fetus floating inside her, and distract-edly moved Ilan's hand around and around on her stomach, once told me that at twelve he vowed that every moment in his life would be full of interest and excitement and meaning. I tried to tell him that was impossible, that no life could be only climaxes and peaks all the time, and he said, "Mine will be, you'll see."

We both liked jazz, Ilan remembered and smiled onto Ora's neck. We used to go to Bar-Barim in Tel Aviv, to hear Arale' Kaminsky and Mamelo Gaitanopoulos, and then, on the bus back to Jerusalem, we'd always sit in the back row and scat sing our way through the whole ses-sion, and people would get annoyed but we didn't care.

I only knew your dad from the age of sixteen, Ora thought. Now maybe I'll know what he was like as a child.

They lay there for a long time, close to each other, and talked silently to Ofer.

One day, when he was about five—Ora writes in a leftover page of the blue notebook—*Ofer stopped calling us "Mom" and "Dad" and started calling us "Ora" and "Ilan." I didn't mind, I even liked it, but I could see that it really bothered Ilan. Ofer said, "How come you're allowed to call me by my name, and I'm not allowed to call you by yours?" And then Ilan said something to him that I remember to this day: "There are only two people in the whole world who can call me 'Dad.' Do you know how great that is for me? And think about it: Are there that many people in the world who you can call 'Dad'? Not really, right? So do you want to give that up?" I could see that Ofer was listening, and that it spoke to him, and ever since then he really did always call him "Dad."*

"What are you writing?" Avram asks, propping himself up on one arm.

"You scared me. I thought you were asleep. Have you been watching me for a long time?"

"Thirty, forty years."

"Really? I didn't notice."

"So what were you writing?"

She reads it to him. He listens, his heavy head tilted. Then he looks up: "Does he look like me?"

"What?"

"I'm asking."

"If he looks like you?"

And for the first time, she describes Ofer to him in detail. The open, large, tanned face, the blue eyes that are both tranquil and penetrating, and the eyebrows so fair you can hardly see them, just like she used to have. The wide, lightly freckled cheeks, and the slight, ironic smile that dispels the severity of the rounded forehead. The words tumble out of her, and Avram swallows them up. Sometimes his lips move, and she realizes that he is memorizing her words, trying to make them his, but it occurs to her that they will never really be his until he writes them down himself.

She is embarrassed by her fluent gush of speech, but she cannot stop because this is exactly what she needs to do now: she must describe him in minute detail, especially his body. She must give a name to every eyelash and fingernail, to every passing expression, to every movement of his mouth or hands, to the shadows that fall on his face at different times of day, to each of his moods, to every kind of laughter and anger and wonderment. This is it. This is why she brought Avram with her. To give a name to all these things, and to tell him the story of Ofer's life, the story of his body and the story of his soul and the story of the things that happened to him.

She holds up a finger. "Wait. What did I just think of? Umm . . ." Her fingers play in the air, trying to birth a vague spark from it. "It was something of yours that I remembered. What was it? Oh, of course!" She laughs. "You once had this idea, you wanted to write a story, in the army, just before you started the one about the end of the world, remember?"

"About my body." He smiles, then snickers, quickly belittling, dismissive.

But Ora won't let him off the hook. "You thought of writing a sort of autobiography, where every chapter is about a different part of your body—"

"Yes, an *autobodyography*. It was silly . . ."

"And you let me read the chapter about your tongue, remember?"

He waves both hands in protest. "Leave it, really, such nonsense."

"It was horrible. It was slander, not autobiography. Honestly, Avram, if you ever need a character witness, don't invite yourself."

He laughs an unpleasant, dishonest laugh, as if wanting to appease her without really acquiescing. Something jackal-like flashes in the depths of his eyes, reminding her of how twisted and cruel he could be with himself when the evil spirits tormented him. And she suddenly yearns for him, an unbearable yearning, a sharp, blazing longing for him, for all of him.

He says: "Look at us, we're two old people now."

"Just as long as we don't grow old before we grow up."

He looks at her for a long time, reading her thoughts. His gaze is steady and strange, with no ill intentions. On the contrary. It seems to her that he has only kind, tender thoughts for her now. "Ora."

"What?"

"Can I join you for a bit?"

"Where?"

"No, never mind."

"Wait! You mean . . . ?"

"No, only if you—"

"But are you . . . Wait, now?"

"No?"

Her body starts to agitate and flutter in the sleeping bag. "You mean . . ."

He nods with his eyes.

"My place or yours?"

Avram wriggles out of his sleeping bag and stands up, and she opens her zipper and spreads her arms out to him: "Come, come, don't say anything, just come here already. I thought you never would." He collapses into her sleeping bag, heavy and dense, and their bodies are stiff and stammering, wrapped in too many layers of clothes and awkwardness. Their hands stutter and bump and pull back, and it's not working, that much is already clear, it's not right, it's a mistake, they shouldn't even go back to that place, and she's afraid of what will happen if she forgets Ofer for a moment, if he is suddenly abandoned without protection, and she knows exactly what is going through Avram's mind: the criminal returning to the scene of the crime—that's what is in his twisted brain right now. "Don't think," she moans into his ear, "don't think anything." She presses her fingers on his temples, and Avram is on top of her, his heavy bones, his flesh, and he rams his body against hers with immense force, as if fighting to break through himself even before he can break into her, but she isn't ready yet, either. "Wait, wait." She moves her mouth away from his wandering lips. "Wait, you're crushing me."

For several moments they are like two people who have struck up a conversation and are trying to remember—not who the other person is, but who they themselves are. But then, here and there, behind an opened button, an unhooked clasp, their scents rise, tongues taste, fingers slip between a shirt and pants, and suddenly skin, warm and alive, skin against skin, skin in skin, and here is a mouth, an eager and sucking and sucked-on mouth, and Avram moans: her mouth, her beloved mouth, and only then does he remember, and his tongue touches her lips lightly, probing, testing, wondering. Ora freezes: It's nothing, she reminds him silently, just two millimeters. But something does feel more wilted. He licks and sucks lightly, carefully, gently. Something has fallen asleep there, that's all, but it's warm, and it's hers, it's the pain imprinted on her, and his healing powers rise up. It's her, with everything she now is.

The dog scampers around them and yelps, trying to shove her face in between them, sniffing longingly. Then, shoved away, she sprawls nearby with her back to them, and a shivering furrow of insult plows through her fur. Avram's hand, spread wide, supports Ora's back and tightens and gathers her into him. "Wait, slowly now, give me your hand, give me." A hand on a breast, softer and larger than it was. Yes, they both feel it, she knows through his hand. "Your sweet breasts," he whispers into her ear, and she interlaces her fingers with his and wanders around her body with him. "Feel it, feel this," and everything is broader and fuller, a woman, "touch, feel how soft," yes. "You're velvet, Ora'leh." "Suckle on me." A long silence. But it is then that they are both transported, and Neta flies through Avram's head: Where are you, Nettush, we have to talk, listen, we have things to talk about; and Ora for an instant is with Ilan, the touch of his hands, the bones of his wrist, their tanned skin, the power contained in them. She used to run her finger over his wrists and feel as though she were touching a heavy iron key, the secret of his masculinity. But then the Character, Eran, also pops up in her mind, with his lips that turn pale with passion for her, with his feverish, crazed pleas: Now wear this, now put this on—how dare he show up here? And then, to her surprise, two long thumbs smooth over her body, full lips flutter, dark, plum-like, and where did they even come from, and she tightens her whole body toward Avram, "Come, you, you," and Avram responds immediately, back from his wanderings, she remembers him by the signs, the tight grip, his head burrowing in the round of her neck, his hand softly cupping her head as though she were a baby—Ora whose head must be protected—and his other hand strokes her stomach, clinging to it with excited fingers, and she smiles, his hunger for the belly of a woman, soft, large, full (she always felt it in his fingertips, and could almost guess by the way his fingers touched her stomach, could almost draw the figure of the fantasy woman he truly desired), and now she can finally give him something of that, not just the taut, boyish drum skin she had back then. He is grateful, she senses it immediately, his entire flesh exalts her funny little stomach, which has found a use after all, and his mouth is hungry for hers, and his fervor, it's all familiar and beloved, a huge wave of longing breaks between them. *We*, she wails in her head, a she-wolf of many udders and nipples, and Avram sucks on them all. Here we are! she rejoices, squirming beneath him. This is how we are, and always have been, and this is how we put thigh to thigh, and our feet interlace, and our hands, and all the corners of our bodies, even the most remote, elbows, ankles, behind the knees, carnivalesque excitement, and Ora whispers something in his ear, and then reaches the tip of her tongue to the tip of his tongue, a sting of moisture from within her, and they both ignite, and his blacksmith's arms carry her, and her head drops back as though decapitated, and together they thrash the earth beneath her, and he is at her neck, his teeth on the artery, grunting and groaning, and she, "Don't stop, don't stop," let him gallop and bellow and drum her with his loins to the earth, and he is one and he is with her, there is no other woman with them, only he and she now, a man and a woman going about their business—that's what he used to tell her: "Now we're a man and a woman going about our business," and he would tempt her with the madness of his strange, formal language, and the way he turned his back on the whole world, and with one thrust he would release her from the torture of thinking about Ilan, just a man and a woman going about their business. Now too, there is no world outside their body, no breath outside their breath, no Ilan, no Neta, no Ofer, no Ofer, no Ofer, yes, yes there is an Ofer, if Avram and Ora are like this then there is an Ofer, there is, there will be, there will be an Ofer, leave Ofer now, release him for one minute . . .

Hours go by, slowly. As though they have been preserved in some distant cellar, in jars of pickled time. They fall asleep and awake and return. They cross expanses, plains, absences, insults, longings, and regrets. And again he slows down, he slows and stops exactly at the moment she wants him to, so they can gather strength together. A quiet circle breathes heavily in the eye of the storm, and they curl up inside it, and Avram is quiet, perhaps asleep, dissipated, contracting inside her, and she remembers his deep, steep dive, now he is a prehistoric ocean creature, a fish with one half fossilized, turning over inside her, diving into her depths, and now he is there, now he will not move for a moment, he will just slowly throb, resting among the corals of her flesh, hallucinating inside her, and she waits, she waits, and he starts to move again, very slowly, and she moves with him, her lips against his shoulder, very focused, she remembers him fat and heavy and clumsy, and the dance that emerges from him, and now slowly his scent will change, she starts to smile, it's a scent that only Avram has, and only in these moments, and you cannot describe it in words.

"One day, not now, one day," she murmurs afterward, playing with the curls on the back of his neck, "you'll write about our walk."

They lie naked under the sky canopy as the wind caresses them with soft brushes.

"I wanted so badly to be filled up with you," she says.

The dog is lying closer to them now, but she does not submit when Ora invites her to come closer, to be stroked by her free hand, and she does not look directly at the two bodies whitening in the moonlight. When her gaze meets them, she runs a tongue of discontent over her lips.

"What?" He wakes from a doze of repletion. "What did you say about the walk?"

"I'll buy you little notebooks, like I used to, whatever you need, and you'll write about us."

He laughs in embarrassment. His fingers tap a light rebuke on her neck.

"About me and you," Ora says gravely, "and about how we walked, and about Ofer. Everything I told you." She takes his right hand and kisses his fingertips, one after the other. "And don't stress about it. For all I care, you can take a year, two, ten, however much you need."

Avram thinks it will be a miracle if he ever writes anything more complex than a restaurant order again.

"You just have to remember everything I'm telling you. What do you have such a big head for? Because I'll forget, I know I will, and you'll remember everything, every word. And in the end, you'll see, we'll give birth to a book." She laughs softly at the twinkling stars.

"Do you know that Ilan went to look for you?" she murmurs into his shoulder.

"When?"

"Then."

"When the war was over?"

"No, at the beginning."

"I don't understand. What . . . ?"

"He got all the way to the Canal—"

"No way."

"From Bavel. He just walked off the base."

"That can't be, Ora, what are you talking about?"

"I'm telling you."

His back hardens under her hand, and Ora is amazed at her stupidity: all she had in her mouth were the pleasurable murmurs and purrs of afterward, and then this came out.

"On the second day of the war, or the third, I can't remember."

Avram sits up abruptly, his nakedness still soft and anointed in her. "No, that can't be, we'd already lost the Canal." He searches her face for clues. She is still dizzied by the sweetness of her body, still fluttering yet already abandoned. "It was all full of Egyptians. Ora, what are you saying?"

"But we still had a few strongholds, no?"

"Yes, but how could he . . . There was no way to get to them, the Egyptians were twenty kilometers into our territory. Where did you come up with this?"

She turns her back to him, hunches into a ball, and curses herself. Twenty-one years I waited with this, so why now?

"Hey, Ora?"

"In a minute."

Why now, after they made love? Which demon had spurred her to ruin it? But the fact that we slept together, she tells herself firmly, was so good, and it was the best thing we could do for Ofer. "Just don't regret it!" She turns to him and her heart sinks, because it's there, that same expression she saw in his face after the last time, when they conceived Ofer. His face has fallen, emptied out.

"I don't regret it, it's just that you're suddenly laying this story on me."

"I didn't . . . I didn't think I was going to tell you. It just came out."

"But what is the story?" he whispers.

"He left Bavel with the water tanker, on the second or third day. Forged a transit order and left. He got all the way to the HQ at Tassa. And from there he hitched a ride in a jeep, I think, with a Canadian or Australian TV crew. A cameraman and a reporter, two crazy guys in their sixties, and they were high, you know those disaster freaks."

"But what was he thinking?" Avram wonders feverishly, and Ora gestures: I'm getting there.

"The jeep ran out of gas in the middle of the desert, so he set off alone, on foot, at night, no map and almost no water, and all around him—well, you know."

No, Avram says voicelessly, tell me.

What she heard from Ilan one morning twenty-one years ago, she now tells Avram in detail—she remembers quite a bit, in fact—finally bringing the story full circle.

Ilan walked. He was scared of the roads and walked only on the sides, through sand that was sometimes knee-high. Every time he saw a vehicle, he fell flat and hid. All night he walked alone among the charred remains of jeeps and APCs, smoldering tanks and cracked fuel tankers. Egyptian armored vehicles passed him twice. Then he heard a wounded Egyptian soldier crying, begging for help, but he was afraid of traps and didn't get close to him. Here and there he saw a charred body with black stumps sticking up and the head bent backward, mouth agape. A burned helicopter with its propeller missing was pinned into the side of a dune; he couldn't tell if it was ours or theirs. Soldiers still sat inside, leaning forward, looking very intent. He walked on.

"He just walked. He didn't even know if he was heading in the right direction. You asked what he was thinking, and he wasn't. He walked because he walked. Because you were there at the end of the road.

Because only by chance were you there instead of him. I don't know, I think I would have done the same thing. Maybe you would have too, I don't know."

Because that's exactly the way she's walking here, Avram thinks and tries to stop the mounting tremors in his body. She is walking because she is walking. Because Ofer is there, at the end of the road. Because she's decided that this is how she will save him, and no one will dissuade her from that. "I wouldn't do that," he says angrily, buttressing himself against what her story is piling up on top of him, closing in on him from one minute to the next. "I wouldn't have gone out to find him like that, I'd have been scared to death."

"Yes you would have. That's exactly the kind of thing you would have done." An act of greatness, she thinks. A misdeed.

"I'm not so sure," he hisses through gritted teeth.

"And I'll tell you something else. It was exactly because of everything he'd learned from you over the years that he knew it could be done."

What he remembered from that night, Ilan told her only once, at daybreak. He squeezed her suddenly from behind, as if in his sleep, trapped her between his arms and legs, and emptied the story into her spasmodically. Now it was her turn to do the same to Avram. She hadn't meant to tell him, Ilan had made her swear she would never, under any circumstances, in any situation, tell him. But maybe, she thinks, Ilan didn't know the story would burst out of *him* either, a moment before Ofer was born. And besides, it was enough. Enough with the secrets.

Ilan kept walking. It started to get light. Every so often he had to hide in some bushes, or in the shady folds of sand dunes. His eyes and nose filled with sand. His teeth were gritty with sand. A soldier with a cushy job in Intelligence, armed with an SKS, no bullets, no gear, one water canteen.

He lay down to rest in a ditch and must have fallen asleep, because when he opened his eyes there was a guy in glasses sitting next to him, gesturing for him to be quiet. He was a tankist from Brigade 401 and his tank had been hit, killing his entire crew. He'd pretended to be dead when the Egyptians had looted the tank. So these two, with one water canteen and a torn map, navigated for several hours—in total silence because they were afraid of Egyptian commando units—until they reached the coast and saw an Israeli flag, shredded and bedraggled but still flying from the broken, sunken roof of the Hamama stronghold.

The whole time she talks, Avram frantically runs his thumbs over his fingertips, as though he has to count them over and over again. I'm not, he murmurs to himself, it can't be. What is she babbling about?

"It's a fact. It happened."

"Ora, listen, don't play with me about this."

"Have I ever played with you?" she answers angrily.

"Hamama was one kilometer from my stronghold."

"One and a half."

"And how come he never told me anything?"

"Didn't you ever tell him anything?" she'd asked Ilan back then.

"If I'd reached him, he'd know. I didn't, so I didn't tell him."

Even without touching Avram, she can feel what is occurring inside him. She pulls up her sleeping bag over her nakedness.

"I don't understand!" he almost yells. "Explain to me again, slowly, how did it happen?"

"Think about it. On Yom Kippur he was in Bavel. They already knew that the strongholds were falling and there were loads of casualties. There were horrible rumors. And also, he listened in on the Egyptian networks and heard—"

"What do you mean 'listened in'?" Avram jumped up, furious. "He wasn't a radio operator, he was a translator! Who gave him permission to intercept networks?"

"I don't know if anyone 'gave him permission.' He probably found an unmanned scanner, and in between translation shifts he sat and played with the frequencies. You can imagine what kind of chaos it was there in the first few days."

"This is just impossible." Avram shakes his heavy head. "I don't know why you would tell me something like this."

He suddenly remembers Ilan the teenager, scanning the old radio in Avram's house for Willis Conover's jazz program on the Voice of America. His green eyes narrow, his long fingers gently turn the dial. Avram gets up and starts to pull on his clothes. He cannot hear this news with nothing on.

"Why are you getting up?"

"I have to know, Ora. Did he hear something on the network?"

"Wait, I'm getting there, let me—"

"Did he hear me?" His eyes gape.

"I can't do it like this." She gets up and also dresses quickly. "With—you—pressuring—me—like—this!"

"But what could he have done there?" Avram yells, one leg hanging out of his pants. They fumble around, each hopping on one foot, battling rebellious pants and shouting, and the dog barks fearfully. "What was he looking for?!"

"*You!* He was looking for you!"

"Is he an idiot? What is he, Rambo?"

They sit down breathlessly, facing each other.

"I need some coffee." Avram gets up and gathers wood and twigs in the dark. They light a fire. The night is cold and seething. Birds screech as in a dream, toads croak with thick voices, mongooses churr. Dogs bark in the distance, and the bitch scurries around, restlessly watching the dark valley. Ora wonders if she can hear her pack barking. Perhaps she regrets leaving them.

"Listen, they wanted to court-martial him after the war," she says quietly. "But in the end they let it go. The circumstances. The chaos. They dropped it."

"But he barely knew how to shoot! What was he thinking? Didn't you ask him?"

"I did."

"And what did he say?"

"Well, what could he say? He said he was mostly looking for someone to shoot him."

"What?"

" 'Someone to do him a favor,' " she quotes. "What are you looking at? That's what he said."

At ten a.m., Ilan and the tankist reached the Hamama stronghold on the banks of the Suez Canal, opposite the city of Ismailia. For the first time, they saw the Egyptians crossing the Canal en masse, not far away, streaming into the Sinai Peninsula. They stood staring. It was hard to believe the scene. Ilan told her, "Somehow it wasn't frightening. We felt like we were watching a movie."

They called out to the soldier watching them from the tower near the gate, waved a white undershirt, and asked him to let them in. A short burst of fire came from the stronghold, and they ran and fell to the ground, spread their arms out in front of them and kept shouting. The gate opened a crack and a frightened-looking officer with an Uzi aimed at them peered out. "Who are you?" he yelled. Ilan and the guy replied that they were Israelis. The officer screamed at them not to move. "Let us in!" they begged, but he wasn't in any hurry. "Where are you from?" They gave him their unit numbers. "No, where in Israel?" "Jerusalem," they both replied, and glanced at each other. The officer considered this, signaled for them not to move, and disappeared. The earth below their feet trembled. Behind their backs they could hear the hum of Egyptian tanks. "Where d'you go to school?" Ilan hissed without moving his lips. "Boyer," the guy said, "a year below you." "You mean you know me?" Ilan exclaimed. The soldier smiled. "Who didn't? You were always with that other one, the fat guy with long hair who jumped off the tree." The gate swung open and the officer motioned for them to approach slowly, on their knees, with their hands up.

Ghosts with bloodshot eyes gathered around them. Filthy ghosts covered with white dust. From all ends of the stronghold they closed in around the two new guys. They silently listened to their report on what they'd seen on the way. The stronghold commander, a tired, worn-out man twice Ilan's age, asked what he was doing in this area. Ilan looked him in the eye and said he'd been sent from Bavel to remove classified information and secret equipment from Magma, and asked when he could go there. The soldiers gave one another sideway looks. The commander just grimaced and left, taking the tankist with him. A fat reservist with a blunt look turned to Ilan and said in a drawl, "Forget about Magma. Those guys are done for. And even if by some miracle anyone's still alive there, the Egyptians are throttling them from all directions." Ilan was astonished. "Then why doesn't someone go help them? Why doesn't the Air Force take out the Egyptians?" The soldiers snickered. "The Air Force? Forget it," said the fat reservist. "Forget everything you know about the IDF." The others mumbled in concurrence. "You should have heard the guys from Hizayon crying over the radio," said a blond soldier with a soot-blackened face. "Depressed the hell out of us." Ilan whispered: "Crying? They really cried?" The fat guy said, "They cried, and they cursed us for not coming to help. Don't worry, we'll be crying soon, too." Another soldier, with a bandaged arm hanging in a filthy fabric sling, said, "We know how it goes now, all the stages." A short, dark-skinned sergeant piped up: "You hear everything here. You hear it right up to the last minute, right up to when they shit themselves. Live broadcast." A squat reservist added, "We've gone through it with a few strongholds by now." They all talked at Ilan together, interrupting each other. Their voices had no colors. Ilan sensed they were taking advantage of his presence to talk to one another through him.

He turned away and staggered over to a corner and sat down on the floor. He looked around and did not move. His brain was empty. Every so often someone came up to him and tried to engage him, asked what he knew about the war and about the situation in Israel. The medic forced him to drink some water and ordered him to lie down on a stretcher. He lay down obediently and must have fallen asleep for a while. He soon awoke when an earthquake shook the ground and a cloud of dust thickened the air. A faint alarm rang out somewhere in the distance, and then came hurried footsteps from all directions, and panicked shouts. Someone tossed him a helmet. He stood up and walked around the bunker, confused, from wall to wall, amid the commotion of a disturbed ants' nest. He felt as if he were walking very slowly through a fast-forwarded movie and that if he reached out to the soldiers dashing around him, his hand would go right through their bodies.

"Ora."

"What?"

"When did he tell you all this?"

"The morning Ofer was born."

"What, in the delivery room?"

"No. We were still at home. Before we left for the hospital. Very early in the morning."

"He just woke you up and started telling you?"

She blinks, trying to understand why the details are so important to him, amazed at how, just like in the old days, his soothsaying instincts have awakened. "Look, it was the first and last time I heard the story."

"Then how do you remember everything?"

"I can't forget that morning. Every single word." She looks away, but he spies, he scans, sharp and keen, and she knows: he can feel something. He just doesn't understand what.

. . .

The bombardment stopped. People calmed down, took off their steel helmets and flak jackets. Someone made Turkish coffee and handed Ilan a cup. He stood up, walked mechanically to the commander, and asked if he could go back to his base at Um Hashiba now. People poked their heads up over maps and transceivers and looked at him as if he were crazy. They repeated his question to one another. "You're a real space cadet," they scoffed. "The only way you leave this place is with broken dog tags in your mouth."

"And that's when he finally grasped what he'd gotten himself into," Ora said.

"I didn't know," Avram whispers, pained.

Ora thinks: Wait till you hear how much you didn't know.

"They stuck an Uzi in his hand and asked if he knew how to shoot it. He said he'd done target practice six months ago. They smiled disdainfully and sat him down by some device. I think it was something for night vision—"

"SLS," Avram murmured. "Starlight scope, we had one at Magma, too."

"—and they told him to snap out of it because the Egyptians were coming and it would be rude to greet them in that state. 'Cause at that point they were still joking around."

He couldn't see anything through the telescope and probably didn't know how to use it, but all night he heard shouting in Arabic, very close, and large objects splashing in the water, and he realized the Egyptians were still crossing. Shells fell constantly and shook the stronghold. Every so often he told himself: Avram is dead. My friend Avram is dead, his body is close by. But even though he kept repeating the words, he still couldn't feel their meaning. He couldn't feel simple pain or even bewilderment at not feeling pain.

They sit quietly, both their hearts suddenly speeding up, beating down the questions that will not be asked. What did you think, Ora? What did you think when we called you and told you to take a hat and two pieces of paper? Did you really have no clue what you were drawing? And what did you secretly hope? Which name did you want to pick out of the hat? And had you known then what would happen—no, don't ask that question. Still, he has to, he has to know for once: Had you known what would happen, which name would you have wanted to pick?

At four in the morning someone took over his position. Ilan ran out to the bunker and a shell flew past his head. Horrified, he shrank into one of the pigeonholes in the side of the trench. "Where's the latrine?" he yelled at a bearded soldier hunched nearby in the moat, his whole body shaking. "Wherever you take a shit, that's the latrine," the guy groaned. Ilan felt as if his pants were about to fill up any second. He tore them down, and for a few blessed moments forgot about everything—the war, the shelling, Avram whom he'd lost—and focused entirely on emptying his bowels.

When he got to the war room afterward, the silence terrified him. Someone signaled for him to climb up the lookout point and look west. And there he saw a massive carpet of white and pale yellow moving toward the stronghold like a tidal wave floating through the desert.

"Theirs," a soldier spat out. "Probably twenty tanks. All the guns are at us."

And the bombardment began. Tanks fired, a battery of mortars that appeared on a distant hilltop fired, and an Egyptian Sukhoi flew over and dropped bombs. The air and the earth shook. Everything in front of Ilan's eyes shook. People and concrete walls and tables and transceivers and weapons. Every object diverged from its natural shape and hummed wildly. A new discharge of diarrhea surged in Ilan's bowels. He turned and ran to his pigeonhole.

"The world's dead," muttered a young redhead in military long johns as he ran past, and Ilan dimly realized it might be time to write letters— or something like that—to his parents, and to Ora and Avram, and then he realized he'd never write anything to Avram again. Not notes in class, not lewd limericks, not ideas for recordings or Ephraim Kishon quotes or quasi-Talmudic interpretations of *Fanny Hill*. There would be no more songs in Rashi script describing the charms of their female classmates, nor long conversations in sign language during class, right in front of the teachers. No sweet dreams about the ultimate Israeli movie—a *neon-realist* film—which Ilan would direct based on Avram's screenplay. No rhymed letters full of horny cogitations, like the ones that flew among the various bases to which they were each sent, already stamped with circles of ink for the censor's drool spots. No messages— transmitted in code that was unbreakable because it was based on their own secrets and trivia—which they sent each other over the military teleprinter. Gone were their joint voyages of discovery to the new continents of Bakunin and Kropotkin, Kerouac and Burroughs, and Fielding's *Tom Jones* and *Joseph Andrews*, or Druyanov's *Book of Jewish Jokes and Wit.* Finished were the jokes, Ilan finally realized, the witticisms, the repartee, the rude puns, the comprehension with one glance, the deep, dark, mutual identification between two spies in enemy land, two only children and what always linked them together, beyond the hysterical laughter to the point of tears.

That was it. He would no longer have anyone to marvel with at *On Aggression* and *Thus Spoke Zarathustra*, which they read to each other out loud in the valley of Yafeh Nof, perched on a rock known as "the elephant tusk." And whom would he argue with, while running through a hole in the fence of the Bahad 15 base in the middle of the night, about Moshe Kroy's concepts or the blues chords encoded in Beatles songs? Who would dramatize and sketch and record with him on the clumsy Akai tape recorder the stomachachingly exhausting arguments between Naphta and Settembrini from *Magic Mountain*? There would be no more quotes from the sacred poetry of David Avidan and Yonah Wallach or from *Catch-22* or *Under Milk Wood*—a song of praise for the human voice, from which Avram could recite entire pages by heart. And who else in the world would manage to drag him to the offices of *Yedioth Aharonot* in Tel Aviv for a meeting with the editor in chief, who was surprised to discover that they were only boys, and that the idea to which they had alluded in their letter—"which, if permitted, we may unfurl in your honor's ears solely in a face-to-face meeting"—namely that once a month the entire newspaper should be written by poets ("all the sections," Avram explained gravely to the astounded editor, "from the main headline down to the sports and ads. Even the weather")? Only with Avram would he live a whole life, parallel to their own and hidden to all, in the smoky rooms of *DownBeat* magazine, which they stole every month from the Music Academy's library, and with which they carefully planned their nightly entertainment at Carnegie Hall, Preservation Hall, and the jazz dens of New Orleans, and fantasized about new jazz albums, and books they could not get in Israel, though they could entertain wild conjectures about their content—Duke Ellington's *Music Is My Mistress* drove them crazy for weeks, based solely on the reviews and the ads and the title. And who would dig through Ginsburg on Allenby Street with him, looking for secondhand instruments? Who would buy for him, with money he did not have, Stan Getz and John

Coltrane albums, and open his ears to the political protest of jazz and blues, which he had never detected or imagined before Avram? No one in the world would cheerfully call him "progeny of languid seed," or "misbegotten Adullamite," or "gout-ridden vesicle." And who else would thrash out with him the finer points of the Hebrew language and its Greek borrowings? Who would compliment him after a brilliant move in backgammon by yelling, "Mighty is your roar, O lion!"?

There would be no rowdy competitions to recite the Ayalon-Shen'ar Arabic-Hebrew dictionary by heart, and therefore, no one would hit him with *tadahlaz:* "to dally in the corridors, of parliament etc." (of course Ilan had to remember the "etc."), or slip him, in a crowded elevator, *nahedah*—"a maiden with rounded, full breasts." Gone were their Arabized Hebrew and Hebraized Arabic: he could not call bottles *bakabik* instead of *bakbukim*, or birds *tzapafir* instead of *tziporim*, or condoms *kanadem* for *kondomim*, or buttocks *aka'ez* for *akuzim*. And who would there be to immerse him in a bubbling cauldron, pass him with the call of the wild, carry him through a storm in his talons, and shuffle him off this mortal coil?

He went back to the war room just as the Israeli tanks flanked the Egyptian tanks and set two of them on fire. The soldiers throughout the stronghold cheered and hugged. They waved excitedly at the Israeli tanks and began to prepare for their rescue. When the forces disappeared over the sand dunes in pursuit of the unharmed Egyptian tanks, a heavy, toxic silence spread through the stronghold. The soldiers stood with their arms suspended awkwardly, mid-wave.

A few moments later, a wounded Egyptian soldier climbed out of his tank with flames shooting up from his shoulders. He jumped off the tank and started running around with his hands held high, until he finally collapsed facedown, convulsed, and eventually stopped moving. He lay there in strange surrender as the flames engulfed his body. Four Egyptian APCs showed up and discharged a few soldiers in camouflage fatigues, who looked at the stronghold and consulted. The stronghold commander gave an order, and everyone who had a weapon started shooting. Ilan, too. The first shot, his only one in the war, punctured his eardrum and scarred him with a constant ringing sound. The Egyptian soldiers jumped back into the APCs and retreated. Ilan pulled a water canteen out of an abandoned gear belt and gulped down almost the entire contents. His knees were shaking. The thought that he could have killed a person, and that he really wanted to, ripped off a layer of film that had been covering him since he began this journey.

The commander called him over, said he didn't care where he'd come from, but from now on he was under his command. He told him to circle through the lookout positions and take care of anything the men asked for. Over the next several hours, Ilan hauled crates of ammunition, jerry cans of water and generator fuel, and sandwiches churned out by the medic. Together with a thick-bearded, reticent soldier, he dismantled a MAG from an APC in the yard and helped erect it on the northern post. He gathered more and more "administrative material," papers and forms and activity logs, and burned them in the yard.

When he stopped to pee, a thought came to him. He went up to the APC, untied and rolled back the camouflage net, and peered in at the pile of instruments. He stood looking at them for a long time. Suddenly he jumped up as though someone had slapped him and ran as fast as he could to look for the Intelligence NCO. He dragged him back to the APC and explained what he wanted to do.

The NCO stared at him, then laughed loudly, cursed him, and yelled that HQ would kick his ass if anything happened to any of the instruments. In the same breath he added that in an hour or two they'd have to douse the whole thing with gasoline and burn it anyway. Ilan said, "Just gimme one instrument for an hour, that's all." The NCO shook his head and crossed his arms over his chest. He was a big guy, taller and broader than Ilan. Ilan said quietly, "We're all going to die. Why would you cheap out on me for one lousy VRC?" The NCO tied the camouflage net back on the APC and whistled to himself. When he finished, he turned and saw Ilan still standing there. "Get lost," he hissed, "there's nothing for you to do here." Ilan said, "Half an hour, you can time me." The NCO turned red. He snarled that Ilan was getting on his nerves, and besides, the transceiver at Magma had been destroyed ages ago, so there weren't any transmissions coming out of there anyway. Ilan smiled and asked pleasantly, almost sweetly ("Well, when Ilan wants something . . . ," Ora says, and Avram nods), "Just tell me one thing. What other instruments do they use in the strongholds?" The NCO, thrown by Ilan's friendliness, muttered that Magma probably had a few PRC-6s, but there was no chance anything was left there. Ilan asked if *this* scanner could pick up a PRC-6 frequency. The NCO shoved Ilan's hand off the instrument, fastened the net again, and growled that if Ilan didn't get lost, he was done for. Ilan, with his usual coolheadedness, smiled again and said that if the NCO gave him an instrument now, just for an hour, he promised, he swore, not to tell the Egyptians when they came that he was the Intelligence NCO.

"What did you say?" the NCO blurted. Ilan pinned him to the APC with his arms, and repeated his offer face-to-face. The NCO's eyes darted around in search of help, but Ilan could already see the wheels in his mind moving like a very simple abacus. "You're fucked up," the NCO panted in his ear, "you're an asshole, a spy, this is treason." But he spoke in a whisper that disclosed the results of his calculations. Ilan let go. They stood facing each other. "Where did you come from?" the NCO whispered hoarsely. "Who are you, anyway?" Ilan flooded him with his green eyes and shamelessly mimed fingernails being torn out and electrodes being hooked up to his balls. The guy moaned. His lips moved silently. All this lasted maybe ten seconds. The NCO could no longer deal with such a terrifying scenario and voluntarily gave in. Without a word, he undid the camouflage net and extracted a VRC device. He placed it on a small wooden table outside the war-room bunker and turned to leave. Ilan grabbed his arm and asked: "Are you sure this can pick up a PRC-6?"

"No," the NCO mumbled, avoiding Ilan's eyes like a hypnotist's. "It's not even in the right range."

"Then make it in the right range."

The NCO swallowed and hooked up the instrument with a wire to the only antenna that hadn't yet collapsed. Then he pulled out a screwdriver, removed the instrument lid, dug through its innards, and expanded the frequency range. When he finished, he got up and walked away without looking at Ilan, his arms hanging by the sides of his body and the back of his shirt soaked with sweat.

As Ora talks, Avram slowly pulls his sleeping bag around his body like a cocoon. Only his white face peers out.

"Ora?"

"What?"

"He told you all that?"

"Yes."

"The morning Ofer was born?"

"I told you—"

"What was it, some kind of urge he suddenly had, before the birth? To tell you all this?"

"I guess. Ask him."

"Just like that, out of the blue, you were sitting there, chatting over your morning coffee, and he started telling you about—"

"Avram, I don't remember all the details."

"You said you couldn't forget anything about that morning."

"But what difference does it make now?"

"It's just interesting, don't you think?"

"What?"

"That right before Ofer's birth, he decided. It's a bit strange, after all."

"What's so strange?"

"That he chose that time—"

"Yes, that time. Don't you understand?"

His eyes scan hers. She looks straight at him without hiding anything. She gives it to him: herself and Ilan, and Ofer in her stomach. He looks and sees.

"Hello hello hello hello," came a ghostly voice, exhausted and despondent, and Ilan jumped up in his chair, losing the signal when he did so. He carefully moved the dial again. His finger suddenly trembled uncontrollably, and he had to fold it in and use his wrist to turn the dial. He'd been sitting there for two hours, almost without moving, only his index finger rolling the dial with paper-thin moves as his eyes scanned the lawn of signals: thin green blades that sprouted and withered intermittently on the little screen. "Hello hello hello," a distant voice whispered weakly again. "Hello, hello . . ." The voice faded, disturbed by the breezes of radio noise, someone from Ismailia shouting in Arabic at a squad commander of Sagger missiles. Ilan tried to calm down and convince himself he'd been wrong—there was no way to identify a single voice in this hellish commotion. He carefully turned the dial through Egyptian and Israeli radio networks, a concoction of hysterical yells, engine hums, falling shells, orders and screams and curses in Hebrew and Arabic, until suddenly, from the depths, the weak and desperate voice emerged again: "Hello hello, answer already, you fuckers." Ilan's hair stood on end.

With both hands he held the earphones to his head and heard it, word for word: "Where is everyone? You scurvy-ridden eunuchs, may my spirit haunt you at night!" He tore the headphones off and ran to the war-room bunker, burst into a debriefing, and yelled, "There's a soldier in Magma! I heard him, I got him on the radio, he's alive!"

The commander gave him one look and hurried after him, without even asking who gave Ilan permission to deploy secret interception equipment. Trembling, Ilan put the headphones over the commander's ears: "Listen, he's alive, he's alive." The commander leaned on the desk with two fists, listened, and his forehead wrinkled as his face changed expressions. Ilan thought quickly: Maybe I should explain that this is how Avram always talks; he even considered adding that they had to rescue him *despite* his talk.

Years later—Ilan told Ora that dawn, the day Ofer was born—he still tormented himself for being so embarrassed about Avram in front of the commander. When he told her, Ora suddenly realized that Avram, in the way he spoke, the way he acted, and his entire being, was always exposing a vaguely embarrassing, private secret that everyone kept. She remembered how he used to joke, "I always say out loud what everyone isn't thinking." The commander let out a pent-up breath, straightened up, and said, "Okay, it's that kid, we know about him, but we thought he was gone." He took the headphones off and asked, "Who gave you permission to open up a position?"

Ilan seemed not to have heard and asked in a choked-up voice: "You know about him? Why didn't you tell me?"

The commander furrowed his brow. "Who are you, anyway? What makes you think I have to report anything to you?"

Ilan turned very pale and seemed unable to breathe, and the commander sensed his distress and changed his tone. "Listen, calm down, sit down, we can't do anything for him for now." Ilan sat down obediently. His limbs were weak, and sweat poured down his face. "On the first and second days he drove the whole network crazy," said the commander as he glanced at his watch.

"What did he do?" Ilan whispered.

"Oh, he just wouldn't stop blathering and shouting for us to come and get him out. And he's wounded, too. Lost a hand or a foot or something, I can't remember. Truth is, he kept giving so many vivid descriptions, we just stopped hearing it, and then he disappeared off the airwaves just like everyone else over there, and we thought that was it. So it's commendable that he's lasted this long, but forget about reaching him. Get that out of your head."

"Get what?" Ilan whispered.

"Him," the commander said, raising his eyebrows in the direction of the scanner, which once again emitted Avram's voice, now sounding strangely joyous as he trumpeted Duke Ellington's "Take the 'A' Train" through his lips.

The commander started to head back to the bunker, but Ilan grabbed his arm. "I don't understand. What do you mean, we can't? He's a soldier in the IDF, isn't he? So what do you mean 'we can't'?"

The commander gave Ilan a cautionary look and slowly released his arm from his grip. They faced each other as Avram's voice wafted between them, announcing, in English, a competition between Russian and American big bands, and asking his listeners to send in postcards and vote for their favorite.

The commander was a short and doleful-looking man. His face was covered with floury dust. "Forget it," he said gently. "I'm telling you, forget it. We can't do anything for him right now. He's surrounded by the entire Egyptian army, and we have zero forces out there. Besides, listen to him," he added in a whisper, as though he feared Avram could hear him. "He's beyond caring where he is, believe me." As if to confirm this, Avram burst into a long, screeching yodel that sounded horrifyingly alien, and the commander quickly flipped the dial and replaced Avram's screech with the sounds of orders and gunshot and Artillery Corps tracking points that briefly sounded, even to Ilan, logical in their own way, legal tender under these circumstances.

"Wait!" Ilan ran after the commander as he left the room. "Has anyone been able to talk to him?"

The commander shook his head and kept walking. "At first, yes. On the first day he had one good transmitter, but it stopped working, and he doesn't seem to know how to put the PRC in receiving mode."

"He doesn't know?" Ilan asked in horror. "How could he not know? All he has to do is listen, doesn't he?"

The commander shrugged his shoulders as he walked. "I guess the instrument's screwed up. Or else the guy's screwed up." Then he stopped abruptly, turned to Ilan, studied him closely, and asked, "What's your deal with this guy? You know him?"

"He's from Bavel. Intelligence."

The commander turned grave. "That I didn't know. Not good. We'll have to send word on."

Ilan brightened at this spark of interest. "Listen, we can't let him get caught, he knows lots of stuff, he knows everything, he has a phenomenal memory, we have to get to him before they do—"

He fell silent at once. He wanted to bite his tongue. Something foreign and tortuous flashed in the commander's eyes, and Ilan realized that he himself might have handed down a death sentence for Avram at that very moment. He stood there, stunned by what he had done. In his mind's eye he saw an Israeli Phantom diving down over the stronghold to destroy the security risk hidden among the ruins of Magma. He ran after the major and danced around him, behind him, in front of him. "Try to save him!" he begged. "Do something!"

The commander lunged at him and lost his temper for the first time. "If he's from Intelligence, why doesn't he shut up?" He grabbed Ilan's shoulders and shook him, shouting: "Is he an idiot? Doesn't he know they're listening in on all the networks? Doesn't he know they're pinpointing every fart they pick up in the whole sector?"

"But you heard him," Ilan whispered in despair. "I guess he isn't really—"

"Leave him there, I told you!" the commander shouted, and the veins on his neck bulged. "Get off the frequency, pack up the scanner in the APC, and get the hell out of my face!"

The commander walked away, waving his arms angrily, but Ilan no longer knew what he was doing. He run after him again, blocked his way, and stood forehead to forehead. "Just let me listen in on him. At least let me hear what he says."

"Negative," the commander hissed, amazed at Ilan's impudence. "You have three seconds to get the hell out of my—"

"But we have to!" Ilan groaned. "At least so we'll know if he's giving them anything about Leech—"

"What's that?"

Ilan held his face very close to the man and whispered something.

There was a silence. The major blinked, put his hands on his waist, and studied a flaw in the walls of the trench. 'Leech' was always beyond any argument or objection. "I can't spare the men," he finally snarled.

"I'm not one of your men," Ilan reminded him. They took a step back from each other.

"You *and* your Intelligence can choke on it," the major whispered. "You've really fucked us. You've murdered everyone here. Go on, get out of here, do whatever you like, I'm washing my hands of it."

"Hello, hello? Anyone left?" The voice returned when Ilan put the headphones on. They were still warm from the commander's touch. "Why doesn't anyone answer . . . What is this, are you playing with me? Over, over, over," Avram mumbled hopelessly. "God damn this fucking machine. Does it work? No? How am I supposed to . . . Hello? Man, this blows. Fuck!"

He must have hit the instrument. Ilan pulled a chair over and sat down with his back to the room. He forced himself to calm down and think rationally: Avram is in the stronghold, one and a half kilometers from here. He seems to be alone, injured, and slightly unstable, and an Egyptian Intelligence listener could locate him at any minute and send soldiers over there.

Ilan found that his attempt to stick to logic made him even more anxious.

"And I need clean water and bandages," Avram mumbled, exhausted. "This thing stinks. It's a rag . . . Hello? Hello? Can't hear. Why would you hear, you assholes. Well, if you don't hear, you'll soon smell, with this wound. Gangrene for sure, fuckit."

Shut up, Ilan begged him. He pressed his legs together and pleaded: Just hide there and shut up.

Silence. Ilan waited. More silence. He breathed a sigh of relief. The silence continued. Ilan leaned forward, his eyes darting nervously at the flickering display. "Where are you, why did you disappear?" he murmured.

"Plant, this is Peach." A new voice rose dimly over a rattling engine sound. "We've been hit on Lexicon 42. We have casualties. Requesting evacuation."

"Peach, um, this is Plant. Copy. Sending evacuation momentarily, over."

"Plant, this is Peach. Thanks, waiting, just hurry 'cause it's kind of a mess here."

"Peach, this is Plant. We are handling, we are handling, out."

"Shakespeare, for instance, is immortal," came the weak murmur again. "Mozart, too. Who else?"

Ilan's finger jumped. He still could not control his initial reaction every time he picked up Avram's voice. His skipping heart had shuddered the frequency. The signal line shrank back into bushes of analog greenery, and Ilan swore at himself furiously with some of Avram's juiciest curses.

"Socrates is immortal too, I think. Don't know him well enough. I started reading a little this summer, but I couldn't get through it. Who else? Kafka? Maybe. Picasso for sure. Then again, the cockroaches will survive, too."

A foreign voice came over the frequency in Arabic. "Division 16 lookout to Bortukal. Sighted Jewish tank hit at Kilometer 42, over."

"Hello, hello, answer me, you sons of bitches, you quislings. You left me here to die? How could you leave me to die?"

"Bortukal to lookout. On the way to Jewish tank, Allah willing we'll be there in five."

"Dear listeners," Avram suddenly said in a grotesquely seductive whisper that shocked Ilan. "Hurry up and get here, 'cause soon there won't be any Avram left for anyone."

"Plant, this is Peach, still don't see the evacuation. Situation here is bad. Over."

"Peach, this is Plant. Don't worry, everything under control. Evacuation at yours in seven, and if needed we can call in the blues, over."

"Thanks, thanks, blues would be great, just hurry, I have two matchsticks with severe injuries, over."

"This is your beloved Avram." His voice wove into the frequency again. "This is Avram begging you to hurry and save him before he lies with his forefathers, who, incidentally, adamantly refuse to lie with him, claiming his injury is considered menses—"

"I heard you found that guy from Magma," said a grinning Yemenite soldier as he walked past Ilan. "He's shooting the shit again, is he? We thought he'd turned in his gear by now, if you know what I mean."

"So you heard him, too?"

The soldier snorted and a demonic flash in his eyes cracked through the mask of dust on his face. "Who didn't? Totally hysterical. Cursed us, threatened us. Berserk. What are you laughing at?"

"No, nothing. Did he really threaten you?"

"Even General Gorodish wouldn't talk to a grunt like that. Move over, lemme hear." He leaned on the table, flipped one side of Ilan's head-phones out, and held it to his ear. He smiled and nodded as he listened. "Yeah, that's him all right, blah-blah-blah. Belongs in the Knesset."

"He's been that way the whole time?" Ilan asked, although he knew the answer.

"No, at first he was okay. Balls of steel. He was careful on the radio, talked in hints, used code names. I think he even got through to the BG at Tassa, gave him info."

Ilan imagined how quickly Avram would have adopted military lingo, making it sound like his mother tongue. He could hear him intoning in a deep voice, "Negative, um, negative, over," and delightfully picturing the astonished look at HQ ("Anyone know this kid running the show at Magma on his own?").

"But you're on a PRC-6," the soldier jibed. "This thing's like a walkie-talkie; I don't get how you even found him."

"Someone set it up for me."

"It's for internal communications, anyway, for inside the stronghold. It's just a shoddy hunk of metal, not for these ranges."

"Are you a radio operator?"

"Can't you see?" He smiled and pointed at his big ears.

"How long can it keep transmitting?"

The solider pouted as he considered the question, and finally de-creed: "Depends."

"On what?"

"On how many batteries it has, and how long till the penny drops on the other side that they have one of our guys alive."

In the background, Avram sang vigorously, *"My sukkah is a delight— with greenery and lights!"* and the radio operator hummed along with him, bobbing his head to the rhythm. "Listen to him. Thinks he's on *Sesame Street* or something."

The song broke into a groan of pain. Avram disappeared for several seconds and Ilan searched feverishly, fiddling with the needle, slamming the radio—and that was when he realized that the sharp ring he kept hearing wasn't coming from the scanner but from his ear, because of that one shot he had fired. When he found Avram again, there was no trace in his voice of that terrifying cheerfulness, only a quiet, docile murmur: "I don't remember, leave me alone, my brain's fried. I wanted to tell you . . . what did I want to say? Why did I even come? What am I here? I don't even belong in this place."

Shoulder to shoulder, ear to ear, the radio operator and Ilan stooped over the device. The radio operator said, "He's got a chick on his mind, you hear him?"

"Yes."

"Poor guy. Doesn't know he'll never see her again."

"And there's no food," Avram groused, "only flies, a trillion of them. Fuck you, you sucked out all my blood. I have a fever, touch here, and there's no water, and they won't come, hello . . ."

"His problem," the soldier said, "is that he's keeping it turned on."

He always keeps it turned on, Ilan thought to himself with a smile. Avram would have liked that.

"Hello, you urethra-less, testes-scalded . . ." Avram blathered on, but the desire was gone, and the words dropped from his mouth empty and dry. "For God's sake, you've had your fun and games, I get it, now come and get me already, I want to go home."

"What's his deal?" the soldier asked with a grimace. "D'you understand him?"

"I understand him," Ilan replied.

Avram whispered, "Hey, maybe you've got a connection at the Egyptian commando?"

The soldier moaned, "Man, it's bad enough he's calling them over, now he's spreading his legs, too."

"Maybe your aunt from Przemysl happens to have gone to school with the grandmother of Wicked Akid Khamzi from Regiment 13?"

Ilan made a hopeless attempt: "D'you think we really can't send over a force to—"

The radio operator flipped the headphone back on Ilan's ear, got up, and looked at him for a long time. "What'd you say your name was?"

"Ilan."

"Okay, listen up, Johnny. Take the headphones off—take them off now—and get over him. Forget him. *Khalas.* Just erase that he ever was. He never was."

"Forget him?" Ilan scoffed. "Forget Avram?"

"You're better off making a clean cut." Then he caught on. "Wait a minute, you know him?"

"He's a friend."

"A friend-friend or a how's-it-going friend?"

"Friend-friend."

"Forget what I said," the soldier mumbled and walked away.

"Scorpion, this is Butterfly. Sighted flock of Saggers on your right, five hundred range. Fire, fire all means, over."

"Plant, where the hell is the aerial support you promised? You keep saying 'copy' and 'on the way,' and nothing's happening. They're killing us here! I have one dead, one wounded, over, over."

"Who at his predestined time and who before his time; who by water and who by fire; who by sword and who by beast."

"Hello! What's wrong with you? Yom Kippur was two days ago."

"In the name of Allah most gracious and most merciful, to all units, Division 16 continues across the Canal according to plans. No serious resistance so far, inshallah we will continue to victory."

"Abir, this is Duvdevan, in response to your question, maybe fifty men still alive along the border, one here, a couple there."

"Plant, they're coming at us, why don't you answer?"

"Who by strangulation and who by stoning, who will rest and who will wander, who will live in harmony and who will be harried."

"Jewish pilot injured in bushes near two five three."

"Your orders are: be prepared, maintain radio silence, wait for them to come and rescue him, and only then, fire with all means, over."

"And my mother, even though you don't deserve to hear about her, you fuckers, abandoners of your brethren—"

Ilan pressed the sides of the machine until his knuckles turned white.

"My mother," Avram croaked, "she's already dead, gone in a flash. But she always . . ." He made a strangled sound. "She was always patient with me, I swear on my life." He giggled. " 'On my life,' what a great expression! On-my-life—do you understand what that means? On-my-life! *Lechayim!*"

Then another long silence, punctured by grating chirps. The green signal shrank, quivered, and split, then expanded and climbed up again.

"I used to run down Bezalel Street with her," Avram continued, and now he sounded so weak that Ilan slumped over on the radio. "We lived near the *shuk* when I was little . . . I don't remember, don't remember if I told you. How come I can't remember anything? Don't remember faces now, I can't remember Ora's face . . . Just her eyebrows. All her beauty is in her eyebrows."

His breathing was belabored. Ilan could feel him burning up and his consciousness rapidly slipping away.

"And with Mom we used to run down Bezalel, all the way to Sacker Park, anyone know it? Hello?"

Ilan nodded.

"She used to hold my hand, I was maybe five, and we ran all the way down, then back up, and we'd run until I got sick of it."

He gurgled and fell silent. The background noises died down, too. A strange, terrifying silence pervaded the entire sector. Ilan imagined that everyone on both sides of the Canal had stopped for a moment to listen to Avram's story.

"And you know how when you're a kid, and some grown-up plays with you, you're always afraid of when they'll get sick of you? When they'll look at their watch, when they'll have something more important to do than be with you?"

"Yes," Ilan said. "Yes."

"But Mom, she never got sick of it before I did, not with anything. I knew that no matter what, she'd never stop a game before me." He was floating through a mist. His voice was bare and thin like a child's, and Ilan felt as though he was seeing Avram naked, but he couldn't stop. "That's something that gives you strength for your whole life. That's something that makes a person happy, isn't it?"

A gaunt and extremely agitated religious soldier bumped into Ilan's chair and asked him to help pack up the religious paraphernalia. He blinked and smiled mechanically every few seconds. Ilan got up from his scanner. When he stretched, he realized he hadn't moved for over an hour. He knelt down by the soldier and filled an empty ammunition crate with Bibles, prayer books, yarmulkes, a havdalah wine goblet, an army-issue menorah, boxes of Shabbat candles, and even a fragrant *etrog* for Sukkoth. The religious guy held the *etrog* up, then buried his face in it and inhaled the citrus scent with a wild sort of passion. He told Ilan in a broken voice that his child had been born right after Yom Kippur. The brigadier general himself had radioed to give him the news, but since he wasn't trained to listen over the encoded phone, he wasn't entirely sure if it was a boy or a girl, and he was embarrassed to bother the BG. God willing, he'd be fortunate enough to see his son or daughter. If it was a boy he'd name him Shmuel, after General Gorodish, and if it was a girl, Ariela, after General Sharon. He kept blinking as he talked, and his face changed expression rapidly, and all that time Ilan heard Avram calling out to him in his mind, imploring him, but still he kept encouraging the soldier, deriding himself for feeling so relieved at being free for a few moments from having to sit by the scanner and listen to Avram fade away.

Shells fell very close to the stronghold. The soldier sniffed the air and grimaced. "It's NBCs!" he yelled. He dragged Ilan to a large iron cabinet with a label that read *Nuclear-Biological-Chemical Gear—Open Only in Emergency*. The soldier broke the lock with his Uzi butt and the door swung open. Inside, from top to bottom, were empty cardboard boxes. The soldier looked at them and started to scream and hit his head and stomp his feet. Ilan walked back to his listening post and put the headphones on.

"So how many more minutes do you think Avram has until his belly is cleaved? His soft, hairy belly, which he so loved to run his paws over? His belly that served him as storehouse and granary—"

"Stop," Ilan said. "Stop it!"

"Because Avram, funny as this may sound, was actually planning to hang around for at least another forty or fifty years, he was planning to live to be an old man, a dirty old man. He was still hoping to fondle the occasional breast and thigh, to travel the world, devour the expanses, donate a kidney or an earlobe to the needy, bathe in earthly delights, write at least one book that would truly tremble on the shelf—"

Ilan shook his head. He took the headphones off and stood up. He walked through the trenches until he reached a lookout post with a view of the old Ismailia hospital. Two reservists were sitting with their feet up on the sandbags as though they were relaxing on a cruise ship. They'd both been in the Six-Day War during their regular service and looked old to Ilan. He nonchalantly considered the fact that he would not live to reach their age. They were complacent and jovial and assured Ilan that the Sixth Fleet was on its way, and soon the "A-rabs" would regret the minute they'd thought all this up. Then they broke into an uproarious and grating duet of "Nasser Is Waiting for Rabin." Ilan sniffed the air and realized they were drunk—probably on cheap army wine. When he looked behind, he found a few empty bottles hidden among the sandbags.

He left them and stood staring at the blue water and the green gardens of Ismailia. Not far away, an endless convoy of Egyptian jeeps was crossing a bridge over the Canal. A massive torrent of humans and vehicles swarmed past, very close to the stronghold, not even bothering to stop and take it over. Ilan thought about the movie *The Longest Day*, which he'd seen twice with Avram. He felt that the various bits of reality he'd known could no longer be pieced together, and he simply stopped ruminating.

The shells pounded, and the steel netting holding down the rocks started to tear. Shattered pieces of stone began flying. The stronghold's protective layer was wearing down, and the air was ash, soot, and dust. Ilan stood there, unable to look south toward Magma, but he guessed that the smoke he could see curling around from the corner of his eye was coming from Avram's location. He wondered if there was any way to force the commander to send a few soldiers to rescue Avram, but he knew there was no chance. The commander wouldn't send any of his men on a suicide mission. He felt his way back to the war-room bunker. His eyes were red and teary, and he had trouble breathing. On the way he passed his little table and glanced at the scanner. He couldn't sit himself down there.

Inside the stifling bunker, someone remembered the manual air pump. It barely made any difference, and the noise—a feeble jackal's howl—added to the gloom. A smoldering Egyptian MiG plummeted to the ground, and a parachute opened up as it fell. Paltry cheers came from some of the lookouts around the bunker. The pilot parachuted right onto the Canal bank and limped over to the bridge. Egyptian soldiers hurried over to him, embraced him, and seemed to shield him from a possible hit from the direction of the stronghold. The Israeli soldiers watched in gloomy silence. There was a spirit among this Egyptian gang that aroused their envy. Ilan scrubbed his filthy face with his fingers. Through all the thousands of hours he'd listened to Egyptian soldiers on the listening devices in the underground bunker at Bavel, and through all the days and nights he'd translated their conversations and been privy to their military routine and their trivial moments, their gags and lewd jokes, and their most private secrets, he had never felt how much they were real, living people, flesh and blood and soul, as sharply as he felt now, watching them hug their pilot friend.

"But I did," Avram tells Ora. It's the first time he's spoken for a long time. "I was more enthusiastic about the whole listening thing than any of the other radio operators, even the senior ones. It drove me crazy that you could listen freely to anyone who opened his mouth. And the fact that you could hear what people were saying to each other behind closed doors." He laughs. "Well, I was less interested in the military secrets, you know. I was all about the stupid things, the little intrigues among the officers, the jabs, the gossip, all kinds of hints about their private lives. There were two radio operators from the Second Army, fellahin from the Delta, and I realized at some point that they were in love, and they were sending each other innuendos over the official network. That's the kind of thing I was looking for."

"The human voice?" Ora suggests.

An Israeli F-4 Phantom burst onto the sky, swooped over the stronghold, and fired from both guns. No one moved. The plane's roar filled up the entire space. It filled Ilan's body too, wreaking havoc on it. A heavy glass ashtray danced madly across a table, then fell off and shattered on the floor. In the yard, the Jerusalemite tankist who had arrived at the stronghold with Ilan stood drinking coffee. His wide eyes peered up at the sky over the lip of his mug. His glasses shimmered, the plane tilted slightly toward him, and Ilan watched as his body was split diagonally from shoulder to waist and his two halves were pitched to opposite ends of the yard. Ilan doubled over and threw up. Others next to him vomited, too. A few soldiers waved their fists in the air, cursing at the Air Force and the entire IDF.

Then the Egyptians blanketed the skies with a red-orange carpet of antiaircraft fire. Every so often, the trail of a plummeting missile emerged. The Phantom capered among them, but suddenly flames leaped up from its tail and it spiraled down in loops of thick black smoke. The soldiers tracked it silently until it crashed to the ground. Not a single parachute opened up. Everyone in the stronghold looked away from one another. When Ilan glanced back at the yard, he saw that someone had covered the fallen soldier's remains with two separate blankets.

"What's up with your buddy?" the dark-skinned radio operator asked. "Have you given up on him?"

Ilan couldn't understand what he was saying.

"The guy from Magma. It's a good thing you dropped that."

Ilan stared at him and his vision suddenly cleared. He took off running.

"Hello, hello, anyone hear me? Hello? I'm alone here. They killed everyone yesterday, or the day before. Twenty guys or so. I didn't know them, I got here a few hours before all hell broke loose. They killed them in the courtyard, took them out and shot them like dogs. Some of them they beat to death. The radio operator and I hid under some barrels of diesel that rolled over on us. We pretended to be dead."

Something had changed, Ilan noticed immediately. Avram sounded lucid and businesslike. He was talking as if he knew for certain that someone was listening, thirsty for his talk.

"I heard our guys crying. They begged the Egyptians not to kill them. I heard two guys praying, then they were gunned down in the middle. The Egyptians left and didn't come back. There's shelling all the time. I don't think you can even get into this room now. It's all destroyed. I can see that the rods holding up the doorway are completely bent."

Ilan shut his eyes and tried to see what Avram was describing.

"Up until the first evening I was with the radio operator. He lay maybe two meters away, badly wounded, with one radio on him, and another little one next to him, and loads of batteries. He must have had at least eighty, I know because he kept counting them, he had this obsession with counting the batteries. He was hurt in his leg, and me in my shoulder. I caught some shrapnel from a grenade that blew up when the place caught fire. It's sticking halfway out of me. I can touch it. If I don't move, it doesn't bleed. Just hurts. That's such a crazy thing. There's iron inside my body. Hello, hello?"

"Yes, I can hear you," Ilan said softly.

"Whatever. The radio operator lost a lot of blood. He kept bleeding. I don't know his name. We hardly talked, so that if we got taken hostage we wouldn't know too much about each other. After a while I could see he was really not doing well, he was shaking. I tried to cheer him up, but he couldn't hear me. At some point I crawled over and put a tourniquet on his thigh. He was talking rubbish. Hallucinating. He thought I was his kid. Then his wife. The radio still worked, and I talked to some officer at Tassa, a pretty senior one, I think. I explained what was going on here, I told him what the army had to do. He promised help was on the way and that the Air Force would send a helicopter to evacuate me. That night, I don't know when, the radio operator died."

Ilan found that Avram's sudden sobriety was harder on him than the delirious chatter. He had the feeling that Avram was completely exposed now, without any insulation to protect him from what was ahead.

"After that I dug in the earth a bit, until I fell into a hole underneath. I fell maybe one meter, on my back, with the radio and all the batteries. I can't even sit up here, so I just lie with the fucking radio on top of me, and there's no chance of anyone hearing me from this hole, but I can turn from side to side and even roll a few feet in either direction. I stacked up some sandbags to let some air in, but it's dark as Egypt—"

He paused, then added with a weak sigh: "Dark as Egypt, get it?"

Ilan gave an encouraging laugh.

"And I've got the shits like you wouldn't believe. I don't know what's left to shit anymore. I haven't had any food and barely any water for three days. Hardly slept, either. I can't stand to think that they'll kill me in my sleep.

"Just not in my sleep, dear God."

He was slipping again, Ilan knew.

"I guess they don't want to stop here, the Egyptian commando. They'll come back later to finish off the job. You think so? Dunno. What do I know about it? First they'll probably blow the whole thing up, then they'll come in to search. Bombing is better, no? Go out with a bang. This is so screwed up. It's unbelievable, I keep . . ." He let out a sudden laugh. "No, I mean, really, what am I doing here? Why me?"

Ilan cringed. He knew Avram was going to talk about the lots now.

"Hey, Ora, Ora'leh, where are you? Just to touch your forehead, to draw your eyebrows and mouth with my finger . . . You drove me so wild."

Ilan put his hands over his mouth.

"Listen, I've had this idea for a while. It's a great idea. I haven't told you, or Ilan . . . Hello? Anyone left in the galaxy? Hello, humanity? Ilan?"

Ilan jumped out of his seat in terror.

"They burned the whole stronghold," Avram whispered in a panic. "With the people, the equipment, the kitchen, our backpacks, everything they could see. They walked around with flamethrowers and set fire to it all. I heard them. Everything was burning. My hands and face are burned from the heat, I'm all black with soot. They burned my notebooks, too. A whole year of work gone. The whole last year, my idea, that's it, all gone. Fuckit. Every spare minute I had on the base, on leave, driving to the base, you saw what I was like this year. Seven notebooks. Shit. Thick notebooks, two hundred twenty pages each one, all ideas—"

His voice broke and he started to cry. He talked and cried. It was hard to follow. Ilan got up and stood listening to Avram sob. Suddenly he ripped the headphones off and threw them aside.

The Egyptians stepped up their fire. Shells of 240mm mortars fell constantly. The lookouts shouted warnings: boats carrying unidentified equipment were stealing onto the shore right beneath the stronghold. A cool breeze of fear blew through the trenches, the lookout positions, and the rooms, and then the boats began to hose them with water. At first it was a relief. The jets flushed out the dust that had thickened the air everywhere—bunkers, coffee cups, sinuses—but after a while the bottom of the stronghold began to cave in. The soldiers on the lookout points shot at the boats with every available weapon and tossed grenades. The boats left, but the stronghold had sunk slightly on one side and looked like a crooked, bitter sneer.

The commander convened all the soldiers in the war-room bunker. Ilan found a corner and sat down on the ground. Avram's voice sawed on inside his head, whispering, hallucinating, pleading for his life. The soldiers and officers sprawled along the walls. They avoided one another's eyes. Now that the soupy dust had been sprayed with water, the air was unmistakably thick with a terrible stench of shit, a tangible sediment of terror. A soldier who looked as if he was around fifteen, with soft, smooth cheeks, lay next to Ilan with his eyes closed, curled up and mumbling quickly, devotedly. Ilan touched his leg and asked him to say a prayer for him. Without opening his eyes, the boy said he wasn't praying. He wasn't religious at all, he was just reciting chemistry equations. That's how he used to quiet himself before his matriculation exams, and it always worked. Ilan asked him to say a few equations for him.

The soldiers and officers sat with their heads bowed. Outside, the desert roared—a massive, injured beast that lurched up and died down with every strike. Ilan constantly thought he could hear the Egyptian soldiers breaking down the stronghold gate. His brain produced their voices vividly. They pounded on the gate with the butts of their rifles. Then came the explosions, just beyond the wall, and their cheers after bursting in. There was shouting in Arabic, and shooting, and yelling and pleading in Hebrew, which slowly died down. A metallic taste spread through Ilan's mouth, freezing and dulling his upper teeth and his septum. "It won't hurt, it won't hurt," mumbled the young soldier. His eyes were shut tight, and a patch of wetness spread over his pants.

Ilan feverishly tried to remember something he'd once invented as a boy: the happiness method. How did it go? He used to divide himself up into different parts, separate regions, and whenever he was unhappy in one part, he'd skip to another. It never really worked, but at least he'd had that inner skipping sensation, and something like the momentum of his own private ejection seat, which could propel him for a few moments over his parents' divorce, the parade of new men who started visiting his mother, his father's abominations with his female soldiers in front of the whole world, the forced move from Tel Aviv to Jerusalem, the hated school, the horrible boredom—three days and nights every week at the transport base his father commanded. Once, on guard duty with Avram under the antennas on the northern cliff of Bavel, he'd half jokingly told him about his method, making fun of the child he used to be, but he'd sensed Avram's converging revulsion and attraction.

Avram had looked at him then as though he'd discovered something new, something very dark. He'd questioned Ilan in great detail about the method and demanded to know all the nuances of the mechanism, how he had come up with the idea and the different sensations at each stage. After luring him on mercilessly, he'd arched his eyebrows and grinned. "You know what the next stage is, right?"

Ilan had smiled wearily. "What? What's the next stage?"

"After you divide yourself up into lots of little squares, you can't fit into any of them anymore!" Avram conveyed an excitement that may or may not have contained slight mockery. "I'm telling you, I've never heard of a more elegant way to commit suicide! And without anyone noticing!"

. . .

The landline phone connected to the division HQ rang, and a familiar voice came through. The speaker did not identify himself, but he didn't have to. He told the soldiers he was planning to reach their area with an entire division and rescue everyone trapped in the strongholds. They looked at one another, then slowly stood up and stretched out. Feet stomped, blood started flowing through dulled limbs again. "Arik is coming!" the soldiers told one another, savoring the words. They gradually sped up their movements and went back to their positions throughout the stronghold. Even Ilan repeated the line to himself and to others: "Arik is coming. Arik's gonna screw the Egyptians. Arik will save Avram and me. One day we'll laugh about all this."

"Because you won't ever be mine anyway, you're Ilan's," Avram's voice said as soon as Ilan put the headphones back on. "And me, I've got this imprint of you, from the first minute I saw you, and every other girl will always be just a substitute. That was clear from the start, so what do I have to look forward to? People make such a big deal out of their lives. What I'm worried about now is just the thermal discomfort, you know, those goddamn flamethrowers. Truth is, I've never liked *shawarma*. I don't want to die, Ora."

He laughed, he cried, and he talked to Ora, describing her body and the two of them making love. As usual, he was bolder in his imagination than he'd ever really been with her.

Ilan listened, and that morning, the day Ofer was born, he told Ora what he'd heard, for the first and last time. They never spoke of it again. She lay with her back to him and did not move. He lay close to her and quoted Avram. She heard Avram through his lips. "He was so delirious," Ilan said. She didn't say a word. He waited. He said nothing and asked her nothing. She lay silently. Ilan reached out and pulled down her underwear. She did not move, did not resist. At most she said his name with slight hesitation. Then he was inside her with all his force. Had he asked her whether the lovemaking was just Avram's fantasy, she would have told him the truth. He didn't ask. He entered her. She did not respond. She took him inside her. Her senses perked up, warning her against what she was doing, but she found that her body was eager to take him. She thought of how she had to protect the fetus inside her, but her body responded wildly, hungry for him. His arms and thighs closed in on her. His mouth burned, he bit the back of her neck, he almost went right through her. Even many years later she found it hard to believe that she'd done it. Her belly swayed, and the boy Avram had planted in her body rocked around inside her, waiting to be born, but for a few moments Ilan and she were only a man and a woman going about their business.

This is so the boy can be born, she sensed at the time, through her fog of self-sedation. And so that Ilan can be his father, and so that Ilan and I can once again be man and woman to each other.

"Hello, hello, this is the Voice of Free Magma. It's the third night. Or fourth? I've lost my sense of time. I got out of the alcove before. There was total silence here for a few minutes, so I crawled out. First time since this started. I could barely move. I thought maybe the battle was over and they'd gone back to the other side of the Canal. I guess that's not exactly the case. I think it's still going on, at least in my area, 'cause I peeked out and saw them still crossing the Canal, masses of them, hard to believe, and I didn't see a single one of our forces."

He sounded completely lucid again.

"I searched the stronghold, and apart from the radio operator I saw three other bodies, all our men, in Bunker 2, totally scorched. At first I thought they were tree trunks, I swear, but then I got it—why would there be trees here? It's the reservists from the Jerusalem brigade. When I got here on the eve of Yom Kippur, I went right down to the edge of the Canal with my notebook. It was completely quiet, and I thought everything they'd scared us with at Bavel was bullshit. I found a barrel to lean on, and I sat with my back to the water and wrote a bit, just to acclimate myself faster. And these three guys were on the look-out post above me, and they made a whole production over my writing, and I fought with them, we almost came to blows. Now I feel bad. The way they looked, I think they were executed together. Maybe they tied them to each other and then shot. What was I going to—

"Everything's falling apart here. Iron rods, rocks, nets, bent and melted Uzis. I think I saw an Egyptian flag above the stronghold. I found three cans of meat loaf, one hummus, and one sweet corn. And most important, two bottles of water. I can't eat the meat. I'm done with meat for the rest of my life.

"I also filled two helmets with dirt, to cover my latrine. Now that I have food, I'll probably go back to running my bowels on full speed, ha-ha.

"Bottom line, I'm back in my cage. I crawled in here, lay down again in the dervish-sucking-himself position. If I only knew how to operate this lousy machine, damn it! Anyone there? Hello . . .

"I just hope it doesn't hurt. I wish I could lose consciousness. Before, after I saw the guys in there, I tried to strangle myself with my own hands, but I started coughing and I was afraid someone would hear.

"I just hope they don't torture me first. A guy like me is their bread and butter. I keep seeing pictures flash by. And it's a shitty movie.

"Good thing they don't have a lot of time to waste on me.

"But how much? A minute? Three? How long could it take?

"Just do it quickly. A bullet to the head.

"No, not the head.

"Then where?

"Okay, come on already. Come on, you sons of bitches! Fucking Egyptians—sideways-walkers!"

He yelled as loudly as he could. Then Ilan heard two ringing blows and figured Avram had slapped himself.

"Ilan," Avram said suddenly in a voice so close and tender that it sounded like a casual phone call, "you'll probably marry Ora in the end. Way to go, you stud. Just promise me you'll name your son Avram, d'you hear me? But with the 'h'—Avra*h*am! Father of many nations! And tell him about me. I'm warning you, Ilan, if you don't, my ghost will haunt you at night in your bed and bruise your reed."

Then he laughed. "Listen to this! Once, before the army, I went to Ora's house in Haifa, and her mom made me take my shoes off, you know her, but my socks were so stinky, I hadn't changed them for maybe a week, you know me, and she sat me down in the living room, on the fauteuil, to find out who I was and what I was plotting to do with her daughter, and I was so nervous about my socks that I started telling her that when I was seventeen I'd decided to be a Stoic, and then I was an Epicurean for a while, and now I'd been a Skeptic for a few months. I gave her a whole speech so she wouldn't notice the stench. Just a silly story. But tell it to Ora, and to the boy, to Avraham, and you can all laugh about it, why not.

"Enough," he pleaded. "Come on, come on, whoever you are."

"Seven notebooks, Ora—d'you get that? It was a fantastic idea. Listen, I was thinking of a series, not just one play. Three at least. One hour each. And no compromises. For once, I was going to do something huge, something like our old friend Orson's *War of the Worlds*. The end of the world, I was thinking. That's the idea, see? But not because of an alien invasion or an atom bomb. I was thinking about a meteor strike, and everyone knows exactly when it's going to happen. 'Cause the whole idea is that the end date is known, see? Every person in the world knows exactly when—

"It kills me that I can't tell you this. How am I going to write something without getting your confirmation, without your enthusiasm? Listen, listen, listen to me," he talked on, but his breath was heavy.

Whenever he described a new idea to Ora or Ilan, Avram was a bundle of excitement. The heat radiated from him. Ilan tried to imagine him in his underground hovel, moving his hands and legs excitedly.

"And all of humanity knows that exactly on such and such date they will be destroyed. Not a single living thing will survive, not even animals or plants. No one gets off the hook, no exception committees, no board decisions. All of life will evaporate.

"Seven notebooks those fuckers burned!" he shouted again with sincere astonishment. "How could they screw me like that?

"Listen, the clocks will only show the time left until the evaporation. And when someone asks what time it is, it'll only have one meaning: How long left until—

"Get it? Wait, there's more."

Ilan ran his tongue over his lips. Avram's excitement had begun to infect him. He could see Avram's inner light, which made him almost beautiful.

"For example, the museums will take their pictures and statues out of the galleries and warehouses. All the works of art. Everything will be out on the streets. Just think, Venus de Milo and *Guernica* leaning on a fence outside a plain old house in Tel Aviv, or Ashkelon, or Tokyo. All the streets will be full of art and everything people have ever painted or sculpted or created. The great masters, alongside grannies from the art class at the Givatayim community center. Nahum Gutman and Renoir and Zaritsky and Gauguin, next to drawings by kindergarten kids. There'll be pictures and sculptures everywhere, clay, iron, plasticine, stone. Millions of art works of every kind, from every age, from ancient Egypt and the Incas and India and the Renaissance, all out on the streets. Try to see it, try to see it for me. In the squares, in the tiniest alleys, on the beach, in the zoos, everywhere you look there'll be some work of art, doesn't matter what, a kind of massive democracy of beauty—

"And maybe—what do you think?—regular people can take home the *Mona Lisa* for one night. Or *The Kiss*. D'you think that's too much? Wait, wait, o ye of little faith, I'll convince you . . ." Avram smiled, and Ilan ached, feeling the burn of a private joke between Avram and Ora.

Ilan could see the look on Avram's face when he was testing out a new idea. All his force would narrow into a spark of light in the depths of his eyes, one hovering glow, and at the same time his face would take on a remarkably corporeal expression, making him look almost suspicious, as though he were guessing the weight of some dubious goods he'd been handed, and then the eruption: the glow would ignite, a smile would spread, his hands and arms would open wide. "Come on, world!" Avram would bray. "Fuck me hard!"

"Well, there is one big issue I haven't completely solved yet," Avram murmured to himself, focused and distracted at once. "Will people dismantle all the frameworks of their lives, like their families, or will they want to leave everything just like it is right up to the last minute? What do you say? I'm also wondering if people will start telling each other nothing but the truth, right to their faces, 'cause time's running out, you know? There's no time."

"In this kind of situation," he mumbled after a few moments of silence, "even the most trivial thing, like the illustration on a can of corn, or like a pen, or even that tiny spring inside a pen, suddenly looks like a work of art, doesn't it? The essence of all human wisdom, of all culture.

"Shit, no pen. Now. I'd really start writing it right now. Now I feel like I'm right there."

Ilan got up and hurried to the bunker. He dug through some drawers and found a few papers the Military Rabbinate had given out for Yom Kippur. They were printed on both sides, but they had wide margins.

"Sweet Queen Elizabeth," Avram sang over the radio. Ilan wrote.

"My queen, my sweet queen.

"How I wish to protect you from the impending disaster.

"Kings must die slowly, my queen,

"With the heavy toll of bells,

"With flower-strewn carriages,

"With a dozen pairs of black horses."

He sang and breathed into the mouthpiece. It was hard to follow. The tune was only an awkward hum, a recitation full of pathos and air, and Ilan distractedly began to ponder the musical score that could go with the song.

"But!" Avram croaked, and Ilan could have sworn he was waving his hand up high. "Perhaps we shall kill you slightly before, beloved Queen Elizabeth.

"An expressionless servant will hand you a goblet,

"So that we can see you off appropriately,

"We will lay you down to sleep three days before the rest of us,

"In a coffin of ebony,

"(or mahogany).

"So that you shall not suffer the shame

"Of common, faceless death,

"With crude screams of fear,

"With the stinking farts that we might emit in our final moments.

"And also, my queen, my queen,

"So that the noble thoughts of you

"Do not prevent us from dying cheaply,

"As we deserve to."

Avram stopped and let the last few words echo, and Ilan unwittingly thought: Not bad for a start, but a little too Brechtian. Kurt Weill was also in the neighborhood, and maybe Nissim Aloni, too.

"These kind of scenes, you see, Ora. I had dozens, maybe hundreds, in the notebooks. Fuck them. How am I going to reconstruct—

"Listen, there's a line that Ilan and I like. Maybe I should say *liked*, because one of us, and regrettably that would be me, has to start practicing the past tense: I was, I wanted, um . . . I fucked, I wrote—"

His voice broke off and he started weeping softly again. It was hard to understand what he was saying.

"It's a line written by the great Thomas Mann in *Death in Venice*," he continued after a few minutes, and his voice was rigid and strained again, a poor imitation of his joking and acting voice. "It's a great line, you have to hear it. The writer guy, the old one, whatshisface, Aschenbach, he had 'the artist's fear,' you know? 'Fear of failing to achieve his artistic goals—the concern that his time might run out before he had given fully of himself.' Something like that. I fear, my darling, that due to the circumstances my memory is limp, and so is everything else. When they hang you, at least you're promised one good ejaculation, but somehow I don't think that's the arrangement with a flamethrower—

"Hang on—

"What should we do about prisoners? Let them go? Let out murderers and thieves and rapists? How can you keep someone in prison in that state? And what do I do with death-row inmates?

"And schools?" he asks after a painful silence. "I mean, there's no point in teaching anymore, or preparing anyone for the future when it's obvious they don't have one, they don't have anything. Besides, I imagine most kids would leave school. They'd want to live, to be inside life itself. On the other hand, maybe the adults will go back to school? Why not? Yes, that's not bad." He giggled in delight. "There'll probably be loads of people who want to reconstruct that time in their lives.

"This rag stinks to high heaven, but at least it's stopped bleeding. Hard to move my arm. The excruciating pain has come back in the last few minutes. Fever's going up, too. I'm dying to take my clothes off, but I don't want to be naked when they come. Mustn't give them any ideas."

He was panting like a dog. Ilan could feel him willing the story to trickle back into him, to revive him with its touch.

"And children will get married at nine or ten, boys and girls, so they'll have a chance to feel something of life."

Ilan put down his pen and rubbed his aching eyes. He saw Avram lying on his back, underground, in the little womb he'd built for himself, while the Egyptian army swarmed around him. Invincible Avram, he thought.

"They'll get little apartments, the kids, and they'll run their own lives. In the evenings they'll go walking in the squares, arm in arm. The adults will look at them, sigh, and not be surprised.

"Lots of things are coming to me now.

"It's all alive in front of my eyes.

"Hey!" Avram suddenly exclaimed with a peal of laughter. "If anyone's listening, write down this idea with the kids for me! I don't have a pen, what a bummer."

"I'm writing," Ilan mumbled. "Go on, don't stop."

"Maybe the governments will start drugging the citizens, in small doses, without their knowledge. Through the water supply? But why? What does that give me?

"To blur the fear?

"Have to think about that."

Ilan remembered that Avram always joked that if he had a good idea, he was capable of working on it even inside a blender.

"He was right, that Chinese guy," Avram said wondrously. "There's nothing like the proximity of a flamethrower to sharpen your mind.

"And people will get rid of their cats and dogs.

"But why? Pets give comfort, don't they?

"No, think about it. In their state, people can't give love to anyone. They have no reserves.

"So it's an age of total egoism?

"I don't get it . . . You mean people become completely wild? Gangs on the streets? Absolute evil? *Homo homini lupus est?*

"No, that's too easy. It's trite. I want to maintain the frameworks. Especially toward the end. That's the power of it. That will be the power of a story like this, that people still manage to somehow keep the—"

He muttered, intermittently excited and fading, and Ilan struggled to keep up, and knew that no one had ever opened up to him like this before, not even Ora, not even when he slept with her. As he scribbled, something was being written inside him: a new, cool, lucid knowledge that he himself was not a true artist. Not like Avram. Not like him.

"And I forgot to tell you that babies will be abandoned, too.

"Yeah, yeah, parents will abandon their babies.

"Why not—my dad did it when I was five.

"Holy shit, there are so many possibilities. One year, man, one whole year I was stuck with this. It kept not working, it just stuttered and seemed unrealistic and hackneyed, and now, all at once—"

Ilan wrote it all down. And he knew, with total acceptance, that if he got out of there alive he would have to look for a new path. What he had thought of becoming, he would never be. He would not make movies. He would not make music, either. He wasn't an artist.

"So let's say the women will give birth in secret, in all kinds of hiding places, right? Out in nature, or in garbage dumps, parking lots, and they'll just run away from the newborns? Yes, that's it . . . Parents simply cannot tolerate the sorrow.

"This whole part is still a little weak.

"I can't imagine what it's like, parents. Parents and children, I can't figure out families.

"That's the awful thing, that people will have time to understand the exact meaning of everything that's about to happen to them.

"On the other hand, and the other, and the other"—he was awake again now, alive—"it's a kind of condition where you can suddenly fulfill all your dreams, all your fantasies. There's no shame, you see? And maybe there's no *guilt*, either." He gave a quiet but triumphant laugh, as though finally acknowledging some profound, private shame to himself.

Ilan leaned his head on his arm, pressed the headphone to his ear, and wrote quickly, every word.

"Why not? Why not?" Avram whispered, as though arguing with himself. "Did I get carried away? And what would Ilan say? That I'm full of hot air again?

"It's a good thing I have enough balloons for all his pins." He laughed.

Ilan laughed too, then grimaced.

"No one will feel guilty about what they are. And there will be a time, not for long, a month is enough, or a week, when every single person will be able to completely fulfill what they were meant to be— everything their bodies and souls have offered them, not what other people have dumped on them. God damn this all!" he roared. "I wish I could sit down and write it all now. Such light, such massive light, God."

He sighed, after a brief pause. "And every sight, every landscape or face, or just a man sitting in his room in the evening, or a woman alone in a café. Or two people walking through a field, talking, or a boy blowing bubble gum. There will be such splendor in the smallest thing, Ora'leh, and you'll always see it, promise me that.

"Though I walk through the valley of the shadow of death," Avram whispered, "I will fear no evil, for my story is with me.

"And I have to decide if they'll even use money—

"Well, we can leave that for later—

"There is no later, you idiot.

"Hello, Israel, homeland? Do you even exist anymore?"

The transmission was getting weaker. Perhaps the battery was dying. Ilan's foot tapped incessantly.

"I wish they'd come already," Avram moaned. "I wish they'd shout out their *Itbach al Yahud* and burn it all."

He breathed heavily. Ilan could no longer tell when Avram comprehended his situation and when he was disoriented.

Avram was sobbing uncontrollably now. "Everything's going to die. All the thoughts and the ideas I won't be able to write now, and my eyes will be burned, and my toes also.

"Ilan, you asshole," he whispered through his sobs, "this idea is yours now. If I don't come back, or if I come back in a decorative urn, do whatever you want with it. Make a movie out of it. I know your mind."

Some disturbances came over the radio, as though someone were rocking heavy objects in the background, behind Avram.

"But listen, it has to start like this, this is my one condition: A street, daytime, people walking quietly. Silence. No noise at all, not yelling, not whispering. No soundtrack. Among the walking people, a few stand on crates here and there. And then the camera narrows in on a young woman standing, let's say, on a laundry tub. That's what she brought with her from home. A red laundry tub. She stands there hugging herself. She has a sad smile, she smiles into herself—"

Ilan clutched the headphones. He thought he could hear human sounds in the background.

"And she doesn't even look at the people standing around her. She just talks to herself. And she'll be beautiful, Ilan, I'm warning you, eh? With a pure forehead and perfect eyebrows, the way I like, and a big, sexy mouth, don't forget. Anyway, you know who she should look like. Maybe you can use her?"

There was no doubt now: the Egyptians were inside the stronghold. The transmitter's microphone had picked them up, but Avram still hadn't noticed.

Avram laughed. "She can't act to save her life, but she'll just need to be herself, and she knows how to do that better than either one of us, right? And you'll shoot her face, we don't need anything more, you know? Just her face, and that happy, naïve smile—"

The sounds grew louder. Ilan stood up. His left foot was stomping madly, and his hands crushed the headphones against his temples.

"Wait a minute," Avram murmured, confused, "I think there's some-one—

"Don't shoot!" he shouted in English. Then he tried Arabic: "*Ana bila silakh!* I'm unarmed!"

Ilan's ears filled at once with shouts in throaty Arabic. An Egyptian soldier, who sounded no less startled than Avram, was screaming. Avram pleaded for his life. One shot was fired. It may have hit Avram.

He screamed. His voice was no longer human. Another soldier arrived and called out to his friends that there was a Jewish soldier there. The frequency bubbled with a medley of shouts and commotions and blows. Ilan rocked back and forth and murmured, "Avram, Avram." People walking by looked away. Then came a very close burst of fire, one dry sequence, and then silence. The sound of a body being dragged, and again curses in Arabic, and loud laughter, and one more single shot. Then Avram's transmitter went silent.

The commander gathered all the soldiers again in the war-room bunker. He said it didn't look like anyone was coming to rescue them, and they had to try to get out on their own. He asked for their opinions. There was a quiet, friendly conversation. People talked about the duty to save lives. Others feared that in the army, and in the country, they would be seen as cowards or traitors. Someone mentioned Masada and Yodfat. Ilan sat among them. He had no body, he had no spirit. The commander summed up and said he was planning to notify Arik Sharon immediately that they would leave that night. "What if Arik says no?" someone asked. "Then they'll slap us with a five-year prison term," one guy said, "but we'll be alive."

The landline wasn't working, and the officer used the two-way radio and asked to speak with "the boss." He said the situation was hopeless and he'd decided to leave. There was a short silence, and then Arik said, "Excellent, you leave and we'll try to hook up with you on the way." The soldiers listened as Arik said, "Do whatever you can." He stopped, and you could hear the cogwheels running in his mind. Finally he sighed and said, "Okay, then, um, goodbye, I wish you well . . ."

The religious soldiers recited the evening prayers before leaving, and a few other soldiers joined them. Then everyone prepared for departure. They filled their canteens and made sure they didn't rattle. They emptied their pockets of change and keys. Everyone had a weapon. Ilan got a bazooka in addition to his Uzi. "An anti-tank pipe," they explained. He didn't know how to operate it. He didn't say a word.

At two a.m. they set off. In the light of the full moon the stronghold looked like a ruin. It was hard to believe that this lopsided enclosure had protected them all those days. Ilan avoided looking left, toward Avram's stronghold.

They walked in two rows, at some distance from one another. At the head of Ilan's row was the commander, and at the head of the other one was his deputy. Next to the commander walked a soldier who was born in Alexandria. If they ran into Egyptian forces, he was supposed to shout that they were Egyptian commandos on their way to nail the *Yahud*. The soldier recited his lines to himself as they walked, trying to embody the Egyptian commando spirit. Ilan was somewhere in the middle of the row with his head bowed. They tripped on the sand frequently and fell in silence, quietly cursing.

Suddenly they heard shouts in Arabic. An Egyptian armored vehicle was driving nearby, shining a spotlight to track the sides of the road.

"Turns out we'd walked into an Egyptian parking lot," Ilan told Ora that dawn. His body had quieted down, but he was still enfolded in her and his hands dug into her shoulders. "I even stepped on the blanket of someone sleeping there."

She lay stunned, her flesh still fluttering around his.

"We didn't move, we didn't breathe. The armored vehicle went on. They hadn't seen us. Hadn't seen anything. We lay there, thirty-three men, and they didn't see us. We got up and ran back to the sand to get away from the road." She could feel his warm breath against the back of her neck. "We kept going east and walked all night at a half run. I ran with my gun and the bazooka. It was hard, but I wanted to live. As simple as that."

She wanted him to pull out of her right away. She couldn't speak.

"Then the sun rose. We didn't know where we were, or whether it was our territory or theirs. Or where the IDF was, if it even existed. I saw tire marks in the sand, and I remembered that the IDF only uses APCs with chains, but these tracks were from a Soviet BTR, which the Egyptians used. I told the commander, and we quickly changed course. We walked and walked until we reached a small wadi with hills and mounds, and we sat down to rest. We were dead tired. Tanks were burning on the hills around us. Giant torches. We didn't know whose they were. The whole area reeked of scorched flesh. You can't imagine it, Ora."

She flinched, and he tightened closer to her body. He was barely letting her breathe. The fetus felt as if it was throbbing too quickly. She wondered if it might somehow absorb anything of what Ilan was telling her.

"On the radio they told us they couldn't reach us. We had to wait some more. We waited. After a few hours they told us to try to reach this mountain range. They gave us a code map. We walked until we could see the range straight ahead. But see, the Egyptians are shooting at us all the time, from all the hilltops, and they're not hitting us. It's all miracles. We're walking with bullets whistling past us like in the movies. When we got to the mountain range we realized it was swarming with Egyptians. We thought it was all over."

"I can't breathe this way, Ilan—"

"But a minute later, our tanks arrived and stormed them. A battle started. Gunfire. We just sit on our asses and watch the movie. Everything's on fire. Burning people jump out of tanks. People getting killed 'cause they came to rescue us. We sit on our asses and watch. And we feel nothing—nothing!"

"Ilan, you're really suffocating me—"

"They yelled at us over the radio to shoot up flares so they could see where we were. We shot a flare and they found us. One tank came down from the range, and it's a steep incline, a wall. It came all the way to us. An M60 Patton. An officer sticks his head out the turret and motions for us to come quickly and get in the tank. We shout at him: 'What should we do? How?' And he gestures: Climb up, there's no time. 'You mean, all of us?' 'Get up. Get up!' 'What do you mean get up? Where?' 'Get up already!' And there's thirty-three of us. Ora, what did you say?"

"Ilan!"

"Sorry, sorry. Did I hurt you?"

"Pull out, pull out now."

"One more minute, please, just a minute, I have to tell you—"

"It's not good, Ilan—"

"Listen, just give me one more minute. Please, Ora, that's all." He spoke quickly, firmly. "We climbed up on the tank, every guy grabbed on to something, people glued themselves to the MAG hatches, ten guys crowded into the turret basket, I jumped up on the back and grabbed on to the leg of the guy above me, someone else took hold of my shoes, and the tank rolled. Not just rolled but barreled, in zigzags, to get away from the Saggers, and we barely held on. And the whole time I just kept thinking: Don't fall, don't fall."

This child, Ora thought, the things he's hearing before he's even born.

"The tank is jumping around like crazy," Ilan murmured and clutched her again, convulsing. "Your bones are breaking, you can barely breathe, dust everywhere, stones flying, you just stop up all your holes and just stay alive."

Dust penetrated her mouth, her nose. Yellow desert streams. She choked and coughed. She felt as though the fetus inside her was also shrinking, fighting to turn over, to turn his back. Stop, stop, she groaned inside, stop poisoning my child.

"It went on that way for a few kilometers, stuck onto the tank, and then all of a sudden—that's it. Over. We were out of the line of fire. I could barely let go of the other guy's leg. My hand wouldn't open."

His muscles relaxed. His head plunged onto her neck, heavy as a rock. His fingers slowly disengaged from her body and lay open in front of her face. She did not move. He slid out of her. A moment went by, and then another. He breathed heavily. His face was up against her and he lay in an utterly helpless huddle. A spasm went through her body.

"Ilan," she murmured. Her temples began to throb, and little beads of sweat glistened on her skin. Her body was telling her something. She lifted herself up on her elbow as if she were listening. "Ilan, I think—"

"Ora, what have we done?" she heard him whisper in a panic. "What have I done?"

She touched her wet thighs and sniffed. "Ilan, I think this is it."

HE ASKS ABOUT the deep cracks that had run through the walls even in his day, mainly in the kitchen, but also in the bedrooms. He wonders if the house continued to sag over the years and how she and Ilan dealt with the lintels that protruded from their frames. He asks if the huge bureau that used to be in his room still exists, and she tells him that until the family left the house and moved to Ein Karem, the bureau ruled the room like an old patriarch. The bedroom closet had also stayed. "We hardly touched that house. Just a little work in the kitchen, like I told you, and downstairs in the basement sewing room when the boys got older."

The path is hard going, and the day is very hot even this early. Tabor turns out to be the steepest of all the mountains they've climbed. Sometimes they turn to face down the incline and walk backward. "You let the quadriceps rest and make these two guys here work a little"—Ora pats her rear end with both hands—"the gluteus maximus and the gluteus medius. Let them do their part, too."

As they walk backward, facing Kfar Tavor and the Yavne'el Valley sprawling below, Avram goes through the house with her, room by room. He asks about the sunken floor in the hallway, the redundant step up into the bedroom, and the clumsy water pipes, some of which were exposed. He remembers every fault and defect as well as every beauty spot in that home, as though he'd never stopped walking through it and caring for it. He asks if the manhole in the basement kept overflowing every time it rained.

"That was Ofer's domain. He used to declare flood duty whenever it rained and prepare mops and buckets and rags. Later he got more sophisticated and installed a little pump." Ora laughs. "You should have seen it, with an engine and two hoses. But he solved a problem that I think had started when the house was built.

"He also built a bed for us," she says. She had sensed this was something she should not tell him, but they were in a good mood, and why not?

"He built a bed himself?"

"When he was in eleventh grade, yes. Or was it twelfth?" She stops to catch her breath and leans against a boldly slanting pine tree. "Never mind, I was just thinking about it. Listen to what else I remembered"— she slyly changes the topic because when he asked, she thought Avram had a stab of pain, and she tells him about how Ofer, when he was around three, used to come up to her and announce: "I want to tell you a story." She would say, "I'm listening," and then wait and wait while Ofer stared into some corner of the room for a long time. Then his face would take on a ceremonial look, he'd fill his lungs with air and say in a voice hoarse with excitement: *"And then . . ."*

"And then what?" Avram asks after a moment.

"You don't get it," she says, her peals of laughter rolling all the way to the valley.

"Oh," he says awkwardly. "That's the whole story?"

"And then, and then . . . That's the main point in stories, isn't it?"

"That's even shorter than my shortest story." Avram smiles and leans his hands on his knees, breathing heavily.

"Remind me."

" 'On the day I was born, my life changed unrecognizably.' "

Ora sighs. "And then . . ."

"And then he made you a bed."

"At first it was going to be for him," she clarifies.

She heard him pacing around the house in the middle of the night, and when she went up to him he said something was driving him crazy. He wanted to make a bed, but he couldn't decide which kind, and it kept waking him up. Ora thought it was an excellent idea: the youth bed he'd slept on since he was a boy was wobbly and creaky, almost collapsing under his adolescent weight. "I have all kinds of ideas," he said, "but I can't decide." He blew on his hands excitedly, and repeated that he couldn't sleep. He'd been waking up in the middle of the night for several nights in a row, feeling that he simply had to build this bed, now, and he kept seeing it in his thoughts, but it wasn't really clear yet, it came and went.

He paced around Ora, drummed his fingertips rapidly, and bit his lower lip. Then he stopped and straightened up, and his face looked altered. He crossed the room, practically passing right through her, snatched a piece of paper and a pencil from the table, improvised a ruler, and at three a.m. he started sketching the bed.

She peered over his shoulder. The lines flowed easily and accurately from his fingers, as if they were extensions of them. He murmured to himself and conducted a lively inner debate, and she watched in amazement as a regal canopy bed emerged. But he crumpled the paper in annoyance. "Too refined, too elegant." He wanted a peasants' bed. He grabbed another page and sketched—how beautiful his hands are, she thought, heavy and delicate at once, and those triangular beauty spots on his wrist—and as he did so he explained: "Here, in the frame, all around, I want it to have wooden ties."

"I can help you with that," Ora said cheerfully. "Let's go to Binyamina, to the place where I got *that*." She pointed at the wooden shelf above the sink, which had pots and pans and dried peppers hanging from it.

"You mean, you'll come with me?"

"Sure, we'll go together, and afterward we can spend the day in Zichron Yaakov."

"And I want eucalyptus tree trunks. Four, for the legs."

"Why eucalyptus?"

" 'Cause I like their colors." He seemed surprised at the question. "And here, above the headboard, there'll be an iron arc." He quickly sketched it.

"Ofer spent almost ten months working on that bed," Ora tells

Avram. "There's a forge in the Ein Nakuba village, and he got friendly
with the blacksmith. He spent hours upon hours there, watching and
learning. Sometimes, when I drove him there, he let me see how the
bed was coming along." She draws with a stick in the earth: "This is the
arc, an iron arc over the head. The crowning glory."

"Nice," says Avram and watches her face as she looks at the dirt. An
arc above their two heads, he thinks.

Just before they reach the peak, they sit down to rest among oak and
pine trees. A small grocery store in the Bedouin village of Shibli had
revived them. They'd even found a bag of dog food there, and there'd
been no radio on. Now they gobble down a full breakfast and drink
fresh, strong coffee. The wind dries their sweat, and they enjoy the
clear view of Jezreel Valley's brown-yellow-and-green-checkered fields
and the expanses that roll into the horizon—the Gilead mountains, the
Menasheh hills, and the Carmel range.

"Look at her." Ora glances at the dog, who lies sprawled with her tail
to them. "She's been like that since we slept together."

"Jealous?" Avram asks the dog and lands a pinecone next to her paw.
She defiantly turns her head the other way.

Ora gets up and goes over to the dog. She scrubs her cheeks and rubs
noses with her. "What's up? What did we do? Hey, maybe you miss that
friend of yours, the black one? He really was a hunk, but we'll find you
someone in Beit Zayit." The bitch gets up and moves away a few steps,
then sits facing the valley. "Did you see that?" Ora sounds amazed.

"The bed," Avram reminds her, startled by a flash of insult that ran
through Ora's face. "Come on, tell me about his arc."

Ofer had explained it to her: "At first I made an arc out of two identical pieces, and they were supposed to join up with this rung, here. It
looked pretty good, and technically it worked, but I didn't like it. I just
didn't like it, it didn't work well with the bed I want."

She couldn't follow all the details, but she enjoyed hearing and
watching him as he described his work.

"So now I'm making a different arc, this time from one piece,
and I'm going to wrap iron leaves over it, and it's going to be super-
complicated, but that's just the way it has to be—it *has* to, you know?"

She knew.

He disinfected wormholes in the tree trunks, sealed them with var-
nish, then carved into the center of each trunk at a ninety-degree angle.

" 'This wood is hard, it's resistant,' " she quotes, "but Ofer's strong, he has your arms, kind of thick in this part"—she pats Avram lightly with unconcealed pleasure. "He worked for several weeks on those trunks and finally decided to buy, with his own money—he did it all on his own, apart from driving he wouldn't let us help him at all—a power saw for cutting iron. But that didn't work for what he wanted, and he bought another blade—an aggressive one," she stresses with an expert tone—"and made channels through the trunks. And wait—" She interrupts a question forming on his lips. "He made the little leaves on his own too, from iron, for the arc over the head. Beautiful little rose leaves, twenty-one of them, with thorns."

Avram listens and his eyes narrow in concentration. He strokes his arms distractedly.

"He designed every single leaf right down to the last detail. You would have enjoyed seeing how lovely and delicate they came out. And for the frame, the wood itself was a massive hunk, but it flows in these wavy kinds of lines"—she rounds her hands, and for an instant she feels Ofer himself between them, large and strong and tender—"I've never seen a bed like that anywhere."

There was something alive about it, she thinks. Even in the iron parts there was motion.

"And when he finished making it, he decided to give it to us."

"After all that?"

"We argued with him, we wouldn't let him. 'Such a special bed, you worked on it for so long, why shouldn't it be yours?' "

"But he's stubborn." Avram smiles softly.

"I don't know what happened. Maybe he looked at it when it was done and it frightened him a little. It was huge. The hugest thing I've ever seen."

She swallows down quickly what almost escaped about the bed and its size, and how many people could lie comfortably on it. She shakes the dirt off her hands. Why did she even tell him? She has to get out of this story quickly.

"Anyway, he said that one day, when he got married, he'd build a new bed for himself. 'For now,' he said, 'buy me one.' And that was it. Just a little story. So you'll know. Come on, let's go."

They get up and walk around the nipple of the mountain, avoiding the churches and monastery, then start walking back down toward Shibli. A buzzard hovers overhead, and the white down of sheep's wool clings to a thistle. The bitch hears the village dogs barking and casually comes closer to Ora and rubs against her leg. Ora cannot keep a grudge for even three minutes, and she leans down and strokes the golden fur. "Is that it? Friends? You forgive me? You're a bit of a prima donna. Has anyone ever told you that?"

They walk side by side, Ora scolds and strokes, and the dog flicks up her tail and curls it into a loop and skips lightly around them again. Ora thinks about the night before, and about the night ahead, and looks at Avram's back. Only last night she'd discovered that his eyebrows were not as soft and velvety as she'd remembered. And his fleshy earlobes—Ofer is the only one in the family who has them, and Ilan and Adam always make fun of his Dumbo ears; Ofer won't even let her touch them, but now she knows their touch. Five years, she thinks. It was only five years ago that Ilan and I inaugurated the bed. Ilan was afraid it would creak. He went downstairs to the living room and shouted, "Now!" and Ora, upstairs, jumped all the way up and down the bed like a madwoman. She almost lost consciousness from jumping so hard and laughing hysterically (and not one creak could be heard downstairs).

"I like him," Avram says suddenly.

"What?"

He shrugs, and his lips curl with slight surprise. "He's so . . ."

"Yes?"

"I don't know, he's such . . ." His hands, raised in front of his body, sketch and sculpt Ofer, living matter, dense and solid and masculine, kneading him in an imaginary embrace. Were he to tell her now that he loved her, she would not be this moved.

"Even though he isn't . . ." She starts but changes her mind.

"Isn't what?"

"He isn't—I don't know—an artist?"

"An artist?" Avram sounds surprised. "What does that have to do with anything?"

"Nothing, never mind, forget it. Wait, I didn't even tell you—wow," she lets out a gasp, "you really stunned me with that." She stops and holds his hand to her chest. "Touch here, feel. The way you said, you know, that you like him, and there's still so much I haven't told you about him."

She laughs and shakes her head. "He saved a well, you know. Never mind, I'm just showing off a bit."

Avram responds immediately, a bit insulted: "That's called showing off?"

"Then what is it?"

"It's telling me about him."

She speeds up, walks in front of him, and spreads out her arms. There's so much oxygen she can barely breathe.

"They found a well, Ofer and Adam. They were hiking at the foot of Mount Adar, near Beit Nekofa, and they found a little well that was completely stopped up with mud and stones and hardly had any water. There was just a trickle. Ofer decided he was going to restore it, and for a whole year—d'you get this?—when he came home on leave from the army, he would go to this place. Sometimes Adam went with him—Adam wasn't really into the project, but he was afraid for Ofer to be there alone, it's right on the border, and the two of them would go together."

Avram has already noticed that a warmth spreads through his loins almost every time she says "the two of them."

"They removed the stones and rocks that were blocking the spring, and dirt and mud and silt and roots"—she is so radiant when she talks, and Ofer fills her with life, and now she is certain that it's good, that it will be good, that her crazy plan may work—"and after they cleaned it out they dug a small holding pool, about a meter and a half deep. We spent a lot of time there too, we didn't want them to be alone. We used to go on Saturdays and take food, and their friends went too, and some of our friends—I have to take you there one day, there's a huge mulberry tree over the pool, and Ofer was the foreman and we all worked for him."

"But how? How did he know how to do it?"

"First he built a little model at home. Ilan helped him"—she remembers the feverish enthusiasm that took hold of the two of them and how the house filled with sketches and computations of water supplies, flow angles, and volume, with constant experiments and simulations—"and then, you know, all you have to do is . . ."

"What? What do you have to do?"

"Build it," she explains gravely. "Reinforce walls, concrete, plaster. All the stages. You need a special kind of plaster. Ilan lugged a ton and a half of plaster and sand in his car. And just so you understand, he wouldn't have sacrificed his Land Cruiser for anyone but Ofer. And then he planted a little orchard of fruit trees. We helped him. We took a plum tree, and lemon and pomegranate and almond, and a few olive trees, and now there's a real little oasis there, and the well is alive."

She stretches her arms out and her steps are light: she has so much to tell.

They leave Shibli behind, and the trail crosses through fields and groves, hidden paths rich with cascading greenery that shelters them on either side. Ora drags a little, burdened by some shadow she cannot clearly see, an unfocused pain. The tiny hope from earlier has melted away and seems foolish and hollow.

Avram thinks about Ofer, who is out there now. He tries to picture him there, forces himself to see the streets and alleyways, but there is only one permanent war play in his mind, staged continually in an utterly empty auditorium that he never enters. Avram has five of these auditoriums, all empty and dark, and in each one a different play is performed nonstop—when he sleeps and when he wakes. The plays must always go on, and their sounds are distant and vague when they reach his ears, and he does not go inside.

A new fear trickles into Ora with each step. Perhaps she is wrong. Perhaps she has the whole thing upside down. Perhaps the more stories she tells Avram about Ofer, the less will remain of Ofer's life. And in a state of suffocation she lets out: "I just wonder what kind of person he'll be when he gets back."

"Yes," Avram whispers beside her. "I was just thinking that."

"I can't force myself to imagine what he's seeing and doing there."

"Yes, yes."

"He may come back a completely different person."

They walk on, bowed, dragging heavy weights.

But maybe Ofer's immune now, she wonders. Maybe after the thing in Hebron he can withstand anything. What do I know? What do I really know about him? Maybe he really is more suited to life here than I am.

'Cause if I'd only kept my big mouth shut, she thinks, I might still have a family today. The three of them, Ilan and Adam and Ofer, had warned her so many times. They'd sent a thousand little signals to tell her that there are some situations, some issues, that it's better to keep quiet about. Just put a sock in it. You don't have to pour out a live broadcast of your whole stream of consciousness, right? But only when it was all over did she get it: they were constantly preparing themselves for every situation—*every situation*. And they knew ahead of time, and beyond any doubt, that there would in fact be a "situation." It wasn't difficult to assume, after all, given that Adam and Ofer served there for six years, three each, with patrols and checkpoints and chases and ambushes and night searches and demonstrations to suppress, that it was impossible for a "situation" *not* to arise. It was this annoying, exasperating, male wisdom that made Ora seethe. And the three of them were all decked out in protective gear while she walked around naked, like a little girl. "You're not in Haifa anymore, Dorothy," Adam spat at her during one family argument. What was it about? Something to do with Ofer's problem, or a different matter? Who can remember? And by the time she realized what he was talking about and what he was insinuating, they'd already changed topics. They changed topics remarkably quickly back then, switching the subject like cardsharps when she started up with her business. She wonders what Avram would say about it.

Avram quickly checks in on all his auditoriums: five, like the fingers on one hand. Once there were more, lots more, but over the years he'd managed with great effort to reduce the number. It was beyond his powers to keep them all active simultaneously; it was beyond his means. He scurries back and forth past the row of closed doors, counts them on the fingers of both hands—the second hand is just backup—and pricks up an ear to detect the dull murmur coming from inside, the soundtrack of plays produced continuously, day and night, for twenty-six years now, never losing their novelty. He grabs a line here and a line there; sometimes all he needs is one word to know what point in the plot they're at. Sometimes he wishes he could shut them down for good, turn the lights off. On the other hand, the thought of the silence that would then prevail was utterly terrifying—a hollow sound, the whistling wind of an infinite plunge into the abyss.

He secretly counts his fingers again, running the thumb over each digit. He has to do that periodically, at least once an hour, as part of his duties, his maintenance routine. There's the play about the war, and the one about after the war, with the hospitalizations and the operations, and the one with the interrogations in Israel with Field Security and the Shabak and the Ministry of Defense and the Intelligence GHQ, and the one with Ilan and Ora and their children's lives, and the one about the POW prison, of course, in Abbasiya, which he really should have noted earlier, before anything else, in Auditorium One. He forgot to start with that one, which is not good. The thoughts about Ofer must have thrown him, the thoughts about Ofer who is fighting now. Not good.

He runs over his fingers again. The thumb, the counter, is of course the POW one, which he mustn't insult under any circumstances, and obviously there will have to be a small sacrificial offering for his grave mistake, the unforgivable insult, the hurtful, impudent humiliation he has just caused it. The second one is the war. The hospital and treatments are in Three. And the interrogations in Israel are in Four. And Ora and Ilan's family, Five.

For good measure, he thrusts his hand into his pocket and pinches himself, twisting the flesh of his thigh and digging his nails in, thumb and ring finger, as if into foreign flesh—how dare you, how could you forget to start with the POW prison! Still walking, he falls on his knees and begs the moustached interrogator, the tall one, Doctor Ashraf, the one with the terrifying, sinewy hands. It almost never happens, he explains. It's happened so rarely. It won't happen again. And deeper inside, through the tearing skin: well done, now you're talking, now you understand your mistake. And the dampness is spreading through the fabric and his fingertips.

Ora is holding his face in her hands. "Avram!" she yells at him as if into an empty well. "Avram!" He looks at her with dead eyes. He is not here. He is frantically flitting among his dark auditoriums. "Avram, Avram," she calls in to him, alarmed, fighting, not giving up, she has the power to do it. And he slowly comes back in hesitant waves, rises up and appears again through his pupils, smiles with miserable submission.

"Once every three weeks or so, he'd come home on leave," Ora says. She would pounce on him as soon as he walked through the door, press her whole body against him, then remember to hold her chest away and feel his soft stubble on her cheeks. Her fingers would recoil from the metal of the gun slung over his back and search for a demilitarized space on that back, a place that did not belong to the army, a place for her hand. She would shut her eyes and thank whoever needed to be thanked—she was willing to reconcile even with God—for bringing him home in one piece again. And she would sober up when he gave her three quick slaps on her back, as if she were just a friend, a male friend. With that *thwack-thwack-thwack* he would both embrace her and mark the boundaries. But she was also well versed and would soon drown out the whisper of insult with cheers of joy: "Come on, let's have a look at you. You're tan, you're sunburned, you don't use enough sunscreen. Where's this scratch from? How can you lug all that weight around, are you telling me everyone goes home with a backpack this heavy?" He'd mumble something, and she'd resist reminding him that he always used to take the whole house on his back to school as well. She should have guessed he would end up in the Armored Corps.

He slowly removed his Glilon rifle and fastened the magazines with a thick khaki band. He looked giant, as though the house were too small for him. His shaved head and round forehead gave him a menacing look, and for a fraction of a second she was meekly handing him her identification card at a checkpoint. "But you must be hungry!" she said cheerfully with a dry throat. "Why didn't you let us know you were coming at lunchtime? We thought you'd only get here in the afternoon. You could have at least phoned on the way, so I would have had time to defrost a steak for you."

"To this day I'm still not used to him eating meat," she tells Avram. "At age sixteen or so, he just changed his mind. And the fact that he gave up his vegetarianism was somehow harder for *me* than for him. Do you understand that?"

"Because being vegetarian is . . . what?" Avram asks curiously. "It's special? It's character?"

"Yeah, I guess so. And it's also a kind of cleanness. I won't say purity, because Ofer, even when he was vegetarian he was always"—a moment's hesitation: Should she tell him? Can she? May she?—"kind of *earthy*" (at least she managed not to say "corporeal"), "and I had the feeling that part of his maturation was to turn around all at once, with all his strength, in that direction, to the opposite of vegetarianism, a kind of anti." She laughs awkwardly. "I don't know what I'm saying."

"Anti what?"

"I don't know. Maybe it's more of a *who*."

"Anti who?"

"I have no idea"—but she has a guess—"maybe delicacy? Fragility?"

Avram suggests: "Adam?"

"I don't know, maybe. It's like he decided to be as . . . I don't know . . . as rigid as possible? And masculine. With two feet planted firmly on the ground, and even a little, intentionally, corporeal?"

The day grows hotter and they walk silently, comfortable that way. What has not been recounted now will be told in the evening, or tomorrow, or maybe years from now. Either way, it will be told. They climb to the top of Devorah Mountain and lie down for a snooze on a shady patch of grass. They sleep for almost two hours, exhausted from the mountains, and when they awake they are surrounded by families who've come to spend a leisurely day at this spot looking out onto Mount Tabor and the Gilboa, Nazareth and the Jezreel Valley. Loud Arabic music blares from car radios in all directions, smoky aromas rise up from grills, nimble-fingered women chop meat and vegetables and roll kibbeh on long wooden tables, babies laugh and coo, men smoke bubbling hookahs, and a group of young boys nearby aim stones at glass bottles, shattering them one after the other. Ora and Avram leap to their feet into this vision, amazed at the abyss into which their sleep has rolled them. They have the strange sensation of having let their guard down, and they quickly gather up their backpacks and walking sticks and pass through the revelers without saying a word. They slip away with inexplicable secrecy, the dog with her tail between her legs as well, and they walk down the path toward a nearby Arab village. The muezzin is calling, and the echoes of his voice engulf them, and Avram remembers the muezzin at Abbasiya, with whom he used to sing along in his cell, composing Hebrew lyrics to the tune.

Low and ruddy, the sun hovers over the land, inflaming the colors with one final touch. "It'll be dark soon, we should find a place to sleep," Avram says. The trail markers have been erased, or else someone has intentionally knocked them down or even turned the wooden posts in the wrong direction. "But it's so beautiful here," Ora whispers, and there is shame in her voice, as though she is peeking into someone else's scene. The path, which may no longer be their path—perhaps they have been exiled onto a different route—winds through olive groves and fruit-tree orchards, and a stream runs alongside. Ora feels the bristle of

Sami and their drive with Ofer to the army that day, and Yazdi who had slumped on her, and the woman who had breast-fed him, and the people who sat on the floor in the underground hospital, warming up food on little gas burners. And the man who knelt down and bandaged the foot of a guy sitting on a chair in front of him.

How had she not realized what Sami was going through when he saw those injured, beaten people? She swears that the first thing she'll do when she gets home is call him and apologize. She will describe to him exactly what state she was in that day and will force him, just like that, to make up with her. And if he refuses, she'll explain in the simplest way that they have to make up, because if she and he cannot make up after one bad day, then maybe there really is no chance that the greater conflict will be resolved. As she delves into these thoughts, moving her lips while she enthusiastically plans her conversation with Sami, Avram raises his eyebrows at the hilltop above them, where, behind a rock, a young shepherd is watching them. When he sees they've noticed him, he cups his hands over his mouth and calls out, in Arabic, to another shepherd perched on another hilltop, riding a horse or a mule. That one calls to a third shepherd who emerges on yet another hilltop, and Ora and Avram hurry down the path as the shepherds above them call back and forth. Avram translates for her out of the corner of his mouth: "Who are they?" one shepherd asks. "I don't know," another answers, "maybe tourists?" "Jews," the third determines. "Look at his shoes, they must be Jews." "Then what are they doing here?" "I don't know, maybe just walking." "Jews, just walking, here?" asks the horse-mounted shepherd, and his question remains unanswered. The sheepdogs bark while their owners shout, and the golden bitch gurgles and barks back. Ora pulls her close to her leg and tries to calm her.

One of the shepherds starts to sing, trilling his voice repeatedly, and the others join in from the hilltops. Avram hisses that they should hurry. To Ora the melody sounds like a courting or flirting song, or just crude innuendo aimed at her. They both walk quietly, practically running along the narrow path between the hills that close in on each other until they finally meet at a heap of boulders that blocks their way. At the foot of the massive boulders, on a large straw mat, three heavyset men are sprawled serenely, watching them without any expression.

"Shalom," Ora says and stands still, breathing heavily.

"Shalom," the three answer. On the mat between them are wedges of watermelon and a copper tray with three coffee cups. A *finjan* is heating on a kerosene burner.

"We're hiking," Ora says.

"*Sahtein*—good for you," says the oldest of the men. His face is strong and heavy, with a thick, yellowing white moustache.

"It's nice here," she murmurs, oddly apologetic.

"*Tfadalu*—please," says the man, waving for them to sit down and offering a dish of pistachios.

"What is this here?" Ora asks as she takes a larger handful than she'd meant to.

"We're Ein Mahel," says the man. "There, up top, is Nazareth, the stadium. Where did you come from?"

Ora tells him. Surprised, the men pull themselves up into seated positions. "So far? Are you, *ya'ani*, athletic?"

Ora laughs. "No, not at all. It worked out this way almost by accident."

"Coffee?"

Ora looks at Avram, who nods. They take their backpacks off. Ora finds a bag of cookies she bought that morning at Shibli, and a package of wafer biscuits from Kinneret. The man hands them slices of watermelon.

"But please, just don't talk to us about the news," Ora blurts out.

"Is there some special reason?" the man asks, slowly stirring the coffee in the *finjan*.

"No, no reason, we just want a rest from all that."

He pours coffee into little cups. The man next to him, thick-armed and taciturn, with a kaffiyeh and *agal* on his head, offers Avram a puff from his hookah. Avram takes it. Then a young man, undoubtedly one of the three shepherds who had watched them from the hilltops, comes galloping over on his horse and joins them. He is the grandson of the older man. His grandfather kisses his head and introduces him to the guests. "Ali Habib-Allah is his name. He's a singer, and he passed the first round for a competition they're going to show on your television," the grandfather says, laughing, and pounds his grandson's back affectionately.

"Tell me," Ora asks with a sudden boldness that surprises her, "would you be willing to answer two questions for me?"

"Questions?" The grandfather turns to her with his whole body. "What kind of questions?"

"Nothing, just a little thing," she giggles. "We're doing—actually we haven't really started it, we were just thinking of doing—we met some-one who was doing a sort of little survey, along the way." She laughs nervously again and does not look at Avram. "We thought, I thought, that every time we meet someone, we'd ask them two questions. Small ones."

Avram looks at her in astonishment.

"Which questions?" asks Ali, the boy, his cheeks flushed with excitement.

"Is this for the newspaper or something?" his grandfather asks, con-stantly stirring the coffee, turning the flame up and down under the pot.

"No, no, it's private, just for us." She blinks at Avram. "A souvenir from our trip."

"Ask away," says the grandson, and he spreads his legs out on the mat.

"If you don't mind," Ora says, pulling out the blue notebook, "I'll write down what you say, otherwise I won't remember anything." She is already holding a pen and looks from the old man to the younger one. "Very short questions," she adds, trying to retreat now, to shrink, to postpone the actual questioning, sensing the metallic taste of an ap-proaching mistake. But all eyes are upon her and there's no way out. "Okay, so the first question, it goes like this, what do you most—"

"Maybe it's better if we don't," the grandfather interrupts with a grin. He puts a heavy hand on the upper back of his grandson the singer. "More watermelon?"

"Once every three weeks or so, he would come home on leave," Ora repeats the next day, threading her way back into what came unraveled on Mount Devorah in the afternoon. She remembers how she would fall on him in the doorway, set upon him with insatiable hunger. His giant backpack would block the doorway and Ora would try to dislodge it with both hands and give up. "*Yalla*, come on, unpack now, before you do anything else. Straight into the washing machine. I'll thaw out some meatballs for you, we'll leave the steak for tonight. There's a new Bolognese sauce I want you to try—Dad loves it, maybe you'll like it too—and I have stuffed vegetables, and we'll have a nice salad soon, and tonight we'll have a big meal. Ilan!" she shouts, "Ofer's here!"

She retreats into the depths of the kitchen, brimming with animal happiness. If she could, she would lick him all over—even now, at his age—and scrub off everything that had stuck to him, restore the childhood smells that still linger in her nostrils, her mouth, her saliva. A wave of warmth spills out to him inside her, and Ofer, without budging at all, moves a whole hairsbreadth away from her. She feels it, and she knew it would happen: he seals himself off with that same quick shift of the soul that she knows from Ilan and Adam, from all her men, who time after time have slammed their doors shut in the face of her brimming, leaving her tenderness fluttering outside, faltering, turning instantly into a caricature.

But she will not allow the hurt to bubble up. Not now. And here comes Ilan from his study, taking his glasses off, and he hugs Ofer warmly, measuredly. He is careful with him. Cheek touches cheek. "Stop getting taller already," he scolds. Ofer lets out a tired, pale laugh. Ilan and Ora move around him with a mixture of happiness and caution. "So what's new in the trenches?" "Nothing really, how are things at home?" "Not bad, you'll find out everything soon enough." "Why, did something happen?" "No, what could happen? Everything's just like it was when you left." "Do you want to take a shower first?" "No, later."

He finds it difficult even to let go of the stinking uniform and the dirt that has stuck to his flesh and that, Ora guesses, protects him a little. Three weeks in the field, on patrols, fixing tanks, checkpoints, ambushes. He has a strong odor. His fingers are rough and full of cuts. His fingernails are black. His lips look as if they are constantly bleeding. His gaze is distracted and vacant. She sees the house through his eyes. The cleanliness, the symmetry of the rugs and the pictures and the little knickknacks. He seems to find it hard to believe that such refinement exists in the world. The softness is almost unbearable to him. When she looks at Ilan, she feels clearly how he sees himself now in Ofer's eyes, all nonchalant citizenry, demilitarized, almost criminal. Ilan crosses his arms over his chest, juts his chin out slightly, and murmurs to himself in a deep voice.

Ofer sits down at the kitchen table and holds his head in his hands. His eyes almost close. Gradually, a casual conversation begins to hum among the three of them, crumbs of speech that no one listens to, whose purpose is only to give Ofer a few minutes to adapt, to connect the world he has come from with this world, or perhaps, she thinks, to detach them from one another.

She knows—she explains to Avram—that she and Ilan cannot even guess the effort it takes to erase, or at least to suspend, his other world so that he can come into the house without getting burned in the transition. The thought must pass through Ilan's mind at that moment too, and they glance at each other. Their faces are still full of joy, but somewhere deep in their eyes, they avoid each other like accomplices to a crime.

Suddenly Ofer gets up and stands there rubbing his shaved head vigorously. He slowly moves between the kitchen and the dining area, back and forth, back and forth. Ilan and Ora watch him with sidelong looks; he isn't here, that's obvious. He's walking a different track, one that is imprinted in his mind. They concentrate on slicing bread and frying food. Ilan turns the radio on loud, and the sounds of the midday news program pour into the room. Ofer revives immediately and sits back down at the table as though he had never gotten up. A young soldier from the Jalameh checkpoint is telling the interviewer how she caught a seventeen-year-old Palestinian boy that morning trying to smuggle explosives through in his pants. She giggles that today happens to be her birthday. She's nineteen. "Happy birthday," says the interviewer. "Cool!" the soldier laughs. "I couldn't have thought of a better birthday present."

Ofer listens. Jalameh is no longer in his sector. He served there about eighteen months ago. It could have been him who had found the explosives. Or not found them. After all, that's his job, to stand there so the terrorist blows himself up on him and not on civilians. Ora's breath is short. She feels something approaching. She recites to herself the names of the checkpoints and posts where he's served. Hizmeh and Halhul and Al Jab'ah, those ugly names. And all that Arabic, she thinks as she pads from one foot to the other, with the gurgles and grunts and yammers. Why were Ilan and Avram so into it in high school and the army? She riles herself up even more: I mean, almost every word in that language has something or other to do with tragedy or catastrophe, doesn't it? She shoves Ilan: "Look at how you're chopping those vegetables. Don't you know he likes his salad chopped really fine? You set the table, do me a favor!" Ilan throws his hands up with an obedient smile, and Ora attacks the vegetables. She grabs a sharp knife, swings it, and lands it down furiously to dice Abd al-Qader al-Husseini with Haj Amin al-Husseini and Shukeiri and Nimeiri and Ayatollah Khomeini and Nashashibi and Arafat and Hamas and Mahmoud Abbas and all their kasbahs and Qaddafis and SCUDs and Izz ad-Din al-Qassam and Qassam rockets and Kafr Qasim and Gamal Abdel Nasser. She slaughters them all together: Katyushas and intifadas and martyr's brigades, and the sacred and the sanctified and the oppressed, Abu-Jilda and Abu Jihad, Jebalia and Jabaliyya, Jenin and Zarnuga, and Marwan Barghuouti, too. God knows where all those places are, anyway. If they could at least have normal-sounding names. She sighs. At least if their names were just a little nicer! Feverishly brandishing the knife, she finely chops up Khan Yunis and Sheikh Munis, Deir Yassin and Sheikh Yassin, Saddam Hussein and al-Qawuqji. All they bring is trouble, from the very first minute it's been nothing but trouble with them, she growls through gritted teeth. And what about Sabra and Shatila, and what about Al-Quds and the Nakba, and jihad and the *shaheeds* and *Allahu akbar*, and Khaled Mashal and Hafez al-Assad and Kōzō Okamoto? She pounds them all indiscriminately like a hornet's nest that must be destroyed, and she adds Baruch Goldstein and Yigal Amir, and with a sudden revelation she also throws in Golda and Begin and Shamir and Sharon and Bibi and Barak and Rabin, and Shimon Peres too—after all, don't they have blood on their hands? Did they really do everything they could so she could get five minutes of peace and quiet around here? All those people who razed her life, who keep nationalizing another one of her children every second—she stops when she notices Ofer's and Ilan's looks. She wipes the sweat off her forehead with the back of her hand and asks angrily, "What? What is it?" As if they too are to blame for something. Then she quiets herself. "It's nothing, never mind, I just remembered something, something was getting on my nerves." She dresses the salad generously with olive oil and a quick dash of salt and pepper, squeezes a lemon, and puts the lovely bowl down in front of Ofer, a kaleidoscope of colors and scents. "Here you go, Ofer'ke. An Arabic salad, just the way you like it."

Ofer arches his eyebrows to express his opinion of her curious performance. He is still moving very slowly. His distracted look gets trapped by a newspaper on the table and he stares at a cartoon without comprehending it, without knowing the context. He asks if there was anything on the news this week. Ilan gives him a report and Ofer flips through the paper. He's not interested, Ora thinks. This country, which he is protecting, doesn't really interest him. She's sensed that in him for a while now: it's as though the connection between the outer layer, where he spends most of his time, and the interior one, here, has been severed. "Where's the sports?" he asks, and Ilan extricates the sports section from the recycling pile. Ofer buries his head in it. Ora asks cautiously if he hears the news over there, if he's been following what's going on in Israel. He shrugs one shoulder wearily but also with a strange bitterness: all those arguments, right, left, same difference, who can be bothered.

He gets out of his chair, kneels, unfastens the straps of his backpack, and starts emptying it out. His skull amazes her: so large, full of power, and solid. Such a complex structure of heavy, mature bones. She stands there wondering when he had time to develop bones like that and how this head could have passed through her body. When he opens the backpack, a sharp stink of dirty socks fills the air. Ora and Ilan laugh awkwardly. The smell speaks volumes: Ora has the feeling that if she focuses on it, if she splits it into its filaments, she will know exactly what Ofer has gone through these past few weeks.

As though hearing her thoughts, he looks up at her with a pair of large eyes that are dark with exhaustion. For a moment he is very young again, needing Mom to read him. "What is it, Ofer'ke?" she asks feebly, alarmed at his expression. "Nothing is it," he answers habitually, and forces a tired smile. *Pussycat, pussycat, where have you been?* she thinks. *I've been to Halhul and the kasbah in Hebron. Pussycat, pussycat, what did you there? I lay in an ambush and shot rubber bullets at kids throwing stones.*

"I'm begging you," she'd said to him roughly a year earlier, even before the whole thing happened, maybe a month before. "Don't ever, ever shoot at them."

"Then what am I supposed to do?" he asked with a smirk. He skipped and danced around her, his broad chest bare and red, holding up a filthy khaki undershirt and writhing like a matador avoiding a bull. Every so often he leaned down and planted a light kiss on her forehead or cheek. "Just tell me what to do with them, Mom. They're a risk to people driving along the road!"

"Scare them," she said cunningly, as though she were trying out a new theory of warfare. "Slap them, punch them, anything, just don't shoot them!"

"We aim at the feet," he explained calmly, with that same amused superiority she knew from Adam and Ilan and the military analysts on television and the government ministers and the army generals. "And don't worry about them so much. The most a rubber bullet can do is break an arm or a leg."

"And if you miss and take someone's eye out?"

"Then that someone won't throw stones again. Let me give you an example: one of our guys shot three boys throwing stones at the pillbox this week, *bang-bang-bang*, broke their legs, one each, very elegantly done, and believe me, those kids won't be back there again."

"But their brothers will! And their friends will, and in a few years their children will!"

"Maybe you should aim so they'll never have any children," Adam suggested as he walked by, quiet and shadowy.

The boys laughed with slight embarrassment and Ofer glanced awkwardly at Ora.

She grabbed his hand and dragged him into Ilan's study and stood facing him. "Now! I want you to promise me right now that you will never shoot someone to hurt them!"

Ofer looked at her and the anger began to rise. "Mom, *khalas*, stop it, what are you . . . I have instructions, I have orders!"

Ora stomped her feet. "No! Never, do you hear me? You will never shoot to hurt a human being! For all I care, aim at the sky, aim at the ground, miss in every direction, just don't hit anyone!"

"And if he's holding a Molotov cocktail? If he has a gun? Huh?"

They'd already had this conversation, or one like it. Or maybe that was with Adam when he started his service. She knew all the arguments, and Ofer knew them, too. She had sworn to herself that she'd keep quiet, or at least be very careful. She was always afraid that at the decisive moment of battle, or if he were taken by surprise, ambushed, her words would enter his mind and fail him, or delay his reaction for a split second.

"If your life is in danger then okay, I'm not saying that. Then you try to save yourself any way you can, I'm not arguing about that, but only then!"

Ofer crossed his arms over his chest in Ilan's broad, relaxed posture, and widened his grin. "And how exactly am I supposed to know whether my life is in danger? Maybe I could ask the guy to fill out a declaration of intent?"

She was trapped in the loathsome feeling she always got when he—when anyone—played with her, exploited her well-known lack of debating skills, the rickety assertions that came to her in such moments.

"Really, Mom. Wake up. Hello! There's a war going on there! And anyway, I didn't think you were exactly crazy about them."

"What difference does it make what I think of them?" she screamed. "That's not the point. I'm not arguing with you now about whether we should even be there or not!"

"Well, for all I care, we can get out of there today and let them live their fucked-up lives on their own and kill each other. But at this point in time, Mom, when I have the lousy luck of having to be there, what do you want me to do? No, tell me. D'you want me to lie there and spread my legs for them?"

He had never talked to her that way before. He was burning with rage. Her spirits fell. There must be a winning argument that would counteract all these claims of his. Her fingers spread in a mute scream next to her ears. Wait a minute. She exhaled and tried to gather her ragged thoughts. Soon she'd get it together and clarify to herself exactly what she wanted to say. She'd arrange the words along the right thread, the simple one. "Listen, Ofer, I'm not any smarter than you" (she wasn't) "or any more moral than you" (even the word scared her; secretly she felt she didn't really understand its true meaning, unlike everyone else, who apparently did), "but I do have—and this is a fact!" (she shrieked this in a slightly cheap way) *"I do have more life experience than you!"* (Really? Suddenly this too melted away: Do you really? With everything he's going through in the army? With everything he sees and does, with everything he faces every single day?) "And I also know something that you simply cannot yet know, which is—"

Which is what? What? She could see the flash of amusement in his eyes, and swore she would not react to it. She would focus on the main point, on saving her child from the barbarian standing opposite her.

"That in five years—no, not five: one year! One year from now, when you get out, you'll look at this situation in a totally different way. Wait! I'm not even talking about whether or not it's just, I'm only talking about how one day you will look back at what happened there"—she heroically ignored his sniffle and the smirk spreading over his lips—"and you'll thank me," she said stubbornly; she was a little stuck, and they both knew it, stuck and desperately searching for the elusive winning argument. "You'll see that you'll thank me one day!"

"If I'm still alive to thank you."

"And don't talk to me like that!" she screamed, her face turning red. "I can't stand those kinds of jokes, don't you know that?"

Dad's jokes, they both knew.

Tears of fury came to her eyes. She had almost grasped a brilliant answer in her mind, a logical, organized point, but as usual she lost her train of thought, dropped the stitch, and so she just reached out and held his arm pleadingly and looked up at him: a final argument that was in fact a plea for mercy, if not charity. "Promise me, Ofer, just don't try to hurt someone intentionally."

He shook his head, smiled, and shrugged his shoulders. "No can do, Mom. It's war."

They looked at each other. Their estrangement terrified them. A memory flashed in her mind. That same cold burn of terror and failure from almost thirty years ago, when they took Avram from her, when they nationalized her life. She felt the same old story again: this country, with its iron boot, had once again landed a thundering foot in a place where the state should not be.

"Okay, Mom, enough. What's up with you? I'm just joking. Stop, enough." He reached out to hug her, and she was seduced—how could she not be? A hug of his own initiative. He even held her whole body to him, until she felt the mechanical signal on her back: *thwack-thwack-thwack*.

And throughout the squabble, she tells Avram with her gaze lowered, she actually did have one crushing argument, which of course she didn't tell Ofer, and which she is never allowed to use. Because what was really raging in her was not the eyes or the legs of some Palestinian kid, with all due respect, but rather her absolute certainty that Ofer could not hurt a human being, because if that happened, even if there were a thousand justifications, even if the guy was about to detonate an explosive device, Ofer's life would never be the same. That was it. Quite simply, and irrefutably, he would have no life after that.

But when she took a step back and looked at him, at the strength of his body, at that skull, she wasn't even certain about that.

Now, in the kitchen, he tells them he hasn't changed his clothes or even showered for a week. His speaks tightly, hardly moving his lips, and Ora and Ilan strain to decipher his words. Ora watches Ilan surreptitiously move to the balcony, to close a window or open a door, or just stand there on his own for a moment. She leans over the damp, sticky, greasy pile that has tumbled out of Ofer's backpack and gathers up uniforms, stiff socks, a military belt, undershirts, underwear. When she picks up the mess, sand leaks from pockets, and one bullet and a crumpled bus ticket fall out. She shoves the clothes into the machine and turns the dial to the most vigorous cycle. When the machine buzzes and the drum starts spinning, she feels the first sense of relief, as though she has finally revved up the process of domesticating this stranger.

And he sits at the table laid out for him, his head buried in the newspaper, and he can't find the strength to talk. He hasn't slept for thirty-some hours. There was lots of activity this week, but he'll tell them later. They quickly concur:

"Of course, yes, the main thing is that you're here," Ora says, "we almost lost our minds waiting."

"Mom's been cooking for you all morning."

"Don't exaggerate! Dad's exaggerating as usual, I haven't had time to make anything at all. It's a good thing I baked the brownies yesterday."

"Oh come on," Ilan moans, and presents his argument for Ofer to judge: "She was out shopping all afternoon yesterday. Robbed the greengrocer, looted the butcher. By the way, how's the food over there?"

"Better, there's a new cook and we don't have rats in the kitchen anymore."

"Are you with the same guys from training?"

"More or less. A few new ones came from another battalion, but they're all right."

"And did everyone go home this weekend?"

"Please, Dad, let's talk later. I'm dead tired now."

A strange silence falls on them. Ilan squeezes oranges and Ora heats up the meatballs. A strange boy with a strange smell sits at the kitchen table. Long threads untangle behind him all the way to a place that is difficult to see and hard to think about. Ilan is telling her something. Some minutiae about a deal he's been working on for two years between a Canadian venture-capital fund and two young guys from Beersheba who are developing a way to prevent drunk driving. Everything was ready to be signed, almost a done deal, and then at the last minute, when they took their pens out . . .

The words fail to penetrate her. She cannot act out her role in this play, all of whose actors are real. Her lines are familiar, but the space in which the play is staged—the shell of Ofer's tired, depressed silence—makes everything ridiculous and broken, and eventually Ilan also ebbs away and stops talking.

Standing over the sink, Ora shuts her eyes for a stolen moment, concentrates, and says her usual prayer—not to an exalted God, but the opposite. A pagan at heart, she makes due with little gods, day-to-day icons, and small miracles: If she gets three green lights in a row, if she has time to bring the laundry in before it rains, if the dry cleaner doesn't discover the hundred-shekel note she left in her jacket, then . . . And of course there are her usual bargains with fate. Someone rear-ends her bumper? Excellent: Ofer just won immunity for a week! A patient refuses to pay a two-thousand-shekel debt? Penance! Another two thousand credits for Ofer are recorded somewhere.

From within the unpleasant silence a new round of domestic chatter starts up.

"Where's the onion left from the salad?"

"Do you need it?"

"I was thinking of frying some up with the meatballs."

"And put black pepper on it, he likes black pepper, don't you, Ofer?"

"Yes, but not too much. Our cook is Moroccan, his *shakshuka* sets my mouth on fire."

"So you eat *shakshuka*?"

"Three times a day."

And the strand thickens furtively, slyly, weaving back and forth, and then Adam calls and says he's two seconds from home, he's just stopping to buy the paper and some snacks and they shouldn't start eating without him. The three of them exchange grinning looks—Adam, operating us all by remote control. Ilan and Ora blather on about everything that's changed in the house in the weeks since Ofer left. "He was always involved in all the goings-on at home," she tells Avram on a path near Tzippori that cuts through an open field covered with thousands of brown-orange woolly-bear caterpillars squirming in unison inside their silk cocoons, so that the entire field seems to be dancing. "He always wanted to know about every piece of furniture we were thinking of buying and demanded that we report to him whenever an appliance broke and how much it cost to fix and what the repairman was like. He made us swear we would never, God forbid, throw out any broken appliance, or even the old parts, until he could examine them. When he started the army he even asked us to keep minor repairs for him to do when he was on leave—electrical work, plumbing, stopped-up drains, broken blinds, and yard work, of course." But it seems to Ora that he's a little tired of that now. The mundane defects of the house no longer concern him.

The table is set and the food is ready, and Ilan says something that manages to bring the first spark of a smile to Ofer's face, which they both treat as though it were an ember they have to breathe life into. Ofer tells them they have a cat with two kittens in the pillbox, and he's decided to adopt the mother. He blushes slightly: "I was thinking, you know, just so I'd have something maternal there." He gives an embarrassed laugh, and Ora hovers over the frying pan odors, and here is Adam, finally home. "Everything's cold," she complains, but everything's still steaming hot, and the boys hug, and the sounds of their voices mingle, and they laugh together, a sound unlike any other. "Sometimes, here, on this journey," she tells Avram, "I dream about that sound, and I can really hear the two of them laughing."

Ofer's face lights up when he sees Adam, his eyes follow him wherever he goes, and only now does he seem to understand that he's home, and he begins to awaken from his three-week slumber. And when Ofer awakes, they do, too. The four of them come to life, and the kitchen itself, like a reliable old machine, joins them in tracking Ofer's movements, loyally running in the background, humming with the quiet commotion and the jingle of its unseen pistons and wheels. Listen to the soundtrack, she thinks. Believe in the soundtrack. This is the right tune: a pot bubbles, the fridge hums, a spoon clangs on a plate, the faucet flows, a stupid commercial on the radio, your voice and Ilan's voice, your children's chatter, their laughter—I never want this to end. From the pantry comes the rhythmic whirr of the washing machine, now augmented by the sound of metal clicking; probably a belt buckle, or a screw left in a pocket, but not, Ora hopes, another misplaced bullet, which will suddenly explode and fly at us all in the third act.

One day about a year ago she asked the secretary at her clinic to cancel her next patient. She'd had a rough day, hardly slept all night—"the stuff at home had already started," she says, and Avram listens tensely:

there is something in her voice—and she thought she might pop over to one of the boutiques on Emek Refaim to buy a scarf or a pair of sunglasses or something to cheer her up. She walked down Jaffa Street toward the parking lot where she left her car every day. The street was uncharacteristically still and the eerie silence disquieted her. She wanted to turn around and go back to the clinic, but she kept walking, and noticed that people on the street were walking quickly, without looking one another in the eye. A moment later she herself began to act the same way, lowering her eyes and avoiding people, except to steal secret glances, to scan and sort. Mostly, she looked to see if they were carrying anything, a package or a large bag, or if they looked nervous. But almost everyone looked somehow suspect, and she thought perhaps they saw her that way, too. Perhaps she should let them know that she posed no danger? That they could be calm around her and save themselves a few heartbeats? On the other hand, maybe she should not disclose that sort of information so casually here. She pulled back her shoulders and forced herself to straighten up and look right at people's faces. When she did, she saw in almost every person a note that hinted at some latent possibility—the possibility of being a murderer or a victim, or both.

When had she learned these movements and these looks? The nervous glances over her shoulder, the footsteps that seemed to sniff out their path and make their own choices. She discovered new things about herself, like symptoms of an emerging disease. It seemed as though the others, walking around her, everyone, even the children, were fitfully moving to the sounds of a whistle that only their bodies could hear, while they themselves were deaf to it. She walked faster, and her breath grew short. How do you get out of this? she wondered. How do you get away from here? When she reached a bus stop, she halted and sat down on one of the plastic seats. It had been years since she'd waited at a bus stop, and even this act of sitting on the smooth yellow plastic was an admission of defeat. She straightened up and slowed her breath. In a minute she would get up and keep walking. She remembered that in the first wave of suicide bombings, Ilan had gone with Ofer—Adam was in the army by then—to scout out safe walking routes from his school downtown to the stop where he got the bus for home. The first route was too close to where a terrorist had blown himself up on the 18 bus, killing twenty passengers. When Ilan suggested that Ofer could walk up the Ben Yehuda pedestrian mall, Ofer reminded him of the triple explosion on the mall, where five people were killed and a hundred and seventy injured. Ilan tried to outline a slightly longer route, which would go around the back and come out near the Mahaneh Yehuda market, but Ofer pointed out that this was exactly where a double suicide bombing had occurred: fifteen dead and seventeen injured. And anyway, he added, all the buses from town to Ein Karem go past the central bus station, where there had also been a bombing—the 18 again, twenty-five dead and forty-three injured.

And so the two of them roamed from street to street—as she recounts the story to Avram, she has the horrifying thought that Ofer may still have his orange spiral notebook where he writes the numbers of dead and wounded—and the streets and the alleyways where there hadn't yet been a bombing seemed so foreordained and vulnerable that Ilan was amazed nothing had happened on them yet. Finally he gave up, stopped in the middle of a street, and said, "You know what, Oferiko? Just walk as fast as you can. Run, even."

And the look Ofer gave him—he told Ora later—he will never forget.

As she was contemplating all this, a bus stopped at the station. When the door opened, Ora dutifully got up and stepped in, and only then realized she had no idea what the bus fare was or which route she was on. She hesitantly held out a fifty-shekel note, and the driver growled at her for change. She dug through her purse but couldn't find any, and he hissed a curse, handed her a handful of coins, and hurried her in. She stood looking at the passengers, most of whom were older and had weary, gloomy faces. Some were on their way back from the market, propping crammed baskets between their feet. There were a few high school students in uniform who were strangely quiet, and Ora looked at them all with bewilderment and muted compassion. She wanted to turn around and get off—"I never meant to take the bus," she tells Avram— but someone behind her pushed her farther in, and Ora padded a few steps ahead. Since there were no vacant seats, she stood holding the overhead bar, leaned her cheek on her arm, and watched the city through the window. What am I doing here? she thought. I don't have to be here. They passed the jumble of shops on Jaffa Street, the Sbarro restaurant, and then Zion Square, where a booby-trapped refrigerator had blown up in 1975, killing, among many others, the artist Naftali

Bezem's son, whom she'd known in the army. Ora wondered if Bezem had been able to paint after his son's death. At the YMCA stop, a few seats opened up, and she sat down and decided she would get off at the next stop. She stayed on as they passed Liberty Bell Park and Emek Refaim, and when the bus drove past Café Hillel she said, half out loud, Now you're getting off and going in for a cup of coffee. And she kept going.

It was amazing to her how quiet the passengers were. Most of them gazed out the windows as she did, as though not daring to look at their fellow passengers. Every time the bus stopped at a station, they all sat up a little straighter and stared at the people getting on. The new passengers, in turn, scanned them with squinting eyes. It was a very quick exchange of glances, for a fraction of a second, but there was the wondrously complex labor of sorting and cataloging going on, and Ora stayed on the bus through the Katamonim neighborhood and the Malha Mall, until they reached the last stop and the driver looked at her in the rearview mirror and called out, "Lady, end of the road." Ora asked if there was a bus back to town. "That one over there," the driver said and pointed to the 18. "But run, 'cause he's about to move. I'll honk at him to wait for you."

She got on the empty bus, and her eyes refracted a split-second scene that was torn, shattered, and bloody. She wondered where the safest seat was; had she not been embarrassed, she would have asked the driver. She tried to remember the many reports she'd heard about bus bombings and couldn't decide whether most of them occurred when the terrorist got on the bus, in which case of course it would be in the front part, or whether he went farther inside, and then, once he was standing in the middle of the bus, surrounded by most of the passengers, he called out his *Allahu akbar* and pressed the button. She decided to sit in the back row and pushed away the thought of how the shrapnel and the metal studs would somehow be stopped before they reached her. But after a minute she felt too lonely, and she moved one row forward. Wondering if this simple switch might seal her fate in just a few moments, she met the driver's probing eyes in the mirror. "And suddenly it occurred to me," she tells Avram, "that he might end up thinking I'm the suicide bomber."

After an hour of traveling she was exhausted but afraid to let down her guard. Her eyelids drooped and she fought the urge to lean her head on the window for a quick nap. For the last few days she had felt like a child who discovers, unhappily and too quickly, the grown-ups' secrets. A week earlier, she'd sat down one morning at Café Moment when the place was neither full nor empty, and a short, stocky woman wearing a heavy coat had come in, holding a baby covered with a blanket on her shoulder. She was not a young woman, around forty-five, and perhaps that was what seemed suspicious, because suddenly a whisper of "It's not a baby" flew through the air, and the place turned upside down in an instant. People leaped up, overturned chairs as they fled, knocked over plates and glasses, fought one another to get to the door. The woman in the coat observed the commotion with a baffled look and did not seem to comprehend that it was all because of her. Then she sat down at a table and placed the baby on her lap. Ora, unable to move, watched the woman, transfixed. She unwrapped the blanket, unfastened the buttons of a little purple coat, and smiled at the chubby, sleepy face that peered out. She cooed at the baby: *"Ah-googoo, googoo, googoo."*

The next afternoon—Ora tells him on their way up to the Reish Lakish lookout point, as they step in the footprints of ancient Rabbinic sages on a glaring hot day; the level path winds comfortably through carob and oak trees, and plump cows graze in the distance—she asked her secretary to cancel her next session again, walked to the 18 bus stop, and took the bus to the last station. Since her afternoon was free and she didn't feel like being alone at home, she took the bus back all the way to the first stop, in the Kiryat HaYovel neighborhood, where she changed to another bus and took it back downtown. She got off and walked around for a while, watched the reflection of the street behind her as she window-shopped, scanned the passersby, and forced herself to move slowly.

The next morning, before her first patient, she got the 18 at the central bus station, and this time she sat in front. Every three or four stops, she got off and changed to a different bus. Sometimes she crossed the street and rode the other way. She tried to sit in a different place every time, as though her body were a pawn in an imaginary game of chess. When she realized she was late for her third patient, she had a brief moment of fear that her clinic directors would call her in for another talk, but she postponed the thought to a time when she would have more energy. She was so tired during those days that the moment she sat down she would let her head droop, and sometimes she'd doze off for several minutes. Every so often she would drowsily look up at the people on the bus through a haze. Voices from conversations between strangers and phone calls penetrated her slumber. If they stopped at a station and no one got on, relief would immediately spread through the bus, and the passengers would talk to one another. A heavyset elderly man adorned with Red Army medals who sat next to Ora on one of her journeys pulled a large brown envelope from his shopping basket and showed her an X-ray of his kidney, which had a growth on it. Through the X-ray, Ora could dimly make out two Ethiopian soldiers from Border Patrol checking the papers of a young man who might or might not have been Arab. He kept kicking at the sidewalk.

They stop and take a breath. Hands on waists. Why have we been running like this? they ask one another silently. But something is already kicking at their heels, stirring pins and needles in their souls, and they merely glance at the beautiful Netofa Valley and walk on quickly through a forest of terebinth, oak, and birch trees. Ora walks silently, her eyes on the path. Avram throws her a few cautious looks and his face constricts and closes up from one step to the next. "Look," she whispers, pointing. On the path, at their feet, a crowded series of hieroglyphics emerges, a crosshatch that flows and runs from all directions until it congregates in a cluster of snails on one branch of a bush.

By the second week, some of the drivers recognized her. But since there was nothing suspicious about her, they filtered her out of their minds so they could focus on more important things. She began to identify a few regular passengers and knew where they got on and where they got off. If they talked on their cell phones, or with their fellow travelers, she also knew something about their ailments and their families, and what they thought about the government. An elderly couple drew her attention in particular. The man was tall and thin, the woman very small, shriveled, and almost translucent. When she sat down, her feet swung without reaching the floor of the bus. She always had a bad, phlegmy cough, and the man would worriedly examine her used tissues and replace them with fresh ones. Ora woke up a little every time the couple got on, at the market. They took the bus to the last stop, the way she did, and to her surprise they almost always switched with her to the bus going back and got off at the same station where they had originally boarded, on the other side of the street. She couldn't understand the meaning of their route.

Day after day, for three or four weeks, Ora took the 18 bus and spent at least an hour traveling around the city. She discovered that the bad thoughts loosened their grip on her while she was on the bus. Most of the time she did not have a single complete thought, merely transposing her body from one stop to the next. She grew accustomed to the jolting, the screeching brakes, the potholes, and the religious radio stations blasting their admonitions at full volume. And she realized that Ilan never asked her what she did for long stretches of the day, and she could keep her activities from him. Sometimes, when they sat down for dinner, she would stare at him and silently scream with her eyes: How can you not sense where I am and what I'm doing? How can you let me go on like this?

"Just then, the thing with Ofer happened," she says cryptically to Avram, who has been quiet for a long time. "We had a crazy month, with the constant questionings in the battalion and the brigade, and the inquiries and investigations. Don't ask." She sighs and swallows her saliva. Here comes the moment when I have to tell him. He has to hear it, to know, to judge for himself.

In those days it seemed to Ora that every word she uttered, every look she gave, and even every silence were perceived by Ofer, Ilan, and Adam as a provocation, the premise for a fight. On these bus journeys, she felt a slight reprieve from them, and from herself too, from her strange insistence on bickering with them over and over again, and from her petty, circuitous questions, which were honestly starting to drive her mad. They burst out of her like acidic hiccups every time she so much as thought about what had happened there, when she merely heard the beeps signaling the hourly radio news, or even when she just thought about Ofer. "It's like I couldn't think of him without going through the incident first."

"But what happened?" Avram asks.

She listens inside herself, as though the answer will come, finally, from there. Avram holds his backpack straps with both hands—grips them.

One day Ora left the clinic, apologized distractedly to a couple in the waiting room, and hopped on the 18 bus for a quick ride. When they were near the Mekasher bus depot, she heard a very loud explosion. Then there was a moment of bottomless silence. The passengers' faces slowly foundered and turned to pulp. A powerful stench of excrement spread through the air, and Ora was flushed with cold sweat. People started to shout, curse, and cry, and begged the driver to let them out. The driver stopped in the middle of the street and opened the doors, and the passengers streamed out, fighting one another, kicking and punching to get out first. The driver looked in the mirror and asked, "Are you all staying?" Ora turned back to see who else he was talking to, and there was her elderly couple, huddled against each other, the woman's tiny, almost bald head buried in the man's body as he leaned over her and caressed her shoulder. Their expressions were difficult to describe: a mixture of shock and fear and also terrible disappointment. The radio immediately switched to emergency broadcast format— "First of all, allow me to express my condolences, to wish a speedy recovery to the injured, and to grieve with the families," said ministers and security experts one after the other. The explosion had occurred on a bus going the opposite way, near Davidka Square, which Ora's bus had driven past only moments before. The ambulances were already roaring to Shaare Zedek and Hadassah hospitals.

The next morning, soldiers and policemen manned all the bus stops, and the few passengers were even more nervous, irritable, and suspicious than usual. There were outbursts of anger at anyone who pushed in line, trod on a toe, or bumped into someone. People talked loudly on their cell phones. Ora felt they were using the phones as breathing tubes to the outside world. When the bus passed the site of the attack, there was a silence. Through the window she saw a bearded Orthodox man, a volunteer from the victim-identification unit, standing in a tree-top and using a cloth and tweezers to peel something gently off a branch and place it in a plastic bag. A group of kindergarten children got on the bus in Beit HaKerem, and a few of them were holding colorful balloons. They laughed and chattered and ran around, and everyone stared at the balloons. When one inevitably popped, although everyone could see it was just a balloon, a bitter screech of panic pierced the bus, and a few of the children burst into tears. The passengers, ashamed and exhausted, avoided one another's eyes.

More than once on those circular journeys, Ora realized that if she happened to see someone she knew, she wouldn't know how to tell that person what she was doing there or where she was going. Sometimes she thought to herself: What is this ridiculous behavior? Just think how Ilan and the boys would feel if something happened to you, or if Ofer thought, God forbid, that it was because of him. Or that because of him you wanted something to happen to you. Yet still, for three or four weeks, every single day, a moment would come when she could not stop herself from leaving home or work and walking in a shamefaced, defeated sort of daydream state to the nearest bus stop, where she stood at some distance from the other people—all of whom also made a point of keeping a little distance between themselves—and got on a bus. She would walk into the middle, look dimly at an empty seat waiting for her, and search for her elderly couple, who seemed to expect her by now and who would nod with the forlorn partnership of co-conspirators. She would sit down, lean her head on the window, sometimes doze, and travel for a few stops or a whole route. She never knew in advance how much time she would have to spend on the bus, nor was she capable of picking herself up and getting off until the moment arrived when— without any apparent reason—she sensed relief, release, as though the effect of an injected substance had diminished, and only then could she get off the bus and go on with her day.

As the weeks went by, she was more and more able to summon up the image of the strange old man who had danced and laughed and frol- icked, naked as the day he was born, in front of the soldiers who had finally freed him from the meat locker in the cellar in Hebron. "The building's owner was a wealthy butcher," she explains to Avram, who still does not understand, but he is breathing faster and his eyes dart. And the soldiers, she remembers, were so embarrassed when they talked about it, about his nude dance, as though that was the hardest thing about the whole incident. He made a total idiot out of himself, one soldier told her when he slept over at their house the night before one of the inquiries. His name was Dvir, a kibbutznik from Kfar Szold. Six-five, lanky, stammering, and slightly juvenile. Ora drove him and Ofer to the brigade HQ—

"Wait, Ora," Avram says with a pale face. "I can't follow, who is this old man?"

"The army actually took the case seriously," she says after a few moments of silence, during which they plunge to the ground, suddenly exhausted, and sit on the edge of a pool glistening with large yellow water lilies. The dog keeps jumping into the water, spraying everything around her, urging them to join in. But they do not see her. They sit side by side, hunched over.

Even though Ofer had begged her several times to stop talking about it, at least in public, Ora had to ask Dvir: "But how could you forget he was there?"

Dvir shrugged his broad shoulders. "I don't know, maybe everyone in the platoon thought someone else had let him out."

Ofer sniffed angrily and Ora vowed to keep quiet, not to say another word. She drove on with her brow furrowed and her shoulders hunched up almost to her ears. "But how could you forget a human being?" The words escaped her lips again after a few moments. "Just explain to me how you can forget a human being in a meat locker for two whole days!"

Avram lets out an uncontrolled grunt of pain and surprise. The sound of a body dropped from up high hitting the ground.

Dvir looked at Ofer pleadingly. Ofer said nothing, but his eyes darkened. Ora saw, but she could not stop herself.

"What can I tell you, Ora? It really wasn't right, there's no question about that. We're all eating our hearts out now, but you have to take into account that everyone was busy with their assignments, we're pulling eight-by-eight roadblock shifts that suck your brain dry, and the fact that all of a sudden they took us on an assignment we didn't even know how to do, and we had to keep some families with us in that apartment for two days, in one room, with one bathroom, and kids and old people and all their crying and yelling and whining, and just that is enough to make you lose your shit, and at the same time you have to do lookouts onto the street and the killing zone, and cover for the prima donna snipers, and make sure the Hamasniks don't booby-trap our downstairs doors, so it ended up falling between the cracks."

Ora bit her lip. Mustering up all the restraint she could find within herself, she said, "Still, Dvir, I can't understand how a bunch of guys—"

"Mom!" Ofer yelled. A single yell that cut like a knife. They drove the rest of the way in silence. When they got to HQ, Ofer wouldn't let her wait for him to hear the results of the preliminary inquiry, as she had intended to do. "You're going home now," he announced.

Ora looked at him, at her strong child with the shaved head and the pure gaze, and her eyes brimmed with tears. The question almost burst out again, and Ofer said in a terrifyingly quiet voice, "Mom, listen closely. This is the last time I'm going to tell you. Get off my case. *Get off my case!*"

His eyes were gray steel, his lips iron wire, and his shaved skull a ball of cold fire. Ora shrank back from his power, his hardness, and above all his foreignness, and he turned his back on her and left without letting her kiss him.

She drove off, wild with sorrow, hardly able to see the road. A pelting, dusty rain began to fall, and one of the Fiat Punto's windshield wipers didn't work, and Ilan phoned and she couldn't say more than a few words without shouting the question, and of course he lost his patience too—it's a wonder he kept it for so long—and said he was getting sick and tired of her sanctimonious self-righteousness and that she should really keep in mind that Ofer needed her now, needed her full support.

Ora bellowed, "Support for what? Support for what?" even though she wanted to yell, Support for whom? Because she really wasn't sure anymore.

Ilan softened his voice. "Support for your son. Listen, you're his mother, right? You're the only mother he has, and he needs you unconditionally now, do you understand? You're his mother, you're not some Mother for Peace, okay?"

Ora was dumbfounded: Where had he come up with that? What did she have to do with Mothers for Peace? What did she have to do with those leftist women and their supposedly neutral checkpoint observations? She didn't even like them! There was something defiant and annoying and unfair about them and the whole idea, coming to harass soldiers while they worked. How could you blame those kids, who'd been stuck there to man those checkpoints for three years? Instead of doing that, why didn't they go and demonstrate at the military compound, or go and shout outside the Knesset? She'd always sensed a slightly grumbling weakness about them, with their excessive self-confidence and their total lack of reverence when they faced officers at the checkpoints or debated senior commanders on television panels. If not reverence, she thought, at least they should show a little gratitude, just a tiny bit, for the people who were doing our dirty work and eating all the Occupation shit for us, to keep us safe. As she conducted this confused dialogue with herself, Ilan kept talking softly: "Yes, there was a screwup. It really is awful, I agree with you. But Ofer isn't to blame, get that into your head. There were twenty soldiers in that building and in the periphery. *Twenty*. You can't saddle this whole case on him. He wasn't the commander there, he isn't even an officer. Why do you think he has to be more righteous than everyone else?"

"You're right," Ora murmured. "You're a hundred percent right, but"—and again the question dislodged itself against her will. It had been like that for weeks, she had no control over it, as though her body was independently producing the toxic compound that hiccupped out of her at regular intervals. Ilan was still in control of himself. It was amazing how all the people around her controlled themselves while she was falling apart. Sometimes she even suspected that the three of them were able to control themselves precisely *because* she was crumbling and that in some strange way, upholding some hidden and complicated home economics, she was even conducting her embarrassing, shameful collapse *instead* of them, and perhaps for their sake. Ilan reminded her for the thousandth time that as early as Thursday morning, roughly at four-thirty a.m., nine hours after the old man was put in the room— "was put," he said; she noticed that the three of them had started using the passive voice: "was put," "was left," "had been forgotten"—Ofer had actually asked his commander what about the guy in the room downstairs, and he was told that Nir, the company commander, must have sent someone to take him out by now. At six that evening he'd asked Tom, the operations sergeant, and they'd told him over the walkie-talkie that there was no way someone hadn't let the man out by now.

And then he didn't ask anymore, Ora thought. And Ilan said nothing. Ofer himself had told them he'd somehow forgotten, he had other fish to fry, and Ora realized that perhaps there comes a moment when you can no longer ask that kind of question, because you begin to fear the answer.

Avram listens and thrusts his head lower and lower between his shoulders. She cannot see his eyes at all.

Ilan took a deep breath and said, "What do you want, Ora? Up to now, in all the investigations, the army has even cleared Nir and Tom, because of all the chaos going on around them."

"I don't want anything, and I hope they really do clear all the guys. But still, just explain to me how for two whole days Ofer didn't think to go down and check for himself—"

They'd had this argument many times during the last month, reciting their lines over and over again with growing desperation, and now Ilan yelled, "Enough with this already! Listen to yourself, what's gotten into you? You've become a crazy woman!" And he hung up on her. After a few minutes he called to apologize. They never hung up on each other, and he'd never burst out at her like that before. "But you're really getting on my nerves with this," he said in a weary voice, and she could hear his desire for reconciliation and knew he was right and that they had to unite to get through this together. If matters were not handled sensibly and calmly, the case could deteriorate into a court-martial, rather than just the comprehensive inquiry being held in the battalion and the brigade. And if that happened, it was only a matter of time before it got into the news, as Ilan often reminded her, and those assholes were just looking for an excuse to dig up some dirt. You also had to remember, Ora recited to herself, that ultimately no one had died in that meat locker, and no one had been wounded or even starved, because there were cows and sheep and goats hanging on the meat hooks, and the old Palestinian man had managed to remove the gag they'd tied on his mouth so he wouldn't shout. And thanks to the frequent power cuts mandated by the army in the killing zone, the man didn't even freeze, and in fact at times he was kind of cooking down there—they boiled him and then froze him, then thawed him out again, as she had gradually understood from Ofer's fellow soldiers with whom she was able to talk. Naked and reeking and covered with animal blood, he had rolled around on the floor when they'd finally opened the meat locker's door—Ofer was home by then. "That Friday, at six p.m., he'd been sent home," she murmurs to Avram. "Do you understand? He wasn't even there." And after they opened the door, he started to twitch and convulse on the sidewalk, and it was as if he performed a strange dance for the soldiers as he lay there, banging his head on the sidewalk. He pointed at the soldiers and at himself and cackled horribly, as though for the two days he was locked up he had kept hearing a tremendous joke, and soon he would get his act together and tell it to them. They ordered him to get up and he refused, or maybe he could not stand up. He just stumbled and squirmed at their feet and kept banging his head on the sidewalk and crowing his crazy laugh. Ora resisted telling Ofer's friends, or Ilan and Adam, and Ofer himself, what was on the tip of her tongue: that perhaps going out of his mind was the only way a Palestinian could get through all the checkpoints and the permits and the physical examinations. But that thought was foreign to her too, and it seemed to have been created by her brain against her own will, and for a moment she wondered what would happen if she started having more and more of these outbursts, left-wing Tourette's attacks, and she quickly pulled herself together. After all, she reasoned, you should be grateful to Ilan for being so supportive of Ofer. He had studied the details of the case and reconstructed with Ofer every single minute of those two days, and prepped him carefully before each interrogation and questioning. He'd also talked to a couple of people he knew in the army and elsewhere and had gently pulled a few strings to bring the matter to a quick conclusion, by limiting it to the internal inquiry in the brigade. Ora swore that from now on she would try to control her big mouth. All was not yet lost, and now that she'd had her say, she could finally resume her natural place in the family and once again be mama bear protecting her cub. It was so clear, after all, that she could not keep enflaming this fight for even one more day. Cracks and slits were widening and appearing everywhere, and whenever she looked at Ilan she knew he felt the same way, that he was just as alarmed and no less paralyzed by what was happening to them.

Avram listens and wraps his arms tightly around himself. He feels a frost descend on him in the midst of the blinding light-blue shades of the Tzippori River—the frost of a dark confinement cell, a forehead slammed against stone. Ora, her lips drained of blood, tells him how she and Ilan used to wake up and lie silently next to each other during those nights. They felt that their family was coming apart with remarkable speed; a trampling force that seemed to have been lurking all those years had now burst out and lunged at them with incomprehensible fervor, even with an oddly gleeful vengefulness. Avram contorts his face with intolerable pain and shakes his head, No, no.

With just a little restraint and coolheadedness, she could still stop the deterioration, she thought as she drove and listened to Ilan softly try to placate her. It depended only on her now, on one kind word from her, on her giving up this poison that was bubbling inside her and killing her, too. But suddenly she pounded the steering wheel with both hands and shouted at the phone from the depths of her heart: "How could he not remember? A man in a meat locker!"—she slammed the wheel to the rhythm of her words, and Avram pulled back as though he were the one being hit—"A night and a day, and another night and day—how could he not remember? He remembers every single thing that has to be done, doesn't he? Every leaky faucet, every door handle. He's the most responsible kid in the world, yet he can forget a human being for a whole night and day and night—"

"But why are you picking on *him*?" Ilan had groaned painfully, and she felt that she had finally managed to penetrate a shield. Ilan muttered, as if to himself, "Did *he* initiate it? Did *he* want something like this to happen? Did *he* decide to put that man in there?" Only now did Ora notice that two police cars were flashing their lights behind her and to her left, and the policemen were signaling for her to drive onto the shoulder. Suddenly frightened, she sped up. God knows what she'd done now; she'd only gotten her license back two months ago, after a six-month revocation. "And do I have to remind you again that there was a big operation going on there?" Ilan went on. "There were wanted men, and shooting, and Ofer hadn't slept for forty-eight hours, and only by chance his guys were sent to do a job they weren't even supposed to do and weren't trained for, so what are we even arguing about?"

"But he was there in the building, three floors up, and he ate and drank there and went up and down the stairs." She slid onto the muddy shoulder and drove quickly, hoping somehow to outrun the police. She finally stopped when they closed in on her. "And he talked over the radio at least twenty times with Chen and with Tom, and he had twenty opportunities to ask if they'd let the old man out already, and what did he do?" Ilan did not answer. "Tell me, Ilan, what did he do, our child?" Ora roared hoarsely. She heard Ilan straining to hold his breath and not explode again. Three policemen got out of the two cars and approached. One of them was talking on his walkie-talkie. Ilan said, "You know he meant to go down there and see." She scoffed—an alien, loathsome scoff. "Meant to, yeah, sure. For two whole days he kept meaning to go down, but just when he was most meaning to, they came to tell him there was a ride leaving for Jerusalem, right? And then we all went out to the restaurant, right? And he forgot, right?" She let out an amazed guffaw and held her head in both hands, as though she was only now, for the first time, finding out the true story. "And that whole evening in the restaurant, he didn't remember! Oops, sorry, slipped my mind! Doesn't that incense you?" Ora roared and the veins on her neck swelled. "Tell me, Ilan, doesn't that make you crazy?" "Ora, you're losing your mind," Ilan said, retreating into his sobering tone, the one that observed her with amused wonder, the one he used when they fought, when he let her wallow alone in her bitterness, in the filth that burst out of her. "Just please be careful and keep your eye on the road," he added with that same tone of lawyerly advice. Ora locked the Punto's doors from inside and ignored the cops rapping on the windows, their faces pressed up against the glass. One of them ran a scolding finger over the half of the front windshield that was caked with drops of muddy rain, and Ora laid her head on the steering wheel and murmured, "But it's Ofer, do you understand that, Ilan? It happened to *us*. It's our Ofer. How could Ofer, how *could* he?"

AT FIVE-THIRTY in the morning, at the point where Mount Carmel begins to rise, Ora and Avram disentangle from each other. He folds the tents and the sleeping bags and packs up their two backpacks, and Ora goes to buy some food at a nearby grocery store.

"We haven't been apart for a long time," she says, coming back to wrap herself around him.

"Should I come with you?"

"No, stay here with the stuff. I'll only be a few minutes."

"I'll wait."

"And I'll be back," she adds, sounding uncertain. "I don't know what I'm suddenly afraid of," she murmurs into his embrace.

"Maybe that you'll see what civilization is like and you'll want to stay."

She is uneasy. An obstinate embolus moves inside her body like the undigested remnants of a dream. She stretches her arms and holds

Avram back to look at him, engraving him in her memory. "Now I can see that I didn't give you a good haircut. I'll snip that straggler off today."

He fingers the stray lock.

"And maybe you'll let me shave you, too?"

"Yes?"

"I don't know, it's annoying to see you with a beard."

"Oh, that."

"Yes, that."

"Okay."

"Maybe just a trim. We'll see. We'll just take a little off."

"Don't you think I'm off enough as it is?"

They look at each other. The spark of a smile in their pupils.

"Buy some salt and pepper. And we're almost out of oil."

"And we need batteries for the flashlight, right?"

"And bring some chocolate, I could go for something sweet."

"Anything else, my dear?"

A soft hand travels inside them on its fingertips. Avram shrugs. "I've gotten used to you."

"Watch out, you'll get addicted."

"What's going to happen, Ora?"

She puts a finger to his lips. "First let's finish the trail, and then we'll see what works for us." She kisses him on each eye and turns to leave. The dog looks from Ora to Avram, unsure whether to join her or stay with him.

"Wait, Ora, hold up."

She stops.

"It's good for me to be with you," he says quickly and lowers his gaze to his hands. "I want you to know that."

"Then say it. I need to be told."

"The way you let me be with you like this, and with Ofer, and with all of you." His eyes redden. "You don't know what you're giving me, Ora."

"Well, I'm just giving you back what belongs to you."

They cling to each other again—since she's taller than he, she has to hold her feet slightly apart; it's always been that way—and for some reason she remembers how every time she was about to go and see him in Tel Aviv, during those years when he agreed to meet, Ofer always sensed it. He used to grow restless and gloomy and sometimes run a high fever, as though trying to sabotage their meeting. When she got back he would sniff her out like an animal, demanding to know exactly what she'd been doing. And he always asked, with transparent slyness, whether Ilan knew where she'd been.

Avram holds her to his body, cups her buttocks with both hands, and mumbles that there's nothing like her gluteus maximus and her gluteus medius. "Take care of yourself there, in the store," he says into her hair, and they both hear what he has not said: Don't talk with anyone too much. If the radio is on, ask them to turn it off. Do not under any circumstances look at the papers. Avoid the headlines.

She walks away and pauses a few times to turn around and give him a movie star's long, lingering wave and blow him a kiss. He smiles, his hands on his waist, the white *sharwals* flapping around his body, and the dog sits erect beside him. He looks good, Ora thinks. The new haircut and Ofer's clothes are good for him, and there's something refreshing in the open way he stands and in his smile. "He's coming back to life," she tells herself out loud. This walk is bringing him back to life. What does that say about me? What place will I have in his life when the journey is over, if I have any place at all?

Wait, she thinks, suddenly troubled—why isn't the dog coming with me? But even before she can finish the thought, Avram leans down and pats the dog on her butt, urging her to run along.

An hour later Ora silently unloads her purchases from the Kfar Hasidim supermarket's plastic bags—labeled "Strictly Glatt Kosher"—and divvies them up between the two backpacks: biscuits, crackers, canned goods, packets of bouillon. Her movements are quick and sharp.

"Did something happen, Ora'leh?"

"No, what happened?"

"I don't know. You seem . . ."

"I'm fine."

Avram licks his upper lip. "Okay, okay." And after a moment, "Ora—"

"What is it?"

"Did you hear the radio down there? Did you see a newspaper?"

"There's no radio there, and I didn't look at the paper. Come on, let's go. I'm sick of this place."

They hoist up their backpacks, pass the playground at Kibbutz Yagur, and choose a path with red markers. They soon replace it with a blue one that leads to the Snake River, recently renamed Ma'apilim River, and start climbing up the mountain. The day is still swathed in morning mist, indulging itself and lazily putting off its brightening. The climb soon grows steep, and the two of them and the dog are all breathing heavily.

"Wait a minute," he calls after her, "did someone tell you something there?"

"No one told me anything."

She practically runs up the incline. Stones spark from her heels. Avram gives in and stops to wipe the sweat off. At the same moment, without looking at him, Ora also stops and stands like an angular exclamation point one rocky step above him. Through oak trees and the milky morning vapors, they can see the Zevulun Valley, the suburbs of Haifa, and the Yagur Junction as it comes to life. The pair of towers at the oil refinery in the bay emit plumes of white steam that slowly curl and mingle with the mist. Avram wants to give her something, to quell the sudden irritation bristling around her. If only he knew what to give. Glimmering cars fly by on the roads leading to the junction. A distant train sends out rhythmic sparks of metal and light. But here on the mountain the silence is broken only by the occasional truck horn or the stubborn wail of an ambulance.

"Here, this is how I live," he finally says quietly, perhaps honestly, perhaps as a modest bribe of candor.

"How?" Her voice above him is grating, scratching.

"Like this. I watch."

"Then maybe it's time you went in," she hisses and starts walking again.

"What? Wait—"

"Listen, Ofer's fine," she cuts him off, and Avram rushes after her excitedly. "What? How do you know?"

"I called home from the grocery store to pick up my messages."

"You can do that?"

"Of course you can." Then she mutters to herself, "You can do a lot more than that."

"And? Did he leave a message?"

"Twelve."

She lurches forward again, cutting like a razor. Fine strands of a morning spiderweb graze her face, and she brushes them away angrily. The ghost of an adolescent, grumbling girl flashes in her movements.

"At least until last night he was fine," she reports. "The last message was from eleven-fifteen." She glances at her watch. Avram looks to see how high the sun is. They both know: eleven-fifteen is good, but meaningless now, like yesterday's newspaper. As soon as he was finished leaving the message, an hourglass turned over somewhere, and the timer started from zero again, with no advantage to hope over fear.

"Wait, why didn't you just call him on his cell phone?"

"Him?" She shakes her head, giggles nervously. "No, no way." She half turns her head to him, like a doe to a hunter, and asks wordlessly, with her desperate eyes: Do you really not understand? Do you still not get it, that I can't, I absolutely can't, until he's home?

The path grows difficult and stubborn, and Avram is anxious. Ofer is suddenly so close, his voice still echoing in Ora's ears. Even his clothes, which swathe Avram, rustle as though Ofer's spirit blows through them.

"But what did he say?"

"He said all kinds of things. Joking around. Ofer, you know."

"Yes," Avram says, smiling to himself.

"What do you mean 'yes'?" she spits. "What do you even know about him?"

"Whatever you tell me," Avram replies in bewilderment.

"Yes, stories. Stories we have plenty."

He sinks into himself as he walks. Something happened, that's obvious. Something bad.

As far as the eye can see, stalks of sage soar in purple and white, campions glow in a rosy hue, and buttercups take over the red shift from aged, shedding poppies. Pine needles are dotted with beads of dew. The sound of bells tinkling: a herd passes nearby, lambs tremble on spindly legs, the bellies of pregnant sheep dangle, almost touching the ground. Ora glares at Avram as he gazes at the udders and bellies, and for a moment he is embarrassed, as though caught red-handed at something.

They walk on, panting and groaning up the vertical path. Avram is restless, almost frightened. They'd shared a night of total love, and it seemed their bodies had finally been able to trust again and to believe they would not be separated for many years to come. All night they'd made love and slept and talked and dozed and made love and laughed and made love. Neta had come and gone, leaned in and faded away, and with his body he had told Ora about her. A rare tranquillity had engulfed him, and as if in a dream he had imagined them swinging him between them, very slowly, from one to the other. When he lay by her side afterward he felt happiness return to him with slow steps, like blood to a deadened limb.

"One thing I know, which I never imagined," he said during one of those hours, with her head resting on his chest.

"Hmmm?"

"You can live an entire life without purpose."

"Is that what this is?" She lifted up on her elbows and looked at him. "Without any purpose at all?"

"Once, when I was still the dearly departed me, if you'd told me this was what I could expect, a whole life of this, I'd have done myself in on the spot. Today I know it's not that terrible. That you certainly can. I'm living proof."

"But what does that mean? Explain it to me. What do you mean, a life without purpose?"

He pondered. "I mean that nothing really hurts you and nothing really makes you happy. You live because you live. Because you happen not to be dead."

She managed to resist asking what he would feel if something happened to Ofer.

"Everything passes in front of you," he said. "It's been that way for ages."

"Everything?"

"There's no desire."

"And when you're with me like this?" She moved her hips against him.

He smiled. "Well, there are moments."

She turned over and lay on him. They moved slowly against each other. She arched her back a little and opened to him, and he did not enter. He was happy this way, and he wanted to talk.

"And lots of times I thought—"

She stopped moving abruptly: something in his face, in his voice.

"If you have a child, say," he mumbled quickly, "that's a purpose in life, isn't it? That's something worth getting up for in the morning, no?"

"What? Yes, usually. Yes."

"Usually? Not always? Not all the time?"

Ora thought back to some of the mornings this past year. "Not always. Not all the time."

"Really?" Avram asked wonderingly. "But I thought . . ."

They lay silently again, moving over each other's bodies carefully. His foot curled over her shin, his hand caressed the back of her neck.

"Can I tell you something weird?"

"Tell me something weird," she hummed and held her whole body against his.

"When I got back from there, right? When I started to understand what had happened to me, you know, all that"—he waved his hand dismissively—"I suddenly realized that even when I'd had it, I mean the desire, and a purpose in life, I somehow, in some recess, always knew it was only borrowed. Only for a limited time." He paused. "Only till the truth emerged."

"And what is the truth?" she asked, and thought: the two rows of hitters. The cruel decree.

"That it's not really mine," said Avram stiffly. He propped himself up on his arms and gazed at her intently. "Or that I don't even deserve to have it," he added, like someone deciding to confess to a horrible crime at the end of a trivial questioning.

A notion flitted through her mind: And if he has a child?

"What happened?" Avram asked.

"Hold me."

If he has a child, she thought feverishly, his own child, whom he'll raise. How did I never think of that? Of the possibility that he will be a father one day—

"Ora, what's up?"

She breathed into his neck. "Hold me, don't leave me. You'll walk with me all the way home, right?"

"Of course. We're walking together, what are you—"

"And we'll always, always be together?" She tossed him the fragment of a sentence that had suddenly floated to the surface of her memory, a promise he'd sent her by telegram on her twentieth birthday.

"Until death us do join," he completed the sentence without hesitation.

And then, at that moment, Avram felt that Ofer was in danger. He had never known the sensation before: something dark and cool slashed his heart. The pain was intolerable. He held Ora hard. They both froze.

"Did you feel it?" she whispered in his ear. "You felt it, didn't you?"

Avram breathed into her hair, mute. His body was bathed in cold sweat.

"Think about him," she whispered and clung to him with her whole body until she put him inside her. "Think of him inside me."

They moved slowly, gripping each other as in the eye of a storm.

"Think about him, think about him!" she cried out.

"Listen," she says angrily a few hours later, on the path from Yagur up to the Carmel. "He left me a message yesterday. Ofer. 'I'm okay, the bad guys not so okay.' "

"Didn't he ask where you were, where you'd disappeared to, how you were doing?"

"Yes, of course, several times. He's a terrible worrier. The biggest worrier of all of us. And he always has to know"—she doesn't feel like telling him anything now, but it tumbles out of her anyway, so that he'll know this too, so that he'll remember—"he has this need, it's really compulsive, ever since he was a child, to know exactly where each of us is, so no one will disappear on him for too long. He needs to hold us all together—"

She stops talking and remembers how, as a child, Ofer used to get scared every time an argument broke out, even a tiny one, between her and Ilan. He would dance around and push them at each other, force them to be close. How, then, did he end up being the reason we broke up? she wonders. She lurches forward again in a sudden surge, butting the air with her forehead, and Avram wonders if Ilan left her a message, too. Or perhaps it was Adam who called and said something that hurt her.

The dog rubs up against him as though to strengthen him and to seek refuge from Ora's fury. Her tail droops and her smile is gone.

"What was it you said? 'I'm okay, the bad guys—' "

"The bad guys not so okay."

Avram repeats the words silently. Tasting the arrogance of youth, he thinks—

But Ora is already muttering out loud what he was thinking: " 'Back in Pruszkow, they didn't say things like that.' "

Avram throws up his hands: "I can't win with you! You know it all."

His attempt at flattery falls flat. She sticks her chin out and lopes ahead.

In the shift logs kept by the translators at Bavel, he had written a regular column entitled "Our Town of Pruszkow," in which he logged his reports using the trembling, suspicious grumblings of the shtetl-dwellers Tzeske, Chomek, and Fishl-Parech. An Egyptian MiG-21 transferred from Zakazik to Luxor, a Tupolev grounded due to rudder problems, battle rations issued to commando fighters—all these were adorned with churlish, defeatist, and bitter commentary from the three elderly Pruszkowites invented by Avram. He constantly expanded and enriched their characters, until the base commander uncovered "the Jewish underground," as Avram called it, and sentenced him to a week of night-guard duty next to the flag in the parade courtyard, to strengthen his nationalist convictions.

"But Ora," he says, to exploit quickly the sweetness of memory that might be softening her heart toward him.

"Well, what is it?"

With a stifled grunt, almost sobbing. Without even turning her face to him. Are her shoulders trembling or is it just his imagination?

"Were there any other messages?"

"A few, nothing important."

"From Ilan, too?"

"Yes, he deigned to call, your friend. Finally heard what was going on here, and all of a sudden he's terribly worried about the situation in Israel, and even about my disappearance. Imagine."

"But how did he know you—"

"Ofer told him."

Avram waits. He knows there's more.

"And he's coming back to Israel with Adam. But it'll take them a few days, he's not sure when they'll get on a flight. They're in Bolivia now, on some salt flats." She sniffs angrily: There's enough there for all my wounds.

"And Adam?"

"What about Adam?"

"Did he also leave you a message?"

She stops, amazed, and realizes: I can't believe it.

"Ora?"

Because only now does she remember that Ilan said Adam sent his regards. She was so caught up with herself, with what she was doing, that she almost forgot. He specifically said, "Adam says hi." And she'd forgotten that. Adam is right, he really is. An unnatural mother.

"Ora, what happened?"

"Never mind, forget it." She's almost running again. "There weren't any important messages at my place."

"Your place?"

"Leave me alone, okay? What's with the interrogations? Just leave me alone!"

"I'm leaving," he murmurs, with a sinking feeling in his gut.

A cloud of gnats accompanies them, forcing them to breathe through their noses and keep quiet for a long time. Avram notices exposed tree roots surrounded by mounds of damp earth: there were wild boars here last night.

Later, they come across a big dark rock with letters carved deep: *Nadav*. A stone next to it reads: *A grove in memory of Captain Nadav Klein. Fell in the War of Attrition in the Jordan Valley. 27 Sivan 5729. July 12, 1969.* Across the way, among pine needles and pinecones, a monument and a plaque: *In memory of Staff Sergeant Menachem Hollander, son of Chana and Moshe, Haifa, Kfar Hasidim. Fell in the Yom Kippur War in the battle for Taoz on 13 Tishrei 5734, at the age of 23.*

A short while later there is a huge concrete relief depicting the entire Canal region in 1973, marked with *Our Forces' Positions*—Magma is there too, so tiny—and through the long, serrated leaves of a group of cactuses, they see gilded statues of a doe and a lion, and a monument bearing the names of eight soldiers who fell in the battle for the Suez Canal on May 23, 1970. Ora looks out of the corner of her eye to make sure Avram is able to cross these hurdles of memory in one piece, but he seems to be troubled only by her now, and she wonders how to tell him, where to start.

She walks too fast for him to keep up. The dog stops every so often, pants, and looks questioningly at Avram. He shrugs his shoulders: I don't get it, either. From the main road of Usafia, opposite the Shuk Yussuf greengrocers, they turn to follow the marker down a path that leads through a sparse grove of pine trees. The earth is covered with mounds of trash and filth, tires, furniture, old newspapers, shattered televisions, dozens of empty plastic bottles.

"They throw this stuff here on purpose," she hisses. "I'm telling you, it's their twisted revenge on us."

"Whose?"

"Theirs." She sweeps her arm broadly. "You know exactly who."

"But then they're just making their own place dirty! This is their village."

"No, no, inside their houses it's all sparkling, glimmering, I know them. But everything on the outside belongs to the state, to the Jews, and it's a commandment to junk that up. That's probably part of their jihad, too. Look here—look at this!" She kicks an empty bottle, misses, and almost falls on her rear end.

Avram cautiously reminds her that Usafia is a Druze village, and they're not obligated by the jihad commandment. "And anyway, when we came down from Arbel, and also near the Kinneret, and at the Amud River, we saw piles of trash, totally Jewish trash."

"No, no, it's their protest. Don't you understand? Because they don't have the guts to really revolt. I honestly would respect them a lot more if they just came out against us openly."

She's feeling bad, Avram senses, and she's taking it out on them. He looks at her and sees her face turn ugly.

"Aren't you angry at them? Don't you have any anger or hatred about what they did to you there?"

Avram thinks. The old man from the meat locker comes to his mind, lying naked on the sidewalk, banging his head against it, twitching in front of the soldiers.

"What do you have to think about for so long? Me, if someone did to me a quarter of what they did to you, I'd run them down to the corners of the earth. I'd hire mercenaries to take revenge, even now."

"No," he says, and runs a vision of his tormentors in front of his eyes: the chief interrogator, Lieutenant Colonel Doctor Ashraf, with his sly little eyes and his sickeningly flowery Hebrew, and the hands that tore Avram to shreds. And the jailors in Abbasiya, who beat him whenever they could, who were drawn to torture him more than the others, as though something about him drove them crazy. And the two who buried him alive, and the guy who stood on the side and took photographs, and the two men they brought in from outside—Ashraf told him they were trucked in especially for him, two guys from death row, rapists from a civilian prison in Alexandria—even them he doesn't hate anymore. All he feels when he thinks of them is insipid despair, and sometimes simple, raw sadness at having had the misfortune to end up there and see the things he saw.

The path seems to be trying to shake off the filth, curving sharply to the left and spitting them out into the Cheik riverbed, then descending and plunging into the belly of the earth. They have to watch their steps because the rocks are slippery from the morning dew and the path is crisscrossed with sinewy tree roots. The sun dances through the foliage in tiny pieces of light.

How come Adam said hi to me? she wonders. What happened that made him do that? What is he feeling?

Oak trees and terebinths and pine trees, grandfathers and grandmothers by the looks of them, lean in from both banks of the riverbed, and ivy tumbles down their branches. Here and there is an arbutus, and then a massive pine tree on the ground, hewn, its pinecones dead and its trunk turning white across the path. In unison, Avram and Ora look away.

Next to a dried-up reservoir filled with giant, blighted reeds, two tall boys with unkempt hair come toward them. One has thick, dark dreadlocks, while golden curls tumble from the other's head, and they both wear tiny yarmulkes. Their faces are welcoming, and they carry large backpacks with sleeping bags rolled on top. Ora and Avram are experts at these encounters by now. They almost always say a quick "hello," lower their eyes, and let the other hikers pass. But this time Ora greets the boys with a broad grin and takes off her backpack. "Where are you from, guys?" she asks.

The boys exchange somewhat surprised looks, but her smile is warm and inviting.

"Feel like a little coffee break? I just bought some fresh biscuits. Kosher," she adds piously with a glance at their yarmulkes. She chatters and giggles with them, abounding with motherly warmth and a certain flirtatiousness. They accept her invitation, even though only an hour ago, on Mount Shokef, they'd had coffee with a doctor from Jerusalem who'd asked them all sorts of funny questions and written their answers in a notebook. Ora tenses up.

At her request, after a moment's hesitation, they tell her what the doctor had told them when they sat down for coffee with him— "amazing coffee the guy makes," the dark one notes. It turns out that he and his wife had planned for years to make this journey together as a couple, all along the trail, from the north down to Taba, almost a thousand kilometers. But his wife got sick and died three years ago—the boys interrupt each other, excited by the story, and perhaps by Ora's transfixed look—and before she died she made him swear that he'd still do the hike, even on his own. "And she was always looking for something else for him to do along the way," the golden-curled boy adds with a laugh. "In the end she had this idea"—the dark one snatches the story from his friend's mouth—"that every time he met someone, he'd ask them two questions." It seems as though only now, recounting the story, the boys allow its true meaning to penetrate them.

Ora smiles but she is hardly listening. Deep inside, she tries to picture the woman. She must have been very lovely, with a ripe, glowing beauty, spiritual yet corporeal, with flowing, honey-colored hair. For a moment she forgets her troubles and clings to this stranger—Tammi, Tamar, he'd called her, Tamyusha—who had tried, on her deathbed, to find that "something else" for her man. Or some*one* else, she thinks, and smiles with affection and subtle appreciation for this woman who knew her husband so well (that shirt of his, honestly, it looked like a tablecloth in an Italian trattoria) and equipped him with two questions that no woman could resist.

The two boys gather branches and straw. They light a fire and place a charred *finjan* on the embers and offer their collection of tea leaves. Ora takes more and more food out of her backpack. "Like a magician's hat," she laughs, delighting in her horn of plenty. Avram watches with some concern as she spreads out everything she bought that morning in the supermarket. Cans of hummus and *labaneh*, cracked green olives, a few pitas, still warm and soft. She urges them to taste everything, and they gladly comply. They haven't had a meal this good for ages, they say with their mouths full. They boast of their frugality on the trip, of how industriously they are managing their little household, and she watches affectionately as they gobble down the food. Only Avram feels slightly out of place.

They compare notes on the long route from the south and from the north. Helpful advice and important information flow back and forth about surprises and obstacles waiting for both parties on the way. Ora thinks it was good that she left her phone number on the note for that man. If he calls, she can deliver the pages he'd written in her notebook.

Eventually Avram warms up. After all, the trail is like a home for him too, and to his surprise he even senses a hikers' camaraderie that he's never known before. And perhaps he, like Ora, enjoys the boys' healthy appetites, and the fact that they are dining at his table, so to speak, and it seems completely natural to them. This is the way of the world: impoverished youngsters, frugal and ascetic by necessity, should occasionally enjoy the generosity of affluent adults they meet on their paths, and in this case, of a friendly, decent-looking couple—despite Avram's flapping white *sharwals* and his ponytail tied with a rubber band—a man and a woman who are no longer young but not yet old, and are surely parents to grown children, perhaps even grandparents to one or two little ones, who have taken a little vacation from their full lives and set off on a short adventure. Avram is excited to tell them about the steep climb to the peak of Tabor, and the rock steps and the iron pegs on the ascent to Arbel, and he has some advice and a few warnings. But almost every time he wants to say something, Ora beats him to it and insists on telling the story herself, embellishing slightly, and suddenly it seems to him that she wants to prove at any cost how good she is at animating young people and speaking their language. He dwindles as he watches her, all bustling chumminess, as clumsy as an elbow in a rib, her conduct foreign and grating, until it occurs to him that she is doing this to spite him, that she is still angry at him about something and that she is defiantly pushing him, step by step, out of the little circle she has woven around herself and the two boys.

And he does retreat. He extinguishes his light and sits inside himself in the dark.

The young boys, who live on the settlement of Tekoa, sense nothing of the silent battle being fought so close to them. They talk about the wonders of the road from Eilat—the Tzin River at sundown, the daffodils in the cisterns of the Ashkelon River, the ibex at Ein Avdat—and Ora explains that she and Avram are only planning to go as far as Jerusalem. "Maybe one day," she says, and her gaze wanders off, "we'll do the southern part of the trail too, all the way to Eilat and Taba." The boys grumble about the military practice zones in the Negev, which push the trail away from the wadis and mountains to plain old roadsides. They warn Ora and Avram about the Bedouins' feral dogs—"they have tons of dogs, those people, make sure you protect yours," and the conversation circles around, and suddenly Avram feels something hovering over his face, and when he looks up he sees that it is Ora's gaze, a tortured, disconnected stare, as though she is suddenly seeing something new and extremely painful in him. He reaches up distractedly to brush a crumb from his face.

As they talk, they discover that Jerusalem is about ten days' walk away. "It might take you a bit longer," the boys say.

"It'll zoom by at the end," laughs the curly-haired one. "From Sha'ar HaGay you'll start to feel the pull of home."

Ora and Avram flash each other a look of alarm: Only ten days? What then? What after that?

"Ora, wait, you're running."

"This is how I walk."

It's been this way for a few hours. She's been walking wildly, gritting her teeth. Avram and the dog trail behind, not daring to come close. She stops only when she can no longer walk, when she is literally falling off her feet.

They had passed the Alon Valley, Mount Shokef, chives, cyclamens, poppies. Then suddenly they saw the sea. Ora had been waiting for this moment since the beginning of the trip, but now she didn't stop, didn't even point to the sea, her love. She kept on walking, lips pursed, grunting with the effort, and Avram straggled behind her. The walk up the Carmel was harder than the Galilee mountains. The paths were rockier, strewn with felled trees and invaded by thorny bushes. Titmice and jays hovered above them, calling to one another excitedly. They accompanied the walkers for a long way, passing them off to each other. When evening fell, they both stopped for a moment in front of a giant pine tree that lay in the middle of the path with a gaping crack. It was flooded with rays of dying sunlight, and a peculiar purple radiance glowed from between its thin leaves.

They stood looking at it. A glowing ember.

They started walking again. Avram began to feel that he too was seized with disquiet whenever they lingered even for a moment. The fear had started to nag at him. A new fear. When we get to the road, he thought, maybe we'll take a bus. Or even a taxi.

The Rakit ruins, the Yeshach caves, and a cliff looming brazenly above. They walked down among huge rocks, grasping on to tree roots, grottoes. Over and over again, Avram had to climb back up and carry the dog, who whimpered at the rocky channels. They kept walking when it got dark, as long as they could see the path and the markers. Then they slept, briefly and nervously, and woke in the middle of the night, just as on the first nights of the trip, because the earth was humming and rustling constantly under their bodies. They sat by the fire that Avram lit and drank the tea he made. So terrible was the silence and what filled it. Ora closed her eyes and saw the little street leading to her home in Beit Zayit. She saw the gate to the yard, the steps up to the front door. Again she heard Ilan saying that Adam said hi. In Ilan's voice she could hear Adam's concern. His compassion. Why was he worried about her all of a sudden? Why did he feel sorry for her? She leaped to her feet and started packing the dishes, shoving them haphazardly into her backpack.

They kept walking in the dark, with only the light of the moon, and then the sky began to brighten. For a few hours they had not said a word. Avram felt that they were running to reach Ofer in time, the way you dash to rescue someone from the ruins of a building: every second counts. It's not good that she's quiet, he thought. She isn't talking about Ofer. Now is when we have to talk about him, when she has to talk about him. We have to talk about him.

And then he started talking to himself, silently. He repeated stories about Ofer, things Ora had told him, trivia, little moments, word for word.

"Just tell me he's okay," he growls into the blinding sun. With a sudden lurch, he overtakes her and blocks her path. "Tell me nothing happened to him, that you're not hiding something from me. Look at me!" he yells. They both breathe heavily.

"I only know up to the night before last. As of then he was fine." The sharpness is gone from her face. He senses that something has happened to her in the last hour, somewhere between the tea and sunrise. She looks tattered and stooped, as though finally defeated after a prolonged battle.

"Then what's wrong? Why have you been like this since yesterday? What did I do?"

"Your girlfriend," Ora says heavily.

"Neta?" The blood rushes out of his face. "What happened to her?"

Ora gives him a long, miserable look.

"Is she all right? What happened to her?"

"She's fine. Your girlfriend is fine."

"Then what?"

"She sounds nice, actually. Funny."

"You talked to her?"

"No."

"Then how?"

Ora trudges off the trail and into a tangled thicket. Dragging past thistles and shrubs, she trips as she walks, and Avram follows her. She climbs up a little crag of tall, gray rocks, and he follows. And suddenly they're inside a small crater, where the light is dull and shadowy; the sun seems to have gathered up its rays from this place.

Ora plunges onto a rock ledge and buries her face in her hands. "Listen, I did something . . . It was wrong, I know that, but I called your apartment. I picked up your messages."

He straightens up. "My apartment? Wait, you can do that, too?"

"Yes."

"How?"

"There's a code, a general one, the manufacturer's default option before you set it yourself. It's really not that complicated."

"But why?"

"Don't ask me."

"I don't understand. Wait—"

"Avram, I did it, and that's that. I had no control over it. I dialed home first, and then my fingers just jumped to the numbers."

The dog comes over and nestles between them, offering Ora her warm, padded body, and Ora puts her arms on the dog. "I don't know what came over me. Listen, I'm really . . . I'm so ashamed."

"But what happened? What did she do? Did she do something to herself?"

"I just wanted to hear her, to hear who she is. I didn't even think—"

"Ora!" he practically bellows. "What did she say?"

"You had a few messages. Ten, and nine are from her. There's one from your boss at the restaurant. They're finishing the renovations next week, and he wants you to go back to work. He really likes you, Avram, you can feel it in his voice. And there'll be a housewarming party that they—"

"But Neta, what about Neta?"

"Sit down, I can't do this while you're standing over me like that."

Avram doesn't appear to hear her. He stares at the gray rocks protruding all around him. Something in this place is closing in on him.

Ora rests her cheek on the dog's body. "Listen, she called about a week and a half ago, maybe more, and asked you to call her back immediately. Then she called a few more times and asked . . . No, she just said your name. 'Avram?' 'Avram, are you there?' 'Avram, answer me.' That kind of thing."

Avram kneels down in front of her. His head is suddenly too heavy to bear. The dog, with Ora hunched over her, turns to him with her dark, soft eyes.

"Then there was one message where she said"—Ora swallows, and her face takes on a childish, startled expression—"that she had something important to tell you, and then . . . Let's see, yes, the last message is from the evening before last." She laughs nervously. "That's exactly the same time Ofer left his last message for me."

Avram is hunched, rounded into himself, ready for the blow—he won't be taken by surprise.

" 'Avram, it's Neta,' " Ora says in a hollow voice, her eyes fixed on a spot beyond him. " 'I'm in Nuweiba and you haven't been home for ages and you won't call back your loving ones—' "

Avram nods, recognizing Neta through Ora's voice.

Ora continues lifelessly, as though her entire being is operated by a ventriloquist. " 'A little while ago I thought I might be slightly pregnant, and I didn't have the courage to tell you, and I came down here to think about what to do, and organize my thoughts, and of course in the end I'm not, as usual, it was a false alarm, so you have nothing to worry about, my love.' And then there was a beep."

He stares at her. "What? I don't understand. What did you say?"

"What's not to understand?" Ora rouses from her trance and sharpens her knives at him again. "What exactly don't you understand? Did I say anything not in Hebrew? Do you understand the word 'pregnant'? Do you understand 'false alarm'? Do you understand 'my love'?"

His mouth drops. His face stiffens with immeasurable wonderment.

Ora abruptly turns away from him and the dog. She hugs herself and rocks back and forth. Stop this, she orders herself. Why are you attacking him? What did he do to you? But she cannot stop. Back and forth she rocks, finding pleasure in pulling this molten thread farther and far-

ther out of her innards and unspooling herself until she disappears completely—if only. And poor Neta—*and of course in the end I'm not, as usual,
it was a false alarm*—and suddenly Ora knows how Avram and Neta
sound when they talk to each other, she knows their music, and the soft
playfulness, exactly the way he used to fence with Ilan, and the way Ilan
still does with the boys, with that same lightning-fast wit that Ora herself is no longer capable of and in fact never was. *False alarm*, Neta had
giggled. But does he even realize how much she loves him, and how
much she is suffering?

He grunts. "I still don't understand what you're angry about."

"Angry?" She flings her head back and lets out a toxic spray of
ridicule. "Why would I be angry? What do I have to be angry about?
On the contrary, I should be happy, right?"

"About what?"

"About the mere possibility," she explains with a serious face and a
dizzy sort of matter-of-factness, "that you may have a child one day."

"But I don't have a child," he says sternly. "Other than Ofer I have no
child."

"But maybe you will. Why not? Men your age can still do it, after
all." She regains her senses for a moment and almost falls into his arms
to apologize for the madness that took hold of her, for the narrow-
mindedness, for the smallness of her soul. Because more than anything
she wants to say how good it would be for him to have a child and what
a wonderful father he would be, a full-time dad. But then another flam-
ing sword turns every which way inside her, and she jumps up with an
astonished realization: "Maybe you'll even have a girl. Avram, you'll
have a girl."

"What are you talking about?" He gets up quickly and stands facing
her. "Neta said she wasn't, that she just thought she was." He reaches
out to embrace her and Ora flows through his arms and crumples into a
large pit in the rock. Her hands cover her mouth as though she is sucking a finger or trying to stifle a scream.

"Come on, let's keep walking." He kneels beside her and speaks
rhythmically, confidently. "We'll walk all the way to your house, as far
as you want me to walk with you. Nothing's changed, Ora, get up."

"What for?" she whispers helplessly.

"What do you mean what for?"

She looks at him with tearful eyes. "But you'll have a girl."

"There's no girl," he says tersely. "What's the matter with you?"

"I suddenly get it, it's suddenly tangible for me."

"I only have Ofer," Avram repeats insistently. "Listen: you and I, together, have Ofer."

"How do you have Ofer?" she says, snorting into her hands. Her eyes flit emptily through the air. "You don't know him, you didn't even want to see him. Who is Ofer to you? Ofer is just words to you."

"No, no." In his distress he shakes her, hard, and her head bobs forward and back. "No. You know that's not true anymore."

"But all I've told you is words."

"Ora, don't you happen to have . . ."

"What?"

"A picture of him?"

She looks at him for a long time, as though failing to grasp the meaning of his words. Then she digs through her backpack and pulls out a small brown wallet. She opens it without looking and holds it out to Avram. In a small plastic window is a picture of two boys with their arms around each other. It was taken the morning Adam joined the army. They both have long hair, and Ofer, young and skinny, hangs on his older brother, enveloping him with his arms and his gaze. As Avram looks at the picture, Ora thinks she can see every feature in his face begin to stir uncontrollably. "Avram," she says softly. She puts her hand on his as he holds the picture. She steadies it.

"What a beautiful boy," Avram whispers.

Ora shuts her eyes. She sees people standing on either side of the street that leads to her house. Some of them have already gone into the yard, others are standing on the steps to the door. They wait for her silently, eyes lowered. They wait for her to pass them and walk into her house.

So that it can begin.

"Talk to me. Tell me about him," she murmurs.

"Tell you what?"

"What is he for you?"

She takes the wallet and puts it back into the backpack. For some reason she cannot bear to have the picture so exposed to light. He does not dare resist, even though he would like to sit there and look at it more and more.

"Ora—"

"Tell me what he is for you."

Avram feels a burning need to get up and leave this place, get out of the shadows of this strange little crater with the craggy gray rocks. Across the way, a sun-kissed strip of green stretches out between two jagged cliffs, and here they are in the shade, too much shade.

"I can't hear you," she whispers.

"First of all . . . First of all, he is your child. That's the first thing I know about him, that's the first thing I think about him."

"Yes."

"That's what I always think about him: that he's yours, with your light and your goodness, and the things you've always given him, his whole life, the way you know how to give. Your abundance, your love, and your generosity, always. And that is what will protect him everywhere, there, too."

"It will?"

"Yes, yes." Avram looks beyond her and presses her limp body to him. She feels cold, and her breath is shallow.

"Tell me more, I need you to tell me."

"And you let me hold him together with you. That's what it is. That's what I see. Yes."

Her face grows distant and weak. She seems to be falling asleep with her eyes open, in his arms, and he wants to wake her, to breathe life into her. But something about her, something in her vacant gaze, her gaping mouth . . .

"And it's like," Avram struggles, "like you're trying to take him with you somewhere, alone, but he's too heavy for you. And he's asleep the whole time, right?"

Ora nods, understanding yet not understanding. Her fingers move, weak and blind on his forearm, distractedly feeling the edge of his sleeve.

"It's like he's been anesthetized," Avram murmurs. "I don't know why, I don't fully understand it. And then you come to me and ask me to help you."

"Yes," she whispers.

"The two of us have to take him somewhere, I don't know where, I don't understand why. And we hold him together, between us, all the time. It's like he needs both of us to take him there, that's it."

"Yes."

"Only the two of us can take him there."

"Where?"

"I don't know."

"What's there?"

"I don't know."

"Is it good?" Ora rustles desperately. "Is it a good place there?"

"I don't know."

"What is this, what are you telling me? Is this a dream you had? Did you dream about him?"

"It's what I see," Avram replies helplessly.

"But what is it?"

"We're both holding him."

"Yes?"

"He's walking between us."

"Yes, that's good."

"But he's asleep, his eyes are closed, one of his arms is on you and the other on me."

"I don't understand."

Suddenly Avram shakes himself off. "Let's get out of here, Ora."

She moans. "This isn't good. He has to be awake the whole time. Why is he sleeping?"

"No, he's asleep. His head is on your shoulder."

"But why is he asleep?" Ora shouts and her voice cracks.

Avram shuts his eyes to wipe the scene away. When he opens them, Ora is staring at him in horror.

"Maybe we were wrong," she says, and her face is strained. "Maybe we got it all wrong, from the beginning. This whole path, all the walking we did—"

"That's not true! Don't say that, we'll walk, and we'll talk about him—"

"Maybe the whole thing was the opposite of what I thought."

"Opposite how?"

She slowly turns her palms out. "Because I thought that if we both talked about him, if we kept talking about him, we'd protect him, together, right?"

"Yes, yes, that's true, Ora, you'll see—"

"But maybe it's the exact opposite?"

"What? What's the opposite?" he whispers.

Her body flutters at him. She grips his arm: "I want you to promise me."

"Yes, whatever you want."

"That you'll remember everything."

"Yes, you know I will."

"From the beginning, from when we met, when we were kids, and that war, and how we met in isolation, and the second war, and what happened to you, and Ilan, and me, and everything that happened, yes?"

"Yes, yes."

"And Adam and Ofer. Promise me, look me in the eye." She holds his face in both hands. "You'll remember, right?"

"Everything."

"And if Ofer . . ." Ora slows down and her eyes glaze over, and a new wrinkle, vertical and deep and black, suddenly runs down between her eyes. "If he—"

"Don't even think that way!" Avram grabs her shoulder and rocks her wildly.

She keeps talking, but he does not hear. He holds her to him and kisses her face, and she does not surrender to him and his kisses, all she gives him is the shell of her face.

"You'll remember," she murmurs through his shaking. "You'll remember Ofer, his life, his *whole* life, right?"

They sit for a long time, hidden away in the small crater. Holding each other like refugees from a storm. The sounds slowly return. The hum of a bee, the thin chirp of a bird, the voices of workers building a house somewhere in the valley.

Then Ora detaches her body from his and lies down on her side on the rock ledge. She pulls her knees into her stomach and rests her cheek on her open palm. Her eyes are open yet she sees nothing. Avram sits beside her, his fingers hovering over her body, barely touching. A light breeze fills the air with the scents of *za'atar* and poterium and a sweet whiff of honeysuckle. Beneath her body are the cool stone and the whole mountain, enormous and solid and infinite. She thinks: How thin is the crust of Earth.

DECEMBER 2007

I BEGAN WRITING *this book in May of 2003, six months before the end of my oldest son, Yonatan's, military service, and a year and a half before his younger brother, Uri, enlisted. They both served in the Armored Corps.*

Uri was very familiar with the plot and the characters. Every time we talked on the phone, and when he came home on leave, he would ask what was new in the book and in the characters' lives. ("What did you do to them this week?" was his regular question.) He spent most of his service in the Occupied Territories, on patrols, lookouts, ambushes, and checkpoints, and he occasionally shared his experiences with me.

At the time, I had the feeling—or rather, a wish—that the book I was writing would protect him.

On August 12, 2006, in the final hours of the Second Lebanon War, Uri was killed in Southern Lebanon. His tank was hit by a rocket while trying to rescue soldiers from another tank. Together with Uri, all the members of his tank crew were killed: Bnayah Rein, Adam Goren, and Alex Bonimovitch.

After we finished sitting shiva, I went back to the book. Most of it was already written. What changed, above all, was the echo of the reality in which the final draft was written.

DAVID GROSSMAN

A NOTE ABOUT THE AUTHOR

David Grossman was born in Jerusalem. He is the author of numerous works of fiction, nonfiction, and children's literature. His work has appeared in *The New Yorker* and has been translated into thirty languages around the world. He is the recipient of many prizes, including the French Chevalier de l'Ordre des Arts et des Lettres, the Buxtehuder Bulle in Germany, Rome's Premio per la Pace e l'Azione Umitaria, the Premio Ischia—International Award for Journalism, Israel's Emet Prize, and the Albatross Prize given by the Günter Grass Foundation.

A NOTE ABOUT THE TRANSLATOR

Jessica Cohen was born in England, raised in Israel, and has been living in the United States since 1997. She translates contemporary Israeli prose, as well as commercial material from and into Hebrew. Her published translations include David Grossman's award-winning *Her Body Knows*, and critically acclaimed works by Yael Hedaya, Ronit Matalon, Amir Gutfreund, and Tom Segev. Her translations have appeared in *Words Without Borders*, *Two Lines*, and *Zeek*.

A NOTE ON THE TYPE

This book was set in Janson, a typeface thought to have been made by the Dutchman Anton Janson. It has been conclusively demonstrated that these types are actually the work of Nicholas Kis (1650–1702).

Composed by Creative Graphics, Allentown, Pennsylvania
Printed and bound by Berryville Graphics, Berryville, Virginia
Designed by Maggie Hinders